THE SEVENTH SIGIL

MARGARET WEIS
AND
ROBERT KRAMMES

A TOM DOHERTY ASSOCIATES BOOK
NEW YORK

THE SEVENTH SIGIL

Edited by James Frenkel

Maps by Ellisa Mitchell

A Tor Book
Published by Tom Doherty Associates, LLC
175 Fifth Avenue
New York, NY 10010

www.tor-forge.com

ISBN 978-0-7653-6953-6

Our books may be purchased in bulk for promotional, educational, or business use. Please contact your local bookseller or the Macmillan Corporate and Premium Sales Department at (800) 221-7945, extension 5442, or by e-mail at MacmillanSpecialMarkets@macmillan.com.

First Edition: September 2014
First Mass Market Edition: December 2015

Printed in the United States of America

0 9 8 7 6 5 4 3 2 1

To the battle between the horsemen and the sheep herders at Gen Con that introduced to me two very dear friends.

—Margaret Weis

For my dear friend Margali, with heartfelt thanks. And in memory of Tom Smith and Ellen Sloan, I miss you both . . .

—Robert Krammes

ACKNOWLEDGMENTS

Father Jacob is recalling Romans 1:20, the Bible, when he is considering how a creator reveals Himself.

The song the Trundler sailors sing in chapter four is from an old chanty sung by riverboat sailors known as "One More Day."

Sir Henry quotes the great statesman David Lloyd George, Earl of Dwyfor, in chapter twenty-six.

Franklin Sloan quotes *The Works of John Owen*, English Nonconformist church leader and theologian in chapter twenty-eighty and the Puritan clergyman, Stephen Charnock, from *Discourses upon the Existence and Attributes of God*, in chapter forty-six.

Julian de Guichen and General Dwight D. Eisenhower were thinking along the same lines in the quote in chapter forty-one.

—Margaret Weis

I want to thank Jim Hart for listening to my frequent cryptic questions and helping me come up with some answers, and especially for his enormous help creating the religious structure of the Bottom Dwellers.

And Margali Thomas for her help with proofreading.

—Robert Krammes

Freya
Isle of Narris
Isle of Harris
Upper Alten
Verdin
the Midlands
Bley
Lake Garendil
Grafton
Slopford
the Glaie River
Glenham
Kerringdon
Ilwick
West Aulkin
East Aulkin
Port Fahey
Khendrun Island
Tarth
Fort Upton
Lowland
Haever
Whithaven
Longbow Highway
Barthen Moor
Olgen River
East Watch
Hempstead
Waight
Aeber
Dunham
100 miles
the Eidan Moors
Fourchester
Trellingham
Dought Crossing
the Westlands
Blue River
High Ridge
Woostenbroke
Lower Alten
Lake Elizabeth
Port Crighton
North Milton Island
South Milton Island

Rosia

Dragon Lands
Milasceau
the Dragon Duchies
Dragon Lands
Caltreau
Duchy of Caltreau
Duchy of Reinholt
Reinholt R.
Upper Ker Grech River
Ciel-et-terre
Ker Grech River
Mountains
Westfirth
County Alfor
County Defor
Ellif Province
Oscadia Mountains
St. Agnes
Lente River
Martini Province
Bay of Faighn
Duchy of Piette
Jeandieu River
Vailpointe
Lake Fulmeau
Easguard
Royal River
County of Marjolaine
Fulmeau Province
New Evreux
Duchy of Almice
Brighan Province
Evreux
Drie Mountains
Kharun Dir Desert
Aurun River
Eudaine
County Cheauval
Duchy of Bourlet
Duchy of Oskae
Argonne
The Wildes
Capione
County Galiar
Strait de Domcaido

the Fortress

Main Dock
Bridge
Main Doors
Officers' Quarters
Infirmary
Gun Emplacements
Cannon Emplacement
Privies
Stairs to the Lift Tanks
Combat Powder & Shot Magazine
Mess Hall
Main Barracks
Powder Magazine
Main Armory
Kitchen
Food Storage
Privy & Wash Room
Common Space for Dragons
Cold Storage
Main Barracks
Store Room
Gun Emplacements
Gun Emplacements
Back Door
Cargo Dock
Gun Emplacement

1

I have resisted the calls of many in the Arcanum to install a standing army within the Citadel. I fear such an army could too easily be misused for political purposes.

—Sister Marie Elizabeth, first provost of the Arcanum

The wyvern-drawn prison carriage transported Stephano de Guichen and Rodrigo de Villeneuve to a makeshift wharf located only God and the Arcanum knew where. The terrain was isolated, rockbound. A yacht painted black and marked with the symbol of the Arcanum was the only boat docked at the wharf. The rain had let up and now the sun shone through gray, trailing mists. The time must be somewhere near midafternoon. Only about an hour had passed since Stephano and his friend were accosted by the monks of Saint Klee, placed under arrest, and carried off in chains.

The carriage landed. The monks ordered Stephano and Rodrigo, both still in chains, to descend, then escorted them to the black yacht.

They had been charged with heresy. They would be taken to the dungeons at the Citadel, the home of the Arcanum, the priests who enforced Church laws. The Citadel was a fortress located on a mountain surrounded by the waters of an inland sea. If anyone had escaped from the Citadel's dungeons, they had not lived to tell the tale.

Two monks sat in the driver's box of the yacht. One was the driver, operating the helm and handling the two wyverns. The other rode along as guard.

"We're dangerous criminals," Stephano remarked bitterly to Rodrigo.

His friend said nothing, might not have even heard him. Stephano regarded him with concern. Rodrigo walked with his head bowed, seemingly oblivious to what was going on around him. He wasn't even watching where he was going. He stumbled blindly over the uneven ground.

"We'll prove our innocence, Rigo," Stephano said to him.

Rodrigo bleakly shook his head. He knew as well as Stephano that those who went into the dungeons of the Citadel never came out.

The monk who had accompanied Stephano and Rodrigo ordered them into the yacht. The entrance was located behind the driver, which meant they had to climb up on the box to make their way inside.

The driver stood to allow them to pass. Stephano hoisted himself up on the box—not easy to do with his hands shackled. Rodrigo followed more slowly, missed his step and nearly fell. The monk caught him and assisted him through the door. Once his prisoners were safely inside, the monk entered and shut and locked the door behind him.

Stephano had been in Father Jacob's black yacht. It was luxurious, homey with a table, comfortable chairs, and beds. The interior of this yacht was bare, stripped down. The only furnishings were benches that had been built into the bulwarks, a table—bolted to the deck—a chair and several storage lockers. The portholes were covered by iron bars. This yacht was designed for prisoner transport.

The driver shouted at the wyverns, and the black yacht lifted smoothly into the air.

"If you give me your word as gentlemen that you will not cause trouble, I will remove the manacles," said the monk.

Rodrigo held out his hands. Stephano was about to tell the monk to go to hell.

Rodrigo, seeing Stephano's obdurate expression, said, "Don't be a fool. Look at your wrists."

Stephano looked down. His wrists were cut and rubbed raw from the manacles. And he had to admit he felt helpless without the use of his hands.

"You have my word," he muttered dourly.

A blue spark sizzled from the monk's fingers, and the lock on the manacles clicked. The manacles popped open and fell to the floor. The monk did the same for Rodrigo, then pointed to the benches, silently indicating they were to sit there.

Stephano sat down and rubbed his wrists. Rodrigo eased himself down on the bench and lay motionless, staring up at the ceiling. He was deathly pale. Stephano rested his hand on his friend's shoulder.

"Everything's going to be all right, Rigo. These charges that we conspired with Father Jacob and Sir Ander are ludicrous. There's been some sort of mistake. We're innocent."

Stephano spoke loudly, aiming his words at the monk, who had taken a seat facing his prisoners in the yacht's only chair.

Rodrigo closed his eyes.

Stephano sat forward and continued his argument.

"These charges make no sense! The idea that either Father Jacob or Sir Ander are heretics is absurd and the notion that we conspired with them against the Church is more absurd still! Sir Ander is a Knight Protector, a man of honor, a true knight, dedicated to his faith. We met him and Father Jacob at the Abbey of Saint Agnes. They were there to investigate the murders of the nuns. When the Bottom Dwellers attacked them, their yacht was damaged and we towed them to Westfirth for repairs. That's all there was to it."

The monk remained unmoving, seemingly deaf.

"You're wasting your breath, my friend," Rodrigo said in a listless tone. "The monks of Saint Klee are the guardians of the Citadel, sent to arrest us and deliver us safely to the inquisitors. They don't care if we are guilty or innocent."

"They *should* care," Stephano said angrily.

Rodrigo gave a wan smile and again closed his eyes. The monk sat upright in his chair, watching Stephano and Rodrigo without appearing to watch them. Stephano had heard stories about the monks of Saint Klee, the guardians of the Citadel.

Saint Klee had been a man who taught that life was sacred and that one should subdue a foe, if possible, rather than kill him. To this end, the monks of Saint Klee had, over the centuries, developed specialized magicks designed to subdue their victims. Stephano could attest to the magic's effectiveness. His body still tingled from the spell they had cast on him, which had left him twitching and writhing on the floor.

This monk was short, lean, and spare. He wore the traditional red robes of the monks of Saint Klee. His long curly black hair was tied in a knot at the back of his head. He spoke with an Estaran accent. The other two monks in the driver's box wore the same red robes. They were both built the same—all bone and muscle and gristle. The only difference was that one had sparse graying hair and one had brown.

Stephano, feeling the need to move about, started to stand up. The monk jumped to his feet. Stephano hurriedly raised his hands to show he meant no harm.

"I gave you my word, Brother!" said Stephano, annoyed. "I just want to walk around a little, stretch my legs."

The monk considered, then nodded and settled himself again.

Stephano paced aimlessly around the yacht's only room, then walked over to look out one of the iron-barred windows. He was aware of the monk's eyes on him the entire time and he was tempted to ask if the monk thought he was going to try to rip out the bars, smash the glass, and hurl himself to his death on the ground far below.

The yacht was flying just beneath cloud level. Below, Stephano could see a walled city and outlying homes and farm fields spread over lush hillsides. A large river meandered among the hills. By the sun's location, he could tell they were sailing south. There were no other walled cities in this part of the country. The city must be Eudaine, on the banks of the river Conce.

A flash of lightning followed quickly by a crack of thunder startled him; then came a deluge. Rain poured down in a gray curtain, drumming on the roof and rolling down the windowpanes. The yacht's interior grew dark as clouds closed in.

A lamp stood on the table. The monk apparently liked to sit in the gloom, however, because he did not light it. More thunder rumbled and the yacht rocked with the gusting wind. The storm was worsening.

Rodrigo had not moved and Stephano feared he might slip into melancholia and never come out. He needed some way to distract him, rouse him from his dark thoughts. Stephano went back to sit beside him.

"Rigo, we need to talk," he said. "It's about my mother."

Rodrigo opened his eyes and sat bolt upright to stare in

astonishment. The subject of Stephano's mother was forbidden by Stephano, who disliked thinking about her, much less talking about her. He was now driven by recent events to do both.

"I'm listening, but just remember, so is our friend," Rodrigo said with a glance at the monk.

Stephano gave a shrug.

"He probably knows everything anyway. D'argent showed me the will that states I am my mother's legitimate heir."

"I know," said Rodrigo. "I saw it. What about it?"

"I don't believe it. It's a fraud. To be my mother's heir, she and my father would have to have been married."

"Then that must be the case. My dear fellow, your mother's will was drawn up by lawyers, signed and attested with her signature and the signatures of witnesses. How could it be a fraud?"

"According to my grandfather, my father never saw or communicated with my mother after I was born. He never talked about her; never uttered her name."

"Your grandfather must have been wrong. You have to face facts, my friend," said Rodrigo. "Upon your mother's death—which sad occasion we all hope will not happen for many, many years—you will become one of the wealthiest men in Rosia, maybe in all the world. The riches of the crown are said to be nothing compared to those of your mother."

Stephano brushed wealth aside. "D'argent said that he told me about my mother's will on her orders, because she fears she might not return. I am worried about her, Rigo. Seems strange to say, since I have always hated her."

"You could ask Sir Ander—" Rodrigo began.

"When we see him in prison?" Stephano said drily, forgetting that he was supposed to be keeping Rodrigo's mind off their current predicament.

Rodrigo paled a bit, but he rallied.

"What I was going to say is that *once we are freed,* you can ask Sir Ander if he knows anything about your parents being married. He was a good friend to both of them."

Stephano thought this over. "I think Sir Ander *does* know something. He tried to tell me back at the Abbey, but I wouldn't listen. I resented the fact that he was friends with my mother, and I accused him of being disloyal to my father's memory. But maybe—"

He was stopped in midsentence by the shrill shrieking of the wyverns. The next moment, a fiery blast hit the yacht, throwing Stephano and Rodrigo off the bench and dumping the monk out of his chair.

"Were we struck by lightning?" Rodrigo asked.

"Not unless lighting is green," said Stephano grimly. "That was a blast of contramagic! Keep down."

Rodrigo flattened himself on the deck.

The monk twisted catlike to his feet. He cast Stephano a warning look.

"Stay where you are, sir," the monk ordered, finally speaking. "Don't move."

The monk hurried to the window. Stephano had no need to move. Looking past the monk's shoulder, he could see armed men riding gigantic bats flying out of the rain clouds.

"Bottom Dwellers," said Stephano.

"Dear God!" Rodrigo groaned. "First we're arrested and now demons are attacking us! Could this day *get* any worse?"

The riders appeared to be aiming their fire at the driver. The wyverns were shrieking in terror at the sight of the giant bats, and he was having difficulty controlling them. The yacht rocked and pitched, making it hard to stand. Stephano could see at least a dozen more bats emerging from the storm clouds. He doubted if even the legendary monks of Saint Klee could fight off such numbers.

The monk remained standing in front of the window, gazing out at the bat riders, who now had the yacht surrounded. Stephano waited tensely for another attack, which likely would send the yacht plunging to the ground. But nothing happened; no more blasts.

"They are trying to force us to land," Stephano said.

"Why?" Rodrigo asked in muffled tones. He lay face down on the deck with his arms covering his head. "Why not just blow us out of the sky?"

Stephano shook his head. He spoke to the monk's back. "Do you know why, Brother?"

"They want the yacht," the monk replied. "They don't want to damage it. And they want to capture us alive."

Stephano wondered why at first and then he recalled what Father Jacob had told him, about how the demons had tortured the nuns of the Abbey of Saint Agnes before they killed them. He started to say something, glanced at Rodrigo, and was silent.

The high-pitched screams of the wyverns were growing louder and more frantic. The Bottom Dwellers, wearing demonic-looking helms, flew alongside the yacht—a strange and hideous escort. The monk walked over to a bench and reached underneath it to draw out what appeared to be an ordinary wooden walking staff. Stephano guessed it wasn't ordinary and that it wasn't a staff. The monk returned to the window.

"I can help you fight them, Brother," said Stephano. "Give me a pistol. I know you rely on your magic, but you must have weapons stored somewhere on board."

The monk made no answer.

"I gave you my word as a gentleman I won't try to escape," Stephano promised.

"Mine, too," said Rodrigo from the deck. "If you have some silk I can cover it with constructs to defend against contramagic—"

"Rigo!" Stephano said sharply. In a lower voice he added, "Don't talk about contramagic! You're in enough trouble already!"

The monk was keeping watch out the window. He smiled faintly.

"We also know how to defend against contramagic, Monsieur Rodrigo. Father Jacob warned us to be prepared."

"Then why are they charging us with heresy?" Stephano asked angrily. "None of this makes any sense."

The monks launched their own attack. Bright, fiery red light reflected off the gray clouds, then another blast of green contramagic shook the yacht. Bats screeched; the wyverns screamed. Stephano caught a glimpse of a bat and its rider tumbling out of the sky trailing smoke.

"Please stand back, Captain," the monk ordered.

Placing himself directly in front of the iron-barred window, the monk raised the staff. The wood began to glow. A blast of red light streaked from the staff and struck the porthole. The glass exploded. The iron bars glowed red hot. The bat riders saw their danger, but it was too late to flee before the fiery wave hit them, immolating the two bats and their riders, consuming them in white flame.

"Good thing we didn't try to escape," Rodrigo remarked, shuddering.

The wind gusted, sending rain rushing through the broken window. The monk glanced over his shoulder at Stephano.

"The pistols are stored in a compartment in the bulkhead just above your head, Captain."

Stephano looked, but he could not see a compartment. The monk spoke a word and blue magical light illuminated the wall, revealing a secret cabinet.

"The pistols are loaded," the monk continued. "I will have to remove the warding constructs—"

A bat rider appeared outside the shattered window, and another bat rider swooped down beside him.

"Brother, duck!" Stephano warned.

Green fire blasted through the window. The monk cried out and reeled backward. Blood and rain streamed down his face. He staggered and Stephano caught hold of him.

"Rigo, light the lamp!" Stephano ordered, lowering the wounded monk to the deck. "Bring it over here. And keep your head down!"

Rodrigo activated the lamp's magic with a word. Crouching low, he brought the light to Stephano. Rodrigo took one look at the monk's face in the lamplight and sucked in a horrified breath.

"Oh, God!" he whispered.

One of the monk's eyes had been pierced by a large, jagged splinter of wood. The other eye was dark with blood.

"I can't see!" The monk started to lift his hands to his face.

"Lie still. Don't move," Stephano said to the monk. Taking hold of his hands, he gently lowered them. "I'll get help."

Green light flared, and Stephano could feel the yacht take another hit and make a stomach-dropping dive. Stephano and Rodrigo froze, helpless. Finally the driver managed to bring the yacht under control and they leveled out. Stephano breathed a sigh of relief.

"Rigo, stay with him. I'll go fetch the others."

Stephano started to stand up, but Rodrigo seized hold of his arm, dragging him back down.

"Look!" Rodrigo held the lamp over the monk.

A large stain, black against the red of the monk's robe, was slowly spreading over the monk's chest. Stephano tore open the monk's robes to examine the wound. The lantern wavered. The beam of light stabbed all around the yacht's interior.

"Stop shaking, Rigo. Hold the lamp steady," Stephano ordered curtly.

Rodrigo swallowed and made a valiant effort to hold still. A projectile of some sort had entered the monk's chest. The monk's head lolled, and his body went limp.

"He's dead," said Stephano, as he sat back on his heels.

The gray clouds reflected the green and red of the flaring attacks as the yacht rolled despite the driver's struggles with the wyverns. His fellow monk was still alive, still fighting. Another flash of red light accompanied by an extremely loud explosion was followed by the sound of a bat screeching in its death throes.

"They won't be able to hold them off," said Stephano. He stood up, then staggered across the deck to the cabinet, nearly falling as the yacht took another hit. "Rigo, I need those pistols. Can you see the warding constructs he was talking about?"

Rodrigo lurched toward Stephano, stumbled and crashed into him. "I can see them, but they're—"

"Good! Work your magic and get rid of them."

"I can't," said Rodrigo, keeping one arm braced against the bulkhead.

Stephano glared at him in frustration. "Damn it, Rigo, you have to!"

"You saw the kind of fancy magic these monks use!" Rodrigo protested. "It would take me a week to unravel—"

"Hush!" Stephano ordered.

Rodrigo froze. They could both hear the sounds of a desperate struggle right outside the door. They heard another blast, loud screams, and the shrieking of fear-crazed wyverns. And then they could feel the yacht begin to descend. No more red flares of light. The fight was apparently over.

"What's happening now?" Rodrigo whispered. "Can you tell?"

Stephano could see through the hole the tops of trees rising up to meet them.

"They're going to try to land," said Stephano.

Rodrigo gulped. "What do we do?"

"I have an idea," said Stephano, thinking as he spoke. "Block the door with that crate!"

"Is that going to stop them?" Rodrigo asked. "The crate's not very heavy."

"No, but it will slow them down."

Rodrigo dragged the crate across the deck and pushed it against the door. Stephano retrieved the lamp. Holding it, he placed himself directly in front of the gun cabinet.

"Get behind me," he ordered Rodrigo. "Out of the line of fire."

"Meaning you're going to let them shoot at you. You can't be serious!"

"Not shoot at *me*. Shoot at the cabinet and destroy the magic. It's the only way to break those damn constructs. When the magic is gone, you yank open the cabinet and grab two pistols. One for you and one for me."

Rodrigo blanched. "Me! You know I can't hit anything!"

"You can hardly miss at this range," said Stephano grimly. "Just make sure to point the barrel at the bat rider, not at me. Or yourself."

Rodrigo groaned. "Oh, God!"

A bat rider tried to open the door, only to find it blocked. He struck the door with something, probably his foot. The first blow shifted the crate. The second knocked the door open.

From his vantage point, Stephano could see two Bottom Dwellers in the driver's box. One was driving the yacht, trying desperately to calm the wyverns and not having much luck. The other bat rider stood warily in the doorway. He wore the demonic-looking armor and was carrying one of the short-range green fire weapons.

Stephano waved the lamp back and forth to draw the man's attention. He shouted, raised his hand as though he held a pistol, and took aim.

Startled, the Bottom Dweller shot at him.

Stephano leaped to one side. Fiery contramagic streaked past him and struck the cabinet right where he had been standing. The warding constructs flashed blue, then started to disappear as the green-glowing contramagic ate away at them.

Rodrigo desperately tried to open the cabinet. The magical constructs were broken, but he discovered a manual lock. Such locks were generally no problem for Rodrigo, who was accustomed to doing a little harmless snooping around the palace. Judging by his muttered imprecations, he was having difficulty with this one.

The Bottom Dweller drew a second weapon and aimed it at Rodrigo. Stephano flung the lamp and hit the soldier in the arm, disrupting his aim. The lamp broke, plunging the cabin into darkness

"Rigo!" Stephano called urgently.

"Got it!" Rodrigo cried.

A small sizzle of blue electricity flared around the lock, sparks flew, and he pulled open the cabinet door. Several pistols were mounted on one of the cabinet walls, along with powder flasks, and ammunition. Rodrigo took down a pistol and tossed it to Stephano, who caught it and dove for cover underneath the table. He hoped the monk had been right when he'd said the pistols were loaded.

Barely taking time to aim, Stephano pulled back the hammer of his pistol and fired, just as the bat rider fired his weapon at him.

The soldier grunted in pain and clutched his leg as green light flared, and a wave of heat washed over Stephano. The wooden tabletop went up in flames. Stephano beat a hurried retreat, crawling across the deck. He knew he had at least hit the Bottom Dweller, but unfortunately, not critically. Even as blood was running down the man's leg, he was reloading his weapon.

Rodrigo, white-faced, held a pistol in his shaking hands. "Don't make me kill you! Don't make me! Don't make me!"

The Bottom Dweller raised the weapon and aimed it.

"Rigo! Shoot!" Stephano yelled.

Rodrigo shuddered, closed his eyes, and pulled the trigger.

The gun went off. Rodrigo fell over backward and the Bottom Dweller staggered as the bullet slammed into him. Stephano dashed across the deck to the cabinet and grabbed another pistol. He turned to shoot, caught a glimpse of tree limbs flashing past the window and realized that the yacht was falling much too fast. With a horrific, wood-splintering crash, the yacht slammed into the trees, flipped over on its side, and went tumbling, rolling through the branches. Tree limbs snapped and cracked.

Stephano lost his grip on the pistol and crashed into what had once been the ceiling and was now the deck. The yacht continued to fall. Rodrigo slid on his belly past Stephano. The body of the dead monk tumbled past Rodrigo. The Bottom Dweller slammed into the table, which was bolted to the deck and was the only object in the yacht that wasn't in motion. Then the terrifying plunge through the trees suddenly ended. The yacht came to a bone-jarring stop.

Stephano lay on his back, too shaken to move. Dim light filtered through the wreckage. He looked for the door and saw it hanging open above him. Through it he could see nothing but leaves and branches. The yacht shifted and shuddered and Stephano sucked in a breath, expecting another fall. The yacht was apparently only settling, for it stopped moving.

"Rigo," Stephano called softly.

"I'm here . . . I think . . ."

Stephano looked over his shoulder to see his friend lying on his belly, his arms outstretched, his feet against the blood-spattered wall.

"Are you all right?"

"I bit my lip," Rodrigo said plaintively. "And my arm hurts. What about you?"

"Bruises and cuts, nothing serious. Where are we?" Stephano asked, still whispering. "Can you see out the window?"

Rodrigo gingerly turned his head.

"I think we're on the ground. The yacht is tilted at an angle, leaning against a tree trunk."

Stephano was about to try to raise himself off the deck when he heard sounds coming from outside—a groan and someone moving about. Whoever had been flying the yacht—presumably a Bottom Dweller—was still out there.

"Lie still!" he hissed at Rodrigo.

Stephano shifted his head to locate the gun cabinet and silently swore. The pistols were there, mounted in the gun cabinet, but he couldn't reach them. The cabinet was now about twelve feet above his head.

"Odhran!" the driver—he assumed the man was the driver—called.

Stephano was startled. Gythe had claimed the Bottom Dwellers spoke to her in the language of the Trundlers, and this one had a Trundler name. He recognized it because one of Miri's innumerable cousins was called Odhran. Stephano cast a glance at the Bottom Dweller in the cabin. His body was wrapped, unmoving, around the table.

The driver called again more urgently, *"Odhran, cabru le!"*

Stephano knew a few words that he'd picked up from Miri. These words were among them, good words to know in any language: "I need help!"

Rodrigo's eyes were wide.

"What do we do?" he mouthed.

"Play dead," whispered Stephano.

"I can do that," Rodrigo muttered. "I'm halfway dead from fright already."

Stephano kept looking at the door, his eyes half closed, peering out through his eyelashes.

The Bottom Dweller said something else, something about his legs. Stephano wasn't sure, but he thought the man was pinned inside the driver's box. A head appeared in the open doorway. The Bottom Dweller had removed his helm and his large eyes squinted in the dim light, trying to see. When he saw the body hooked on the table legs, he groaned and shook his head.

He called Odhran's name for a third time, then muttered something and shifted his attention to Stephano and Rodrigo. Stephano closed his eyes and held his breath.

A flapping of bat wings came from outside the yacht. The Bottom Dweller drew back his head.

"Captaen! Thar anseo!"

Through the open door, Stephano could see a mounted bat rider hovering in the air above the yacht.

"There's another fiend outside," Stephano told Rodrigo softly. "Don't move!"

"Don't worry!" Rodrigo gasped.

The bat rider descended, out of Stephano's view. He could hear the man outside, talking to the driver. Stephano had trouble understanding, but he caught enough to gather that the driver was trapped inside the box and the captain was attempting to free him. The latter asked about Odhran, to which the driver said something Stephano couldn't hear due to the rustling of leaves and cracking of branches. After a lot more noise, the captain was successful in freeing his comrade, and the next thing Stephano knew, both men were peering inside the door.

Stephano closed his eyes. The captain called Odhran's name again, and Stephano waited tensely for him to climb into the yacht to investigate. After several heart-pounding moments, the captain drew back from the door and said something to the driver.

Stephano recognized the word, *marbh*. Dead.

The captain left the doorway.

"I can't stand this. I'm going to be sick," Rodrigo murmured.

"No, you're not," Stephano whispered savagely. "They're still out there."

He waited a moment, listening. "I think they're leaving. Don't move yet."

Watching through the open door, he saw the bat rise from the ground, now carrying two riders. Stephano waited until the bat was out of sight, then drew in a breath. He didn't realize until then he had stopped breathing.

"Can I be sick now?" Rodrigo asked. He was in pitiful condition, his face smeared with soot and blood from where he'd bitten his lip, and his jaw swollen and bruised. When he moved his left arm, he winced.

Stephano could feel a large lump growing on his forehead, and realized that a painful gash across his nose was bleeding profusely.

"Wait until we get out of here," he said, as he helped Rodrigo to his feet.

Kicking aside some broken boards, they crawled out of the wreckage. Once out in the open, Rodrigo ducked behind a tree, and shortly after, Stephano heard the sound of retching.

When Rodrigo returned, pale and disheveled, he was cradling his left arm.

"Is it broken?" Stephano asked, concerned.

"I don't think so. I'm going to have an unsightly bruise," he added.

He paused a moment, clearly distraught.

"Did I kill that wretched demon, Stephano?" he asked finally. "My eyes were closed. I couldn't see."

"I don't know, Rigo," said Stephano, who was fairly certain Rodrigo's shot had by some miracle actually hit the fiend. "Everything happened at once. If you did, you saved us. He would have killed us."

"I know," Rodrigo said quietly. "But still . . . he was some demon mother's son."

He sighed deeply, wiped his face again and looked around. "Do you have the faintest idea where we are? All I see are trees."

"The yacht flew over the city of Eudaine not long before we were attacked," said Stephano. "We can't be far from there. We were flying south, and we can tell by the position of the sun which way is west. So if we start walking that direction—"

"Stephano, look," said Rodrigo suddenly, pointing to a tangle of green leaves and gray branches and a splash of red.

The body of the monk of Saint Klee lay in a heap a short distance from the yacht. The body must have been thrown from the yacht when it struck the trees.

"We need to do something for him. We can't leave him here. We should bury him," said Rodrigo, his voice breaking.

"We have no tools to dig a grave," said Stephano.

He walked over to the corpse. Taking off his coat, he draped it over the monk's ravaged head. "God rest your soul, Brother, and give you peace."

"Amen," Rodrigo said softly.

He slumped against the trunk of the tree. Stephano eyed his friend with concern.

"Sit down and rest. I'll search the yacht. There must be

food and water on board." He glanced at Rodrigo. "We don't want to spend the night here, I'm thinking."

Rodrigo shivered. "With two dead men? God forbid. But I've thought of a problem, Stephano. We gave the monk our word of honor as gentlemen we wouldn't escape."

"I think he would release us from that promise," said Stephano. He was silent a moment, then said somberly, "We will have to go to the monks, tell them where to find his body."

"That means they'll arrest us again!" said Rodrigo. He looked back at the corpse lying beneath Stephano's coat and sighed. "You're right, of course. The poor fellow must have a proper burial. I suppose the monks will bury the demon, as well. We should leave them a note, tell them his name was Odhran. Strange that his armor didn't go up in flames, like the first demons we encountered."

"Good thing for us it didn't," said Stephano grimly. "The same happened with the Bottom Dwellers that died on Braffa. Their armor didn't destroy the bodies. I wonder why."

"Maybe because they're not taking time to add the magical constructs that caused it to catch fire," said Rodrigo, adding in thoughtful tones. "That could be significant."

"For what reason?" Stephano asked, trying to sound interested.

His mind was on other things, such as wandering about lost in the wilderness without food or water. He was glad to see Rodrigo thinking about something else, taking his mind off their terrifying experience. "I'm going inside the yacht to look around. Keep talking."

Stephano made his way back to the wreckage of the yacht, shifted some tree branches and climbed inside. Rodrigo's voice floated through the cracks.

"They went to great lengths to make us think they weren't human. They were fiends from hell with faces out of nightmares and bodies that were destroyed by magic fire. They wanted to demoralize, terrorize. But now they don't care. And maybe they've stopped caring because it doesn't matter anymore. The flaming corpses, the murder of the nuns, the attack on Westfirth, the destruction of the Crystal Market, the seizure of the Braffan islands and the attempt to bring down the palace—they are rushing headlong toward some dire ending."

Stephano considered this highly likely. "All the more reason I need to go ahead with my plan to take the fight to them. That assumes, of course, we're not languishing in some dungeon."

Rummaging about, he found blankets, a bag of dried sardines, complete with the heads; dried fruits that were so shriveled up he couldn't recognize them; and bread that looked as if it had been baked sometime during the Dark Ages. If this was what the monks lived on, no wonder they were so thin.

He also found a water skin filled with tepid water. He hauled his finds out of the yacht, then walked over to where Rodrigo was sitting and handed him the water skin, figuring he'd tell him about the unappetizing-looking food later.

Rodrigo took several sips of water and seemed to feel better. Some color returned to his face.

"Do you feel up to walking? We have about two hours before dark," Stephano said.

"I'm ready," said Rodrigo, rising a little unsteadily to his feet. He cast a gloomy look about. "There are certainly a *lot* of trees."

"I think that's why they call it a forest," said Stephano.

He and Rodrigo set off, gauging their direction by the sun that every so often would break through the clouds. Their progress was slow, for they had to make their way through the dense undergrowth, climbing over fallen logs, pushing through brush and bushes. Both of them were soon bruised, battered, and exhausted.

Stephano called a halt when they reached a small stream. Rodrigo built a fire, using his magic to light the kindling.

"Reminds me of being marooned on that damn island," he remarked.

He eyed the food with a shudder and said he wasn't hungry. Stephano persuaded him to eat something, to keep up their strength. They huddled near the fire, for as the sun went down, the night was growing cold.

"How far do you think we are from Eudaine?" Rodrigo asked. "How long will it take us to get there?"

"I don't know," said Stephano. "Several days? Maybe a week."

"What if we keep walking and walking and we never find our way out?"

"That's not going to happen," said Stephano.

Rodrigo pressed him. "You're certain?"

"Mostly certain," said Stephano with a smile.

Rodrigo sighed.

The woods were now dark outside the circle of the firelight, filled with shadows and strange night noises. Stephano banked the fire. They wrapped themselves in the blankets and tried to burrow down among the leaves.

"Keep talking," said Rodrigo. "Whenever I close my eyes, I see that poor monk's face. What do you think our friends are doing now?"

Dag, Miri, and Gythe had been in the alley outside Stephano's house, waiting for him and Rodrigo, who had walked into their kitchen and straight into an ambush. Their friends had watched, helpless to save them, as the monks took them away.

"They will all be sitting around the kitchen table," said Stephano. "Dag will be forming schemes to break us out of the Citadel. Miri will be fuming, sweeping, cleaning like she always does when she's upset. Gythe will be trying to keep the Doctor from licking the butter and Benoit will be telling them how he could have fought off the monks single-handed if it hadn't been for his lumbago."

Stephano smiled at the thought of the crotchety old steward.

"Maybe our friends will come looking for us . . . ," said Rodrigo with a tinge of hope in his voice.

Stephano had to squelch it.

"They won't try to find us, Rigo. Because no one knows we're lost."

2

I must confess that studying what I am forbidden to study gives me a delightful thrill of wickedness.

—Rodrigo de Villeneuve, journal

Miri was fuming, as Stephano had pictured her, bustling about, unpacking trunks, taking out Rodrigo's collection of books and stacking them on the table. She folded Stephano's baldric and carried it upstairs to his room, along with his dragon pistol and his father's sword. She was very pale when she returned.

Gythe knelt on the hearth, toasting bread over the fire. Dag sat at the table, drinking a mug of ale. Benoit was in his chair by the fire, muttering imprecations on the head of the grand bishop. The cat, Doctor Ellington, was perched on a chair, considering a raid on the butter, which sat temptingly on the edge of the table.

None of them had spoken in a long time, and the silence was tense. When Miri slammed a book down on the table; the sudden noise caused all of them to jump, and sent the cat fleeing to the pantry.

Miri rounded on Dag and fixed him with a scathing glance. "You have to *do something,* not just sit here swilling beer while Stephano and Rigo are being carried off to prison!"

"We have been over this, Miri," Dag said carefully, setting down his mug. "Just what would you have me do?"

Miri glared at him, still fuming.

"I don't know," she said. "*You're* the military man. Come up with a plan."

Dag cupped his hands around his mug and stared morosely into the dissolving foam. "We have to face the facts, Miri. There's nothing to be done. Where they've gone, we can't follow."

"I don't believe that," Miri snapped. She took the last of the books out of the trunk and began stacking them on the floor. "We've been in lots of tough situations before and we've never let one of them defeat us."

Dag raised an eyebrow. "Sir Henry left us marooned on an island."

"But we got off the island!" Miri said triumphantly. "We never gave up the fight. You've given up before this fight has even started!"

Dag was silent. Miri eyed him, exasperated, then went back to her work. She needed to keep busy. Having removed all of Rodrigo's books from the trunks, she began pulling out his shirts with the thought of washing them. She straightened and sniffed the air.

"Do you smell smoke?"

Miri turned to look at Gythe. Her sister was staring into the flames, her thoughts a world away. The bread at the end of the toasting fork was blazing merrily.

"Mercy's sakes, Gythe!" Miri gasped. "You're supposed to be toasting the bread, not burning down the house!"

Gythe opened her blue eyes wide. She thrust the flaming lump of bread into the ashes in the grate, putting out the fire. Giving Miri a small smile of apology, she went to the pantry to cut more bread.

Miri stood with her hands on her hips, staring after her. "What is wrong with that girl? She's up in the clouds somewhere."

"Same thing's wrong with her that's wrong with the rest of us," Dag muttered. "She's upset about Stephano and Rigo."

"I think it's more than that." Miri took out one of Rodrigo's shirts, frowned at it. The lace was starting to come off the cuff. She set it to one side for mending. "Here's an idea. We go to the king and plead with him for their release."

"First, the king didn't arrest them. The Church did that," said Dag. "Second, the king has no love for Stephano. His Majesty would be just as glad to let him rot. Third, we're two Trundlers and a mercenary. We couldn't get anywhere near the palace, much less gain an audience with the king. If his mother were here, she could help. But she isn't."

"It's just like the countess to disappear when we need her. Where is she?" Miri demanded in frustration. "Did Stephano know?"

Dag shook his head. "He didn't want to talk about it. Did you ask Benoit? He visits the palace and talks to her on a regular basis. Perhaps she told him something about where she was going."

Miri looked over at the elderly retainer. He sat slumped over, his head in his hands. He seemed very old, pale, and woebegone.

Miri shook her head. "This has been a shock to the poor man."

Leaving her work, she went to Benoit and rested her hand gently on his shoulder.

"Do you know anything about the Countess de Marjolaine?" she asked gently. "Where she could have gone? We need her to help Stephano."

"I tried to go to the palace to see her a few days ago

when the monks first came," Benoit said in a shaky voice. "They caught me sneaking out. There's nothing we can do. Nothing."

He groaned and closed his eyes and sat back in his chair. Miri studied him closely. Benoit was advanced in years, though his exact age was hard to determine. He had served Stephano's father, Julian de Guichen, and after his death, he had served Stephano. Benoit always claimed to be suffering from some complaint or other, generally whenever there was any work to be done. The old man could be spry enough when he chose—only a few hours ago he'd come running into the alley to tell them the terrible news about Rodrigo and Stephano.

Miri was worried about him. This time, Benoit did not appear to be malingering. His usually ruddy complexion was gray and sallow and his breathing was raspy. When she put her hand to his forehead his skin was clammy. She felt his pulse and looked over at Dag, her brows drawn together in consternation.

"What's wrong?" Dag asked softly.

"I think it's his heart!" she whispered.

Dag rose to his feet in alarm.

"Benoit, you don't look well," Miri said in coaxing tones. "Dag is going to help you to bed."

"I'm fine, truly!" Benoit said in feeble protest. "I'm just a bit short of breath. A glass of the master's brandy . . ."

"I'll bring you some brandy and a potion I want you to drink," said Miri. "Now go along with Dag."

"Maybe I will lie down . . . just for a bit," said Benoit, allowing Dag to assist him. "I need to be rested when the master and Monsieur Rodrigo return."

Dag helped the old man to his bedroom, which was on the ground floor across the hallway from the kitchen.

"Gythe, put the kettle on," Miri ordered.

Gythe did not move. She was sitting in a trancelike state, once more staring at the flames.

"Gythe!" Miri shouted.

Gythe started and dropped the toasting fork.

"Where's the bread? You've been toasting nothing but the fork! What is the matter with you?" Miri demanded.

Gythe shook her head and shrugged.

Miri gave up the argument. "Benoit's having problems with his heart. I'm going to fix him a potion and I need hot water. I want you to put the kettle on."

"Is he all right?" Gythe asked worriedly, her hands forming the words she could not speak.

"I hope so." Miri eyed the trunks that Dag had hauled into the kitchen. "Now where did I pack my herbs?"

Gythe filled the kettle. Miri located the trunk in which she had packed her herb jars wrapped for safekeeping in some of Rodrigo's handkerchiefs.

"Maybe it's a good thing Rigo's not here," Dag observed on his return. "If he knew you'd used his precious handkerchiefs to wrap up your jars, *he'd* be the one having heart palpitations."

Miri tried to smile, but without success. Dag regarded her with concern.

"I'm sorry, Miri. Honestly, I've been racking my brain trying to think of some way to help our friends. They're being taken to the dungeons in the Citadel! No one ever escapes from that terrible place. I don't see a way."

Miri tossed one of the handkerchiefs onto the laundry pile and began taking out her jars, arranging them on the kitchen counter. Each jar was neatly labeled. Finding the one marked FOXGLOVE, she carefully measured out a small portion. Gythe hung the kettle over the flames.

"We'll rescue them," said Miri, waiting for the water to boil.

Dag shook his head in exasperation. "Miri, they're not in the city jail. We'd need an army and even then—"

"Then we'll get an army!" said Miri tersely.

They waited in uncomfortable silence for the water to boil. Gythe brought over the kettle and poured the steaming water into a mug. Miri added the foxglove and other herbs and stirred them as she sang below her breath. It was an old, old song, handed down from one Trundler healer to another. Perhaps the song was magic, as Rodrigo had once theorized. Miri didn't know. All she cared about was that her healing potions worked. When her song reached the end, the potion was finished. She handed the mug to Gythe with orders that Benoit was to drink it all. He could wash it down with a bit of brandy if he liked.

Dag wrinkled his nose at the smell. "He won't drink it."

"Gythe will see to it. If anyone can get that cantankerous old man to take his medicine, she can," said Miri, wiping her hands on her apron. "And now I'll heat up more water to start the laundry. Will you haul the tub in for me? It's in the backyard. What are you doing? Let go of me!"

Ignoring her protests, Dag marched her forcibly to a chair next to his.

"Sit down. That's an order. You're exhausted. And you need to eat something."

"The laundry—"

"Will wait," said Dag. "Working yourself to death isn't going to help Stephano and Rigo."

Sitting felt good. She hadn't realized how tired she was.

"I'll rest, but only for a moment."

Dag sliced what was left of the bread. Miri began to sort through Rodrigo's books that were stacked on the table, thinking she could put them into some sort of order. Most of them had to do with magic and were so complicated she got a headache just reading the titles. One extremely thick volume was *Magic and Metaphysics, Existence, Objects and their Properties, Space and Time, Cause and Effect, and Possibility.* Another was *Magical Epistemology.* Finding one well-worn book that had no title stamped on the cover, Miri opened it, curious. The book was apparently Rodrigo's journal, for the pages were filled with his flamboyant handwriting and diagrams. He had written the title on the first page, even going so far as to embellish it was fanciful drawings. Miri stared at the title and felt her throat constrict.

"Dag, you need to see this," she said.

Hearing her altered tone, he looked up from his work. "What's wrong now?"

In answer, Miri shoved the book across the table. Dag picked it up, opened it to the first page. He shook his head, then flipped through the pages. His expression grew grim.

"Good thing the monks didn't find this!"

"What do we do with it?"

"Burn it," said Dag dourly. "And then bury the ashes."

He shoved the book back to her.

"But . . . there's a wealth of knowledge in here," said Miri, turning the pages. "Knowledge that is valuable."

"Knowledge that will get Rigo burned at the stake," Dag retorted. "If we don't burn it, we should at least hide it. You never know. The monks might come back—"

He was interrupted by the sound of wyverns screeching, the clatter and thud of carriage wheels landing on the pavement, and the voice of the coachman shouting at the wyverns. The noise came from directly outside the house. Someone knocked on the door and rang the bell. Dag reached for his pistols.

"Hide that damn book!" he ordered.

"Where?"

Miri looked around the kitchen. Finally, in desperation, she dashed into the larder and shoved the book into the flour barrel.

"Go to Benoit's bedroom," Dag told her. He loaded a pistol and handed it to her. "Stay with him and Gythe."

Miri started toward the hall on the run. The knocking continued and was now accompanied by a voice.

"Stephano, open the door!"

Miri caught her breath in relief. She knew that voice.

"It's D'argent!" she called. "What should I do?"

Dag lowered his pistol, but didn't put it away. "Find out what he wants."

Miri ran to the entry hall. She had never met the countess's man of affairs, but he had often visited Stephano and she knew him by sight. Despite being friends with Stephano for many years, no one else in the Cadre of the Lost had ever met D'argent, though they had all heard of him. Whenever D'argent came to the house, he brought a message from Stephano's mother and since her messages were generally not welcome, Stephano would meet with D'argent privately, if he chose to meet with him at all. He and Stephano and Rodrigo met upstairs in the parlor, leaving his friends downstairs in the kitchen. As Stephano had often explained, he wasn't ashamed of his friends; he was ashamed of his mother. Miri went to the front door and peered out the peephole.

D'argent wore a dark cloak. He carried a leather satchel in one hand, while he held on to his hat with the other. The rain had stopped for the moment, but the wind was brisk. The driver stood by the carriage door. The wyverns were snapping at each other.

Miri unlocked the door and opened it a crack.

"Monsieur D'argent . . ."

D'argent stared at her, startled and confused.

"I am sorry, madame. I was expecting Benoit. Is Stephano here?"

Miri hesitated, then she opened the door wide and invited D'argent inside. As he entered, looking uncertain, Miri stared intently up and down the street. The rain clouds hung low in the sky. The evening was gray and dismal. No one was out in this weather. The street was empty. She shut the door and locked it and turned back to D'argent, standing in the entry hall.

D'argent touched his tricorn hat. "You have the advantage of me, madame. I do not believe we have met."

"I am Miri, sir. Miri McPike."

D'argent smiled. "One of the Cadre of the Lost. Stephano speaks of you often. I need to talk to him and Rodrigo on a matter of some urgency—"

He noticed suddenly that she was carrying a pistol.

"What's wrong?" he asked.

"You better come with me, sir," said Miri. "I would take you to the parlor, but there's no fire. We're sitting in the kitchen. If you don't mind—"

"I will join you there," said D'argent.

"Are you certain, sir? I could light a fire . . ."

"Please, do not trouble yourself," said D'argent. "Something is wrong. Stephano is expecting me. Where is he? What has happened?"

"It's a long story, sir. Let me take your cloak and hat. I'll put them by the fire to dry out. Shall I take that?" She indicated the satchel.

"No, thank you, madame."

D'argent kept hold of the satchel and followed Miri to the kitchen.

"This is Dag Thorgrimson," said Miri, performing the introductions.

"I feel I know you, Sergeant Thorgrimson," said D'argent, advancing to shake hands.

"I feel I know you, too, sir," said Dag, frowning.

D'argent gave a wry smile. "I can well imagine what Stephano has told you about me. I am his friend, though he may not believe it." His smile vanished. "Now, tell me what is wrong. First, where is Benoit?"

"He suffered a great shock that affected his heart," said Miri. "I gave him a potion and sent him to bed. My sister, Gythe, is with him."

"The matter is not serious, is it?" D'argent asked worriedly.

"I don't think so," said Miri. She laid the pistol on the table. "He's a tough old bird."

"He is, indeed," said D'argent. "So what has become of Stephano? He hasn't gone after his mother yet, has he? I told him I would bring him the money—"

"Stephano has been arrested," said Miri.

"Arrested!" D'argent repeated, clearly stunned. "Stephano? Who arrested him? On what charge?"

"The monks of Saint Klee, sir," said Dag. "They arrested him *and* Rodrigo. The charge is heresy. They've taken them to the Arcanum."

"Heresy! Oh, my God." D'argent's tone was exceedingly grave. "This is bad. Very bad indeed. I met with them only a few hours ago. When did this happen?"

"The monks were waiting for him and Rigo here in the house, sir. They'd been holding Benoit prisoner for days. He tried to warn Stephano that it was a trap, but by that time, it was too late."

D'argent placed the satchel on the floor. "You better tell me the whole story."

Dag pulled out a chair, intending to offer it to D'argent, only to find it already occupied by Doctor Ellington. Smelling food, the cat had decided to once more favor them with his presence. Dag removed the cat, brushed cat fur off the chair, then offered it to D'argent.

Miri left to reassure Gythe and Benoit, who would have heard the commotion at the door. She returned to report that Benoit was sleeping. His breathing had improved and his pulse was stronger.

"I am relieved to hear this, at least," said D'argent. "Tell me what happened."

Dag repeated what Benoit had told him.

"Stephano guessed something was wrong. He told us to wait in the alleyway with the cart, while he and Rodrigo went inside. The last we saw, sir, the monks were taking them away in a wyvern-drawn yacht. The crest of the Arcanum was on the doors."

D'argent shook his head, baffled. "I still do not understand why he was charged with heresy!"

"According to Benoit, the monks claimed that Stephano and Rigo conspired with a priest, Father Jacob Northrop, and a Knight Protector named Sir Ander Martel to commit heresy."

"I know Sir Ander," added D'argent, now deeply troubled. "I know the reputation of Father Jacob. Both of them are good men, men of faith. I don't understand any of this."

"There was another charge involving Rodrigo, sir," said Miri. "They said he was conspiring with the enemy, Sir Henry Wallace."

"That charge is trumped up. He was Wallace's hostage," Dag added.

"But there is something else, sir. The monks don't know yet, but they might find out . . ." Miri looked at Dag. He gave a reluctant nod.

"You better see this, sir."

Miri went into the larder and returned with the book. She wiped the flour off the cover with a damp rag and handed it to D'argent. He opened the book to the first page.

Thoughts on Contramagic.

D'argent paled. "God have mercy!"

He flipped through some of the pages, pausing occasionally to read Rodrigo's notations and entries. "This is . . . this is amazing."

He looked up at Miri. "Monsieur Rodrigo writes that he devised a way to form a bridge over the ruinous contramagic spells on your boat. Is that true? Did his magic work?"

"It did, sir," said Miri. "We could not have sailed off the island otherwise. Not only that, but when we were attacked by Bottom Dwellers at the refinery where we found the crystals, the Tears of God, that you came to pick up at the dock, Rigo protected the pinnace with a magical construct that deflected the contramagic or some such thing. I don't come close to understanding."

"Thank God in heaven the monks did not find this!" D'argent said earnestly. He closed the book gently. "This would seal his fate."

"Dag is right. We should burn it," said Miri reluctantly. She picked up the volume.

"No! Wait!" D'argent cried urgently. "I've just had a thought. Give the book to me. This book might be what we need to set Rodrigo and Stephano free!"

Miri frowned and kept hold of the book. "What are you going to do with it, sir?"

"I don't plan to take it to the grand bishop, if that's what you fear," said D'argent, smiling. "I plan to take it to the king."

"I don't see how that helps, sir," said Dag. "We both know King Alaric hates Stephano."

"I wish I could tell you," said D'argent. "I am sworn to secrecy."

"You need to tell us, sir," said Miri, respectful, but firm. "Or the book goes into the fire."

D'argent hesitated. "You must tell no one."

"You can trust us, sir," said Dag with quiet dignity.

"The lift tanks that keep the palace floating in the air were sabotaged by contramagic. It is eating away at the magical constructs that charge the lift gas. The crafter engineers are doing what they can to stave off disaster, but they know nothing about contramagic. Unless a way is found to stop the contramagic, the palace will crash to the ground. The loss of life, the devastation this would cause is incalculable. Such a disaster could plunge the country into chaos."

"You have the crystals we found in Braffa, sir. You could put them in the lift tanks," Dag suggested.

"I had the same idea when Stephano first told me about them," said D'argent. "I took them to the palace. The engineers thought they would work. But when they put the crystals in the lift tanks, nothing happened. They said it was because the crystals rely on the same magical charge as the lift gas."

"You are right, sir. Rodrigo *could* help!" Miri said excitedly. "He knows how to build a construct that will bridge the contramagic. That is what he did on the *Cloud Hopper*."

"Exactly what I was thinking," said D'argent. "I will need to show the book to the king as proof."

Miri and Dag held a silent consultation, then Dag nodded and Miri handed the book to D'argent, who opened the satchel and placed the book inside.

"My only concern is that the king will free Rodrigo and not Stephano. I don't suppose Stephano was studying contramagic?" D'argent asked, half jesting and half in earnest.

"No, but I can give His Majesty a reason to free Stephano," said Dag. "He has an idea on how to carry the battle to these Bottom Dwellers, sir. An idea on how to sail down below the Breath."

"Which means Stephano ascribes to Father Jacob's theory that these people are survivors of the sinking of the island of Glasearrach," D'argent said. "Father Jacob explained this notion to the countess. She found it credible, but, let us be honest, it is just a theory. We have no proof."

"*We* have proof, sir," said Dag. "Our Gythe has talked to them."

"She talked to the Bottom Dwellers?" D'argent was amazed. "How did she do that?"

"My sister and I are Trundlers, sir," said Miri, "and she is a savant. I don't pretend to know how, but she hears their voices. They frighten her. They told her they live at the bottom of the world and that those of us who live in the world Above are to blame for their suffering."

"I fear I can hardly tell His Majesty that your Gythe hears voices," said D'argent drily. "I will tell him about Stephano's plan, however. I have an idea he might be interested in it. Can you describe his thinking to me?"

Dag did so in a few words. D'argent listened closely, asking for clarification on a few points. "I remember hearing of this battle, the Siege of the Royal Sail, for it was the last battle fought by the Dragon Brigade before it was disbanded. Where is this fortress?"

Dag gave the location. "Our crafter saw to it that the fortress survived the fall relatively intact. Good thing for me. I was inside the walls when it hit the ground."

D'argent started to close the satchel. He paused, then took out a purse that he handed to Miri.

"What is this for?" she asked suspiciously.

"You and the sergeant and your sister should go somewhere far from here. Evreux is not safe for you. The grand bishop has not had you arrested yet, but the very fact that you are in this house puts you in danger."

Dag and Miri exchanged glances.

"Thank you for your concern, sir, but we won't leave Benoit—"

"I will send the countess's personal physician to tend to him," said D'argent.

"And we won't leave without first knowing what's going to happen to our friends. Besides," Miri added with some asperity, "we can't go to our boat. The countess had it impounded."

"She rescinded the order," said D'argent with a faint smile. "You will find the *Cloud Hopper* where you customarily dock. If you won't leave the city, at least leave this house, go to the boat. I will meet you there."

"That's probably a good idea," said Dag, looking at Miri. "Especially since Gythe has been so upset. She might feel better away from here."

Miri nodded. "We'll wait for the physician and then we'll go."

"I hope to meet with His Majesty immediately, perhaps even tonight," said D'argent. "I will bring news as soon as I can."

Miri accompanied D'argent to the door.

"What about Father Jacob, sir?" she asked. "Can the king do anything to help him and Sir Ander?"

"His Majesty has no authority to intervene in Church matters. The grand bishop exerts control over them," said D'argent, shaking his head gravely. "Father Jacob has been walking a dangerous path for some time now."

Miri sighed and went to fetch D'argent's cloak and hat.

"I will give the physician a letter," D'argent told them. "Ask to see it before you allow him inside. Don't open the door to anyone else."

Miri accompanied D'argent to the carriage. Evening

had fallen and the lamplighter was making his rounds. The driver opened the door and D'argent entered. Then the driver mounted his box, plied the whip and worked the magic that caused the carriage to rise. On his command, the wyverns clawed their way into the air. Miri watched the lights of the carriage disappear swiftly among the low-hanging clouds. She looked again up and down the sidewalk, dark now except for the pools of light shining from the streetlamps.

She reported back to Dag. "I didn't see anyone."

"You wouldn't," said Dag grimly. "You don't see the monks of Saint Klee unless they want you to see them. I think D'argent is right. We should leave. We're not safe."

He shut the door and locked it. They returned to the kitchen. Miri started to pack up her herb jars back into the trunk. Dag stopped her.

"We can't take anything with us. We'll have to go on foot, make sure we're not being followed."

"You're right, of course," said Miri. "I wasn't thinking."

She bleakly looked around at the clothes she'd meant to wash, some hanging over the backs of chairs, others in a pile on the floor. The books were scattered over the table, along with mugs and plates, silverware and cutlery.

"You go stay with Benoit," said Miri. "Send Gythe to me. At least I'll leave this place clean for Stephano and Rigo. When . . . when they come home."

Her voice caught in her throat and her lips quivered. She picked up one of Rodrigo's shirts and stood smoothing the fabric. Dag said nothing, but she felt his hand rest on her shoulder. His touch lasted only a moment; relations between them were still strained and probably always would be.

"They'll come home, Miri," said Dag.

She felt comforted. She drew in a breath and managed a smile. "I know they will."

Dag went to fetch Gythe. Miri hung the kettle over the fire and while she was waiting for the water to boil she began to fold shirts. Gythe came to help her and reported that Benoit was still asleep. His breathing was now normal and some color had returned to his cheeks.

The physician arrived just as Miri finished washing the dishes. He presented the letter from D'argent, and Miri escorted him to Benoit's room. The physician examined Benoit, listened to his heart. Miri described the potion she had given him.

"You administered the proper treatment," said the physician. "I do not think the heart has been damaged. The patient experienced palpitations due to the shock. With rest and continued care he should soon be able to return to his duties. I propose that we take him to the hospital and keep him there for a few days. The nuns will care for him."

Miri was disposed to think highly of the physician, especially since he had approved her treatment. She was reluctant to abandon Benoit, even though she knew nothing would please the old man more than lying in a hospital bed all day, ordering the poor nuns about.

"I don't like to think of leaving him to the care of strangers," she said to Gythe. "I believe we should stay."

Gythe took hold of Miri's hand, squeezed it tightly and began to gesture.

"We have to go to the boat, sister!" Gythe said. "I am afraid to stay here. The monks will come for us! We should leave now. Please, Miri, I want to go home!"

Miri stared at Gythe worriedly, taken aback by her sister's outburst. Gythe was truly frightened. Miri could feel her sister trembling.

"All right, Gythe. We'll go back to the *Hopper*. Hush, child, don't fret."

Gythe nodded and suddenly flung her arms around

Miri and hugged her tightly. Then she turned away and began to adjust the coverlet, drawing it snugly over Benoit's shoulders to prepare him for his trip to the hospital.

When the horse-drawn carriage arrived, Dag lifted the old man and placed him inside. Miri tucked blankets around him. Benoit slept through the entire procedure. The physician settled in by Benoit's side and Miri kissed the old man on the forehead. She watched as the carriage rolled down the street, moving slowly so as not to jar the patient.

Miri folded the clothes and put them back into the trunks as Dag packed away Rodrigo's books, then Gythe laid a protective magical construct over the trunks. Miri carried the clean dishes to the pantry, where she found Doctor Ellington with telltale traces of gravy from the remains of the meat pie on his whiskers. Miri handed the cat to Dag. Taking the lamp, she made a final tour of the house to see that all was right.

Dag and Gythe and the Doctor waited for her outside the back door. Miri stood in the shadowy kitchen.

"We were going to come home and everything was going to be right. And now everything's gone horribly wrong," Miri said softly.

She blew out the lamp, set it on the kitchen table, and joined the others. Turning the key in the lock, she handed the key to Dag, who hid it behind a loosened brick in the wall. Wrapped in dark cloaks, the three slipped out of the garden and into the alley.

The clouds had rolled away over the distant mountains. The stars gleamed, and the full moon was so bright they could see their own shadows.

The three walked in silence, none of them in the mood for talking. Miri and Gythe moved quietly, their leather slippers making almost no noise. The sound of Dag's heavy boots crunching on the gravel seemed to reverberate through the night. Seeing Miri wince, Dag grimaced and shrugged. There wasn't much he could do.

Miri was worried about Gythe. She walked with her arms folded beneath her cloak, her head down, paying no attention to where she was going. She would have fallen into a trench filled with water if Miri hadn't caught her and dragged her around it. Gythe cast her sister a grateful glance and smiled. Something about Gythe's smile made Miri uneasy.

She took hold of her sister's hand. "Tell me what is wrong, Gythe. You can tell me anything. You know that."

Gythe's eyes were shadowed with sorrow. She slid her hand out of her sister's grasp and hurried on ahead.

Miri's heart ached. Gythe had never before kept secrets from her. She had changed so much, Miri hardly knew her. She was no longer the hurt and fearful child. She was a "woman grown" as Dag had once said, making her own decisions, leading her own life.

She wondered if Gythe still fancied herself to be in love with Brother Barnaby. Such a love was hopeless, as Miri had often tried to point out. The monk was deeply committed to God. Miri shook her head. Hopefully Gythe would soon come to her senses, forget this nonsense about being in love.

The alley brought them to Haymarket Street, which would lead them by a meandering route to the harbor where the *Cloud Hopper* was docked. As they were leaving the alley, Miri cast a brief glance over her shoulder. She caught a glimpse of movement, a shadow seen and then gone.

"Dag! Someone's following us!" Miri whispered.

"Hush! I saw them," Dag said quietly. He took hold of her arm and propelled her forward. "Keep moving."

3

I cannot ignore their silent pleas.

—Gythe McPike

Miri left their route to Dag, who always laughingly boasted that he kept a map of Evreux in his head. He knew every street, every side street, every byway and alleyway and how they all connected. He led them to the harbor by a circuitous way that he hoped would throw off their pursuers, all the while behaving innocently, as though he had no idea they were being pursued.

Miri was familiar with the major thoroughfares, the area around Stephano's house and around the docks, but that was the extent of her knowledge. She was soon lost amid the tall buildings, the tangle of alleys, mewses, parks and courtyards. She could tell by the moon and stars that although they often veered off in one direction or another, they kept moving south, toward the harbor.

"I think we lost them," Dag said finally.

They had stopped about a block from the *Cloud Hopper.* They stood in the shadows of a warehouse, taking the precaution of observing the boat before they approached.

"Who was following us? The monks?"

Dag shook his head in perplexity. "If it was the monks,

they wanted us to know we were being followed. The monks of Saint Klee would have never been so careless as to let us spot them."

"Who else could it be?" Miri asked.

Dag gave a wry smile. "Maybe a jealous husband looking for Rigo."

"I'm serious," Miri said irritably.

"Honestly, I don't know, Miri," Dag said with that overly patient tone that made her want to hit him. "Whoever it was, we've lost them."

Miri sighed. "I'm sorry I snapped at you. It's just . . . I'm tired of this way of life, Dag. I used to think our adventures were fun and exciting. Not anymore. Everything that's happened lately—being stranded on that island, fighting for our lives at that refinery, and now Stephano and Rigo gone, maybe forever." She shivered. "I am afraid all the time. I don't want to live in fear."

"This has been hard on all of us," Dag said.

"Has it?" Miri retorted, adding bitterly, "You and Stephano seem to thrive on dodging bullets. One day one of them is going to find you. I don't want to be around when that happens."

Dag said nothing. He petted the Doctor on his shoulder to keep him from howling and kept watching the *Cloud Hopper.* Gythe linked arms with her sister, resting her cheek on Miri's shoulder in silent sympathy and looked at her with eyes that seemed to plead for her to understand.

Understand what? Miri had no idea and she was too tired and upset to delve deeper into one of her sister's fey moods.

The street that ran along the dock was lined with warehouses and businesses that provided services used by the boats and barges that plied the channel. The streets were busy during the day, nearly empty at night. The sounds of laughter and music could be heard, coming from one of the taverns.

Moonlight bathed the boat, washed out all the hull's bright colors. The sails were down, the balloon hung limply from its tethers. If anyone had sneaked on board, the person was hiding in the darkness.

Gythe tugged on Miri's sleeve, pointing to her feet and to her belly. "My feet hurt from walking. I'm tired and hungry."

"*You're* the one who set the bread on fire," Miri reminded her crossly.

Gythe made a face, pursing her lips and thrusting out her chin, mimicking a child's pout. Miri couldn't help but smile.

"I doubt there's any food on board," she said. "The constables probably ate everything."

Gythe looked so horrified that Miri began to laugh. She was pleased to see Gythe behaving much more like her old self.

"I think it's safe," Dag announced.

Miri eyed him. "You say it's safe and yet you're checking to make certain your pistols are loaded."

"I'm only taking sensible precautions, Miri," Dag answered. "You two should wait while I go ahead—"

"It's my boat," Miri stated. "If there's danger, I'll deal with it. Come along, Gythe."

She crossed the street, the wind ruffling her cloak behind her. Gythe ran after her. Dag, sighing, hurried to keep up with them, his boots thudding on the pavement.

Miri examined the *Cloud Hopper,* worried that her beloved boat might have been damaged while it was in the impound yard. Her gaze went to the masts, the furled sails, the sagging balloon. Everything appeared to be shipshape. In fact, as she drew closer, she could smell the odor of fresh paint and she saw that their old patched balloon had been replaced with a new one. Miri sniffed. She supposed the countess meant the repairs as an apology. Miri was not inclined to be mollified.

"You stay here with Dag," she told Gythe.

Gathering up her skirt, Miri jumped nimbly from the dock onto the deck, deaf to Dag's pleas for her to lower the gangplank so that he could board and search the boat.

Miri walked the familiar deck, glad to be home. Placing her hands on her hips, she called out, "If anyone is hiding on my boat, you better show yourself now! I warn you. I'm not in the mood for more surprises this night!"

She lit the lamp that hung on a hook over the binnacle. With the lamp in one hand and a belaying pin in the other, she went down the stairs that led below deck. She shined the light into the cabin shared by Rodrigo, Stephano, and Dag when they were aboard, then searched the cabin she shared with Gythe and inspected the galley and the storage room.

Returning to the upper deck, she lowered the gangplank.

"No one lurking about," she reported to Dag as he came on board. "You can put your pistols away."

He cast her an exasperated glance, but was wise enough to keep his mouth shut. Dropping the Doctor onto the deck, Dag clumped down the stairs, probably going to see for himself. The cat dug his claws into the wood, stretched, and took a turn around the deck.

"The larder's stocked with more food than we can eat in a year," she told Gythe, as her sister came on board.

Gythe stood gazing around in amazement, taking in the fresh paint and the new sail. "Who did this?"

"The countess, I suppose," said Miri. "Her way of apologizing."

"Countesses don't apologize," Dag said, coming back on deck. "Not to people like us."

"Find anyone hiding under the beds?" Miri asked archly.

Dag gazed at her a moment, then shook his head. He was obviously upset with her, but, as usual, he was going to keep his anger bottled up inside. Dag had to understand. The *Cloud Hopper* was her boat, her responsibility.

"Gythe, haul up the gangplank," she said.

"What about D'argent?" Gythe signed worriedly.

"It's too late for him to come tonight. I'll fix us something to eat. Dag, you'll find your bedding and some of your clothes in your cabin."

She was heading below and Gythe was about to draw in the gangplank when they heard the sounds of horses' hooves and the rattle of a carriage driving over cobblestones. The carriage pulled up in front of the *Cloud Hopper.* Before the driver could reach the door it opened and D'argent sprang out.

"Good news!" he called.

"About time," Miri said, trying to sound curt. She had trouble keeping her voice from quivering. "Come on board, sir. Gythe, fetch the Calvados."

D'argent hurried up the gangplank. The night was warm, the air still. They sat at the table on the deck beneath the stars, the mists of the Breath curling around them.

Gythe brought the bottle of the famed Trundler liquor. Dag carried mugs. D'argent politely refused Miri's offer to dine with them, saying he still had work to do and he had to return to the palace. He did accept a glass of Calvados.

"God knows I need this," he said. He seated himself, took off his hat, and rested it on his knee. He raised his glass. "A drink to His Highness, Prince Alaric Renaud."

"Why are we drinking to him?" Miri asked.

"Without His Highness, I would most likely be the bearer of bad news," said D'argent. "I will tell you what happened. Upon arriving at the palace, I sent a message to His Majesty, saying I needed to meet with him on a matter of the utmost urgency. The king granted me an audience. When I arrived in the audience chamber His Majesty was not alone. Prince Renaud was there, as well."

"The prince is lord admiral of the navy," said Dag, frowning in puzzlement. "Why was he there?"

"His Majesty is under a great strain," D'argent replied gravely. "If the countess were here . . ."

D'argent did not elaborate. He had no need. They knew enough of palace intrigue from Rodrigo to fill in the words he had not spoken. Alaric needed someone to tell him what to do. He generally turned to the countess. Since she was not here, he had summoned his son.

D'argent continued. "I explained to King Alaric how Rodrigo had come up with this method for bridging the damage caused by the contramagic. I showed him the book, Rodrigo's drawings and notations. His Majesty was appalled and shocked by the very thought of using contramagic, and at first refused to look at them."

D'argent sighed and toyed with his glass of Calvados. "To speak bluntly, the king is overwhelmed. He did not believe in the existence of the Bottom Dwellers or contramagic. He has since learned that contramagic is about to bring down his palace and that the Bottom Dwellers are responsible."

"How did he find out about the Bottom Dwellers?" Dag asked.

"His Highness is, as you say, lord admiral in charge of the northern fleet. Somewhere between Rosia and Travia, his flagship, the *Hornet,* became separated from the rest of the fleet in a thick fog. Catching a single ship alone, the Bottom Dwellers apparently thought they had found easy prey, for they attacked with only a small force. Too late they learned they were attacking a royal naval flagship. The battle was short. The *Hornet* killed or drove off the enemy and even managed to capture one alive. The prisoner talked proudly of his people, how they lived at the bottom of the world, how their leader, a man named Saint Xavier, was destined by God to destroy us."

Miri looked at Gythe. The Bottom Dwellers had told her much the same. She should be smiling in triumph, saying, "I told you so!"

Gythe didn't seem to have heard. Doctor Ellington had jumped in her lap and she was stroking his fur and gazing vacantly at the boardwalk shining silver in the moonlight.

Where is she? Miri wondered. What is wrong with her?

I'll give her a dose of cod liver oil before bed, Miri decided, and turned her attention back to D'argent.

"Prince Renaud studied Rodrigo's drawings. The prince is a crafter, a rather gifted one. He understood at once that Rodrigo's plan to save the palace could work. Encouraged, I told him about Stephano's idea to renovate the old Fort Ignacio and sail it Below, carry the war to the Bottom Dwellers. His Highness knows Stephano from the days of the Dragon Brigade and spoke quite highly of him. I had heard from the countess that the prince did not agree with his father's decision to disband the Brigade. Be that as it may, the prince is intrigued by the plan."

"So what was decided?" Miri asked eagerly.

"Prince Renaud is a cold, dispassionate man; a man of wisdom and intelligence. In that, he takes after his grandfather," D'argent added with a wry smile. "The prince persuaded His Majesty to write a letter to the grand bishop, urging him in the strongest words possible to free Rodrigo and Stephano."

"A letter? Is that all?" Miri was dismayed.

"Mistress Miri, that is everything," said D'argent, smiling. He picked up his hat and rose to his feet. "And now I must return to the palace to wait for the letter so that I can arrange for its immediate delivery. Thank you for your hospitality."

He was walking down the gangplank, when he turned back to speak to them. "I forgot to mention. I have news of Benoit. He is resting comfortably, so you need not worry about him. I again urge you to leave the city. The grand bishop won't receive the letter until tomorrow at the earliest. You might still be in danger."

"We plan to leave at dawn," said Miri. "Not safe to sail at night."

"Likely you'll see Stephano before we will," Dag added. "Tell him we'll meet him at the fortress. If something goes wrong, you can send a message to us there."

D'argent promised he would. He wished them a safe journey and took his leave. Miri gazed after him, her brows drawn together, her lips pursed in a frown.

"Nothing but a letter." She shook her head in disappointment. "Seems the king could do better—issue a writ or a decree or something."

"There's politics behind it," said Dag. "You can be sure of that."

"You think they'll be set free?" Miri was dubious.

"D'argent seems to think so and he should know. God knows I don't," Dag said.

Gythe lifted the Doctor from her lap and handed the cat to Dag.

"I'm going to fetch supper," she signed. "The larder is filled with good food for a change."

She smiled at Miri to let her know she was teasing.

Miri offered to help, but Gythe told her to rest. She served cheese, apples and figs, dried beef, and ale. The cheese was Guundaran, imported. The figs came from the Aligoes Islands. The ale was excellent—nut brown and slightly bitter. Dag drank two mugs of it, proposing a toast to D'argent and another to absent friends.

Gythe went below soon after eating, saying she was going to wash up. Miri watched her go with concern.

"She nibbled at her food and barely touched her ale," said Miri.

"She's worried about our friends," said Dag. "I'll take first watch."

Even as he spoke, he gave a great, jaw-cracking yawn.

"You haven't had a good night's rest in a month," said Miri. "I'll keep watch. You go to bed. I can't sleep anyway. Something's wrong with Gythe. There's that monk, Brother Barnaby. She claims she hears him talking to her. You know she thinks she's in love with him."

"You need Rigo for help with such stuff as that, Miri," said Dag, clearly uneasy. He yawned again. "I guess I will turn in. Wake me when you need me to take over."

Miri promised she would. Dag hauled in the gangplank and then clomped down the stairs. She heard him rummaging about the cabin, arranging the pallet on which he slept. Unlike Stephano and Rodrigo, Dag didn't like sleeping in hammocks. After a while, she heard his rumbling snore.

Miri went to the galley to help Gythe with the washing up. Instead she found her sister asleep, snuggled in bed with Doctor Ellington draped over her feet.

Miri smiled and washed the dishes. Going back on deck, she sat down in a chair in the moonlight. The *Cloud Hopper* was securely moored with ropes aft and forward. The air was calm, fresh-washed after the rain. The boat rocked slightly with the faint eddies and currents of the Breath.

Miri had assumed that worry and anxiety would keep her awake and she was startled to rouse from a nap she had never meant to take. She didn't feel well. Her head seemed to swell. Her hands and feet tingled. She stood up to go wake Dag, but she was sick and dizzy and couldn't walk straight. She staggered across the deck, fetching up against the helm.

She clung to the brass panel, trying to keep herself upright. She knew dimly that she'd been drugged and she fought against the effects of the narcotic as long as possible.

She lost her grip on the brass panel and her hold on consciousness at the same time.

Gythe lay in bed, staring into the darkness, making herself wait until she was sure the potion she had mixed into the ale had done its work. The potion was harmless—some herbs and a little song, sung beneath her breath, that would induce sleep. The bitter taste of the ale concealed the taste of the herbs. Judging by the sound of his snoring, the potion had worked on Dag.

Gythe worried about Miri, who had not drunk that much ale. She listened closely, and when she could no longer hear her sister stirring about on deck she decided she had waited long enough.

She gently moved the Doctor, petting him to keep him quiet. The cat grumbled, but didn't wake. Gythe put on her soft slippers, then donned her clothes—the traditional Trundler garb of pantaloons and skirt and blouse. She stealthily slipped on deck, fearful of finding Miri awake and angry.

She found Miri asleep on the deck beneath the helm. Gythe gazed at her sister and her eyes filled with tears. She resolutely blinked them away. Lighting the lamp, she held it high and swung it back and forth three times. She waited, then swung the lamp three more times. Staring intently into the darkness, she saw an answering light, moving back and forth.

She hung the lamp on its hook and ran back downstairs. She gave the Doctor a blessing and a kiss on the top of his head. Stopping at the door to Dag's cabin, she drew a good luck sigil on it, silently thanked him and begged his forgiveness.

The sound of hoofbeats sent her hurrying up on deck. Three men on horseback waited in front of the boat. One of the men dismounted and walked closer, watching her expectantly.

Gythe was suddenly terrified, and couldn't move. Her heart seemed to fill her throat. The man was wearing a cloak, but she could see beneath it glimpses of the demonic armor worn by the Bottom Dwellers. Gythe stared at him, trembling so she had to put her hand on the table to support herself.

The man was not wearing a helm. His face glimmered white in the moonlight. His eyes were dark. His hair was long and lank and might have been red in color, though the moonlight made it seem gray.

"You are Gythe," the man said.

He spoke the Trundler language, though with an odd accent. The words sounded thicker, older.

Gythe managed a little nod.

"I am Patrick. Brother Barnaby sent me."

At the sound of the monk's name, Gythe felt her fear ease.

"Are you ready?" the man asked. "We should not linger."

His voice was deep and harsh, but she was no longer afraid of him. Gythe bent over Miri and kissed her. Her tears fell on Miri's face. She reached into her pocket, took out the note she had written, and laid it on the deck beside Miri.

"I am sorry! I am so sorry. I hope you understand!" Gythe told her sister silently.

Patrick gave an impatient cough. Gythe rose to her feet.

She did not lower the gangplank, but jumped nimbly from the boat to the dock.

"You will ride pillion with me," he told her.

Gythe nodded to show she understood. Brother Barnaby must have told the men she was mute, for Patrick didn't seem surprised that she didn't audibly respond. He picked her up and was about to lift her onto his saddle.

"Let her go!" Miri ordered, her voice slurring. "Or I will blow off your head."

Gythe turned to see her sister clinging to the rail with one hand and aiming a pistol at them with the other. The pistol wavered in her shaking hand.

"She thinks you're abducting me!" Gythe signed frantically. "Let me go to her. I'll explain—"

"There is no time!" said Patrick.

"She *will* shoot you!" Gythe clutched at him, trying to make him understand. "Please!"

"Go on then. But be quick."

Gythe ran to the boat. Miri kept the pistol aimed at the men.

"Come back on board—"

"Miri, stop!" Gythe pleaded. She pointed at the men and then placed her hand on her heart. "You are wrong. You don't understand. They came to fetch me. I have agreed to go with them."

Miri slowly lowered the gun. She stared, bewildered, and then shook her head violently. Her red hair was as dark as blood in the moonlight. She dropped the pistol onto the deck and made a clumsy leap off the boat for the dock. Gythe caught hold of her and steadied her. Miri clung tightly to her, digging her nails into her arm.

"You're not going!" Miri said thickly. "I won't let you!"

Gythe shook her head and gently wrested her arm out of her sister's grasp.

"You can't stop me. Our people need me. They need

my magic. They need my songs," Gythe signed, putting her fingers to her lips.

"Then I'm coming with you," said Miri.

"We have no time to waste, Gythe," said Patrick angrily. "Leave her."

"I'll scream for the constables!" Miri said shakily. "I'll wake up the city. Take me with you or I'll scream bloody murder."

"Bring her, then, if she wants to go," said one of the men impatiently. "Just be quick about it!"

Miri took a step, staggered and fell. Gythe helped her walk to the horses, and one of the men lifted Miri into the saddle. She was limp, her head lolling, the drug taking hold again. The man called Patrick mounted, then pulled Gythe up to sit behind him. The men spurred their horses and galloped down the street.

Gythe looked back at the *Cloud Hopper.* Poor Dag. He would wake up alone with no idea what had happened. She sighed, then turned away.

They rode most of the night. Leaving Evreux, they struck out along an old rocky coastal road, now seldom used. Travelers preferred the new toll road that had been constructed to connect the capital to the northern provinces. Gythe jounced on the horse's bony backside and soon came to envy her sister, who had fallen into a drugged sleep and was feeling no pain. They reached their destination as the sun's light was just beginning to turn the sky gray. The men reined in their horses on a bluff overlooking the shoreline. Below was a small military encampment.

A ship was moored there: one of the strangest looking sailing vessels Gythe had ever seen. The ship was half again as wide as a cargo vessel, with two full decks and a forward half deck. A double row of masts allowed for the heavy ship to carry six balloons—three main lift balloons and three smaller balloons for ballast. Open hatches provided access to the lower deck.

A large number of people were gathered on the dock. Many were soldiers, wearing the demonic armor. Others were apparently prisoners, huddled together in a group apart from the soldiers, their hands bound.

"That is the ship that will carry us Below," Patrick said, helping Gythe dismount. "A troop transport."

Miri was awake now, staring around in bewilderment. She suddenly twisted, turning to search fearfully for Gythe. Catching sight of her sister, Miri half jumped and half fell out of the saddle and started to run to her.

"Gythe! Don't be a fool! Don't let them take you!" Miri cried.

"Keep her quiet!" Patrick cautioned.

Gythe caught hold of her sister and put her fingers to Miri's lips. Gythe pointed to the troops gathered on the shoreline beneath the rise.

"They must not see us!" she signed.

Miri stared at the soldiers in a daze, not seeming to comprehend. She looked back at her sister. "Where are we? Who are these men? What is going on?" Her voice rose with each sentence.

Distressed, Gythe once more touched Miri's lips, begging her to speak softly. Patrick watched this exchange, then came over to deal with the situation himself. Miri drew back, regarding him with cold hostility.

"Go away! Leave us alone," she told him.

He ignored her and spoke to Gythe.

"I will tell the guards you and your sister are savants. Xavier decreed that we are to round up savants, bring them Below. I think Brother Barnaby explained this to you."

"Brother Barnaby!" Miri sucked in an angry breath. "So you are running away to meet him! I might have known."

Gythe looked at her sister helplessly, not knowing how to explain.

The other men were growing nervous.

"Patrick, they're starting to load the ship. We have to go."

"If these two are going to cause trouble, leave them," another said angrily.

"There is still time for you to change your mind, Gythe," Patrick said. "I can give you one of the horses—"

Miri seized Gythe's hand. "We will go home. Won't we, Gythe?"

Gythe couldn't move, unnerved by the sight of the ugly, strange-looking ship with its many balloons and double row of masts and the cries of the prisoners in chains. She was suddenly appalled, aghast at what she was doing. She wanted to hide her face in Miri's skirt, as she had done when she was a child in trouble. She wanted to go home, wanted to feel safe and protected in her sister's sheltering embrace.

But she had promised Brother Barnaby she was coming. He had tried to dissuade her. When he had described the suffering of the people of Glasearrach, he had not meant for her to come help them. That had been her decision. Her people needed her. She could do something good with her life.

On the dock below, the sailors were starting to prepare the ship for sailing, singing an old Trundler sea chantey.

Oh, have you heard the news, me Johnny
One more day
We're homeward bound tomorrow
One more day

The song was an old, old song, one sung for generations. Their songs were her songs: the songs she hummed to keep up her courage, the songs she had taught to Brother

Barnaby when he was afraid and in pain. The songs bound her to her people. They needed her help. She had promised she would come.

Gythe gave Miri a gentle kiss.

"I must go. I am sorry," she said, touching her heart.

She withdrew her hand from Miri's grasp and walked over to stand beside Patrick.

Miri stood dumbstruck. She tried to speak, but her words clotted on her tongue. Gythe couldn't bear to see the pain and she turned away.

"Here, mistress," said Patrick, handing the reins of his horse to Miri, "you can ride back—"

"I won't leave her," Miri said, her voice trembling with her resolve. "You are my sister, Gythe. If you are determined to go, I want to go with you."

Patrick looked to Gythe. "It's up to you, mistress."

"We are both coming," Gythe signed, taking hold of Miri's hand.

Patrick cast a dark glance at Miri, apparently not pleased, but there wasn't much he could do. He took a length of rope from his saddle and cut off two long pieces.

"You and your sister must appear to be our prisoners."

Gythe held out her hands. Patrick tied the rope around her wrists, binding them tightly. He went over to Miri, who flushed in anger and was about to refuse, until she caught Gythe's eye. Miri bit her lip and held out her hands.

"Obey the guards," Patrick instructed them. "If you cause trouble, the guards will beat you. I can't do anything to help. I would be putting your lives and mine in danger. You understand?"

Gythe indicated she did. Patrick lifted her onto the horse. He picked up Miri, seated her behind Gythe. Taking the reins, he led the horse down the hill toward the camp and the waiting ship. A soldier caught sight of them and hastened toward them, his weapon raised at the sight of the Patrick and his men who were still wearing their cloaks.

Patrick drew aside his cloak, revealing his armor. The soldier lowered his weapon.

"What is this?" the soldier asked, frowning. "More prisoners?"

"Savants," said Patrick. "By order of our blessed saint."

"Send them with the rest."

The other prisoners were being loaded onto the boat. Patrick escorted Miri and Gythe to the gangplank that extended from the dock to the ship, spanning the Breath.

"Where are they taking us, Gythe?" Miri asked as they crossed the gangplank. "Where is this ship bound?"

Gythe looked down over the edge of the plank that spanned the emptiness between shore and ship. The mists of the Breath swirled and eddied in pale silken colors of orange and pink. Far below the mists the Breath thickened to gray fog, cold and blinding. Far below that lay the sunken island of Glasearrach.

Gythe looked back at her sister.

No need to say more.

Dag woke to blinding, eye-searing sunlight and a feeling that his head was stuffed with cotton wool. His mouth was so dry his throat hurt. After a few failed tries he managed to stand upright, bumping into the walls as though the boat was heaving and rocking.

He couldn't imagine what was wrong. He would have said he had the king of all hangovers, but he had drunk only two mugs of ale.

"The countess buys only the best," he muttered to himself.

The boat bobbed gently with the morning breeze. Dag paused to steady himself before he attempted to climb the three stairs that led to the deck above. He navigated those and stumbled out into the sunlight.

He squinched his eyes to see against the dazzling sun. The boat was still moored to the dock.

Odd, he thought, Miri had wanted to sail with the dawn.

"Miri," he called, wincing as pain shot through his head. "I'm sorry I didn't take my turn at watch. You should have wakened me—"

He stopped talking and peered around. Miri should have been shouting at him, punching him in the arm, calling him a lazy slug and other things not so nice. The only sounds he heard were the voices of the workers on their way to the warehouses and shipyards.

"Miri?"

When Dag finally managed to open his eyes without squinting, he saw that he was the only one on deck, except for Doctor Ellington. The cat wound around Dag's ankles and meowed loudly, announcing that it was past time someone fed him. Dag picked up the cat, so as not to step on him, and put him on his shoulder.

Miri had been exhausted. Thinking that she had given up keeping watch and gone to bed, Dag went back down below. The corridor seemed pitch dark after the bright light above. Groaning with the pain in his head, he made his way along the corridor to the cabin where Gythe and Miri slept.

The door was open, slightly swinging back and forth with movement of the boat. Dag looked inside. The bed was empty, the sheets rumpled, the blanket thrown about. A cold draft of fear ran through Dag's veins, acting better than any elixir to clear his head. Miri hated an unmade bed worse than spiders.

"Miri! Gythe!" Dag's voice echoed through the boat.

No one answered. The Doctor meowed loudly and jumped from Dag's shoulder. The cat ran to the galley, where the smoked fish was kept. Dag followed, his fear catching in his throat. He looked into the galley, telling himself he would find Miri and Gythe there, though he knew perfectly well he wouldn't.

The galley was empty. The Doctor hopped onto the barrel of smoked fish. Dag took the hint and fed the cat, then searched the boat again. Miri and Gythe were gone. Going back on deck, he noticed what he should have noticed immediately. A pistol, lying on the deck near the rail.

Dag examined the weapon. The pistol was loaded, but had not been fired. He knew now with a sick feeling in his gut that something terrible had happened to Miri and Gythe during the night.

They'd been abducted. He'd been drugged. That was the reason for the pounding head and the fact that he had slept like a dead man.

But who had taken them? Had the monks come during the night to arrest Gythe and Miri? That made no sense. How would the monks have managed to slip the drug into his ale? They were stealthy, not invisible! And why arrest the women and leave him?

Dag thought back to the mysterious, shadowing pursuers who had followed them from Stephano's house. He had assumed he had lost them, but perhaps he hadn't. He searched the deck, thinking he might find another clue, and discovered a note.

His name and Miri's name were written on the front.

Dag stared at it in wonder. He recognized the handwriting—Gythe's childish scrawl. Few Trundlers could read or write. Miri, being a loremaster for her people, had taught herself to read and she had insisted her sister learn. The moment Miri would bring out the lesson books, Gythe would disappear. Miri had waged a constant battle trying to teach her sister and had finally given up. Gythe knew the rudiments of both reading and writing, but that was about all that could be said.

With a shaking hand Dag picked up the note and opened it. He sat down, trying to puzzle out the message. Gythe had never bothered to learn punctuation.

I hope the potion did no harm I have gone where I am needed you cannot follow so don't try go to abby sant agnes you are needed pleese forgive me I luv you both not forgetting the Doctor and Stefano and Rigo luv Gythe

He let the note slip through his fingers to the deck. He could make a pretty good guess as to what must have happened. Gythe had drugged both him and Miri in order to sneak off the boat during the night. Miri must have wakened, grabbed the pistol, and gone after Gythe.

He lowered the gangplank and went out into the street to try to pick up their trail. He found signs that horses had waited out in front of the boat. He gazed up and down the street that was crowded with horse-drawn carriages, riders on horseback, horses pulling wagons. He gave a snort and returned dejectedly to the boat.

Dag had to face the brutal truth. He couldn't find them. He had no way of knowing where they were. If they were on horseback, they had a long head start. They could be anywhere in Rosia by now.

He picked up the note, read it again and again.

The Abbey of Saint Agnes. Gythe told him to go there. He "was needed." Dag didn't want to leave Evreux now, fearing he might miss Gythe and Miri if they came back. Then again, the Abbey was his only clue. Perhaps Gythe was traveling there and she wanted him to meet her. As for what had become of Miri, he had no idea. Hopefully she was with Gythe and they were both safe.

Dag pulled up the gangplank and raised the sails. He shouted at a passerby, who obligingly cast off the ropes for him. Taking his place at the helm, Dag put his hands on the constructs, sending magical energy into the lift tanks and the balloon. He steered the *Cloud Hopper* down the channel and out into the Breath, heading southward toward the ill-fated Abbey of Saint Agnes.

4

Sleeping on the ground in the forest, I hear the growls and see the eyes of predators watching me from the darkness. I might as well be back in the palace.

—Cecile Raphael, Countess de Marjolaine

The Countess Cecile de Marjolaine was one of the wealthiest, most powerful people in all the courts of all the nations of the world. Her network of agents was second only to that of Sir Henry Wallace, spymaster of Freya. She was whispered to be the shadow ruler of Rosia. King Alaric generally did what she advised him to do. Those times he acted against her advice and willfully pursued his own course of action, he came to regret it.

Cecile resided in a suite of elegant rooms in the royal palace given to her by the king. She lived in the palace eleven months out of the year, traveling to her family estate and spending one month in the summer there to manage her business affairs, meet with her steward and her tenants, and escape the heat of the city. At the age of fifty she was still considered one of the most beautiful women in Rosia. Her exquisite gowns were copied by women from Rosia to Travia, her hair was always perfectly coiffed, and her magnificent collection of jewelry was legendary.

Cecile thought of all this as she sat in the post chaise traveling at breakneck speed along the highway, expecting at every moment that they would overturn. Her cloak was wet, mud spattered and travel worn. The plain, serviceable woolen gown she had chosen to wear was in need of a good scrubbing, as was its mistress.

She had not had time for a proper bath in the week since this journey had begun. She had been forced to bathe in the washbasins of the inns along the route, giving herself what her old nursemaid would have called "a lick and a promise." Her hair was twisted into a braid, wound up, and pinned in the back beneath a wide-brimmed hat, a hat that was anything but fashionable, but well designed to protect from the elements. And her only jewelry was a plain gold band on her left hand.

Her companion was a Knight Protector, Sir Conal O'Hairt. They rode in pursuit of a woman named Eiddwen, a practitioner of blood magic also known to the Arcanum as the "Sorceress"; her supposed nephew, the Conte Osinni, a murderer whose hands were steeped in blood; and Sophia, princess of Rosia, a fifteen-year-old girl who fancied herself in love.

Cecile and Sir Conal had been following the three for what seemed an eternity of days and nights, shaken and jounced in the small, lightweight post chaise, the fastest conveyance for traveling overland.

Cecile was both pleased and amazed that they were still on Eiddwen's trail. She had been surprised to discover Eiddwen and her companions were making the journey by road when they could have traveled far more swiftly in a wyvern-drawn carriage. Sir Conal had pointed out that while wyvern flight would be faster, Eiddwen would have to stop every day to rest and feed the wyverns. Traveling overland permitted her to keep going day and night.

That is precisely what Eiddwen had done. She and her

companions stopped at posting inns used by the mail coaches only for short periods of time to eat and change horses. Cecile knew this because Sir Conal asked about their quarry at every tollgate and every posting inn. These stops slowed their own progress, but allowed them to keep track of the three.

"I do not understand it. Eiddwen is making no effort to throw off pursuit," Sir Conal had said after four days on the road. "She has taken the princess of Rosia, for God's sake! She must know that the king would have the entire army out searching for her."

"Eiddwen warned the princess to tell no one. We are fortunate that Sophia disobeyed and wrote me of her plan to elope. I left a message for the king that his daughter is safely with me at my estate." Cecile gave a bitter smile. "Even if His Majesty did find out about the elopement, Eiddwen knows he would not dare risk a public scandal by sending people to pursue the couple. He would hush the matter up and pray to God that Sophia returns honorably wed. And we must remember, Sir Conal, Eiddwen sabotaged the palace before she left. She expects to hear any moment that it has fallen from the sky."

"I've been expecting to hear that, too," said Sir Conal gravely.

"In that regard, no news is good news," said Cecile. "If the palace had crashed, we would hear of it even in this remote part of the world."

They rode on, day after day. The route they were taking was leading to the dragon duchies. Eloping couples such as the conte and the princess generally traveled to the part of the realm that was under dragon law. There they could be married without parental consent or Church interference.

Cecile had assumed that Eiddwen would soon leave the main highway, turn aside to her true destination, wherever that might be. She could not believe that this was truly an elopement.

But as they drew nearer and nearer to the duchies, Cecile began wondering if she had been mistaken. Perhaps this young man really *was* planning to marry the princess. Such a marriage would be horrible; the young man was a murderer. Cecile found herself almost praying for this outcome. A marriage could be annulled.

After five days on the road, she and Sir Conal spoke hopefully of catching up to them. A tollgate keeper had said the three had passed through his gate only a few hours ahead of them. They continued their pursuit with renewed vigor when the sky grew dark, the wind strengthened, and rain poured down in torrents. The road became a river of mud in which the horses slipped and staggered, causing the post chaise to slide into a rut. The wheel struck a rock; Sir Conal managed to save the carriage from overturning, but at the cost of a broken wheel. Their journey was delayed two days while they waited for the local wheelwright to make a new one.

When they were back on the road, they came to a crossroads. The highway to the dragon duchies ran east. The other road continued north, a route far less traveled. Here they found out that their fears were confirmed. Eiddwen had not gone to the dragon duchies. The people at the posting inn on the eastern road had not seen the three, nor had the gatekeeper at the tollhouse.

"They must be traveling north," Sir Conal reported.

Cecile sank back in the carriage, fear and misery almost overwhelming her. She had known all along that this was an abduction.

Sir Conal climbed back in the driver's seat. "The road leads into the western slopes of the Oscadia Mountains."

"Where can they be going?" Cecile wondered, puzzled.

"And why?" Sir Conal asked.

He cracked the whip and the chaise lurched forward.

They picked up the trail of the three after several days of weary traveling. The road was little used, the only posting inn along this route in a village at the end of the mail route. Sir Conal drove the post chaise into the yard and dismounted. As he held open the door for Cecile, she descended and looked around in dismay.

"The end of the road," she murmured.

The village of Alsac was located in the rolling foothills of the mountains. From her vantage point, she could see flocks of sheep and goats spread out over bright green hills set against a backdrop of darker green pines. Smoke rose from the chimneys of the few houses scattered about the landscape. The road ended in the carriage yard of the inn. From here a pony trail led into the mountains. She studied the trail ahead. It wound up into the foothills, the terrain slate gray and forbidding.

The innkeeper, seeing a private post chaise and well-dressed, if travel-worn guests, came out personally to greet them. Sir Conal gave the innkeeper their standard story, how they were searching for Cecile's runaway niece.

"I remember the three quite well," said the innkeeper readily. "Two women and a young man. I remember because a gentleman had been waiting three days for them. He had flown here on griffin-back and he had two griffins with him. I had to find room in the stables for the beasts. The older woman seemed surprised to see him. They had a long talk. The three stayed the night and the next morning the older woman and the young man flew off on the griffins."

Sir Conal and Cecile exchanged startled glances.

"But what became of the young woman?" Cecile asked. "My niece. She and the young man were going to be married."

The innkeeper regarded Cecile with sympathy. "I think

you must have been mistaken about that, madame. The young woman left in company with two monks. She is taking the veil, joining a convent."

Cecile stared at the man, incredulous. "That is not possible. We cannot be talking about the same young woman."

"I am not likely to be confused, madame," said the innkeeper. "They were my only customers at the time. The young woman was fair complected, about fifteen, and in possession of a small dog, which the monks allowed her to take with her. She called the dog Bandit."

"That is Sophia," Cecile said dazedly. "I . . . I need to sit down."

Sir Conal gripped her arm. "Come inside, my lady. This has been a shock."

The innkeeper fussed over her, treating her with solicitous kindness. He led them to the inn's common room and shouted loudly for the serving girl to stir up the fire. Sir Conal escorted Cecile to a chair. She sat down and rested her head in her hand.

"I think we should stay here the night, my lady," said Sir Conal in a low voice. "We need to find out what is going on."

"That was my thought, as well," said Cecile softly. "You go tend to the horses. I will be fine."

"Are you certain?" Sir Conal asked worriedly.

"Hearing about Sophia was such a shock it took my breath away," said Cecile. "I am much better."

Sir Conal gave her a comradely pat on the shoulder and whispered, "Find out what you can from the serving girl. I'll talk to the stable hands."

He hurried away.

Having lived most of her life in the royal court, Cecile was well aware that servants make the best spies. People tend to view their servants as just another piece of furniture. They forget they are present, forget they have eyes and ears. Servants can blend into the background, and have been known to listen at doors, peer through key-holes.

Cecile kept her head bowed and observed the serving girl from beneath lowered lashes. The girl was young, about fourteen. Her cap was crooked, her brown hair straggled out from underneath. Her apron was torn, stained and rumpled where she used it to wipe her hands. She was looking at Cecile with wide eyes, her hands plucking at her apron.

"You seem poorly, mum. Can I fetch you something?"

Cecile lifted her head and smiled. "What is your name, child?"

"Anna, my lady." The girl dropped a pretty curtsy.

"Could you fix me a posset, Anna?" Cecile asked.

Anna flushed in confusion. "I'm sure I'd be glad to, my lady, but I don't know how. I could ask Cook—"

"We don't need to bother Cook. Bring me milk, brandy and honey, a pitcher, two mugs and I will show you."

When Anna departed, Cecile took off her damp cloak and moved her chair closer to the fire. She felt chilled to the bone. She tried to make sense of the news the innkeeper had told them. Eiddwen and that young man departing on griffin-back, leaving Sophia in the company of monks! From what the innkeeper said, Eiddwen had been surprised to see the man with the griffins. This journey was unexpected. Where had she flown in such haste? And why abandon Sophia when they had gone to so much trouble to abduct her? Had the purpose been, all along, to bring her here? To monks? Try as she might, Cecile could not think how any of this made sense.

Anna returned with the ingredients for the posset. She hung the pot over the fire and, under Cecile's direction, poured in milk and honey and began to stir it with a wooden spoon.

"You must scald the milk, but be careful not to let it

burn," said Cecile. "When the milk starts to bubble around the edges, you will know it is the right temperature."

The fire was low. Scalding the milk would take some time.

"I understand from the innkeeper that my niece was here," Cecile continued. "A pretty young woman of about fifteen. Her name is Sophia. She has a little dog."

"Yes, mum," said Anna, her gaze on the milk.

"Can you tell me how my niece seemed? Was she all right? I am worried about her. She ran away from home. Her parents are extremely upset."

Anna's cheeks grew red. She cast a fearful glance at the door that led to the entryway where the innkeeper stood at his desk. Biting her lip, she kept stirring.

"I'm not supposed to talk about the guests, mum."

"I feel a draft," said Cecile. Walking over to the door, she told the innkeeper she was feeling unwell and asked that no one disturb her. He promised she would be left in peace. Cecile smiled at him and then shut the door. "The room stays warmer this way, don't you think?"

"Yes, mum," said Anna, stirring the milk assiduously.

Cecile drew her chair close to the girl.

"Please, Anna," Cecile said softly and persuasively. "I am sick with worry for Sophia. You may talk to me. I will tell no one. Was that the name of the young lady? Sophia?"

Anna looked at her, looked again at the closed door, and seemed more at ease.

"Yes, mum. That was what they called her. She was here in this very room," Anna said, barely speaking above a whisper. "She didn't want to be, neither. I served supper and Sophia didn't eat enough to keep a dickey bird alive. That's what Cook said when I took back her plate still full of food to the kitchen."

"Who was with the young lady?"

"There was a woman they called Eiddwen. She said

she was the young lady's companion, but *I* thought she acted like her jailer. There was a young man, too. His name was Lucello. I didn't like him, though Cook thought he was very good-looking. I think the milk is ready, mum."

"Well done, Anna," said Cecile warmly. "Pour the milk in the pitcher, then into the mugs, carefully now. Then add the brandy."

"Cook said some cinnamon and clove would be good." Anna sprinkled the spices carefully on top of each mug of frothy, steaming milk. "Who is the other mug for, mum?"

"It was for my friend, Sir Conal, but he is still with the horses and this will get cold. I do not like it to go to waste. Perhaps you would like to drink it, Anna?"

"Oh, I couldn't, mum!" said Anna, even as she glanced longingly at the fragrant milk.

"Please, I insist," said Cecile.

She handed the mug to the girl. Anna sat nervously on the edge of a chair. She took a tentative sip of the milk. Her eyes grew wide. "This is ever so good, mum!"

"I'm glad you like it, Anna," said Cecile. "Tell me more about Sophia. The innkeeper said she was going to join a convent. She left with two monks."

Anna drank more of the posset. Her face grew flushed. She began to talk freely, without reservation.

"The young lady didn't want to go to no convent, mum."

"How do you know, Anna?"

"A man flew here on a griffin. First time I ever seen a griffin, mum," said Anna. "They're fearsome beasts. The lady called Eiddwen brought him in here and they talked while I served supper. He told her that orders had changed. She was to go to Freya. Something about a saint and drummers having to stay home because the storms were so bad. She was to send the savage to the monastery."

"Savage?" Cecile repeated, perplexed. "What savage?"

"I think that was the word they used. They meant the young lady."

"Savage," Cecile murmured to herself. Then she understood. "Savant! Was that the word?"

"It might have been, mum. This milk is awfully good!"

Cecile sipped the posset. "What happened after that?"

"Eiddwen and the young man, Lucello, and the man with the griffin finished their meal and left the room. Eiddwen told Sophia to stay put, she wouldn't be gone long. The moment they left, Sophia asked me if there was a back door. I nodded my head and she picked up her little dog and told me to take her. Before we could leave, that Lucello came back. He caught hold of Sophia and twisted her arm, hurting her. Then he took the little dog away from her and said he was going to kill it! I was so frightened, mum. I couldn't move."

Anna's eyes filled with tears. She put down the mug and wiped her nose with the tip of her apron.

"What happened then?" Cecile prompted her.

"The poor young lady fell to her knees, mum. She begged him not to hurt the little dog. She said she wouldn't make trouble. She would go where they told her. He threw the little dog on the floor and dragged the young woman into the yard. There were two monks on horses. They had brought a horse for Sophia to ride. Lucello took the little dog and shoved him in a gunny sack and tied it to her saddle. The dog howled somethin' frightful."

"Anna, is there a convent near here?" Cecile asked.

"No, mum. There's some old monastery up in the mountains, but no convent. I told Cook and she wondered about that, too."

The sound of footsteps approaching and a knock on the door caused Anna to set down the mug, hurriedly wipe the telltale signs of milk from her mouth and run for the kitchen. The innkeeper entered with an apology to tell

Cecile her room was ready. She followed the innkeeper up the stairs.

Cecile looked at the bed with its straw mattress and shabby wool blanket. She thought of her bed chamber in the palace, her bed with the finest cambric sheets, the embroidered silk coverlet, the goose-down pillow . . . and smiled ruefully.

Sir Conal met her in the hallway outside her door. His expression was grim.

"What did you find out?" Cecile asked, alarmed.

"We can't talk here," Sir Conal said in a low voice. "Come admire the view."

They left the inn and walked to a promontory overlooking the countryside. The sky was blue with only a few puffy clouds. The air was chill even in the sunlight. Cecile wrapped her cloak more closely around her. She told Sir Conal what Anna had told her.

"Sophia left with two monks," Cecile said in conclusion. "And there is no convent anywhere around here."

"They traveled the road north," said Sir Conal. "I found fresh hoofprints, three horses. The stable hand said he heard Eiddwen tell the men they were to take the young woman to the monastery of Saint Dominick's without delay."

"But why a monastery?" Cecile asked, baffled. "That does not make sense."

"The north road is used only by shepherds and the monks from the monastery. That has to be their destination."

"I have never heard of a Saint Dominick."

"I asked about him," Sir Conal said. "The stable hand was glad to oblige. His story is quite curious. It seems that back in ancient times, a man and his son discovered the Gates to Hell. The man opened the gates, letting demons escape into the world. The man made a deal with the Evil

One for the demons to serve him. A priest named Dominick opposed this man, who retaliated by sending the demons to murder the priest and tear down his church. Dominick stood in the door of the church and, calling on God to help him, he sent the demons and the evil men who summoned them back to hell."

"You are telling me that the Gates of Hell are located in the Oscadia Mountains," said Cecile drily.

Sir Conal did not return her smile. "Local legend has it that during the Dark Ages, demons came down out of the mountains and laid siege to the village. The church sent monks to fight them and drive them back through the gates. The monks built a monastery at the site to watch for demons and adopted Saint Dominick as their patron saint."

Cecile felt the blood chill in her heart. "Demons . . . Eiddwen . . ."

"I, too, made the connection, my lady," said Sir Conal gravely. "But I cannot fathom what Eiddwen and Sophia and the Bottom Dwellers have to do with a monastery hidden in the mountains."

"The man who came to give Eiddwen her orders referred to Sophia as a 'savant.' And Eiddwen told the monks to take the 'savant' to the monastery."

"Is Her Highness a savant?"

"She is quite gifted in magic. A natural talent, so the priests said when they examined her. She could well be a savant."

"And what do you make of Eiddwen and Lucello flying to Freya?" Sir Conal asked. "On orders from some saint. And all that about drummers and storms. I have no love for Freyans, but if that woman is headed their way, I feel sorry for the poor devils."

Cecile remembered Father Jacob warning that the Bottom Dwellers were a threat to all the nations of the world. He had said that the night a bomb using contramagic had nearly killed them. Was Freya somehow connected with Eiddwen sabotaging the palace and abducting the princess? Eiddwen did nothing without a reason. As Sir Conal said, the Freyans should beware.

"Sophia knows now that Lucello never meant to marry her," said Cecile, returning to the problem at hand. "She knows his true character. She tried to escape, but he caught her. He threatened her, saying that if she didn't cooperate, he would kill Bandit. She must be terrified."

Cecile had to clamp her teeth on her lips to check her emotions.

"We will find her, my lady," Sir Conal replied with quiet reassurance. "The road is too rocky and narrow for the post chaise. I will purchase riding horses and supplies. We can leave tonight, if you are not too tired."

"I am not tired." Cecile smiled at him. "Thank you, Sir Conal. I do not know what I would do without you."

Sir Conal O'Hairt was not a handsome man. He was short of stature, of stocky build, with bull-like neck and shoulders. The Knight Protectors were a group of knights assigned to guard priests of the Arcanum, who were often sent on dangerous missions. Sir Conal had served in this capacity for many years until he had begun having difficulty with his knee. He now trained new members of the Knight Protectors in combat.

Cecile had been dubious about him at first. They were undertaking a perilous journey and he was a forty-year-old knight hampered by a bad knee. Sir Ander had recommended Sir Conal and since Sir Ander was one of the few people in this world Cecile trusted, she had taken Sir Conal into her service.

During the long, exhausting, and sometimes seemingly hopeless journey, she had come to appreciate the knight's cool and confident demeanor. He dealt with each crisis swiftly and calmly. Best of all, he was invariably cheerful, enlivening the journey in the rattling and uncomfortable post chaise with stories of his childhood growing up among the Trundlers and tales of his adventures as a member of the Knight Protectors.

"You are staring me out of countenance, my lady," said Sir Conal, grinning.

"I am sorry," said Cecile. "Please continue. You were saying something about the monks."

"No one in the village knows much about them or their monastery, except that it is very old," Sir Conal continued. "Two monks drive a wagon to town twice yearly to pick up supplies. The monks have been coming to the village as long as anyone can remember. They never engage in idle chatter. They speak only as they find it necessary to convey their needs.

"As for the road itself, the stable hand tells me it is winding and narrow, used mostly by sheep and goat herders. Their shelters are scattered along the way. They've moved the flocks down out of the mountains for the coming of winter, so we should find the shelters available for our own use."

Cecile sighed deeply. "They left with Sophia days ago . . ."

"Take heart, my lady," said Sir Conal, patting her hand. "We know the princess is alive and that these two monks are taking pains to keep her safe and unharmed, even letting her keep the little dog."

"They are using the dog to control her," Cecile returned bitterly.

"That is a good sign, my lady," Sir Conal said. "Wherever they are taking her, for whatever reason, they want her alive and unharmed."

Cecile understood what he meant. Threats against Bandit would make Sophia far more tractable than threats against herself. Because she was subject to painful, debilitating headaches, the princess appeared fragile and frail. Living with chronic pain had given her a core of strength and fortitude. Witness the fact that she had dared to try to flee her captors.

To keep up appearances, Cecile and Sir Conal returned to the inn and ordered supper. Once they had eaten, Sir Conal left to purchase horses. Cecile shut herself in her room. She bathed as well as she could, considering the washbasin itself was none too clean. Then she wrote a letter to D'argent, wondering even as she wrote it if D'argent was still alive.

She had urged him to leave the doomed palace. He had refused as politely as one could refuse a countess, saying she would need him to remain at his post. When the letter was written, she went downstairs and slipped it in the mailbag to leave with tomorrow's post. Returning to her bed, she lay down on it, fully dressed, and worried about Sophia until weariness overtook her and she fell asleep.

Cecile woke to a quiet knock on the door. Moonlight had managed to make its way through the dirty window, casting a pale glow around her room.

"I have the horses, my lady," Sir Conal said softly.

Cecile gathered her things and joined him. The hour was late, the inn quiet. The innkeeper had retired to his chambers in the back and the servants had gone to their beds. Cecile and Sir Conal slipped down the stairs as silently as they could.

"The horses are not much to look at," Sir Conal warned her, as they walked into the stable yard. "But they will suit our needs admirably. My lady, may I introduce Jean and Pierre."

The two were mountain ponies, short and sturdy, with shaggy manes and rough coats. They were outfitted with odd-looking high-backed saddles made of wood over colorful blankets with ropes for bridles. The ponies appeared to be in good health, bright and alert.

Cecile was an experienced horsewoman, having ridden since childhood. She bred her own horses and regularly rode to the hunt with the king, as well as riding for her own pleasure and exercise. Her favorite horse, Warrior, was a proud, fiery stallion, black with a white blaze, who stood sixteen hands. She smiled at the contrast.

"I am pleased to meet you, Pierre," said Cecile, feeding the pony an apple.

"They are sure-footed, bred for the mountain trails. Just what we need," Sir Conal said as he rubbed Jean's shaggy forehead. "I'm a bit dubious about the comfort of the wooden saddle, but the owner assured me we would grow accustomed to it. That loop of rope is the stirrup, my lady. I am afraid you must ride astride."

"I generally ride astride. I cannot abide sidesaddles." Cecile kilted her skirts, thrust her foot into the loop, and pulled herself into the strange-looking saddle. She glanced down at her skirts that were hiked to her shins. "I trust your sense of propriety will not be offended by seeing my ankles, Sir Conal."

"God made the ankle as he made the moonlight, my lady—for us to admire," Sir Conal returned gallantly.

He loaded the supplies—blankets, food, water, powder and ammunition—dividing them between both ponies. When they were ready, Cecile gave Pierre a gentle kick in the flanks and the pony obediently ambled off, his pace unbearably slow. When she gave him another kick to encourage him, he shifted his head to look back at her in mild rebuke, letting her know he knew his business. He continued at his same deliberate pace.

"I could wish they were faster," said Cecile, thinking of the many miles that lay between them and the princess.

"We can't help Her Highness if we break our necks, my lady," said Sir Conal. "Or if the ponies break theirs."

Cecile gave Pierre a pat on the neck in apology and counseled herself to be patient.

With the moon to light their trail, they rode far into the night, stopping when they came upon a shepherd's hut. Sir Conal slept outside the hut with the ponies. Cecile wrapped herself in her cloak and slept inside, thinking, as she did so, that the hut's dirt floor was cleaner than her room in the inn.

The next morning, Cecile performed her ablutions in a cold, clear mountain stream. She sat on the creek bank, minding the ponies while Sir Conal searched the road ahead for signs of the princess and monks. Every muscle in Cecile's body was sore, especially the parts that came in contact with the wooden saddle. Sitting down was painful, but then so was standing.

Sir Conal returned and called out a cheerful good morning. Cecile carried water back to the campsite and mixed it with dry oatmeal in a tin pot. Sir Conal ate with relish. Cecile had no appetite, but she forced herself to eat the lumpy, congealing mass to keep up her strength.

"You are a born campaigner, my lady," Sir Conal said in admiring tones, watching her choke down the cereal. "You make the best of what God sends and no grousing."

"If it was God that sent this oatmeal, I may never forgive Him," said Cecile. "What did you find?"

"Nothing, I fear, my lady," said Sir Conal. "The ground is too rocky."

"We don't know they came this way," said Cecile, discouraged.

"We know they started out on this road," said Sir Conal. "I see no reason why they would leave it."

The journey into the mountains was slow and treacherous. Cecile came to bless the sure-footed little ponies and even to admit the usefulness of the wooden saddle. The high back supported her when the trail seemed to ascend straight into the sky, and the high pommel kept her from falling over the pony's neck when they rode straight down.

No one had purposefully constructed this road. It had been ground into the mountain by centuries of hooves and boots and it was pitted and gouged, strewn with rocks and sheep droppings. Well-worn trails used by the herders branched off from the main road, meandering over grass-covered slopes. Shepherds must have tended their flocks here back in the days of the Sunlit Empire.

Despite the uneven terrain, the ponies kept their footing, nimbly picking their way among the rocks and climbing the steep grades with ease.

The plodding rhythm and swaying motion lulled Cecile, made her drowsy. She must have nodded off, for she came to herself with a start when Sir Conal suddenly brought Jean to a halt.

"What is the matter?" Cecile asked, tugging on the reins. "What is wrong?"

"Wait here, my lady," said Sir Conal.

He climbed off the pony and walked over to the side of the road. Cecile leaned forward in the saddle to try to see what had attracted Sir Conal's attention.

The road curved around a stand of pine trees, then made a steep plunge down into a gorge where a small stream trickled over the rocks. The road crossed the shallow water and continued crawling snakelike up the side of the mountain.

Near the pine trees, Sir Conal bent down to examine something. Rising, he walked a short distance among the pines, keeping his gaze on the ground. Cecile lost sight of him. She sat on the pony, her hands tightly clenched over the reins. He reemerged and went down to the stream, still searching the ground, then left the stream and walked back up the steeply sloping road to meet her.

"You had best come see this, my lady."

"You found something!" Cecile dismounted and hurriedly accompanied him to the pines trees.

Sir Conal pointed to the ground, indicating a blackened patch on the stone and a few bits of charred wood. "People camped here recently. You can see where someone built a fire. If you will water Jean and Pierre, I will keep searching."

Cecile led the ponies to the stream and filled her own water skin. She walked a bit to ease the stiffness and soreness and to marvel at the breathtaking beauty of this wild and desolate land. She had entered a world of sharp angles and stark contrasts: bright sun and chill air, blue sky above and gray and green below, patches of snow in the midst of summer. The world had never seemed so vast as when viewed from this close to heaven, or so small. The air was thin and brittle and tasted of pine.

She was roused from her musings by a low whistle indicative of astonishment. She turned to see Sir Conal examining his boot. He began to laugh and motioned her to join him.

He looked up at her with a smile and pointed to the bottom of his boot. "You will be pleased to know I just stepped in dog droppings, my lady."

Cecile stared at him a moment, wondering what he was talking about. Then she gasped in understanding. "Bandit!"

"The little dog was here, my lady," said Sir Conal with satisfaction. He pointed to a patch of mud. "These are his footprints and those of his mistress."

He conducted a wide-ranging search, walking all around the campsite. Cecile watched tensely as Sir Conal shoved aside sticks and pine needles with the toe of his boot.

"This campsite is old," he said. "Probably a favorite resting place for shepherds and monks traveling to and from the monastery. Trees provide shelter. There is a stream nearby. Down through the years, people have built fires in this location. You see how they rolled boulders near the fire to use as benches— Ah!"

Sir Conal must have caught sight of something out of the corner of his eye, for he picked up an object and brought it over to her, holding it in the palm of his hand.

Rubies set into leather sparkled in the sunlight.

"Bandit's collar!" Cecile said softly. She added, with a catch in her throat, "I gave this to Sophia to help her keep track of him. He was constantly getting lost—"

And now Sophia was the one who was lost. Cecile pressed her lips together and held fast to the collar. "What a pity this cannot tell us where to find *her*!"

"In a way, it has, my lady," said Sir Conal. "Note that the collar was unfastened. It did not come off by accident. Her Highness took it from the wee dog and left it here deliberately."

"I am certain you are right, Sir Conal," said Cecile. "This means she is alive—"

"And that she is free to move about. She is still with the monks, apparently. I found their tracks in the mud as well. Both of them are wearing boots that have been recently patched, if that is of any interest."

Cecile rested her smooth white hand on Sir Conal's rough, broken-knuckled, sun-browned hand.

"You are a good and true friend, Sir Conal," she said, pressing him warmly. "I bless Ander every day for bringing you to me in my time of most desperate need."

"I am proud to be able to serve you, my lady."

Cecile thought he would kiss her hand as would any courtier. Instead, to her pleasure and surprise, Sir Conal shook her hand—a frank, firm handshake as between two comrades.

Cecile kilted her skirts, mounted the shaggy pony, and they continued on their journey. She held fast to Bandit's collar and promised him an entire tray of iced cakes the moment he and his mistress were safely back home.

5

My duty is to work in the shadows so that the light may shine more brightly on those in the sun.

—Dubois

D'argent was in the office of the Countess de Marjolaine, waiting to receive the king's letter of pardon for Stephano and Rodrigo. Once D'argent had the letter in his possession, he would leave in haste to deliver it personally to Monsieur Dubois—the grand bishop's confidential agent and one of the few people who could gain immediate access to His Eminence.

D'argent had tried to distract himself from worry by working on the accounts—noting down figures in a massive ledger, adding, subtracting, moving numbers from one column to another. Cecile's holdings were extensive, her wealth immense, her business affairs complex. D'argent couldn't keep his mind on his work, however, and after his third mistake, he gave up, shut the ledger and put it away.

He could hardly make a mistake sorting mail, though, so he began to go through Cecile's massive amount of correspondence, answering those missives that required immediate reply, putting away those that could wait, and reading those that came from her network of agents around the world.

The news from her agents was universally bad, almost all of it regarding the Bottom Dwellers. D'argent was forced to admire the genius of their strategy. With only a few ships and a limited number of troops, they had managed by a series of carefully calculated strikes to spread fear and panic among nations, hamper trade, cripple economies. All the while, if Father Jacob was right, they were using their contramagic to destroy the magical constructs that kept buildings standing and ships aloft.

As he was working, a kind of shudder went through the palace, tilting the floor and sending a miniature porcelain shepherdess sliding off the table. A crash came from the balcony, a thud from one of the interior rooms. D'argent grabbed the desk, his heart beating fast. He had become so involved in his work he had forgotten that the palace might at any moment crash into the lake below. This time, the palace settled, righted itself. D'argent breathed a little easier and hoped the king would hurry with that pardon. These shudderings and lurchings were growing worse.

He made a quick inspection of the countess's rooms to see what had been damaged. A rose tree on the balcony had tipped over, a painting in the music room had fallen off a wall. He righted the rose tree and left the painting on the floor. No sense in rehanging it when the palace was only going to shake again.

He returned to the office to find Marie Tutolla, Cecile's lady's maid, waiting for him. Marie had been with the countess forty years, Cecile having brought Marie with her when she came to the palace at the age of sixteen. Marie was agitated, unnerved. She stood at the edge of the desk, clutching something in her hand.

"Marie, are you all right?" Dubois asked, concerned. "Did you fall? The shaking was quite bad that time."

In answer, Marie glanced uneasily at the door. "Are we alone, sir? Is the young secretary here?"

"I sent the viscount home on extended leave. What is it?" Dubois asked, suddenly tense, alert. "What is wrong?"

Marie held out a trembling hand. "A letter, sir." She paused, drew in a breath, and added in a husky voice, "It's from her ladyship. For you."

D'argent's pulse quickened. He took the letter, sat down, and examined it. He recognized the countess's handwriting immediately. The paper was plain, the sort carried by a dry goods and sundry store, such as anyone traveling might purchase.

"Did you open it?"

"No, sir," said Marie. "I wanted to show you. Someone else did."

D'argent could see what she meant. The sealing wax had been loosened, probably with a hot knife, and then replaced. A clumsy job by someone obviously unfamiliar with such delicate work.

D'argent scanned through the letter and smiled. Whoever had opened the letter must have been thoroughly bored by the contents. The letter gave D'argent instructions for Cecile's dressmaker, her hatmaker, her glover, her cobbler, her jeweler. She placed orders for a dozen silk stockings, three new hats in the latest Estaran fashion, seven pairs of silk gloves, emerald earrings as a gift for the princess. Cecile was chatty in her letter, interspersing her orders with details of her journey.

The letter was long and difficult to read, for the countess was a careless writer, crossing out paragraphs, amending others, scratching through words. He showed the letter to Marie.

"What do you make of it?"

She read through it. "This is all wrong, sir. My lady

writes a neat, pretty hand. This looks to have been written by some silly schoolgirl. And here, this cobbler my lady names. She said she would never again do business with him. And she wouldn't be caught dead wearing the 'latest Estaran fashion.' This is code, isn't it, sir?"

"A very simple code," said D'argent.

He didn't tell Marie, for he didn't want to add to her worry, that this was Cecile's emergency code, used only in the most dire circumstances since anyone with moderate skills in code breaking could solve the cipher with relative ease. She hadn't had time to devise anything more elaborate.

The first items the countess requested him to purchase were four silk handkerchiefs. D'argent searched through the letter and copied down the fourth word in each of the first four paragraphs. He stared in astonishment: Freya, Eiddwen, Henry, warn.

"What does it mean, sir?" Marie asked, reading over his shoulder.

"I think it means that Eiddwen has traveled to Freya and that I should warn Sir Henry Wallace to be on the watch for her," said D'argent.

"Freya's the enemy, sir!" said Marie, sniffing.

"They *were* the enemy," said D'argent.

He read the next item on the list: seven pairs of leather gloves. He searched for every seventh word in the first seven paragraphs.

"Princess, demons, monastery, saint, Dominick, Oscadia."

Marie frowned. "Are you sure you have that right, sir?"

D'argent counted again and came out with the same result. "It would seem the princess and demons have something to do with a monastery of Saint Dominick in the Oscadia Mountains."

"I never heard of a Saint Dominick," said Marie.

"Neither have I," said D'argent. "Given the vast number of saints in the calendar, however, that is not surprising. But . . . a monastery of all places!"

"Perhaps her ladyship has taken refuge there," Marie suggested.

"Perhaps . . . I will do what I can to find out. When do you start on your journey?"

"This afternoon, sir," said Marie. "I don't feel right about leaving. I don't mind the danger. I want to be here, in case there should be any news of her ladyship."

"I understand, Marie," said D'argent. "But we have said publicly that the countess and the princess have traveled to the family estate. People would think it strange that her lady's maid is not in attendance. They might start asking questions."

"I told my friends that I was staying behind to supervise the packing. There was a lot to pack, since the countess didn't know when she would return . . . if ever . . ."

Marie had to stop to wipe her eyes. "I'm sorry, sir. I didn't mean to give way like this."

"We need to be strong, Marie, and put up a bold front," said D'argent. "Act as if nothing is wrong."

"I know, sir," said Marie with a faint smile. "I generally do my crying at night when no one can see me. You will let me know if there is news, sir?"

"You have my word," said D'argent.

After Marie left, D'argent read and reread the letter, wondering if there was some clue he had missed. He was deep in thought when the door opened and Prince Renaud walked in. Startled by the sudden intrusion, D'argent jumped to his feet, hurriedly shoving Cecile's letter beneath a stack of papers dealing with accounts.

"Your Highness . . ."

"For the pardons," said Prince Renaud, holding out two

letters. "One for Captain de Guichen and one for Monsieur Rodrigo de Villeneuve."

He stopped, staring about the room that was simple yet elegant, and beautiful, with understated colors of lavender and blue, and pale wood panels carved with delicate curves. The room was faintly fragranced with perfume. The prince suddenly seemed to realize he had committed a most serious breach of etiquette.

"Sorry for barging in like that," Prince Renaud said, frowning. "Rude of me. Should have knocked. Keep forgetting I'm not back on my ship."

"I apologize for the fact that the servants were not on hand to greet—"

"Quite," Prince Renaud interrupted. "I need to have a word with you in private, D'argent. I need you to carry a private message to Captain de Guichen. I did not approve of my father's decision to disband the Dragon Brigade. The noble dragons are furious with us and they have a right to be. They refused to see the delegation my father sent to try to restore relations. My hope is that when Captain de Guichen returns, he will meet with the noble dragons. He has friends among them who might be willing to overlook the past and aid us in this time of crisis."

"I am sure he will be honored, Your Highness—"

"I like his idea for taking the fight to the enemy," Renaud continued. "I have dispatched work crews to the fortress to start repairs. I trust Captain de Guichen will not take that amiss."

"I am certain—"

"Good." Prince Renaud handed over the letters and left the room as abruptly as he had entered.

D'argent locked up Cecile's correspondence in a box with special magical constructs to deter spies. Tucking the pardons into an interior pocket of his coat, he grabbed his hat and his cloak and left the palace, ordering his carriage driver to take him to the inn known as Canard à Trois Pattes, the "three-legged duck," where Dubois had taken lodgings.

He found Dubois pacing the inn's stable yard. D'argent jumped from the carriage. He handed Dubois the pardons, which Dubois shoved into a leather dispatch bag.

"I have a message for Stephano from the prince," said D'argent. "To be given in person, not in writing."

He related his conversation with Prince Renaud.

"Well, well, well," was Dubois's murmured remark.

"One thing more," said D'argent.

He took hold of Dubois's elbow and steered him to the far end of the stable yard, out of the way of the bustle of arriving guests, out of earshot of the servants.

"I received a letter from the countess," D'argent said, speaking in an undertone though it was doubtful if anyone could have overheard him, since a carriage had rolled into the yard, disgorging a matronly female with five shrill-voiced and giggling young women. "She is on the trail of the princess's abductors. She writes that Eiddwen has traveled to Freya. The countess says we should send a warning to Sir Henry Wallace."

Dubois looked so astonished his eyebrows seemed likely to fly off his head. "A message to Sir Henry." He muttered something about, "Strange bedfellows."

"In addition," D'argent continued, "the countess mentioned a monastery called Saint Dominick's in the Oscadia Mountains. Have you heard of it?"

"Never. Are you certain? Saint Dominick?"

"That was the name," said D'argent. "I don't know what it means. All I know is that this monastery has some connection with the princess and 'demons.' I am assuming she means Bottom Dwellers. Her Grace would not have mentioned it otherwise."

"A monastery. Odd, isn't it," Dubois said after a moment's contemplation.

"Damn odd," said D'argent. "It's all damn odd. Godspeed, monsieur. A safe journey. I wish there was something His Majesty could do for Father Jacob."

Dubois gave a deep sigh. "There is nothing. A sad business."

"Have you found out anything more about the charges against him?"

Dubois shrugged, which either meant he couldn't say, he wouldn't say, or he didn't know. With a vague smile and a bobbing bow, he took his leave.

D'argent returned to his carriage, climbed inside and told the driver to take him back to the palace. He wondered, as he went, how Stephano and Prince Renaud would get along. He hoped they might actually like each other.

Back at the inn, Dubois wrote a letter addressed to one of his agents in Freya. Inside the first letter was another letter addressed to Henry Wallace, Naval Club. He gave his agent instructions to destroy the first letter and deliver the second to the Naval Club. Dubois was taking precautions. Although the countries were not at war, it would never do for him to be caught corresponding directly with the Freyan spymaster. Yet he had to warn Sir Henry that Eiddwen was traveling to his country. Since the woman had already tried once to assassinate Wallace, Dubois could rest assured that he would take the threat seriously.

Dubois pondered, wrote a few more lines and posted the letter within a letter. After that, he hastened to the stables where the griffin he had hired was saddled and waiting.

Dubois climbed on the back of the griffin. The beast's

handler assisted Dubois in settling himself in the small saddle where he would ride behind the handler. He did not like traveling by griffin-back, and did so only when he considered the matter one of utmost urgency.

He donned the helm, similar to that worn by dragon riders, though lighter in weight, since this helm was made of leather rather than steel. Then he wrapped himself in his cloak, and indicated he was ready in the same tone a man might have used prior to mounting the scaffold.

The griffin's handler strapped Dubois into the saddle, an extremely uncomfortable affair placed over the lion body's bony hind end. Then the handler shouted to the griffin. Dubois gripped the reins. As the beast spread its wings Dubois closed his eyes. He hated this part.

The griffin bounded off the ground, seeming to leap straight up, inspiring Dubois to cling with all his strength to the saddle. Although he was strapped in, he was certain he was going to fall. He didn't open his eyes again until he felt the griffin level off.

Many riders found the speed of griffin flight exhilarating and thrilling. Dubois instead found it stomach-churning and terrifying. He hunched his shoulders against the blasting wind and commended himself to God.

The journey from Evreux to the Citadel took a day and a half on griffin-back, with a stop overnight in Eudaine to change griffins. Dubois dismounted, hobbled about a bit to restore the circulation to his legs, and immediately mounted a fresh griffin. Dubois arrived at the Citadel just as the sun was setting.

As the griffin brought them close to the Citadel, they flew near one of the guard towers, to allow the guardian monks of Saint Klee to identify the visitor. Dubois raised his helm so that they could see his face. The monk on duty appeared to give them more than usual attention. At last the monk raised his hand in permission. The griffin landed in the large open area at the base of the mountain fastness that was the Citadel

Immediately on his arrival, Dubois sent a message to the grand bishop, requesting an audience. He then began to wend his way up the stairs that had been carved out of the side of the mountain until he reached the guest halls, located near the summit.

The Citadel was comprised of a great many buildings, from the magnificent cathedral at the top of the mountain to the stables and wharves and warehouses at the bottom. The Citadel was a self-contained community, with a hospital, a library and the infamous Library of the Forbidden, dortoirs for the priests and nuns who lived and worked in the Citadel, the chapter house, halls for dining and for study, quarters for the lay brothers and sisters who acted as servants, and the house of the provost, located near the cathedral.

The various structures occupied the different levels, all connected by a series of stairways and ramps and surrounded by protective walls and guard towers. Gardens and courtyards adorned the grounds and provided areas where the inhabitants could rest and relax.

As Dubois ascended the stairs and strolled past the gardens, he cast sharp, curious glances at those he met and saw immediately that something was amiss. Dubois had been in the Citadel many times, but few ever paid much attention to him, mainly because he took great care not to garner attention. Still, they were welcoming, always giving him a cheerful greeting, a friendly nod.

This time, no one greeted him or even looked at him. People were deep in whispered conversation, their heads together, their expressions grave or troubled. No one was working in the gardens or strolling the ramparts, despite the fact that the summer evening was warm, with a splendid sunset to admire. If people met, they huddled together, spoke a few moments, then walked on, expressions grim.

Dubois was intrigued. The Citadel had recently come under attack by the Bottom Dwellers, leaving several buildings badly damaged; some people had been wounded and a few were killed. The attack had happened weeks ago, however, and the priests and nuns of the Arcanum were not the sort of men and women to go about bewailing their fate. They left tragedy and loss in God's capable hands and carried on with business.

Dubois guessed this upset had something to do with Father Jacob. He needed to talk to someone, find out what was going on before he met with the grand bishop. He saw many people he recognized, but no one he trusted.

Walking past the hospital, he caught sight of a short-statured nun walking rapidly, with a brisk and no-nonsense air about her. Dubois was elated. He could not have asked for a better informant. Sister Elizabeth was the surgeon who had operated on Father Jacob. She was one of the few people in the Arcanum who actually liked the irascible priest.

She walked with her lips tight, her brows knitted. Dubois accosted her, hat in hand.

"Sister Elizabeth, forgive me . . ."

"Eh?" Sister Elizabeth stopped, startled to find him in her path. She lifted her gaze to his face. Her frown increased. "I know you. You work for the grand bishop."

She skirted around him. Dubois hurried after her.

"My name is Dubois, Sister. I have heard a rumor that Father Jacob has been arrested. Is this true? Can you tell me under what circumstances?"

"Ask your friend the grand bishop," said Sister Elizabeth, glowering.

Dubois could move more quickly than people gave his

pudgy body credit for and he managed to dodge around her and place himself squarely in front of her, forcing her to stop or run over him.

Still holding his hat in his hand, Dubois said softly, "I am a friend to Father Jacob, Sister. I know you to be his friend, as well. Possibly I can help. I need to know what is going on."

Sister Elizabeth regarded him intently. Dubois met her gaze with openness and frankness. She pursed her lips, then gave a little snort.

"You best be careful going about saying you are Father Jacob's friend. That could get you arrested." She eyed him again. "You don't know what has happened?"

"I arrived only this past hour," said Dubois. "I have not yet spoken with the grand bishop. I would like to help Father Jacob if I can. I believe his work to be of immense importance."

Sister Elizabeth stood silent, her hands folded in the sleeves of her black habit. The wind ruffled the wimple around her face.

"You are limping, monsieur," she said suddenly.

Dubois followed her gaze to see two monks of Saint Klee approaching. He understood and immediately started to groan and rub his calves.

"Muscle cramps," Sister Elizabeth added. "I can help you find ease. Where are you bound?"

"I have rooms in the guest hall, Sister."

"I will walk with you."

The monks of Saint Klee passed by, neither of them glancing at Dubois. As he and Sister Elizabeth walked to the guesthouse, he could see signs of the recent attack. The smell of burning lingered in the air. He noticed repair work had been started. The guesthouse had been on the fringes of the battle and had suffered little damage. Some tiles were being replaced on the roof and ruined trees had been replanted. No one was at work today, however. Usually bustling with activity, the guesthouse was empty, silent.

"The grand bishop asked all our guests to leave," said Sister Elizabeth, answering Dubois's unspoken question. "He told them the Citadel might come under attack again and that remaining here was dangerous. I am surprised *you* were permitted to land."

She eyed him curiously, clearly wondering why he was here.

"*Will* the Citadel be attacked?" Dubois asked, changing the subject.

"God Himself is the only one who knows. I suppose it is possible," said Sister Elizabeth. "But that is not the true reason he ordered the guests to depart."

Dubois did not think it was. She led him into a courtyard with benches beneath shade trees and an ornamental fish pond filled with darting orange fish. Sister Elizabeth sat down on a bench, put her hands on her knees, and faced him.

"The grand bishop ordered the provost removed from office. The provost is, to all intents and purposes, under arrest," she said. "Montagne has taken sole control of the Church."

Dubois was not easily astonished. He knew the depths to which humans could sink, and the heights they could attain. He had viewed the remains of the murdered nuns at the Abbey of Saint Agnes. He had witnessed the fall of the Crystal Market, seen the gutters running red with blood. He had thought that nothing in life could shock him and yet, at this astounding news, he felt the need to sit down.

He stared at her dumbfounded.

"You didn't know any of this," Sister Elizabeth said.

"I . . . I did not," Dubois murmured, shaken. "I heard

only that Father Jacob had been arrested. Was his arrest the cause of the rupture?"

Sister Elizabeth glanced around to make certain no one was near. "One day, not long after the attack, the provost and the grand bishop were alone in the provost's office. Their voices were raised in anger. Walls are thin. The provost's staff heard everything. The provost said he would not be a party to Father Jacob's imprisonment. The grand bishop said he would have the provost removed from office. The provost countered that he could be removed only by a vote of the Council of Bishops. The grand bishop countered by disbanding the Council."

"He can't do that," said Dubois.

"Who is going to stop him?" Sister Elizabeth returned.

Dubois had no answer to that. "What has happened to Father Jacob? What are the charges against him?"

"During the attack on the Citadel, he broke the rule and entered the Library of the Forbidden," said Sister Elizabeth. "No one knows what happened in the Library except the monks of Saint Klee, and they're not talking. Father Jacob and Sir Ander fled the Citadel during the attack. They were apprehended in the dragon duchies and brought to the Citadel under guard by the monks of Saint Klee. After that, Father Jacob and Sir Ander both vanished."

"They would be in the prison, wouldn't they?" Dubois asked, startled.

"One would think so," said Sister Elizabeth darkly. "As Father Jacob's physician, I demanded to examine him. I said I needed to make certain he is not suffering any lingering effects from his head injury. I was not permitted to see him. After that I talked to one of the lay brothers who takes meals to the prisoners. He said that neither Father Jacob nor Sir Ander are in any of the prison cells."

Dubois frowned.

Sister Elizabeth tapped him on the knee.

"You are the first person who has been permitted to enter the Citadel since the Council was disbanded. Everyone in the Arcanum has been placed under Seal. So how did you manage?"

Sometimes parting with information gained information. In this instance, Dubois wasn't revealing anything that wouldn't shortly be known to everyone in the Citadel anyway.

"I am here on behalf of two men who have also been arrested and brought here: Captain Stephano de Guichen and Monsieur Rodrigo de Villeneuve. Perhaps you have seen them . . ."

Sister Elizabeth shook her head. "These men you mention are not here."

"They must be," said Dubois, dismayed. "They were arrested in Evreux. Their friends saw the monks of Saint Klee take them away."

"I wonder . . ." Sister Elizabeth frowned, looking thoughtful. "Did the arrest take place a week ago?"

"Yes," Dubois replied. "Why?"

"I heard a report that a group of monks who left for Evreux to make an arrest did not return. They should have been back days ago. Search parties are going out to look for them."

"Good God!" Dubois exclaimed. "I hope nothing has happened to them. His Majesty has granted royal pardons to these two. Monsieur Rodrigo is wanted—is urgently needed—at the palace."

"May God save and keep them," said Sister Elizabeth. She glanced toward the courtyard, and something she saw made her start. "Merciful saints, there is Father Pietro! The grand bishop has sent him to fetch you. I must leave before he catches me. He will want to engage me in conversation and he's the most boring man that ever drew breath."

Dubois turned his head to see a priest entering the courtyard. His gaze fastened upon Dubois whose coat and hat, though they were plain and drab colored, stood out markedly amid the black cassocks and habits.

"Are you Monsieur Dubois?" the priest called across at him. "I am Father Pietro. I have been sent to escort you to the grand bishop."

"He will want to tell me all about the life of the latest saint he is studying," Sister Elizabeth said, standing up and smoothing the skirts of her habit. "The man is a font of worthless information."

"Speaking of saints, Sister," Dubois asked offhandedly, "do you know anything about a Saint Dominick?"

"Never heard of him," said Sister Elizabeth promptly. "Ask Father Pietro. He holds a degree in theology *and* is a doctor of divinity, as he will be certain to tell you."

"Thank you for your help, Sister," said Dubois.

"I hope you can talk some sense into Montagne," Sister Elizabeth added in a low mutter.

She waved at Father Pietro. "I would love to hear about Saint Whosit, Father, but I have to hurry back to the hospital."

"Saint Whosit?" Father Pietro repeated, mystified. "I have never heard of him. I must look him up in the calendar.

"I am Father Pietro," the priest said to Dubois again, as if fond of hearing his own name. "I have been assigned to act as secretary to the grand bishop. I hold a degree in theology *and* I am a doctor of divinity."

Dubois hid his smile and said something polite.

"The grand bishop has granted you an audience," Father Pietro continued with the air of one conferring a great honor. Clearly he had taken Montagne's side in this ecclesiastical war. "I will escort you."

"I am glad for your company, Father," said Dubois gravely.

They wended their way through the gardens to an old building that had once been the Hall of Offerings, as the financial arm of the Church was called. When the priestly accountants and clerks had moved into a new and more secure building on a lower level, this building had been given to the grand bishop and his staff for their use when he was in residence. He lived in a house nearby. Once the home of Saint Denis, second provost of the Arcanum, the house was furnished with its own small chapel. Montagne could worship in private, work and dwell in isolation. What dread secret was he fighting to protect? Dubois wondered as he and Father Pietro approached the hall.

"This building was constructed during the time of Grand Bishop Alonzo Diego of Estara," Father Pietro stated sonorously. "You will note the elaborate architraves, which were a hallmark of the period. Also the ashlar—"

"You are a font of information, Father," said Dubois.

Father Pietro bowed with satisfaction.

"I myself am writing a small volume on the monasteries of Rosia," Dubois continued with a modest air. "I came across a reference to an old monastery in the Oscadia Mountains dedicated to Saint Dominick. I can find no one who can tell me anything about this monastery. Perhaps you know something of it?"

"Saint Dominick the Keeper," said Father Pietro at once. "He lived in the time of the Sunlit Empire when the Church was sending missionaries into remote parts of Rosia. He died a martyr defending his flock from an attack by fiends summoned by the ruling Brovaighn family, who had made an alliance with the Evil One."

"Why is he called the Keeper?" Dubois asked.

"Because he was the Keeper of the Gates of Hell,"

Father Pietro explained. "The story tells that at the behest of the Brovaighns, the ground split open and an army of fiends poured out. Saint Dominick drove them back and died fighting them. His holy blood spilled on the rocks and sealed the ground shut."

"And so the monastery that bears his name dates back to that time?"

"No, no," said Father Pietro officiously. "The monastery to which *you* refer was founded five hundred years ago during the Dark Ages. I am not certain why the monks chose to name it in honor of Saint Dominick. His miracle occurred in the region of Blenheim. Nowhere near the Oscadia Mountains."

"The monastery is still active?" Dubois asked.

"It is still on the Church rolls," said Father Pietro as they walked up the steps leading to the entrance. "I know nothing more beyond that. The grand bishop is within. I will announce you."

The gray walls of the hall were covered in ivy, their sharp lines softened with age. Trees as old as the building surrounded it, shading it from the sun. The lead-paned windows had not been replaced by the more modern mullioned variety.

The grand bishop was the only official currently occupying the building. He had not brought any members of his staff, cutting himself off from everyone except Father Pietro, who was so self-absorbed he had no idea he was being used merely as an errand boy. The interior of the hall was cool, silent, and smelled of dust. The floor creaked as they walked down a corridor. Doors leading to other offices were closed. The office of the grand bishop was located at the far end.

Father Pietro knocked softly on the door, then opened it to say, "Monsieur Dubois is here, Eminence."

"Very well," said Montagne. He did not sound pleased.

Father Pietro hovered near. "Should I remain, Eminence?"

"No, Father. Return to your studies."

Father Pietro shut the door and left. Dubois could hear his footfalls creaking down the corridor. Despite that, the ever-cautious Dubois opened the door to make certain the priest had really, truly departed.

Satisfied they were alone, Dubois shut the door and turned around. He was so surprised by what he saw that he was jolted out of his usual complacency. Dubois stared in dumbfounded astonishment.

Ferdinand de Montagne was a big man, in his middle years, well above average height at six foot five, with broad shoulders, a wide girth. He had always been in excellent health, save for a tendency to dyspepsia due to a fondness for wine and rich food.

Dubois would not have recognized the man. Montagne had lost weight. His skin was sallow. His hair was grayer, thinner and his eyes were bloodshot and watery. He was seated at a large desk, engaged in writing something in a small book, a task he would have ordinarily assigned to a member of his staff.

"Eminence," said Dubois, bowing. "I fear you have been ill."

"The food they serve in this place is abominable. I cannot keep anything down. What do *you* want, Dubois?" Montagne growled. "Be brief. I am busy."

He held his pen poised above the paper, his finger marking his place. He regarded his agent with deep suspicion.

"As always, I am your faithful servant, Eminence," said Dubois with quiet reassurance.

Montagne swallowed. He lowered his gaze, then slowly laid down the pen. Moving his hand from the book, he sat back in his chair. A muscle in his neck twitched. He closed his eyes and rubbed them.

"I know you are, Dubois," said Montagne wearily. "Sit down. I assume you have heard what has happened."

Dubois spread his hands. "Everyone is talking . . ."

"Of course, they are. Fools! They know nothing. They should trust me! Why don't they trust me? I am trying to save the Church!"

He sighed. "But you did not come for that. Why are you here?"

Dubois reached inside his coat and drew out the letter from the king. Rising to his feet, he laid the letter in front of Montagne, who recognized the seal with at first surprise and then anger.

"What is this?"

"A letter from the king."

"I can see that! Since when have you become Alaric's courier?"

"If Your Eminence will read the letter, I will endeavor to explain."

The grand bishop pressed his signet ring onto the seal; the magical constructs set into his ring caused the king's seal to open. He read the letter. Dubois watched the man's expression grow dark. Montagne reached the end, then tossed the letter onto the desk with contempt.

"Ineffable twaddle," he stated. "Lift tanks failing due to contramagic. Alaric must be desperate to concoct such a ridiculous tale. As for releasing Captain de Guichen and Monsieur de Villeneuve . . ."

He stopped talking and fiddled with his pen.

"I heard they never arrived," said Dubois.

"No secret is safe from you," said the grand bishop caustically. "We presume they attempted to escape. The criminals will be found, however. We have sent out search parties."

"I hope they *are* found," said Dubois gravely. "We badly need Monsieur Rodrigo. The king is telling the truth about the lift tanks, Eminence. I myself discovered the contramagic constructs that are causing the lift tanks to fail."

Montagne's index finger rapped on the table. He regarded Dubois intently. Dubois met the grand bishop's gaze without flinching.

"How the devil do you know what contramagic looks like, Dubois?" Montagne demanded.

"I had seen such constructs before, Eminence. They were on the bomb that exploded in the library of the archbishop in Westfirth; the bomb that nearly killed Father Jacob, Sir Ander, the countess, and myself. As Your Eminence knows, God gave me the ability to remember what I see with remarkable accuracy. The constructs were contramagic. Father Jacob said so at the time and, after undertaking some research on my own, I believe him. Just as I believe the magic that destroyed the Crystal Market was contramagic. The disastrous effect is being felt worldwide, Eminence. You cannot arrest *all* the crafters . . ."

Montagne's face turned livid, his brows contracted, and his eyes glittered. Dubois had the feeling that his own arrest was imminent. Nevertheless, he pressed on.

"Your Eminence, think of the terrible political implications of this disaster for the Church. If the Sunset Palace falls from the heavens, the result will be catastrophic. Untold numbers of people will die. King Alaric is prepared to claim publicly that *you* had it in your power to save the castle and the city from destruction. He will produce a copy of this letter. He will produce witnesses. He will claim that you were jealous. The scandal would be—"

"Enough!" Montagne said through gritted teeth.

His jaw clenched, his hand clenched. He breathed hard and swallowed several more times, grimacing as though the taste in his mouth was bitter as alum. At length, he took a fresh sheet of paper, wrote something on it, signed it, sealed it.

"I am pardoning Captain de Guichen and Monsieur de Villeneuve at the king's behest. I hope they can find a way to save Alaric's damn palace."

"Thank you, Eminence," said Dubois with his bobbing bow. "I understand that no one is being permitted to leave the Citadel. I will require a letter of authorization, giving me permission to do so."

The grand bishop muttered something. Taking another sheet of paper, he wrote out the authorization.

As Dubois approached the desk to pick up the letter and the pardons, he stole a swift glance at the page of the book the grand bishop had been reading. The passage he had marked referred to the authority of the grand bishop in regard to the Council of Bishops. Montagne must be endeavoring to justify his action in disbanding the Council.

"Is there anything I can do for Your Eminence?" Dubois asked.

"I wish there was, Dubois. I wish there was," said Montagne heavily. "Close the door behind you."

He gestured in dismissal. Dubois bowed and left the office, walking down the creaking hall. He thought of the man sitting alone in this large and silent building, an embattled man, under siege, and he felt deep and profound pity.

Dubois took possession of his room in the guesthouse. Locking the door, he sat down and read through the letter that authorized him to leave the Citadel. Montagne had scrawled his signature below.

Dubois studied the letter, then dipped the pen in the ink and began to write. He had developed a talent for forgery over the years; a useful skill for an agent. He had room to remove a period and add only a few words, but that was enough.

> *M. Dubois is granted permission to depart the Citadel after he has interrogated the prisoner, Jacob Northrop.*

Dubois inspected the forgery carefully. Satisfied that even Montagne might be fooled into thinking he had written the note, Dubois let the ink dry, then set forth on his mission.

6

You can lock truth in prison, but she will always find a way to escape.

—Father Jacob Northrop

People the world over shuddered at the mere mention of the dungeons of the Citadel. They told tales of the torture chambers; the dark oubliettes into which men disappeared forever; the chill, dank cells where prisoners in chains hung from the walls; the diet of moldy bread and rat meat.

In truth, the Citadel prison was clean, well kept. The cells were not exactly comfortable, but they were open to the light and air. Prisoners were allowed to take daily exercise in a courtyard. They were fed three times a day and given water for drinking and for washing.

The prison was situated about halfway down the mountainside, built on a promontory that jutted out into the inland sea. Walls surrounded the prison on three sides. The fourth side was guarded by the sea and a bone-breaking drop to the rocks below. Three small guard towers overlooked the prison courtyard. The complex was not very big, consisting of the cell block and two small outbuildings—one where the prison guards resided and one for supplies. The monks of Saint Klee were responsible for overseeing the prisoners.

Only the worst of the worst were locked up in the prison. Those men and women who were placed "under Seal," but who had not committed any crime, were housed in the guesthouses. A person might be placed under Seal for any number of reasons. Father Jacob had placed the sailors who had first encountered the Bottom Dwellers at the Abbey of Saint Agnes under Seal to interrogate them about what they had seen and heard. Those sailors had long since been released. Dubois considered it telling that Father Jacob and his Knight Protector, Sir Ander Martel, both had been locked up in prison—the worst of the worst.

Dubois stopped at the entry gate to show his credentials and to submit to a search. He was armed with a portable writing desk, which he opened at the monk's behest. The desk contained nothing more dangerous than pen, ink, and paper.

"I am here at the request of the grand bishop to interrogate Father Jacob," said Dubois.

He handed the monk the grand bishop's order. The monk read it through twice and lingered, frowning, on the last sentence.

"Father Jacob is not here," said the monk.

"Then take me to him, Brother," said Dubois.

The monk hesitated. "I must seek the approval of the master."

"Of course, Brother," said Dubois.

If the master in turn sought approval by going to the grand bishop, Dubois was in trouble. He waited with outward complacency and inward tension.

The master of the monks of Saint Klee was a tall, spare man with iron-gray hair, all bone and muscle. He regarded Dubois intently, giving no hint of what he was thinking. The master's face was gaunt, his cheeks hollow, his eyes deep set, dark and unreadable. His expression never changed. He registered no emotion. Dubois could not tell what the man was thinking and he felt a little flutter of his pulse, a little qualm in his gut. The master might be here to do his bidding or to escort Dubois to his own prison cell.

The master made a gesture indicating Dubois was to accompany him into the prison. The master walked with long strides, and Dubois, with his short legs, had to hurry to keep up. He was expecting to go to the cell block and he was startled when the master entered another door, one that led into the courtyard where the prisoners exercised.

The master crossed the courtyard. Dubois, hampered by the unwieldy desk, puffed along at his side. They came to a small building where the monks who guarded the prisoners lived when off duty. The building was a square blockhouse made of stone. Slit windows faced out over the inland sea.

Dubois now had a good idea of what was going on. The master opened the door of the residence. Inside was a common room used by the monks for prayers, meditation, and studies. The central feature was a shrine to Saint Klee. A statue of the saint, notable for his long, blond hair, stood on an altar. A candle always burned in his honor.

A door sealed with elaborate constructs stood at the end of the room. Dubois was impressed with their intricacy. The master removed them, then ushered Dubois through the door. What had once been the monks' sleeping quarters had been transformed into two prison cells. There were no walls, only iron bars, so that the guard would be able to see the prisoners at all times. There were no windows. Each prisoner had a bed and a chamber pot.

A monk seated on a stool near the door rose at the entrance of the master. He and the monk exchanged glances and the monk departed, leaving Dubois and the master alone.

"Father Jacob Northrop," said the master, indicating the prisoners. "Sir Ander Martel."

Sir Ander had been lying on his bed reading a book. Seeing Dubois, the knight closed the book, dropped it on the bed, and rose to his feet.

One of the Knight Protectors, charged with protecting the lives of the members of the Arcanum, who were often sent on dangerous missions, Sir Ander Martel was about fifty years of age and, Dubois knew, had been traveling with Father Jacob for twenty of those years. Dubois wondered on what legal grounds Sir Ander was being held. Knight Protectors were assigned to their charges; they had no say in the matter. If Father Jacob had committed an act of heresy, could Sir Ander be held complicit? A pretty legal problem.

Sir Ander was a well-built man, tall, with a military bearing. Not long ago, he had saved Dubois's life when a contramagic bomb was tossed into the room in which they were meeting. He had warned Dubois and the others in the room to take cover, then picked up the bomb, and threw it out the door a mere second before it exploded. Dubois gave Sir Ander one of his little bows to show he remembered and was grateful. Sir Ander frowned.

"Father," he said in warning tones, "we have company."

In his midforties, Father Jacob was of medium height. His hair had once been brown, but was now almost completely gray. He had worn the tonsure, but that was starting to grow out. Normally clean-shaven, he had a stubbly growth of gray beard. A Freyan by birth, he had fled his homeland after the Reformation to come to Rosia. He was what people called a savant—a crafter born with magic at his fingertips, as the saying went. He was undoubtedly one of the most brilliant wielders of magic in the world . . . and probably the most eccentric.

Dubois was considerably disconcerted to see Father Jacob crawling on his hands and knees on the floor of his cell with a piece of chalk. Moving nearer, he saw that Father Jacob was drawing the sigils of a construct. Dubois looked around in astonishment to see the priest had covered most of the walls and floor with constructs. The magic made no sense to Dubois. As he watched, fascinated, Father Jacob uttered an exclamation of irritation and with his sleeve rubbed out what he had just drawn.

All this time, the master waited, not moving. This was nettlesome to Dubois. The master's presence stood in the way of his important business here. He needed to speak to Father Jacob in private.

He bowed to the monk. "Thank you, Master. You need not stay, I need to be alone with the prisoner."

"That is not possible," said the master. "A guard must be present at all times. Given the prisoner's skill as a savant, no cell could hold him. The only way we can ensure Father Jacob will not break out is to keep him under constant surveillance. I will be present."

Dubois was annoyed with himself. He should have foreseen this. Most prisons used magical energy drains in cells where they kept crafters. The magic was built into the walls and drained the energy of any construct the prisoner might use to try to break out.

A drain would not work with a savant such as Father Jacob, who did not need to inscribe a physical construct. He used his mental powers to fuel his magic, which made it all the more puzzling to Dubois to see Father Jacob on the floor drawing magical constructs that were seemingly harmless.

"We offered Father Jacob and Sir Ander the opportunity

to swear by their faith in God that they would not try to escape," the master continued. "Both men refused, stating that they have not been given a chance to defend themselves at a public trial and that they thus believe their imprisonment to be unjust."

No, there could not be a public trial, Dubois thought with an inward sigh.

He eyed the master, wondering what was going on in the mind behind that inscrutable face. Where did his loyalties lie? The monks of Saint Klee claimed to be loyal to God and God alone. Dubois hoped that was true. He decided upon a compromise.

"Perhaps you could wait in the outer room during my interrogation, Master. You would be able to react swiftly if the prisoners tried to escape. I can easily call for your help."

The master regarded Dubois in silence. Dubois endured the scrutiny, thankful he had a clear conscience. He would not otherwise have wanted to sustain that soul-piercing stare. Apparently satisfied, the master walked into the outer chamber, although he left the door open. Dubois would have liked to have closed it, but having won a small victory, he did not want to continue the fight.

Dubois took the small stool usually occupied by the guard and dragged it in front of Father Jacob's cell. Dubois perched on the stool, placing the small writing desk on his knees. He cast a glance outside the door, then opened the lid to the desk and took out pen, ink, and paper.

"This man is Dubois, the bishop's creature, sent to interrogate you, Father," Sir Ander said bitingly.

Father Jacob looked up from this work. Sitting back on his heels, he wiped his hands on his cassock, the black of which was now gray from chalk dust. He smiled broadly.

"Monsieur Dubois. Good to see you again. I am glad you have brought implements for writing. I would like very much to tell you all I know and to have my words set down on paper."

"May I ask what you are doing, Father?" Dubois asked, studying the constructs.

"He's doing his best to ensure that we are burned at the stake," said Sir Ander bitterly. "Don't say a word, Father."

"My dear Ander, I've committed so many crimes, broken so many laws that a few more won't matter. I am studying contramagic," said Father Jacob.

Dubois felt the hair on the back of his neck raise. He glanced uneasily out the door. The master was kneeling at the shrine of Saint Klee, perhaps praying for the souls of them all.

Father Jacob noted his glance and gave a slight shrug. "The grand bishop will never set me free. I might as well work on contramagic. Someone has to study it, although I fear the knowledge we obtain will be too little, too late."

Dubois could almost feel the flames of an inquisitor's fire roasting his feet. He had already seen enough to be branded as a heretic, however, so he might as well proceed. He placed the paper on the desk and set the jar of ink in the small holder built into the top of the desk. He smoothed the paper, but did not pick up the pen.

"What have you discovered, Father?" Dubois asked.

"That the Church's doctrine against contramagic is all wrong," said Father Jacob with asperity. "Contramagic isn't evil any more than night is evil. Night is the opposite of day. Contramagic is the opposite of magic."

He got down again on all fours and pointed to a magical construct that he had drawn near the bars of the cell.

"Observe this." Father Jacob indicated the sigils of the construct. "Contramagic uses the same six basic sigils we study as children: earth, air, water, fire, life, death."

"But they are backward," said Dubois.

"You are a keen observer," said Father Jacob, gratified.

"In contramagic, the sigils are the mirror image of their counterparts, with some subtle differences. The sigils are combined to form constructs differently, in ways I find quite ingenious. But, you are correct. They are, in essence, the same basic six only backward."

"So what makes contramagic work?" Dubois asked. He still had not picked up his pen.

"I will show you," said Father Jacob. He tapped his finger on the floor. "Do you recognize this construct, monsieur?"

"It was on the bomb that nearly blew us up," said Dubois.

"Do you recognize the sigils that make up the constructs?"

"I do. All except that one," said Dubois, pointing.

"Excellent, monsieur!" Father Jacob said with pleasure, as though praising a gifted student. "That is the 'seventh sigil.' Contramagic adds a seventh sigil to the basic six."

Father Jacob shook his head sadly. "Despite the fact that I can re-create it, I still cannot make it work."

Dubois was intrigued. He looked at the constructs that were scrawled all over the floor and the walls. They reminded him of the mathematical problems he had studied as a child. He could now see the mysterious seventh sigil in all of them, placed at random, sometimes at the beginning, sometimes in the middle, sometimes at the end.

"None of these constructs do anything," said Father Jacob, frustrated. "This seventh sigil is a mystery. Until I figure out what it represents and how it fits in with the other six, I cannot recreate the contramagic."

"Just as well," Sir Ander said drily. "You'd probably blow us up."

"The saints knew," Father Jacob continued, ignoring his friend. "The books I obtained from the dragons talk of the *roed* and the *raeg*. Saint Marie and the others learned about contramagic from the dragons. They wrote it all down."

He cast a stern glance in the direction of the master. "The monks confiscated the books before I could study them. I need access to those books!"

He turned back to Dubois. "The grand bishop trusts you, monsieur. Speak to Montagne! Convince him of the urgency!"

Dubois shook his head. "I am sorry, Father. What you ask is impossible. The books would now be in the Library of the Forbidden."

Father Jacob was very grim. He muttered the word "Fools" under his breath, gazed down at the constructs with a shrug and a sigh. He rose to his feet.

"But you did not come here to talk about contramagic, Monsieur Dubois," said Father Jacob. "You came to interrogate me. I am happy to talk."

He walked over to stand near Dubois. Sir Ander shook his head and started to go back to his bed and his reading.

"Sir Ander, if you please," said Dubois. "I ask you to hear what I have to say."

Sir Ander looked at him, frowning. Dubois shifted the stool to be able to speak to both men in a hushed voice.

"Gentlemen, we are facing disaster," said Dubois. "The future of the monarchy literally dangles by a thread. You are acquainted with a woman called Eiddwen, known to you as the Sorceress?"

Father Jacob's face darkened. "I am, monsieur, to my sorrow. What has she done now?"

"She has sabotaged the Sunset Palace."

Father Jacob's face grew darker still. "Tell me all, monsieur."

Dubois described how Eiddwen had assumed a false identity and taken up residence in the royal palace, bringing with her a young man she termed her nephew. Dubois had now identified him as her protégé in blood magic, a murderer known as the Warlock. He went on to tell how Eiddwen had placed contramagic "bombs" on the lift tanks and how the engineers were working frantically to keep the palace from crashing into the lake.

"What about the king and the people who reside there? Do they know the danger?" Sir Ander asked, shocked.

"Most of the members of the nobility left for the summer," said Dubois. "The king knows the danger and he remains, much to his credit."

"What about Eiddwen?" Father Jacob demanded. "Has she been apprehended?"

"There is worse news, if that is possible, Father. Before she fled, Eiddwen abducted the princess, Sophia."

He related how the Warlock had ingratiated himself with the princess and persuaded her to elope, claiming they were going to the dragon duchies, how Eiddwen accompanied them as "chaperone," and that the Countess Cecile de Marjolaine had discovered the elopement and gone after them to rescue the princess.

"Tell me she did go alone!" Sir Ander said, alarmed.

"She did not, sir," said Dubois. "A friend of yours is traveling with her. A Knight Protector named Sir Conal O'Hairt."

"Thank God!" said Sir Ander fervently.

Dubois continued: "The countess discovered news of them and wrote to her aide, Monsieur D'argent. The letter was in code, of course. First, she said that Eiddwen has gone to Freya. She asked him to warn a . . . um . . . mutual acquaintance."

Father Jacob was grave. "Did you?"

"I did, Father. I thought it was important that he should know."

Father Jacob nodded. "God help my countrymen."

"What else did the letter say?" Sir Ander asked.

"The next part of the letter was more difficult for

D'argent to understand. He believes the countess was trying to tell him that the princess is being taken to a monastery dedicated to Saint Dominick the Keeper. It is located in the Oscadia Mountains."

"I have never heard of such a monastery or that saint," said Father Jacob.

"Have you, Sir Ander?" Dubois asked.

Sir Ander shook his head. "Dominick the Keeper. Keeper of what?"

"Keeper of the Gates of Hell," said Dubois.

He related the story. "The monks were sent to drive the fiends back and seal the gate," he said in conclusion.

"What was the date this monastery was built?" Father Jacob asked abruptly.

Dubois was startled. "Around the year 25 DT, when the Dark Ages were nearing an end. Why?"

Father Jacob clasped his hands behind his back and began to pace the small cell, talking to himself. Dubois strained to listen.

"So we have a monastery dedicated to Saint Dominick the Keeper of the Gates of Hell founded in the mountains of Oscadia. A strange place to build a monastery. A strange choice for a saint. A strange time to build it, when the Church had few resources and was struggling to survive. A strange tale of fiends attacking a village."

He walked back and forth the short distance between the iron bars and the wall. Dubois looked at Sir Ander, who could only shrug.

"It makes no sense to me," he said.

Father Jacob stopped pacing. He stared into the distance, past the iron bars, past the prison walls, perhaps down through centuries. Suddenly he whipped around, his cassock shedding chalk dust. He came close to the bars of the cell, clasped them with his hands so hard that his knuckles were white.

"God help us, Monsieur Dubois! If what I fear is true, the Church has committed an unspeakable crime."

Dubois picked up the writing desk and drew his stool near Father Jacob. Sir Ander had moved as close as the bars of his cell would allow.

"What do you suspect, Father?" he asked.

Father Jacob shook his head. His lips were pressed tightly together, his brows were lowered and his expression was grim.

"Let us postulate that by some means survivors from the sunken isle of Glasearrach made their way to the surface. They did not travel by ship, but on foot."

"That would mean they would have to climb up from the bottom of the world! How would that be possible?" Dubois was skeptical.

Father Jacob shrugged. "We know that rivers such as the Safelle flow into sinkholes and from there become subterranean rivers, running beneath the ground, carving through the rock, forming vast caverns. It is not beyond the realm of possibility that an intrepid explorer could travel up from Below through such caverns, reaching the surface by following the course of the river."

"God makes all things possible," said Dubois, still not entirely convinced.

He began to jot down the information, using a code he had developed himself.

"Let us assume this is what occurred," Father Jacob continued. "Survivors from the doomed island reach the surface. They are ecstatic. They can save their people from a life of darkness and hardship by bringing them back to the world. They find the nearest village and tell their story. Sadly, their story was a tale that must never be told."

Dubois's hand started to shake. He dropped a blot of ink on the paper. He glanced at the door, wishing himself on the other side of it. Wishing himself on the other side of the world. Too late. He knew too much already.

Sir Ander was shaking his head in disbelief. "Think about what you are saying, Father! You are accusing the Church of having knowledge that people were alive on the island at the bottom of the world and that the Church did nothing to help them."

"I am accusing the Church of worse than that," said Father Jacob grimly. "Consider this: The Church used contramagic, which they had proclaimed to be a tool of the Evil One, to sink the island. They expected everyone on that island to die. Their secret would never be revealed. But now they are confronted with survivors who will tell the tale.

"How could the Church explain that they had essentially conspired with the Evil One to kill countless innocents? They could not do so. The Church made up a story about fiends escaping from the mountain. They sealed up the entrance and built a monastery on the site, commanding the monks to guard the Gates of Hell."

"I don't believe it," said Sir Ander harshly.

"I do," Dubois said in an unhappy whisper. He crumpled up the paper on which he had been writing. "I have long known the grand bishop has been guarding some dark and terrible secret, a secret that is destroying his health, eating him up inside."

"Montagne has allowed countless people to die rather than risk revelation," said Father Jacob sternly, not bothering to lower his voice. He added with a sigh, "I wonder if he knows the monks of Saint Dominick have failed in their duties."

"What do you mean?" Sir Ander asked.

"The Bottom Dwellers found their way up once," said Father Jacob ominously. "They could find it again."

"You are saying they came back to the monastery!" said Sir Ander, aghast.

"That is the only reason I can see that they would be taking the princess to the monastery, though I cannot fathom why they want her. Perhaps to hold her hostage."

"But if that is true, Cecile and Sir Conal could be walking into an enemy camp! And I have no way to warn them!" Sir Ander exclaimed in agony.

"They are in God's hands, my friends, as is the princess," said Father Jacob. "Have faith. He will keep them safe."

"Why do you think Eiddwen is going to Freya?" Dubois asked.

"To bring death, mayhem, chaos, and destruction," said Father Jacob in dire tones.

"You have encountered this woman before, Father," said Dubois urgently. "*You* know how to stop her."

Father Jacob looked back at the walls, the constructs of contramagic. "I *failed* to stop her, Monsieur Dubois. I am not sure I can or if anyone can—"

"Certainly we cannot stop her from a jail cell," said Sir Ander caustically.

Shrugging resignedly, Father Jacob kilted up his robes, picked up his chalk, and went back down on his knees, scrawling more constructs on the floor.

Sir Ander stood watching him in frustration. "We have to do something, Father! Drawing pictures isn't going to help!"

"Unless you can find a way to break out of a prison from which no one has ever escaped, Sir Ander, I will continue to draw my pictures," said Father Jacob.

Sir Ander muttered something best not repeated and flung himself on the bed. Lying with his hands beneath his head, he stared at the ceiling. Dubois cleared his desk, putting away his writing tools and the ink. He picked up the desk and, bidding Father Jacob and Sir Ander farewell, headed for the door.

The master stood blocking the way.

Dubois was not surprised. He was in possession of a terrible secret. The grand bishop might just skip prison and go straight to execution. Dubois waited several agonizing moments.

"Go with God," said the master.

Dubois stared at the monk in astonishment. The monks of Saint Klee never spoke without reason. They did not make idle chitchat or toss out offhanded blessings.

The master unlocked the door and held it open. Dubois passed through the door and into the sunlit courtyard.

"Well, well, well," said Dubois.

He left the prison, deep in thought, wondering what he should do. He knew what he needed to do. The question was whether he had the courage to do it.

Compared to his fellow spymasters—Sir Henry Wallace and the Countess de Marjolaine—Dubois led a relatively quiet life. He had never assassinated anyone, had never worn a disguise or sailed off in a pirate ship, or ever endured a cannonade. No one had ever challenged him to a duel or laced his coffee with arsenic.

He had been shot once, but that was by accident, and he had almost been blown up by a bomb. Both of these terrifying experiences had served to reinforce Dubois's notion that it was better, healthier, and far more comfortable to avoid having adventures.

In this instance, however, Dubois was stymied. He could send an agent, but he dared not trust even his most loyal agent with such a critical and delicate mission. Dubois was planning to commit high treason and, if his plans worked out, high treason would be only the first of many crimes.

He left the Citadel in haste, flying on griffin-back to the city of Eudaine where he took rooms at an inn. He first wrote a letter to D'argent, apprising him that Captain de Guichen and Monsieur Rodrigo had never reached the

Citadel. He urged D'argent to seek them out. He enclosed the grand bishop's release and dispatched the packet to the palace by swift courier.

This done, Dubois ate a good meal, drank an unpretentious wine, made his arrangements, said his prayers, and went to sleep.

The next day, Dubois set out alone on what might be his first, last, and only adventure.

7

One can find winning in the losing.

—Johan Alfheisen

The carriage stopped in front of Stephano's house. D'argent stepped down. He paused a moment before entering, arranging his thoughts. He had to tell Benoit about Dubois's letter, relating the grim news that Stephano and Rodrigo and the red monks who had arrested them had never arrived at the Citadel.

The old man was still in his sickbed, recovering from what the physician termed an "incident" with his heart. D'argent had been receiving daily reports from the physician, who said that Benoit was making steady improvement. Indeed, the physician had said the old man was well enough to return to his duties. Benoit had proclaimed himself too ill, however. He remained in his bed while the Sisters of Mercy read to him, played cribbage with him, brought him his meals, and fluffed his pillow.

D'argent had been of two minds whether or not to tell Benoit that Stephano had disappeared. He worried that he might cause a relapse, but he needed to find out if Benoit had heard anything, if Stephano had contacted him.

D'argent had been in touch with the monks of Saint

Klee, being so bold as to travel to their monastery in Evreux to talk to their master. She had agreed to meet with him, but refused to answer his questions about Stephano and Rodrigo. She would not even admit that her monks and their prisoners were missing. Frustrated, D'argent had showed her a copy of the king's pardon.

"If you find Lord Captain de Guichen and Monsieur de Villeneuve, please be aware that your monks have no right to take them into custody. I would be grateful, however, if your monks render them aid should they require it and that you would immediately inform me that you have recovered them."

The master had said nothing. She had merely bowed. D'argent had finally given up and left in extreme ire.

D'argent took hold of the door knocker that was in the shape of a dragon and knocked quietly. A boy about twelve, acting as servant, answered the door. He took D'argent's hat and cloak and escorted him through the darkened, quiet house to the patient's room. D'argent found Benoit sitting up in bed, surrounded by every comfort from books to a bowl of fruit on the nightstand. A nun fussed over him.

"The patient is progressing nicely, sir," she said in answer to D'argent's question. "He ate every bit of his dinner—a cold breast of boiled chicken and some custard for dessert and a mug of small ale."

Benoit looked very meek, but when the sister wasn't looking, he grimaced and shook his head. D'argent expressed his relief on hearing the good news.

"He will enjoy a visit, sir," the sister continued, adding severely, "Mind you, Monsieur D'argent, do *not* allow the patient to cozen you into giving him brandy. He is permitted one small glass before bed and that is all."

Benoit lay back in the bed and the sister arranged the coverlet. He thanked her feebly as she picked up the dinner tray and departed the room, her wimple floating behind her. The moment she left, Benoit threw back the coverlet and hopped nimbly to his feet.

"Let me pour you a brandy, sir," he said, hurrying to the table on which stood the cut crystal brandy decanter. "A gift from her ladyship. As fine a brandy as I've ever tasted."

"Benoit!" D'argent exclaimed, shocked. "You should be in bed!"

"Bah! I'm quite well or I would be if the sister would let me have food fit for a man. Small ale and cold boiled chicken!" Benoit grunted in disgust. "One would think I was a babe in arms! Do you know what they feed me for supper, sir? Gruel! That's what! It's a wonder I'm strong enough to walk."

D'argent declined the brandy, saying that he never drank strong spirits in the middle of the day.

"Then I will take a snifter, sir, if you don't mind," said Benoit. "I find it soothes the stomach."

He poured himself a large glass, returned to his bed and settled himself comfortably. D'argent remembered the sister's instructions, but he knew quite well that Benoit wouldn't listen to him.

"Have you heard word from the master and Monsieur Rodrigo, sir?" Benoit asked eagerly. "I was so thankful to hear His Majesty had pardoned them. I've been expecting them home any day."

D'argent pulled up a chair and sat down.

"I have not, Benoit. I came to ask you the same."

The old man regarded D'argent intently. He sat bolt upright, almost spilling the brandy.

"Something's amiss, sir! Something's happened to the master!"

"Please, don't excite yourself, Benoit," said D'argent. "We know nothing for certain yet. They are missing. The monks and Stephano and Rodrigo never reached the Citadel."

Benoit sank back among the pillows with a groan.

"Can I do something?" D'argent asked in concern. "I'll fetch the sister—"

"No, sir, no!" Benoit said. He gestured feebly at the brandy decanter. "Another glass, sir. To aid me in recovery from the shock."

D'argent hid a smile as he poured another glass of brandy and brought it to the old man. As he did so, he was aware of the sound of someone knocking on the front door and voices as the servant answered. The boy entered a moment later.

"A man to see you, Monsieur Benoit. He gave no name, sir," said the boy, adding indignantly. "He told me it was none of my business. I left him waiting on the front stoop."

"Are you expecting a visitor?" D'argent asked.

Benoit shook his head.

"I will deal with this," said D'argent.

As he was leaving, he saw Benoit's hand dart beneath his pillow, take out a loaded pistol and hide it beneath the counterpane. D'argent opened the door and stared in amazement so great he took an involuntary step backward.

One of the largest men D'argent had ever seen stood on the stoop. His massive shoulders spanned the doorway, and he was so tall that he would have to bend down to enter. He was bald and wore no hat; D'argent guessed there were few hats that would fit this giant. His neck was thick with muscle. He wore a flannel shirt with an open collar, leather breeches, a leather weskit, thick, sturdy brogues, and a red kerchief tied around his neck. He was perhaps in his early forties. He stood straight, his hands clasped in front of him, his feet spread wide.

Two men on the sidewalk behind him seemed almost identical to their leader. They had the appearance of stevedores, and yet there was a gleam in their alert brown eyes and an assured, confidence in their carriage that told D'argent there was much more to these men than was revealed on their very large countenances.

"Good day, gentlemen," said D'argent. "How may I assist you?"

The man on the stoop was clearly the eldest. He looked D'argent over and then said imperturbably, "I am here to see Benoit."

"He is indisposed," said D'argent gravely. "I would be glad to deliver a message—"

"My message is for Benoit, sir. I'll thank you to take me to him." The man smiled pleasantly. "I make an unsightly lawn ornament, but you should know that I'm prepared to stand here all the rest of the day and into the night."

He jerked his thumb. "As are my brothers."

The brothers were quiet, reserved, respectful. D'argent did not feel threatened, though any one of them could have picked him up and tucked him under a massive arm. Yet they meant what they said. They would stand patiently outside the house until he complied with their request or doomsday arrived, whichever came first.

Excellent men to have by one's side in a crisis, D'argent realized. The sort of men who might once have served with Stephano at some point in his military career. The sort who might be serving him still.

"May I tell Benoit your name?" D'argent asked.

"The Han brothers," said the man shortly.

"Is that all?" D'argent asked.

"That's enough," said the man.

"Please wait here."

D'argent left the man on the stoop and went to speak to Benoit.

"The . . . er . . . Han brothers are here," said D'argent.

Benoit looked wary. "Tell them the master isn't home."

"The one who talked to me asked to see you. Should I let them in?"

Benoit considered, frowning. "So long as you don't allow those young giants anywhere near the pantry. They ate a week's provisions in one sitting the last time."

Smiling, D'argent returned to the door. The three had not moved.

"Come in, gentlemen," D'argent said.

The Han brothers trooped into the house, crowding the hall to such an extent that D'argent was forced to flatten himself against the wall. The three gazed steadily at him.

"And who would you be, sir?" the first asked.

"My name is D'argent. I am in the employ of the Countess de Marjolaine."

The three absorbed this information in unblinking silence. One glanced back at the carriage emblazoned with the countess's coat of arms, which was waiting in the street, as if to confirm the information.

"I'm Johan," said the first. "This is Mohan and Aelfhan. What's the matter with old Benoit?"

"He had a bad spell with his heart. He is better, but he should not have any excitement," D'argent warned.

Johan nodded gravely. "I'll see Benoit now, if you please, sir." He glanced at his siblings. "You stay here. Keep the watch."

His two brothers posted themselves at windows, drawing aside the curtains slightly to see the street. Mystified, D'argent led the eldest through the hall to Benoit's room. Johan stooped his head and went through the door sideways to accommodate his shoulders. Benoit regarded the man with narrowed eyes.

"Well, Johan, and why have you come? The master's not home."

"I'm sorry to see you laid low, sir," said Johan, rocking back on his heels. "I heard Stephano and Rigo were taken prisoner by the red monks."

"Hauled away in irons like common criminals," Benoit said heatedly. "What brings you here?" He added hurriedly, "You're too late for dinner."

Johan smiled, but didn't immediately answer. He turned to regard D'argent in frowning thoughtfulness, then turned back to Benoit.

"This man says he's the countess's man. More to the point, is he a man to be trusted? Stephano's told me—"

"Never mind what the master's told you," Benoit interrupted impatiently. "D'argent's a good friend."

Johan found this acceptable.

"I'll give this to you, Monsieur D'argent. I'm thinking you'll know what to do."

Reaching into his shirt, Johan drew out a letter and handed it to D'argent. Recognizing the handwriting, he opened the letter hurriedly.

"It is from Stephano," he said to Benoit.

"I knew it!" Benoit said triumphantly. "Is he all right? What about Monsieur Rodrigo?"

D'argent scanned the letter swiftly. "They are both fine. The Arcanum's yacht was attacked by Bottom Dwellers. They killed the monks, the yacht crashed, and Stephano and Rodrigo suffered cuts and bruises, nothing worse. He writes they are in danger and in need of money—"

Benoit looked dour. "That's the master for you. In danger and in need of money. Well, there's no help for it. I best go pull him out of his scrape." The old man started to climb out of bed. He gestured to Johan. "Hand me my trousers, young giant—"

Both D'argent and Johan hurried to restrain Benoit.

"You rest, sir," said Johan, gently easing the old man back down into bed.

"Do not trouble yourself, Benoit," said D'argent. "I will go to them at once."

Benoit grumbled and argued, but in the end allowed himself to be persuaded to remain in bed. He settled back among the pillows and held out his empty snifter. "Could you fetch me a drop, young giant? I feel my heart a bit fluttery."

Johan took the crystal snifter. The fragile stemware that was Rodrigo's pride and joy disappeared in his large hand. For a big man, his movements were graceful and deft. He poured a small amount of the brandy into the snifter and carried it back to Benoit. The old man glared at the small amount, but drank it swiftly, aware, D'argent was sure, that the sister would be back soon. He handed the snifter back to Johan and ordered him to "wash away the evidence."

"See to it the master doesn't get himself arrested again, sir," Benoit called to D'argent as he was leaving. "My heart can't take much more of this."

D'argent promised he would. He found the sister having her tea in the kitchen and sent her to Benoit. The boy brought D'argent's hat and cloak. Johan escorted him outside.

"My brothers and I are available if you need our help, sir. We think a good deal of Stephano and Rigo."

The two brothers silently nodded their agreement.

"Thank you, but that will not be necessary. I am pleased to have met all of you." D'argent held out his hand to each brother in turn. They shook his hand solemnly. He left massaging bruised knuckles.

As his carriage rolled away, D'argent looked out the window to see the three Han brothers walking down the sidewalk, shoulder-to-shoulder. Probably how they went through life. D'argent leaned back in the carriage and recalled what he knew of the participants in the Lost

Rebellion—the ill-fated cause, led by the Duke de Bourlet, that had cost Julian de Guichen his life.

He remembered what he had been trying to recall, that the wife of the Duke de Bourlet had three nephews. She was the daughter of the Earl of Thorlburg of Travia. The three fought with the duke and were believed to have died in the battle. They were said to have been very tall, well built. Described as "young giants."

The letter directed D'argent to the walled town of Eudaine on the Conce river. The Arcanum's yacht would have flown over the town on the way to the Citadel, which was some two hundred miles to the east. The town was surrounded by rolling hills and thick forests.

Eudaine, one of the oldest towns in Rosia, had been established on the river long before the rise of the Sunlit Empire. For centuries, the people had made a living fishing the river, selling wool, fur, and leather.

The ancient wall that surrounded the town was now more picturesque than functional. The population had long since spilled over the wall into the surrounding countryside. The townsfolk had torn down the old gates that had once been locked up every evening at sundown.

Now people came and went as they pleased, although since the attack in Westfirth there had been some talk among the city leaders about building new gates. Merchants had protested that locking up the town would be bad for business; the matter was left unresolved.

D'argent's carriage landed in a stable yard outside the town wall. When men came to unharness the wyverns and lead them into the stalls, D'argent gave orders to feed and water the beasts and have them ready to depart before sunset.

The heart of Eudaine was Cathedral Square, a large

open area of flagstone in front of the cathedral. The square was easy to find. The cathedral was the largest building in town, with spires that rose above the fabled wall. By long established custom, all the businesses in Eudaine closed their doors at noontime. People either went home to nap in the afternoon or dined in the restaurants and cafés around Cathedral Square.

D'argent strolled impatiently about the town. When the enormous clock on the cathedral chimed noon, he followed the instructions in Stephano's letter and took a seat near the statue of Saint Sebastian, the patron saint of fishermen. He had not waited long when two men approached him. They looked like tramps, seedily dressed in dirty coats and shabby wide-brimmed hats, which they kept pulled down low over their eyes.

D'argent did not like the looks of them. He was glancing about for a constable when he was startled to hear one speak his name.

"D'argent! What the devil are you doing here?"

"Good God! Stephano!" D'argent exclaimed.

"Hush! Not so loud," said Stephano, glancing around. He eyed D'argent uncertainly. "I expected Benoit."

"He couldn't travel," said D'argent. "His heart. He's fine," he added, seeing Stephano's alarm. "I thought it best if I came instead."

D'argent looked at the second man, who was standing behind Stephano. The hat covered the man's face to such an extent D'argent wasn't certain who was beneath it. He looked questioningly at Stephano.

"Is that . . ."

Stephano nodded.

"Monsieur Rodrigo, I am so glad—" D'argent began.

"Don't speak my name!" Rodrigo whispered, ducking his head. "Someone from court might recognize me wearing these deplorable rags. I would never live down the shame. Bad enough you have to witness my degradation. Swear you will say nothing of this. Nothing!"

"I swear," D'argent promised.

Both men were injured. Rodrigo had a cut lip, his jaw was swollen and bruised. He had his arm in a makeshift sling. Stephano had a large lump on his forehead and a gash across his nose.

"I am so glad to see you both," said D'argent, gripping their hands with unusual emotion. "When I heard that the yacht had not arrived at the Citadel, I feared the worst. What happened?"

"We can't talk here," said Stephano. "Did you bring money? I was thinking we could travel to the dragon duchies. I have friends among the dragons who will let us live there while we plead our case with the grand bishop."

D'argent smiled. "I have brought money, but more than that, I have brought good news. You need not travel to the dragon duchies, nor fear being arrested. At the request of His Majesty, the grand bishop has granted you both pardons."

Rodrigo forgot he was hiding his face and looked up at D'argent in slack-jawed amazement.

Stephano frowned. "I don't understand. Why would the king intervene on our behalf?"

"Never mind why!" Rodrigo flung his arm around D'argent, clasping him in a crushing hug. "Thank you, dear D'argent! Thank you! Thank you!"

"Let us have some dinner and I will explain," said D'argent, extricating himself with some difficulty from Rodrigo's embrace.

D'argent chose a café located in the shadows of the cathedral, selecting a table in the back beneath a large oak tree. A fine claret soothed Rodrigo's feelings with regard to his shabby clothes.

"Tell me what happened," said D'argent.

"The yacht was attacked by bat riders," Stephano replied. "The monks never had a chance. The Bottom Dwellers seized the yacht and tried to sail it. The driver lost control and the yacht crashed into the forest somewhere south of here. We survived by playing dead."

"We've been walking ever since," said Rodrigo. "Once we came to the river, we followed it to this town. I won't tell you how we've been living. It's been ghastly."

Both men ate voraciously, devouring a meat pie between them and asking for seconds.

"I'll say one thing for the Church, they build a damn fine yacht," Stephano remarked, finally leaning back and throwing down his napkin. "It survived the crash mostly intact; saved our lives."

"We need to send a message to the red monks, tell them the location so they can find the body of their comrade," said Rodrigo somberly. "We didn't have any means to bury him."

Rodrigo sighed and pushed away his plate. Thinking it was time to change the subject, D'argent reached into his pocket and drew out the pardons. He handed one paper to Stephano, who took it doubtfully and began to read. Rodrigo read his and looked at D'argent with amusement.

"So first I am to be burned as a heretic for studying contramagic and now His Majesty wants me to use my studies on contramagic to save the palace. I do *so* love intrigue."

Stephano read his pardon through once, read it through again, and looked at D'argent.

"The grand bishop has pardoned me at the desire of His Majesty." Stephano's expression darkened. "The grand bishop arrests me for no reason and the king pardons me for no reason. This doesn't make sense."

"Politics," said Rodrigo in knowing tones. "It's not supposed to make sense."

"Alaric wants something in return," said Stephano grimly.

He tossed the paper contemptuously on the table. Rodrigo snatched it up and held it close to his breast.

"What if he does? Would you rather be thrown into a dungeon for the rest of your life?"

"I might," said Stephano.

"The king *does* want you to do something for him, Stephano," D'argent admitted. "I told the king about your idea for taking the battle to the Bottom Dwellers. His Majesty was impressed. He agreed to give you money and men to repair Fort Ignacio, and placed soldiers under your command. He would like for you to put your plan into operation as swiftly as possible."

"My plan . . . ," Stephano said, bewildered. "How did you know about my plan?"

"Your friend, Dag, told me. I met him and your other friends back at your house. They are safe. They returned to the *Cloud Hopper*. They know about the pardons. Dag said to tell you they would meet you at the fort."

Stephano had tilted his chair back, listening with his arms crossed, his gaze fixed intently on D'argent. He brought his chair forward, landing with a thunk. Shoving aside his cutlery, he leaned his arms on the table.

"I will not say you are lying, monsieur, for I know you better than that. But you are not telling me all the truth."

D'argent ordered another bottle of claret. "I am not?"

"King Alaric hates me because I am my father's son. Alaric is a man who clings to his hatred. He would happily toss me in a hole and forget about me. You cannot persuade me that he willingly granted me my freedom. My mother might have persuaded the king, but she is not in the palace. I am beholden to someone else. Who is that person? You?"

"No, Stephano, not to me," said D'argent. "I am merely your mother's man of affairs. The person you have to thank is Prince Renaud."

Stephano was completely taken aback. "Prince Renaud! The lord admiral? How would he— I don't understand."

"The prince is acting as adviser to his father during this time of peril," said D'argent, choosing his words carefully. "You will be reporting directly to him. I had a private conversation with the prince before I left. He did not agree with his father's decision to disband the Dragon Brigade. He will discuss the matter with you when he comes to inspect the fortress."

Stephano stared at D'argent. "I . . . I don't know what to say."

" 'Thank you, Your Highness,' would be appropriate," said Rodrigo.

"Do you know the prince?" D'argent asked.

"I met him once, briefly, at a ceremony," said Stephano. "I never served under him, but I know those who have. He is said to be a hard man, a martinet when it comes to discipline. But he's intelligent—unlike his dolt of a father—and a skilled naval officer. No one likes him, but everyone respects him."

Stephano drank his claret in thoughtful silence, then said, "If I am to pursue this plan with the fortress, I must abandon my search for my mother. Have you heard from her? Is she safe? Do you know where she is?"

D'argent had known Stephano would ask this question and had determined how to respond. He knew that if he told Stephano about the letter the countess had written, gave Stephano the location and told him of Father Jacob's theory that she and Sir Conal were in danger, Stephano would go in search of her and abandon his plan to attack the Bottom Dwellers. Stephano was wrong when he said

D'argent would not lie to him. D'argent was perfectly capable of lying when there was need.

"I have heard nothing from your mother," he said. "You have a duty to your country now, Stephano. Your mother would want you to act on your plan."

Stephano twirled his glass and brooded.

D'argent continued: "I have been reading the reports from your mother's agents. The Bottom Dwellers are launching an all-out assault. The Estaran coast is in flames. Travia is on the verge of economic collapse. The Bottom Dwellers hold the refineries of Braffa, as you know. The Freyans attempted to recapture them, but their navy was defeated in a terrible battle."

"I wonder if Sir Henry Wallace survived," Rodrigo mused.

"If he didn't, we can be grateful to the Bottom Dwellers for something," said D'argent drily. He continued more somberly. "We must find a way to stop this foe. To be brutally honest, the world is losing this fight. The Bottom Dwellers won't expect an attack on their home base. Your plan to carry the battle to the enemy may be our only chance."

"And that chance is a slim one," said Stephano. "I have no idea if we can even survive the descent."

D'argent paid the bill and the three left the square. Stephano walked with his head down, his arms folded. He was obviously still worried, still having doubts.

"Your mother is a strong woman," said D'argent, reading his thoughts. "She can take care of herself."

"If anything, I would be worried about those who try to cross her," Rodrigo added.

Stephano half smiled and then said bitterly, "I made no secret of my loathing for my mother. I still do not know what happened between her and my father, how they came to be married. But I know enough to be ashamed of the way I treated her and I fear I will never have a chance to tell her. I would not want her to die thinking me a wretched, selfish, ungrateful child."

D'argent thought of the danger into which the countess and Sir Conal were unknowingly walking and his heart failed him.

"Your mother loves you, Stephano," he said, but he said it with a catch in his voice. "You two wait here. I will go see to the carriage."

He hurried off, feeling Stephano's troubled gaze on him.

8

A lady should always rise to the occasion.

—Lady's Book of Deportment and Propriety

Sir Conal and Cecile followed the road for several days. They rode long hours, not stopping until darkness fell and they could no longer see the trail. Sir Conal found other sites where the three had made camp. Pointing to Sophia's footprints and those of the little dog, he noted that the princess appeared to purposefully walk in muddy patches, in the hope, he said, that someone was searching for her.

"Do you think her abductors know they are being followed?" Cecile asked worriedly.

"I have wondered the same," said Sir Conal. "I do not believe they do. They keep to the trail and make no effort to conceal their campsites."

Cecile smiled, as he intended. He was glad that his logic made her feel better. Despite his belief that the abductors had no idea they were being pursued, Sir Conal deemed it prudent that he and Cecile should take turns sleeping and keeping watch.

"I am not being very chivalrous, asking you to stay awake while I slumber, my lady," said Sir Conal, half jesting, half in earnest.

"I am surprised at you, Sir Conal," Cecile returned, with mock rebuke. "The truly chivalrous man would remain awake three nights running, then pitch headfirst off his horse and break his neck, leaving me to fend for myself."

Sir Conal laughed, as she intended.

Cecile would take first watch, promising to wake Sir Conal after midnight. She had never required much sleep. She often stayed up late into the night to read or write letters.

Making herself comfortable against a tree trunk, Cecile would smile to think what the courtiers of the royal palace would say if they could see the elegant Countess de Marjolaine sitting under the stars on a cushion of pine needles, a loaded pistol beneath her hand, listening to the sound of Sir Conal's snoring and the quiet snufflings of the ponies.

The thought would come to her every night that she was happier in the wilderness, eating stale bread and dried meat, than enduring the rigors and subtle dangers of a royal banquet. She had never known until now how much she truly detested her court life: the intrigue, the pettiness, the jealousies, the rivalries. Here she feared being ambushed. There she lived daily with the fear of being stabbed in the back. If it were not for her fear for Sophia, Cecile would have been at peace.

She and Sir Conal continued to follow the princess and her abductors. The farther they traveled, the more difficulty they had following the trail. More than once the road dumped them in a ravine or left them stranded on an outcropping of barren, windswept rock. Sir Conal would have to spend precious time searching for where the road picked up again. Once, they came to a place where several trails meandered off from the road. These trails wound down the mountainside and appeared to be well traveled.

"They don't lead to the village," said Sir Conal, puzzled. "They are not used by shepherds. We have left sheep-grazing land far behind us. I wonder where they go and who walks them."

On the fourth day, they were riding slowly along the torturous, winding trail when, topping a rise, Cecile looked through an opening in the pine trees and called sharply for Sir Conal.

"The monastery," she said, pointing.

Drawing out his spyglass, Sir Conal peered through it. His expression grew grim. He handed the glass to Cecile.

The monastery, located at the edge of the tree line, was simple in design, consisting of one main building made of stone and several outbuildings of wood, all surrounded by a stone wall. The stone wall was low, only six feet high, designed to keep out beasts rather than men. A wicket gate set in the wall provided entry.

The main building was rectangular in shape, plain and unadorned except for a tall bell tower. The monks had not built a cathedral, nor was there a church that Cecile could see. What appeared to be a small shrine stood with its back against the mountain about half a mile from the main compound. The shrine had no spires, no steeple. Two large wrought-iron gates in the front stood open. The monastery was busy. People were everywhere, walking from the main building to the shrine, milling about the gate.

Cecile stared until her eyes began to ache from the strain. She lowered the glass.

"Those are not monks," she said. "They are soldiers."

"I fear you are right, my lady," Sir Conal agreed. "Judging by the account Sir Ander sent to the Mother House, these soldiers are the same as those who attacked the Abbey, Westfirth, and the Citadel."

"Bottom Dwellers," said Cecile, adding in soft dismay, "There are . . . so many of them."

The shaggy pony, Jean, bent his head to nibble grass. Cecile sat in the wooden saddle and gazed at the monastery, the bustling activity going on all around it.

"Is this a military base, Sir Conal? Out here in the middle of nowhere? That doesn't make sense."

"I doubt it, my lady. Ships can't navigate safely in these mountains," said Sir Conal. "The place is too small to billet an army and, as you say, it doesn't make sense. What would be the point? Yet the fiends do appear to be well established here. By the looks of it, the soldiers have been occupying the monastery for some time."

"And that is where they have taken the princess," said Cecile.

"So the signs indicate, my lady," said Sir Conal.

Cecile sat in silence for a long time, gazing at the monastery through the gap in the pine trees.

"I wonder what they did to the monks who lived here," she asked with a shiver.

"Best not to think of that, my lady," Sir Conal replied somberly.

Both of them again sat in silence. The ponies grazed, unconcerned over the strange affairs of men.

"What do we do now, Sir Conal?"

"The two of us cannot storm a fortress," he said. "I suppose all we can do is return posthaste to Evreux and report what we have discovered."

"That will take weeks. And what becomes of the princess? You said yourself warships cannot navigate through these mountains. We could come back here with army, but that would cost even more time . . ."

An idea came to mind. She considered it, studied it logically, rationally as she would have studied a business proposition. Once she had made up her mind, she set her jaw in resolve and clamped her hands determinedly over the pommel of the saddle. Her brows contracted. She straightened in the saddle, her back rigid.

"I have a plan, Sir Conal."

"I thought you might. I saw that look in your eye," said Sir Conal.

"You won't like it . . ."

Sir Conal chuckled. "I'm not likely to naysay you, my lady. I'll wager when you give him that look, even His Majesty quakes in his boots."

Cecile glanced at him in some astonishment and then began to laugh. She couldn't remember when she had laughed like this. Given the danger and her fear for Sophia, Cecile was almost ashamed of herself.

"You should laugh more often," said Sir Conal approvingly.

"Apparently I laugh only in the face of desperation and despair, Sir Conal," said Cecile.

"And what is your plan?" he said.

"The two of us *are* storming the fortress."

Sir Conal nodded complacently. "And how do the two of us accomplish that, my lady?"

"We knock on the gate," Cecile replied. "And demand entry."

The trail leading up to the monastery was so narrow that Sir Conal and Cecile had to ride single-file. Sir Conal, mindful of the soldiers that would be keeping a watch on them, wanted to take the lead. Cecile refused, saying that their deception would be more believable if she took the lead.

"They will see a woman and her male escort," Cecile told him. "That reminds me, do not call me 'my lady.' "

"Very well, my lady—" Sir Conal caught himself,

flushed and shook his head. "That won't be easy. What should I call you?"

"I will be Cecile. You will be Conal. As Eiddwen's agents, we can be secretive about our backgrounds."

"You realize, my . . . um . . . You realize, Cecile, that if Eiddwen is in that fortress, she will be able to identify you as the Countess de Marjolaine. I doubt if she will give us a hearty welcome."

"We heard Eiddwen left the party." Cecile frowned.

"For all we know, she flew here."

Cecile's color heightened, her lips pursed. Sir Conal had the impression she was not accustomed to people arguing with her.

"I was merely pointing out the danger, Cecile," he said. "Forewarned is forearmed, as the saying goes."

Cecile relaxed. "I thank you, Conal. I am both forewarned and forearmed." She gestured to the small gun he had given her, which she carried in her boot. "Let us proceed."

As they rode, Sir Conal kept watch on the monastery. He caught a glimpse of the sentry in the bell tower, a shadowy figure, barely visible. Too late to turn back. The sentry would have alerted the gate guard that someone was approaching.

Sir Conal made certain the three pistols he carried were loaded, including and especially the one pistol that did not rely on magic, a gift from Sir Ander.

The world had been blessedly unfamiliar with contramagic at that time. Contramagic could cause a pistol set with magical constructs to explode in one's hand. Father Jacob's foresight had led to Sir Ander ordering these pistols. The fact that Cecile had paid for them had come as a pleasant surprise to Sir Conal's friend.

Sir Conal knew the secret of Sir Ander's love for Cecile de Marjolaine; a hopeless love that had driven him eventually to become a Knight Protector. Sir Conal had not quite understood. He was fond of women and had loved many of them in his lifetime. The idea of allowing one to break his heart was impossible to fathom.

He understood a little better when he finally met Cecile de Marjolaine. She had graced the world for nearly fifty years, yet her beauty still took his breath away. He came to know her well during their journey and his admiration for her grew. He was not tempted to fall in love with her. He admired her courage, her intelligence, her fortitude, her determination and resolve. He could have gazed all the day long at her perfectly carved face, the rose-stained cheeks and marble-white skin. He would have laid down his life for her with never a qualm.

But Sir Conal loved the living. And although Cecile de Marjolaine walked and talked and breathed, she was dead inside. She had died the day her beloved husband died. Like the pagan women of old, she was buried in his grave.

Sir Conal watched the woman who rode ahead of him, her head high, never wavering, and thought to himself that he could not have asked for a braver, more courageous and trusted comrade.

The gate stood open. The gate guard was backed by two soldiers, both of them wearing the leather armor decorated with knot work and strange-looking constructs. They were not wearing the demon-faced helms Sir Ander had described. They carried weapons—tubelike guns that shot green balls of magic-destroying fire. The weapons were on their backs, not in their hands. Although they were watchful and wary, they seemingly did not consider this woman and her escort a threat.

Sir Conal had never seen one of the Bottom Dwellers, and although he had read the reports, he was amazed by the sight of these men with their sickly looking, pale complexions and large eyes. The reports said that they were sensitive to bright light, and even though the day was gray and overcast, one of the soldiers was wearing spectacles made of smoky colored glass.

Cecile brought her horse to a halt and summoned Sir Conal imperiously to help her dismount. He climbed off his own pony and limped over to Cecile, leaning far more heavily on his cane than was necessary. He rested the cane against the flanks of the patient Pierre, reached up and helped Cecile to dismount, his hands clasping her around the waist. The two exchanged glances, all was going well so far.

Cecile alighted on the ground. She did not thank him, but walked off, leaving him with the horses. She strode past the soldiers as if they weren't there, her skirt swishing, her cloak billowing in the wind. The soldiers were so astonished that for a moment they didn't react. Cecile was halfway into the courtyard beyond before the guards stopped her, ranging themselves in front of her.

Sir Conal, leading the ponies, arrived in time to hear Cecile say angrily, "Let me pass. My business is urgent."

The guard said something in a foreign tongue. Cecile frowned at him, unable to understand. Sir Conal stared at the soldier in amazement. He did understand. The language the soldier was speaking was the Trundler of Sir Conal's childhood. The man's accent was heavy and the words were pronounced somewhat differently, but Sir Conal had no difficulty making out what the guard had said.

He wondered if he should reveal that he knew the language. If people thought he could not understand them, they would be more apt to speak openly in front of him. Then he saw the guards were eyeing him curiously and he guessed what they were thinking. He had all the physical characteristics of a Trundler. Anyway, he wasn't much good at lying.

Limping forward, he said to Cecile, "The guard asks you to state your business."

"Tell him I am here to see Eiddwen," said Cecile.

Sir Conal complied, translating her words.

"My father was a Trundler," he added by way of explanation. "I was raised a Trundler. As were you, I gather."

The guard grunted and muttered something to his fellow, their voices low enough that Sir Conal could not make out what they said. He did not think it was complimentary, however, for their looks were not friendly.

Cecile cast him a veiled glance of concern, wondering what was going on. She continued to play her part, however. Frowning, angry at being thwarted, she said in frozen tones, "I am one of Eiddwen's agents. I know she came here. Tell this fool again that I have an urgent message for her."

Sir Conal translated. Their fate rested on the playing of this card—Eiddwen. Cecile was betting that Eiddwen was a person of importance, a person who garnered respect, perhaps even generated fear.

The name *did* appear to have an effect on the guards. Sir Conal could hear something of what they said and they were both uneasy, uncertain how to react. As they were conferring, a woman who had been walking past the gate caught sight of them and stopped to watch.

The guard conferred briefly with his comrade, then did what soldiers had done from time immemorial—handed this problem off to his superiors.

"Fetch the *ceannasal*."

"He's sent for the commander," Sir Conal translated.

The soldier wearing the smoky glasses left on the run. The woman continued to stare at them. She was wearing a russet-colored mantle over a plain gown. The soldier, passing by her, paused to make a hasty obeisance, touching his hand to his forehead.

She is someone of importance, Sir Conal thought. He wondered if her sudden interest in them was good or bad.

The guard permitted Cecile and Sir Conal to enter the gate, gesturing to a stone bench outside the tiny gatehouse and inviting them to be seated. Cecile remained standing with her arms crossed, her expression cold and forbidding. Sir Conal eased himself onto the bench with a sigh and looked curiously around the compound.

The main building was across the unpaved courtyard and off to his right. He figured it must have served as a dortoir for the monks with cells for sleeping, rooms for study, and a common room. A new addition had been added to this building—additional housing. Soldiers and more men and women wearing mantles could be seen emerging from both buildings.

The two wooden outbuildings must hold supplies and provide shelter for the animals. He could hear a cow lowing and caught a whiff of the pigsty.

The shrine with the wrought-iron gates was about a half mile away. Now that he was closer, he could see that the shrine was built flat against the cliff. The shrine was tiny and yet numerous people kept entering, far more than would have fit into the small space. He could only conclude that the shrine must open up into a cave. He found this perplexing. Mankind had not worshipped in caves since the ancient days. He could not remember that Trundlers had ever worshipped in caves or anywhere else for that matter.

The guard sent to fetch the officer was running toward the shrine, not the main buildings, and Sir Conal took note of a large numbers of soldiers gathered around the shrine's entrance. They lounged about as though they were awaiting orders. The soldiers were heavily armed and appeared prepared for a fight.

"Only two soldiers at the main gate," Sir Conal said to

himself. "Yet there must be twenty or more outside that shrine, along with their commander."

The woman with the russet mantle continued to linger nearby, keeping them under observation. Sir Conal glanced obliquely at the woman and then looked away. He wondered what Cecile made of this, but dared not ask. These men probably spoke only Trundler, but he didn't want to risk it.

Another soldier, presumably the *ceannasal,* emerged from the shrine to speak to the soldier from the gate. He seemed, by his body language, to be highly annoyed. At first he made a gesture of refusal and then he changed his mind and began walking rapidly toward the gate. He wore the same leather armor as the soldier, but the knot work was more elaborate, perhaps marking his rank. As he passed the woman, he gave her a swift salute. She gave a cool nod in return.

The captain walked with long, impatient strides. Sir Conal was relieved to see the *ceannasal* appeared more angry at being interrupted in his work than concerned about their presence.

The *ceannasal* walked straight up to Cecile. He was a young man, in his thirties. He must have been here for some time. His complexion was no longer dead white, but had gained some color from the sun. He flicked a glance at Sir Conal and, seeing the cane, dismissed him as a servant. The *ceannasal* did not introduce himself, but came straight to the point.

"You have business with Sister Eiddwen." The *ceannasal* spoke Rosian, though with such a heavy accent Sir Conal could barely understand him. "What business do you have with her?"

"I hope you take no offense, sir, but my business with her is confidential." Cecile was polite. Her manner made it clear that she considered him an underling. "My orders are strict. I am to report to no one except Eiddwen. If you know her, sir, you know that those who disobey her do so at their peril."

"I know her." The *ceannasal* grunted.

He glared at Cecile, not in anger, but in frustration, as if trying to figure out what to do with her.

"Attendant Eiddwen is not here. She has been dispatched to Freya. I can send a messenger to her."

Cecile was distraught. "My information is highly secret. I can tell no one!"

"Then I cannot help you."

The *ceannasal* turned on his heel and strode off, taking the guard in the smoky glasses with him.

Cecile looked after him blankly, then angrily ordered Sir Conal to help her with the horse's bridle. As the two bent to the task, she asked him in a whisper if he knew what was going on.

"Something important, by the looks of it," Sir Conal whispered back. "The commander has no time for the likes of us, that's certain. Now what do we do? It seems we've reached a dead end."

"Perhaps not," Cecile murmured.

The woman in the russet mantle was coming forward to meet them. Cecile straightened up to find the woman at her shoulder.

"I am Steward Allie," the woman said. She spoke excellent Rosian with barely the trace of an accent. "I am one of the *Leanai Scath*, the Children of Shadow. I could not help overhearing your conversation with the commander. I know Attendant Eiddwen. Perhaps I can be of help."

Cecile introduced herself and Sir Conal, describing him as bodyguard and companion. He bowed as he regarded the woman curiously. She was of medium height, thin, middle-aged, and with an air of one who is accustomed to being obeyed.

"I *must* speak to Eiddwen," Cecile was saying, sounding desperate. "I am one of her agents. I was told to meet her here."

"Eiddwen was supposed to come to the monastery with the new savant, the princess of Rosia. Saint Xavier changed her orders, however, sending her on a mission to Freya. I apologize for the commander's rudeness," Allie added, sighing. "As you are aware, Fulmea the first is fast approaching. Our saint is attempting to prepare for the launch of the invasion fleet . . ."

Invasion fleet! Sir Conal was rocked to the core of his being. He had difficulty arranging his face to look as if this news were old news. The words resounded in his head. The Bottom Dwellers were planning to launch an invasion fleet. Good God in heaven! He dragged his attention back to Allie with difficulty.

". . . and now word has come that the rebels have attacked the outpost guarding the foot of the *Bhealach Ardaitheach.* As you can imagine, our commander is under considerable strain. You said you have urgent news for Eiddwen?"

Cecile had absorbed the information with cool aplomb and swiftly took advantage of it. "I have acquired knowledge regarding the invasion. I fear I can say no more. Could I ask what became of the young woman, the savant you mentioned? I heard rumors that Eiddwen's companion, Lucello, was quite taken with her. Did he travel with Eiddwen or remain here with the savant?"

Allie was disdainful. "I did hear that Lucello had formed a romantic attachment to the girl while they were in the royal palace. If so, he soon conquered it, for he traveled to Freya with Eiddwen. As for the princess, she was sent

Below to Saint Xavier. He has great hopes for her, or so Eiddwen told me."

"Hopes in regard to what?" Cecile asked. "I must confess that I never understood . . ." She hesitated, embarrassed.

"Our saint's orders regarding female savants?" said Allie. "He read somewhere that savants have the magical ability to stop wizard storms."

"Indeed," Cecile murmured. "I wondered."

"I am certain we hope that this is true," Allie said, sounding skeptical.

Cecile shot a swift glance at Sir Conal. This idea of savants stopping storms explained why Eiddwen had taken such care to keep Sophia alive and even why she had been permitted to keep Bandit. This saint needed Sophia's cooperation.

"Do you know Attendant Eiddwen well?" Allie asked.

The question was couched in friendly tones, but Sir Conal sensed a trap. He shifted his hand slightly to be closer to his pistol.

"I doubt if anyone truly knows Eiddwen well," Cecile replied with a faint smile.

Allie nodded in grave understanding. Sir Conal relaxed.

"You speak a true word there," she said. "I have known Eiddwen since she was a little child. Even then, she was withdrawn, solitary, remote. She was an orphan, you know, chosen by our saint for her talent in magic."

"He chose wisely," Cecile said. "Speaking of our saint, I believe that since Eiddwen is not here, I should deliver my information to him. Where will I find him?"

Sir Conal could not believe he had heard right. He gave a meaningful cough, warning she had gone too far. If Cecile understood, she ignored him.

"Saint Xavier is Below," Allie replied. "He was supposed

to ascend to witness the downfall of his foes after the fleet launched. He is prevented from leaving Glasearrach by the storms and the rebel attacks."

Allie regarded Cecile uncertainly. "Your information must be of the utmost importance for you to risk such a journey."

"I cannot overstate the value," said Cecile earnestly. "My news could make the difference between defeat and victory."

She studied Allie intently, as if debating whether or not to trust her. Making up her mind, Cecile drew near to Allie. "I fear our invasion plans may have been discovered!"

Allie drew back to stare at her in alarm. "Certainly Xavier must know! You will need your horses to make the journey. Fetch them, then meet me back here. I will make arrangements. You cannot travel in those clothes."

Allie hastened off, returning to the main building.

Sir Conal and Cecile walked back to where the ponies were tethered.

"We could ride off now and no one would stop us, my lady," Sir Conal remarked. "The commander won't waste the manpower to chase after us."

"You are right, Sir Conal," said Cecile. "We could. But we won't. Will we?"

She regarded him with a slight smile.

"No, my lady," said Sir Conal, returning her smile. "We won't."

Returning with their ponies and their dwindling supplies, they had to wait only a few moments before Allie came hurrying to meet them. She carried two mantles, one yellow gold and one a brownish green.

"The gold denotes you as a steward, Cecile, and will gain you access to the saint. The green is worn by the warders. Your bodyguard should wear it."

The mantles were long, sleeveless, hooded cloaks made of coarse wool. Sir Conal had to turn the garment upside down before he located the arm holes.

"You said the way is perilous, Mistress Allie," said Sir Conal. He flexed his arms in discomfort. The mantle was tight through the shoulders and the wool against the back of his neck made his skin itch. "What perils do we face?"

"The rebels have attacked military bases and outposts such as the one that guards the *Bhealach Ardaitheach* and they are targeting those of us who are members of the *Leanai Scath,* those closest to our saint."

"So these mantles will put us in danger," said Sir Conal, hoping he had an excuse to remove it.

"You will be in more danger without them," Allie returned. She looked them up and down. "Everyone you meet Below will know you are not a Bottom Dweller. You are too well fed. I cannot leave the monastery now, not with everything that is going on, or I would travel with you. The mantles are enough to indicate you are under the protection of a high-ranking priestess. Come with me. I will take you to the *Bhealach Ardaitheach.*"

"What does that mean?" Cecile whispered.

"Ascending Way," said Sir Conal.

Whatever the Ascending Way was, it was located in the shrine, seemingly, for that was where Allie was taking them. People stared as they passed, some with mere curiosity, others openly hostile. No one said anything to their faces, although Sir Conal heard some comments and mutterings after they had passed. He tried to imagine what life would be like living at the bottom of the world. Allie had said he looked "too well fed." Likely these men and women resented anyone living up here in the sunshine, even those who were supposedly on their side. Everyone in the monastery appeared to hold Sister Allie in high esteem however, some bowing, others touching their foreheads. Soldiers saluted.

They arrived at the shrine to find the *ceannasal* posting soldiers at the gate and inside the shrine itself. He frowned at the sight of Cecile and Sir Conal.

"Where are those two going?" he demanded, stopping them.

"They are going to Saint Xavier," Allie replied. She added haughtily, "On my authority."

"They are on their own, then," said the *ceannasal* curtly. "I don't have the men to guard them."

"They are aware of that, Commander," said Allie with a touch of asperity. "Have you any more news about the rebel assault on the outpost?"

"It wasn't an assault," returned the *ceannasal* bitterly. "These cowards don't want to fight. They just want to kill. They struck in the night, murdered anyone they could find, set fire to a few buildings and vanished."

"So the outpost is still manned?"

"Of course, it is," said the *ceannasal.*

"Do you really think the rebels could strike us here?" Allie asked, looking with amazement at the defensive preparations underway. "That seems hardly likely."

"I am taking no chances, Steward," said the *ceannasal.*

Sir Conal was leading the ponies and he looked about for a trail or a road. The name Allie used, Ascending Way, seemed an odd term, even among Trundlers. He could see nothing beyond the gray stone of the side of the mountain and he had no idea where he was supposed to go.

"Where are we bound?" he asked Allie.

"Inside the shrine," she replied.

"What do I do with the ponies?"

"Bring them, of course. As I said, you will need them to make the descent."

Sir Conal and Cecile exchanged startled glances. The soldiers guarding the gate parted to permit them to pass. These soldiers were wearing the demonic-faced helms, prepared for battle. Sir Conal could not see their eyes, but he had the distinct impression their looks were not friendly. Crossing a tiny courtyard, they entered the shrine of Saint Dominick.

The five-hundred-year-old shrine was constructed of marble blocks that must have cost the monks considerable toil to haul to this site. Built into the side of the mountain, the shrine was small, simple, and elegant in design. There had been six windows, three to a side, made of stained glass. Much of the glass was broken now and had not been replaced. A double door made of wood banded with iron was propped open. Above the door, carved into the stone, was the motto, I STAND WITH GOD. Below that was written, SAINT DOMINICK THE KEEPER. The words had been defaced with a hammer and chisel.

A statue of the saint stood to one side of the shrine. The saint was holding the scripture in one hand. His other was extended in a warding manner, keeping the demons out of his church. Someone had knocked off the saint's head and scrawled crude Trundler words all over his body.

Sir Conal entered the shrine, only to find that Jean and Pierre were having nothing to do with it. The ponies balked in the doorway, shaking their heads and stamping their hooves. Cecile bribed them with dried apples, while Sir Conal pushed them from the rear and finally the ponies clattered over the doorstep.

Sunlight streamed through the broken windows. A single aisle ran down the middle. Two rows of pews made of wood lined either side. An altar railing stood at the end of the aisle. The altar was gone, as was the stone wall behind it. The wall had been breached, blasted apart. Large chunks of broken stone and mortar marked where the wall had once stood. The wall had been constructed of several layers of both stone and brick, further reinforced by concrete, iron bars, and magical constructs.

Sir Conal stared at the wall. The hair rose on his arms and neck and a cold shiver went up his back. Some inkling of the truth was starting to occur to him. He could feel Cecile shudder. Again they exchanged glances and he saw disbelief in her eyes.

Beyond the remnants of the wall was a large cavern, illuminated by an eerie green light that shone from constructs carved into the walls. Armed soldiers guarded what appeared to be the entrance to an underground stairway. Green light flowed from the passage into the main chamber.

"You said the journey was long," Cecile said, a slight quaver in her voice. "How far must we travel?"

And where are we going? Sir Conal wanted to ask, but he kept silent. He feared he already knew the answer.

"The distance has never been measured, but I would guess it to be just under two hundred miles. With the ponies, the journey down the stairs should take you about six days. There are waypoints along the route where you can rest and find food and water for yourselves and your beasts. At the end of the *Bhealach Ardaitheach* is the outpost where you will take transport to the holy city of Dunlow, the residence of Saint Xavier."

"Thank you for your help, Steward Allie," Cecile said. She was very pale, gazing in shock at the entrance.

Allie mistook Cecile's pallor for fear, for she added reassuringly, "This part of the journey will be safe enough. All who ascend the stair must be sanctioned by our saint. Despite what the *ceannasal* says, I do not believe the rebels would dare attempt an attack. Still, you should remain vigilant."

The soldiers watched in silence as Cecile and Sir Conal

walked slowly through the cavern, leading Jean and Pierre. The ponies were nervous; not liking the darkness, the dank, damp smell of the cavern, or the strange green light. Allie accompanied them to the entrance. Looking inside, Sir Conal saw stairs carved out of rock that sloped down into darkness.

Far, far down.

The monks of Saint Dominick who had been posted in this monastery to keep out the Evil One and his demons had failed.

"May Saint Xavier walk with you and keep you safe," said Allie. "Here is the entrance to the *Bhealach Ardaitheach*."

"Enter the Gates of Hell," said Sir Conal softly.

9

Prince Alaric Renaud attended the Academie Royal d'Equitation *at age six until age fourteen when he obtained his commission in the navy as midshipman . . .*

—Excerpt from *Baronetage of Rosia*

(Anonymous note written in the margin: The fact that King Alaric sent his sons away from home at an early age was the best thing that could have happened to them!)

Stephano and Rodrigo returned home to find the nuns had departed. Benoit was out of bed and able to resume his duties around the house, which meant that he was once more seated in his comfortable chair by the kitchen fire. He was pleased beyond measure to see them, and even got out of his chair to tell them so. He was not, however, able to be of any assistance to them. Rodrigo was shocked to learn they would have to heat their own bathwater.

"The physician warned me that I should not work too hard, sir," said Benoit, returning to his chair with a pint of ale, which he maintained the doctor had prescribed.

"I doubt there'll be much danger of that," Stephano said drily.

He and Rodrigo attempted to fend for themselves that

night. But after Rodrigo nearly scalded himself in the bath and Stephano broke one of the family serving bowls, Benoit rose from his chair in ire, demanding to know if they wanted to send him to an early grave. He restored order to the household, then returned to his chair. Stephano, watching Benoit, was truly concerned to see how slowly he moved and how he stopped repeatedly to catch his breath.

That night Stephano said to Rodrigo, "We need to bring in someone to help him."

"He won't like it," said Rodrigo. "But we need to do something. I have severe burns on my posterior."

"I'll think of something," said Stephano.

The next morning, as they fixed their own breakfast under Benoit's supervision, Stephano made his suggestion.

"I was thinking that I could hire the Widow Bellard to come cook and clean while you are on the mend."

Benoit frowned and shook his head. "I don't like the idea of strangers mucking about the house, sir. Pawing through Master Rodrigo's silk undergarments."

"The widow does our laundry. She's already on intimate terms with Master Rodrigo's undergarments," Stephano said.

"And consider this, Benoit," Rodrigo added, "no one makes a beef pie like the Widow Bellard. Juicy and succulent with a soupçon of red wine and those little pearl onions . . ."

"That is true, sir," Benoit admitted.

"She would be under your supervision," Stephano said persuasively. "Receiving her orders from you."

"I will take on the widow under advisement, sir," said Benoit.

The Widow Bellard arrived that very morning. A good-natured woman, she cheerfully tolerated Benoit's officious supervision, assuring him that she would handle Master Rodrigo's silk undergarments as gently as she would a newborn babe. The two discovered a mutual love of gossip, which proved a blessing to Benoit, who had not been able to leave the house and was desperate to hear the latest news.

"They say, Monsieur Benoit," said the widow, "that the Freyans sabotaged the palace and it's going to fall right out of the sky."

Stephano and Rodrigo were at that moment coming down the stairs, dressed in their finest, for they were on their way to the palace. They looked at each other in alarm. Thus far, word of the danger to the palace had been kept quiet.

"Does Benoit know the truth?" Rodrigo asked in a whisper.

Stephano shook his head. "D'argent kept it from him. Didn't want to upset him."

Benoit was responding with a disdainful snort. "Stuff and nonsense. I am a frequent guest at the palace. The Countess de Marjolaine sent her personal physician to attend me."

"Did she now?" the widow stated, impressed.

"If such a disaster were imminent, I would have been informed. The master himself would have told me. He takes me into his confidence on all matters of importance. Needs me to tell him what to do. He daren't make a move without speaking to me."

Rodrigo had to put his hand over his mouth to keep from laughing. Stephano grinned and shook his head.

The widow was not to be talked out of her news. "I am quite certain this is true, Monsieur Benoit. My late husband—God rest him—has a nephew who is a metalsmith crafter. He works as an apprentice for the company who built the lift tanks in the palace and *he* heard it from his master, who was summoned to the palace to see if there was something he could do. I was at the butcher's this morning and he had heard similar reports. People say Her Majesty and the princess have fled in terror, along with most of the gentlefolk."

Stephano looked grim. He turned to Rodrigo. "If word of this spreads through the city, God knows what will happen." He took a step toward the kitchen. "I should say something to the widow, tell her it's not true—"

Rodrigo caught hold of his friend. "Thereby you will immediately confirm her worst fears. We can't do anything. I'm surprised the secret lasted as long as it did, given the number of people who knew it."

The elegant wyvern-drawn carriage bearing the crest of the de Marjolaines, which D'argent had sent to pick them up, landed on the street outside Stephano's house. Leaving Benoit and the widow to their gossip, Stephano and Rodrigo stepped into the carriage. Rodrigo was meeting with the engineers and Stephano had a meeting with the prince. Both men were in a solemn mood as they sat on the fine leather seats, gazing out the windows at the floating palace. The pink-tinged clouds and orange-golden mists of the Breath drifting past the walls created the illusion that the palace glided through the azure sky.

"What are we going to tell Benoit about the palace?" Rodrigo asked after long minutes of silence.

"The truth, I suppose," said Stephano.

"You should send him away from Evreux," said Rodrigo. "Just in case it does crash. Send him to your estate."

Stephano smiled. "You know as well as I do, that cantankerous old man won't leave."

Stephano had never before admired the marvel of the magic that kept the palace suspended above the shining lake. He had visited the palace only when his mother forced him to go and he had hated every moment, seeing only the ugliness, the intrigue and scandal, deception and lies.

Now his mother was gone on a mysterious, dangerous mission, leaving a will that had named him her heir. The palace was a melancholy sight to him. He pictured the grand edifice falling from the sky, the devastation as it plunged into the lake, the horrific loss of life as the deep lake overflowed its banks and sent flood waters pouring into the city. His Majesty often claimed God held the Sunset Palace in His divine hand. If so, God's grasp was feeble and shaky.

As the carriage landed in the portico reserved for noble visitors, Stephano descended and looked out at the ships of the royal navy keeping guard. A dozen ships of the line, each with two full decks of cannons were on station above the palace, along with an equal number of frigates. A half dozen barges were loosely moored around the walls, ostensibly to haul supplies, but in reality to accommodate any last-minute evacuation. He could hear from every ship the ringing of the bells and the squeals of the bosun's pipe calling the sailors to their morning chores.

He was too early for his meeting with the prince, so Stephano accompanied Rodrigo to the lowest level of the palace where the engineers were working day and night to keep the palace afloat. Stephano had never been to this level and he gazed in awe and amazement at the cavernous chamber and sixteen massive lift tanks that ranged around the walls.

"Do you think your bridging technique will work?" Stephano asked.

"I don't know," said Rodrigo. "I won't know until I inspect the damage."

"You realize the palace could fall down with us inside it," Stephano said.

"Precisely why I took champagne with my breakfast," said Rodrigo with a smile.

The chief engineer caught sight of them. Assuming they

were two dissolute noblemen come to gawk and gape, he came charging over.

"Gentlemen," he said in a stern voice, "you have no business down here. I must ask you to leave—"

"I am Monsieur Rodrigo de Villeneuve," Rodrigo began, then was stopped by a sneeze.

The engineers moving back and forth among the tanks were stirring up a considerable quantity of dust. Taking out a silk handkerchief, Rodrigo dabbed at his nose, adding in muffled tones, "You are Master Henri, I presume. I believe you have been told of my coming. I might possibly be of some help."

Master Henri was a large man with a full, black beard. His face was drawn and haggard, his clothes filthy from crawling about under the lift tanks. He eyed Rodrigo, wearing his fine court clothes and his best perfume, and scowled.

"Thank you, sir, but we can do without your sort of help—"

He was speaking to the dusty air. Rodrigo had walked past him. Going over to the first lift tank, he began asking questions of the engineers, who were eyeing him uncertainly. Master Henri started after him with the grim look on his face of a man prepared to remove Rodrigo by bodily force. Stephano intercepted him.

"Rigo is smarter than he looks," Stephano said.

"I heard that," Rodrigo called.

"Seriously, Chief, he knows what he is doing," Stephano told the worried engineer.

Master Henri eyed Stephano, who was wearing his Dragon Brigade uniform coat with the insignia marking him an officer, and was somewhat mollified.

"Monsieur D'argent *did* vouch for him . . ." Master Henri walked over to the lift tank to confront Rodrigo. "What do you want to know, sir?"

Rodrigo and Master Henri and the engineers began discussing sigils and constructs. They leaned close to stare at the paint on the tank, at least that was all Stephano saw. Crafters would see the glowing lines of the magic that were keeping the tank operational. Or, in this instance, the broken lines of constructs being destroyed by contramagic.

"You are using the crystalline form of lift gas, the Tears of God, inside the tanks now?" Rodrigo asked.

"Yes and that is all that is keeping the palace in the sky," said Master Henri. "But those crystals require magic to work. We have not been able to stop the destruction of the constructs, and once they are completely gone . . ." He finished his sentence with a shrug and a heavy sigh.

Rodrigo investigated the tank closely, even to the point of spreading his handkerchief and getting down on his knees, risking injury to his best pantaloons and silk stockings. He rose slowly to his feet, silent and thoughtful, and gave a bleak shake of his head.

"What's the matter?" Stephano asked. "Can't you build a magical bridge like you did to save the boat?"

"My dear fellow, a bridge that spans a river must be firmly anchored to both riverbanks," said Rodrigo. "On the *Hopper,* magical constructs were in place on either side of the patches of destroyed magic. I was able to anchor the bridge to the parts of the magic that had not been affected. Here, there is so little magic I have nothing with which to work."

"Then . . . you can't save the palace?" Stephano was aghast.

"The damage to the lift tanks is extensive," Rodrigo said somberly. "I don't know, Stephano. I have to think about it. You should go to your meeting. From what I hear, HRH doesn't like laggards. I'll meet you here—or on the ground, in case I fail to fix the magic."

"That's not funny," Stephano growled.

"It wasn't meant to be," said Rodrigo.

A footman guided Stephano to the rooms occupied by His Royal Highness, Prince Renaud. Stephano had never been in this part of the palace, where the royal family lived and worked. He had never had any reason or inclination to come here and he wasn't comfortable being here now.

His Majesty, King Alaric, hated Stephano, who returned the favor. Alaric had goaded the Duke de Bourlet into rebelling and had then mercilessly crushed the rebels. His soldiers had killed the duke and captured Julian de Guichen, and then Alaric sent Julian to a cruel and agonizing death as a traitor. Stephano's mother had managed to keep her son alive and even to gain him a commission as an officer in the Dragon Brigade. She had not been able to stop Alaric from disbanding the Dragon Brigade after only a few short years, forcing Stephano to resign or accept a reduction in rank and duty as a low ranking officer aboard a naval ship.

Stephano followed the footman through the elegantly furnished, silent and empty halls. The king had sent his queen to the summer palace, along with her servants and ladies-in-waiting and other members of the nobility who had been encouraged to go with her.

Stephano did not see the king, a blessing for which he was grateful. He was fairly certain he would have said or done something to get himself arrested again. The prince's chambers were in another part of the royal quarters, some distance from the king's. The footman handed over Stephano to the prince's personal manservant—a sailor who served the lord admiral when he was aboard his ship, who had been transferred to the palace. Having expected to be forced to languish for hours in the antechamber, Stephano was surprised and pleased when the sailor took him immediately to see the prince.

Entering Renaud's study, Stephano felt that he had walked into the admiral's quarters on board ship. Gone were the end tables, settees, love seats, and fainting couches generally found in any room in the palace. The few pieces of furniture in the room were utilitarian: desk, chair, chart table, bookcase. The floor was bare, all the carpets had been taken up. Paintings of landscapes and hunting scenes had been replaced by charts and maps. An enormous bay window provided the prince with a view of his ships on patrol in the skies around the palace

Stephano felt at ease the moment he entered the room. He had not been disposed to like Prince Renaud, simply because he was King Alaric's son. He was starting to think he had made a mistake.

The prince had his back turned, and was staring intently at one of the large wall maps. The servant announced Stephano, who was faced with a quandary. Did he salute the lord admiral or bow to the prince? He didn't think he could do both at once. He chose the lord admiral. Stephano stood stiffly at attention and saluted.

"Lord Captain Stephano de Guichen—" Stephano began.

The prince made an impatient gesture, cutting him off. "Tell me, Captain, will this friend of yours be able to keep the palace from smashing into the lake?"

Stephano was taken aback. He had heard that the lord admiral was blunt-spoken, disliking what he termed "tittle-tattle." Stephano had not expected him to be quite so blunt.

"Rodrigo says the damage is extensive, Your Highness. He is not certain he can do anything to stop the fall." He hesitated, not wanting to give advice to his prince, yet feeling he should say something. "The palace is in imminent danger of crashing, sir. Your importance to your country in this critical time cannot be overstated. Perhaps . . . if you were to return to your ship—"

"I will not leave my father," said Renaud. "And he will not leave the palace. He would not have people say that he basely fled in the face of danger."

As if the palace was listening, a tremor ran through the building. A map fell from the wall, and a flag on a stand behind the desk toppled over. Stephano grabbed hold of the back of a chair to steady himself. The prince, probably accustomed to the rolling of his ship, had no difficulty keeping his balance. He and Stephano tensely waited for calamity. After a few seconds, the palace righted itself.

Stephano drew in a shaky breath; Renaud merely raised an eyebrow and gave a slight shrug. Stephano wondered how the prince could be so calm. He couldn't imagine living day and night with the knowledge that at any moment your house might plunge to the ground and disintegrate.

"You and your father should leave, sir," said Stephano. "If anything happened, our country would be left leaderless during a time of peril. People would not think the less of either of you—"

"Wouldn't they?" Renaud demanded wryly. "Isn't the captain supposed to go down with his ship?"

"I've always said that was the waste of a good captain," said Stephano.

Prince Renaud's upper lip gave a little twitch, which for him was tantamount to a smile. "I must say, I agree with you."

He walked over to pick up the flagpole, put it back in place. He ran his hand over the Rosian flag, bright with its red rose inside a gold sun that blazed on a field of white. He smoothed the folds.

"I know you despise my father, Captain," said Renaud abruptly. "Perhaps you have good reason. Still, you cannot say that he is a coward. He chooses to remain here so that the people will not lose faith in their monarch. I am certain you have heard the rumors around town that his grandiose palace is doomed—impossible to keep something like this secret. People are watching to see if their king will flee, if he will save himself at the cost of the lives of his subjects. They will see their king defiant, battling his enemies to the end."

Stephano said nothing, merely bowed. He had been rebuked, but not harshly. Renaud walked over to another map that was still hanging on the wall and motioned for Stephano to join him.

"I hear you were in Braffa," Renaud continued. He jabbed his finger at one of the islands. "D'argent says that you fought the fiends at this refinery. Tell me about the battle. The time will come when we will have to take back these refineries."

Stephano described the fight, and then he and the prince discussed the Braffan situation. The prince was especially interested to hear about Sir Henry's armored gunboat, although he grimaced when Stephano mentioned the name of the Freyan spymaster.

"I would give a great deal to see that man dangling at the end of a yardarm," said Renaud.

They next went on to discuss Fort Ignacio and Stephano's plan to take the battle to the Bottom Dwellers.

"I've been to see this fortress of yours," said Renaud, adding, to Stephano's amazement and displeasure, "I have a few ideas."

Proud of his plan, Stephano was prepared to dislike the prince's ideas. But Renaud's suggestions on repairing the fort proved to be sound; he brought up several problems Stephano had not foreseen and indicated how they might be solved. Stephano was grudgingly impressed.

"You will not mind that I ordered the stonemasons and

crafters to begin work already," Renaud continued. "I have also sent along a barrel of the crystals, the Tears of God. Time is of the essence, Captain. I have information from a prisoner we captured that the Bottom Dwellers are preparing to launch an invasion fleet."

"Monsieur D'argent told me that you had taken one of these people alive, sir," said Stephano. "Given the fact that they are ready to kill themselves rather than be captured, I am surprised that he talked."

"Actually we had trouble shutting him up," said the prince drily. "He was eager to spew out his hatred. He told us proudly about his so-called saint's plans for our destruction. You have seen their black ships. You know that one of them destroyed the *Royal Lion* with a single blast."

"I saw the *Royal Lion* go down, sir," said Stephano grimly. "A terrible sight."

"They have a fleet of those bloody black ships ready to launch," said Renaud. "The fleet will target Rosia, destroy the coastal cities, then strike at Evreux, expecting to hit a population demoralized and in chaos after the fall of the palace."

"What about allying with Freya, Your Highness?" Stephano asked. "The Bottom Dwellers have no love for them, either. Perhaps we could combine forces: the enemy of my enemy is my friend."

"Frankly I consider the enemy of my enemy to still be my enemy," Renaud returned caustically. "The moment Wallace heard we were under attack, he would no doubt urge his queen to take advantage of our weakness and invade. Besides, I think Sir Henry has his own worries. The prisoner bragged that Freya would fall 'without a shot being fired.' "

Stephano made a mental note to send a warning to Sir Henry. Stephano would never admit it, but he'd developed a grudging liking for the man. Wallace was a patriot with an abiding love for his country. Stephano could sympathize and admire that.

"The main problem that I see, Your Highness, is that we have no idea where to find the sunken island."

"I considered that myself, Captain. The island was here before the sinking," said the prince, jabbing the location on the map with his finger. "I have consulted several scientists who study the Breath and they all agree that the island must have traveled straight down. The winds and currents of the Breath are not strong enough to have blown such an enormous landmass off course."

Stephano conceded that this theory seemed likely.

"The scientists also agree that your descent be will dangerous, Captain," said Renaud. "And extremely unpleasant. Our prisoner spoke of bone-chilling cold, impenetrable mists, the inability to catch one's breath."

"If these people can survive the ascent, we can survive going down," said Stephano.

He thought back to the time the damaged *Cloud Hopper* had started sinking into the Breath. He remembered the cold, the dankness, the fog. He remembered himself and Dag, walking the deck, unable to see each other when they were standing face-to-face. The memory brought another thought to mind.

"My lieutenant, Dag Thorgrimson, served in that fortress during the assault and he knows it well. You must have met him there, Your Highness. He was going to travel to the fort more than a fortnight ago."

Renaud shook his head. "The fortress was deserted when I arrived, Captain. No one was there."

Stephano was puzzled. "That is strange. I wonder what happened . . ."

The prince shrugged. The matter was not his concern.

"What about the Dragon Brigade?" Renaud asked abruptly.

Stephano flinched. Touching that subject was like touching an open, bleeding wound.

"The Brigade was disbanded, Your Highness," said Stephano, adding coldly, "By your father."

"I am aware of that, Captain," said Renaud impatiently. "You are understandably bitter, as are the dragons. Their help would be invaluable to us."

"It would, sir," said Stephano. "I would go so far as to say the dragons might make the difference between victory or defeat."

"*I* cannot go to the dragons and formally ask for their help. Diplomacy and all that. You could go, Captain de Guichen. The dragons like you and respect you. They would listen to you."

"The dragons would be risking their lives, sir. I would need to offer them something."

"The thanks of a grateful nation wouldn't be enough, I suppose," said Renaud.

Stephano grinned. He liked this man.

"No, sir, I'm afraid not."

"Tell them the king is willing to discuss bringing back the Dragon Brigade."

"Only discuss, sir?" Stephano asked.

"That is the best I can do, Captain. My father is not well. The threat to the palace came as a severe shock to him. I did not want to upset him by pressing him on this matter. And now I believe we have concluded our business," said Renaud. He rang for the servant. "If you have need of anything, please contact me."

"Thank you, Your Highness," said Stephano. "I will keep you informed of our progress."

He saluted. The prince's sailor servant escorted Stephano from the royal chambers. As he was winding his way through the halls, Stephano noticed a room with the door partially opened. Curious, he glanced inside and was startled to see King Alaric. His Majesty was standing in front of a window, leaning his head against the glass, gazing down at the ground below. His face, seen in profile, was grim and gray.

Alaric's proudest accomplishment, the magnificent floating palace, the star that shone with his glory and greatness, was either going to fall out of the sky or be lowered ignominiously to the ground. This palace, with cracks in its walls, broken windows, toppled chimneys, squatting in the lake, would forever be his legacy. Perhaps Alaric was hoping the palace would fall and take him with it.

Stephano gently and quietly shut the door. Alaric might have been a hated and detested foe, but every man had a right to keep his misery private.

The prince's servant escorted Stephano from the royal chambers and offered to take Stephano to his destination. Stephano preferred to be alone with his thoughts and dismissed the sailor, saying he must have duties to which he must attend. The sailor saluted and left him in a hallway. From there, he was on his own in the vast palace. Rodrigo knew every closet, every boudoir, every secret passage. Stephano was soon thoroughly lost. He wandered about, traversing corridors, walking down flights of stairs, only to find they were the wrong stairs and he had reached an exit. He had to retrace his steps.

His mind was not in the palace. He was mentally inside the fortress, anticipating problems, working to solve them, and wondering what had happened to Dag, Miri, and Gythe. The last D'argent had spoken to them, they were intending to travel to the fortress, a journey that should have taken only a few days. He had assumed they were there and had not worried about them. Now he wondered what had happened.

At last he found a corridor he recognized. His mother's rooms were at the end of the hall. He went there, hoping to talk to D'argent, and found him closeted with the grand bishop's agent, Dubois.

Both men rose to greet him. Stephano noted that they had been speaking with their heads together, their voices low. He wondered uneasily what was going on.

"Your meeting with the prince went well?" D'argent asked.

"It did," said Stephano. "I leave for the fortress this very day. Have you talked to Rigo?"

D'argent shook his head.

Stephano was uncomfortable. He wanted to talk to D'argent in private, but he couldn't think how to convey his need. Both men were gazing at him, waiting for him to speak.

"What is it, Stephano?" D'argent asked at last. "Can I help?"

"I fear I am in the way," said Dubois, starting to sidle toward the door.

"No, wait," said Stephano. "You have access to the Freyan court, Monsieur Dubois. I need to send a message to someone in Freya." He paused, then said, "Sir Henry Wallace."

D'argent and Dubois exchanged startled glances and Stephano guessed immediately that Wallace had been the topic of their discussion.

"I might be able to assist you, Captain," said Dubois. "You do not need to write your message," he added, as Stephano was starting to pick up a pen from the desk of the countess. "I have an excellent memory. What is your message?"

Stephano explained how the prince had captured a Bottom Dweller.

"The prisoner said that Freya would fall without a shot being fired," said Stephano. "I don't know what he meant, but Wallace should be warned. The man saved my life. It's the least I can do."

"I will see to it that Sir Henry receives your message, Captain," said Dubois.

Stephano thanked him, bid farewell to D'argent, and departed. As he left, he heard Dubois say, "Our information is confirmed."

So he wasn't bringing them news at all. He should have known. He shrugged and hurried off, realizing too late he should have asked if they knew the way to the lift tanks. He wandered about until he bumbled into the kitchen. Here he enlisted the help of a scullery maid, who led him to the chamber where the lift tanks were located.

He found Rodrigo crawling on the stone floor, drawing constructs with a piece of chalk. The engineers stood gathered around him, watching in respectful, if baffled, silence. Catching sight of Stephano, Rodrigo stood up and brushed himself off. His clothes were covered in dust, his hair straggled down his face and one cheek was smeared with chalk dust.

"I have a solution," he said to Stephano.

"Thank God!" Stephano exclaimed.

"You had much rather thank me, not God," said Rodrigo. "I won't be able to stop the palace from falling, but I can keep the constructs working so that we can lower the palace slowly and steer it clear of the lake."

"That is excellent news. You are a genius, Rigo."

"I know. How did you fare with HRH?"

"I am to proceed as planned," said Stephano cautiously, not wanting to talk with others present. "I'm leaving for the fortress today. I was hoping you could come with me."

Rodrigo shook his head. "I have to say here. I'm the only one who can do what I do. I may be here for days, in fact. If you could send Benoit with a change of clothes—"

The palace shuddered and lurched, only a slight jolt this time, but enough to cause everyone to look exceedingly grim.

"There is a lot to be said for a nice quiet prison cell," Rodrigo remarked.

"Rigo, saving Alaric's palace isn't worth risking your life—"

"I'm doing my patriotic duty," said Rodrigo lightly. "Sacrificing my pantaloons in the service to my country."

Stephano eyed his friend. "See to it that you and the palace and your blasted pantaloons survive."

"I'll do my best," said Rodrigo. "Give my love to Miri and Gythe, Dag and the Doctor. I'll join you as soon as I can."

As Stephano was leaving, he glanced back over his shoulder to see Rodrigo, chalk in hand, down on his knees in the dust.

Arriving home, Stephano found Benoit peering out the window, watching for him. The old man's face was creased with worry.

"A letter for you, sir," said Benoit, holding it in a trembling hand. "Arrived shortly after you left. Sergeant Dag's handwriting. His news is urgent. You should read it at once."

"How can you tell it's urgent unless you read it?" Stephano demanded.

"It *looks* urgent, sir," said Benoit.

Stephano took the letter and glanced at the seal. "It's been opened."

"Has it, sir? I'm sure I don't know who would do such a thing. Where is Master Rodrigo?"

"He is staying at the palace," said Stephano, opening the letter. "You need to take him a change of clothes."

"You left Master Rodrigo in the palace!" Benoit cried, shocked. "The bloody thing is going to fall out of the sky!

And what's going to become of us when the palace does fall, that's what I want to know?"

"Just . . . go pack some clothes for Rigo," said Stephano in exasperation. "Old clothes!"

"And then there's that letter," said Benoit unhappily. He called back, as he began to climb the stairs. "Always bad news, letters!"

Stephano leaned his back against the wall, with his foot to brace himself, and opened the letter. Another letter fell out. This letter was creased and folded, the ink almost faded. The first was from Dag. Stephano noted with astonishment that it was dated at least a fortnight ago and had been written from the Abbey of Saint Agnes. The letter had been a long time in transit. Since the destruction of the Abbey, hardly anyone stopped at their pier anymore. Dag must have had difficulty finding someone to carry it.

Dag wrote letters as if he were making a report to an officer. He gave only the facts, and did not embellish the account or add many details. Consequently the letter was brief and jumped straight to the point.

Sir,

I'm writing this in the hope that you and Rigo have been set free. I have bad news. Gythe ran off with the Bottom Dwellers. She drugged me, but even so, I should have done something to try to stop her.

Miri is with her, I think. I searched for some trace of the two of them, but couldn't find any.

Gythe left me a note, which I have enclosed. In it she told me to go to the Abbey. I did as she said, thinking I might find her here. I didn't find her, but I did find the three young dragons: Petard, Viola, and Verdi.

They went back to their home to discover that their home was no longer there. The Bottom Dwellers had either killed or driven out the elder dragons and set fire to the island. The three young ones had nowhere to go and so they came back to the Abbey to talk to the dragon brothers, Hroal and Droal. The young ones are fired up and they want to fight now.

Petard wouldn't tell me, but I suspect he's been communicating with Gythe. He may know where she is.

I'm leaving for the fortress as ordered, sir. I don't know what else to do. I'm sorry I failed you, sir.

Dag

P.S. I'm taking the young dragons with me.

Stephano read Dag's letter in bewilderment. He had to read it again and yet again and even then it made little sense. Gythe and Miri with the Bottom Dwellers! That would be bad enough, but it seemed Gythe had gone with them of her own free will. He opened the note and between the creases and the wear, managed to make out the writing.

I hope the potion did no harm I have gone where I am needed you cannot follow so don't try go to abby sant agnes you are needed pleese forgive me I luv you both not forgetting the Doctor and Stefano and Rigo luv Gythe

Stephano sank down on a bench. The Bottom Dwellers had been communicating with Gythe or so she had claimed, saying she could hear their voices in her head. Stephano had not taken her seriously. She had claimed she could hear Brother Barnaby talking to her, as well, and Sir Ander had written to tell Stephano that Brother Barnaby had died in the attack on Westfirth.

Either the voices were real and they had lured her away to God only knew where or Gythe was insane. At least, wherever she was, he hoped Miri was with her.

Stephano's first impulse was to rush off and search for them. He had to reason with himself, view this problem with cold, dispassionate logic. Dag had not been able to find them. Stephano was not likely to succeed where Dag had failed.

He loved Miri; he had loved her for a long time. He had made up his mind to ask her to marry him. And now he had to face the terrible truth that she and Gythe had gone and he had no idea where. He might never have the chance to tell her. He might never see them again, might never know what had happened to them.

Stephano dropped the letters to the floor and let his head sink to rest in his hands. He sat a long time in bleak despair until after some indeterminate interval a hand gently rested on his shoulder and gave him an awkward, comforting pat. Stephano was reminded of the time he had returned home after his father's execution.

"They're in God's hands, sir," Benoit said brokenly.

Stephano rested his hand gratefully on the old man's hand and blinked back tears.

"I hope He takes better care of them than I have," said Stephano.

He rose from the bench and went upstairs to pack.

10

I used to think a man's love for his family made him weak, vulnerable. I have since come to believe such love gives him the strength of angels.

—Sir Henry Wallace

The Southern Expeditionary fleet had sailed to Braffa with the goal of achieving Sir Henry's greatest triumph—Freya's acquisition of the Braffan refineries. Unfortunately, when Sir Henry arrived at the refineries, he discovered that they had been seized by the Bottom Dwellers. Frustrated that his plans had gone awry, Sir Henry and his friend, Captain Alan Northrop, commander of the privateer gunboat, the *Terrapin,* had joined the Freyan naval fleet in an attempt to recapture the refineries.

Before they even reached Braffa, Bottom Dwellers ambushed the fleet. Two black ships and their bat riders sank seven Freyan ships of the line and seriously damaged many of the rest. The flagship, HMS *Invincible,* might have been lost except for the heroics of Captain Northrop aboard the *Terrapin.* When the flagship's balloons caught fire, threatening the main gun deck and the powder magazine, Alan steered the steel-plated gunboat between Admiral Baker's flagship and the black ships of the Bottom Dwellers, engaging the black ships to allow the flagship time to limp away.

The *Terrapin* suffered several direct hits from the green beam weapons mounted on the prows of the black ships. The steel plating absorbed the force of the blasts, but while there was not much structural damage, except for one of the air screws that had been hit by enemy fire and disabled, some of the crew succumbed to the intense heat generated by the green beams.

The gunboat was nonetheless able to respond. It pounded the black ship with one broadside after another until the Bottom Dwellers were forced to retreat. The only injuries aboard the *Terrapin* were several sailors with cracked skulls and broken limbs and burns suffered by those who happened to be standing too close to the hull when the green beam struck the metal plates.

With the flagship in tow, the *Terrapin* escorted what remained of the Freyan naval fleet back to Freya. Admiral Baker was wounded in the battle, having suffered severe burns on his hands and face when he pulled flaming sailcloth off one of his lieutenants. When his flagship put in for repairs at Port Fahey, the admiral and the most seriously wounded sailors were carried on litters from the ship to the city's hospital.

Sir Henry and Alan visited their friend before they sailed on to dock in Haever to repair the damage. They found Admiral Baker in considerable pain, though Sir Henry guessed the pain came more from the losses Randolph had suffered than from his burns. The admiral's face was swathed in bandages that left only his eyes and the tip of his nose and his mouth visible.

"They say you will recover, Randolph," Sir Henry told his friend. "I'm afraid, though, you'll be left with some nasty scars."

"Bah! I was never that pretty to begin with," Admiral Baker mumbled dismissively.

He reached out with his bandaged hand and with an effort that obviously gave him pain, he gripped Sir Henry's arm.

"The butcher's bill was over a thousand men dead," Randolph said, his voice quivering with anger. "Destroy these fiends, Henry! Do whatever it takes. Destroy them!"

"I will, my friend," said Sir Henry earnestly. "So help me, God, I will!"

Sailing at night, the *Terrapin* moved at a crawl worthy of its namesake back to its secret moorings in a junkyard in the Freyan capital city, Haever, to replace the *Terrapin*'s damaged air screw.

Once it was daylight, the crew immediately began work. Captain Northrop had canceled their shore leave, but none of the men grumbled. Their mood was grim and somber, for they had seen seven ships go down in flames, and many of their comrades were dead. The sailors worked with a will, hoping to go back out to fight and sink the heinous black ships.

The odd-looking gunboat resembled its name—HMS *Terrapin,* encased in a shell consisting of magically enhanced steel plates.

Sir Henry, Captain Northrop, and the inventor of the magical steel, Pietro Alcazar, walked around the gunboat inspecting the damage in a cold, drizzling rain.

"Look at this, sir!" said Alcazar, pointing to one of the plates on the starboard side. The smooth steel plate was marred by a crater about the size of a man's head. "This took a direct hit. And see how well it fared!"

"Only a dent," said Sir Henry.

"I'd call that more than a dent," returned Alan heatedly. "It's a great bloody hole!"

"Imagine the great bloody hole the green beam would have left in the hull if it were made of wood," Sir Henry said drily. "There would be nothing left."

Alan grunted and scowled.

"The point is this, gentlemen," said Alcazar, almost dancing in his excitement. *"The constructs are still there!"*

He gazed at them expectantly. Both men stared at him blankly.

"So the bloody constructs are still there?" Captain Alan demanded. "So what?"

"Sir, they were hit by a green beam weapon and the constructs are still there!" Alcazar repeated.

Alan shook his head.

"Good God!" Sir Henry exclaimed in sudden understanding. "He's right, Alan. This is of the most vital importance!"

"You know what he's talking about?" Alan asked.

"I do," said Sir Henry. "Father Jacob explained it to me."

Alan's lip curled in a sneer.

"Hate your brother all you like, Alan," Sir Henry said. "But you must admit that Jacob is brilliant. He's probably the only person in the world right now who has studied contramagic. As he explained it, the moment contramagic constructs hit ordinary magical constructs, they start breaking them apart. The contramagic will eventually obliterate them to the point where there's nothing left."

He jabbed his finger at the steel plate. "The constructs are still there! Whereas, if you look at the damaged air screw that was made with ordinary steel, you will find that the constructs have been completely obliterated."

"That is the God's honest truth, Captain," said Alcazar.

"I can see the constructs on the steel plate. They were weakened by the hit, but not destroyed."

He traced the constructs with his hand for Sir Henry who had no talent for magic and thus could not see the magical sigils strung together. "Those fiends would have to hit this spot with that beam over and over again before they could punch through this steel."

Alan put his hand in the crater, running his fingers over the construct. He was a crafter, though not nearly as talented as his savant brother, Jacob.

"He's right. I can still detect the magic. Looks like your grand experiment paid off, Henry," Alan said.

"For all the good it will do us," Sir Henry muttered.

Alan regarded his friend with surprise. Seeing Sir Henry's embittered expression, Alan dismissed the excited Alcazar, sending him to work replacing the magic on the broken air screw.

"I thought you'd be pleased, Henry," said Alan when the two men were alone.

"And what happens when the black ships appear off the coast of Haever, Alan? These fiends could arrive any day and how will we defend our homeland? We don't have time to outfit every ship in the navy with magical steel plates!"

"You think they will invade Freya," Alan said.

"I do, indeed. Thus far, they have hit Rosia, Travia, and Estara and yet left us alone. They're plotting something dire. I sent a message to Her Majesty when we landed at Port Fahey, urging her to order the ships patrolling the Aligoes to sail for home. We're going to need them to defend the coast, though I fear they will arrive too late."

The drizzle had turned into a downpour, and water dripped off their tricorn hats. They turned up the collars of their greatcoats and shoved their hands into their pockets to keep warm. As the buildings of Haever disappeared behind a curtain of gray, the sailors donned their oilskin coats and hats and kept working.

"That begs the question, Henry. Why *haven't* the Bottom Dwellers attacked Freya?" Alan asked, pondering. "All they've done is knock down one guard tower. The attack on the fleet was an attack of opportunity. They haven't struck at our heart."

"I am hearing rumors from my Evreux agents that the Sunset Palace has been sabotaged. They expect it to fall from the skies."

"By God, if that happens, Rosia will be in chaos," said Alan, adding wistfully, "If half our ships weren't grounded, we could sail in and pick up the pieces."

"Don't you think I know it!" Sir Henry said. "The world is at war, Alan, and the world is losing."

They walked in silence, squelching through puddles. Henry was lost in his gloomy thoughts, hardly watching where he was going. Alan nudged him and he looked up, peering through the rain to see a tall, lanky, stiffly upright figure walking purposefully toward them.

"Here comes the inimitable Franklin Sloan," said Alan. "No doubt he has brought the carriage. What do you say, Henry, to dinner at the club in front of a roaring fire? Some of the Woostenbroke port to lift the spirits. *And* a shave and a change of clothes. You don't want to go home to your wife looking like you've been carried off the battlefield."

"An excellent idea, Alan," said Sir Henry, cheering up at the mention of his beloved Mouse. "Especially as she believes I have been in Travia these past few weeks conducting trade negotiations."

They increased their pace, hurrying to meet Mr. Sloan halfway.

"I received your message, sir," said Mr. Sloan. "I am

extremely sorry to hear about Admiral Baker. I trust he will recover?"

"So the physicians tell us," said Sir Henry. "How fare Lady Anne and my son?"

"Both in excellent health, sir," said Mr. Sloan. "The boy has grown a great deal. I daresay you will not recognize him. He is already cutting a tooth. Nurse Robbins assures me he is quite advanced for a child his age."

"The captain and I will dine at my club, Mr. Sloan, and I will change my clothes there. Tell Lady Anne that I have returned from a successful mission to Travia and I will be home tonight in time for tea."

"She will be most pleased to hear that, sir," said Mr. Sloan.

The three men boarded the carriage. Once they were out of the rain, Mr. Sloan reached into an inner pocket and drew forth two letters.

"This came for you this morning, sir," said Mr. Sloan, handing over the first. "Sent to your home. From Mr. Yates."

"How is Simon?" asked Alan.

Simon Yates was an old friend from university, one of the "Seconds" as they termed themselves, for all of them were second sons. Simon was the inventor, the analytical and scientific thinker of the group. He had been looking forward to a lucrative career as an attorney in the royal chancery until the four were drawn into helping to solve a mystery involving the attempted assassination of the crown prince.

Simon had been shot and nearly killed during the pursuit of the assassin. The bullet had severed his spinal cord, leaving him paralyzed from the waist down. Although he couldn't walk, he could still think, as he liked to say. He now worked for the intelligence branch of the Freyan government.

Sir Henry opened the letter, glanced through it, and

grinned. "Typical Simon. He says: 'Glad to hear you are home safe. Need to talk. You and Alan. Urgent. Tomorrow. Ten. Simon.' "

"The *Terrapin* slipped back during the dead of night to its secret berth in a junkyard. We haven't been docked more than a couple of hours. How did he know we were home at all, much less safe?" Alan demanded. "You didn't tell him, did you, Mr. Sloan?"

"I have not seen Mr. Yates for several months, sir," said Mr. Sloan.

Sir Henry chuckled. "You should know Simon by now, Alan. His giant brain works day and night. Mr. Sloan, take a note to Mr. Yates. We will meet him at that crazy floating house of his at ten."

"You'll have to find out where his house is moored and make certain it is going to stay put, Mr. Sloan," Alan stated dourly. "I've no desire to spend half the day in pursuit of the damn thing like we did the last time."

Mr. Sloan promised that he would find the current location of Welkinstead, as the house was known, named for the brilliant, eccentric woman who had designed it. He handed over the second letter.

"This arrived for you at your club, sir. Hand-delivered."

Henry took the letter, glanced at it. He did not recognize the handwriting. Opening it, he read it once, then read it again. He frowned deeply.

"Son of a bitch."

"What is wrong?" Alan asked, astonished. His friend almost never swore.

"Listen to this," said Sir Henry. He read the letter aloud, 'E staying with friends, sabotaged dwelling, fled. Now believed to be in your area. Beware.' "

"Who is 'E'?" Alan asked. "Do you know?"

"Unfortunately I know all too well," said Sir Henry in grim tones. "E is for Eiddwen."

"What does the letter mean about sabotaging a dwelling?"

Sir Henry gazed down at the letter, thoughtful. "Do you remember when we were in Capione, at her house? We found Dubois there and he recognized her masquerading as a duchess in the royal palace—"

Alan gasped in sudden understanding. "Eiddwen sabotaged the royal palace of Rosia! I wonder what she did to it?"

"Simon will know. We will ask him tomorrow."

Alan turned the letter over. "Who sent this, do you suppose?"

"Look at the signature."

"What signature?" Alan peered at the letter again. "It's not signed."

"The small drawing of the bee in the lower left hand corner. That warning came from the agents of the Countess de Marjolaine. Probably D'argent."

"But she's your worst enemy!" Alan protested. "The countess would be happy to see you gutted, your head on a pike. Why would she warn you?"

Henry flung himself back in the seat, crossed his arms and stretched out his legs. He frowned down at his boots. "What I told you before, Alan. The world is at war. And the world is losing. Freya and Rosia are going to have to stand together in this."

"Eiddwen has tried before to have you assassinated, my lord," said Mr. Sloan. "You should request police protection. Not so much for yourself," he added hurriedly, seeing Sir Henry shrug. "I fear for Lady Anne and your son."

Henry was immediately concerned. "A good suggestion, Mr. Sloan. Tell the police to station constables outside my house. And find out if the detectives have investigated any particularly gruesome murders lately. Murders that might be related to blood magic."

"Yes, my lord."

Alan was grim. "I remember that blood-splattered wine cellar in Capione. The woman is a monster. Why do you think she's here?"

"As we were discussing, Freya has been spared," said Henry. "The Bottom Dwellers have dealt serious blows to Braffa, Travia, Estara, and Rosia. I fear that now it is our turn."

Eager to see his wife and child, Henry hurried through dinner at his club, bathed and shaved in the rooms he kept there, and changed into clothes more suited to a diplomat than to a spymaster. He left Alan to enjoy his own pursuits, offering to pick him up in the carriage tomorrow to visit Simon.

The city home of Sir Henry Wallace was located on Regent Street. His neighbors tended to be those who had earned their fortunes and their titles, not inherited them. The four-story house, built of red brick with a gleaming white door and white-framed windows, was elegant and unassuming, as suited a diplomat, a statesman, and adviser to his wife's aunt, the queen. One would never know that inside this modest dwelling lived one of the most powerful and most dangerous men in the kingdom.

Henry noted with approval two constables strolling up and down the sidewalk in front. They saluted him as he stopped to speak to them.

"Thank you for keeping an eye on things, Officers."

"Our pleasure, sir," said one. "We have a man stationed around back, as well."

Sir Henry nodded and went to the door. The footman met him, took his cloak and hat, and told him that Lady Anne was waiting for him in the drawing room.

"Has Mr. Sloan returned?" Sir Henry asked.

"No, my lord," the footman replied.

"He must be having trouble finding Simon's house," Sir Henry said to himself with a chuckle.

He instructed the footman to let him know when Mr. Sloan arrived and then hurried up the stairs to greet his wife. The drawing room was located on the second floor. Small and intimate, the drawing room was where the master and mistress could "withdraw" from the world, spend quiet time together. It was situated in a corner of the house, with two windows—one facing the street, the other overlooking the small area of grass, trees, and neatly trimmed hedges that separated their house from the home of their neighbor.

The room, done in shades of rose and mauve, had been designed and furnished to Lady Anne's specifications. He opened the door softly to find her seated by the window, reading a book. She was so absorbed she did not hear him enter. He stood gazing for a moment, taking the time to let the fragrance of fresh-cut flowers blot out the remembered stench of blood and gunpowder and death. Henry cherished his house as an island of peace and refuge in a sea of danger and tumult.

When he stepped inside and shut the door, Lady Anne looked up, dropped her book to the floor, and ran to him with open arms. He embraced her and held her fast.

Lady Anne Wallace was much younger than her husband. She was slight of build, shy and withdrawn, with brown hair and large brown eyes. She and her wealth had been a gift to Henry from the queen in thanks for his service to his country. Henry had been astonished to discover that his wife was in love with him and even more astonished when he realized that he himself had fallen in love with her.

"I will ring for tea," said Anne, emerging from the embrace with pink cheeks and mussed hair.

"How is little Harry? I want to see him."

"He is fretful. Nurse Robbins says he may be cutting a tooth, though I think two and a half months is too early. I'll have her bring him down," she said, as she rang for the servant.

The tea arrived at the same time as Nurse Robbins entered carrying young Henry Alan Randolph. The baby had indeed grown considerably, even in the weeks he'd been gone. Red-faced and bald, he was chewing determinedly on one of his fists and was covered in drool. Henry insisted on holding him, to the dismay of Nurse, who hovered near, expecting disaster.

Holding the baby around the waist, Henry began tossing him gently into the air. Young Harry, far from being upset, gurgled and laughed. Shocked, Nurse Robbins started to intervene.

"Go to the kitchen, Nurse, and have your tea with the other members of the staff," said Anne. "We'll bring Harry up in time for bed."

"If you're certain, my lady . . . ," said Nurse Robbins in dubious tones.

She lingered at the door, in case they changed their minds. Henry made a face at her, and Nurse Robbins sniffed indignantly and fluttered out of the room.

"Silly old cow," said Henry.

"Don't offend her, dear. She is quite good with Henry and good nursemaids are hard to find. Should I pour you some tea?" Anne asked.

"Not just yet," said Henry. "I'm going to reacquaint myself with my son." He tucked the baby in the crook of his arm. "What a brave boy he is. See how he looks at me. He couldn't possibly remember me. Any other baby would be screaming its head off."

"He knows his father," said Anne, pleased

"I really believe he does," said Henry.

Holding the child in his arms, he stood near his wife's chair, gazing out the window, thinking that he was never so happy as here. He glanced behind to see his wife picking up the teapot.

Blinding green light blazed into the room. The light was brighter than the sunlight, illuminating every part of the room. Henry stood stock still, staring. Ann half turned, gazing in astonishment at the brilliant light.

"Merciful heaven—" she began.

Henry grabbed hold of her arm and dragged her out of the chair, overturning the tea table and spilling the tea.

"We have to get out of here!"

Anne stared at him, frightened. "Henry, what—"

"We have to get out of here *now,* my dear," Henry repeated. "Hold Harry."

He thrust the baby into his wife's arms. Anne clasped her son tightly. She was frightened, but calm. She had no idea what was going on, but she trusted her husband to deal with it. Henry put his arm around her and they ran for the door. He had his hand on the door handle and was starting to open it when he heard a rumbling sound and felt the house give a great shudder.

Plaster fell from the ceiling, covering them in dust. Henry could hear the wooden beams in the ceiling creak and groan. The house was starting to collapse.

He pushed Anne ahead of him out the door and onto the landing. Screams and cries were coming from the kitchen where the servants were gathered, having their tea.

"Get out!" Sir Henry bellowed. "Run!"

His warning echoed through the house. The servants' hall was below street level. He hoped they had heard him and that they would all escape before they were buried alive.

He put his arm protectively around his wife and child,

holding them close as they hurried down the stairs. The front door was two flights lower. He could see it through the dust and falling plaster. A great rending and snapping sound came from overhead. Henry glanced up, saw the ceiling give way. He hunkered down, shielding his wife and son with his body as a huge wooden beam crashed through the ceiling and onto the stairs.

Dust and debris cascaded down on top of them. Henry was aware of objects striking him, but he was so concerned about his wife and child he scarcely felt the pain. He held Anne tightly. She pressed close against him, covering the baby's head with both her hands and bending over him. Henry could feel her trembling, but she remained calm, murmuring soothing words to the baby. Little Harry was in a frenzy; frightened of the noise and objecting to being half smothered.

When the debris quit falling, Henry opened his eyes and blinked away the dirt and grit. The beam had landed on the stairs right in front of them, missing them by a hand's breadth. He looked up to see a gigantic hole in the ceiling. Cracks appeared in the wall, and windowpanes had broken, the glass falling inside and out. The house continued to shake. Any moment it might tumble down on top of them.

Henry assessed the situation. The wooden beam lay across the stairs, blocking their way. The stairs were covered in broken glass and rubble. Henry stood up, shaking off bits of plaster.

"Stay down," he warned his wife.

She remained crouched on the stairs, holding the baby protectively, shielding him with her own body. She gave Henry a smile, letting him know she had faith in him. He wished he felt as confident. Putting his shoulder against the beam, he tried to shift it. The beam was heavy, firmly wedged against the wall.

"It won't budge," he said to his wife.

Now he could smell smoke and hear the crackle of flames. Something somewhere close had caught fire. The smoke was growing thicker. Through it, he could see flashes of orange. The fire was spreading rapidly.

Lady Anne was coughing. She drew her handkerchief from her pocket and covered the baby's mouth and nose.

"Sir Henry!" a voice called from the front door. "Where are you?"

"Mr. Sloan! Thank God! The main stairs!" Sir Henry shouted, choking in the smoke. "Up here!"

"Don't go in there, Mr. Sloan!" Henry heard one of the constables cry. "It's too dangerous. The house is going to fall down!"

"If you do not want to lose your hand, sir," said Mr. Sloan sternly, "I suggest you let go of my arm.

As Mr. Sloan ran into the entryway a chunk of the ceiling fell, hitting him a glancing blow on the shoulder. He made his way through the rubble to the stairs, paused a moment to tie a handkerchief around the lower part of his face, and began to climb, his boots crunching on broken glass. He hurled aside larger chunks of debris.

The staircase rocked and lurched. A section of the balustrade broke off and fell to the floor below. For a heart-stopping moment, Henry feared the staircase would give way beneath them. Lady Anne gasped and closed her eyes, clinging to her child and whispering prayers. Henry grabbed hold of the beam to keep from falling. Mr. Sloan braced himself, his hand against the wall.

When the staircase stopped moving and the dust cleared, Henry saw that it had come loose from the wall and was canting sideways, leaning precariously. The entire staircase could go at any moment. As luck would have it or perhaps because of Lady Anne's prayers, the shifting of the stairs had opened up a small gap between the beam and the wall. Henry looked back to see the orange glow brightening. He put his hand over his nose and mouth and crouching low to escape the smoke, clasped his wife in his arms.

"When Mr. Sloan comes, my dear, hand him the baby, then crawl out under the beam."

"What about you?" Anne asked, regarding him anxiously.

"I will be right behind you."

Mr. Sloan continued to climb the stairs, moving slowly and carefully so as not to trigger another shift until he finally reached them.

"Take the baby, Mr. Sloan!" Henry told him. "And Lady Anne!"

Anne thrust the child through the gap underneath the broken beam. Mr. Sloan grasped the baby and did what he could to assist Anne, whose long skirts hampered her ability to crawl through the gap herself.

Henry coughed and tried to hold his breath. A loud crash came from outside. He guessed that a chimney had toppled.

Anne was finally through the gap. She tried to walk and swayed dizzily, the smoke making her light-headed. Mr. Sloan took hold of Anne around the waist. Carrying the baby, he assisted her down the stairs. Henry crawled through the gap and hurried after them, slipping and sliding in the debris.

He caught up with Mr. Sloan and his wife and child. The stairs quaked and shook beneath their feet. They made it to the ground level and dashed through the entryway and out the front door. Mr. Sloan, carrying the baby, ran ahead of them. Henry was the last out, helping his wife. Once out, her strength gave way and she fell. Henry gathered her up in his arms on the run.

Behind him, he could hear the house crumble. Bricks and mortar cracked, wood beams splintered, and glass shattered. Flames shot out one of the upper windows, as another chimney crashed to the ground. Then, with a horrendous snapping and creaking sound and a deafening boom, the house vanished in a cloud of dust and debris that roiled across the lawn, driving back a crowd of gawkers.

Henry's own strength gave out. He could feel his knees start to buckle and he was still carrying his wife. One of the constables saw his trouble and came to his aid. Lifting Anne gently in his arms, the constable lowered her to the grass.

"Let me see her. I'm a physician," said a man who looked vaguely familiar. He smiled to see Henry looking at him confusedly and added, "I am your neighbor, Sir Henry. The next house over. I was in my carriage, heading out on my rounds when I heard the explosion and came to see if I could help."

He knelt beside Anne, loosened her stays, felt her pulse and listened to her lungs.

"How is she?" Henry asked anxiously.

"She has suffered no ill effects, my lord. She is already starting to come around."

Anne's eyes fluttered and opened. She looked at Henry and her brow creased. "Little Harry? Where is he?"

"He is fine," said Henry, smiling in reassurance. "He is with Nurse Robbins."

The nurse, her face streaked with tears and grime, was holding the baby in her arms, rocking him soothingly.

Anne breathed a sigh of relief. "Did all the servants escape?"

Henry took hold of her hand and brought it to his lips. "I'll find out. You are not to worry."

"Our house?" Lady Anne asked with a catch in her throat.

"Gone, my dear," said Sir Henry. He added cheerfully. "We'll find another."

"Henry, what happened?" Anne asked softly, grasping his hand tightly. "I saw a strange green light and then the house shook—"

"I think the house was struck by lightning," said Henry.

"Lightning, Henry?" Anne looked into his eyes and faintly smiled.

She didn't believe him, but her faith and trust in him was implicit. Henry's heart swelled with love. He realized how close he had come to losing her and his little son.

"My dear Mouse! Take care of yourself and our boy," he said in a choked voice.

He kissed her on the forehead and left her in the physician's capable hands. He rose to his feet to find Mr. Sloan at his elbow.

"How are you, sir?" Mr. Sloan regarded Sir Henry in concern. "You are bleeding."

"Am I?" Sir Henry asked vaguely.

He hadn't realized until now he was hurt. He looked down to see blood on his shirt. His head ached and he felt a throbbing pain in his back near his right shoulder.

"Cuts and bruises, nothing serious," he said dismissively. "We need a quiet place to talk."

"The physician's carriage, my lord," said Mr. Sloan, indicating a black phaeton standing near the curb. "He was leaving for his rounds when he heard the explosion. I do not think he would mind if we used it."

"An excellent idea, Mr. Sloan."

He motioned for Mr. Sloan to join him inside the small phaeton. The open-air carriage did not keep out the noise or the acrid, sickening smell of smoke, but it did offer them a modicum of privacy.

"Your orders, my lord," said Mr. Sloan.

"Take Lady Anne and my son to the palace. Tell Her Majesty what happened."

"What *has* happened, my lord?"

"The house was hit by a green beam weapon," said Henry grimly. "I think you know who ordered the attack."

"Do I tell Her Majesty the truth, my lord?" Mr. Sloan asked. "Do I tell her about Eiddwen?"

Henry mulled this over. "Yes, you had better do so. The queen should be prepared. Have the palace guards keep watch on my wife and child around the clock."

"Yes, my lord. Where will you be?"

"I'm going to my club. After you have Lady Anne settled and you have spoken to the queen, meet me there."

"I have news for you, my lord, that may have bearing on this attack," said Mr. Sloan. "I was coming to tell you. The police recently discovered the body of a young woman who had been tortured and murdered. She was a prostitute, so they did not investigate as thoroughly as they might have. The description of the wounds on the victim is consistent with those on the bodies found at Capione."

Sir Henry pressed his lips together, gave a tight nod and muttered, "Eiddwen."

"If there is nothing more, my lord, I will order your carriage for Lady Anne."

"Thank you. You are armed, Mr. Sloan?"

Mr. Sloan drew aside his coat to reveal his pistol. "I have another in my boot, my lord."

The crowd of gawkers was growing, drawn by the arrival of the horse-drawn fire engine that rattled and clanged along the street. Henry waited with his wife until Mr. Sloan brought the carriage around. Henry was able to assure her that all the servants had escaped without harm. Once his wife and his child were safely inside the carriage, attended by Nurse Robbins and Mr. Sloan, Henry turned to deal with the inevitable questions.

He had refused to speak to the two constables who had been outside his house until his wife was gone. They came forward along with a news reporter who had chased after the fire engine in hopes of getting a story. When the reporter attempted to sneak up behind the constables, one of them caught him and angrily ordered him to remove himself, going so far as to threaten him with his nightstick.

"I am pleased to see you gentlemen are not hurt," Sir Henry said to the constables.

"No, my lord. Thank you, my lord. We saw the light and heard the blast and, seeing as how there was nothing we could do . . ."

"You took to your heels," said Sir Henry. "Quite wise."

The constable was flustered, but not to be deterred from his pursuit of the truth. "We were wondering if you could tell us what happened, my lord."

"What did you men see?" Sir Henry countered the question with a question.

"Bright green light, my lord."

"A *beam* of green light, my lord," said his partner, elaborating. "Like a beam of light shining from a bull's-eye lantern."

"That's right," said his partner. "Only brighter."

"A beam of green light," Sir Henry repeated, pursing his lips. "You will forgive me if I find that hard to believe, Officers."

"You must have seen it, my lord," said one.

"As it happens, I was facing away from the window at time," said Sir Henry blandly. "All I know is that one moment my lady wife was pouring tea and the next moment our house was falling down around our ears. I remember thinking at the time we'd been hit by lightning. Did this green light shine from the sky?"

"Well, yes, my lord," said one.

"A clear blue sky," his partner added. "Not a cloud in sight."

"I've heard of such phenomena before. They call it heat lightning or something," said Sir Henry. He put his hand to his forehead. "Forgive me, Officers, but I really am not well. My head is throbbing. I cannot think clearly. I am worried about my wife who has gone to stay in the palace with her aunt, the queen. Please excuse me, but I really must be on my way."

"Yes, my lord," said the constable resignedly. He touched his hat. "Thank you, my lord. I hope your lady wife is going to be well."

Mr. Sloan had thoughtfully ordered another carriage for his master. Henry was glad to climb inside, away from the onlookers, the noise, and the smell of smoke and the dust that still hung in the air. He started to pull down the shade, then paused to take a last look at his home—a smoldering pile of rubble being doused with small streams of water from the fire hoses.

He thought of those terrifying moments on the staircase, holding his wife and little child in his arms. He had been in desperate and dangerous situations before, but he had never known such cold, bowel-twisting terror as when he feared that any moment they might be crushed to death in the collapse of the building.

He shut the curtains as the carriage rolled off down the street, then sank back in the seat and closed his burning eyes. A single tear slid down his thin cheek. He gritted his teeth and tried to keep another tear from falling.

11

I have my brain. Legs are superfluous . . .

—Simon Yates

As the sun was setting, Henry arrived at his club, the Naval Club. Membership was exclusive to naval officers, and though Henry had never served in the navy, he had worked in the admiralty and was a member of the committee that approved naval funding. He was also either generally feared or admired and when Admiral Baker and Alan had proposed him for membership, not a single member had voted against him.

The doorman welcomed Henry with an understanding look and murmured sympathy. Apparently news of the disaster had spread. Henry avoided the sitting room and the library, where members would be reading the evening papers, drinking brandy, and talking about him. He went immediately to his private room to bathe, examine his injuries, and change clothes. He was standing half naked in front of a mirror, peering over his shoulder at an ugly bruise on his back, when there came a banging on the door. Alan bounded into the room.

"Henry, I just heard what happened! Are you all right? Lady Anne? Your son?"

"We are all fine," said Henry. "I sent Lady Anne and little Harry to the palace under the care of Mr. Sloan."

"Some of the chaps were saying you were dead." Alan flung himself into a chair and mopped his brow. "That's a nasty cut on your head. You should have the healer take a look."

"Nonsense," said Henry. "Patch it up, will you? There are some plasters in that drawer."

Alan cleaned the wound and applied a sticking plaster. Henry grimaced as he shoved his arm into the sleeve of a clean shirt, drawing it tenderly over his injured shoulder.

"Are you hungry?" Alan asked.

Henry shook his head. "I could use a brandy."

Alan poured two large brandies into cut crystal snifters. Henry drank the first in a single gulp. Alan poured his friend another.

"Do you want something eat?"

Henry shook his head. "Not here. Too many damn fool questions. We'll dine out."

Alan was silent a moment, seemingly embarrassed. Then he could contain his curiosity no longer.

"If you'll forgive a damn fool question, Henry, what happened?"

Henry smiled. "I forgive a damn fool question from you." Motioning his friend closer, he said in a low undertone, "The house was hit by a green beam weapon."

"Good God!" Alan exclaimed, regarding Henry in horror. "The Bottom Dwellers. They tried to kill you!"

"And nearly succeeded," said Henry drily.

"A green beam weapon . . ." Alan sipped his brandy, frowning in puzzlement. "How is that possible? The alarm would have been raised if any of their black ships had been sighted in the skies above Haever."

"It wasn't a ship," said Henry.

"What was it then?"

Henry drank his brandy, gazing unseeing at his reflection in the mirror. He set the empty snifter down.

"Eiddwen."

Alan sucked in a breath and let it out in a muttered curse. Rising to his feet, he walked to the window and drew the curtain closed.

"Blasted female could be anywhere out there."

"But she couldn't have fired the green beam weapon from anywhere. Judging by the angle of the beam, I would guess she was shooting at the house from a rooftop of a nearby building."

Henry reached to his waistcoat, drew out his watch, only to find that it had stopped working at precisely the moment the house had begun to collapse.

He placed the broken watch on his nightstand.

Early the next morning, in a gray and cloudy dawn, Henry and Alan, accompanied by Mr. Sloan, flew on griffins to the site where Henry's house had stood. The neighborhood was quiet at this early hour. Only the servants were awake, going about their duties. The street was otherwise empty. Gawkers would doubtless arrive later in the day, but for now, nobody impeded their grim task.

The three men flew over the wreckage, viewing it from various angles before landing. They left the griffins to rest on the ground, their wings folded, waiting patiently for their return, and went to more closely examine the wreckage.

Henry had been too shaken, too worried about his wife and child to pay much attention to the destruction yesterday. This morning he had ascertained from Mr. Sloan that Lady Anne and Little Harry were well, both recovering from the shock. Lady Anne had sent Henry her love and begged him to be careful.

Henry frowned at the last.

"I fear she does not believe your explanation of the house being hit by lightning, my lord," Mr. Sloan told him. "I am convinced that Lady Anne knows more than we realize."

"My clever little Mouse," Henry said, smiling proudly. "She is a brave and intelligent woman."

"Indubitably, my lord," Mr. Sloan agreed.

Henry gazed at the wreckage in awe. The back wall and a portion of the north wall of his four-story house were all that remained standing. The rest of the dwelling was nothing more than an enormous pile of bricks, charred and cracked beams, plaster, pulverized furniture, and shattered glass.

The silence was awful, broken only by horrible creaking sounds as the pile settled. The smell of burning filled the air.

"You're certain it was a green beam weapon, Henry?" Alan asked. "This looks like a bomb exploded!"

"Green light, bright as the sun, blazed through the window," said Henry. "I knew what it was the moment I saw it. Still, we need proof. Mr. Sloan is going to examine the debris. You know what you are looking for, Mr. Sloan?"

Mr. Sloan went to the front of the house, picked up what was left of a brick and studied it closely. He tossed it back on the pile and picked up another. He examined bricks, splintered pieces of wood, and slivers of glass. He studied them from the front, the back, and the sides.

Henry cleaned off a stone bench in what had once been the garden, then sat down. Folding his arms, he extended his legs and fixed his gaze upon Mr. Sloan. Alan sat down beside him, but he was almost immediately back on his feet, pacing restlessly.

"Good God, Henry, how can you be so nonchalant?

That bloody female has now tried three times to have you killed!"

"Third time's a charm, as they say," remarked Henry.

"Don't joke about it," said Alan angrily.

"What would you prefer me to do, Alan? Break into tears? Go into hiding? We're not yet certain it was a green beam weapon. I have only the evidence of my own eyes and it is possible I could be mistaken."

"True," said Alan caustically. "The possibility exists that God struck you with a thunderbolt."

Henry smiled. "We always assume God is on the side of Freya. He might be Rosian for all we know, in which case he would have no compunction about smiting me. Ah, Mr. Sloan, what have you found?"

"First, my lord, may I say it is my firm belief that God is on the side of Freya."

"Good to know that God is a patriot, Mr. Sloan," said Henry gravely.

"As to the attack, you were right, my lord. The house was hit by one of the Bottom Dweller's green beam weapons. When the green beam hit, the contramagic destroyed the constructs that are in the mortar, the wood frames, the glass. In addition to that, the tremendous heat from the beam destroyed the magical constructs in the bricks, which caused the walls to collapse."

"My next house will be built without magic," said Henry.

"I fear that might be difficult, my lord."

"I fear so, too, Mr. Sloan. Speaking of which, you should send the servants to our country estate until we can find a suitable house to let here in the city. Lady Anne and my son will remain in the palace under guardianship of Her Majesty. I trust they will be safe there . . ."

His words died away. The thought was in his mind, in the minds of them all, that none of them was safe anywhere.

"So where the devil did this green beam come from?" Alan asked after a moment.

"I've been thinking about that. The weapon could have been mounted on a roof," said Henry. "The Bottom Dwellers did something similar when they attacked me in Westfirth. Do you agree, Mr. Sloan?"

"I do, my lord," said Mr. Sloan. "From what you describe, you observed the beam striking the upper level of the house near where you were standing."

"If that is the case, the Bottom Dwellers would have been relatively close by," said Alan. "Otherwise buildings would obstruct the view and they wouldn't be able to get a clean shot. If we flew over the area, we might find some evidence."

•

The three men waited until the morning sun burned off the fog, then once more mounted the griffins and set out, flying low over the rooftops of neighboring buildings. Their search did not take them long. Only a few blocks from Henry's house they saw an odd-looking object on top of a building that had once, according to the faded sign, housed a wheelwright's business. The three landed the griffins on the roof and went to investigate.

Mr. Sloan picked up the object and held it up for inspection.

"That looks like a mount for a swivel gun," said Alan. "Only bigger."

"Is there magic on it, Mr. Sloan?" Henry asked.

"There is, but I do not recognize any of the constructs that were used in the manufacture of this thing," said Mr. Sloan. He held it gingerly. "If I were to hazard a guess, I would say they might well be contramagic."

"Look at this," said Alan, who had been snooping around in a corner.

He picked up a metal disk with a crystal gleaming in the center. "There's three of these things over here. What do you suppose they are?"

"I have no idea, but treat them carefully, Alan," said Henry. "Mr. Sloan, take charge of them."

Mr. Sloan placed the three disks in his leather satchel.

"Looks to me as if whoever was here had to beat a swift retreat," said Alan. "They carried off the weapon, but they were in such a hurry they left behind the mount and the ammunition."

"They also forgot these, my lord," said Mr. Sloan.

Reaching down, he picked up a pair of leather gloves and brought them over for closer inspection.

The gloves were soft leather, finely made, and far too small to fit their hands.

"Those are a woman's gloves," said Alan in a low voice. "Dog's bollocks, Henry! Eiddwen fired that weapon herself! She took the gloves off in order to trigger it and didn't have time to put them back on."

The three men looked at each other. Henry's brows came together. Mr. Sloan was grim.

Alan and Henry left the griffins on the roof in the care of Mr. Sloan and descended the stairs of the empty structure. They reached the street level and went looking for the constable who regularly patrolled this area.

They found him walking his beat. He touched his hand to his hat in a polite salute.

"Constable, I am interested in purchasing this building." Henry indicated the former wheelwright's establishment. "I was wondering if you had received reports of any trouble with vagrants."

"Odd you ask, sir. We don't get many vagrants in this neighborhood. Never had a problem until yesterday afternoon," the constable reported. "I was walking my beat when I saw a flash of bright light on the roof. I thought it strange, sir. Had a kind of green tinge to it. I started to go up to investigate, when I heard the clanging of the fire bells and one of the other constables comes running. Seems that a house exploded and the captain wanted all of us to report to him there. I was just going to check the building today to see if the vagrants had cleared out."

"No need, Constable," said Alan. "We've been up there. Nothing is amiss."

"As for the bright flash of light, I've heard the house was hit by lightning," Henry added. "Perhaps that was what you saw."

"I did hear that same report, sir. That must have been it. To think I saw it!"

The constable touched his hat again and walked off, marveling. Henry and Alan went back inside the building and began climbing the four long flights of stairs that led to the roof.

"Now we know why Eiddwen left in such haste," said Alan. "She was afraid the constable would return to investigate." He drew out his watch. "We should make haste ourselves or we're going to be late for our meeting with Simon. We'll have to travel by air to get there. That blasted house of his has floated off to other side of the river. And we can't take the griffins. Simon has nowhere to stable them."

"We will send Mr. Sloan back to the club with the griffins and take a hansom cab," said Henry. "Mr. Sloan can meet us at the house."

They continued to climb.

"Henry," said Alan after a pause to catch his breath, "if Eiddwen wanted to kill you, why did she go to all this trouble? Why blow up your house when she could have just as easily blown off your head with a gunshot?"

"I've been thinking about that myself," said Henry. "She wanted to utterly destroy me, kill me and my wife and my child. Level my house, my 'safe haven' from the world. And if I, by some miracle, survived, she hoped to put the fear of God in me."

"Did she, Henry?" Alan asked, struck by a note in his friend's voice. "Did she put the fear of God in you?"

"I must confess she did, Alan," Henry admitted after a moment. "Last night as I lay in the darkness, remembering those horrible moments when I thought I was going to lose all that I loved, I told myself I would pack up my wife and child and leave Freya, leave this life of intrigue, travel to some safe haven . . ."

"If what you say is true about these Bottom Dwellers, Henry, that they are waging war on the world, nowhere is safe from them," said Alan.

"Which is what I realized when I woke up this morning," said Henry. "And now we must go see if we can locate Simon."

Given that Rosia's beautiful floating palace was considered one of the wonders of the world, Freyans claimed to possess another wonder. Or if not a wonder, then certainly one of the world's oddities: a flying house.

Welkinstead, the flying house of Simon Yates, had once belonged to Dame Winifred Ufford. A gifted crafter, renowned scientist, and artist, she was described by polite society as "eccentric." She had designed her house to fly because she "was sick and tired of looking out the window at the same old thing day in and day out."

Her house didn't exactly fly. It "drifted with panache," as Dame Winifred was fond of saying.

The original house was a marble villa. As the family grew and styles changed, they had added new wings without any seeming rhyme or reason. The most unique renovation came from Dame Winifred herself, who had introduced powerful magical constructs that fortified the supporting structure of the home. The installation of lift tanks and several ship's balloons allowed Welkinstead to rise up off the ground and go floating about the city. When Simon inherited the house, he added sails and air screws so that he could steer the contraption, rather than allow it to drift at will.

Dame Winifred had become acquainted with Simon and his friends, the Seconds, during the famous incident when a young Henry had foiled an assassination attempt against the prince regent. The lady had taken a liking to Simon, saying their minds worked the same way.

"Both of them are crackpots," Alan had stated at the time.

When Simon had suffered his debilitating wound, Dame Winifred had designed a special magical chair for his use and brought him to live with her in her wondrous house. At her death, she bequeathed the house and her immense wealth to him.

Simon Yates was insatiably curious. He read voraciously, spoke every major language in the world and many of the more obscure languages, and subscribed to every newspaper, pamphlet, and gazette. He received so much correspondence from his many informants that the post office had assigned one person to do nothing except sort his mail and deliver it to wherever his house happened to be at the time.

His genius was such that he could take all the disparate bits of information he absorbed, shuffle them about in his brain, and start connecting them. He used his talent to thwart plots, solve crimes, catch criminals, and discover information vital to the government, all without ever leaving his chair. He had proven himself so valuable that Henry called Simon Yates "Freya's secret weapon."

Arriving at the house, which was currently drifting

over the Parliament building, Alan and Henry stepped out of the wyvern-drawn carriage onto a pier that served as the front porch. They knew better than to knock or ring the bell. Simon's manservant, Mr. Albright, would have observed their arrival and would be waiting at the door.

Mr. Albright was a tall man, standing well over six feet, with a muscular build, and the straight, upright stance of a military man.

After the death of the eccentric Dame Winifred, Simon had been left alone to shift for himself in the vast house. Although he had protested that he was quite capable of managing on his own, Henry had been determined to hire a suitable manservant for his invaluable friend.

"If you insist on foisting a manservant on me," Simon had said, "then you must find someone who won't speak to me. I can't abide idle chatter. And I don't want anyone who will 'tidy up' or muck about with my things. And he must be completely and totally discreet. You know that I deal with a lot of sensitive information. If you can find someone like that, which I very much doubt, then I will consider him."

Mr. Sloan had recommended Mr. Albright as someone who would suit Simon's exacting criteria.

"Allistar Albright is known for his laconic manner, sir. We served many years together in the same regiment and I doubt if I have heard him say seven words in all that time," Mr. Sloan had said.

Simon had interviewed Mr. Albright, found him suitable, and grudgingly agreed to give him a trial. Mr. Albright had been with Simon ever since.

Entering the house was tantamount to entering a museum ("or a freak show," Alan had once remarked). Dame Winifred had traveled extensively and every room contained objects acquired on her journeys. Beautiful, valuable paintings adorned the walls, every one of them tilted at a crazy angle due to the movement of the house. Stuffed animals lurked in dark corners, occasionally lunging unexpectedly at startled visitors when the house was hit by a high wind. The lady collected chandeliers. Hundreds of them hung (and sometimes fell) from the ceilings, their crystal prisms casting rainbows on the walls and filling the air with faint chiming sounds.

Ornate wooden chests contained collections—of butterflies, eggs, rare beetles and glass eyeballs. Barometers of various types were scattered about, as well as instruments designed to measure barometric pressure, rainfall, and wind speed. The walls were lined with bookshelves filled with books. Having acquired more books since, with no room on the bookshelves, Simon had taken to stacking the overflow of books on the floor. The stacks of books generally toppled over whenever the house moved and had to be put to rights about once a week.

Accompanied by the silent Mr. Albright, Henry and Alan navigated their way around the furniture and stuffed animals, both of them keeping a wary eye on the chandeliers that swayed gently with the motion of the house. They knew exactly where to find Simon and climbed the stairs to the second floor to his office. He worked here by day and most of the night, for he required only about four hours of sleep a day.

The office was enormous, taking up most of the floor. The only other rooms on this floor were a small bedroom and the water closet. The kitchen had once been on this floor, but the lady, having arranged for all her meals to be delivered, had converted it to a scientific laboratory, and Simon had continued the arrangement for himself and Mr. Albright. Simon ate little and rarely paid attention to his food, for he always read while dining.

Simon's wheelchair, which the lady had designed, could roll across the floor or glide through the air. When the three arrived in his study, he propelled the chair over to greet them, reaching out to shake hands.

"My dear Henry," said Simon, "I heard about your house exploding. Hit by a green beam, wasn't it? You are damn lucky you survived. That female, Eiddwen, must be behind it. She's back in the country along with her deranged, depraved young man."

Henry cast an amused glance at Alan.

"I said you would know. How did you find out? I heard word only yesterday."

"The two were staying in the George under false names. I suspected her when I heard the news about your house. I sent several of my agents around to the hotels with her description. The two have fled, of course. No forwarding address. You know she tried to destroy the Sunset Palace."

"I heard something—" Henry began.

"She sabotaged the lift tanks. Engineers are trying to save it, but my people tell me it's only a matter of time before the palace crashes into the lake. I don't like it. Not one bit. Alan, I'm glad to hear the damage to the *Terrapin* was minimal. Alcazar's steel works as advertised. Sit down, sit down."

Simon Yates was in his forties, of an age with Henry and Alan. He wore his sandy blond hair cut short so as not to have to fool with it. That, and his light blue, bright, eager eyes made him seem younger. He was always cheerful, never melancholy; never moped about, whined or felt sorry for himself. He had his work. He had his friends. And, as he was wont to say, he had humanity to entertain him.

He led the way to his desk, steering his chair through a veritable forest of filing cabinets made of polished wood with brass fittings. Each cabinet was designated with a series of numbers and letters that made little sense to anyone but Simon. He had created this method for keeping track of all the information he collected. And though it was a mystery to everyone else, he could lay his hands on any document, paper, letter, or journal stored there within minutes.

His desk was in a turret room located off the main chamber. Surrounded on three sides by glass, the room currently provided a magnificent view of the city of Haever and the mists of the Breath.

An enormous telescope in one of the windows allowed Simon to get a close-up look at just about anything he desired. A large chart table stood alongside his desk, on which he had spread out a map. Behind the table was a slate chalkboard.

Simon steered his chair to his desk, which was the size of six ordinary desks put together and had been built especially for him. Henry had no idea what the top of the desk looked like, for he had never seen it. It was covered with papers a foot deep arranged in neat, orderly piles, tied up in ribbons of various colors.

Henry and Alan sat down in chairs located on either side of Simon. This way, he could show them any document to which he referred. Mr. Albright, silent and unmoving, stood hands folded, in his usual place in a corner of the room. He reminded Henry of one of the stuffed animals.

"I will explain why I sent for you," said Simon. "You must bear with me a moment."

"We always bear with you, my friend," said Henry.

Simon grinned appreciatively and continued. "I could give you report after report. Every other country in the world has been hit by the Bottom Dwellers. Every country except Freya. They have yet to strike at our heart."

"Alan and I were saying the same thing yesterday," said Henry.

"Eiddwen did not come back just to knock down your house, Henry." Simon pointed to a pile of documents.

"Alan, toss over that bunch of newspapers, the ones tied with the green ribbon that are on top."

Alan did as he was asked. Simon removed the ribbon and set it aside.

"I used green, you'll note. I thought that an appropriate color for the Bottom Dwellers." He held up a newspaper. "From the court records of the twelfth circuit, published in the *Lowland Gazette*. I will summarize. A farmer was plowing his land when he struck a large boulder partially buried in the ground. The blade of the plow broke. Are you following me so far?"

He eyed Alan, who had yawned.

"Broken plow," said Alan. "Tell me quickly what happens next. I'm not sure I can stand the suspense."

"This gets better," Simon promised. "The farmer swore in court he had been plowing the same field for years and never saw the boulder before. He claimed that the boulder had been placed there by a road crew the county had hired to repair the road a few miles from the farmer's land. The farmer said the crew had dumped the boulder in his field. He sought restitution for his plow in county court. Wait, wait," said Simon, seeing Alan yawn again. "Here comes the interesting part.

"When asked how he knew the boulder had been put there by the road crew, the farmer testified that the boulder was covered with strange markings."

Henry sat forward in his chair, suddenly interested.

"The farmer attributed the markings to the road crew. The crew foreman stated that his crew had not dug up the boulder, they had not put any markings on it, nor had they dumped the boulder in the field. He swore under oath. The judge agreed and the farmer's suit was defeated."

Henry frowned and put the tips of his fingers together.

Alan was puzzled. "Could I ask—"

"No, you can not," said Simon. "What you can do is

look at the map of Freya I have spread out on the table and note the location of Lowland. You see it marked there with a green pin."

Alan and Henry dutifully noted the location of the green pin.

"Next we have an article written by one Alberta Higgenbotham that appeared in the *Slopford Herald*—"

"You're making that up," said Alan. "No town would name itself 'Slopford.'"

"Indeed I am not. The town was named for the Slopfords, a highly respected family of long standing. Now sit there and be quiet. The article is titled: 'Spirits Active in Our Community.'"

Alan groaned and flung himself back in his chair.

"Mistress Higgenbotham is a well-known medium in the area, who claims to be on familiar terms with the local ghosts and spirits. She was riding in her wyvern-drawn carriage one day, when she looked down and saw several large boulders placed at regular intervals around the fields.

"Believing this could not be a natural phenomenon, she landed her carriage to investigate. She found—note this—'*strange markings on the boulders.*'"

Simon looked at Henry as he spoke.

"She states: 'These markings were undoubtedly placed there by spirits attempting to communicate with us, the living.' Mistress Higginbotham writes that she is 'organizing a tour to visit the site, during which she will attempt to speak with the spirits. Picnic luncheon will be provided.'"

Simon paused to see what effect this had on his readers. Henry's frown deepened. He placed the tips of his finger to his lips.

"Boulders with strange markings," said Alan. "I fail to see—"

"Look at the map," said Simon. "Note the location of

Slopford. It's marked with another green pin. Next we come to the account in another paper of the sighting of the legendary 'Ogre of the Barthen Moor.' The ogre was seen walking the moor in the middle of the night. Listen to the description: 'a face that was evil, like a fiend from hell.' We even have a drawing made by a witness."

Simon handed over the newspaper clipping.

"Bottom Dweller," said Henry grimly. "Wearing one of their demonic helms."

"I'll be damned!" Alan gave a low whistle and regarded Simon in admiration and wonder.

"Note the location of Barthen Moor on the map. The green pin. Next I have here a story in the Hempstead paper about a magistrate accusing local hooligans of dressing up as fiends from hell and roaming about the fields at night. They terrorized a shepherd and scattered his flock. The lads denied it, but they did admit they had spent the evening drinking their own homemade distilled spirits and couldn't actually recall what they had done. Note the location of Hempstead on the map."

Henry rose from his chair, walked over to the map, and stood staring down at it. "Alan, hand me that green ribbon."

Taking the ribbon, Henry stretched it from one green pin to the other. The ribbon formed a curved line. "I see more green pins. What else have you found?"

"A police report from Glenham-by-the-Breath. The body of a young man was found in one of the lakes. Fishermen dragged up the body in their nets. The young man had died a horrible death, it seems. There was evidence he had been tortured, his body drained of blood."

Henry found Glenham-by-the-Breath's green pin on the map and extended the ribbon.

"One hundred miles away, in the village of Dunham, police reported finding the body of a young woman in a burning barn. The fire had been set deliberately to cover the murder. Neighbors were able to extinguish the fire before it could do much damage. The police found signs that the young woman had been tortured. I sent for the coroners' reports in both instances."

"I'm guessing the killings are remarkably similar to that string of murders in Capione," said Henry.

"I see we were thinking along the same lines," said Simon.

"You sent people to investigate these boulders."

"I did better than that," said Simon. "I went myself."

Alan and Henry stared at their friend in astonishment. They had never known Simon to leave his beloved house.

"You must consider this important," said Henry at last.

"I consider it to be of the greatest importance," said Simon gravely. "Albright, it is time for the next post delivery. If you will go fetch it—"

Mr. Albright silently walked off, heading for the large mail basket, which was located at the rear of the house. The basket was the repository for newspapers and reports from his agents that arrived at all hours of the day and night. Mr. Albright emptied the basket several times a day and sorted through its contents, arranging them according to Simon's instructions before bringing them to him.

Simon continued. "While you two were battling Bottom Dwellers in Braffa, Albright and I visited Slopford, which, by the way, is a charming little town. I went to Hempstead and Dunham and Barthen Moor—every place you see a green pin. I found the boulders with the strange markings, all of them located in remote spots. In some instances, where it had not rained recently, I discovered what appeared to be bloodstains on the boulders or on the grass around them. I made a copy of the markings, which were roughly the same on every boulder. Turn the chalkboard around, Alan."

Alan complied, turning the chalkboard so that it faced

them. He and Henry walked over to stand in front of it, studying the odd-looking markings.

"I'm no crafter," said Henry at last. "But those lines look like magical constructs."

"They are," said Simon. "I am moderately skilled in crafting, as you know. Those are definitely magical constructs. They are like no constructs I have ever seen before—"

"But I have," said a voice.

The three men turned, startled. Alan drew his pistol. Mr. Albright came barreling into the room, scattering the mail in all directions, and jumped in front of Simon, who glared at him.

"Albright, we have discussed this predilection of yours for protecting me," Simon told him tersely. "You are *not* my bodyguard. Return to your post. I cannot see our visitor."

Mr. Albright did not move. Simon glowered and tried to shift his chair. Mr. Albright had him penned behind the desk.

"Who the devil are you?" Alan demanded.

He had his pistol aimed at their visitor—a short, pudgy man wearing a long cloak, carrying his hat in his hand. He stood at the end of the desk gazing intently at the chalkboard. He looked travel worn and weary.

"Don't shoot," said Henry. "I know him. He is Monsieur Dubois, agent for the grand bishop of Rosia."

"All the more reason I should shoot him," Alan growled.

"Please do not do anything in haste, Captain Northrop." The speaker was Mr. Sloan, hurrying up to stand alongside Dubois. The tall secretary loomed over the little man. "When I stopped by the Naval Club to see if there were any letters, I found Mr. Dubois. He recognized me and said he had an urgent matter to discuss with you—a matter of life and death. I took the liberty of bringing him with me."

"There now," said Simon. "All is well. You can go back

to your corner, Albright. And please do not let this happen again."

Returning to his post, Mr. Albright exchanged an oblique glance with Henry, who gave a small nod of satisfaction. Mr. Albright's eyelids flickered in response.

"The man's a filthy spy!" Alan was saying angrily, still aiming the pistol. "I say we shoot him anyway."

"We're not shooting anyone, Alan," said Henry impatiently. "Put your gun away. I know Monsieur Dubois. We may be enemies, but I believe there is mutual respect between us."

Dubois gave a little bobbing bow. "I respect you so much, Sir Henry, that I have flown by griffin-back all the way from the Citadel to speak to you." His gaze shifted to the chalkboard. "But first, tell me about those most interesting constructs."

"First *you* tell me what they are," Simon parried.

"They are contramagic," said Dubois.

Henry gave a soft gasp. Alan lowered his pistol.

"I thought so," Simon said triumphantly. "How do you know?"

"Because, as I said when I walked in, I have seen such constructs before, Monsieur Yates."

"Where?"

"On a bomb," said Dubois. "A bomb that very nearly killed me."

12

All of us were born second sons, which means we had to make our own way in the world. I make certain to always thank my elder brother.

—Sir Henry Wallace

"You are speaking of the bomb that was meant to kill Father Jacob in Westfirth," said Henry. "You and the Countess de Marjolaine were with him at the time, according to the report I received."

"Your intelligence is accurate, as always, my lord," Dubois replied. "We were together in the library at Westfirth listening to Father Jacob tell us what he had learned about the Bottom Dwellers. A man we now know to have been a Bottom Dweller—a priest known as Brother Paul—threw the bomb into the room." He pointed toward the fireplace. "It was as big as that coal scuttle. The constructs glowed a bright green. The Knight Protector, Sir Ander Martel, picked up the bomb and threw it out of the room into the hallway, where it exploded."

"Pardon me, Monsieur Dubois, but you must have seen the constructs on that bomb for only seconds," said Simon.

"A great many seconds too long, monsieur," said Dubois gravely.

"I can imagine," said Simon. He pointed to the board. "But how can you be certain these constructs are the same constructs on the bomb?"

"God has gifted me with an unusually accurate memory, Monsieur Yates," said Dubois. "For example, if you were to blindfold me, I would be able to name in order all of these piles of documents on your desk *and* tell you what is written on the documents in my sight."

Simon cast a skeptical glance at Henry for confirmation.

"Dubois's talents are quite extraordinary," Henry replied. "He came near to capturing me when I was trying to smuggle Alcazar out of Westfirth."

"You have the devil's own luck, my lord," said Dubois, shaking his head in admiration.

Henry smiled. "If Dubois says these constructs are the same constructs as those on the bomb, you can trust his judgment."

"One question, Monsieur Yates, did you find blood at any of these sites?"

"I did," said Simon. "Blood magic used in conjunction with contramagic."

"Indeed," said Dubois, looking pleased to have his suspicions confirmed. "The two make quite a potent combination."

"And that is why Eiddwen is here," said Henry. "The Sorceress; the expert in murder, torture, and contramagic."

"So all this means the boulders are bombs like the one that almost blew up Dubois?" Alan looked from Dubois to Simon to Henry. "That makes no sense. Why would the Bottom Dwellers go to all this trouble to blow up some farmer's pumpkin patch?"

"Why indeed?" Simon muttered.

He rolled his chair over to the map with the pins and

the ribbon stretched between them and gazed at it with a look of great concentration.

"But this is not the reason you have flown all this way in such haste, Dubois," Henry said.

"I believe it might be, my lord, though I had no idea of any of this when I started." Dubois removed his hat and sat down in a chair. He passed his hand over his brow. "I am considerably fatigued. Perhaps a glass of wine?"

"We could all use a drink," said Alan firmly. "And I don't mean wine. Where do you keep something stronger, Simon?"

He did not answer. He was gazing at his map, his brow furrowed, muttering to himself.

"He can't hear you," said Henry. "He's miles away in Slopford. You will find a bottle of aquavit in the bottom drawer of the first file cabinet there to your left."

"I took the liberty of bringing sandwiches," said Mr. Sloan. "I thought perhaps you gentlemen might be hungry."

"You anticipate my every want, Mr. Sloan," said Henry. "Fetch the sandwiches."

"I strive to please, my lord."

Mr. Sloan went back downstairs and returned with a large basket containing sandwiches, cheese, apples, and walnuts, and several bottles of wine. Alan found the bottle of aquavit and glasses in a cabinet. Henry cleared space on the desk, and Mr. Sloan served the meal. Mr. Albright munched on a sandwich in his corner.

While they were eating, Henry explained to Dubois how Simon had discovered the series of boulders with the strange markings and the deaths related to the use of blood magic. Dubois listened closely. He was obviously as puzzled as the rest of them. He declined the aquavit, but gratefully accepted a glass of wine. Having eaten little supper the previous night, Henry ate with a keen appetite.

Mr. Sloan fixed a plate for Simon, but he remained focused on his map.

When they had finished the meal, Mr. Sloan cleared away the plates but, at Alan's insistence, left the bottle of aquavit on the table.

"Now, Dubois, if you are feeling restored, tell us why you have come—"

Henry was interrupted by a gasp from Simon.

"Merciful God in heaven!" He shifted his chair around to face them. "Look at this!"

They left their chairs to gather around the map table.

"As you know," Simon continued, "the city of Haever is built on a shelf that juts out from the continent, the reason we are blessed with such excellent harbors. Alan, slide that serving tray under the map. Good. Now I'll adjust the map so you can see what I'm talking about. We will say the table is the continent of Freya. The part of the map on the serving tray is Haever."

Simon placed the map on the serving tray and ordered Alan to slide the tray out beyond the edge of the table.

"Note the location of the boulders with the contramagic markings. They form a semicircle that extends from the north of the shelf at Glenham-by-the-Breath to the southern portion of the shelf at Dunham. The city of Haever is here, in the center. Please observe what happens when I simulate exploding all these boulders."

Simon spoke a few words. The pins caught fire, as did the ribbon connecting the pins. The fire spread to the parchment on which the map was drawn. Smoke filled the room. Mr. Sloan hastened to open a window.

"For God's sake, Simon," Alan said, waving his hand above the map to dissipate the smoke. "Are you trying to asphyxiate us?"

"Watch!" Simon said with grim urgency.

As he spoke, the magical fire burned through the map

and started to burn the serving tray. Alan dropped it with a curse. The tray and Haever and its environs fell to the floor.

The five men stared in silence at the smoking remains of the map. The room was so quiet that one could hear the sounds of traffic drifting up from the street below. A breeze blew in the window, wafting away the smoke and ruffling some of the papers on Simon's desk. Mr. Sloan quietly closed the window. Simon was the first to speak.

"Let us say that each of these boulders is a bomb. As sappers bring down the wall of a fortress by placing bombs at intervals and then setting them off simultaneously, the Bottom Dwellers plan to blow up a portion of the continental shelf, sending Haever and its many thousand inhabitants—including our queen, her cabinet and ministers—plunging into the Breath."

"As we sent their island plunging into the Breath," Dubois remarked in a soft voice.

"Thus the Bottom Dwellers have their revenge," said Simon. "The disruption in the Breath would be catastrophic. Storms would sweep the world, producing another Dark Age, one that might never end."

Alan recovered from his shock with the help of another glass of the potent liquor. "You've given us a good scare, Simon, but let's be sensible. Contramagic or not, these fiends couldn't possibly blow off a piece of a continent!"

"They could do so in exactly the same way they destroyed the Crystal Market in Evreux," said Henry. "Resonance. Several crafters reported hearing a drumming sound right before the collapse. Others talked about the crystal bricks shivering beneath their hands."

"Your intelligence is good, Sir Henry," Dubois murmured. "I congratulate you."

"It's a matter of geology," Simon explained. "About forty years ago, miners digging for iron ore discovered a flaw in the bedrock, a fault that runs for several hundred miles along a north–south axis, approximately three hundred yards below the surface. Scientists examined the fault and determined it was stable. They advised, however, that the mines be closed, so as not to disturb it. The bombs are placed directly along the fault line."

"Eiddwen must have learned of this," said Henry.

"Of course. It was in all the papers," said Simon, shrugging. "Let us say that the same contramagic used to bring down the Crystal Palace creates a harmonic wave that causes tremors around the fault line. The weight of the shelf would cause it to break off. Almost a third of Freya would slide into the Breath."

Alan was skeptical. "Henry, do you honestly believe this is possible?"

"The fact that Eiddwen has traveled to Freya tends to support the theory," said Henry. "She is here to set this in motion. The question is, how do we stop her?"

"Simple," said Alan. "We fire the *Terrapin*'s cannons at the damn boulders. Blow them up."

"That is your solution for every problem," said Henry, exasperated. "Blow it up."

Simon interceded between the two men. "I'm afraid that isn't the solution for this problem. We have no idea how contramagic behaves, especially when it's combined with blood magic. Destroying the boulders might well set in motion the very destruction we seek to prevent. Note that the boulders do not yet extend to the very edge of the continent. Eiddwen and her troops are probably working on placing those devices right now."

"Then send in the army," said Alan. "Hunt her down and shoot her."

"Killing her would alert the Bottom Dwellers to the fact that we have discovered their plot, and could make them decide to detonate the boulders they have in place.

Even if the blast didn't cause the shelf to break off, the resulting earthquakes would spread death and destruction throughout the land."

"So what do we do?" Alan demanded, exasperated. "Let her blow us all to kingdom come?"

Dubois had remained so silent until now, Henry had forgotten him and was startled to hear him speak.

"There is one person who has made a study of contra-magic *and* blood magic *and* who understands Mistress Eiddwen and her tactics," said Dubois. "You know of whom I speak, Sir Henry."

"We all know, and you can go to hell!" said Alan, his face flushing.

"Be quiet, Alan," said Henry. "You refer, of course, to Father Jacob, Monsieur Dubois."

"I do, my lord," Dubois replied. He cast an uncertain glance at Alan, who had crossed his arms and was glowering at the rest of them. "Father Jacob is the reason I am here. He is being held in prison in the Citadel—"

"The best place for him," said Alan. "He should have been imprisoned years ago. Let him rot."

Ignoring Alan's outburst, Dubois said, "We need Father Jacob, Sir Henry. We need his advice and his counsel, his unique skills and his knowledge of the enemy to stop this catastrophe. I have tried to persuade the grand bishop to release Father Jacob, but His Grace refuses. I fear, in fact, that he could order Father Jacob to be executed. His Grace is . . ." Dubois hesitated, then said softly, "His Grace is not well."

Henry regarded Dubois thoughtfully, trying to figure what the grand bishop's agent was *not* saying. Henry Wallace had two major enemies in this world. One was King Alaric of Rosia and the other was Grand Bishop Montagne.

"You came here to ask me to help free Father Jacob," said Henry.

Alan gave a mirthless laugh. "You've wasted a trip, my friend."

Dubois remained silent, his gaze on Henry.

"Simon, what do you think?"

"This man, Dubois, is right, Henry," said Simon. "I'm sorry, Alan, but I've read your brother's work and he's brilliant. If I had my choice of any of the top scholars in the world to help us with this calamitous situation, I would choose Jacob Northrop."

"You can't be serious about rescuing him, either of you," said Alan, his voice rising as he spoke. He was shaking with rage. "Jacob is a goddamn traitor. He doesn't give a damn about Freya and he is being held a goddamn prisoner in the goddamn dungeons of the goddamn Citadel! You have all lost your bloody, goddamn minds!"

There was an embarrassed silence. Simon smiled and gave a little shrug. Dubois affected to be admiring the view out the window. Mr. Sloan coughed politely.

"I forget that you are a fundamentalist, Mr. Sloan," said Alan, calming down. "I beg your pardon for my language."

"You were in the grip of strong emotion, sir," said Mr. Sloan. "I take that into consideration."

"Alan—" Henry began in a conciliatory tone.

"Good God almighty, you're going to do it," Alan exclaimed in disbelief. "You're planning to break into the Citadel, which no one in the entire history of mankind has ever done, to free that treacherous bastard."

"Indeed I am, Alan," said Henry calmly. "And, what's more, you are going to help me."

13

Fort Ignacio was a marvel of modern magical engineering.

—Father Antonius of the Arcanum

While Sir Henry and his friends were plotting a jailbreak, Stephano traveled to the fortress on griffin-back. Not so long ago, he would have never been able to afford hiring a griffin for the journey. More intelligent than wyverns, with a much better temperament, griffins were swifter than wyverns, their flight smooth and even. They were strong and could fly long distances without stopping to rest or eat.

Griffins were costly to maintain, however, because they worked on their own terms. They refused to be harnessed to any sort of conveyance. They detested being penned up in stables. Though they might deign to be put up in a stable for a night or two, they preferred to live in their own communities high in the mountains. A hostler who offered griffins for hire often kept a "runner," a young griffin in training who lived on the premises and would carry word to his fellows in the mountains that their services were needed. Griffins accepted payment in cattle and swine.

Long ago, in an ancient time, griffins and dragons had

once gone to war, battling over territory and food. The battles had ceased when the dragons moved out of their caves into their own realms and became increasingly involved with humans. Like dragons, griffins had their own language, but unlike dragons, they refused to communicate with humans except on the most basic level. The relationship between griffins and dragons these days was one of wary tolerance.

Stephano was keenly aware of this tense relationship when he drew near the fortress and saw his three wild dragon friends flying in slow, wide, sweeping circles above it. He wondered what the wild dragons thought of griffins, if they had ever encountered griffins on their island. He hoped the wild dragons did not view the griffins with hostility. Stephano had money now, but he didn't want to have to pay for a dead or injured griffin.

The wild dragons saw him immediately, but they seemed not to recognize him. The youngest one, Petard, flew to investigate the stranger approaching the fortress. When Stephano waved and shouted to him, Petard gave a loud answering hoot, turned a somersault in midair, and dashed off to alert the others.

The female dragon, Viola, flew to greet Stephano, accompanied by the large dragon, Verdi, with her scapegrace younger brother, Petard, trailing behind.

Viola had been Stephano's partner, the dragon he rode. The leader among the three, she was steady, brave, and he had thought that they had formed a bond . . . until the battle with the Bottom Dwellers at the refinery in Braffa, when Viola and the other dragons had refused to fight.

Stephano had been angry until he had later learned why they had fled. Apparently, these young dragons had been sent by their elders to try to learn more about the Bottom Dwellers and the contramagic that was having such a devastating effect on them. After they left the battle, the three dragons had flown back to their home, but according to Dag, when they reached home, they'd found it destroyed. Their families were gone.

Stephano had named Viola for the rare, beautiful purplish blue cast of her scales. She was thirty feet long, sleek and swift. Stephano could read her emotions from the tilt of her head on the long, graceful neck, and the expressive eyes that could be opened wide and gleaming with joy or hooded and dangerous.

Viola's head drooped, and she glanced at him sidelong, not directly. She circled, but didn't come near. Stephano thought he understood how she felt: She had betrayed his trust and was ashamed and contrite.

Verdi was watching Viola, matching her reactions. Stephano got the impression that Petard would have rushed to greet him, but when Viola cast the youngling a stern glance, Petard meekly fell into formation behind her. Stephano was relieved to note that none of the dragons seemed at all interested in the griffin he was riding.

Stephano removed his helm and called to Viola and the others, keeping his tone deliberately joyful, letting them know he was glad to see them.

With that, everything changed. Viola's eyes shone, and the three wild dragons spread their wings and flew toward Stephano so fast that they alarmed the griffin. Screeching in warning, the beast went into a steep and unexpected dive that caused Stephano to nearly lose his grip on the reins . . . and his lunch. With his eyes smarting in the blasting wind, he yelled at the dragons to keep their distance and ordered the griffin to land.

As Stephano descended, he had a chance to observe the fortress from the air. From a distance, Fort Ignacio could be easily taken for an odd stone formation, a mound made of rock jutting up out of a field. Likely one reason it had remained undisturbed for all these years. Those traveling in this part of Rosia—and they would be few, since the land was mostly unclaimed wilderness—would take no particular notice of one more hillock among many.

As he flew closer, he could see clearly that this was no natural formation. Three stone walls encircled the stone mound, one near the top, one in the middle, and the largest at the bottom. He noted with interest the gun emplacements were on the lowest level and thought it would be wise to mount swivel guns on the middle and upper walls. As he drew ever nearer, he could see the stonemason crafters reinforcing and repairing the walls. Prince Renaud had told him he had already sent crafters and others to start work on making repairs to the fort.

Dag, having once served inside Fort Ignacio, had likened the fort to a skep—a beehive made of straw, shaped like a dome with the wide portion at the bottom. The fort had been constructed years ago by Estaran stonemason crafters, who had burrowed through the solid stone, transforming it into living areas: The main barracks, officers' quarters, privies, food storage, infirmary, kitchen and mess hall collectively formed a ring around the innermost part of the fort. The center of the dome contained the main armory and powder magazine. Between the two, a large space was being hollowed out and cleared for the dragons to rest when they hit the near-liquid part of the Breath, and would have to shelter inside. They could fly on their own most of the way down, but Stephano was concerned about them flying through that environment.

This assumed that Stephano could persuade the dragons to fly with him. A large assumption.

As Stephano drew nearer, he saw Dag standing on the ramparts on the upper level. Dag must have heard Petard's hooting and looked to see what was going on. He waved at Stephano, then left to descend the stairs, to meet him outside the main gate.

After the griffin landed, Stephano thanked the beast and dismissed it. The griffin flew off, pointedly ignoring the dragons, who in return paid him no heed. The three circled overhead, preparing to land.

Stephano took off his helm and ran his hand through his sweat-dampened hair, walking swiftly to meet Dag, who was just emerging from the fortress's main gate.

At the sight of Dag, Stephano checked an exclamation of dismay. He was shocked at Dag's appearance. The big man had lost weight and his hair, which he wore in a short, military cut, was showing gray at the temples. He looked haggard and sleep deprived.

Stephano knew, of course, that his friend had been working day and night with the crafters to restore the fortress. He noted the lights they had rigged to enable them to work well into the night. But he didn't think long hours alone could account for Dag's altered appearance. His military friend thrived on hard work. He must be blaming himself for Gythe and Miri's disappearance and, worse yet, assuming that Stephano blamed him as well.

Dag was standing in the shadow of the fortress, waiting for his arrival. The three dragons had landed some distance away, eager to see Stephano, but he had to reassure Dag before he visited them.

"Good to see you, sir," said Dag stiffly, starting to salute.

"The hell with that," said Stephano. He grabbed Dag's hand and pressed it warmly. "It is good to see you, my friend."

Dag shook his head. "Don't call me friend, sir. I don't deserve it."

"Dag, listen to me," said Stephano, keeping hold of Dag's big hand. "I don't blame you for what happened with

Miri and Gythe. I don't hold you responsible. You shouldn't hold yourself responsible. Gythe drugged you. You had no way of knowing what she was planning. And likely no way of stopping her, even if you had known."

"I'm not sure, sir. Gythe had been acting strangely. She kept to herself, didn't hear us when we talked to her. She seemed to be hearing *their* evil voices. I'm sure they lured her away. I should have known!"

"But you didn't," said Stephano, practical and matter-of-fact. "Dag, answer me this: How many men in this whole wide world ever know what any woman is thinking?"

Dag gave a wan smile. "I know you're trying to help, sir. But it's still my fault."

Stephano gave up. Dag had not forgiven himself for an incident that had happened years ago when he'd ordered men to go on what had ended up being a deadly mission. Despite the fact that he could not have foreseen an ambush set to catch him and his men, he still blamed himself for their deaths.

"I don't suppose you've heard any news of Miri and Gythe?" Stephano asked.

Dag shook his head. "No, I haven't. You, sir?"

"Nothing." Stephano rested his hand on Dag's shoulder. "But no matter where they are, we'll find them."

"That we will, sir," said Dag with grim certainty. "I won't rest until I have."

"I'm going to greet the young dragons," said Stephano, glad to end this conversation. He was uncomfortable talking about Miri, even when all he did was think about her. "You get something to eat. You're starting to look like a skeleton."

"I haven't had much appetite lately, sir. The prince sent his own cook from the flagship. The food's actually good."

"Only the best for His Highness," said Stephano drily.

"About the young dragons, sir," said Dag. "They have a surprise for you."

Stephano was wary. "A good surprise or a bad surprise? I've had enough bad surprises."

"You'll find out, sir," Dag said with a smile.

Stephano stood gazing up at the fort. He vividly remembered the immense size of the fortress, the thickness of its walls. He and the Dragon Brigade had fought a hard battle until they finally forced the men inside to surrender. The memory brought back thoughts of his former dragon partner, Lady Cam, and her death. He shook his head, banished the thoughts, and went to meet his new partner.

The three dragons were lined up as he had often seen them on the island, with Viola in the center and the two males on either side. She was eager and excited, now that she knew all had been forgiven between them. Her head tilted slightly, her tail thumped the ground.

Stephano called out, "I am pleased you have returned, Viola. I am very sorry to hear about your homeland."

Viola opened her mouth and spoke slowly and haltingly. "Thank you, Captain Stephano."

Stephano stopped to stare at the dragon in amazement. Although he knew the wild dragons understood what he said to them, they had never spoken anything other than the dragon language; nor had they ever evinced any interest in learning how to speak a human language.

"Viola, that is wonderful!" said Stephano warmly. "I am pleased you are learning my language!"

"Learning," said Viola. "Hard."

"Cap-tain," said Petard, crowding his way forward, bumping his sister.

"Ste-phan-o," said Verdi slowly. "Dag. Gythe."

Viola shot him a warning look. Verdi ducked his head.

Petard regarded Stephano with grave solemnity. Petard had been Gythe's partner, and the two had been very close.

"What about Gythe?" Stephano asked sharply. "Do you know where she is? Is she safe? Is Miri with her?"

"Safe," said Viola cautiously.

"You have heard from Gythe!" Stephano said excitedly. "I know the two of you could communicate mentally. Tell me. Where are Gythe and Miri?"

Viola glanced back uneasily at Petard and Verdi. Clearly, Petard was unhappy, his head down, his mane flattened along his spine, his eyes hooded. Verdi stood stoic, solemn, silent.

"Please, help me," Stephano pleaded. "If you know, tell where to find my friends!"

Viola again repeated, "Safe."

Stephano was frustrated. Either the dragons didn't know or they weren't telling. At least Gythe and Miri were safe—presuming Viola knew the meaning of the word.

Petard fetched a sigh that rippled over his body from his head to his tail. Lifting his wings, he glanced longingly into the sky.

"Fly?" Viola said eagerly.

"You should rest. We will be making a long flight into the dragon realms. You three can meet your cousins."

He thought they would be pleased. But the young dragons seemed to be thrown into a panic by this news, fluttering their wings and tossing their heads. They had met only two civilized dragons, Hroal and Droal, the brothers who guarded the sorrowful ruins of what had been the Abbey of Saint Agnes. Stephano guessed the three must have heard disparaging stories about their civilized cousins from their elders.

He felt he should say something reassuring, but he had his own doubts about this reunion with the civilized dragons. The two factions had not parted on good terms and even though the rift had occurred centuries before, the long-lived dragons had long-lived memories.

"Speaking of families, I heard from Dag about what you found when you returned to your island. I am sorry, very sorry. You couldn't find any trace of them?"

"Fire," Viola said sadly. "All gone. Alive? Dead?" She shook her head.

Stephano returned to the fortress to find Dag had assembled all the workers: crafter masons, carpenter crafters, and engineers, to meet Stephano.

"They were told they were readying the fortress to defend this part of the coastline," said Dag softly to Stephano. "Prince Renaud offered them an extra week's wages if they finished the work ahead of schedule. They've been working two shifts, day and night."

"Excellent," said Stephano, pleased.

After they met with the workers to discuss the repairs and answer any questions they might have, Stephano asked Dag to give him a tour of the fortress. During his days as a mercenary soldier, Dag had been hired by the Estarans to serve as a sergeant in Fort Ignacio, which they knew was going to come under attack by the Rosians. The Estarans had laid claim to the southern part of the Rosian continent for centuries and had established the fortress to test Rosian resolve.

"The Estarans snagged a small island drifting in the Breath off the coastline and magically altered the natural landscape," Dag explained to Stephano. "Crafters smoothed the jagged rocks of a mountain into an inverted bowl shape, adding the walls and guard towers."

In addition, they had tethered four smaller free-floating islands to the main fortress, added walls and gun batteries, turning them into redoubts. Suspended at the end of heavy iron chains, the redoubts could be extended to provide a better field of fire and keep the enemy from landing troops on the main fortress.

"I remember," said Stephano, adding grimly, "I wish I didn't."

"I agree, sir," said Dag, shaking his head over his own memories. "That was a war both sides lost."

"Considering it fell a thousand feet through the air, the fortress appears to be in pretty good repair."

"The main body of the fortress remained intact, though, as you can see, most of the walls and towers collapsed."

"And you lost the redoubts," said Stephano.

"One was destroyed in the siege," said Dag. "The other three broke free when the fortress hit the ground. Two came down God knows where. The fourth almost fell on our heads. You can see what's left of it over there. We're using the stone to repair the walls."

"You were damn lucky you survived," said Stephano, looking over the walls at what was left of the redoubt: a large crater filled with rubble.

"I owe my life to our crafter, Father Antonius," said Dag. "He guided the fortress down, doing his best to slow the descent and alter the angle at which it fell, minimizing the force of the impact. Our biggest challenge now is sealing the doors and windows so that we can survive the freezing cold and the powerful, treacherous currents we'll face in the Breath."

"When do the workers expect to be finished?"

"In a few weeks, sir," said Dag. "Maybe sooner."

"Would you be free to leave, travel with me for a few days?" Stephano asked.

"Yes, sir," said Dag, brightening. "I'm really not needed. Thus far my main job has been to keep the masons from fighting with the carpenters."

"Good. We'll make the wild dragons happy. I believe they are eager for an adventure."

"Where are we going?" Dag asked.

"The dragon realms," said Stephano. "His Royal Highness has authorized me to try to reform the Dragon Brigade."

"Congratulations, sir!" said Dag. "That's wonderful news."

"There are a lot of 'ifs' before that happens. *If* I can find any of the former members and if I do, will they set aside their anger and agree to come fight to save us after we insulted them and drove them away? I haven't forgiven Alaric for disbanding the Brigade," Stephano added grimly. "I don't see why they would."

"The dragons must know by now that the Bottom Dwellers are a threat to them," said Dag. "If what the wild dragons tell us is true, the contramagic is killing their young."

"Maybe the wild dragons can convince them," said Stephano. "Although that could be another problem. The wild dragons and their so-called civilized cousins haven't spoken in hundreds of years."

They were standing on the ramparts of the upper wall, watching the three young dragons. Ignoring Stephano's suggestion that they rest, they had taken to the air to practice their battle maneuvers: diving straight down toward the ground, pulling up at the last moment, twisting and turning to avoid fire from an imaginary foe.

The sunlight glittered on their scales, and with their speed and grace, they were a beautiful, even awe-inspiring sight. Few of the workmen had ever seen dragons in action and a number of them stopped to stare, bringing down the wrath of their foremen upon them.

Stephano grinned. He could understand the workers' reaction. Even he found it hard to tear his attention away from the dragons. Watching them, he thought of a question he had been meaning to ask Dag. "What happened on the dragons' island? All Viola would tell me was 'fire.'"

"According to what they told Hroal and Droal, the young dragons returned home to find that the island had been torched. They discovered bat corpses and the body of a dead dragon," Dag said. "The body was so charred, they couldn't tell who it was. The young ones searched for their clansmen, but the island was deserted. That's why they came back to us. They had nowhere else to go."

"Suitable members for the Cadre of the Lost," Stephano remarked.

"I wish we *were* a cadre again, sir," said Dag heavily. "Doesn't seem right without Miri and Gythe. I even miss that plague sore, Rigo, though if you tell him I said so, I'll deny it."

"We'll be together again," said Stephano confidently. "I feel it in my bones."

Dag grunted. "You always get like this, sir."

"Like what?" Stephano asked, startled.

"Happy," said Dag dourly. "When you're about to go into action, you get happy."

Stephano looked at the dragons wheeling in the sky, then at the towering walls of the fortress, and he thought of the possibility of putting the Dragon Brigade back together.

"We're going to take the fight to the Bottom Dwellers, Dag," said Stephano. "We're not going to play defense any longer. We're going to avenge the murdered nuns, the sailors aboard the *Royal Lion,* and all those who died in the Crystal Market. We're not going to let them destroy the voice of God. They're going to hear God roar."

"You also wax poetic," said Dag, grumbling.

Stephano laughed. He was about to suggest that Dag

show him where to find the mess when the young dragons began to hoot. Both men turned to see what was happening. Two dragons, one of them unusually massive, were flying toward the fortress from the northwest.

"That's Droal, sir," said Dag, squinting against the sunlight. "I never saw the other."

Stephano stared intently. "By God, it's Lord Haelgrund! He was a member of the Dragon Brigade. I haven't seen him in years."

"I wonder how he knew you were here," said Dag.

"Droal must have told him and brought him to meet with me."

Stephano watched the two dragons approach. Haelgrund, a young dragon who could fly swiftly for his size, was deliberately slowing his flight to allow the elderly Droal to keep pace with him.

"Odd coincidence," Stephano said, troubled. "Here I am thinking about flying to the dragons to discuss reinstating the Brigade and Haelgrund comes looking for me."

"You don't sound as if you think this is a *good* coincidence, sir," said Dag with a sidelong glance.

"I don't," said Stephano.

Droal and Haelgrund landed in a field, and then the wild dragons landed nearby, keeping their distance. They were glad to see Droal, but appeared wary of the stranger, especially such a large stranger.

Haelgrund was seventy-five feet from his head to the tip of his tail, with the long, arching neck that marked him a dragon of noble blood, and vivid green scales. Lady Cam had once confided to Stephano that the female dragons of the realm considered Haelgrund a fine specimen of dragon manhood. Stephano doubted he had taken a mate. Dragons generally did not mate until they were closer to three hundred.

Stephano was interested in the reaction of the wild dragons, who had probably never seen a dragon this enormous. Viola was clearly impressed, because her eyes were open wide. Verdi, his eyes narrowed in displeasure, was not happy to see Viola admiring the newcomer. Hearing Verdi growl loudly, the irrepressible Petard gave a hoot of laughter, causing Viola to whip her head around to glare at him. Petard fell meekly silent, though Stephano thought he saw a gleam of mischief in the young dragon's eye.

Haelgrund, who would have learned about the wild dragons from Droal, now regarded the three curiously. His attention focused immediately on the lovely Viola. She noticed his admiration, but pretended not to, averting her head and preening her spikey mane.

Haelgrund turned back to Stephano and lowered his head to the ground, putting himself almost at Stephano's eye level.

"Captain! My friend!" said Haelgrund in a rumble of emotion, extending a huge front foreclaw. Stephano placed his hand on the scales of the dragon's foreleg, a show of friendship between human and dragon.

"I have missed you, Haelgrund," said Stephano. "I've missed everyone in the Brigade."

"We've missed you, Captain," said Haelgrund, his eyes flickering. He seemed wistful. "I hope you understand why I couldn't come to visit you. After your king insulted us—"

"I understand," said Stephano. "Trust me, my friend, I understand all too well."

Haelgrund shifted his gaze to the young dragons, glad to change the subject. "Who are your friends, Captain? Please introduce us. Sergeant Droalfrig has told me all about my wild cousins."

Stephano performed the introductions. Viola was shy and flustered, bobbing her head, fluttering her wings and curling her tail. Verdi, seeming offended by the presence of the very large stranger suddenly in their midst, was sullen and rude. Petard was very friendly, and immediately began bombarding Haelgrund with questions about past battles. Viola silenced her brother with a hiss.

"We need to talk, Captain," said Haelgrund quietly. "In private."

Stephano and Haelgrund walked away from the others into the open grasslands that surrounded the fortress. Dag visited with Droal, while the young dragons nervously watched Stephano walk off with the large dragon.

"Do you ever hear from Belmonte?" Haelgrund asked abruptly.

Francois Belmonte had been Haelgrund's rider. The two had been close.

"He sent me word that he was moving to Estara where he had family," Haelgrund continued. "I thought perhaps you might know something more."

"I haven't kept in touch," said Stephano. "Lieutenant Armand tried to organize a reunion a couple of years ago, and he sent me an invitation, but I didn't reply. I don't expect many of the others did either. Best to forget and move on."

Haelgrund nodded his massive head. As they walked together in silence fraught with memories, the ground shook with the dragon's heavy footfalls.

"How did you know where to find me?" Stephano asked at last.

"Sergeant Droalfrig has been keeping the Duke of Talwin informed about your exploits, Captain," said Haelgrund.

Stephano was startled, then realized he shouldn't be.

Lord Haelgrund's family were minor nobility, owing fealty to the Duke and Duchess of Talwin, and Haelgrund was a dragon of means. His family owned lands that contained iron and tin mines, along with vast stretches of virgin timberland. Once the dragon families had employed humans to work and manage these assets. But after the dragons had angrily left the royal court, humans had left dragon lands in fear. Stephano suspected that the mines must be closed now, the logging operations ended.

Haelgrund had moved out of the family dwelling when he was one hundred, having built his own house on the bluffs of the Ker Greeh River not far from the duke's estate.

"Droal visits me whenever he comes to report to the duke. He told us about the attacks by these . . . what does he call them . . . Bottom Dwellers. People who live at the bottom of the world." Haelgrund shook his head in wonder. "Hard to believe."

"What does the duke think?" Stephano asked.

"That you humans made a pig's breakfast of things," Haelgrund said bluntly. "First you sink this island and plunge the world into the Dark Ages. Five hundred years later, these Bottom Dwellers return from the dead to seek their revenge."

"*We* weren't the ones who sank their bloody island, but I don't suppose that matters to them," said Stephano. "Of course they have a right to be angry, but that doesn't excuse slaughtering people *and* dragons in cold blood. You heard from Droal what they did to the families of the wild dragons. And *I've* heard about how the contramagic is killing your young."

"The drumming," said Haelgrund. "We wondered what it was, where it was coming from. Now we know. Those living on the bottom of the world are using the drumming to generate waves of contramagic to disrupt the magic in our world. Only the most magically sensitive humans can hear it, for the sound is very faint. We hear it, however, and we have discovered that when the drums beat, the resonance disrupts the delicate balance of magic and contramagic in our bodies. The contramagic surges and our hatchlings die."

"Contramagic in your bodies!" Stephano stared at Haelgrund, amazed. "Dragons have contramagic inside them? No dragon ever said anything about contramagic to me."

"Because you humans would not have understood," said Haelgrund bitterly. "You banned any talk of contramagic. Your grand bishop would have banned us if he knew. Dragons are a mixture of magic and contramagic. One balances the other. We thought it best to keep silent."

"So why are you telling me now?"

"The Bottom Dwellers requested an appearance before the Gathering," said Haelgrund. "They are proposing a nonaggression pact between themselves and the dragon realms."

Stephano stared, stunned. "How did this happen?"

"It seems these bat riders have established a base of operations at some old monastery in the Oscadia Mountains. We discovered it and, although the base isn't on dragon lands, it is close enough for the council to be concerned. The duke and I flew to speak to them, find out what was going on."

"Did they fight?"

"Frankly, Captain, life has been so deadly dull with no humans about that I would have welcomed a fight. No such luck, however. The bat riders were pleased to see us, and said they had no war with dragons, only with humans. They asked if they could present their claims and grievances before a meeting of our Supreme Council."

"Do you mind if I sit down?" Stephano asked. "I need to think about this."

"Not at all, Captain," said Haelgrund, politely offering the use of the tip of his massive tail as a seat.

Stephano sat down on the smooth scales that were warm in the sun. He'd been given so much information he was having trouble sorting it all out. Bat riders in a monastery in the Oscadia Mountains made little sense to him.

"Did the duke ask them why they had built a base in such a remote location? It's too far from any major human population center to be of use militarily."

"The duke didn't ask. I wondered about that myself," said Haelgrund. "I wanted to question these people, but you know the duke. He declared it wouldn't be polite. Something else I wondered: Where are the monks that used to live in the monastery? There weren't any around. The duke did ask about that. The Bottom Dwellers said they found the monastery abandoned."

Stephano pondered. Given the intelligence the prince had gained about the planned invasion, he could understand the Bottom Dwellers wanting to keep the dragons out of the war. Peace talks, negotiations . . .

"I don't like this, Haelgrund. You dragons discover this secret base and suddenly, out of nowhere, they want to talk peace. You can't trust these humans. As you said, they are killing your young."

Haelgrund grunted. "The duke finds it hard to trust *any* humans these days. His Grace is nothing if not fair, however. He wants to hear both sides of the conflict, but he doesn't want someone from the royal court. He sent me to ask if you would meet with the council to present your side of the argument."

"Me? I'm not a diplomat!" Stephano protested. "I'm a soldier. I'd say the wrong thing. I *always* say the wrong thing. You should invite the minister of Dragon Affairs."

"The duke wants you, Captain. You are one of the few humans His Grace trusts. He also asked the grand bishop to send a priest, Father Jacob Northrop, but he received no reply."

"That's because Father Jacob is in prison for talking about contramagic," Stephano said, rubbing his temples.

Dragons and contramagic. Humans and contramagic. Bat riders suing for peace with the dragons, all the while killing their young. Trying to unravel this tangle was giving him a throbbing headache. He decided that, after all, perhaps he was the person who should speak to the Gathering. And this would be a good time to reunite the wild dragons with their long-lost cousins, if he could manage to make that happen.

"Very well. I'll come," said Stephano. "To be honest with you, Haelgrund, I was planning to travel to the dragon realms to recruit some of the former members of the Brigade to join us in the fight."

Haelgrund heaved a sigh that ruffled the long grass. "After the insult of disbanding the Brigade I doubt His Grace would permit it. And if we make peace with these Bottom Dwellers . . ."

"Would you fight with me again?" Stephano asked.

"In the twitch of a tail," said Haelgrund promptly. "I don't mind telling you, Captain, these people make my scales creep. Perhaps it's the giant bats. I could never abide bats, not even the little ones. But . . ."

Haelgrund did not finish the sentence.

Stephano glumly finished it for him. "But only if the duke sanctioned it."

"He is my liege lord, Captain," said Haelgrund apologetically.

Stephano rose to his feet. "When is the Gathering being held?"

"Four days from now. We'll have to do some fast flying to reach the site in time."

Haelgrund's admiring gaze shifted to the wild dragons.

"I hope you will bring that beautiful female with you. Such remarkable coloring! I have never seen a dragon like her."

"I will bring her," said Stephano, grinning. "She's my partner."

14

The decision by King Alaric to disband the Dragon Brigade is deeply insulting to those of our kind who have loyally served and in many instances sacrificed our lives for our country. Hence the decision made by the noble dragons families to withdraw from the royal court to reconsider our place in the Rosian empire.

—Aerdinail, Duke of Talwin

The journey to the dragon realms took three days. They flew north along the eastern side of the Kartaign Mountains, then crossed Rosia's central plains and headed east until they reached the Jeandieu River Valley. They followed the river east, crossed Lake Fulmeau and then turned north along the eastern edge of the Oscadia Mountains and the mountaintop city of Ciel-et-terre.

Stephano elected to take rooms in the city for the night near the large, natural amphitheater where the dragons held public meetings of their council, as humans knew it. Dragons referred to it as an open Gathering. Closed Gatherings—those open only to dragons—were held in an ancient, secret location in the mountains. Stephano and Dag took rooms in the Dragon's Foot inn, one of the few businesses in Ciel-et-terre that had not closed its doors.

"The city's name means 'sky and land,'" Stephano told Dag. "Ciel-et-terre claims to be the city nearest the sky."

"Looks to me like the empty city near the sky," Dag remarked.

"Thank you, King Alaric," said Stephano caustically. "The last time I was here, nine years ago, this city was thriving: crafters, laborers, innkeepers, priests and barmaids, artists and musicians; children underfoot, dragons in the skies. Now this city feels like it's near death, if not already dead."

Haelgrund had offered to take the wild dragons hunting for deer in the forests, promising to return in time for the meeting, which was scheduled to start at noon.

Since their return, the wild dragons had seemed almost pathetically eager to please Stephano and intent on proving to him that they would not fail him now as they had failed him at Braffa. Viola was contrite, Verdi practically groveled, and even the impetuous Petard was subdued. Stephano missed their fiery spirit, their stubborn independence, their need to do things their way, never mind that their way sometimes ended badly.

"I fear our wild dragons are now 'civilized,'" Stephano said to Dag as they walked the silent streets to their inn. "I don't think I like it. I can't figure out how to tell them to go back to the way they were."

"I think we should be grateful for the peace and quiet, sir," said Dag. "They're like rowdy children. On their best behavior now, but it won't last long."

"Since when did an old bachelor like you become an expert on children?" Stephano asked, scoffing.

"Six younger brothers and sisters, sir," said Dag.

"You never told me that!"

"Why do you think I left home to join my father's regiment at the age of eight?" Dag said with a grin and a shake of his head.

The Dragon's Foot, located in the center of the city, had been popular with the members of the Brigade. Stephano remembered the owner and was sorry to hear he had died. He expressed his condolences to the widow, who was now running the inn.

"I don't know how much longer I can keep the dear old place open, Captain," the widow confided in Stephano and Dag as she showed them to their rooms. "You and your friend are the first guests to stay here in months. I've let go all my staff. The only reason *I* stay is because my Franco is buried in the churchyard. We visit every day. He'd miss me if I was to go."

Stephano looked out his window. The hour was mid-morning, when the streets should have been noisy with people coming and going. The only movement that he could see was last year's dead leaves swirling about the lamp-posts, blown by the wind coming down out of the mountain peaks.

"Why did everyone leave?"

"After the Brigade was disbanded, the dragons were angry, sir. A rumor started that the dragons were going to attack the city."

"That's nonsense!" said Stephano.

"You and I know that, Captain," said the widow sadly. "My Franco told the people they were fools, but they wouldn't listen. The dragons didn't help. Some of them made it clear that humans were no longer welcome in their realms.

"To be sure, sir, there's some dragons who have relented. The Duke and Duchess of Talwin, for example. She's fond of music and invites musicians to stay with her. And there are a few people who remain like myself—maybe twenty or thirty of us. Father Louis tends to our souls. He visits with the duke to talk theology. And the duke has kept on some crafters and masons who do repairs. And then there's Marcelle, who runs the tavern."

"I remember Marcelle," said Stephano warmly. "He was so fat he could barely squeeze behind his own bar."

"You wouldn't recognize him now, Captain. Gone to skin and bones. I'm almost glad my poor Franco isn't around to see what has become of his city." The widow wiped the corners of her eyes with her handkerchief. "He was a leading citizen, a member of the assembly. Watching his city die a slow death would have broken his heart."

Stephano and Dag bathed and changed their clothes. Stephano brushed his Dragon Brigade coat and helm and polished his boots. He carried his ceremonial sword, which had been a gift from those under his command. Rodrigo had pawned the sword when the Cadre was in need of funds. After receiving money from D'argent, Stephano had at last been able to reclaim it.

Dag, too, was wearing the uniform of a Brigade officer. Stephano had found it in the same pawnshop where his sword had been in hock.

At first, Dag had been reluctant to put it on. "I wasn't an officer in the Brigade, sir."

"You are now," said Stephano. "Seriously, Dag. I want you for my lieutenant in the newly formed Dragon Brigade." He gave a wry smile. "Even if, as seems likely, the Brigade is going to consist of only two humans and three dragons."

About noon, a little before the sun was nearing its zenith, Stephano and Dag set out for the amphitheater, glad to leave the quiet, depressing city behind. They found Haelgrund and the three wild dragons sunning themselves in the tall grass of one of the fields outside the city walls. The wild dragons were excited, daunted, and nervous about meeting the duke and the rest of their noble cousins.

The Gathering of Dragons was made up of eight noble dragons, both male and female. Since dragons mated for life, if the male dragon died, his mate inherited the estate and was required to attend gatherings as head of the household. Each dragon acted as representative for those dragons, such as Lord Haelgrund, who swore fealty to him or her.

Stephano was nervous about appearing before the Gathering. As he said, he was no diplomat, was prone to blunt speaking, and was impatient with formal occasions. He smiled inwardly, thinking how utterly astounded Rodrigo would be if he knew Stephano was going to address dragon royalty.

The amphitheater was a natural land feature, a dry lake bed on the outskirts of the city. The lake had been created by the worldwide storms that raged during the Dark Ages; the lake had long since dried up, leaving behind the shallow, circular bowl.

The dragons had chosen this spot for the Gatherings and other events, paving the bottom with flagstone, and as an accommodation for the comfort of human guests, adding stone benches on one side of the facility. There once had been a throne for the special use by the Rosian king, but that was removed when Alaric had so insulted dragonkind by disbanding the Dragon Brigade.

When Stephano and Dag arrived, the dragons were already seated at compass points around the circle. The highest ranking dragons—the two dukes—sat at the head, north, with the six dragon counts ranged around the perimeter, each at his or her proper station.

"I've told your young friends not to worry," said Haelgrund as they ambled toward the amphitheater. "The

Gathering members are keen to reestablish relationships with our wild cousins. I've coached the younglings on how to behave, how to bow, how to address the dukes as 'Your Grace' and the counts as 'Your Excellency.' I warned them not to stamp their feet or thump their tails. And they must ask to be excused if they need to relieve themselves—"

"I'll remember that," said Stephano drily.

Haelgrund hooted with laughter.

Viola moved stiffly, holding her head up, keeping her neck curved at what she thought made her look as noble as possible, though in truth she looked terrified. Petard slunk along with his belly on the ground, looking as though he had committed some awful crime, and Verdi slogged along, grim and resolute.

Not entirely trusting the Bottom Dwellers, Stephano had insisted that the wild dragons should be saddled and ready to ride. Haelgrund had protested, saying that the duke wouldn't like it, but Stephano had been adamant. He was wondering now if that had been a bad decision.

"Everyone is here," announced Haelgrund. "Except the Bottom Dwellers. I don't see any signs of them."

They had topped a ridge overlooking the amphitheater. The two dukes were in their places, talking to each other. Haelgrund stopped on the rim of the amphitheater. "I'll keep the wild dragons with me, Captain, until the duke asks to speak to them. You should go now. You sit on the stone bench to the right of the Duke of Talwin. I would suggest that Sergeant Thorgrimson remain here with me."

Stephano felt his stomach lurch.

"Steady as she goes, sir," said Dag, regarding him with concern. "You look a little peaked."

"I can't remember the bloody speech," Stephano said, panicked. "I've been composing the damn thing for the last two days and now it's flown clean out of my head."

"You'll do fine, sir," said Dag. He caught hold of Stephano as he was about to descend into the amphitheater. "This will be the first time we've ever been able to talk to these fiends. I was thinking, if you could find a way, you could ask them about Miri and Gythe. They might know something."

"I've been thinking the same," said Stephano. "I'll see what I can find out."

"Good luck, sir," said Dag. "I'll keep an eye on the young ones."

Stephano walked down into the amphitheater, moving as stiffly as Viola. He carried his hat under his right arm and his left hand was on his sword to keep it from banging against his leg. To reach his seat he had to circle around the noble dragons, who were sitting with their tails curled over their feet, their wings folded, their manes flat and smooth along their necks.

He had met several of them before. One, the Countess de Colvue, had been in the Dragon Brigade, where she had met her mate. The count had died in the Battle of Daenar. He could see her eyes warm when she saw him; he felt a little better knowing he could be certain of at least one ally in her. The others watched him with interest and curiosity, except for the Duke of Talwin, who scanned the sky and said something to the Duke of Whitcliff. Stephano guessed the duke was annoyed that the other humans had not yet arrived. He pulled out his watch. The meeting had been slated to commence at noon and it was already a quarter past the hour.

Good, thought Stephano, taking a seat on the cold stone bench. The enemy will start at a disadvantage.

The dragons waited several more moments, but there was no sign of the Bottom Dwellers. The duke was clearly irritated. He shifted his gaze to Stephano.

"Lord Captain de Guichen, you are welcome."

The duke introduced the noble dragons, who inclined their heads. The countess said she hoped they would have a chance to visit after the meeting. Then the duke summoned the wild dragons, who crept forward, manes prickling and wings trembling.

The duke greeted them cordially, assuring them all the dragons were pleased to be reunited with their cousins. The young dragons were pleased, but appeared too embarrassed to respond. Introductions over, the duke looked once more for the Bottom Dwellers. The sky remained empty. He glowered and glanced at the other duke, who rumbled something about proceeding with business.

The duke requested Stephano to approach, so Stephano complied, advancing with a bow.

"These people who call themselves the Bottom Dwellers have informed us that they are about to declare war upon your people, Captain," the duke stated. "They claim they have serious cause for grievances against the governments of the world, and I must say I agree with them. They have requested that we dragons stay out of the war. They have said they have no quarrel with us. We were not a party to the tragedy that befell them, the sinking of their island."

"Your Grace, honored members of the Gathering, the dragons are in this war whether they like it or not," said Stephano. "Lord Haelgrund has told me about the drumming, how it disrupts the contramagic balance. These people are killing your young."

The duke's mane quivered, his eyes narrowed. "I have heard this theory before. A priest spoke of it to the duchess. I know some here believe it." His gaze went around the circle of dragons. "I, for one, do not. Lord Haelgrund informs me, Captain, that you would like to reinstate the Dragon Brigade and that you have been urging the former dragon members to join you humans in your fight."

Stephano cast a sidelong glance at Haelgrund, who gave him a wink.

"The question is this, Captain," the duke continued, "why should dragons involve themselves in a war that has nothing to do with us? You may speak."

"First, Your Grace," said Stephano, "I want to say to the Gathering that I bring with me with an apology from His Highness, the Crown Prince, Alaric Phillip Renaud for disbanding the Dragon Brigade. I am authorized to tell you on his behalf that the crown never meant to insult the dragons and he hopes you will take your places once more as valued citizens of Rosia."

With the sun blazing down on the stone, Stephano was sweating in the wool coat with its fancy embroidery, gold buttons, and large cuffs. He would have liked to have wiped the perspiration from his face, but feared that would be rude. He waited silently for a reaction. He had chosen his words carefully, but he sensed the dragons were skeptical.

The duke twitched the spikes on his head and expressed the collective thought: "Why didn't this apology come from the king?"

Stephano had known this was going to be the question and he had no good answer. He couldn't tell the truth, which was that the palace had been sabotaged and that the king had fallen into some sort of melancholia. The sabotage of the palace was still, officially, a secret.

Nor could Stephano tell the dragons what he considered to be closer to the truth—that King Alaric was a stubborn bastard who would never admit he'd been wrong. Stephano was not a diplomat, but he was a fencer. Turning aside the opponent's stroke with his blade, he went on the offensive.

"The Bottom Dwellers have already attacked dragons." He gestured to the wild dragons. "The Bottom Dwellers drove out their families, set fire to their homes. Their talk of peace is a ruse, a pretense—"

"Captain!" Dag bellowed a warning.

Stephano whipped around. Dag would never be so impolite as to interrupt him during this important meeting unless there was an emergency. The young dragons were upset, rumbling among themselves and thumping their tails, which they had been told specifically *not* to do. Dag pointed to the sky. A black ship, accompanied by hordes of bat riders, was sailing out from a gap in the mountains. The Bottom Dwellers with their lethal green beam weapon were bearing down on the assembled dragons.

Their talk of peace is a trap! Stephano realized.

He could see their plan clearly. The Bottom Dwellers had lured the leaders of the dragons to one place. They planned to attack, destroy all the ruling dragons in one swift blow and throw the dragon realms into chaos.

"About damn time they arrived," the duke rumbled.

Stephano turned around in shock to see the noble dragons rising slowly and ponderously to greet those they considered to be their guests.

He had a split second to decide what to do. Should he try to convince the noble dragons that they were soon going to be noble sitting ducks? Or should he prepare to take action? If the Bottom Dwellers were truly here to negotiate and he went looking for a fight he would anger the duke, and destroy his chances of bringing the dragons into the war.

Stephano decided that angering the duke was better than allowing the Bottom Dwellers to wipe out the entire dragon hierarchy. He broke into a run, leaving the amphitheater by dashing in between the countess and the Duke of Whitcliff.

As Stephano ran past the countess, he yelled, "Ambush!"

She looked from him to the Bottom Dwellers, then shifted her gaze to the duke. Her eyes narrowed as her mane rose. Stephano kept running. He didn't have time to wait to see if she would join him.

The young dragons were preparing for battle. Dag had taken his cue from Stephano and was climbing up onto Verdi's back and strapping himself into the saddle. Once he had settled in, he drew out his spyglass and clapped it to his eye, training the glass on the black ship.

"They're manning the green beam weapon, sir!" he shouted.

Stephano swore beneath his breath and ran toward Viola. Haelgrund intervened, blocking his way, clearly upset.

"Captain, what are you doing? You can't attack these people. They're here to negotiate. The duke is furious!"

Stephano didn't need to be told that. The duke's angry boomings echoed down the mountainside.

"Better furious than dead," Stephano said. "The fiends are here to kill. Look for yourself, Haelgrund. If they were truly here on a mission of peace, they wouldn't be manning their weapon!"

Haelgrund shifted his head to gaze at the black ship. He would be able to see the Bottom Dwellers clustered around the cannon, but whether he would act or not, Stephano couldn't guess. He didn't have time to argue. He circled around Haelgrund to where Viola crouched in the tall grass, waiting for him. He climbed up onto her foreleg and from there into the saddle and strapped himself in. He and Dag had both loaded their weapons before they set out. He drew his pistol. Dag had his new rifle.

Dag raised the visor of the helm. "What's the plan, sir?"

"I wish to God I knew," Stephano returned, putting his helm on his head.

He forced himself to take a breath and think. The bat riders, flying in advance of the black ship, would attack with their green contramagic fireballs. Those might wound the dragons, but they were not likely to be lethal. The green beam weapon could kill with a single shot.

"Target the ship!" Stephano yelled.

He looked behind at Petard, who was flapping his wings, snaking his neck and roaring in rage.

"Petard!" Stephano shouted.

The young dragon didn't hear him. Viola hooted a command and Petard looked at him.

"Petard, we're flying for the ship!" Stephano called. "Keep us covered!"

Petard bobbed his head and opened his mouth in a grin, showing his fangs. Stephano had no idea if the young dragon understood him or not. He wished Gythe was here. She had been Petard's rider. The next moment Stephano was glad Gythe was not here. The likelihood of them surviving this lopsided battle was slim.

Stephano lowered his visor and gave the signal to fly. Viola spread her wings, raised her body, and bounded off the ground, propelling herself into the air with her powerful hind legs.

In the amphitheater, the dragons were in turmoil. Haelgrund was speaking to the duke, forcefully, to judge by the way his neck was stretched forward. The countess had joined Haelgrund. The other dragons were peering uncertainly into the sky. Huddled together, they made an ideal target.

Stephano set his jaw and held on fast while Viola clawed her way into the air. Dag, mounted on Verdi, was behind him. Petard flew ahead. Without a rider or a saddle to encumber him, the young dragon had taken swiftly to the skies, angrily bellowing challenges.

Stephano sighed. That wasn't what he'd meant by keeping him and Dag covered. At least Petard had caught the attention of the bat riders. Leaving the black ship, they flew straight toward the young dragon.

Stephano smiled grimly. He doubted if the bat riders had ever fought a dragon before. Petard waited, as Stephano had taught him, until the riders were within range, then opened his mouth, sucked in a breath, and unleashed a blast of fire. He incinerated the lead rider and his bat and sent the other two bats flapping off wildly to avoid the blaze.

Stephano pointed emphatically toward the ship, signaling they were to ignore the riders and head straight for the weapon. Dag raised his hand to indicate he understood. Stephano took a brief moment to look back down on the ground. Haelgrund and the duke were still arguing, and the others were hovering nearby. Some, like the countess, gazed upward, watching the battle.

He couldn't afford to spare them any more attention. He and Viola were coming up on the bat riders. Having seen the fate of their comrades, the riders chose to fire from a distance. They were using the small handheld weapons, not the ungainly cannon-type weapons they had used at the attack on the Abbey.

He braced himself as Viola raised her left wing, dipped her right, and soared past the bat riders. Stephano clung to the saddle, staring straight down at the ground that began to spin beneath him. Green fireballs whizzed past him. Viola righted herself, climbing. Now the ground was gone and the sky was spinning.

Stephano caught a glimpse of Petard bearing down on the bat riders, then heard a roar and felt the heat of fiery breath. A bat and its rider plummeted out of the skies, and then Viola straightened out and resumed her course toward the ship.

Verdi was slower and less maneuverable than Viola,

but his breath was far more explosive and he had learned to belch a great glob of fire, then blow it like a deadly soap bubble toward his foes. The blaze incinerated only those in front of him, however, and the bat riders were flying at him and Dag from all directions now.

Stephano shot at one of the bat riders, and then ducked down in the saddle as a green fireball blazed overhead. The next fireball actually struck the saddle. Stephano had no way of knowing if Viola, too, had been hit; He didn't see how she could avoid it, being such a large target.

Petard was doing his best to drive the fiends away, and Dag and Verdi were under heavy fire. All the while, the black ship was holding course, sailing for the dragons on the ground. Stephano was close enough he could see the green beam weapon swiveling about to take aim. He and Viola were still too far away to stop it. He drew his dragon pistol, urging Viola closer.

Braving the fireballs, Dag stood up in the saddle, aiming the rifle, hoping for a lucky shot that would disable the weapon. Verdi flew as steady as he could, while Petard swooped and blasted at the bat riders. Stephano yelled to Viola and they flew over to help.

Dag fired his rifle and then ducked back down to reload. He hit one of the Bottom Dwellers, who jerked, spun and went over backward, but he missed the gun. Two others continued to man the weapon, and the green beam streaked into the amphitheater. Stephano left the fight to Viola and looked worriedly down at the dragons.

Thick, ugly smoke rose from the amphitheater, obscuring his view. He caught sight of a dragon sprawled on the ground, a mass of blood and bones and burning flesh. Stephano could not tell who had been killed, nor could he see what the other dragons were doing.

"Hopefully they now realize the Bottom Dwellers aren't here to talk," Stephano muttered.

A green fireball burst in front of him, half blinding him. The Bottom Dwellers shooting from the ship were using the long guns that had a greater range. Petard was everywhere, diving, swooping, breathing fire, forcing the bat riders to keep their distance, though in his enthusiasm, he once came too close to Viola and scorched her, causing her to snarl at him.

Viola herself was doing an excellent job, as was Verdi. Both dragons were keeping their focus on the ship, not allowing themselves to be drawn off into fighting the bat riders. Stephano could see the blackened scales on Verdi's flanks where he had been hit. The wounds did not appear severe, but that was deceptive. The contramagic would eat painfully at the dragon's flesh and scales, doing extensive damage.

The dragons were closing in on the ship. Viola opened her mouth, her jaws gaped, her eyes blazed. Verdi roared in rage. Petard flew in fast, hooting with joy. The Bottom Dwellers lining the rails saw death flying toward them. Some broke and ran. Others held grimly to their task.

The green beam weapon was mounted on the forecastle, a raised deck on the bow of the ship, manned by only two Bottom Dwellers now that their third lay in a pool of blood.

Stephano and Viola would fly in first, hitting the gun with dragon fire from above, then Petard would follow. Viola started to attack, but was forced to veer off as her little brother dove in ahead of her. Crazed by battle, without a rider to guide him, Petard flew straight at the green beam weapon. Opening his jaws, he sucked in his breath.

A man whose clothes were covered in blood shoved aside the soldiers and took charge of the weapon himself. He aimed the green beam at point-blank range at Petard, who was so excited he didn't see his own danger. Viola strained against the harness, longing to swoop in to save her brother. Stephano held her back and even she seemed to realize there was nothing she could do. She couldn't set fire to the gun without hitting Petard.

Before the man could shoot, Petard breathed a gust of fire that sent flames rippling and flowing over the forecastle like molten lava. The dragon was so close he had to make a mad scramble to avoid crashing into the burning ship. His wings flapped wildly, his legs paddled the air, and he nearly flipped over backward. His tail struck the burning forecastle, smashing it to fiery splinters.

The captain bellowed orders to come about and retreat. Viola hissed angrily at Petard, who gave her a wide grin. Stephano signaled to Dag that they were going in for the kill. Here was his chance to remove at least one black ship from the fight.

Stephano and Dag and their dragons were about to launch their attack when Haelgrund suddenly appeared in front of Stephano, flying so close he almost clipped Viola's snout.

"Stop!" Haelgrund roared.

Stephano tapped on his helm to indicate that he couldn't hear.

"Stop!" Haelgrund roared again. He glared at Viola and repeated the word in the dragon language.

Confused, Viola looked back at Stephano. He yanked off his helm in anger.

"What are you doing, Haelgrund? Get out of my way!"

"The duke orders you to stop, Stephano," said Haelgrund. "I need not remind you that you are in dragon territory and subject to dragon law."

Seething, Stephano gave the signal to break off the attack. He could do nothing except watch as the crippled black ship, trailing smoke, limped off for the safety of the mountains. Dag must have guessed why Stephano called them off, for he and Verdi turned back. Viola had to bark loudly and forcefully at Petard, who was happily pursuing the ship. At first Stephano didn't think the young dragon was going to obey. Truth be told, he hoped he wouldn't.

Viola shouted something, and whatever threat she made worked, for Petard veered around. He was clearly outraged, demanding to know what was going on. Viola had only to indicate Haelgrund with a jerk of her head. The big dragon said something stern. Petard shrank, his mane flattened. He flew over and tried to hide behind Verdi.

Stephano was too angry to speak, and Haelgrund understood. He kept darting sidelong glances at Stephano as they headed back toward land.

"Who died?" Stephano asked at last.

"The countess," said Haelgrund. "She threw herself in front of the duke. Saved his life."

Stephano shot Haelgrund a grim glance.

"I'm sorry, Stephano," Haelgrund returned. "I don't agree with the duke. You know I don't. I said we should kill the bastards. He was adamant. He maintains you attacked these people without provocation when they had come to seek peace."

"Balls!" said Stephano furiously. "You saw the black ship making preparations to fire. This was an ambush!"

"I told the duke, but he wouldn't listen. He's in a terrible state. He blames you for the death of the countess. You have to leave the dragon realms immediately. He will let the wild dragons stay here, since they were only obeying your commands."

Viola gave a snort that sent flame shooting out of her nostrils and curled her lip, showing her fangs.

"The wild dragons are coming with us," said Stephano.

"I'm sorry, Captain," Haelgrund said again and flew off.

"I couldn't understand what he was saying, sir," said Dag, "but I'm guessing we're not going to be reforming the Dragon Brigade."

"You guessed right," said Stephano.

He looked down at the body of the countess on the ground. The other dragons were gathered around the shattered, bloody corpse. They would burn her body, then gather her ashes and give her to the sky.

"The duke be damned. We will pay our respects," said Stephano. "She was my comrade."

He ordered Viola to swoop down low, flying over the body as he stood braced in the saddle and saluted. Dag did the same, and then Petard, his flight a little wobbly, flew overhead as well.

The duke watched them, his mane bristling, but made no move to stop them. The countess had been a member of the Dragon Brigade and deserved the honor. The duke kept a baleful eye on them, however, making certain they flew off.

"Where are we headed, sir?" Dag asked.

"Back to the fortress," said Stephano. "We have a war to wage."

15

We are the light that will banish the darkness.

—The Children of Flame

Miri had always been the pilot of her life. She stood at the helm; she was the navigator. As she sailed the *Cloud Hopper* through the clear skies and the storms, so she had always guided her own destiny. But now, Miri was no longer at the helm. Gythe had taken over, and she and Miri were prisoners on board the Bottom Dwellers' ship, sailing into darkness and fog and cold that struck through to the bone.

The little sister who had always depended on her was steering their lives into the unknown. Miri knew Gythe had some plan in mind, but she refused to tell her.

"The less you know, the better," Gythe signed to her sister. "If we are captured, you can say truthfully you didn't know anything."

"Captured!" Miri repeated, frightened. "Gythe! Tell me what is going on!"

But Gythe would only shake her head, leaving Miri feeling helpless and, for the first time in her life, alone.

Gythe affected being a prisoner herself, having made up a story about how she and Miri had been abducted. Miri kept up the pretense, afraid to do anything else. The

Bottom Dwellers had taken three other prisoners besides Miri and Gythe, all of them women. They treated the prisoners harshly, keeping them locked in the hold and threatening them with beatings if they made trouble. Huddled together in the cold and the darkness, with barely enough food to keep them alive, the women were certainly not inclined to cause trouble.

But while the Bottom Dwellers might threaten them, it was clear that they wanted to keep them alive. Their captors provided wool blankets and thick coats to protect against the cold, and though their rations were meager, Miri saw that the prisoners ate as well as their guards.

"Why take these three women?" Miri asked, puzzled.

"They are all savants," Gythe replied.

Miri would later learn during the voyage that one woman was a baker, who used her magical talent to make wondrous confections served at the royal palace. Another woman was studying to be a crafter-priest, and the third woman was a milliner who rarely used her extraordinary magical talent because she did not want to appear "different."

"Why do the Bottom Dwellers want savants?" Miri asked. "What does Brother Barnaby have to do with this? What is he doing down Below? I thought he was dead! I don't understand."

Gythe would give her no answer, except to say, "The Bottom Dwellers will not harm us or the others. Tell them not to be afraid."

"Tell *me* not to be afraid," Miri snapped.

Gythe cast her a hurt look. Miri sighed deeply. "I wish you would trust me with your secret, Gythe."

Gythe clasped her sister by the hand and gave her a remorseful kiss on the cheek.

"The secret is not mine to tell . . ."

Shut up in the hold belowdecks of the troop ship and unable to see outside, Miri lost track of the days. She spent most of her time wrapped up in a blanket, huddled together with Gythe, trying to keep warm as the ship sank down into the Breath. She knew the ship had broken through the chill, thick mists of the Breath when she heard the sailors cheering and calling out to each other that they would soon be home.

The cheers did not last long, though. The ship sailed out of the Breath and into a wizard storm. Fierce winds and rain tossed around the large, heavy ship as if it were the little *Cloud Hopper.* Thunder cracked and roared. The prisoners were sick from the erratic motion, as were some of the soldiers and members of the crew, according to the sailor who brought them their daily ration of food and water.

Having been born sailing the Breath, as the saying went, Miri and Gythe were not subject to the sickness that plagued the other prisoners. They made the women as comfortable as possible. Sick and miserable, the women lay on pallets and groaned, when they weren't heaving into buckets. The hold reeked of the stench. One day, desperate for a breath of air that wasn't tainted by the smell of vomit, Miri opened the door of the hold.

The guard glared at her and ordered back her inside.

Miri begged him: "I just want to let in some fresh air."

The guard seemed hesitant, but then he caught a whiff of the smell and relented.

The door to the hold was at the bottom of a flight of stairs that ended in a closed hatch at the top. As she watched, one of the sailors pulled the hatch open to go into the hold. The fierce wind blew the hatch out of his hand, and rain pelting down through the open hatch drenched Miri. She didn't move, but just wiped the water from her face and breathed in the rain-fresh air as she gazed, awestruck, at the flaring pink and purple lightning that swept across the sky.

The sailor called to the guard to come help him. Miri, seeing they were absorbed in their work, sneaked out of the hold and climbed the stairs. Battered by the wind and rain, she peered up onto the deck.

The ship was riding out the storm with only very small staysails to maintain steerage. Heavy weather lines had been added to the balloons to keep them from being swept away by the savage winds. Sailors staggered against the blasting rain, hanging onto thick lines stretched above the gunwales to keep from being blown overboard.

Miri knew what it was like to be caught in a wizard storm, though she had never faced one of this magnitude. She watched the captain and the helmsman fighting to maintain control and despite herself felt sympathy for them.

Hearing the guard yelling at her, Miri hurried back down the stairs. The sailor shut the hatch, cutting off her view and the flow of fresh air, and the guard angrily ordered her to go back into the hold. Miri did as she was told, and when she was back in the hold she found Gythe waiting for her.

"A wizard storm," Miri said. "Like the one that nearly sank us and the *Sommerwind*."

"Worse, much worse," Gythe said, her hands trembling as she signed. "There is evil in this storm."

The ship rocked and lurched, knocking her to her knees and flinging Miri into a bulkhead. On the deck above, something fell with a loud crash. They heard feet pounding and commands being shouted.

"Stay down," Miri said, crouching. "Safer than trying to stand."

"Such storms were once very rare Below," Gythe told her. "They happen constantly now, making life unbearable. That is why they want savants."

"To control the storms." Miri shook her head. "It's not possible."

Gythe gazed at her intently. "Yes, it is. You know it is."

"I know you sang a song and that other storm stopped." Miri glared at Gythe, angry and frightened. "I know Rigo claimed you had something to do with it, but he never said what, and you never told me!"

"Because you never asked!" Gythe's hands flashed.

She rose to her feet, bracing herself on the pitching deck by leaning against the bulkhead.

"We will be landing soon. You must follow my lead, do whatever I do, even if you do not understand. Promise me." Gythe put her hand on her heart.

"Why should I trust you, when you won't trust me?" Miri asked bitingly.

Gythe gazed at her with unblinking calm and repeated, tapping her heart. "Promise."

"I don't know you anymore, Gythe!" Miri said, bewildered. "Who are you?"

"I am who I need to be. They are right. We abandoned them, but not anymore. Promise!"

Gythe's hand was a clenched fist over her heart.

"I promise," said Miri. "You know that."

Gythe gave a curt nod and left, going back to nurse their patients.

Miri remained crouched, shivering in her wet clothes and wondering bleakly how this misery and terror was going to end.

Still battered by storm winds, the ship made a perilous landing that left everyone onboard bruised and shaken. The man named Patrick and the other soldiers took charge of the prisoners, once more binding their wrists. Miri saw Gythe and Patrick exchange glances, as the soldiers escorted the prisoners off the ship.

"Where are we?" Miri asked.

"You are at the bottom of the world," Patrick replied. "The town is Port Gaotha Baile. We stand on the sunken island of Glasearrach."

Miri stood on the dock, gazing at her surroundings. She could not guess the hour. The sun was hidden by gray clouds. For the moment, the wizard storm had abated and only a light rain fell. But the cool air was thick with humidity, and she could see little through the gloom.

Ships were ghostly in the fog, sails and yardarms appearing then vanishing. She could see vague outlines of low buildings and hear people passing by: the wheels of carts, the clopping of hooves. Voices were muffled and indistinct.

I am standing on Glasearrach, Miri thought in disbelief.

The doomed island and its inhabitants and the disaster that had befallen them had been a tale told over a bottle of Calvados as the last glimmers of day faded from the sky. Her cousins would sing the old songs about the Pirate King, a terror and a scourge to the rest of the world, but a hero to the Trundlers.

"Stop gawking," said Patrick, giving her a shove. "Get in the wagon before the storm breaks."

Gythe followed, tugging Miri along. Two wagons, drawn by two thick-necked, short, stout horses stood near the dock. The wagons were made of wood, closed against the elements, with a door and two small windows with wooden shutters.

"Where are you taking us?" Miri demanded, stopping and refusing to move.

"Get in the wagon," Patrick said again, this time harshly. "You two will come with me."

Gythe flashed Miri a warning look and again put her hand on her heart, reminding her of her promise.

The other three women stood huddled together, clasping hands, gazing around in fear and bewilderment. Miri at least knew where she was. These poor women didn't know anything, for they couldn't understand the language. Miri was going to go offer what comfort she could, but Patrick stopped her. Pointing to the other women, he told the guard to load them in the first wagon.

"Why are you separating us?" Miri asked.

"You ask too many questions," Patrick said.

Gythe tugged on Miri's sleeve and gave her a reproachful look as she climbed inside the wagon. Miri heaved a sigh and followed. The interior was stark and plain with benches that ran along each side—a prison wagon.

Patrick told the driver they were ready, then he entered the wagon and shut the door just as another wizard storm swooped down on them.

The wind rose, howling. The rain came down in torrents. Lightning crackled and thunder roared. Patrick had left the window open to let in the air, and the rain was blowing inside. Miri slid across the bench and reached for the shutter to pull it closed. Outside the lightning was almost continuous, spreading in eerie, luminous sheets across the clouds.

Without a word, Patrick roughly shoved her aside and slammed the shutter.

"Stay put," he said.

Patrick closed the other shutter, leaving the interior of the wagon dark and stuffy. The wagon jounced over cobblestones for a time and then, judging by the sounds of the horses' hooves splashing through mud, the paved road ended. Miri was desperate to know where they were being taken, what was going to happen to them. She had promised Gythe she would keep quiet, but she found the strain unendurable. She couldn't sit docilely in a corner, hurtling through the darkness into the unknown. She blurted out the words before she could stop herself.

"Please, Patrick, tell us where you are taking us."

To her surprise, he responded, "To the Temple of the Xaviers in the capital city of Dunlow. If you do what Xavier asks, you will not be harmed."

Miri was relieved to learn something, although she had no idea who this Xavier was or why they were going to a temple. Since Patrick seemed in a mood to talk now that they were alone, she pressed on.

"What does this Xavier want with us?"

"He needs savants to stop the storms."

"And what happens to us if we don't?" Miri asked.

"Xavier's brother, the Blood Mage, has been killing the savants who failed, sacrificing them in ritual magic to aid the drummers."

Miri sucked in her breath in dismay and reached out to clutch at Gythe in the darkness. Gythe clasped her hand in reassurance.

"Trust me," Gythe seemed to say silently, pressing Miri's hand warmly. "Have faith in me."

"I want to, Gythe," Miri whispered. "But it is hard!"

The journey in the wagon was much like the journey in the ship: dark and uncomfortable. The lashing rain stopped eventually, blowing itself out as if the storm had given up in sheer exhaustion. When Patrick opened the window to let in fresh air, Miri looked out to see a watery sun flit among the clouds. The sun's weak light cast a pale, gray illumination on a bleak, barren wilderness and the low green mountains that rose in the distance. The wagon pulled off what passed for a road and rolled to a stop.

Patrick told them they could leave the wagon, walk about for a bit. Miri rose stiffly, grateful for the break. She stepped outside to see the driver and the guard keeping watch, scanning the road, their weapons at the ready.

"What are they watching for?" Miri asked. "Wild beasts?"

"An attack by the resistance, the *Leanai Lasair,*" Patrick answered. "Our wagon bears the emblem of Saint Xavier, their sworn enemy. For your own well-being, do not venture far."

He walked off. Miri kept a watchful eye on him. When he passed by Gythe, the two exchanged glances. He raised his eyebrow and kept moving, going to confer with the driver. Gythe folded her arms and gazed out at yet another storm. Clouds gathered, cutting off the tops of the mountains.

Patrick and the guard and the driver were talking together, their eyes constantly scanning their surroundings, fearing a rebel attack. The horses, splashed with mud up to their withers, waited patiently. The sun was slowly being swallowed by the clouds.

A sudden, startling thought came to Miri. She didn't know if the thought was a comfort or increased her fear. She had not been able to see the markings on the wagon in the gloom. Miri studied the crest—an "X" for Xavier entwined in a series of seven knots, green against red.

Leanai Lasair. Trundler for "Children of Flame."

Miri made her way through the mud to her sister, who was looking out over the landscape slowly dissolving in the rain.

"Patrick is a member of the resistance, isn't he?" Miri said softly. "He is one of the Children of Flame. And so are you. That is why you are here."

Gythe looked up into the sky. Lightning flickered on the fringes of the storm clouds.

"They want to bring back their sun," Gythe said, speaking with her hands. "I can help."

Miri felt a flood of relief and then smiled ruefully at herself. They were still in danger, but at least she was no longer stumbling about blindly.

Gythe turned her gaze to Miri, placed her hand on Miri's lips. "You must keep our secret."

"I will," Miri promised. "And I will help, if I can."

"Get back inside!" Patrick shouted. "The storm is coming!"

Together, in silence, they splashed back through the mud, reaching the wagon just as the storm broke.

They traveled through the night, braving the rain and the wind, blasts of lightning and ground-shaking thunder. Miri fell into an uncomfortable sleep. She was jolted awake when the wagon lurched to a stop, tilting sideways and nearly throwing her off the bench. She could hear the driver shouting at the horses. The wagon did not budge. The driver yelled for Patrick.

Patrick had trouble opening the door in the buffeting wind and when he finally did, the rain blew inside, stinging her face. He was gone a moment, then returned to tell them that the wagon was stuck in a mud hole and they would have to get out.

Miri and Gythe stood huddled together in the driving rain that penetrated their clothes and soaked them to the bone. Miri would have offered to help, but realized that it would seem strange for a prisoner to want to assist her captors. She tried to forget her discomfort by watching the dazzling lightning display: pink and purple bolts streaking among the clouds or spiking to the ground. Patrick and the guard heaved and strained to free the wagon wheel from the muddy rut that held it, while the driver lashed the horses, urging them to pull.

After much fruitless effort, they gave up. Patrick told Miri and Gythe to get back in the wagon. They would have to wait until the driver brought someone back to help. Shivering in their soaked clothes, Miri and Gythe pressed together for warmth as the wagon shook and rattled.

The storm ended at last. Day dawned bleak and dismal. Patrick doled out a small portion of food.

"How long do you think we might be stranded here?" Gythe signed.

Patrick shrugged. "This road goes to Dunlow. It was once a main road that carried lots of traffic. The storms make traveling hazardous now, as you can see. The guard and the driver have gone for help. Hopefully we will be here no more than a day. Maybe two."

He opened the window. The pale sun floated in a pinkish orange sky.

"How do you and your people live like this?" Miri asked somberly.

She ate the small portion of bread slowly, to make it last.

"Before the storms began, our lives were hard, but they were bearable," said Patrick, munching on his own hunk of the hard, stale loaf. "We had learned down through the years what crops would grow in the limited amount of sunshine that filtered through the Breath. We helped each other. We stopped cursing our fate. We taught ourselves to be content, to enjoy life."

Miri smiled. "You actually answered my question."

Patrick smiled faintly in return.

"Your sister told me you guessed our secret, that we are part of the resistance."

"What does the resistance do?" Miri asked. She hesitated

before saying, "And what do you expect Gythe to do to help your cause?"

"We want our lives back," said Patrick. "Xavier caused these storms with his war. He says we will go Above and live in the sunlight. Glasearrach is our homeland! We have raised our families here, going back generations before the sinking. We do not want to leave nor do we seek revenge. Xavier must be stopped."

"How did he cause the storms?"

"Xavier's grandfather learned that blood magic enhances contramagic. His father was a blood mage and so is his brother. He was the one who came up with the idea of using the temple drummers and their blood magic to bombard your world with contramagic. The Blood Mage claims that the contramagic will silence the voice of your God and bring your people to their knees. What he did not tell us was that the drumming is going to bring us to our knees."

"The clash of magic and contramagic is stirring up wizard storms," said Gythe.

"Over time the storms have grown worse and worse. Now the magic rages out of control. The storms are almost constant. Crops drown in the fields. Our children are starving. What food we do manage to grow goes to feed Xavier, his drummers, and his army."

"But why does he want savants?" Miri asked. "Why does he think they can stop the storms?"

"He conceived the idea from some book sent to him by one of his agents Above. He read that these same wizard storms ravaged your world during what you call the Dark Ages. Four saints prayed for a miracle and the storms ceased. Xavier investigated and found out that the saints were savants. That gave him the idea.

"Unfortunately, Xavier has not found any saints among the savants he has taken prisoner," Patrick concluded drily. "The savants he has brought have done nothing. He can't afford to feed prisoners who are useless so he gave them to his brother, the Blood Mage."

"So you brought Gythe here to be murdered," Miri said.

"*I* did not bring her here," Patrick said sternly. "She volunteered. She claims she can quell the storms. If she does, then Xavier will keep her alive."

"And if she doesn't, she will be sacrificed in some unholy ritual!" Miri returned angrily. She rose to her feet. "Gythe, come along. We are leaving."

Patrick made no move to stop her. She knew why when she opened the wagon door and a gust of wind and rain drove her back inside. Grimly, she held on to the door and turned to her sister.

"Gythe! I said we are going!" Miri shouted over the wind.

Gythe shook her head. She sat with her feet on the bench, her arms around her knees.

"Gythe!" Miri cried, both a plea and a command.

Patrick shut the door. Outside the wind howled. The wagon rocked and shook. Miri sank down on the bench.

"You should try to get some sleep," said Patrick.

16

The church punished us for studying contramagic, then begged us to tell them how to use its power. I am sad to say that the four of us, who had remained fast friends through many trials and sorrows, could not agree on what we should do. Certainly the evil they sought to fight was very great. In the end, two of us remained silent and remained imprisoned. Two revealed the secret and were set free.

—Confessions of Saint Marie

Miri woke to the sound of voices. For a moment, she was groggy and disoriented, wondering where she was. The sight of Patrick leaving his seat to open the door brought everything back. He returned to say that the driver and the guard had come with help and that she and Gythe needed to leave the wagon.

Another dreary, sunless day had dawned, the second day they had been stranded. Miri and Gythe stood in the mud and watched six men drag, shove, pull, and push the wagon until they finally managed to free it. She and Gythe climbed inside and the weary journey began again. Patrick was silent, gazing out the window at the bleak, barren mountains.

Gythe cast Miri pleading glances, asking her to understand.

Miri pretended she didn't see. She gazed out the window until the rain started again and Patrick closed the shutters.

She dozed uneasily as the wagon squelched through the mud, and jolted to alertness only when the motion of the wagon changed. The wheels were now rattling over cobblestones again.

"The city of Dunlow," said Patrick. "We have arrived at our destination."

The wagon traveled along streets that appeared to turn and twist, for the wagon was continually shifting direction. At last, it came to a stop. Patrick opened the door. The latest storm was drifting off. The rain was falling in a drizzle instead of torrents. Miri climbed out of the wagon and onto a cobblestone street.

People muffled in heavy wraps against the rain hurried about their business. A few stared at the wagon and its passengers. Most cast furtive glances and then looked quickly away.

The driver told Patrick to keep watch on Miri and Gythe, and walked off, saying he was going to make arrangements for their admittance to the temple.

Miri looked around. Patrick had told them a little about Dunlow, the old capital of Glasearrach. Located in the foothills of a ridge of mountains called the Spine, because they formed the backbone of the island, Dunlow had been a prosperous city prior to the sinking, known for its fine merino wool and the famous Dunlow brick, renowned for its unusual creamy color. The brick came from the clay pits to the north and was once shipped around the world. Dunlow had also been a market town. Crops from the surrounding farms had fed the entire island.

Miri looked down a wet street and saw a hodgepodge

of dwellings and businesses, all made of the famous brick. Like the Trundler floating cities, Dunlow was divided into neighborhoods, each of which was home to a single Trundler clan. In the old days, the clan leaders led the city. The clans had managed to live together fairly peacefully, with only the occasional blood feud.

Miri's uncle claimed that their clan had been one of the leading clans in Dunlow, all lost with the sinking of the island.

"I am amazed Dunlow survived," Miri remarked to Patrick.

"The coastal villages were destroyed by the contramagic beams that struck the island," Patrick replied. "Almost everyone perished. Those who did not die in the burning rubble succumbed to the cold as the island sank into the Breath. The residents of Dunlow were more fortunate. Saint Xavier the First ordered the people to flee to the caves in the mountains and there they managed to survive the descent through the Breath.

"The island fell slowly. The contramagic that had killed us proved our salvation. The Breath boiled and bubbled and thickened. The island came to a soft landing in a mixture of sea and swamp. The survivors waited," Patrick continued, his voice hardening. "They waited in the endless night for their people to come rescue them. But no one did. Eventually they realized they had been forgotten."

His voice was tinged with bitterness that Miri realized must have lasted centuries, passed down from parent to child.

"Is that why your people have targeted Trundlers?" Miri asked. "Is that why they attacked Trundler boats, murdered people like our parents? Because you thought your people had abandoned you?"

"You *did* abandon us," said Patrick grimly.

"Our people had no way of knowing anyone had survived!"

"They knew," said Patrick.

"How?" Miri demanded. "How could they know?"

"Those early people were determined to find a way to get back to the surface. A man named Alan MacGregor finally succeeded. He discovered a river that he theorized must have its source in the world Above. He and two of his sons made the arduous and treacherous journey, climbing the rocks along the banks of the river. Eventually, after many months, they reached the surface. They found themselves in a large cavern in the Oscadia Mountains."

Miri stared at him. "I have heard nothing of this tale. No one has."

"There is a reason you have not heard," Patrick said. "Alan and his sons were jubilant. They climbed down out of the mountains and made contact with some villagers. He and his sons were pale, gaunt and haggard, half starved. They spoke a strange language. The superstitious villagers thought they were demons from hell and fled in terror, running to tell the local priest.

"The priest was a wise man and he knew they were not demons. He understood some Trundler. He listened to their tale and believed them. He wrote to his superiors what he considered was good news—people on Glasearrach had survived the sinking. The grand bishop himself traveled to the mountains, saying the Church wanted to help. Alan and his sons went back to the cavern, planning to return to Below to bring the joyous news. They never arrived and everyone on Glasearrach assumed they had failed."

"But if they never arrived, how do you know what happened?" Miri asked skeptically.

"Centuries later, an explorer came across traces of

Alan MacGregor's campsite. He and his party followed Alan's route and climbed to the surface. When they reached the cavern, they found three skeletons, the remnants of the arrows that had killed them, and Alan's journal. He and his sons had been murdered and sealed up inside the cavern. Nearby was a monastery, built to guard the 'Gates of Hell.' "

Miri stared at him, aghast. "You are saying the grand bishop killed them? But why?"

"To stop our people from returning to tell our tale," said Patrick. "To stop us from pointing accusing fingers at a church that talks loudly about mercy and forgiveness while hiding hands drenched with blood."

"If this is true," said Miri slowly, "then what happened to your people is a terrible tragedy."

She was about to add that this didn't give them the right to murder her parents or the nuns of Saint Agnes or the children in the Crystal Market. She remained silent, thinking.

Down through the centuries, Trundlers had lived by their own laws, refusing to obey the laws handed down by others. Trundlers were fiercely loyal to their clans. The right of a Trundler to demand blood justice for an injury done to him or to a clan member was sacrosanct. Miri had taken part in her own share of blood feuds when the honor of the McPikes had been challenged.

She considered the terrible lives these people had been forced to lead, trapped at the bottom of the world, knowing that they had been abandoned. Perhaps they had a right to don demonic armor and fly off on giant bats to seek their revenge.

But blood feuds had rules. Her uncle had taught her that. Before going to war, the clans would meet to air their grievances. The Bottom Dwellers could have done the same, but instead they had resorted to murder.

Her thoughts were interrupted by the return of the driver with word that they could proceed. The temple warders were expecting them.

Patrick escorted them down the street toward a destination obscured by the downpour. As they walked, Miri mused on how it seemed that time had stopped for Dunlow the day the island sank. The old, old buildings were probably much the same now as they had been all those centuries ago, except that they were dirtier, shabbier. The cream-colored brick was stained with soot and was now black or dingy gray.

She could see a few lights in the windows, but, for the most part, the buildings were dark. The people who had dared venture out in the storm carried lanterns or torches that smoked in the rain. Their faces were pale and thin, pinched with hunger.

An oppressive silence hung over the city, dark as the storm clouds. People did not speak, not even to each other. They walked with their heads bent and shoulders hunched, wrapped in private misery. There was little traffic on the streets, no laughter of children playing. The only sound was a distant rumble of thunder.

"I want you to see something," said Patrick softly. "Look to your left, through the gap in the buildings."

At first Miri couldn't see anything, but then a sheet of lightning spread across the sky. She saw ships riding at anchor, their yardarms silhouetted against the lightning. The ships were large and so numerous she couldn't count them. She could see men working on them, climbing among the rigging, even in the storm. An armada of black ships.

"Xavier's fleet," said Patrick. "They are going to invade your homeland. You may be safer down here."

Miri stared at the fleet, lagging behind, until Patrick ordered her sharply to keep up.

The street and the rows of buildings came to an end at a large courtyard paved with ornamental stone. In the center she could see Xavier's crest—the *X* with the knot work—done in mosaic.

"Beyond the courtyard, behind that brick wall, is the Temple of Saint Xavier," said Patrick. "His soldiers are watching us. From now on, you are my prisoners."

They walked across the vast and empty courtyard. Miri could feel the eyes on her. Patrick steered them toward a large, iron-banded wooden gate that pierced the brick wall. Torches mounted in iron sconces on either side of the gate smoked and flickered.

"Keep your hands in sight," Patrick warned. "Make no sudden moves. The guards are suspicious of everyone these days."

Miri and Gythe walked with their hands visible outside their cloaks. Patrick kept close to both of them, herding them in front of him. Two soldiers emerged from a small guardhouse that stood to one side of the gate, providing shelter from the incessant rain. Miri could see two more inside.

"What is your business?" one of the soldiers asked Patrick.

"These are the two savants, Captain," said Patrick, prodding Miri in the back. "They are expected."

Whatever the captain was going to say was interrupted by the arrival of a crude-looking carriage marked with Xavier's crest. The fast-moving carriage came to a stop in a flurry of splashing water and mud. Startled, the captain barked an order and raised his weapon. The two soldiers in the guardhouse ran out with their weapons. Patrick grabbed hold of Miri and Gythe and drew them near the guardhouse.

The wagon's driver raised his hands in the air to show he was unarmed.

"What is the password?" the captain barked.

"The love of Xavier," said the driver, adding, "My passengers are *Leanai Scath.* They bear important tidings for our saint."

The captain gestured. The driver descended and hurried to open the carriage door.

A tall woman with a regal bearing stepped out. She wore a gold-colored hooded mantle that was wet and mud splattered. Accompanying her was a man with an upright, soldierly bearing, wearing a green hooded mantle. He kept the hood pulled low over his face. The man walked with a limp, leaning on a cane.

"Leanai Scath," said Patrick. "The Children of Shadow." He spit on the pavement.

The man and the woman approached the gate. The captain ordered his men to stand down and advanced toward the two.

"Steward," he said, saluting the woman. "How can I be of service to you?"

"I seek admittance, of course," said the woman in disdainful tones. "Why else we would have risked our lives to come here?"

Miri started. The woman spoke in Rosian! The captain of the guard stared at her blankly, not understanding. The woman's companion, the man leaning on the cane, translated her words into Trundler.

The captain was embarrassed. "I have not received any orders from the saint regarding visitors."

"I want to see your superior," said the woman coldly.

Again, her companion translated.

The woman folded her hands in front of her and gazed expectantly at the captain. He turned to one of his soldiers.

"Fetch Warder Roarke," he ordered.

The captain had forgotten Patrick and his prisoners and

Patrick made no move to remind him. He stayed by the wall, keenly observing the two visitors, probably hoping to discover their business.

They did not have to wait long. The soldier returned, accompanied by a man wearing a green mantle. He was of middle height, with the same pale complexion as the others Miri had seen in the city, but his face was rounder and he generally appeared better fed. He regarded the newcomers with suspicion.

"I am Warder Roarke. Who are you? I was not told to expect visitors."

"I am Steward Cecile and this is Warder Conal, my bodyguard. I come at the behest of Attendant Eiddwen," said the woman. "I am her agent. I bring an urgent message to our saint."

Warder Conal was going to translate, but apparently this needed no translation. At the name Eiddwen, the warder immediately became more respectful.

"What is the message?" Warder Roarke asked. "I can take it."

Steward Cecile cast him a cool glance. "I am to deliver it to our saint in person."

Warder Roarke glanced sidelong at the captain, who gave a nod.

"You and your bodyguard are most welcome, Steward," Warder Roarke said. "I am sorry I had to question you. I hope you will not take offense. The rebels would like nothing better than to try to defile this sacred precinct—"

"I understand, Warder," Steward Cecile replied graciously. "The outpost at *Bhealach Ardaitheach* was attacked by rebels shortly after our arrival. We were fortunate to have escaped with our lives."

She and her bodyguard entered the gate, accompanied

by Warder Roarke. Miri was intrigued. The name Eiddwen was of Trundler origin, meaning "blessed, holy."

"Who is this Eiddwen?" she asked Patrick in whisper.

"Pray you never know," Patrick answered grimly.

Once the steward and her companion had entered the gate, he led Miri and Gythe forward. The captain waved them on through.

The Temple of Xavier was a long, low building with only one story. The walls were constructed of roughhewn blocks of granite. The roof was formed of timber beams fitted together. The temple had no windows. Double bronze doors provided admittance. Soldiers at these doors scrutinized them closely before permitting them to enter the temple. Once inside, Patrick took a torch from a basket and lit it. The bronze doors closed behind them, leaving them in darkness so thick the flaming torch did little to light it.

Miri gagged and put her hand over her nose and mouth. "What is that stench?" she asked, her voice muffled.

"Blood," said Patrick dispassionately. "The drummers perform the blood magic rituals in the drumming circle in the center of the temple. My brother was one of their sacrifices. He was only twelve. The soldiers took him from our house. 'In the holy name of Xavier,' they said. We could do nothing to stop them."

"Oh, my God!" Miri whispered, horrified.

Gythe pulled back, shaking her head, refusing to enter.

"We have to go this way," said Patrick. "The building where the savants are housed is in the back of the enclave. We must pass through the temple to reach it. Do not worry. We will not enter the place where the drummers sit. No one is permitted to enter that chamber except the drummers and the Blood Mage."

Miri took hold of Gythe's hand, keeping close to her.

They looked inside the chamber. Now that her eyes were becoming accustomed to the darkness, she could see long rows of benches. A single candle burned on an altar. The chamber was empty. No one about. The only sound was the rain drumming on the roof.

"The drummers are not dealing death today," said Patrick.

They entered a narrow corridor that ran alongside. Portraits hung on the walls. Each portrait had beneath it a small altar lighted by a wick floating in a bowl of oil. The portraits were painted by different artists and were of varying quality. Some were new, others old and faded.

"The family of Meehans," said Patrick. "Beginning with Xavier the First."

He paused before an old, old painting of a young man in priest's robes. The young man's head was shaved in the tonsure. He might have been about eighteen. His face was earnest, intense, devout. He held a book in his hand marked with seven sigils. Miri recognized six of them, the ancient sigils of earth, air, fire, water, life, death. She had never seen the seventh and wondered what it was.

"He was both our savior and the one who caused our downfall," said Patrick, gazing at the portrait. "He and his friends discovered contramagic. The seventh sigil."

"What is the seventh sigil?" Miri asked curiously.

"Despair," said Patrick. "So Xavier taught our people."

"Despair?" Miri repeated, startled.

Earth, air, fire, water, life, death all bound by the seventh sigil: despair. Joy, hope, happiness erased. In the end, only despair. Miri was appalled. She glanced at Gythe, who was gazing at the seventh sigil with a frown. She gave a little shake of her head.

Patrick moved on to another portrait, hanging opposite that of the young priest.

"His brother, Ian," said Patrick. "The Pirate King."

Ian Meehan, the infamous Pirate King. His face bore the same intensity of expression as his brother's. But whereas Xavier's eyes glowed with devotion, his brother Ian's eyes blazed with arrogance and ferocity.

"Our songs still tell of him," said Miri. "He is a hero to our people."

"A hero who imprisoned his brother, Xavier, and tortured him until he revealed the secrets of contramagic," Patrick said caustically. "Ian used those secrets to build the first contramagic weapons that set ships ablaze, killed countless numbers, and led the nations to sink our island in order to destroy him."

Miri glanced at Gythe. Her cheeks burned. One of her favorite songs lauded the triumphs of the Pirate King.

"What happened to him?" Miri asked.

"No one knows. Some say he died fighting. Others say he basely fled," Patrick replied. "No one ever heard of him after the sinking. In desperation, the survivors turned to his brother, Xavier, to lead them. His family has ruled ever since. Now we have Saint Xavier the Fourteenth."

His lip curled as he spoke.

"Why 'saint'?" Miri asked curiously. "Our people do not follow the teachings of any church."

"The grandfather of our current Xavier proclaimed himself a saint, saying he would lead our people out of hell to the light Above. There was once light down here," Patrick added in softer tones. "Glasearrach was not hell. Not until the Xaviers made it so."

They walked on down the silent corridor, passing generations of Xaviers keeping watch with their painted eyes on the blood-tinged darkness. Miri began to understand her sister, why Gythe felt the need to help these people.

"When do the rebels plan to strike?" she asked.

"When the invasion fleet sails. Xavier and the Blood Mage will leave with them. We plan to strike then."

Patrick stared at her intently, his eyes gleaming in the torchlight.

"The ships cannot sail until the storms stop."

"That is why I have come," said Gythe.

"What if the fleet didn't set sail?" Miri asked.

Patrick and Gythe looked at her, startled. Miri flushed. She hadn't meant to say that out loud.

"I mean—what if the fleet and Xavier and this Blood Mage were destroyed before they could sail? What if you had an ally to fight with you?"

Patrick gave a disdainful snort. "What if horses could fly through the air?"

But Gythe knew what Miri was thinking. "Stephano!" She signed eagerly. "Dag's fortress!"

Patrick stared at them, frowning. "I don't understand."

"It would take too long to explain," said Miri. "And there are too many problems. I don't think it would work."

But the idea lingered in her mind.

They continued down the hall, leaving the painted Xaviers behind. A door stood at the end. Patrick started to open it, only to find it jerked out of his hand.

Their driver entered in a gust of wind and rain. The wind slammed the door shut behind him. He came to a halt on seeing Patrick. The driver cast an alarmed glance at Miri and Gythe.

"Haven't you delivered them yet? You should make haste. The Blood Mage is in the prison."

Patrick looked alarmed. "Why? What's going on?"

"Those two newcomers," he answered. "They were arguing with Warder Roarke. He sent for the Blood Mage."

He hurried off down the corridor.

"Make haste!" Patrick said.

He yanked open the door. The wind slammed Miri in the face.

But at least the air is fresh, she thought gratefully. She drew in a deep breath to rid her nostrils of the sickening scent of blood.

The door opened onto a yard that gave evidence of having once been grass-covered and pleasant. Now it had become a sea of mud washing up against the walls of outbuildings that ranged around the enclave. Lights shone in many of the windows of the largest building and Miri could see people moving about inside. No one was outside in the storm. The yard was empty except for themselves.

"The drummers live there," said Patrick, indicating the large building as he hurried them along.

The rain was once more coming down in torrents, falling in cascades off the flat roof. The lightning was blinding. Thunder boomed constantly. Patrick indicated a small building that looked like a storehouse.

"That is where they house the savants. Keep your mouths shut and let me do the talking."

The building was made of cement with a thatched roof. The few windows were barred and shuttered. They ran toward it, squelching and slipping in the mud.

Patrick pounded on the door and shouted his name. A soldier opened the door partway, to keep out the rain. They squeezed inside, entering a poorly lit guard room that was crowded with people: two soldiers, a tall man dressed in lurid crimson robes, the woman in the golden mantle, and the man with the cane. Miri had forgotten their names.

The room was small. Eight of them were a tight fit. The man in the crimson robes cast an annoyed glance at the newcomers.

"Why are you here, soldier?"

"I am delivering two savants, Blood Mage," said Patrick in respectful tones.

The Blood Mage made an impatient gesture. "I will deal with you later. Go stand in that corner and wait."

Patrick crowded Miri and Gythe into a corner, warning them with a glance to keep silent. Pressed against the wall, Miri peeped out from around Patrick's shoulder.

The Blood Mage was tall, thin, with dark hair that was starting to gray at the temples. His face was gaunt, narrow, and disfigured, covered with strange-looking scars that crisscrossed his skin like spider webs. Miri realized, after a horrified moment, that these scars were magical constructs, deliberately cut into his flesh. His large eyes burned with a fanatic passion, frightening in its intensity. Miri felt Gythe's hand clasp hers.

"The savants we have thus far received have not had any effect on the storms. My brother was not pleased," the Blood Mage was saying.

"What happened to them? Where are they?" the woman in the gold mantle asked.

"Our saint honored them by giving them to me. I permitted them to sacrifice their lives in the aid of our cause," the Blood Mage responded.

Miri shivered. Gythe pressed close to her. The woman compressed her lips, as though keeping a grip on some strong emotion. A frown line creased her forehead.

"You are aware that Eiddwen sent one of the savants as a personal gift to the saint," she said sternly. "A very special young woman. I trust she has not been sacrificed. Eiddwen would not be pleased."

The eyes of the Blood Mage flickered.

"That would be the young woman with the dog. You can report to Mistress Eiddwen that we have treated her well. Even to the extent of allowing her to keep her pet."

"I am relieved to hear that," said the woman.

"I regret to say, however, that she has been ill," the Blood Mage added.

"Ill? What is wrong with her?"

"She has terrible headaches, so bad she cannot lift her head from her pillow. I brought in a healer to tend to her."

"Is she inside this cell? Open the door," said the woman. "I want to see for myself."

The Blood Mage appeared to consider, then relented.

"Do as she asks."

The guard took a key from a hook on the wall and unlocked the door. Miri could not see from where she was standing, wedged in behind Patrick. But she could smell the misery that had been inside the room: the stench of fear, sickness, and slop pails. She heard what sounded like a dog's yelp, hurriedly smothered.

"This is a disgrace," said the woman angrily. "The room is filthy. No wonder the girl is sick. Where is the healer? I want to speak to him."

The Blood Mage raised his voice and called sharply, "Brother Barnaby!"

"Barnaby!" Miri gave a soft gasp. She turned to stare at Gythe, who avoided her gaze.

Miri muttered beneath her breath and, giving Patrick an impatient shove, managed to maneuver her way around him so that she could see.

A chamber, once used for storage, had been turned into a holding cell for the savants. A lantern burning at the far end of the room lit the interior. The room was a mess. Straw pallets were strewn about the floor. Someone had draped cloth over lengths of string tied to hooks in the ceiling like curtains, to provide a semblance of privacy. Most of these had been torn down.

"What happened here?" the Blood Mage asked the soldier.

"There was a struggle, Sorcerer," the soldier replied. "The last group of savants. When it came time to take them to the temple . . ."

He did not finish the sentence. Miri wondered if those savants had been the three women with them on the ship. Due to the delay with the wagon, she and Gythe had arrived late. Since they were not here, she guessed, heartsick, that they had been murdered.

The dog yelped again. The sound came from the far corner of the room, behind one of the few blankets that was still left hanging. Miri assumed that this must be the girl in question, the special savant.

"Brother Barnaby," the Blood Mage repeated, impatiently.

"I am sorry, Sorcerer," said Brother Barnaby, drawing the blanket aside. "I did not hear you the first time."

Miri stared, appalled. Brother Barnaby had changed so much that if the Blood Mage had not spoken his name, she would not have recognized him. The young monk was emaciated. His robes hung from his shoulders. His ebony skin had gone gray, his face was thin and pinched. He came forward, walking slowly, his head down, his eyes lowered. He kept his hands folded in the tattered sleeves of his tattered brown robe.

"Who is this man?" the woman asked.

"A monk we captured during the attack on Westfirth," the Blood Mage replied. "I generally sacrifice the priests of the false god of those Above. I find their blood is quite powerful. My brother asked me to spare this one. He is skilled in healing. When the girl fell ill, I summoned him to help."

Brother Barnaby came to stand meekly before them.

"The steward has questions about the girl, Brother," said the Blood Mage.

"She was suffering from an extremely painful headache," Brother Barnaby replied. "I applied a cooling poultice. She is sleeping now."

He briefly raised his eyes and fixed the woman with an

intense gaze. The woman met his gaze, steadfast, unwavering.

"I would like to speak to her," said the woman. "I will report her condition to Eiddwen."

Brother Barnaby looked to the Blood Mage for permission. He nodded.

"I will take you to her," Brother Barnaby said.

The woman in gold entered the room. The man with the limp followed behind. The Blood Mage stood in the doorway, watching them, his expression thoughtful. He spoke to the soldier in a low voice.

"They may stay as long as they want. When they leave, I want them followed."

"Yes, Sorcerer," the soldier said obediently.

The Blood Mage departed, going out into the storm. The soldier cast a disgruntled glance at his companion.

"I don't like it. Spying on friends of Attendant Eiddwen. We'll be the ones to catch hell if she finds out."

He turned around and saw Patrick, standing with Miri and Gythe.

"New arrivals," said Patrick, reminding him.

The soldier gestured. "Take them inside the cell."

Once inside the chamber, Miri felt the darkness and the walls close in around her.

"What is going to happen to us?" she asked in dread.

"That depends on Gythe," Patrick replied. "If you need to get a message to me, Brother Barnaby knows how."

"He is one of us," Gythe signed.

Brother Barnaby—part of the resistance? Miri looked at the monk, who was guiding the steward and her companion among the scattered pallets. They moved slowly, due to the man's limp.

The soldier slammed the door. A key turned in the lock. Miri gazed fearfully around the dark and dismal room. "It stinks of death," she said.

Gythe tugged on her sister's hand and pointed toward the sick girl.

"Perhaps you can help her."

"She has Brother Barnaby," Miri snapped. "Tell me again that you didn't come here because of him, Gythe. Tell me that finding him here is a remarkable coincidence."

"Whatever I say, you won't believe me!" Gythe gestured angrily.

She picked her way among the pallets and went to join Brother Barnaby and the others. Miri hesitated, but not for long. She needed something to do, something else to think about beside the fact that she was locked up in prison.

Miri could not see the patient, only a rumpled blanket and a lump underneath it. Suddenly a dog's head popped out. He began barking in excitement. A girl, frail and slender, threw off the blanket and tried frantically to hush him.

"No, Bandit, don't bark!" the girl begged. "You must be quiet or they will take you away from me!"

The dog broke free of her grasp and ran straight to the woman in gold. He began to leap on her, jumping up and down and barking loudly.

"Bandit! What are you doing?" the girl cried, distressed. "Come here this instant!"

The woman picked up the dog in her arms and carried him back to the girl. She knelt down beside her and spoke a name, "Sophia!" in a voice filled with love and anguish.

The girl stared at her and then gave a cry of joy. The woman dropped the dog and took the girl in her arms, weeping over her and murmuring broken words of comfort.

Miri watched in astonishment. Whoever these two were, they meant something to each other. Brother Barnaby knew nothing, apparently. He was looking on in bewilderment. The man with the limp watched in quiet satisfaction.

The girl, Sophia, sagged in the woman's arms, her head lolling. Bandit whimpered and began to lick her face.

"Sophia!" The woman tried to rouse her. She looked urgently around for Brother Barnaby. "Please, you must help her!"

The monk bent over Sophia, felt her pulse. "She has fainted. She has eaten almost nothing since they brought her here."

"Gythe, fetch some water," said Miri, coming to join him as he knelt by the bed.

"You will find a pitcher and a cup on the floor over there," said Brother Barnaby. He rested his hand on Sophia's forehead. "She is already beginning to come around."

Gythe returned with the water. Brother Barnaby lifted Sophia, who was blinking her eyes dazedly. Miri held the water to her lips.

"Thank you for coming with Gythe, Miri," Brother Barnaby said softly.

"I don't want your thanks," Miri retorted. "This is your fault! You brought her here. If anything happens to her, I'll never forgive you." She eyed the monk grimly. "Your God will never forgive you!"

Sophia drank a sip or two of water and the color began to come back into her cheeks. The woman took off her golden mantle and made a bundle of it, using it as a pillow for Sophia.

"My lady . . . ," Sophia began.

"Hush, now, you must lie quiet," said the woman.

She settled down beside Sophia, supporting her with her arm. Sophia gazed up at her anxiously.

"Is my father safe, Countess? Eiddwen told me what

she had done! She said my father and everyone would die—"

"We discovered her plot in time, Your Highness," said the woman in soothing tones. "The engineers are taking measures to undo the damage she caused. You must not worry. All will be well."

"Your Highness!" Miri repeated. She looked at the woman and then back at the girl. "Who is she? She called you 'Countess'? Who are you?"

"You speak Rosian!" said the woman. She regarded Miri curiously. "I heard the guard say you are savants like Sophia. What are your names?"

"I am Miri McPike," said Miri proudly. "And this is my sister, Gythe. We have nothing to hide. Who are you?"

The woman's eyes widened in astonishment.

"Miri . . . ," she repeated in wonder. "And Gythe . . . You have a boat, the *Cloud Hopper*."

Miri drew back, frowning in suspicion. "How do you know us, Lady?"

"I know you well, Miri, though we have never met," said the woman with a faint smile. "I am the Countess de Marjolaine. Stephano's mother."

17

We warned the church of the consequences should they unleash a barrage of contramagic into the world. We foresaw that the disruption of the Breath would cause deadly wizard storms to plunge the world into a hundred years of darkness.

—*Confessions of Saint Marie*

Miri sat back on her heels, stunned. "Countess de Marjolaine!"

She had never met Cecile de Marjolaine, Stephano's formidable mother. He rarely spoke of her and when he did, his comments were bitterly harsh.

Miri had heard the countess described as a great beauty. Cecile was not beautiful now, except for her eyes, which were of a remarkable blue, large and clear and fearless. Her face showed her age, with lines of worry and care, and of weariness. Her clothes were travel worn and stained.

"My lady, how do you come to be here?" Miri asked in bewilderment.

"I could make the same inquiry of you, Miri McPike," Cecile responded with a faint smile. She suddenly leaned forward to ask eagerly, "My son! Is he with you?"

Miri shook her head. "The last we saw of Stephano, he was being arrested by the Arcanum. He is not there!" She added hurriedly, "Your man, D'argent, obtained a pardon from the king."

"What did my son do to get himself arrested this time?" Cecile asked. She could smile now that she knew he was safe.

"According to D'argent, he and Rodrigo did nothing more than talk to Papa Jake—I mean, Father Jacob Northrop. He, too, was arrested. But Rodrigo devised a plan to save the palace and D'argent went to the prince to have them both released."

"The inimitable Monsieur de Villeneuve," Cecile said.

Sophia was cuddling Bandit and resting her head on the countess's shoulder. "My poor father! He must be so angry. Is he very upset with me for running away, Countess?"

"Hush, my dear!" said Cecile softly, soothing her. "Your father loves you dearly. He could never be angry with you."

"But he must be dreadfully worried about me," said Sophia with a sigh. "And it is all my fault!"

"He does not know you ran away. He believes you are with me at my estate. Your father has so many cares, I didn't want to burden him. When you and I return, we will find a way to explain."

"You are so good to me, Countess," said Sophia, nestling against her. "And I don't deserve it. I was a fool to believe Lucello's lies."

"You were not the only one to believe his lies, my dear," said Cecile softly. "He and Eiddwen made fools of us all."

"She is really the princess," said Miri, struggling to understand the enormity of their situation. "The Princess Sophia of Rosia. What is she doing *here*?"

"She was abducted by an evil woman and her cohort. I came here in search of her," said Cecile. "That reminds me, Your Highness, Sir Conal found something that belongs to Bandit and something else that belongs to you."

She reached into a bag and drew out the collar set with the magical stones. Sophia smiled at the sight of the dog collar and summoned Bandit who, unlike his mistress, did not appear pleased to have the collar restored. He squirmed and wriggled until Sophia bribed him with a morsel of bread to hold still.

"Sir Conal," said Miri. "Is he the man with you?"

Miri turned to look at the man with the cane. He was standing next to the door and had his ear pressed to it, listening.

"Sir Conal O'Hairt, a Knight Protector," said Cecile.

Miri lowered her voice to a whisper. "Do these people know they have the princess of Rosia as their prisoner?"

"I must assume Eiddwen took her for a reason," Cecile replied. "At first I thought she wanted her as a hostage, but now I am not so certain. I was told they need savants to stop these wizard storms. Where did they get such a notion?"

"From the writings of the saints, my lady," said Brother Barnaby. "Saint Marie relates that she and her friends came together to pray to God to stop the terrible storms that were ravaging the land during the Dark Ages. We know from history that they succeeded in lessening the severity, though the storms raged on for years. It is common knowledge that Saint Marie and the others were savants."

"I've told them I don't know anything about wizard storms or about being a savant!" said Sophia, trembling. "All I know is that I am afraid. They murdered the others. One of the women said she heard they were going to be sacrificed in some sort of horrible ritual, and they fought when the soldiers came for them. But they had no weapons, and the guards beat them and dragged them away. I thought they would take me, too, but they left me alone. Oh, Countess, I want to go home!"

Sophia buried her face in the countess's shoulder. Bandit howled in shared misery.

Gythe knelt down beside Sophia, took her hand and held it tightly. She touched Sophia on her forehead, smoothing the fair hair with a gentle touch.

Sophia lifted her head and gazed at Gythe, first in astonishment, then in dawning understanding. She stopped trembling.

"You do not speak, Gythe," said Sophia softly. "Yet I can hear your voice. How is that possible?"

"You are both savants," said Brother Barnaby. "Father Jacob was a savant. I served him for many years. He says that the minds of savants can do wonderful things."

"My lady!"

Miri turned to see Sir Conal gesturing to the countess. Cecile glanced at Sophia, uncertain about leaving her.

"I will take care of her, my lady," Gythe indicated her offer by grasping hold of Sophia's hand.

The countess thanked Gythe. Rising from the pallet, she walked over to join Sir Conal. Miri boldly went along, although she hadn't been invited, determined to know what was going on. Brother Barnaby followed at a more discreet distance.

Sir Conal cast Miri a cool, appraising glance, then looked at the countess, raising an eyebrow.

"You may speak freely," said Cecile. "This is Mistress Miri McPike, a friend of my son's. That is her sister, Gythe."

She looked back to where Gythe and Sophia were sitting close together, talking quietly, with Bandit lying between them.

"Yes, Sir Conal, what is it?"

"I have been eavesdropping on the soldiers. It seems we are to have a visitor. Saint Xavier is coming to see us tomorrow morning. I am not certain what this means—"

"I can tell you, sir," said Brother Barnaby, coming forward.

"I believe you know my friend, Sir Ander Martel, Brother," said Sir Conal with a smile.

"I have that honor, sir," said Brother Barnaby, his expression brightening. "How do you know Sir Ander?"

"He is my best friend. He has spoken of you many times, Brother," said Sir Conal. "He feared you were dead. He will be immensely relieved to find out you are alive. Now tell us about Saint Xavier."

"He will come to test Gythe and the princess, to find out if they can stop the storms. They will be safe enough for the time being. But I fear for you and the countess. You are both in danger, sir. Xavier is very close to Eiddwen. If she denounces you, he will have you arrested and put to death."

They were keeping their voices low, but not low enough, apparently, for Sophia overheard them.

"Countess, you must leave!" she cried fearfully. "I will be safe here on my own. Truly. I have Bandit to protect me."

Cecile looked with fond amusement at the little spaniel, who was at that moment lying upside down with all four paws in the air, begging to have his belly scratched.

"Much as I applaud Bandit's courage, I would not think of leaving you, my dear," said Cecile. "Not after I have traveled to hell to find you."

The countess tried to speak lightly, but her voice broke. She paused a moment to clear her throat, then said briskly, "You should go, Sir Conal. The risk to me is minimal. By pretending to be a friend of Eiddwen's I trust I can convince this Xavier to let me stay. But I fear I cannot make the same claim for you."

Sir Conal smiled and shook his head. "I would not be much of a Knight Protector, my lady, if I failed to protect you."

"The countess is right, Sir Conal," said Brother Barnaby earnestly. "As a Warder, your job would be to act as escort to the steward to her destination and then leave when your services are no longer needed. If you behave in any way out of the ordinary, Xavier will become suspicious of both you *and* the countess. You would be putting her in danger, as well as yourself."

Sir Conal listened with a grave expression on his face. "I understand you, Brother. But if I did leave, where would I go?"

"I have friends, sir, who would be glad to shelter you," said Brother Barnaby.

"And who are these friends who would risk their lives for me?"

"Men and women who are loyal to their country, sir," said Brother Barnaby softly.

"Ah!" Sir Conal gazed at the monk intently. "So that is the way the wind blows."

"I don't understand," said Cecile.

"The good brother has friends in the resistance, my lady," Sir Conal whispered.

"Is this true, Brother?" Cecile asked. Her eyes were bright with hope, her face flushed. "We heard about the resistance movement on our way here. We were hoping to contact the rebels to see if they could help us."

She turned back to Sir Conal. "And now we have our chance! You must do as Brother Barnaby suggests, my friend. Meet the rebels, make arrangements for us to escape."

Sir Conal was not convinced. "I am still loath to leave you and the princess."

"Let us be sensible, Sir Conal," said Cecile, clasping his hand. "You cannot help us if you are dead."

Sir Conal laughed, a cheerful, welcome sound in this dismal place. Miri warmed to him. Leaning on his cane, the knight made a gracious, if somewhat awkward bow.

"As you command, my lady. I will be sensible. How do I contact these friends of yours, Brother?"

"The guards believe you to be a warder, sir, one of the Children of Shadow. They will let you leave without question, though they will likely send someone to follow you."

"I can shake off pursuit," said Sir Conal.

"I will give you directions to a tavern called the Goat's Head. It is not far, about two miles from here. Ask for Liam. Tell him you are looking for 'Ander.' He will know I sent you and he will arrange a safe place for you to stay."

"The code word is Ander, is it," said Sir Conal, smiling.

"When I found myself a prisoner, I drew upon the lessons Sir Ander taught me, sir," said Brother Barnaby. "He says that when we encounter evil, we cannot let God fight the battle alone. That is why I joined the resistance."

"Sir Ander has always spoken of you highly, Brother Barnaby," said Sir Conal, reaching out to shake hands. "Now I know why."

Brother Barnaby looked pleased, if embarrassed by the praise. He gave the knight directions to the tavern.

"You should leave now, sir," he added. "The guards will start to wonder why you are staying so long."

"Farewell, my lady," said Sir Conal, his voice soft with emotion. "God keep you and Her Highness in His loving care."

"Good-bye, Sir Conal," said Cecile. She gave him her hand. "My guardian and my friend."

As Sir Conal started to walk to the door, Miri noticed his limp had much improved. On impulse, she joined him.

"I'm coming with you," she said.

He glanced at her in surprise.

"Oh, I'm not trying to escape," Miri assured him. "I need your help. When you go through the door, I will be right behind you. I have to talk to the guards."

"That could be dangerous, mistress," he said, not trying to dissuade her, merely providing her with information.

"I don't think so," Miri replied. "This Xavier needs savants. He's gone to a lot of trouble to bring us here. The guards won't harm me. I was thinking we could work together. I will keep the guards occupied while you slip away."

"A sound plan, mistress," Sir Conal said.

"Just call me Miri," she said.

"And I am Conal, a fellow Trundler. Ready, Miri?"

She nodded. Sir Conal beat on the door with his fist and shouted for the guards.

The key rattled in the lock. As the door swung open, Sir Conal started to walk through, moving slowly, leaning heavily on his cane. Miri bounded past him.

One of the guards raised his weapon.

"Get back inside or there will be trouble," the guard ordered.

"There *will* be trouble, but the trouble will be for *you*, not me!" Miri said tartly.

As she talked, she kept an eye on Sir Conal, who was quietly making his way toward the door.

"The warder told us that Saint Xavier is visiting tomorrow. When he comes, he will find his chosen savants living in conditions not fit for pigs. I want water, soap, mops, and brooms."

"She's right," one said. "We'll get the blame."

"We are not responsible!" the other said, scowling. "Warder Roarke is in charge of the savants."

"Then send for him."

"He will be annoyed . . ."

While the two argued, Miri shot a glance at Sir Conal. He winked at her, quietly opened the door, slipped out, and shut it. The guards never noticed he had gone.

The argument ended with one of the guards leaving to talk to Warder Roarke. The other took hold of Miri and shoved her roughly back into the prison.

"Don't count on it," he told her and shut the door.

But a short time later, he opened the door and came inside hauling buckets of water, soap, brooms, rags and mops. Miri and Gythe and Brother Barnaby began cleaning. Much to Miri's dismay, Cecile joined them.

"My lady, let me carry that," Miri said, shocked to see the countess lifting a slop pail. "You should not do such work."

"Nonsense," said Cecile, refusing Miri's offer. "We all need something to do to keep fear at bay."

"I will help Gythe with the pallets," Sophia offered.

She and Gythe beat and shook out the unused pallets and then stacked them in a corner, a job made more difficult by Bandit, who kept jumping on them. Cecile helped carry out the overflowing slop buckets and then she got down on her hands and knees and began to scrub the floor.

"If Stephano ever again says one word against his mother I will slap him silly!" Miri said to herself.

The cleaning took some time. As she worked, an idea was slowly simmering in Miri's mind. She had rejected it outright as being impossible to achieve and far too dangerous. But her brain continued to mull it over and at last she had to admit to herself that while her plan was still dangerous, it was no longer impossible.

When the cleaning was finished, Miri sought out Brother Barnaby, who was wringing water from the rags and spreading them out to dry.

"Brother, I need to speak to you," Miri said.

"Certainly, mistress," said Brother Barnaby, giving her his full attention.

"*Did* you tell Gythe to come here?" Miri asked, frowning. "Knowing she would be in danger?"

Brother Barnaby shook his head. "The idea was her own, mistress. I tried to dissuade her from coming." He gave a gentle smile. "Your sister is very determined."

"But how did you come to be here?"

"I was taken prisoner at the battle of Westfirth. They captured many priests at that time. They brought us to the temple. They tortured us, asking for information about books written by the saints. At first, I didn't know why. Now I believe they were searching for a way to end these storms."

He spoke calmly of his capture and torment, giving no hint of the pain and suffering he must have endured. His robes were torn in places and Miri could see weals left by the lash on his back, and ugly scars on his chest and arms.

"What happened to the other priests?" Miri asked.

"The Blood Mage took them," said Brother Barnaby. "I presume they were sacrificed in a blood magic ritual."

"How did you survive?" Miri recalled something the Blood Mage had said. "You helped these fiends; the same demons who tortured you and murdered the innocent!"

"They are not fiends, mistress," said Brother Barnaby. "They are God's children."

Miri snorted. "Go on with your story. What about Gythe?"

Brother Barnaby held out his hand, palm up.

"Do you remember when your sister inscribed that construct on my hand—the Trundler sign of friendship. It must have been magical, because when I was alone in the darkness of my cell, in pain and afraid, she sang to me. She sang the old Trundler songs to comfort me and to help me endure the pain. I began to sing with her to keep my spirits up. My captors heard me singing and I think they felt a kind of kinship to me. Most of these people are not evil. They have to make a living, support their families."

"By knocking down our buildings and murdering nuns," said Miri.

Brother Barnaby sighed. "Some are fanatics, that is true, consumed with hatred and rage. In a way, we have had our revenge. The prisoners from Above brought with them a virulent fever. It swept through the prison, striking down guards and prisoners alike. Their healers were at a loss, having never encountered such an illness. I was familiar with typhoid fever and able to treat those who had caught it.

"When some of the Children of Shadow and temple soldiers fell ill with the fever, one of the guards I had treated told Xavier I could help, and he ordered my release from prison. I was treating one of the soldiers, Patrick, and he marveled that I could help my enemy. I told him of my beliefs, and he in turn told me about the resistance, how he and his comrades wanted to stop the war and raise their families in peace. He asked me to join their cause.

"At first I refused. I am not a warrior. But then, when I was treating some of the drummers, I heard them describe the blood magic ceremony and Xavier's plans for the world Above. He intends to plunge the nations into darkness and chaos as retribution for what we did to the people of Glasearrach."

Brother Barnaby looked away, his eyes dark and shadowed. "I knew I could never face Sir Ander or Father Jacob if I did nothing to try to stop Xavier and his evil brother."

"Who are these drummers?" Miri asked. "What do they do?"

"They use blood magic to enhance the power of contramagic, then blazon the magic into the Breath so that its force destroys our magic and takes down buildings, as they did with the Crystal Market."

Miri was dubious. "People banging on drums. From down here. How is that possible?"

"I'm sure Father Jacob could explain," said Brother Barnaby. "I cannot. All I know is that the Blood Mage and his drummers celebrated when word came from their agents that the Crystal Market had fallen. When the invasion fleet sails, they plan to take down many more structures. The drummers boast of being able to destroy continents."

"Stephano must know about this!" Miri muttered.

"I beg your pardon, mistress," said Brother Barnaby. "I didn't hear you."

"Never mind. Patrick told me that when Xavier and his soldiers are gone, the rebels will attack the temple and other military posts throughout Glasearrach. The resistance needs Gythe to stop the storms so that the fleet can sail. But if the invasion fleet sails, Xavier will launch his war against our people," Miri said, trying to puzzle this out. "The rebels must know this."

"The rebels do not care what happens to the world Above, mistress," said Brother Barnaby somberly. "You can hardly blame them. They want to end the suffering of their people here Below."

"And if Gythe doesn't stop the storms, the Blood Mage will butcher us," Miri said, sighing.

She looked at Gythe and Sophia, who were playing with Bandit, laughing at the antics of the little dog. The countess paced the floor, her troubled gaze often resting on Sophia. And in the morning . . . Xavier would come to test them.

Miri made up her mind. "Gythe, Your Highness, put the dog down and come over here. Sit down on that pallet. Countess, please join us. Brother Barnaby, tell them what you told me."

"The guards could be watching us," said Brother Barnaby. "They can observe us through that small window in the door. We should seem to be doing something, otherwise they will think we are conspiring."

"Which is what we are doing," said Miri.

"We can play a round game," Cecile suggested. "How, Why, When, Where. One of us thinks of an object. The rest of you must ask questions to try to figure out what it is. You can only ask, 'Why do you like it? When do you like it? Where do you like it? How do like it?' "

Miri and Gythe exchanged glances. Gythe made a face.

"We know this game," said Miri. "Rigo made us play it when we were stuck on that island. Countess, you start."

Cecile said she was thinking of an object. The others asked questions and she responded. The asking of questions took a considerable amount of thought. During the intervals, Brother Barnaby told in a low voice all that he had told Miri.

"I saw the invasion fleet," said Miri softly. Aloud she said, "I guess the object is a bucket."

"Very good. Miri, it is your turn. I believe you have already thought of something," Cecile added with a flicker of her eyelids.

Miri smiled, taking her meaning. "I have!" she whispered. "Someone needs to warn Stephano about the invasion fleet and bring him to Dunlow to destroy it. Gythe and Sophia will stop the storms—"

Gythe interrupted with strong gestures. "And *you* will go warn him?" She jabbed a finger at Miri. "You cannot sail through the wizard storms! It is too dangerous!"

"That didn't stop *you* from bringing us down here," Miri retorted.

Gythe's hands fell to her lap, and her eyes welled with tears. She suddenly flung her arms around Miri in a fierce embrace. Miri held her close, thinking how hard it would be to sail away and leave her sister behind. In all their years, they had never been separated.

"We are playing a game," Brother Barnaby reminded them in warning tones. His eyes went to the prison door.

"When do you like it, Miri?" Cecile asked loudly. She said in an undertone, "You can take Sophia with you."

Miri shook her head. "The risk to Her Highness would be too great. First I will have to escape from the temple, which will not be easy, and then I will be sailing the Breath in a small boat."

Miri knew the perils. No one better, for she had been sailing since she was tall enough to reach the helm. The odds of surviving a journey through the bone-chilling cold and fierce storms in a small boat were against her. She did not want to elaborate on the danger, however, for fear Gythe would refuse to let her go and Brother Barnaby would refuse his help.

"I would not want to be responsible for the life of Her Highness," Miri concluded.

"And yet, I believe that Sophia's life will be in greater danger if she stays here. She will go with you," said Cecile, softly but firmly. "Sir Conal will accompany you both."

The countess did not raise her voice. She had no need. She spoke calmly and evenly, in the tone of one accustomed to being obeyed. Miri understood how Stephano found it difficult, if not impossible, to oppose his mother.

"Very well, my lady," Miri said, daunted.

"Bandit wants to know how you like it," said Sophia loudly, holding up the little dog. Dropping her voice, she said, "I'm staying here. Miri says Gythe and I need to stop the storms."

"Your Highness," said Cecile, "you must let me advise you in this matter. I know what is best for you."

"You are undoubtedly right, my lady," said Sophia, flushing. "You risked your life to find me. But if I leave, they would have no reason to keep you alive."

"Your Highness is not to consider that," said Cecile.

"But I must! I have to! I don't want to leave," Sophia said earnestly. "I want to stay with Gythe. She says I am gifted in magic and she can teach me. My entire life has been a waste. I have never been of use to anyone. I can be of use now."

"Your Highness, you must not say things like that," said Cecile.

"But it is the truth, my lady. You cannot deny it," said Sophia somberly. "I have been pampered and petted, dressed up like a doll, told to smile prettily and dance well. If it weren't for you, Countess, I would not even know how to read and write. I don't want to be sent away. I want to be useful. I want to help. You taught me that. You told me that as a member of the royal family, I have duties and responsibilities to my people."

Cecile regarded Sophia with mingled exasperation and fond pride. "I had no idea I was such a good teacher." She reached out to take Sophia's hand. "You had the courage and strength and wit to survive an ordeal that would have defeated many others. I am proud of you."

"Then I may stay?" Sophia asked.

"You are a true princess of Rosia, my dear," said Cecile,

smiling. "You have made the decision to help your people. You do not need my permission."

"Then I am staying," said Sophia.

The sound of a key rattling in the lock brought the conversation to an abrupt halt. The door swung open.

"Time to go, Brother," said the guard.

Miri glanced out the prison's single window. She was startled to see that night had fallen, bringing a deeper darkness to this gray, dreary world.

"I must leave now," said Brother Barnaby. "I will return in the morning."

"Please ask Patrick about a boat," Miri said softly.

"I will," said Brother Barnaby. He hesitated, then asked, "Are you sure you want to do this?"

Miri smiled. "You said yourself, Brother. We cannot let God fight this battle alone."

18

The church was appalled when our predictions of disaster came true. They came to our prison to beg us to intercede with God to save them from themselves. We could not bear to see the suffering of the people.

—Confessions of Saint Marie

Cecile rarely slept much, and tonight Miri was too nervous to sleep. The two had spent the evening improving Miri's plan and finding a way for Miri to escape the temple. Afterward, for the first night in many long and sleepless nights, Cecile went to bed with hope in her heart instead of dread. She fell asleep despite the loud cracks of thunder.

Day dawned as usual without the sun. The guards gave them a meager breakfast of bread and dried meat. Cecile didn't protest the small rations; she knew from her journey across Glasearrach that the guards themselves wouldn't eat much better. At her insistence, the men brought fresh water for their ablutions.

Sophia ate the bread and nibbled at the meat, then fed most of her share to Bandit, who relished the treat. Sophia was in markedly better spirits than the previous day. The women carried out the slop buckets and shook the pallets.

Cecile dressed carefully in preparation for Xavier's visit, arranging her hair and putting on her gold mantle. Then she paced, thinking, wondering, going over their plan in her mind, worrying about what might go wrong. At about midday, the guards opened the door, admitted Brother Barnaby, then left, closing the door behind themselves.

"Xavier is coming," he said, adding in an undertone, "He is not far behind me."

"What about the boat?" Miri asked.

"I spoke to Patrick last night," said Brother Barnaby. "He can obtain a boat, something similar to your houseboat. Trundlers use such boats to sail from Dunlow to the port towns on the coast, taking goods to market."

He started to add something, then fell silent.

"What?" Miri demanded.

"Patrick does not think your plan will succeed. Those from Below who have attempted to sail such small craft into the Breath have either been forced to return or have never returned at all."

"These people live their lives on the ground," Miri said with a disdainful sniff. "What do they know about sailing the Breath? Tell me more about this boat. How much sail does she carry? How many lift tanks?"

His eyes widened at these questions.

"I don't—"

Cecile heard a commotion outside the door.

"Hush!" she whispered. "Make ready!"

The guards opened the door again, and Xavier entered.

Cecile had not been certain what to expect: a madman, a despot, a fanatic. When she saw him, she realized he could not be so easily defined.

Xavier looked to be in his early fifties with dark hair tinged with gray, like his brother's. He wore it cut short, which looked good on him. He was of medium height and build. His eyes were large and gray; he had the pale complexion of all those living Below. He was clean shaven, though the shadow of his beard was blue against his white skin. He wore a sky blue mantle over breeches and a homespun shirt.

He told the guards to leave him and they obeyed, withdrawing and shutting the door.

As Xavier advanced to the middle of the room, he studied each of the women in turn. He seemed interested, not threatening. When his gaze shifted to Cecile, she was surprised. His gray eyes were shadowed, their light obscured by the shadow of some heavy burden.

As she studied him more closely she noted that although he tried to appear austere and aloof, as befitted a ruler, the deep creases around his mouth spoke of bitter resignation, the lines around his eyes of disillusionment.

"This man once believed in miracles," Cecile said to herself. "He doesn't anymore."

Cecile had lived in the Rosian royal court since the age of sixteen and she had visited the royal courts of other nations. Palace intrigue was the same the world over, and the court in Glasearrach was no different. Those who surrounded Xavier might term themselves warders, stewards, or attendants, but they were the same sycophants, flatterers, and obsequious liars who fawned over every ruler.

Alaric believed the lies and basked in the flattery, but she sensed that Xavier saw through the lies to the ugly truth that lay beneath; he could trust no one and that grieved him.

She met his gaze coolly and held it. At the sight of her gold mantle, he frowned slightly. He must be wondering about her, why had he never noticed her among his followers.

Cecile wondered how to deal with this complex man. She wished she had more time to come to know him, especially since she dared not make a mistake in her judgment with the lives of people precious to her at stake. He seemed to be waiting for her to speak and she had no idea what to say. Fortunately Bandit chose that moment to break free of Sophia's grasp. Barking madly, the dog made a dash at Xavier.

He shifted his gaze from Cecile to the dog, though he didn't really seem to see him. Here was a man whose thoughts turned inward, who had withdrawn into himself and shut the doors and bolted the windows.

Gythe caught hold of the spaniel, who was not nearly as hard to grab as the Doctor when he was bent on mischief. She returned the dog to Sophia, who clasped her hand over Bandit's muzzle and told him in frightened tones to be quiet.

Xavier turned to Sophia and spoke to her in Rosian, which told Cecile he already knew something about her. His voice was deep and resonant, an orator's voice, one accustomed to holding an audience in thrall.

"The guards were ordered to give you special treatment, young woman. Why is that? Because you are a princess?"

Sophia paled. She didn't know how to respond.

"Because she is a savant," said Cecile. "You must know this, sir. You ordered Eiddwen to bring her here. As you ordered her to sabotage the Rosian royal palace."

Cecile saw a frown line in his forehead deepen. What she had suspected was true, then. He knew nothing of Eiddwen's orders to sabotage the royal palace. The order had been given in his name.

"And did she succeed?" Xavier asked, more out of curiosity than because he truly cared.

"I pray not, sir," said Cecile earnestly.

"And who might you be, Steward?" He regarded her

gravely. "I was told you came with an urgent message for me."

Cecile slightly smiled. "That was a ruse. I am not a steward, sir, as you must have already guessed. I stole this mantle at the monastery of Saint Dominick's in order to speed my travels through Glasearrach. I am Lady Cecile de Marjolaine of the Rosian royal court. I came to find the princess. Her Royal Highness is my only care, my only concern."

Miri was staring at her in shock, Gythe in horror, and Sophia looked dismayed. All of them must be thinking that she had lost her mind, that by telling him the truth, she was placing all of them in danger.

They didn't understand. Cecile could tell by his questions and the way he looked at her that he already knew she was not who she claimed to be.

A man accustomed to lies can find the truth refreshing. Xavier was interested.

"One of my followers . . . what was his name . . . Paul, I believe . . . He was a spy, posed as a monk. He worked as a courier for the grand bishop. Did you know him?"

Cecile shook her head. "The grand bishop and I are not on the best of terms, sir."

"I am properly addressed as *Naomh,*" Xavier said. "That is Trundler for 'saint.' "

Cecile curtsied. "I am properly addressed as Countess or my lady."

Xavier almost smiled. His deep-set eyes flickered.

"Paul reported that the Princess Sophia was extraordinarily sensitive. He said she heard drumbeats that gave her debilitating headaches. Is that true, *my lady*?"

"I will let Her Highness tell you herself," Cecile replied.

"I can feel the drumbeats inside me, *N-Naomh,*" said

Sophia, faltering over the Trundler word. "The drums pound in my head and my heart. The pain burns like fire."

He was about to say something more when Gythe advanced, making emphatic gesture with her hands and pointing to herself. Xavier stared at her perplexedly.

"What is she doing?"

"She asks to speak to you, *Naomh,*" said Miri, coming forward to stand with Gythe.

"Why doesn't she talk then if she has something to say?" Xavier asked with a flash of annoyance.

"My sister cannot speak, *Naomh,*" said Miri. "She has not spoken since she was a child. She is a savant, like the princess, and myself. She knows what causes the headaches."

Gythe's hands moved.

"She says the same contramagic that creates the wizard storms affects those who are sensitive to magic, causing them pain."

Xavier seized on one word. "Contramagic! How does she know about contramagic? The study of such magic is forbidden."

"How we know is not important," said Miri. "But with such knowledge, Gythe and the princess and I can stop the wizard storms."

"No savants before you have been able to stop them," said Xavier, frowning.

"That is because they did not truly understand the connection between magic and contramagic," said Miri.

"You two are Trundlers," Xavier said abruptly.

"We are," said Miri, lifting her head with pride. "I am Miri and this is Gythe. We are members of the McPike clan."

"You might well have cousins down here," said Xavier. His eyes grew shadowed. "We expected *our* cousins Above to come to our rescue. We cried out to them, but they did not come."

Gythe touched her ears and shook her head. "They could not hear you."

"They heard us," said Xavier grimly. "They wanted us to sink out of their knowledge." And with that, he fell silent.

Miri's eyes burned with anger, and she was about to speak, but Cecile flashed her a warning glance, so she was quiet, biting her lip.

"I have been Above many times," said Xavier at last. "My father took me when I was a young man. I remember standing in the sunshine for the first time. I couldn't see very well; the light hurt my eyes. I wept to see the sunlight. I wept to think of how many hundreds of years we have lived in darkness. I wanted to bring my people to this land of light."

"Why are you attacking us?" Cecile asked softly, wondering, not accusing. "Why start a war? You could have come in peace."

"And what sort of welcome would we have received, Countess?" Xavier asked. He eyed her shrewdly. "The last time our people came to your world in peace, they were murdered."

Cecile had no answer. She twisted the gold ring on her finger.

"We practice contramagic," Xavier continued. "We know many ugly truths about the church. At the very least we would be an embarrassment to your bishop and your king. At the worst, a serious threat. War between our worlds was inevitable. We decided to strike the first blow, that is all."

"Murdering innocent nuns," Miri said, glowering.

"How many innocents died when our island was sunk?" Xavier returned angrily.

Cecile hastily intervened, trying to keep everyone calm. "You want to bring your people into the light, *Naomh*. But if you are victorious, you will destroy the light. Centuries ago, the contramagic that sank your island plunged the world into the Dark Ages. The drumming, if it continues, will have the same effect."

For a moment, discussing the war, Xavier had been passionate, engaged. But now, he retreated back into himself again. He glanced at the window. The morning was dark with rain.

"You already know that," Cecile said in sudden understanding.

"When I was young, I thrilled to hear the drumbeat." Xavier spoke in a low tone, perhaps more to himself than to them. "My brother and I were eager to witness the blood magic ritual. My brother was enthralled, but I was horrified by the blood and the screams of the dying. My father told me those who were sacrificed went to their deaths willingly, proud to be chosen."

He looked up, his eyes shadowed, haunted. "Now, I hear the screams and I know my father was lying."

"Then stop it," said Miri.

"I cannot. I am Xavier." He looked at Cecile, to see if she understood.

Cecile shook her head. If she did, she wanted to hear his thinking.

"I represent all the Xaviers who came before me, who dreamed of the day we would avenge ourselves on those who left us here to die in the darkness. Sometimes I feel their hands," he added softly, "pushing me from behind, shoving me forward. This is their dream, the dream of my people."

His voice hardened. "I will not abandon it."

The thought came to Cecile that ironically, Xavier and his foe, Grand Bishop Montagne, were very much alike:

both were impelled by the same forces from the past to take actions that might destroy what they fought to save.

"I have business I must conduct this day," Xavier said briskly, breaking in on her musings. "You savants will work your magic tomorrow."

Miri cast Cecile an alarmed glance. Tomorrow would be too soon. They would not be ready, either to stop the storm or to arrange Miri's escape.

"We have only just arrived," Cecile said. "We are tired. The princess is not well—"

"Tomorrow," said Xavier, his voice grating. He started to leave, then turned around. "The man who escorted you, Countess, the warder with the limp. Where is he?"

Cecile shrugged. "I have no idea. I lied to his commander, told him I was a steward. He gave the warder orders to bring me safely here. Once he had discharged his duty, he left."

Xavier gazed at her long and steadily, then turned on his heel and walked to the door. Rapping on it, he called out that he was ready to leave. The door opened, and as he started to walk through it, he glanced over his shoulder at Cecile. His expression darkened. He seemed puzzled, perhaps wondering why he had revealed so much of himself.

Cecile knew the reason, even if he did not. "We are fellow prisoners," she murmured.

He left without another word. When the guards had shut the door again, nobody spoke.

"What a strange man," said Miri, breaking the silence. "Not what I expected."

"I don't understand him," said Sophia. "He is a king, like my father. He could stop the killing if he really wanted to. 'I am Xavier.' What does that mean?"

"He is a king, but he is a desperate king," said Cecile. "His rule is crumbling. He knows he has lost the trust of the people. He needs this war to restore the faith of his followers not only in himself, but in those Xaviers who came before him. He must justify their terrible deeds. He is desperate and that makes him dangerous."

She turned to Brother Barnaby.

"I am afraid for Sir Conal. Xavier knows he is not truly a warder, any more than I am a steward. He will send men searching for him. What will happen to him, Brother? Can you and the rebels protect him?"

Brother Barnaby shook his head, troubled. "We can hide Sir Conal for a short time, but as long as he remains here, he is at risk. He should sail back to Rosia with Mistress Miri."

"I'm not sailing anywhere yet," Miri pointed out. "Can Patrick have the boat ready by tomorrow?"

"He will have to," said Brother Barnaby.

"I feel very stupid," said Sophia, blushing. "How can I use magic to stop a storm? I've never practiced magic."

Gythe and Brother Barnaby gazed at her in silent shock.

"Is this true, my lady?" Miri asked, dismayed. "Her Highness has never used her magic?"

"I am afraid it is," Cecile replied. "She and I studied the history of magic, of course, and I taught her how to form constructs. But the practical use of magic is not considered proper work for a princess."

"My mama said it would frighten away a husband," said Sophia. Going to Cecile, she put her arm around her and laid her head on her shoulder. "I don't want a husband. If we ever get back home, I never want to leave."

Cecile held her close and comforted her. Miri muttered something in the Trundler language and ran her hand distractedly through her red curls.

"What are we going to do?" Miri demanded. "Gythe and Sophia must show they can stop the storms, even if only for a little while, or Xavier will give them to the Blood Mage. *And* we need them to divert the attention of the guards so that I can escape."

"Unless . . ." Cecile paused to consider her idea.

"Unless what, my lady?" Miri asked.

"Unless your escape diverts attention from Sophia and Gythe," said Cecile.

She explained her plan. Miri listened and approved.

"I think it could work." Her gaze went to Gythe. "But now I'm not certain I should leave."

Gythe knew what her sister was thinking, for she began speaking, her hands flashing, excited, enthusiastic.

Brother Barnaby translated. "Gythe says you must not worry. She can work the magic. She will teach Sophia."

"She has so much to learn," Miri said in worried tones.

Brother Barnaby smiled reassuringly. "Sophia says she has never used her magic. I believe she has, although she might not know it. She could hear the drumming even when she was in the palace. She can hear Gythe's voice in her mind and Gythe can hear hers."

Miri was still not convinced. "Gythe, when you stopped the storm that was threatening to sink the *Cloud Hopper,* you said you didn't know how your magic worked. How can you teach Sophia what to do if you don't know what you did?"

Gythe laughed, but when she saw Miri's somber expression, she stopped.

"I know now," she signed.

Spreading her arms, she lifted her face, smiling joyously, as though she could see far beyond the prison walls. Blue sparkles of magic danced in the air and she began to whirl around and around like a child playing in the rain. Miri didn't understand, but then she had never understood Gythe. She had, though, come to trust her.

"I have the feeling you are all trying to get rid of me,"

Miri said, but she smiled as she said it. "Brother Barnaby, tell Patrick to have the boat ready tomorrow. And you can tell Sir Conal he can come with me—if he dares."

Gythe clapped her hands and then sat down to talk animatedly with Sophia using a combination of signs and sharing their words in their minds. Miri stood some distance away, watching her sister with pride and affection. Brother Barnaby bade them farewell, saying he had to leave them to help Patrick with the arrangements for tomorrow.

"I will walk with you, Brother, if I may," said Cecile. "I need to speak to you about Sir Conal."

"Of course, my lady."

"I have a task for you regarding him, Brother."

"I will be glad to help in any way I can, my lady," Brother Barnaby replied.

"Sir Conal will not want to leave me, no matter the risk to himself. You must persuade him to go with Mistress Miri. Tell him this mission is of the greatest importance to me."

Brother Barnaby was dubious. "Sir Conal is a Knight Protector and if he is like Sir Ander, my lady, he views his duty as given to him by God. I am not certain I can persuade him."

"And yet, you must do so, Brother. Sir Conal has knowledge of Xavier's military, of the disposition of forces, armaments and the like. Stephano will need such information."

"Sir Conal *does* seem a sensible man," said Brother Barnaby, as they reached the door. "I will carry your message. God bless and keep you, my lady."

He knocked on the door and the guards let him out. Cecile, hearing laughter, turned to see Gythe and Sophia playing cat's cradle. She walked over to watch them, regarding them in wonder.

"I thought they were working on the magic," she said to Miri.

"They are, my lady," said Miri. "Watch."

Gythe had tied the ends of a piece of string together with a square knot. She hooked the string over her thumbs and then her little fingers, thrust the middle finger of one hand into the loop, as the middle finger of the other hand pulled the string to form yet another loop. She began to work the string deftly to form the "cradle," singing softly as she worked.

Sophia watched, fascinated.

"What must I do?" she asked.

"Place your fingers here and here, pinch, and you can lift the string from Gythe's hands onto yours," said Miri.

Sophia did as she was told, taking hold of the "cradle" and transferring it to her own hands. She laughed in delight.

"Now, Your Highness," said Miri, "I want you to picture the strings as magical constructs."

Gythe sang again, and the cradle began to take on a faint blue glow. Sophia stared, entranced. Gythe took the string from Sophia's hands and formed a more intricate net. She nodded at Sophia and sang more loudly, urging Sophia to join in the song, which was about a dog who chased a cat who chased a bird who chased a rat and so on.

"This is for you, Bandit," said Sophia, laughing and starting to sing.

Gythe dropped the string. The blue glowing constructs remained in the air, twined around her hands. Sophia gingerly reached out, touched them, and gasped as she found she was able to manipulate them. The blue glow strengthened, shining brightly.

The tangle of constructs grew, flaring with bright blue

light. Bandit watched the blue glow from a safe distance, his head tilting to one side, then the other.

And then the drumming began.

The drumbeats were slow and irregular at first until the drummers fell into the rhythm. The beating of the drums, coming from the temple, grew louder and louder.

Sophia gave a piercing scream and bent double, clasping her head in her hands and moaning. Gythe dropped the magic. The blue glowing constructs vanished. Bandit gave a piteous howl.

Miri hurried to the princess. "Your Highness, what can I do help you? What does Brother Barnaby do?"

"The potion!" Sophia moaned and fumbled for something beneath her pillow.

She drew out a glass vial with a cork stopper. Her hands shook so violently she could not open it. Gythe took the vial, popped out the cork and sniffed. She wrinkled her nose and handed the vial to Miri.

"Laudanum," said Miri, smelling the bitter odor. "Opium laced with alcohol. Brother Barnaby did not give you that."

Sophia was distressed. She lowered her eyes.

"Eiddwen gave her the potion," said Cecile in grim understanding. "That is how she pretended to help her. She drugged her."

Miri poured the contents into one of the slop pails.

The drumming stopped as suddenly as it had begun, but the silence that followed was almost worse than the beating of the drums. Cecile could hear the rain dripping off the roof of the prison, the low rumble of receding thunder, the grumble of another storm lying in wait on the horizon.

Gythe began to sing again. Sophia brightened, her pain eased. She had a good ear for music. Cecile thought back with a pang to the many times they had played duets together and wondered if those sweet, peaceful hours would ever come again.

Sophia's voice was light and thin. Bandit had no taste for music, apparently, for he started to growl, and Sophia laughed at him. Gythe jumped up and held out her hands to Sophia. The two began to whirl around the room as Bandit chased after them, barking wildly.

Miri and Cecile stood together, watching the young women dance, their hands clasped tightly, twirling until they made each other dizzy.

"I have so many misgivings about leaving," said Miri.

"I know you do," said Cecile.

"What if I fail? What if I die or I'm captured? What will become of Gythe?"

"I will care for her as though she were my own sister," said Cecile. "Do not doubt yourself, Miri. You are courageous and resourceful. I know now why Stephano is in love with you."

Miri blushed crimson and flashed a startled look at Cecile.

"Did he . . . did he say that, my lady?"

"My son does not confide in me," Cecile replied. "But a mother knows these things."

Miri recovered herself. The crimson faded. "You don't have to worry, my lady. I would never marry Stephano. He is the son of a knight and a countess, and I am a Trundler's daughter."

Cecile reached out to brush Miri's red curls off her face, then gave her a gentle kiss on the cheek.

"I would be proud and glad to call you *my* daughter."

19

Our prayers calmed the storms to some extent, but we could not fully assuage God's wrath. Until mankind learns wisdom, I fear eons will pass before harmony can be restored to the song of the universe.

—*Confessions of Saint Marie*

The women were too nervous to eat that morning, much to the delight of the guards, who had a second breakfast. Brother Barnaby arrived early on the pretense of treating Sophia for her headaches.

"Patrick has a small houseboat which he thinks *might* survive the journey through the Breath."

Miri heard the emphasis on the word "might," but pretended she didn't.

"Patrick has made the journey through the Breath many times," Brother Barnaby continued. "He fears—"

Miri fixed him with a warning glance. Brother Barnaby took the hint and said no more. Gythe, though, heard the unspoken words and looked sorrowfully at Miri. Even though Gythe had urged Miri to go, Miri knew her sister was afraid for her.

"Patrick is a soldier, not a sailor," said Miri, sniffing.

"What of Sir Conal? Is he safe?" Cecile asked, deftly changing the subject.

"He is safe for the moment, although we had to shuffle him from one secret location to another. The soldiers are searching for a man matching his description. Since people began hiding their loved ones to keep them from being used as blood sacrifices, the soldiers know where to look," said Brother Barnaby. "Patrick's men will take Sir Conal to the boat. He will be waiting for you, Miri."

Barnaby gave a wry smile. "As you predicted, my lady, Sir Conal did not want to leave you or the princess. Your argument that he had valuable information Captain de Guichen could use finally persuaded him."

"He is a good man," said Cecile.

And then no one had any more to say. The sound of thunder rumbled through the room. Another storm was approaching and with it, Xavier. He would want to see Gythe and Sophia stop one of the wizard storms, as they had promised. Here was his chance.

Sophia was pale and trembling. She held fast to Bandit and talked to him softly, telling him not to be afraid. Gythe was singing snatches of a song. Cecile was braiding a leash for Bandit out of the string Gythe had used for the cat's cradle.

As Miri watched them her courage almost failed her. Her fear was not for herself so much, but for those she was going to leave behind.

"Are we all in agreement?" she asked abruptly. "Do we go through with this? The risks are great."

Gythe motioned with her hands. Sophia answered for them both.

"Gythe and I have practiced the magic," she said in a low voice. "We know what we have to do. And so does Bandit."

She kissed the dog and then handed him to the countess, who tied the leash to his collar. He immediately began to whine and tried to squirm out of the countess's hold.

"I am not certain about Bandit," said Cecile. "But I am prepared." She smiled reassuringly. "The risks are great, Miri, but they are greater if we do nothing."

"Have faith," said Brother Barnaby. "God is with you."

"God isn't going to be the one sailing a rickety houseboat through the Breath," Miri muttered, keeping her voice low so as not to shock Brother Barnaby.

The storm broke, sending rain thudding on the roof and thunder shaking the ground. They almost didn't hear the key turning in the lock, but they all heard one of the soldiers say in warning tones, "Make ready. Xavier's coming!" just before he slammed shut the door.

"He is one of ours," said Brother Barnaby softly.

"One of the resistance?" Miri asked, startled.

Brother Barnaby nodded.

The key turned again in the lock and Xavier entered, followed by a soldier carrying heavy woolen cloaks, which he distributed to the women. Xavier wore a cloak that buttoned down the front with the hood drawn up to protect against the rain. Strange constructs had been sewn into the fabric. Miri thought back to something Patrick had said:

Xavier has survived three assassination attempts. His clothes are steeped in magical constructs. I have heard some people claim he has found a way to inscribe magical protective spells on his flesh.

"It is time," Xavier said. "As with the previous savants, I have assembled people to serve as witnesses. You will perform your magic in the center of the square, where all can see."

This was good; it meant that members of the resistance would be among the crowd.

"You will be in the full fury of the storm," Xavier continued.

"We do not fear the storm," said Miri boldly. "We will command the storm."

Xavier looked at the group and raised an eyebrow. Miri supposed she really couldn't blame him for being skeptical. Gythe was serene, she almost seemed to be in another world. At the other extreme, Sophia was shivering, while trying very hard to be brave. The countess seemed impassive, almost bored. He must be wondering how these few women—his prisoners—could have any effect on the fierce magical storms sweeping over his land.

"We are ready," said Miri.

"Walk with God," said Brother Barnaby softly.

Bandit howled dejectedly.

Xavier accompanied them, allowing Cecile to remain with Sophia, which Miri was surprised to see. Perhaps he had seen the determined look on the countess's face and decided trying to prevent her would not be worth the battle.

Xavier did flatly refuse to allow the dog to come, and Brother Barnaby offered to remain behind with Bandit, whose earsplitting wails were heartrending.

The group of them emerged from the prison into the teeth of a ferocious wizard storm. The wall around the compound sheltered them from the raging wind, but it could not protect them from the driving rain. Their cloaks were soaked the moment they stepped into the courtyard and they were thankful to hurry inside the temple, to gain some respite from the storm.

Miri soon found that walking through the shadowy

corridors of the temple was worse than being out in the storm. The drumming yesterday must have been accompanied by more sacrifices, for the stench of fresh blood seemed to suffuse the air.

Xavier led the way, with Gythe and Sophia following him, their hands clasped. The countess walked directly behind them, staying near the princess, and Miri came last.

With her concentration fixed on what she had to do, she did not notice the foul smell that was making the others gag. She was frightened, but resolute. She did not let herself dwell on the danger of escaping Xavier's forces or flying through the Breath; she would worry about all that when the time came to act.

Xavier briskly led them to the front of the temple, where the soldiers on guard there flung open the doors.

He nodded to his brother, the Blood Mage, who stood on the stairs outside the doors to the temple, his crimson robes whipping in the wind. He was surrounded by a large group of men and women dressed in crimson mantles with drums slung across their shoulders. These must be the drummers who combined blood magic and contramagic in an effort to try to silence the voice of God. The drummers had their hoods pulled over their bowed heads. They muttered among themselves, not appearing at all pleased to be standing, unsheltered, in the fury of the storm.

The Blood Mage turned to the prisoners and regarded them with cold, glittering eyes. Perhaps he was thinking they would soon be within his grasp. Miri shuddered and looked away.

"You will come with me," Xavier said, indicating Gythe, Sophia, and Miri.

He stopped Cecile when she would have gone with them. "You will stay here."

As several guards moved to stand around Cecile, Sophia drew back and cast a frightened glance at the countess.

Cecile gave her a reassuring smile. "I will tell your father how brave you are, Your Highness. He will be proud of you."

Sophia managed a smile. "I will work the magic, my lady. It's just like playing cat's cradle."

Miri risked a glance back and saw Cecile inside the door of the temple raising her hand in farewell. The countess's lips formed the words: "Give my love to my son!"

Miri nodded and, not watching where she was going, stumbled over the hem of her sodden skirt and bumped into one of the soldiers, who ordered her harshly to pay attention.

The wall around the temple sheltered them from the wind. Beyond, in the plaza, they would have no protection. The guards had to struggle to open the gate, pushing against the fury of the wind, and at last managed.

A crowd had gathered in the plaza, waiting in drenched and stoic silence to see if these latest savants could stop the storm. Patrick must be somewhere in that crowd, but Miri despaired of finding him. She could scarcely see anything through the downpour and she doubted if she would have known him anyway. Every person in the plaza was muffled against the rain.

Xavier walked through the gate with an army of soldiers around him and the women following. Once out of the shelter of the wall, they were nearly knocked down by the wind. The storm pummeled them defiantly, as though daring them to try to thwart it. They fell behind. Xavier, forging on ahead, did not seem to notice.

Miri cast a glance back at the Blood Mage. His face bore a slight smile.

"We have to get out there into the plaza!" she gasped.

Gythe took hold of Miri and Sophia and clasped their hands tightly. Looking up into the roiling clouds, Gythe began to sing. Rain struck her face. The wind beat against her slight body. Gythe began to sing the song about the dog.

She sang loudly, encouraging Sophia, who joined in after a moment, spluttering and gulping rain water. Miri knew the song and joined them. Energy tingled through her body. A faint blue glow glimmered around Gythe's hand, twined around Miri's and spread to Sophia's hand. Gythe walked forward, defying the storm, drawing Sophia and Miri with her.

The wind eased and the rain let up. Around her, Miri heard murmuring from the crowd. Led by Gythe, the three women came to the center of the plaza where Xavier was waiting for them.

Miri caught a glimpse of movement. A man standing in front drew back a green scarf that covered his face: Patrick. He lifted the scarf up over his face and faded back among the crowd.

Gythe released Miri's hand.

"Take care of yourself. Tell Stephano and Petard I miss them," Gythe said silently.

Miri needed all her courage and resolve to let go of her sister. She felt as if she were walking off and leaving her soul behind.

"We will come for you!" she said finally.

Gythe smiled and turned to Sophia. The two held fast to each other.

"Stand here," Xavier ordered.

He pointed at the rain-swept mosaic, the first initial of his name, of the names of all the Xaviers. Gythe and Sophia began to sing the children's song about the nine goblins. Miri sang along, pretending to work with them.

The words of the song were in Rosian, and Miri doubted many in the crowd would understand. She could tell by Xavier's frown, though, that he understood. He must be wondering how a song about nine little goblins sitting on a fence could quell a storm.

At first nothing happened. The rain fell. The wind plucked at their cloaks. Then, shimmering "fireflies" of blue magical light began to dance and sparkle around the young women. The fireflies gathered into a swirling swarm that delighted the eye. Children in the crowd pointed and laughed. The adults watched in wary awe. Xavier was still frowning, but he seemed intrigued.

Now the raindrops began to glitter with a bright blue light, falling from the heavens in a shimmering curtain of dazzling, twinkling magic. Xavier was no longer frowning. He was gazing up in awe at the sparkling drops falling on his face. The crowd was silent, spellbound.

A whistle pierced the silence. At the signal, the rebels surged forward. Xavier's bodyguards shouted for him to take cover and fired into the air. As green fireballs burst above them, people began to flee in panic. Gythe and Sophia stopped singing and were staring around in bewilderment.

A man seized Miri around the waist and started to drag her off.

"Kick me," Patrick growled. "You're being abducted!"

Miri screamed and kicked. Xavier ordered his soldiers to rescue the prisoner, but a sea of bodies intervened, rolling over the soldiers and washing them away. At the end of the plaza, the crowd parted, opening a way for them and then quickly flowing in behind them to block pursuit. Patrick held her tightly and soon they were out of the plaza and into the streets of the town.

Miri looked over her shoulder. The plaza was empty,

the crowd melting away. She could not see Gythe or Sophia or Xavier.

Well, she thought, it's done. No going back.

The wind had died and the pelting rain was now only a drizzle. Lightning flickered in the distance, and the thunder sounded subdued. Miri had seen Gythe and Sophia work their magic and force the wizard storm to retreat. She wasn't sure how she felt about that: she'd have to think about it later.

She and Patrick entered a maze of streets and hurried down alleyways into more alleyways. They ran one way, then turned around and doubled back. At last Patrick stopped so that they could catch their breath and see if anyone was following. Miri gasped for air, almost dizzy with the exertion.

The street was empty, the buildings looming over them were dark, though here and there light gleamed through a gap in a curtain.

"The boat is at the edge of town," Patrick said. "I think we've thrown off pursuit for the moment, but Xavier's soldiers will be out in force. We must keep going."

Miri lacked the breath to answer, but she nodded to show she understood. Patrick slowed to a brisk walk, keeping Miri alongside. She wondered what had become of Gythe and Sophia and the countess. It was the countess who had devised the plan of making the escape appear to be an abduction. Xavier would not suspect her or the others of being complicit.

Miri hoped the plan had worked and that they were safe. Sophia and Gythe had not had time to drive away the storms and bring back the sunshine, but they had proven their magic could calm the storms. Xavier would not let the Blood Mage have them. Not without seeing more of what their magic could do.

The pavement came to an abrupt end. One moment Miri had been hurrying down a street surrounded by buildings and the next moment the town seemed to simply stop and she was looking out over a vast plain of rain-flattened grass and mud.

"There's the boat," said Patrick, pointing.

"God have mercy!" said Miri.

The boat was based on an old, old Trundler design that had been modified so that its passengers could survive sailing through storms or, she hoped, the Breath. The gunwales were solid wood and came up to about chest height. The cabins below had small portholes instead of larger windows, and the bridge and helm both were fully enclosed to provide protection from the elements. The mainmast and boom were considerably heavier than the original fittings to brave the winds and the wings had been reinforced.

The boat had been covered by a tarp that now lay off to one side, resting on a crude dock made of slats of wood.

Recovering from the first shock of seeing the strange boat, Miri was both relieved and impressed.

"We might have a chance," she conceded.

As she and Patrick waded out into the mud and wet, stringy, long grass that tangled around their feet Miri noticed several other houseboats in the field. Some rested on their sides, perhaps blown over by the wind. Others were mired so deeply in mud it would take a team of horses to drag them out.

"This area was once a harbor," said Patrick. "Until the storms grew so bad no one could sail."

"My boat seems to be in good shape compared to the rest," Miri observed.

"That's because it belongs to Xavier," said Patrick.

Miri gasped. Now that she looked, she could see the *X*

painted on the sails and the balloon. "We're stealing his boat? Aren't there guards? Won't he discover it's missing?"

"He hasn't used it in years. No one ever comes here anymore. The place is like a graveyard. Don't worry. Xavier would never imagine you would try to escape by boat."

"Because he could not imagine I would be so stupid," Miri stated.

Patrick smiled slightly, then gestured.

"That man, Conal, is on board, waiting for you," Patrick continued. "I'll wait here to cast off the lines."

Sir Conal waved to her. He had already lowered the gangplank. Miri boarded the boat and took a critical look around. The bulkheads were painted in black lacquer, giving it a gloomy air, and the boat's beam was narrower than the beam on the *Cloud Hopper,* but overall, the size was comparable.

"Captain Miri." Sir Conal greeted her with a flourishing salute. "Welcome aboard."

"How much do you know about boats, Sir Conal?" Miri asked, eyeing him. "You being a Trundler, you must have sailed the Breath some in your life."

"You are wondering if I'm going to be a help or a hindrance. I still remember how to splice the main brace and haul on the bowline," Sir Conal replied with a grin. "And I know my port from my starboard. Tell me what to do and I will do it."

"Thank you, Sir Conal," said Miri, relieved. This journey was going to be difficult enough without having to deal with a landlubber. "If you could go below and make certain everything is stowed securely, I will inspect the helm."

The helm had been her biggest worry. If the constructs

were contramagic, this was going to be a very short voyage.

She was pleased to find that the constructs were not contramagic, though they were very old-fashioned, not as elegant or streamlined as those on her boat. After a moment's experimenting, she figured out how the magic worked. The helm responded to her touch. She inspected the rest of the craft. It appeared to be well built, sound. Her uncle would have approved.

Trundlers here Below were not so different, after all.

Sir Conal returned to report that all was secure, the hold was stocked with water and food enough to last a week.

"And blankets and heavy peacoats to survive the cold," he added.

"Are you ready, Miri?" Patrick called. "You should leave now. Another storm is brewing."

Miri put her hands on the helm. Sir Conal was in the bow, waiting for Patrick to cast off the mooring line. He looked at her expectantly. Patrick watched in growing impatience.

Miri had only to move her hands over the magical constructs on the brass helm. Her hands were frozen. She couldn't move a finger. She kept thinking of the perils that lay ahead of them. They would have to sail through wizard storms and endure the mind-numbing cold and the wind currents of the Breath in this ramshackle cockleshell. And if they survived all that, they would surface with no idea where they were and running low on lift gas.

"No going back," Miri said to herself.

She drew in a deep breath and touched the helm. She felt the magic sparkle through her as she channeled the magic and sent it running along the cables, then the familiar thrill of the boat coming to life at her command. Patrick cast off the lines. Sir Conal hauled the ropes aboard and deftly coiled them and stowed them in their proper place. The houseboat rose off the ground.

When Miri felt the wind in her face her fears and worries vanished.

You are born to the Breath, Miri, her uncle always said.

The Breath held no terrors for her.

She was once more at the helm.

20

The answer was always there.

—Father Jacob Northrop

Henry Wallace arrived at Simon Yates's fantastical floating house to find Alan Northrop and Dubois seated at Simon's desk. The men were up to their elbows in gazettes, missives, dispatches, and reports. Mr. Albright silently took Henry's greatcoat and tricorn, hung them in a closet, then silently returned to his corner.

"Any luck?" Henry asked.

Dubois shook his head and flicked open another gazette. Alan flung himself back in his chair and rubbed his eyes.

"My agents, your agents, Simon's agents, Monsieur Dubois's agents—all of them scouring Haever for this Eiddwen and her lover with no result. Admittedly we are hampered by the fact that we have not been able to give our agents any information beyond a vague description of Eiddwen and her young man, both of whom are undoubtedly disguised and have probably separated."

"Do you think we are wrong in pursuing this course of action, Simon?" Henry asked.

"No," Simon said shortly.

Henry coughed. Simon looked up to see them all gazing at him expectantly.

"The two of them will turn up. There *has* to be an explanation for the constructs on the boulders. Speaking of which, another boulder has appeared along the same trajectory I plotted. Another sighting of more Bottom Dwellers."

"We should have had agents there, waiting for them. Have the fiends arrested," said Alan irritably.

"We discussed this, Alan," said Henry patiently. "Eiddwen would hear, realize we were on her trail, and burrow deeper in her hole. We would never find her. If she believes we are living in blissful ignorance, she might grow careless and make a mistake."

Alan bounced up out of his chair and began to pace about the room. Simon raised an eyebrow and glanced at Henry. They both knew what was bothering their friend; it was only a matter of time before he let it out.

"I don't see why the devil we need Jacob!" Alan said angrily.

Henry and Simon smiled.

"Because, Captain, the danger to your country is posed by the contramagic," Dubois answered in his perpetually mild tones. "Your brother has studied such magic. He is the *only* one who has studied it, and the only one who will know how to deal with these bombs."

Alan glowered. "I need a drink. Does anyone else need a drink?"

He uncorked the aquavit, poured himself a tumbler and drank it down in a gulp. Henry reached into his pocket and drew out a document sealed with golden wax and adorned with purple ribbon.

"Speaking of Jacob, I have Her Majesty's writ sealed with the queen's signet ring." He regarded it admiringly. "An excellent forgery if I do say so myself."

"And I have the grand bishop's authorization of safe passage for Sir Henry," said Dubois. "This is *not* a forgery."

He drew out the paper and waved it gently in the air.

"Montagne would like nothing more than to see Henry dangling from a noose," said Alan, scowling. "This is a trap."

"No, it isn't, Alan. I'm bringing Montagne his heart's desire. He would give the Evil One himself safe passage to have what I'm going to bring him," said Henry with a chuckle.

Alan poured himself another drink.

"Did you tell the queen about our theory?" Simon asked.

"I did," said Henry. "Her Majesty was disturbed, of course, and more angry than frightened. I endeavored to persuade her to leave Haever, travel to a place of safety. She refused, saying she would not do anything so cowardly. She did send the crown prince on holiday to the mountains. He had been ill lately. She is telling people he requires pure mountain air."

"What about your wife and child?" Alan asked.

"Mr. Sloan is taking them to Woostenbroke," Henry replied. "I thought that would be the safest place."

He fell silent, his expression dark. No one spoke. They were all thinking that if this plot to break off part of the continental shelf succeeded, there was no telling what might happen. The resultant shockwaves could spread death and disaster throughout Freya. No place would be truly safe.

Their gloomy thoughts were interrupted by the arrival of Mr. Sloan. He entered with his customary grave and solemn mien, bearing a large parcel wrapped in brown paper beneath his arm.

"I have obtained the griffins, my lord," Mr. Sloan

reported. "Admiral Baker loaned us those used by naval couriers. They are admirable beasts, sir. Fast and extremely well trained. Admiral Baker sends his regards. He regrets the fact that he is still laid up in his bed or he would come himself."

"How is old Randolph?" Alan asked. "Are his wounds healing?"

"The admiral is in an extremely bad mood, sir. The physicians tell me that is a good sign. He has sent orders to the fleet as you suggested, my lord. They will be deployed around the Freyan coast. He thinks, as you do, that if the Bottom Dwellers succeed in causing their planned destruction, they will take advantage of the chaos to attack."

"Excellent, Mr. Sloan. What about the luggage?"

"I retrieved the valises with the false bottoms from storage. I packed your court clothes and traveling clothes in the top. The monks' robes are hidden in the false bottoms, along with the weapons and directions for their assembly."

"Well done, as always, Mr. Sloan. What is in the parcel?"

"Captain Northrop's disguise, my lord." Mr. Sloan undid the parcel to reveal the somber clothes of a gentleman's gentleman.

Henry grinned at Alan. "Mind you look sharp, my man. I won't have my servant disgracing me in front of the grand bishop."

"By God, I think you're enjoying this, Henry," said Alan in an accusatory tone. "We're flying into the hangman's noose."

"His Eminence has granted Henry safe passage. As his manservant, you will be safe, as well," said Dubois soothingly. "No one knows you by sight, Captain."

"Except, of course, my brother the traitor!" Alan muttered. He picked up the parcel and stomped off to change clothes.

"You look worried, Mr. Sloan," observed Henry.

"I endeavored to give Captain Northrop instruction on the proper behavior of a gentleman's gentleman, but I fear he is not taking this role seriously, my lord," said Mr. Sloan, sounding aggrieved.

"Alan will rise to the occasion," Henry replied. "He always does. Are the arrangements complete in regard to my family?"

"They are, my lord. I have hired a wyvern-drawn coach, plain, no markings. We will be staying with your wife's cousin, Lord Kerrington, at his hunting lodge."

"Excellent, Mr. Sloan," said Henry. "Make certain that you are not followed. But, of course, you know that."

"Indeed, my lord. You can trust me completely."

"I know I can." Henry reached out to clasp Mr. Sloan's hand. "Godspeed, Franklin. Keep my family safe!"

"I will, my lord," said Mr. Sloan in a low tone expressive of his emotion. "God go with you and Captain Northrop and with you, Monsieur Dubois."

Mr. Sloan departed. Henry took a turn about the room to regain his composure, wipe his nose, and blink away the moisture in his eyes. Simon watched his friend with affectionate concern.

Alan returned, attired in the somber, yet fashionable livery worn by those who served in noble households. This included a curled and powdered wig.

"Your wish is my command, my lord," Alan said with a sweeping bow that sent his wig flying off his head.

Henry was glad Mr. Sloan had departed.

Alan picked up the wig and plopped it on backward, with the pigtail hanging down over his nose. Shaking his head at the antics of his friend, Henry plucked off Alan's wig and threw it in the trash.

"I think we can dispense with this part of the disguise, Mr. North," said Henry, using the name they had chosen for Captain Northrop. "Simon, all we need now are the lock picks."

"I have better than picks," said Simon proudly. "I have keys. Monsieur Dubois was able to provide me with a detailed accounting of the locks on the cell doors. That man's mind is amazing, Henry. He even drew pictures! I was able to determine the type of lock and obtained keys that should fit it. You will encounter magical locks, as well. I have no way of knowing what those might be, but I have included some constructs that could help."

He handed a velvet pouch containing the keys and several papers covered with drawings to Alan, who tucked them into an inner pocket of his coat.

"Everything else you need you will find in the valise," said Simon.

Dubois had been staying with Simon the last two days. He went off to fetch his valise and returned wearing his cloak and hat, his valise in hand. He set the valise on the floor to shake hands with Simon and thank him for his hospitality.

Henry looked around at his friends. "If there is nothing further to discuss, we should depart. Time is of the essence."

"I will have my agents keep searching for Eiddwen," said Simon.

"If they find her, they are to do nothing," Henry cautioned. "Just set a watch on her."

"Understood. They have their orders. I'll be here when you return. Good luck."

"Good luck to us all," said Henry.

He pointed to Dubois's valise on the floor.

"Mr. North, why are you just standing there? Carry the gentleman's luggage. Really, my man, you should know your duties without me having to tell you."

"I beg pardon, my lord," said Alan, groveling. "Forgive me, my lord. It won't happen again, my lord. You're a son of a bitch, my lord."

He picked up the valise and threw it at Henry, who ducked just in time. Laughing, the men grabbed the valises and stowed them in the carriage.

"Here we go," said Alan, settling into his seat. "We are saving the Rosians the time and trouble of capturing us by walking right into one of their prison cells." He nudged Dubois in his waistcoat. "Isn't that right, monsieur?"

"You will have your little jest, Captain," said Dubois mildly.

Inside his own prison cell in the Citadel, Father Jacob sat on his cot in the darkness, staring down at the stone floor. He had drawn six blue sigils—the six ancient, basic magic sigils. The sigils glowed with a faint light.

In the bunk in the adjacent cell, Sir Ander snored. He had long ago learned to sleep during Father Jacob's experiments. The master had taken on the duty of guarding them at night. He sat on the stool by the door, as silent and unmoving as the stone walls behind him.

When Father Jacob bent down to draw six more sigils, the mirror opposite of the first six, the contramagic sigils began to glow with a green light. As he watched, the green glow spread to the blue, eating away at it until the blue glow faded and died.

"The *roed* and the *raeg*," he muttered and shook his head in frustration.

He had advanced far with his studies into contramagic. He could now create a contramagic construct. Nothing complicated—a simple construct such as might be taught to child crafters. He drew six more magic sigils and six more contramagic sigils in a different arrangement. Again the green glow of the contramagic extinguished the blue.

"So, I've proven that," Father Jacob muttered. "Now let's see what happens when I add this."

This time he drew seven sigils. The contramagic sigils glowed. The seventh sigil, the strange sigil that was unlike any sigil Father Jacob had ever seen, remained dark. What was he doing wrong?

"Magic is the voice of God," said Father Jacob, talking out loud, yet softly so as not to wake Sir Ander or disturb the meditations of the master. "Sigils and constructs allow us to interact with God, to use His creation for our own purposes. We have long known that contramagic exists, simply because science reveals to us that every action has an equal and opposite reaction. The church denies such a rational explanation, claiming that contramagic is evil because it is destructive, and therefore contramagic does not come from God, but from the Evil One."

Father Jacob began to pace about his cell, still talking to himself. "Let us say science is right. God holds contramagic in one hand and magic in the other, both of them divine. The *roed* and the *raeg* are both present in the bodies of dragons. They maintain the magic and contramagic in delicate balance. That is why their magic is so powerful—

"Powerful magic . . . Perhaps all of us have contramagic in our bodies . . ." said Father Jacob. He stopped walking to consider this notion. "Perhaps this was the discovery Saint Marie made with the help of the dragons. She and her friends learned how to use both in harmony, so that one would not destroy the other."

The image of God holding magic in one hand and contramagic in the other lingered in his mind. Father Jacob had gone to God with this problem on a nightly basis, making it the subject of prayer, discussion and, it must be admitted, frustrated harangues. Father Jacob had the feeling God was frustrated with him.

"I gave you a mind for a reason," God shouted. "Use it!"

" 'How would a creator reveal Himself but through His creation,' " Father Jacob murmured, quoting words Saint Marie had written. " 'For His invisible attributes, namely, His eternal power and divine nature, have been clearly perceived, ever since the creation of the world, in the things that have been made.' "

He got down on his knees and drew the seventh sigil by itself. God with magic in one hand and contramagic in the other, science proving that every action had an opposite and equal reaction . . .

Father Jacob sat back on his heels.

"I have been a fool. We have all been fools. Heavenly Father forgive us, if You can."

Once more he drew the six basic magic sigils, but this time he formed them in a half circle. He completed the circle with the six basic contramagic sigils—mirror opposites. Then in a trembling hand, he drew the seventh sigil in the center. Only he reversed it, drew it upside down—the mirror image.

Green light shone brightly. Blue light shone brightly. He waited a moment for the usual reaction. Both shone brightly. Neither dimmed or faded or warred with the other.

"What's going on?" Sir Ander asked sleepily. He propped himself up on his elbow, holding his hand over his eyes to block out the light. "You haven't set yourself on fire again, have you?"

"No, my friend," said Father Jacob softly. "All is well. Go back to sleep."

Grumbling, Sir Ander pulled the blanket over his head and rolled over.

Father Jacob remained on his knees gazing at the blue

green light for a long, long time. Hearing a faint stirring, he raised his head to find the master gazing at him. The green and blue glittered in his eyes.

"The seventh sigil is God," said Father Jacob.

21

We met in university and became friends due to the accident of our births, having all been born second sons. Henry was the coolheaded schemer, Randolph the stalwart heart of oak, Alan the daring charmer. I was the brains. We made a damn good team. Still do.

—Simon Yates

Sir Ander woke from a restless sleep to find Father Jacob sitting pensive and silent on his cot, his elbows on his knees, his arms hanging limp. Sir Ander knew the signs. The priest's thoughts were roving far from his prison cell. Looking around at the stone walls, iron bars, and chamber pot, Sir Ander envied him.

He performed his morning ablutions and then began his daily exercise routine. He sometimes wondered dispiritedly why he bothered when all he did was lie on his cot all day.

A fit body equals a fit mind, or so his drill master had dinned into him.

Sir Ander started with knee bends and lunges, did a few rounds of shadowboxing, and then practiced his fencing with an imaginary rapier. All the while he was under constant scrutiny from the master, who never looked at him, but was always watching him.

His routine ended with the arrival of breakfast and the changing of the guard. The master departed and another monk took his place, carrying their meals on trays. The prisoners did not have to subsist on bread and water. They were given the same excellent food that was served to everyone else in the Citadel.

Sir Ander watched as a monk opened Father Jacob's cell door and placed the tray on a desk. The monks of Saint Klee did not engage in idle chitchat or pleasantries, but Father Jacob always greeted them with an annoyingly cheery "Good morning," and today, when he did not speak or even seem to notice the monk's arrival, the monk paused to regard the priest with concern.

"Father Jacob, are you well?" said the monk, the first time the woman had ever spoken to him.

Father Jacob gave no sign he had heard.

Sir Ander began to grow concerned. Father Jacob was an early riser and generally at this time of day he was crawling about on the floor, working with his constructs, spouting theories on magic that gave Sir Ander a headache or watching Sir Ander exercise and making cutting remarks about the knight's lack of skill at boxing.

The monk brought Sir Ander's tray, which she set down on the desk. She cast a questioning glance at the priest, as if to ask Sir Ander what was wrong with him.

"Your guess is as good as mine, Sister," said Sir Ander.

The monk left, shutting and locking the cell door behind her. The guardian monk sat on the stool, silent and watchful.

Sir Ander recalled a bright light coming from Father Jacob's cell in the middle of the night. He vaguely remembered asking Father Jacob about it and being told to go back to sleep.

"Father, what the devil were you doing last night?"

Father Jacob made no response.

Sir Ander shook his head and began to eat his breakfast. Some time later, when the monk came to remove the breakfast trays, she noticed that Father Jacob had not touched his. He didn't even seem to be aware it was there. The monk raised an eyebrow.

"Leave it," said Sir Ander. "He might eat it later."

The monk nodded and was about to depart when Father Jacob called out to her.

"I want to speak to the grand bishop. Tell him the matter is urgent."

The monk bowed and left. Father Jacob stood up and began to pace restlessly back and forth, treading on the chalk drawings of constructs.

"You should eat something," Sir Ander advised. "Oatmeal with honey today. Yours will be cold, but that's your own fault."

Father Jacob stopped to stare at the food tray as if he was just now aware of its existence. He sat down, picked up a spoon, dropped it, and stood up to pace again.

"Were you awake all night?" Sir Ander asked.

"Yes," said Father Jacob.

"Doing what?"

Father Jacob shook his head.

Sir Ander shrugged, poured water into the bowl, stripped off his shirt, and prepared to take a sponge bath. Later, at his insistence, the monk would come to shave him. Although he was a prisoner and perhaps would be for the rest of his life, Sir Ander was not going to give way to slovenliness.

"Why do want to talk to the grand bishop?" Sir Ander tried again.

Father Jacob had stopped walking and was now engaged in staring intently at the floor.

Sir Ander put on his shirt and began to button it.

"Jacob, you're not eating, you're not sleeping. I know the signs. You've discovered something or solved something or developed some new theory. It will give me a splitting headache, but you can tell me about it."

Father Jacob motioned Sir Ander to come as near as he could, given that their cells were across an aisle from each other.

"I am of two minds whether to tell you or not, Ander," said Father Jacob. His tone and his mien were unusually grave. "The knowledge is dangerous. Yet I admit to you freely that I am out of my depth. I would value your advice."

"You know that you can tell me anything," said Sir Ander, deeply moved and now deeply troubled. "Particularly if you believe you are in danger. You can trust me to hold your confidence as sacred."

"Thank you, Sir Ander." Father Jacob drew in a deep breath and let it out with the words in a kind of sigh. "I have identified the seventh sigil that controls the workings of magic and contramagic. I know what it is."

Sir Ander was startled and alarmed. The priest was swimming in deep and dangerous spiritual waters. Sir Ander wasn't certain he wanted to plunge into that dark sea, and yet he was protector and, more than that, friend.

"What is it, Father?" Sir Ander asked steadily.

"The seventh sigil is God," said Father Jacob.

Sir Ander gaped in shock and disbelief. He could not think clearly. He felt the waters closing over his head.

Now that he had shared his burden, Father Jacob felt better. Pulling out his chair, he sat down, tied a napkin around his neck and began to eat oatmeal. Sir Ander, on the other hand, thought that he might never eat again.

"Are you certain, Father? There can be no mistake?"

"None," said Father Jacob calmly. "I conducted the experiment last night. The question is now: Do I tell the grand bishop?"

"No," Sir Ander's voice grated.

"I know you do not like him, Sir Ander, but Montagne is a good man. He is trying to do his best by God and the church. He was not the one who made the decisions that have brought us to the brink of disaster. He was given this terrible secret and told to guard it and that is what he has done."

"He may not have made decisions in the past, Father, but his decisions in the present have cost people their lives," said Sir Ander severely.

"He did the best he could," said Father Jacob. "Poor man. I pity him. He was placed in an untenable situation. In his place, I might have done the same."

"No, you wouldn't," said Sir Ander. "You have faith in God. You would make the truth known and let people wrestle with it and trust God to sort things out. Montagne claims he has faith in God, but he has faith only in himself and now that he's lost control, he can't deal with the result. If you tell him, he will tie you to the stake and start the fire."

"There is a great deal of truth in what you say, my friend," said Father Jacob. "Still . . ."

He shook his head and ate oatmeal.

Sir Ander sat on his cot and watched the priest eat. He had a great many questions, but he waited until Father Jacob finished his breakfast, took off the napkin, and pushed away the empty bowl.

"You said this knowledge is dangerous, Father. Why? The idea that God is the seventh sigil is . . . is natural. Now that I think about it, it seems right. Earth, air, fire, water, life, death, God."

Father Jacob gave a pleased smile. "You are a wise man, Sir Ander. When our forebears heard God's voice and began to pay heed to what He said, they developed powerful magicks using all seven sigils *and* their opposites."

"I wonder what happened?" Sir Ander mused. "How the seventh sigil came to be lost."

"Mankind happened," said Father Jacob grimly. "We will never know, of course, but it is easy to speculate. Some power-hungry soul discovered that by separating out contramagic and removing God from the equation he gained the ability to destroy his neighbors. Small wonder contramagic came to be viewed as a tool of the Evil One."

Sir Ander regarded his friend with admiration and deep concern. Father Jacob had solved an ancient spiritual mystery and made an amazing scientific discovery. Yet he was not elated. He looked weary, careworn, and filled with sorrow, unutterable sorrow.

"What will you do, Jacob?" Sir Ander asked.

The priest sat in his chair with his elbows on the desk, his head leaning on his hands, his fingers rubbing his creased forehead.

"God help me, my friend," said Father Jacob, sighing. "I have been asking myself that question all night. The grand bishop said I would end up destroying the church that I love. He may be right."

Sir Ander pictured what would happen when people began to understand that for centuries the church had lied to them. What would they do when it was proven that contramagic was not evil, that it could be used in positive, constructive ways to make existing magic even more powerful, as powerful as the magic of dragons? King Alaric would most certainly use this as an excuse to wrest the control of magic away from the Church. And that would be just the beginning of the Church's problems.

But with God at its center, could anyone ever truly control magic?

Father Jacob spoke the knight's thoughts aloud. "In time, we will use this newfound power to create untold wonders. But the Church as we know it will fall. People will seek God in the magic, not in the pulpit."

"The prospect is frightening," said Sir Ander.

"All change is frightening," said Father Jacob. He sighed deeply. "This assumes, of course, that mankind survives the coming storm. If the Bottom Dwellers are victorious, they will silence God's voice and drag us into their darkness. That is why I must warn the grand bishop."

"So much for asking my advice," Sir Ander remarked, with a sigh and a faint smile.

The door to the cell block opened and the master entered.

"The grand bishop refuses to speak to me," said Father Jacob.

The master nodded in confirmation.

"Then I must talk with the provost," said Father Jacob urgently. "Father Phillipe will hear me."

The master was an older man, lean and spare, made of skin and gristle and bone. His iron-gray hair was parted in the center and fell to his back, framing his lean, angular face. He never betrayed emotion, and he remained silent, but his silence seemed to speak. Sir Ander rose from his cot and walked over to the cell door.

"I know Father Phillipe to be a just man," said Sir Ander. "He would come if you told him the matter was of the utmost urgency."

"Provost Phillipe is in his dwelling under guard," said the master. "He has been removed from his office by the grand bishop, pending review by the Council."

Father Jacob's shoulders sagged. He sank back down in the chair.

"I give up," he said.

"This is monstrous!" Sir Ander exclaimed, outraged.

"The grand bishop doesn't have the authority to imprison the provost! You know that, Master! How can you obey his commands?"

"The master has taken a vow to God, Sir Ander," said Father Jacob. "He has sworn an oath, the same as you."

Sir Ander realized Father Jacob was right, but he was still upset. He muttered an apology and began to restlessly pace his cell, trying to walk off his anger and frustration.

As the master turned to leave Sir Ander watched him heading for the prison block door—a door that would shut on them and on the truth.

Sir Ander strode to his cell door, grabbed hold of the bars and called out, "The seventh sigil is God!"

"He knows, Sir Ander," said Father Jacob softly. "He was with me in the night."

The master paused with his hand on the latch. He turned to look directly at Father Jacob. Neither man spoke. They gazed steadily at each other. The master opened the door, walked out, and shut and locked the door behind him.

Sir Ander slammed his fist into the iron bars and swore. He pulled back his hand and began to massage his bruised knuckles. Father Jacob picked up a sheaf of paper, dipped his pen in the inkwell, and began to write. After a while, Sir Ander noticed that the female monk had not come to pick up the dishes. He wondered if anyone would ever come again.

"The grand bishop has arrested the provost," he said, shaking his head. "Montagne's lost his mind. What are you doing?"

"Making notes on my discovery," said Father Jacob.

"You realize they'll probably burn them," said Sir Ander bitterly.

"Probably," Father Jacob agreed, as he continued to write.

The following morning, Sir Henry Wallace and Captain Alan Northrop—in the guise of Mr. North, gentleman's gentleman—arrived at the Citadel of the Voice. They were accompanied by Monsieur Dubois, who had sent word ahead by swift courier that he was coming to the Citadel and bringing with him an envoy from Queen Mary of Freya under a guarantee of safe passage. Dubois was careful *not* to mention the name of the envoy. If there was one man in this world Montagne disliked and distrusted more than Father Jacob Northrop, that man was Sir Henry Wallace.

Dubois had no fear of being turned away. Even in the midst of the ongoing crisis, Montagne would wonder what this sudden and unexpected visit might portend.

The griffins landed in the stable yard of the carriage house. The lay brothers who tended the stables came running to take control of the beasts, treating the griffins politely and inviting them to rest in lodgings specially designed to accommodate them.

The three men dismounted, stiff and grimacing after the long ride. They had stopped at an inn during the night to allow Dubois's courier time to deliver his message, and to rest their mounts, but had been up and riding again before dawn.

The monks of Saint Klee came to search them and their belongings to make certain that they were not carrying any weapons into the Citadel. Finding nothing, they said that Sir Henry and his servant were free to go.

Sir Henry gazed around at the fortress mountain in awe and admiration.

"I have never been to the Citadel, though I have seen it often enough in my nightmares," he said to Dubois. "I always feared I would someday languish in a cell here."

"Until they hanged you," said Dubois mildly.

Sir Henry chuckled.

"Your luggage, my lord," said Alan in servile tones, struggling to carry three valises. "The brothers kindly offered to take them to the guesthouse, but I said we preferred to carry them ourselves. If that is quite agreeable to you, my lord?"

"Don't overdo it," Sir Henry muttered.

Alan wasn't paying attention. He had noticed two sisters walking past, coming from the carriage house, peeping around their wimples at the handsome man. Alan swept off his hat and made a humble bow. The sisters smiled graciously; the younger of the two giggled.

"Good God, Alan, must you flirt with every woman you see—even nuns?" Sir Henry demanded.

"All women are fish in my sea," said Alan, watching the nuns depart.

The younger one sneaked another look back at him and blushed when he winked at her. She hurried away.

Dubois took out a handkerchief and mopped his forehead. He was starting to wonder if bringing along Captain Northrop had been the best idea.

"What is the plan, monsieur?" Sir Henry leaned over to ask Dubois in a low voice as they affected to admire the view.

"We will go to our rooms and change. You and I will meet with the grand bishop," said Dubois. "During that time Captain Northrop can assemble the weapons and reconnoiter. You have the map I have drawn for you, sir?"

"I do, monsieur," Alan replied with a bow, neatly catching his hat as it fell off his head.

Dubois sighed as he picked up his valise and reminded

himself that if it came to fighting, he undoubtedly would be very glad to have Captain Northrop on his side. He also thought to himself, sadly, that he now truly understood what it meant when someone was termed a "loose cannon."

Alan carried his valise, as well as Sir Henry's. The three men started the long walk up the side of the mountain.

"Perhaps Captain Northrop could be a little more circumspect," Dubois hinted.

"He's right, Alan," said Sir Henry. "We are here on a mission that could very well get us *all* hanged. None of your daredevil antics."

"Yes, my lord. No, my lord," Alan said meekly. "I endeavor to please, my lord."

He winked at Dubois, who felt his heart sink.

The tension and unrest that existed among the Citadel's inhabitants was still palpable. The Council of Bishops had been thrown into turmoil. Nothing like this had ever happened before. They had called upon legal scholars to try to determine if Montagne had the authority to disband their body. No two could agree. They couldn't talk to him directly. The grand bishop stated he would remain in the Citadel due to concerns for his safety, then refused to allow the bishops to enter the Citadel out of concerns for *their* safety.

Priests and nuns cast curious glances at Dubois and his guests. They knew Dubois to be an agent of the grand bishop, but no one recognized Sir Henry or Captain Northrop. They must be wondering uneasily if Dubois was bringing more trouble.

Dubois wondered that himself. He had wrestled with his conscience. He was, after all, about to break just about every law—secular and religious—on the books. Dubois had come to terms with his better angels. He was saving Montagne from his own desperate act and, by doing so, he was saving the Church to which he had devoted his life. Dubois was not so arrogant as to claim that he was saving God, but the thought lurked in the back of his mind.

As they walked, Dubois noted Sir Henry's swift, sharp gaze darting here and there, taking note of every detail, particularly the Citadel's defenses. Sir Henry observed Dubois observing him and gave a wry smile.

"You realize, monsieur, that you have let the wolf into the sheepfold. Should our two nations ever go to war, I will put this day to good use."

"I considered that, my lord," Dubois replied. "If we are defeated by the Bottom Dwellers, our two nations will struggle to simply survive. If we should be victorious, I doubt we will either of us have much appetite for war."

"Mankind always has an appetite for war, monsieur," said Sir Henry drily. He paused, then said softly, "I used to have such an appetite myself. With the birth of my son, however, my attitude has changed. I would like him to grow up in a world at peace."

Dubois was skeptical.

"That is no doubt why you built the armored gunboat with the magically enhanced steel, my lord. To see to it that peace is kept . . . by force."

Sir Henry laughed and slapped Dubois on the shoulder, nearly sending him reeling into a hedge.

"I like you, Dubois. If you ever grow weary of serving the grand bishop, you must come work for me. Even in a world at peace, I wouldn't mind tweaking Alaric's nose on occasion."

"If His Majesty survives," said Dubois, shaking his head.

Sir Henry cast him a sharp glance. "What news of the palace?"

"I received a letter from Monsieur D'argent. He reports that Monsieur de Villeneuve is managing to keep the lift tanks in operation long enough for engineers to slowly lower the palace to the ground, away from the lake."

"What is Alaric telling the populace? He must find some excuse. He certainly cannot reveal the truth."

Dubois thought back to what D'argent had written:

God knows what His Majesty is thinking. The people can see the palace sinking lower each day, and are growing nervous. Rumors are flying. The king needs to tell them something. Not the truth, certainly, but he could find some plausible excuse for lowering the palace. He will not discuss the matter, however, not even with his son.

Prince Renaud can do nothing with his father. He has asked me several times to send word to the countess, saying that His Majesty needs her. I keep putting him off with various excuses, but Renaud is no fool. He knows something is wrong. As to the countess, I have heard nothing from her since her last letter. I fear that I will never hear from her again.

"His Majesty is considering what to tell the populace," said Dubois. "The matter must be handled delicately."

"He will find it rather late to be delicate when the palace is sitting in the middle of a cow pasture," Sir Henry remarked.

Dubois shrugged and made no comment. He cast a wary glance over his shoulder at Captain Northrop, who was following several steps behind them, as befitted a gentleman's gentleman. The captain was smiling to himself, a dark and devious smile that gave Dubois cold chills.

He drew near to pluck at Sir Henry's sleeve.

"Do you entirely trust Captain Northrop, my lord?" Dubois asked in a whisper.

"I trust him with my life," said Sir Henry promptly.

He glanced back, saw Alan's smile and shook his head.

"Though not, perhaps, with the life of his brother."

22

People like Alan who are unusually lucky are said to have made a pact with the devil. If that's the case, I'm sure Alan will find some way to cheat the devil of his due.

—Sir Henry Wallace

On their arrival at the guesthouse, they found a note from the grand bishop saying that he could spare them a few moments at the hour of one of the clock. Since that hour was not far off, Henry went to change his clothes. He had brought along his finest court apparel and he was soon resplendent in green velvet pantaloons with white stockings, an embroidered satin coat over an embroidered weskit, a white cravat trimmed with lace and lace trim on his cuffs.

He checked to make certain he had the queen's writ with him, went over in his mind the pack of lies he was going to tell the grand bishop, then looked at his pocket watch. Almost time to go.

He knocked on the door of Alan's room and opened it to find his friend was not there. He discovered him outdoors in the courtyard, chatting amiably with a couple of priests. Henry summoned "Mr. North" and Alan, keeping up his role, made his excuses to the priests, saying he had to attend upon his master.

"What did you find out?" Henry asked, when the priests had bowed and departed.

"Quite a bit, actually," said Alan. "Can we talk here?"

"I shall take a stroll about the plaza while I wait for Dubois. Hold my coat," said Henry. "The day's frightfully warm."

"I would be thrilled to hold your coat, my lord," said Alan. "Holding your coat will be the highlight of my day, my lord."

"Go to hell," said Henry, grinning.

"I will go in an instant, my lord," said Alan, grinning back. "If you will show the way."

Henry sat down upon a bench and fanned himself with his hat. Alan took his proper place behind Sir Henry, drawing near to make his report.

"I steered the conversation to these monks of Saint What's It."

"Saint Klee," said Henry. He frowned slightly. "We already have information on the monks from Dubois."

"Forgive me if I do not entirely trust the grand bishop's most trusted agent. I was convinced that Dubois exaggerated their powers, but apparently he was telling the truth. If anything, he underestimated them. These monks are the very devil when it comes to martial magicks. Though it is true that they don't kill a fellow unless they have to."

"They will spare us to see our necks in a noose," said Henry drily. "Let us hope to God Simon's invention works. You make those ready while I'm in my meeting. I'm not sure how long this will take. Montagne will probably keep me waiting to show me what a great man he is."

"Take your time," said Alan lightly. "I've seen several extremely attractive nuns. Oh, for God's sake, Henry, don't look at me like that. I'm only teasing. Here's Dubois coming to see why you are late."

Dubois had emerged from the guesthouse entrance and was standing in the plaza, peering about impatiently. Henry rose to his feet.

"I must go. Help me on with my coat."

Alan dutifully held Henry's coat for him. As Henry was sliding his arms into the sleeves, he said softly, "You are up to something, Alan. What is it?"

"Nothing, my lord," said Alan smoothly. "I plan to spend the afternoon assembling the weapons and studying the lay of the land."

Henry turned to fix his friend with an intense look.

"We are here for our country, Alan. For Freya. The lives of our countrymen hang in the balance. For God's sake, do not do anything rash."

"Me? Rash? I am the soul of prudence," said Alan. "Prudence could be my name."

He patted Henry on the shoulder, smoothing his coat and flicking off a speck of dirt.

"Thank you, Prudence," said Henry.

Alan chuckled. He made a bow with a flourish, then sauntered back to the guesthouse, calling greetings to those he met along the way. Henry kept an eye on Alan as he walked off. He didn't like leaving him to his own devices, but he had no choice. Alan had to assemble the weapons.

Henry commended them all to God, adjusted the lace on his cuffs, and went to join Dubois, who was frowning at his pocket watch and tapping his foot.

As Henry had predicted, the grand bishop kept him waiting in the antechamber, but for only an hour, however, not as long as Henry had anticipated. Henry had used the same tactic himself on occasion, hoping to rattle a visitor, and he took care not to permit himself to become angry or annoyed.

The afternoon was fine, with a slight breeze off the inland sea to cool the air. The chairs in the antechamber were comfortable. Henry relaxed or sauntered about, looking out the window that opened into a pleasant garden. Admiring a rosebush with deep crimson blooms, he thought of his dear Mouse, who was fond of roses. He did not allow himself to think of her long, for he had to keep his mind on business. He could trust Mr. Sloan to keep her and his son safe.

Dubois sat down in a chair, leaned back his head, closed his eyes, and fell into a light doze. A good idea, Henry conceded. They hadn't had much sleep last night and there would be no sleep at all this night if everything went as planned.

Henry sat down, but he could not fall asleep. He was too excited, filled with nervous anticipation.

His main worry was Alan. Intelligent, quick-thinking, loyal, and courageous; Alan, the one man above all others Henry would choose to have at his back in a crisis. But he was also the one man more liable than any other to create a crisis. Alan's saving grace was that he had the devil's own luck.

Henry rose from his chair, walked over to the door that led to Montagne's office, and put his ear to the door. He could hear Montagne talking to someone. By his brief and respectful responses, the someone was an underling, probably a secretary. The thought occurred to him that he and Dubois were alone in an antechamber that should have been crowded with people waiting to see the grand bishop: crafter priests wanting to discuss the rebuilding of the Citadel after the attack; Sisters of Mercy here to report on the wounded; messengers from the king. There was no one even walking in the garden, enjoying the beauty of the day. If it hadn't been for faintly heard distant sounds, Henry would have thought the Citadel had been completely deserted.

Roaming about, he discovered a door that led to an adjoining room. He entered to find a small library and examined the titles on the shelves. They were all theological in nature, of course. He selected one and took it back to his chair. He was absorbed in reading when the door opened. The secretary emerged and said the grand bishop was at leisure to see them.

Dubois was instantly awake and on his feet. Henry took his time, reading a few more paragraphs, just to fluster the secretary, who coughed and repeated again that the grand bishop would see them.

"Fascinating," said Henry.

He closed the book and laid it down on the table.

After carefully adjusting his lace cuffs and arranging his cravat, he followed the grand bishop's agent inside. The secretary announced Sir Henry Wallace and Monsieur Dubois and then left them. Henry could clearly hear the man's receding footfalls.

He focused on them because he was having a difficult time controlling his countenance. Dubois had told him that Montagne had been ill lately. Henry was not prepared for what he found.

He had not attended the Rosian court for well over a year. He knew King Alaric hated him, suspecting him of spying on Rosian affairs and of being involved in sundry crimes, not the least of which was the murder of the Rosian ambassador to Travia.

Henry might have laughed off King Alaric's public sneers and cutting remarks, which were neither very cutting nor very bright, and attended court anyway. The true reason he had decided to stay away from Rosia was that he feared the clever and beautiful Countess de Marjolaine. She had disrupted one of his plots and come perilously close to catching him. She had seen to it that a warrant was issued for his arrest. He had returned to Rosia in peril of his life, sneaking into the country to abduct Alcazar and his magical steel.

Thus it had been a long time since Henry had seen Montagne. The man was so altered in appearance that Henry would not have known him. Montagne did not rise to greet him. Not an insult. Henry doubted if the man could stand up.

Montagne was a big man now gone to almost skin and bones and flab. His cassock hung from gaunt shoulders. His face was an unhealthy sallow color. Yet there was smoldering fire in his eyes when he gazed upon his long-time foe.

"I am sorry to hear you have not been well, Eminence," said Henry, seating himself in a chair directly across the desk from the grand bishop.

Dubois did not sit down, but went to stand at a window, distancing himself from the proceedings.

"I hope you were not injured in the attack of the Bottom Dwellers."

Montagne shot a baleful glance at Dubois.

Henry saw the look and intervened. "I recognized from the extent and nature of the damage that this attack was made by the weapons of this particular foe. I know because they attacked my own manor house."

"Bottom Dwellers," said the grand bishop, his eyes narrowing. "Why do you call them that, sir?"

"Perhaps because that is what they call themselves," said Henry. "We managed to capture and interrogate one of the fiends."

Montagne looked disappointed. He had undoubtedly

been hoping Henry would say something to implicate Father Jacob.

"I am not yet convinced that these so-called Bottom Dwellers even exist," said Montagne, scowling. He glared at Henry. "I think it far more likely Freyans launched this assault."

"You do not really believe that, Eminence," said Henry calmly. "You have received reports regarding the fall of the Braffan refineries to these Bottom Dwellers and the disastrous defeat suffered by our naval forces. Damage we were not likely to inflict upon ourselves."

Montagne glowered.

Before he could speak, Henry continued. "But I did not travel all this way to discuss this enemy."

"Why have you come, then?" Montagne asked.

Henry removed the falsified writ from his inner coat pocket. Rising, he laid it on the desk in front of the grand bishop.

"You recognize Her Majesty's seal, Eminence. I assume you know how to safely remove it," said Henry.

The grand bishop lifted his hand. His fingers began to shake and he hurriedly rested his hand on the desk.

"You had better open it, sir," he said.

Henry obliged by removing the magical construct that had been placed on the purple wax seal. Using the grand bishop's silver letter opener, he slit the envelope and extracted the writ.

The grand bishop picked up the paper and read. Astonished, he looked to Dubois to verify what he was reading. Dubois inclined his head. Montagne dropped the paper on the desk and looked at Henry.

"You know what this says, sir?"

"I have the honor to be in Her Majesty's confidence, Eminence," said Henry.

"Is she serious?"

"Her Majesty, Queen Mary, is always serious, Eminence," said Henry in cold, rebuking tones.

"Yes, yes, you know what I mean," said Montagne. "Is Queen Mary seriously considering abolishing the Church of God's Word and rejoining the Church of God's Breath?"

As Dubois had said, the reunification of the two churches was Montagne's dearest dream. Henry had offered him his heart's desire. Unfortunately, the writ was a ruse. Queen Mary would never consider abolishing the Freyan church, which was flourishing.

"Her Majesty is considering the possibility," said Henry cautiously. "She would require certain assurances."

"Of course, of course," said Montagne, pathetically eager.

Henry went on to propose terms, making them up as he went along. Montagne's face brightened and gained some color. He became animated, effusive, talking about a future that would never come to pass, a future that the grand bishop would soon discover had all been a ploy, a trick. Henry almost felt sorry for the man. When he discovered the truth, the blow would be not only to his body, but to his very soul.

Henry glanced at Dubois, who had remained at the window. His usually mild expression was grave. Henry guessed Dubois was thinking the same. Dubois caught Henry's look and gave an infinitesimal shrug, as much as to say, "Remember the stakes for which we gamble, my lord."

Henry had no need for Dubois to remind him. He kept in his mind the image of his wife and child as he agreed to the outrageous terms.

Montagne was so pleased, he even invited them to tea.

Wondering what Alan was doing and assuming it was probably good that he didn't know, Henry accepted.

After Henry and Dubois had departed, Alan returned to their rooms. Making certain he was alone, and no monks of Saint Klee were hiding in the wardrobe, he locked the door and unpacked the clothes. Removing the false bottoms, he took out the objects, then dismantled the valises, parts of which he used to assemble Simon's weapons: blowguns.

Alan stuffed some of the blowguns with a special powder Simon had concocted. He filled others with round lead shot. He and Henry had both practiced extensively with the blowguns, learning how to fire the projectiles. Alan had developed a great degree of accuracy. He was capable of hitting a rat at thirty paces.

"That could kill a man," Alan had remarked, going over to examine the dead rat.

"For use only in an emergency," Simon had warned.

"Kill a man . . . ," Alan muttered to himself.

Running his fingers over the smooth surface of the blowgun, he smiled.

Weapons assembled, he slid all but one of them under the mattress, just in case some inquisitive monk decided to inspect their rooms. Time to reconnoiter.

He shook out one of the monk's robes, took off his own clothes and struggled into the crimson robes of a monk of Saint Klee. He combed out his hair and wore it loose. His hair wasn't long, falling only to his shoulders. If he kept the cowl over his head, no one would notice.

He had carefully observed the monks at the carriage house and those he had seen along the way, taking note of the way they moved, how they carried themselves. He had questioned Dubois about them extensively and he was confident he could act the part.

He examined himself in the mirror and was pleased with the result. His plan was risky, but Henry had said himself it would be good to ascertain if their disguises would work. Henry had not meant for Alan to test them in advance, but what Henry didn't know wouldn't hurt him.

Alan strapped the blowgun to his forearm, inside one of the flowing sleeves. He gave his reflection a rakish wink, then assumed a monk's impassive expression. Once he felt he had this right, he lifted the cowl over his head, opened the door a crack and peered into the hall. Since they were the only people currently staying at the guesthouse, he did not expect to encounter anyone. Seeing the hall was empty, he exited the door, locked it, and left.

Keeping his hands folded, he emulated the deliberate pace of the monks. He tilted his head slightly downward to allow the cowl's shadow to cover his face. He had committed Dubois's map of the Citadel to memory and knew precisely where he was going. As he walked, he passed several priests and a couple of sisters along the way. Alan was pleased to note that none of them cast him a glance.

He was forced to make a slight detour when he saw two monks coming toward him along the path. The monks of Saint Klee were a small, close-knit community. If they saw his face, they would instantly discover he was an impostor. Fortunately he was near an intersecting path. Turning off, he waited in the shadows of a grove of trees until the monks had walked by, then resumed his walk to the prison complex.

Alan surveyed the walls with their three guard towers. Behind those walls were the notorious dungeons of the Citadel. His gut tightened, and his mouth went dry. He might well end his days inside that building, waiting for the executioner.

Alan smiled grimly. Fear was a dare to himself. The wise course of action would be to go back to their rooms, wait for Henry and Dubois. He had accomplished his mission, studied the route they would need to take tonight and ascertained that their disguises would allow them to pass without hindrance at least as far as the prison gate. Once they reached the gate, they had their weapons.

Alan counseled himself to return. He'd promised Henry nothing rash. Then he decided going as far as the front gate wasn't rash. He'd just see how many monks were on guard.

He continued walking down the winding path that led to the prison. He had not gone far when he heard footsteps behind him and heard a voice call, "Brother!"

Another monk was approaching him, walking swiftly. "Damnation!" Alan swore. He was trapped. The path on which they were both walking was a narrow one, lined with trees and shrubbery. Those offered good cover, except the sight of a monk suddenly bolting into the greenery would alert every monk in the Citadel. He could only stand, grit his teeth, keep his cowl lowered, and keep in mind what Henry often said.

Alan Northrop has the devil's own luck.

This was true. If there was a Travian merchant ship with a hold stuffed with gold sailing anywhere in the Breath, Alan and his pirate crew were certain to stumble across it. Pistols aimed at him point blank invariably misfired. Bullets meant to blow off his head took off his hat. If he was having a romantic encounter, he was out the back door just as the husband was coming in the front.

The devil did not fail him this time.

The monk spoke hurriedly. "I am summoned to the hospital. Brother Anselm is on his deathbed. He brought me into the brotherhood and I would like to be with him, to ease his passing. I am supposed to deliver the prisoners' midday meal. Could you take this for me?"

The monk held out two trays covered with a cloth. Alan did not hesitate.

"Which prisoners, Brother?" he asked, taking the trays.

"There are only the two," said monk. "Father Jacob and Sir Ander."

Only the two. Alan chuckled inwardly.

The smell of fresh-baked bread wafted up from the beneath the cloth. Alan grinned to himself in the shadow of the cowl and proceeded to the prison. He carried the tray carefully, so as not to spill anything.

He wondered suddenly if there was some sort of password he would have to give at the gate. Apparently not, for a monk opened it and silently indicated he was to enter.

One of the monks lifted the cover off the tray to inspect it. He cut apart the loaf of bread and removed the lids on the two bowls to sniff the meat and vegetables. Alan held a silent conversation as he stood silently waiting.

"Checking to see if the bread's been poisoned? Probably not, more's the pity. My brother is fortunate I don't happen to have any arsenic on me today."

The monk replaced the cloth and returned the tray, indicating Alan was to proceed. Fortunately Alan had learned from Dubois that Sir Ander and Father Jacob were being held in the monk's quarters, otherwise he would have blundered into the main cellblock. Instead he headed for the smaller building. As he walked, Alan noted the number of monks and their disposition, the proximity of the gate to the prison entrance and any other details he thought might be useful.

He entered the building, carefully balancing the trays to open the door. Inside was the small shrine to Saint Klee, exactly as Dubois had described.

No one was within the outer room.

That left only the monk who was always on guard duty inside the cell. Dubois had said the master himself sometimes undertook this task. The idea of encountering the head monk was daunting, even for Alan. The master would immediately realize that he was an impostor. Alan was just about to set the trays on the table and make a swift retreat when the door opened.

Alan ducked his head and froze where he stood. Peering out from under the cowl, he breathed easier. According to Dubois, the master was an old man with iron-gray hair. This monk was young and bald.

Alan was about to hand the trays to him and leave, when the devil's own luck was his once more.

"I heard you enter, Brother," said the monk. "You come most timely. If you would take the trays inside and remain with the prisoners a few moments, I will make my daily report."

Alan lowered his head in agreement.

The monk walked past him and out the door, leaving Alan alone.

"Son of a bitch," said Alan.

With a shrug, he carried the trays into the cell block.

He had no clear idea what he was going to do. When they were making their plans, Simon had suggested that if they could find some means to inform Father Jacob and Sir Ander in advance that they were here to break them out of prison, they could work on removing the constructs from their cells. Simon had devised various schemes, but in the end, he had abandoned the idea, saying it was too dangerous.

And here was Alan, strolling into the cell block, ready to astonish his brother.

Ready to kill his brother.

Alan still had the blowgun strapped to his arm. No one

had seen his face. No one would know how Jacob had died, not even the Knight Protector, for Alan would keep his back turned to the knight, his face hidden. Jacob would know in the very last moments who had killed him. That was as it should be.

Henry would be angry. That was putting it mildly. Henry would be furious. But he would understand. Henry was clever. He would find other ways to deal with this Eiddwen female without having to rely on Jacob. Alan wasn't convinced that they needed his brother anyway. Eiddwen was one woman, even if she was a sorceress. At that, he felt a little shiver go up his spine when he remembered the gruesome sight of the bloodstained walls of her wine cellar.

The cells were as Dubois had described them, two cells on either side of a central aisle. Sir Ander was lying on his cot, reading a book. He rose to his feet and walked over to the cell door.

"Lunch is here, Father," he said. "Smells like chicken stew today."

Alan set the trays down on the floor. His brother was seated at a desk writing something. He paused in his work to glance around.

"Chicken stew," he began to say. "One of my favorites—"

Alan removed his cowl.

Father Jacob stopped talking, struck dumb with shock. His pen suspended in midair, he stared in amazement.

"Hello, brother," said Alan.

He walked over to Jacob's cell, his hand on the blowgun beneath his sleeve. Behind him, Sir Ander was demanding to know what was going on.

Jacob sprang to his feet and bounded to the cell door, clutching the bars with his hands.

"Alan! I don't know what fool stunt this is, but you are in terrible danger. You must leave now! At once."

Alan was taken aback by the intensity of his brother's outburst. Jacob's face was pale, the knuckles of his hand white. Alan was reminded suddenly, forcibly, of another time, far in the past, when his older brother had said almost those exact words to him.

You are in terrible danger! You must leave at once.

Almost the same. But not quite.

Shortly after the Reformation, when the Church of the Breath had been outlawed in Freya, Jacob and their father both had been arrested. Jacob had managed to escape. He could have fled to Rosia. In peril for his life, with the guards chasing him, he had come back to warn his sixteen-year-old brother.

"How dare you run off and leave our father in prison?" Alan had cried. "He was arrested because of you!"

"I am the priest, the one they want," Jacob had said. "I came back to tell you that I love you both. Our father will probably not believe it, but that is true. So long as I am in the country, I'm putting you and father in terrible danger. I must leave at once."

Alan let go of the blowgun.

"I won't stay long. I came to tell you and the knight that Henry and I are going to free you. Tonight. Be ready."

"Don't do this, Alan!" Father Jacob said earnestly. "The risk is too great! You know what they will do to you if you are caught!"

Alan shrugged and said with a smile, "Trust me, Jacob, the idea of freeing you is not mine. Henry seems to think you might prove useful. He's the one who has made all the arrangements. I came along for the fun. We will see both of you gentlemen tonight."

He was interrupted by the sound of the outer door opening and footfalls crossing the floor. Alan pulled his cowl low over his face.

"Sit there," said Sir Ander urgently. "On that stool."

The monk entered to find Alan sitting on the stool, his hands folded. The monk silently indicated he would take over. Alan left, stealing one last look at his brother.

Father Jacob was seated in his chair, his gaze abstracted, his expression grave and troubled.

Alan left quickly. Walking back up the path, he wondered where he could find something to eat.

The chicken stew had smelled really good.

23

Our first duty is to God. Our second duty is to man, to save him from himself.

—*Precepts of the Monks of Saint Klee*

"You have the devil's own luck, Alan," was Henry's only remark after Alan related the day's exploits.

Dubois did not take the news so calmly.

"What were you thinking, Captain?" Dubois gasped. "You put the mission in jeopardy! You put us all in jeopardy!"

"Calm down, monsieur," said Henry, fighting a strong desire to pat Dubois soothingly on the head. "As the poet says, all's well that ends well. Everything ended well, didn't it, Alan?"

Henry cast his friend a cool, appraising glance. He and Dubois had returned to their rooms at the guesthouse to find Alan divesting himself of his crimson robes. Removing the blowgun that he had strapped to his arm, he caught Henry's eye and winked at him.

"Of course, everything ended well," said Alan with a negligent shrug. "I'm not in shackles and leg irons, am I?"

"You left Father Jacob in good health?" Henry asked.

"My brother has that sickly prison look about him, but otherwise he is fine. I told him about our plan to set them free. He and his pet knight will be expecting us. And now I must find something to eat. I am ravenous. How did your meeting go with the grand bishop?"

"As you see, neither of us are in shackles or leg irons," said Henry wryly. "Actually our meeting went quite well. We left Montagne ecstatic, envisioning himself lauded through the ages as the man who reunified the Church. I fear it will come as a severe blow to him when he finds out he has been deceived."

He glanced at Dubois to see how he would take this. Dubois was seated on the bed, mopping his face with a handkerchief, still trying to recover from the shock.

Alan dressed again in the livery of a gentleman's gentleman and they went out in search of food. Upon entering the dining hall, they found it deserted. Sister Cook was sorry to inform them that the noontime meal was no longer being served and it was several hours until supper. It was the work of but a moment, though, for Alan to charm the sister with praise of her chicken stew. They soon had all they could eat.

After luncheon, they returned to the guesthouse.

"I am going to take a nap," said Henry. "We have a long night ahead of us. Alan, what are you doing?"

"I thought I'd walk down to the stables to make certain they are taking proper care of our griffins."

"We need griffins for Father Jacob and Sir Ander to ride," said Henry. "Use your charm on the stable hands."

"Use my name, monsieur," said Dubois. "They will give you anything you need without question."

"As you both command," said Alan. "I live to serve!"

He grinned, winked, and started to turn away when Henry called after him.

"No more exploits, Alan." Henry's voice was cool. "Someday the devil won't be watching."

Alan laughed and waved his hand in acknowledgment. Still chuckling, he sauntered off along the path that led down the mountain to the carriage house.

"That man makes my blood run cold," said Dubois, using the handkerchief once again. "Being around Captain Northrop is like being around a powder keg—always waiting for the explosion that will blow one to bits."

"Alan improves upon acquaintance," said Henry, hiding his smile.

The main hall of the guesthouse was dark after the brightness of the sun. Henry observed his companion as they climbed the stairs that led to their rooms. Dubois had loosened his cravat and was fanning himself with the handkerchief.

"You appear nervous, Monsieur Dubois," said Henry, pausing in the hall. "Don't worry. Our plan is sound."

Dubois shook his head. "I confess I am filled with trepidation, my lord. Alas, I am not a man of action like you and the captain."

"I believe you are braver than you think, monsieur," said Henry. "We will meet you at the stables."

"I will have the mounts ready," said Dubois. "We will probably not have time for farewells, my lord. I find it odd to say this, considering that I am Rosian, but I pray that God saves your people from this terrible calamity."

Henry held out his hand. "Thank you for your good wishes, monsieur, and for your help. You and I can never be friends, but I propose we remain the best of enemies."

"I will pray to God to watch over you this night," Dubois said. "Although I fear God Himself can do little with Captain Northrop."

The two men shook hands and parted, each going to

his own room. Henry took off his court clothes and threw them on a chair. That was the last he would see of them. They would be traveling light, so no luggage.

He did not immediately sleep, but stood gazing out the window at the sun sparkling on the waters of the inland sea.

He smiled, thinking again about Dubois's last words to him. A cynical man, a man of science, he did not believe in God. He found himself wishing he could believe as Dubois believed. He longed for the comfort of commending his wife and little son to God's care, the comfort of knowing that a benevolent and loving deity was actually hovering over them. He wished he could believe that God was also taking a personal interest in this night's adventure.

But Henry couldn't worry about what wasn't. At least, he thought, though he might not have God, he had the next best thing. He had Mr. Sloan and Alan Northrop.

The thought sent him to his bed with a smile.

Henry was already awake and changing into the crimson robe when Alan tapped softly on his door. The church clocks had chimed the hour of one. He had left the window open to observe the courtyard bathed in the lambent light of the stars and a bright half-moon.

The Citadel slumbered. The priests and nuns had long since attended evening prayers and were asleep in their cells. The grounds were deserted, and no lights shone in the windows. Accustomed to the bustle of the city, where people roamed the streets at all hours, Henry viewed with alarm the empty sidewalks glimmering palely in the moonlight.

"I knew the place would be quiet," he said to Alan. "But not this quiet!"

"It's like a bloody mausoleum," Alan said in agreement. "I passed Dubois in the hall. He is on his way."

"How did he look? Our Dubois is no adventurer."

"He was so buttoned up in his cloak I couldn't see him. He bobbed his head at me, gave me God's blessing in a voice of doom, and disappeared."

Alan assisted Henry in attaching the first of the blowguns to his arm. "I told them we would need two more griffins. Dubois is right. The moment I mentioned his name, they were eager to give me anything I wanted. Though I wonder what they will say tonight when he wakes them up and orders them to saddle *four* griffins."

"They will do as he orders and keep their mouths shut. I observed him today. Everyone in the Citadel knows he is the grand bishop's agent. He may look like a clerk, but people treat him like royalty. No one will be inclined to question him, especially not these days when Montagne is tossing people into prison willy-nilly."

Henry checked to make certain the blowgun was secure and not liable to fall off his arm, then tested the wrist straps to make certain he could remove it quickly. He and Alan each attached a second blowgun on the other arm. They studied themselves in the mirror, adjusting their robes to make certain they covered the blowguns and the traveling clothes they were wearing beneath.

"I think we are ready," said Henry.

"As ready as we will ever be," said Alan.

He was about to open the door, when Henry clamped his hand over his friend's. He looked at Alan intently.

"You went there to kill Jacob. Knowing how much we need him to stop Eiddwen from destroying our country." Henry's voice held barely masked anger.

"We could deal with that female," Alan said with an attempt at a grin.

"I am disappointed in you, Alan," Henry said.

Alan tried to meet Henry's eye and failed. At last, he lifted his head.

"I didn't kill him. I won't, Henry. You can trust me. I admit that I thought about it, but the old hatred just wasn't there. I must be growing soft."

"Or growing up," Henry suggested.

Alan gave a soft laugh. "God! I hope not!" He looked at Henry anxiously. "Are we friends still?"

"I've put up with you this long," said Henry, smiling.

He opened the door on the empty hall. They walked quietly through the silent corridors and out into the night. Their eyes were already well adjusted to the darkness and they had no difficulty seeing the path. Henry looked up and marveled at the beauty of the clear night sky.

"Did you know there were so many stars? In the city, with all the lights and the fog, we are lucky if we see one or two."

Alan made no response. He was walking with his head bowed, either brooding or playing at being a monk, Henry wasn't sure which.

"He said he wouldn't come with us," said Alan abruptly.

"Who said that? Jacob?" Henry asked, alarmed. "Why not?"

"He didn't want me to risk my life to free him," said Alan. "He was worried about me."

"But he *is* coming," said Henry, a question in his words.

"I think so," said Alan. "We didn't have much time to talk."

Just like Jacob to be contrary, Henry thought.

"We can always hogtie him," Alan suggested.

Henry grunted.

At the sight of two monks walking the ramparts not far from them, Alan and Henry fell silent. They walked along the narrow path, side by side, their shoulders rubbing companionably, preparing once more to go into danger together. Henry felt the usual tingle of excitement, the gut-tightening tension, and a sudden surge of joy. Given a choice, he would not have traded places with anyone this night. He enjoyed danger as some men enjoy opium.

"The prison," said Alan softly. He stopped to point to walls that loomed black against the starlight. "Two monks are posted at the gate. You take one and I'll take the other. When you get inside the compound, turn to your left and keep close to me. I know the way."

Henry nodded. They had been over this plan many times before, but it was their habit to run through the details one final time.

"No lock on the door to the monks' quarters. There is a lock on the door to the cells and padlocks on the cells. You have Simon's keys?"

"In a pouch on my belt."

"I hope this powder of his works," said Alan.

"It works," said Henry, more emphatically than he intended. "I know from firsthand experience."

By way of testing his compound, Simon had thrown the powder into Henry's face, and Henry had spent the next few moments writhing on the floor trying to breathe, then bent over a sink as Mr. Sloan poured water into his burning eyes.

They were within half a block of the prison. From here, the path left the shelter of the trees. Alan and Henry shook hands and then broke into a run. Henry, unaccustomed to running in a skirt, had but one thought: Don't trip on the robe.

The two monks on guard duty saw two of their fellows running toward them. Fearing an emergency, they opened the gate. Alan and Henry arrived breathless.

"Intruders . . . Library of the Forbidden . . . ," Alan gasped. "We fear they may come here next. Try to free the prisoners!"

"Is all well?" Henry demanded.

Before the monk could answer, Alan and Henry put the blowguns to their lips and blew fine, dustlike powder into the faces of the two monks. He knew from experience that the blinding powder would first hit their eyes, making them feel as if their eyeballs were being pierced by tiny hot needles, then fly down their throats.

Both monks fell to their knees, rubbing their streaming eyes, gasping and coughing.

"Go!" Alan said. "To your left!"

Alan and Henry ran through the prison and dashed outside, heading for the small building where the prisoners were housed. Bursting through the door, they entered the darkened room and found a monk praying at the shrine. As he turned his head to look, Alan raised his second blowgun and fired a stone pellet. He hit the monk in the forehead, right above the nose. The monk fell to the floor and did not move.

"Good shot. I'm impressed," said Henry.

Alan shrugged. "I've been practicing."

Henry pulled out the keys and sorted through them hurriedly. Simon had painted a mark on each to tell them apart. While he tried to find the right key in the dim light of a candle burning on the altar, Alan was down on his knees, examining the lock, gazing intently at the magical constructs.

"I can see them," he reported softly. "I hope Simon's friend the burglar was right about this deconstruction technique—"

He touched the lock with his fingers and murmured a few words. Henry kept an eye on the door. "Hurry, Alan—"

"Done!" Alan said softly. "It worked. I will have to remember that spell."

Henry paused a moment to look around. He and Alan

had moved fast and in complete silence. He doubted if anyone had heard or seen anything, but he needed to make sure. The cell where the prisoners slept was quiet. No glimmer of light shone from beneath the locked door.

"Ready," he whispered.

Alan kicked open the door and jumped inside the dark cell with the cry, "God save Queen Mary!"

Startled, the monk on guard duty leaped from his stool, trying to see the intruder as spells crackled from the man's fingertips. Alan dashed into the room, allowing Henry to blow the blinding powder into the monk's face. When the monk reeled, rubbing his eyes, Alan knocked him to the floor, unconscious.

Light gleamed. Henry turned to see Sir Ander, holding a lantern, standing at the door to his cell, ready to go. Father Jacob, on the other hand, was shuffling through papers, tossing some and stuffing others in the breast of his cassock.

"Bloody hell," Alan swore, "what are you doing?"

"Gathering up my research . . . ," Father Jacob said calmly.

"Father, we talked about this—" said Sir Ander.

"You go ahead, Sir Ander," Father Jacob replied, perusing a paper. "I'll be there in a moment."

Alan fixed Sir Ander with a grim look. "You either get him out of here or he can stay and rot."

"I'll deal with him." Sir Ander started to open his cell door. Red fire flared and he snatched back his fingers with a curse.

"Damn it, Jacob! You were supposed to remove the magic constructs on the locks!"

Father Jacob looked up from his work.

"Oh, yes, sorry." He fixed his gaze on the lock and the red fire flickered out. "There you go."

He went back to his papers. Sir Ander touched the cell

door gingerly, and when nothing happened, he opened it and went to Father Jacob's cell.

"Father, you need to unlock your own door."

Father Jacob looked up vaguely. "I opened it weeks ago. There. I'm ready."

Finished with his papers, Father Jacob gave his cell door a push. The lock snapped and the door swung open.

"We can leave now," he said to Sir Ander, who was staring at him in blank astonishment.

Henry had taken up a post at the door leading to the cells, keeping watch for more monks. He thought he had caught a glimpse of movement and stared hard into the night. He didn't see anything, but he didn't like it.

"I suggest you hurry, gentlemen," Henry said coolly.

Alan came up beside him. He looked and sounded disgusted.

"Give me your other blowgun, the one you haven't fired."

"Changed your mind about shooting Jacob?" Henry asked.

"No, but I will if I have to stay around him much longer," Alan replied. "You deal with him."

Henry handed over the blowgun. Alan moved quietly through the room, heading for the entrance. Once there, he looked back and motioned.

"All clear! Hurry up!"

Sir Ander went first, followed by Father Jacob. Henry came last, carefully shutting the door to the cell block behind him.

Hearing Alan swear, Henry turned to see Father Jacob kneeling beside the monk Alan had hit with the stone pellet. The priest had his hand on the monk's neck, feeling his pulse.

"He's not dead, as I feared. Only stunned."

"If I wanted him dead, Jacob, he'd be dead," said Alan, his voice grating. He gazed grimly at his brother

Father Jacob glanced around. He very slightly smiled. "I understand. I am grateful, Alan."

"You can be grateful later. Now move!"

Father Jacob stood up. Henry started toward the door.

"Wait," said Sir Ander. "Someone's here."

Henry froze. Alan whipped around, lifting the blowgun to his lips. He drew in a breath, then let it out in a shocked gasp as the blowgun disintegrated in a shower of glittering red sparks.

A man moved out of the darkness, emerging into the light cast by the candle on the altar.

"Master," said Father Jacob. He made a respectful bow.

Alan was swearing softly, shaking his burned fingers. His hand stole into the pocket where he kept the blinding powder. Henry went to his volatile friend and clasped hold of him firmly.

"Let Jacob handle this," he said in warning tones.

Alan's swearing trailed off. He looked sullen and very grim.

Sir Ander moved to stand protectively in front of Father Jacob.

"He means me no harm, my friend," said Father Jacob.

Sir Ander reluctantly stepped aside.

The master stood calmly, hands folded in front of him. No one moved or spoke. Henry knew they were in trouble, yet oddly, he was neither worried nor fearful. This monk could have dropped every one of them without breaking into a sweat. Henry kept one hand on his friend and watched, intrigued.

"Where are you going, Father?" the master asked.

"I am traveling to Freya," said Father Jacob. "With my brother, Captain Northrop, and Sir Henry Wallace."

Alan drew in a seething breath. "That treacherous—"

Henry dug his fingers into his friend's arm. "Shut up!"

"Alan and Sir Henry believe that the woman known as

the Sorceress is plotting with the Bottom Dwellers to destroy their country. Sir Ander and I have faced her before. They need our help."

The master nodded, his face impassive, expressionless.

"I have spent many days in prayer, Father Jacob. God spoke to me. My way is clear."

In the silence, Henry could hear each man softly breathing. He could hear his own heart beat.

"For too long we have imprisoned truth, Father," said the master. "The lies must end."

Father Jacob shook his head. "Master, I never wanted this. I will go back to my cell. I will stay there for the rest of my life—"

"We are the ones who have silenced God's voice. Go to Freya, Father," said the master. "Stop the evil, if you can. God go with you and your comrades."

The master remained standing by the altar. The light of the candle wavered in a slight breeze blowing gently through the open door.

"I'll be damned! He's letting us go!" Alan whispered.

"Keep still," said Henry. "We're not out of this yet."

Father Jacob stood dejectedly in the middle of the room with his head bowed and his shoulders slumped. Sir Ander was beside him talking to him, softly and urgently. At last Father Jacob heaved a deep sigh and began to walk toward the door. Sir Ander kept close to his side.

"What's happening?" Alan asked in a whisper. "Do you know?"

"I have a good idea," said Henry.

They continued out the entrance, across the courtyard, and through the prison gate. The monks who had inhaled the powder were still recovering, rubbing their streaming eyes and coughing so much that they couldn't stand.

Leaving the prison, the four of them, with Alan in the lead and Sir Ander bringing up the rear, took the winding path that led to the carriage house. Henry found himself beside Father Jacob.

The priest seemed overcome by grief, hardly watching where he was going. When once he stumbled, Sir Henry put out a hand to steady him.

"Thank you for agreeing to help us, Father. For saving a country and its people who sent you into exile, and two men who once tried to kill you."

"That was in the past, Sir Henry," said Father Jacob quietly. "As the scriptures say, 'Forgive, as you hope to be forgiven.' "

"I wouldn't go *that* far," Henry remarked wryly.

Father Jacob smiled, but only barely, then appeared to sink once more into his sorrow-laden thoughts.

"Jacob," said Henry softly, leaning close to whisper. "What did you do?"

"I have destroyed the Church that I love," said Father Jacob.

24

I bear the guilt of ages.

—Ferdinand Montagne, Grand Bishop of Rosia

But what else could I have done? Father Jacob asked himself.

The words sounded familiar and he realized he had asked that same question before, when he had fled his homeland, leaving behind his father, in prison for his son's crime, and a younger brother who vowed to kill him.

"What else could I have done?" he repeated. "I had to go where God led me."

"Where Montagne led you," said Sir Ander.

"What?" Father Jacob asked, stopping to stare at his friend.

"I've been thinking," said Sir Ander. "Montagne chose you of all the other priests in the Arcanum to investigate the attack on the cutter, *Defiant*. He chose you to go to the Abbey of Saint Agnes. In his heart, the grand bishop wanted you to find the truth he could never reveal."

Father Jacob looked up into the heavens, at the myriad stars, the wonders of God's universe.

"You are right, my friend. And in his soul, he dreaded it."

The four men found Dubois waiting for them at the carriage house, with five griffins saddled and ready. He must have sent the lay brothers back to their beds, because he was alone. Unlike wyverns, who would have been in a screeching, clawing brawl by now, the proud and noble griffins waited patiently, cleaning their beaks with their claws, preening their feathers, and talking softly.

Dubois hurried to meet them. He opened his mouth, but whatever he had been going to say was drowned out by the sudden clamor of bells sounding from the towers and echoing throughout the Citadel.

The griffins bounded to their feet, looking around, curious as to the uproar.

"That bastard monk betrayed us!" Alan said angrily.

"The alarm is not for us," said Father Jacob.

"Who is it for, then?" Alan demanded.

Father Jacob did not answer. He had noticed only four griffins were saddled and ready to carry passengers. Dubois had persuaded the fifth griffin to serve as a "pack horse." The griffin was carrying a small trunk strapped onto its back.

"What is in the trunk?" Father Jacob asked.

"The master sent that for you, Father," said Dubois. "He said you would know what it contained."

"The writings of the saints," said Father Jacob. "Taken from the Library of the Forbidden. Montagne did not sanction this, did he, monsieur?"

"You should be on your way, Father," Dubois said.

Henry and Alan were busy checking the harnesses and the saddles to make certain they were securely strapped on. Donning their flight helms, they mounted the griffins and waited impatiently for Sir Ander and Father Jacob. The knight was inspecting Father Jacob's saddle, knowing well that he would never think to do so.

"Sir Ander, I believe these belong to you."

Dubois held out Sir Ander's dragon pistol and the two pistols he'd had specially made that were plain, unadorned, and did not require the use of magic.

Sir Ander took them. He was pleased, but obviously perplexed. "The monks locked those in storage, Dubois. How did you come by them?"

"The master," said Dubois. "He said you would need them."

Father Jacob cast a sharp glance at Dubois.

"I see four griffins saddled and five riders."

"I am not leaving, Father," said Dubois. "My loyalty is to the grand bishop. His Eminence will need me."

"You are a good man, Monsieur Dubois," said Father Jacob. "And a faithful friend."

"Go with God, Father," said Dubois.

Sir Ander hustled Father Jacob to his griffin and assisted the priest, then climbed into the saddle of his own mount. Alan gave the command to fly. The griffins sprang off with their powerful lion hind legs, spread their eagle wings, and soared swiftly up and over the inland sea.

As they circled, gaining altitude. Father Jacob looked down on the Citadel's walls that shone with a faint radiance in the moonlight. A single, solitary light was lit in the window of the grand bishop's residence.

Montagne was awake and could hear the bells. He must know what was coming; perhaps he had always known. A good man, he must suffer for a crime he had not committed.

"God have mercy," Father Jacob said to the air rushing beneath the griffin's wings.

He would never return to the Citadel. No matter what happened, he could never go back. Once again, he was leaving a home, and a family he loved.

And again, he was leaving it in ruins.

Dubois watched the griffins, the wings black against the stars, until they were lost to view. The stable hands had been wakened by the alarm and were quaking in their boots, fearing they would be blamed for aiding criminals to escape. Dubois calmed them.

"Where are the monks of Saint Klee?" he asked. "If those gentlemen had been criminals, the monks would have been pursuing them. As you see, they are not."

The stable hands had to admit his reasoning was sound. He again sent them back to their beds and began the long climb up the mountain.

By now, nearly every person in the Citadel was awake, wondering what was going on. Dubois encountered bleary-eyed priests and nuns, wandering about in their nightclothes. Seeing Dubois, they hurried over to him, asking questions. He lowered his head and pretended he did not hear.

He passed the house of the provost. Lights flared from every window, turning night into day. Members of the Arcanum, summoned from their beds, would be leaving the Citadel with secret orders calling the Council of Bishops into emergency session. That meant sending messengers to Travia and Estara and every other country where the Church had a presence. Given the nature of the crisis, the provost would also send an urgent message to the archbishop of the Freyan church. He, too, would be affected.

Dubois headed for the residence of the grand bishop. A single light shone in the stained-glass window of the small chapel attached to the house.

Dubois found the master and the provost conferring in the darkness in front of the house. Monks of Saint Klee stood some distance away. Dubois kept to the shadows, listening.

"I do not like what we are doing this night, Master," the provost was arguing. "Montagne has made mistakes. He should never have tried to silence Father Jacob. I told the grand bishop the Church could weather the storm that would break when the truth became known. Montagne spoke truly when he said the decision was not his. This secret had been given to him, passed down from one grand bishop to the next. He was trying to save the Church."

"He was trying to save himself," said the master.

Provost Phillipe sighed deeply, an aggrieved sigh as for the death of someone dearly loved. He glanced uncertainly at the lighted window. "I do not like the thought of barging in there and placing him under arrest. He has not been well."

Dubois slipped out of the shadows.

"I believe I can be of help, gentlemen."

"You are Dubois," said the Master. "The grand bishop's agent."

"And his friend," said Dubois gently. "Let me speak to him."

The provost regarded him in thoughtful silence.

"Very well. Come with us."

The master and Provost Phillipe entered the house, Dubois following a few discreet paces behind. Inside, the hall was dark; only starlight, shining through the windows, lit their way. The master carried a lantern, but he did not light it. The still, quiet darkness seemed more suitable. Noisy, bright day would come soon enough.

The chapel was small, intimate. The master silently opened the door. Dubois looked inside to see two rows of well-polished pews and a shrine to Saint Marie. A marble statue of the saint stood in a niche in the wall, behind an altar. A single candle burned on the altar. The candlelight playing on her face made the marble seem alive.

She should feel vindicated, Dubois thought.

But the saint's stone face seemed sorrowful.

Montagne was on his knees before the altar with his back to them, his arms resting on the altar rail, his hands clasped in prayer. When they entered, a shudder passed through his large, heavy frame. He did not turn or lift his head.

Provost Phillipe paused, embarrassed, uncertain what to do, not wanting to disturb a man at prayer. The master took a step forward. The provost stopped him. "The responsibility is mine."

He advanced a few hesitant steps.

"Eminence," he said softly, "I regret—I deeply regret—having to take this action. I ask you to step down as head of the Church until the Council of Bishops can be assembled. Please do not make this difficult—"

The grand bishop made a strange and inhuman sound, a strangled gargle, a rattling in his throat. If there were words in that sound, they were not understandable. He did not rise, nor did he turn to look at them. Provost Phillipe seemed at a loss.

"I will speak to him," said Dubois.

He walked slowly down the aisle. Coming to Montagne's side, Dubois said softly, "Your Eminence, if you come quietly, we can spare you the indignity of an arrest."

Montagne did not move. Dubois felt chilled. Something was wrong. He hurried around the altar rail to view Montagne in the candlelight.

Dubois gasped in shock.

The left side of Montagne's face was horribly contorted, mouth twisted, eyelid drooping. Spittle drooled from the sagging lip. He struggled again to speak and again made the terrible, inarticulate sound.

"Eminence!" Dubois cried. "What is wrong?"

Montagne tried to stand up. His left leg collapsed under him and he toppled sideways. Crashing to the floor, he lay on the carpet. His jaw worked, his body twitched.

"He has suffered an apoplectic fit!" Dubois said. "Send for the physicians!"

The master disappeared while Provost Phillipe remained, standing in the aisle, his hand on the back of one of the pews.

"Can I do something to help him?"

Dubois shook his head. "I think only God can help him now."

He knelt beside the stricken man. Montagne still had his faculties. He reached out a trembling hand. Dubois clasped Montagne's hand in his own.

"I am here, Eminence, by your side."

As Montagne gripped Dubois's hand with a desperate, crushing strength, he fought to speak, his jaw working and his teeth clicking. His body shook with the effort. He managed, through sheer force of will, to blurt out two intelligible words.

"Save . . . her!"

He lifted his eyes. Dubois followed his gaze to the statue of Saint Marie.

"Save her. Save the Church," said Dubois.

Montagne gave a feeble nod and his head sagged to the floor. As he closed his eyes, tears welled from beneath his lids and rolled down his cheeks, falling into the corners of his quivering mouth. He held fast to Dubois's hand.

"I will, Eminence," said Dubois softly. "I will."

25

We are not here because we are meant to be here, but because we choose to be here.

—Stephano de Guichen

Stephano stood on the ruins of a guard tower on the upper level of the fortress, looking down with satisfaction and relief at the work that had been completed on the massive structure.

There had been a time when he didn't think his plan would work. Whatever could go wrong, had gone wrong. The weather turned cold, gray, and rainy, making working conditions miserable. For some reason no one could explain, Dag discovered that twenty barrels that were supposed to contain gunpowder were filled instead with flour. The thought of what might have happened if Dag hadn't checked sent a chill through him.

The worst incident occurred when they had tried to hoist one of the cannons into place. A line broke, sending the three-ton cannon crashing down on top of a section of wall. Fortunately no one was hurt, but the wall had to be completely rebuilt. And Stephano was still looking for a battle crafter, someone who could maintain the magical constructs in the walls, repair and replace any that were damaged by contramagic attack.

Dag had highly recommended his friend, the battle crafter Father Antonius, who was now working for the Arcanum. Stephano sent a request to Prince Renaud, who sent an urgent request by special courier to Provost Phillipe. But the prince's courier was not even permitted to land at the Citadel. Some sort of crisis had arisen there, and the crown did not meddle in matters of the Church. His Highness promised to send one of his own battle crafters from the royal fleet, but the person had not yet arrived.

Apart from lacking a crafter, the work on the fortress was almost complete. The weather had cleared and the sun was shining; better yet, the mists of the Breath were tranquil. The three wild dragons and the old dragon brothers, Hroal and Droal, circled in the bright blue sky above the fortress. As Stephano watched, Viola swooped over to inspect a wyvern-drawn pinnace that was approaching the fortress. She did not come too close, for fear of sending the wyverns into a panic. She must have decided all was well, apparently, for she permitted the pinnace to land.

Stephano hoped the pinnace was carrying the battle crafter and another barrel of the crystal form of the lift gas which was due to arrive today. If all went well, he would be ready to leave on schedule in two days' time.

The thought made Stephano's flesh tingle with excitement, even as his stomach tightened. He planned to sail the fortress into the bone-freezing cold and dense fog of the Breath, with only a general idea of where he was going and no idea what he would find when they got there. And no Dragon Brigade.

He had not heard a word from Lord Haelgrund. Stephano had nursed a secret hope that even after the debacle in the dragon realms, the Duke of Talwin might relent and permit the dragons to join the fight. That hope now seemed to be gone.

Other worries still darkened his outlook: he could find out nothing about Miri and Gythe; and no one could tell him anything about his mother's fate.

He was thinking of his absent friends when he heard footfalls running up the stone stairs. He turned to see a breathless midshipman, a young man of about fourteen. He'd only recently received his naval commission and was extraordinarily proud and extremely eager.

"Lieutenant Dag sends his compliments and requests that you please come at once, Captain," said Master Tutillo, saluting. "He's in the officer's mess."

Fearing yet another disaster, Stephano left in haste. The stairs led down from the ruins of the guard tower to a large open area that extended around the interior of the dome-shaped fortress known simply as the Ring. In the center of the Ring, in the safest part of the fortress, stood a round chamber with thick stone walls that housed both the armory and the powder magazine, well protected from enemy fire. He walked quickly past the kitchen and main mess hall and into the smaller officers' mess.

Stephano arrived to find Dag in company with a stranger wrapped in a long traveling coat, his face hidden by his hat.

"I'm here," said Stephano. "What's the emergency?"

"This," said Dag in grim tones.

The stranger whisked off his hat and held out his arms.

"My dear fellow," said Rodrigo. "Your problems are solved! I have arrived!"

"Rigo!" Stephano hurried to shake his friend's hand. "When did you get here?"

"Only a few moments ago. His Highness sent me in his own pinnace. I'm surprised you didn't notice."

"I saw the pinnace," said Stephano. "Did you bring the extra crystals for the lift tanks?"

"They are being unloaded now, sir," said Dag.

"Excellent! What happened to the palace, Rigo? I take it since you are here in one piece it didn't fall out of the sky."

"Matters were touch and go there for a time," said Rodrigo somberly. "I was able to repair the magic on the damaged lift tanks long enough to bring the castle safely to the ground. The last twenty feet were a bit harrowing. We were operating on only two lift tanks at the end. We missed landing in the lake by just a few feet. The palace suffered considerable damage—cracked walls, paintings falling, et cetera. D'argent says that your mother's rooms survived relatively unscathed."

"Has D'argent heard anything from my mother?"

"I'm afraid not," said Rodrigo. "Any news of Gythe and Miri?"

Stephano shook his head. "How's Benoit?"

"Luxuriating in ill health. He sits in his chair all day long gossiping with the housekeeper. If you ask him to do anything, he puts his hand on his chest, heaves a sigh and says he feels a flutter and he requires a brandy to cure it. He sends his regards, by the way."

Stephano smiled. "That old man will outlive us all. So what is happening in Evreux? What are people saying?"

"Everyone was upset by the fall of the palace, naturally. Rumors spread that the king was dead. The prince put out a statement trying to calm the situation, saying that the palace had been lowered to the ground for routine maintenance. Alaric made an appearance, waving from his balcony. The prince handles all the day-to-day business. His Majesty came to visit us in the lift tank room. Told us we were doing well and to carry on. The poor man looks quite ill."

Rigo fanned himself with his hat. "I'm famished. Any chance of something to eat? Or must I wait for dinner?"

"I have some biscuits and sherry in my quarters," said Stephano. "I hope you can stay to see us off—"

"But that is my good news," Rodrigo interrupted brightly. "I'm coming with you! I heard you were in need of a battle crafter and here I am!"

Stephano cast an alarmed glance at Dag.

"It's official, sir," said Dag drily. "He brought the order from the prince."

Their battle crafter was attired in a lemon-yellow coat over a pale green shirt, green silk scarf tied in a large bow, green gloves, and shiny black boots. Rodrigo smiled and hummed a little tune as he glanced about the mess hall with the air of one who was thinking how he would redecorate.

Stephano ran his hand through his hair. "Rigo, it's out of the question. You don't know anything about battle magic . . ."

"I *knew* you would say that," Rodrigo stated triumphantly. "I told His Highness, 'Stephano will tell me "It's out of the question."' Answer me this: Who saved your lives at Braffa? I did. Who figured out a way to get us off that island? I did. Who kept the palace from crashing to the ground? I did—"

"This is a lot different, Rigo," Dag interrupted impatiently. "We're sailing into battle."

"I am perfectly aware of what you are doing," Rodrigo said in lofty tones. "That is why I am here. Admit it. There isn't a battle crafter in existence who knows as much about contramagic as I do."

"He's right," said Stephano, looking at Dag. "Not even Father Antonius would know anything about contramagic."

"Maybe so, sir," Dag said reluctantly. He cast an agonized glance at the lemon-yellow coat. "But still—"

"Then it's settled," said Rodrigo. "How many mason crafters do you have? I will need all of them. They will have to do exactly as I say, obey my commands to the sigil. Perhaps you should make me an officer. Generalissimo? I've always fancied that."

"You would outrank me," said Stephano, smiling. "And you would be in the Estaran army. How about master crafter?"

"I suppose that will have to do." Rodrigo sighed in disappointment, then cheered up at the sight of two strong sailors struggling to carry a large, heavy trunk. "My wardrobe has arrived! Where should I tell these lads to take my luggage?"

Stephano told them to take the trunk to his own quarters until he could figure out where to stash Rodrigo.

"Shall we have that sherry now?" Rodrigo asked, glancing around. "Don't you find it dark and stuffy in here? Why don't you open a window?"

While Stephano explained that the windows were sealed because the fort would be descending into the Breath, Dag said he would go check on the lift crystals. He departed, muttering to himself in Guundaran with Doctor Ellington at his heels, for Dag did not permit the cat to ride on his shoulder when he was in uniform. The Doctor had been miffed at first, but had gradually grown accustomed to exploring on his own, especially as no one ever scooped him up and stuck him in a storage closet.

Stephano was taking Rodrigo back to his quarters when they were interrupted by Verdi's trumpeting call sounding a warning. Within moments, Master Tutillo appeared in the doorway. He cast a startled glance at the lemon-yellow coat and forgot what he had come to say.

"What are the dragons hooting about, Master Tutillo?" Stephano asked.

"Oh, yes, sir. Sorry, sir." Master Tutillo tore his gaze

away from Rodrigo. “Ship sighted in the Breath. Not one of ours.”

“Rigo, I have to go take care of this. This lad will take you to my quarters. The sherry is on the sideboard. Help yourself. Master Tutillo, meet Monsieur de Villeneuve, our battle crafter. Please make him comfortable.”

The young midshipman’s eyes widened in wonder. He set off down the corridor, accompanied by Rodrigo, who was fanning himself with his hat and asking if there wasn’t some way to pump in fresh air.

Stephano emerged from the dark, cool interior of the fortress into the sunlight. Verdi, Petard, and Viola circled above, a formidable show of force. Three of the sailors he had posted on lookout stood gazing intently into the mists of the Breath through spyglasses.

“I saw a ship out there, Captain,” one repeated. “About five hundred yards away.”

“What sort of ship?”

“Strange-looking vessel, sir. It was there for a moment, then disappeared in the mist. I thought my eyes were playing tricks, but then I saw it again. It was sailing straight for us.”

Stephano looked skyward. Verdi, too, had seen the ship, and that was why he had sounded the alarm. Sailors were already running to man the swivel guns.

“Hold your fire!” Stephano ordered. “No one fires except on my command.”

The fortress was located in a remote area far from the major shipping lanes. Given the storms of the past few days, however, the ship could be a merchant vessel, blown off course. Or it might be a supply ship, though most of the supplies had been delivered by now.

“You say it was sailing this way,” said Stephano.

“Yes, Captain. It was out there, near that buoy.”

The buoy was there to warn ships they were nearing

the coast. Stephano raised his spyglass and looked where the sentry had indicated. He couldn't see a thing for the swirling mist. He swept the area and still nothing. Lowering the spyglass, he looked up at the dragons.

Verdi and Petard were hanging almost motionless in the air. Viola left them and flew into the mists to investigate.

Dag joined him, coming on the run. "I heard the alarm. What's out there, sir?"

"No way of knowing," said Stephano.

Suddenly several sailors shouted and pointed. Viola dove down low, her wings cutting wide swaths in the mists that boiled out behind her. The vessel came into view, rising up out of the mists not ten yards from the main dock.

"Hold your fire!" Dag roared.

The vessel was indeed strange looking, similar in size to a Trundler houseboat, but with high, rounded gunnels, an enclosed bridge, tiny portholes and a short, thick mast. The boat carried no weapons that Stephano could see. As he watched, a woman came out on deck and waved what appeared to be a white flag. When Stephano looked closer, he saw she was actually waving white pantaloons, such as Trundler women wear. The pantaloons fluttered in the wind.

Viola roared a greeting, and Verdi and Petard came streaking toward the boat.

Stephano gasped. "Miri!"

"Good God, sir!" said Dag at the same time. "It's Miri!"

He and Dag left the gun emplacement on the run. Hurrying back inside the fort, they pounded along the corridor, burst through the main gate and out onto the dock.

Stephano could see Miri clearly now. She was wrapped in an oilskin coat and her wet red curls were plastered to her head. She waved to him and smiled.

"Who's that fellow with her?" Dag asked, frowning. "And where's Gythe?"

A man stood on the prow, waiting to throw out one of the mooring lines to the sailors on the dock. Stephano stared, frowning, wondering who this man was and why he was sailing with Miri. The boat drew nearer and Stephano forgot about the stranger. Never stopping to think that if he missed his landing he would fall into the Breath, he leaped from the dock to the deck and took Miri into his arms.

He held her tight, pressing her to his breast. Miri, startled, stiffened at first. Then she seemed to crumple.

"Oh, Stephano! I'm *so* glad to see you!" she cried brokenly.

She held him fast in her embrace and they stood for long moments, just holding each other, with no need for more talking. Each felt their love too deep and too large for words. Stephano tilted back Miri's wet head and kissed her.

"Marry me," he said. "I love you. I have always loved you. Even when I said I didn't, I did."

Miri returned his kiss tenderly, then nestled in his arms.

"I love you, too, Stephano," she said softly. "But I can't think of anything now except Gythe and your mother—"

"My mother!" Stephano gasped.

"And the princess—"

"Princess? What princess?" Stephano demanded, bewildered.

"Princess Sophia of Rosia. Your mother came to find her."

"Came where? Where is my mother, Miri? Where is Gythe? Why isn't she with you? Where have you been?"

"Glasearrach," said Miri wearily. "It's a long story."

Stephano was speechless with astonishment. Her answer

raised so many more questions, he couldn't think which one to ask first.

"We're sailing in a wee bit too close, Mistress Miri," called the man with the limp.

Miri looked, gasped.

"Let go of me, Stephano! We're about to crash into the dock!"

Stephano let go, his hands falling to his sides, nerveless. Miri adjusted the boat's speed, the houseboat veered off just in time, and came floating to a landing. Miri shouted at Stephano to make himself useful and throw out a line. He and the unknown man worked together. Dag and the sailors on the dock caught the lines and secured them.

"Where's Gythe?" Dag bellowed.

"She's safe!" Miri shouted back. "Once I get off this boat and change into some dry clothes, I'll explain everything."

Stephano gazed somewhat jealously at the man, who was wearing an oilskin coat over Trundler-made trousers.

"We haven't been introduced," Stephano said coolly. "I am Captain Stephano de Guichen."

"Sir Conal O'Hairt," said the man. "Knight Protector. I am glad to meet you. I was your mother's traveling companion. She spoke of you often."

"What do you mean 'was'?" Stephano demanded angrily. He fixed the knight with a dark look. "Where is my mother? What has happened to her?"

"Calm down, Stephano," said Miri crisply. "Your mother is safe—for the moment. Though why you should care is more than I can fathom. You never gave a damn about her before."

"Things have changed," said Stephano remorsefully.

He sighed and shook his head, unable to explain what he didn't yet understand.

Miri gave him a smile and a sympathetic pat. "Sir

Conal and I are cold to the bone, wet to the skin, and starving. The sooner you stop talking and help us dock the boat, the sooner we will be ashore and can answer your questions."

Checking his impatience, Stephano helped Sir Conal lower the gangplank. Then he and the knight went below to retrieve a bundle of clothes for Miri and Sir Conal's pistols. Once they disembarked, Stephano introduced Sir Conal to Dag, who appeared to be as amazed and baffled as Stephano. Miri had remained on board to see to it that everything was secure. Before she left, she stroked the helm lovingly.

"You're an ugly thing, *Firinne,* but you saved our lives," she said to the houseboat. "I'm grateful."

Reaching the dock, Miri hugged Dag and gave him a kiss on the cheek. She picked up the Doctor, who had been rubbing around her legs, and hugged him.

"I'm even glad to see you, you flea-bitten beast."

The startled cat apparently thought this unexpected show of affection meant his days were numbered. He gave a startled yowl, squirmed out of Miri's arms, and fled.

"You should say hello to them, too," said Stephano, indicating the dragons flying overhead. "They've been concerned."

Miri looked up and waved. Petard gave a roaring hoot and performed a somersault. Viola and Verdi more decorously dipped their wings.

"I was sorry to hear about their homeland," Miri said. "Gythe told me." Before Stephano could ask, she changed the subject. "Did I see the *Cloud Hopper* sitting in a field as I sailed in?"

"Dag flew the *Hopper* here from the Abbey of Saint Agnes. You see—we knew you'd come back to us."

"You knew more than I did then," Miri muttered. She looked up at the walls of the fortress, towering above them.

"So this is Fort Ignacio. It looks like a skep." She sighed and leaned against Stephano. He could see Miri shivering in her wet clothes. "Take me to my room before I collapse."

As they entered the fortress Sir Conal and Dag lagged a little behind them. Sir Conal was studying the fort with interest, asking Dag questions about its history. Stephano was trying to think where he was going to house his guests.

"You and Sir Conal can both rest in my quarters while I sort out where you're going to stay. Our quarters are a bit tight—"

He was interrupted again by shouts from the lookout and the sound of Verdi bellowing.

"Now what!" he said in exasperation.

"I'll go see what's the matter, sir," Dag offered.

"We might as well all wait here. We'll soon find out," said Stephano.

Sure enough, moments later, Master Tutillo dashed into the room.

"Griffin riders sighted, Captain, flying this way. Four of them."

"Griffin riders," Dag repeated. "Could be messengers from the prince."

"Could be," Stephano said, but he was dubious. The prince would send one messenger, not four.

"Best not to take chances. Give the order to hoist the flags, Master Tutillo. Signal the riders they can land, but I want marines out there to guard them. I'll go see who they are. Dag, stay here with Miri and Sir Conal and find them something to eat. Rigo's turned up," he said to Miri. "He arrived today."

"Rigo! Someone else I never thought I'd be glad to see," said Miri, grinning.

"I'll come as soon as I can," said Stephano. He paused, not wanting to leave her. "God! You are beautiful!"

"Get along with you!" Miri said, laughing and giving him a shove. "Go deal with your latest crisis."

He tore himself away. The landing site was located in the rear of the fortress near the cargo dock. Stephano entered the Ring and continued on his way past the two main barracks that housed the sailors and marines, their privies, and the dry goods store rooms. A corridor led to the dock, which was guarded by two gun emplacements, one on either side

Stephano was in no mood to receive these new visitors, whoever they were, messengers from the prince or not. He wanted to be with Miri, to hear her tale, find out about his mother, and get answers to all the questions that were crashing about his brain.

Stepping from the darkness of the fort into the bright sunlight, he had to take a moment for his eyes to adjust. By this time the riders had landed and the griffins were flexing their wings and keeping baleful watch on the dragons, while the dragons were circling overhead and keeping their own watch on the griffins. Stephano was glad to see the captain of the marines and his men watching the riders.

The four men removed their helms and stood staring at the fort with interest.

"Looks like a bloody beehive," one remarked to one of his companions.

That companion caught sight of Stephano and waved his helm in greeting. The gesture brought back the memory of the other time this man had waved a hat at Stephano.

"Sir Henry Wallace!" Stephano exclaimed blankly.

This was apparently his day for shocking surprises.

"Captain de Guichen," said Sir Henry, coming forward. "We meet again. I am pleased to see you."

"I can't say the same," said Stephano, his voice grating. "You are on Rosian soil. There is a warrant out for your arrest. And you have flown into a restricted area. Give me a reason why I shouldn't order the marines to clap you in irons."

"I believe you have already met my traveling companions," said Sir Henry, unruffled. "Father Jacob Northrop and your godfather, Sir Ander. The gentleman who made the disparaging remark about your fortress is Captain Alan Northrop. He saved your life in Braffa."

Stephano stared, confounded, and turned to Father Jacob.

"I must confess, I am at a loss for words," said Stephano. "The last I heard, Father, you and Sir Ander were imprisoned in the Citadel. Now you are here in the company of a Freyan spymaster and a pirate! I trust someone will tell me what is going on."

Father Jacob smiled. "That is a long story . . ."

Of course, it would be. Stephano put his hand to his temples. His head was starting to ache.

"Monsieur Dubois told us of your plan for the fortress, Captain," Father Jacob explained. "We four agreed that we should meet with you. We propose an exchange of information."

Stephano glanced at Sir Henry. He did not trust him or his pirate friend, and he wasn't sure he trusted the priest.

"I fear I have no information I am willing to exchange," Stephano said coolly. "I am sorry you have traveled all this way for nothing, gentlemen. I bid you a good day."

"May I speak to you privately, Captain?" Sir Henry asked. "I will take only a moment of your time."

Stephano hesitated, then he gave a brief inclination of his head, indicating Sir Henry was to accompany him. As they walked a short distance across the muddy ground, Sir Henry was silent, perhaps considering how to begin. Stephano wasn't going to give him any encouragement.

"This is far enough, sir," he said, turning to confront the Freyan. "Say whatever is it you have to say."

Sir Henry looked back over his shoulder at his three companions, who were regarding the fortress with interest and talking companionably.

"Pirate, priest, soldier, spy," Sir Henry commented. "Sounds like a child's nursery rhyme or the start of a rousing jest, doesn't it?"

"I am extremely busy, sir—" Stephano began in frozen tones.

"But this is not a jest, Captain. Far from it," said Sir Henry gravely. "We have been brought together for a reason. Father Jacob would say we were guided by the hand of God."

Sir Henry turned his gaze toward the fort, where the mists of the Breath twined around the uppermost towers. The dragons flew overhead and the wind ruffled the Rosian flag.

"It is *my* belief, Captain, that our wits, our reason, and our courage brought us to this day, to this place, at this hour. We have important information regarding the enemy you are about to face, Captain de Guichen. I am not being dramatic when I say we hold the fate of nations in our hands."

Brought us together. Stephano thought of Miri, who had traveled from God knew where. And Rodrigo, who had just arrived from Evreux. *This day, this place, this hour.* God's guiding hand? Man's reason? Whichever it was, he decided he needed to take advantage of the opportunity, though he would be very careful about what he shared.

"We have been enemies in the past, sir," said Stephano. "God willing, we will be enemies in the future."

"But for now," said Sir Henry, "we are reluctant allies."

Stephano extended his hand. Sir Henry clasped the hand in his own.

"We might as well be comfortable," Stephano added. "If you gentlemen would consent to join me in my quarters, I can offer you sherry and biscuits."

Stephano escorted his guests to the officers' quarters, a block divided into three rooms: a large room meant for a study and off that two small bedchambers, one for him and one for Dag. Stephano had decided to move out of his bedroom, and give it to Rodrigo, while Dag would give his to Miri. Both Stephano and Dag would bunk in the study. As he herded everyone into the small study area, shoving aside furniture to make room, Stephano looked around at the assembly. Pirate, priest, soldier, spy. Add to that a Trundler, a knight, and Rodrigo. One was not likely to find a stranger meeting of the minds. Or, as Rodrigo said, "a meeting of stranger minds."

Father Jacob latched on to Rodrigo the moment he saw him and the two disappeared into Rodrigo's bedroom and shut the door to discuss magic in private. The bedroom was visible from the study and Stephano tried very hard to ignore the green glowing light he saw seeping through the cracks around the door.

Sir Ander was delighted and amazed to find his comrade and longtime friend, Sir Conal. They kept their voices low. Stephano heard him ask questions about a "monastery." The knight seemed extremely disturbed to hear whatever Sir Conal said in return.

Miri had changed into the dry clothes she had brought with her and was sipping a glass of Calvados when they entered. Sir Henry greeted her with pleasure and Alan Northrop with admiration. Stephano handed around the bottle of sherry. Alan chose to share the Calvados with Miri.

"Now," said Stephano, relaxing. "Will you please tell your tale? Miri, you start."

Miri began by talking of her journey to Glasearrach. She described the invasion fleet and meeting Xavier and the Blood Mage. She told them about the drumming that was destroying the magic here Above and about how Gythe and the princess were being forced to try to stop the terrible wizard storms in time for the invasion.

Miri spoke of finding Brother Barnaby and how he came to be working for the resistance. She told what she knew about the abduction of the Princess Sophia and how the countess and Sir Conal had gone to save her.

The men listened in awe and astonishment. When she spoke of the countess, Stephano kept his head down, his face averted. He was filled with relief to know his mother was safe, proud of her for making the terrifying journey, and consumed by remorse for his former harsh treatment of her. He could have gotten down on his knees to beg her forgiveness. He prayed to God she would live to see him be a better son.

"What is the date Xavier plans to launch this attack against us?" Sir Henry asked.

"Fulmea the first," said Miri. "They will coordinate the invasion with their forces already here. They have something special planned for Freya, according to the countess."

Alan poured himself another drink. "We believe we have discovered the plot. Think of this as Freya." He picked a biscuit, cracked it in half and dropped the crumbs onto the floor.

Sir Henry described the boulders and Simon's theory.

"Seven days," Sir Henry remarked, gazing into his half-empty glass. "Dubois told us about your plan. Can you arrive on the island in time to stop them, Captain?"

"I will have to," said Stephano simply.

Sir Henry consulted his watch. "And now it is time to depart. We need to be in Haever by tomorrow."

Stephano went to fetch Father Jacob and Rodrigo. He found his friend in a daze, dazzled, awestruck by whatever the priest had told him.

"I've seen wonders, Stephano," Rodrigo said softly. "Wonders beyond description. Magic suddenly makes sense."

As the men were putting on their cloaks, Father Jacob extended his hands. "This may be the last time we are ever together," he said. "Let us pray."

Captain Northrop muttered something, which caused Sir Henry to cast him a sharp glance; Northrop subsided.

"The world is changing," said Father Jacob. "For good or for ill, nothing will ever be the same. God grant us strength and courage to defend the innocent and give us the wisdom to face change with understanding, without fear."

Miri whispered something to Father Jacob. He put his arm around her, embraced her and kissed her gently.

"Time to go," said Sir Henry.

Stephano escorted them out of the fortress to where their griffins waited. The Breath was calm this night, and the stars glittered in the heavens. Stephano tried to imagine what it would be like living Below, never seeing the stars, rarely seeing the sun or feeling its warmth on your face.

He was about to find out.

"Captain de Guichen," said Alan, walking up to him. "I wish you luck in your battle, sir. I hope to someday have this fortress of yours in my gun sights."

"At which time, it will be my pleasure to blow you out of the sky, Captain Northrop," said Stephano.

He bade good-bye to Sir Henry and Father Jacob. As they were walking to their griffins, Stephano stopped Sir Ander.

"I need you to answer a question, sir. Were my mother and my father married?"

Sir Ander regarded him in astonishment, taken aback by the suddenness and bluntness of the question. He glanced at the others, who were mounted and waiting impatiently.

"Your mother and father were married the night before your father's execution, Stephano," said Sir Ander quietly. "They spent that last night together in each other's arms."

Stephano could not speak for the emotion that choked him. Sir Ander saw, and put his hand comfortingly on his shoulder.

"Your mother kept the secret to keep you safe," he said. "God willing, you will be able to ask her yourself."

The griffin riders took to the air, flying west, toward Freya. Stephano stood in front of the fortress gazing after them. A single dragon, Verdi, patrolled the skies, keeping watch. The griffins gave him a wide berth.

The world is changing . . .

This day, this place, this hour . . .

Seven days . . .

"And so it begins," said Stephano.

26

We are the warp and the woof of Fate.

—Simon Yates

After a long and weary journey, upon arriving in Haever, the travelers went first to the Naval Club, which had accommodations for the griffins. They were met by Mr. Sloan in a wyvern-drawn carriage.

"Master Yates has invited all of you to stay with him, gentlemen, if that is agreeable."

"I won't sleep in the room with the stuffed bear, Mr. Sloan," Alan stated.

"Master Yates recalled the unfortunate incident with the bear, Captain," said Mr. Sloan. "Saying he did not want any more bullet holes in the wall, he suggested that Mr. Albright and I move the bear to safer quarters."

"Very good, Mr. Sloan," said Alan.

He and Sir Ander both fell asleep in the cab. Father Jacob remained awake, gazing out the window at the lights of the city below.

"How does it feel to return to the country you betrayed?" Henry asked, quietly observing the priest.

"I did not betray my country," said Father Jacob mildly. "I left to serve God."

Henry settled himself more comfortably in the corner of the carriage.

"Alan loves you, Jacob," said Henry. "That's why he hates you so much."

Father Jacob sighed and lowered the curtain, blotting out the lights. "My brother has reason to hate me. I betrayed my family, if not my country. I was young and infatuated."

"In love with God?" Henry suggested.

"You are being sarcastic, but that is what happened," said Father Jacob. "I was in love with God. If I felt a twinge of conscience over the grief I brought to Alan and my father, I told myself I was making the sacrifice to serve the Church."

"Do you still believe that?" Henry asked. "Now that you've discovered the Church's lies and the crimes committed in the name of your God?"

"All of us lose the starry-eyed illusions of our youth. My faith has been dented," Father Jacob admitted. "It is need of repair, but it will be stronger for the mending. What about you, Henry? You profess to doubt the existence of God. Yet every man believes in something."

"Certainly not religion!" Henry gave a brief laugh of disdain. "I've watched your kind brutally kill each other in the name of a deity who preaches love and peace. I find it all ludicrous."

"I think God would agree with you," Father Jacob remarked.

Henry was thoughtful. "If you had asked me a year ago, Father, I would have said I believed in my country. To quote a great statesman: 'Duty and patriotism clad in glittering white; the great pinnacle of sacrifice . . . .' But now I am not so certain. As I stare into the abyss, afraid for the safety of my wife and child, I find the differences between nations I once thought so important seem very paltry."

Henry sat in thought for a moment, then he chuckled. "Though mind you, Jacob, if we succeed in saving the world, I'm going to make damn sure that Freya ends up ruling it!"

They arrived at Simon's house in the middle of the night. Simon was awake, awaiting the arrival of his guests, particularly Father Jacob.

"Father, I am so pleased to meet you at last," said Simon eagerly. "I read your monograph on blood spatters. You have revolutionized the study of criminal behavior."

"Mr. Yates, I have followed your career with interest," said Father Jacob. "Your invention of the direct drive motor and the alteration you made to air screws to provide greater airflow were brilliant, simply brilliant. You must describe to me the thought process behind it."

"And you must tell me what you have learned about contramagic."

"I have cracked it!" said Father Jacob with enthusiasm. "I know how it works and why!"

"Have you? Show me." Simon seized hold of the priest by the arm and started to drag him over to the desk. "As you see, I have been working on—"

Sir Henry forcibly intervened, catching hold of Simon's sleeve. "We are asleep on our feet, Simon. This can wait until morning."

"I have news," said Simon. "But it can also wait until morning. Nothing to be done tonight. I'm afraid I'm a bit short on beds," he added apologetically. "We used to have beds in the guest rooms, but Dame Winifred considered them superfluous. She said they took up room she could use for more important things."

"I am certain Mr. Albright and Mr. Sloan have come to our rescue," said Henry.

"Indeed, my lord. Mr. Albright and I have taken the liberty of making up beds for everyone. The arrangements are not as I would like," Mr. Sloan added, distressed. "I acquired cots, but I confess I had difficulty locating places to put them. You and Captain Northrop are in the guest room on the third level. Sir Ander and Father Jacob will be in the drawing room. I hope you gentlemen will not be discommoded by the presence of the giant lizard. Master Yates assures me the creature has been fed and is not likely to crawl out of the tank. Mr. Albright will show you the way."

"As for me, I'm so tired I could sleep in a ditch," said Alan, yawning. "I bid you gentlemen a good night."

He and Father Jacob and Sir Ander accompanied the silent Mr. Albright to their respective rooms. Henry motioned to Mr. Sloan to speak to him in private.

"How are Lady Anne and little Harry?" he asked. "Have they recovered from the shock of the attack on our house?"

"They were in excellent health when I left them yesterday, my lord. Her ladyship sends her love and you are to be certain to wear your flannel weskit to keep from catching a chill. She adds that your son is now the proud possessor of three teeth."

Sir Henry smiled. "I miss them, Mr. Sloan."

"Yes, my lord," said Mr. Sloan in sympathetic tones. "Do you have further instructions for me, my lord?"

"No, thank you, Mr. Sloan. Go get some sleep. We will see you in the morning."

"Very good, my lord."

Mr. Sloan departed, returning to his lodgings. Henry stood a moment, thinking tender thoughts of his Mouse and his little boy.

"You look exhausted, Henry," Simon said, coming up behind him. "Go to bed."

"I am headed in that direction. What about you?"

"You know me," said Simon, shrugging. "Awake at all hours."

He guided his floating chair over to the desk. Sorting through some papers, he plucked one out of the pile and began reading. Henry observed him with affection and admiration. A prisoner in his own body, Simon never complained, never bemoaned his fate. He was the same man he had always been: eager, curious, inventive, a vibrant force in the world.

"Good night, Simon," said Henry.

Absorbed in his work, Simon gave a vague wave.

The next morning, Henry and the others rose early. After only a few hours sleep, they were all bleary eyed and groggy and welcomed the strong, hot tea provided by Mr. Albright. He also cooked breakfast: rashers of bacon and eggs.

Since the dining table was in use for one of Simon's experiments, which they were forbidden to touch, they ate their meal standing. Mr. Sloan arrived as they were finishing. He joined them in Simon's office.

"I stopped at your club, my lord. You have a letter from your lady wife."

He handed the letter to Henry, who took it eagerly and opened it with impatient haste. He read through it swiftly.

"I trust all is well, my lord," said Mr. Sloan.

"Very well, Mr. Sloan," said Henry.

He slid the letter into his front inner pocket and let his hand linger on it fondly for a moment before turning to business.

"You told us last night you had news, Simon."

"According to my calculations, the Bottom Dwellers need to plant only two more boulder-bombs." He pointed to two locations on the map of Freya that hung from the wall. "Here, and here. The chain will then stretch from Dunham in the south to Glenham in the north. It will be complete."

"Have there been any changes to the boulders?" Father Jacob asked. He turned to Mr. Sloan. "I must assume that you went to investigate them."

"I did, Father," said Mr. Sloan, looking surprised. He exchanged startled glances with Henry. "There were changes. How did you know?"

Father Jacob impatiently waved away the question. "Describe what happened."

"Acting upon Mr. Yates's recommendation, I paid a visit to the boulders closest to Haever," said Mr. Sloan. "I had been to see the same boulders last week. This week, only a few days later, I found the soil in which they were embedded had been recently disturbed. I discovered, buried in the dirt at the base of the boulder, an ordinary glass bottle of the type used by purveyors of cheap wine. I had to look to find it. The bottle would be difficult to detect by the casual observer. The bottle was half buried in the ground. If someone did see it, they would think it was only rubbish."

"You did not touch it, I hope?" Father Jacob asked anxiously.

"No, Father," said Mr. Sloan. "Since I feared what might happen if the bottles were disturbed, I did not consider such a course of action to be wise."

"What are you thinking, Father?" Sir Ander asked. "What are these bottles?"

"Detonators," said Father Jacob. "Do you concur, Mr. Yates?"

"A logical assumption," said Simon, nodding. "Dubois said Eiddwen used bottles to release the contramagic on the lift tanks in the Rosian palace."

"Except that in this instance, the magic is meant to explode," said Father Jacob gravely.

"If that is true, how does she intend to set them off?" Simon asked. "The boulders are spaced across a vast distance."

"Perhaps the last boulder in the chain is the one that will light the fuse, so to speak," Father Jacob suggested. "That would trigger all the others."

"That could be true," Simon agreed. "On the other hand, the possibility exists that the contramagic constructs act like a slow-burning fuse."

"But if that is the case," Father Jacob argued, "the possibility also exists that contramagic—"

"Enough!" said Henry impatiently. He looked from Simon to Father Jacob. "Do either of you gentlemen know how to stop these bombs from blowing up?"

The two men looked at each other. Both shook their heads.

"You must remember, Henry, that we are new to the study of contramagic," Simon said.

"Whereas the Bottom Dwellers have been using it for centuries," Father Jacob added.

"So what do we do?" Henry looked grim.

Mr. Sloan gave a deferential cough. "I believe you need to hear the rest of my report, my lord."

"Of course, Mr. Sloan," said Henry. "I am sorry we interrupted you. Please carry on."

"Thank you, my lord. I traveled to the location where Mr. Yates theorized the Bottom Dwellers would place the next boulder in the chain. I had some difficulty locating the boulder, but I eventually found it in a field. The boulder was blank. No magical spells had been drawn on it."

"When was that, Mr. Sloan?" Father Jacob asked excitedly.

"Yesterday morning, Father. I returned immediately to report to Master Yates."

"Any sign of Eiddwen, Mr. Sloan?" Henry asked.

"No, my lord. I made inquiries. No one matching her description has been seen in the area."

"But she *must* be there," said Father Jacob. "She has work to do and only a short time left to do it."

"We might catch that damn female in the act of placing the constructs!" said Alan. "The griffins are still stabled at the club—"

"No griffins," said Simon emphatically. "I knew you would want to go investigate and I've been thinking of how to proceed. Consider this, Henry: five strangers traveling on griffins suddenly arrive in a small town. You would be the talk of the countryside and alert Eiddwen to your presence, as well as giving rise to all manner of wild rumors and speculations."

"You have a point, Simon," said Henry.

"And then there's the problem of Father Jacob," said Simon.

"Why am I a problem?" Father Jacob demanded.

"Forgive me, Father, but the sight of a priest of the Rosian church will most certainly lead to trouble."

"Of course, Mr. Yates. I should have thought of that. I could wear a disguise," suggested Father Jacob.

"I was thinking that you could appear as a one of our clergymen. Our clerics wear the same type of cassock. The only change would be removing the sash, adding the 'dog collar,' and topping it off with a broad-brimmed, round top hat."

"An ideal solution," said Father Jacob.

"I trust wearing such a disguise would not be counted as a sin, would it, Father?" Simon asked.

"If it is, I will gladly perform penance," said Father Jacob.

"What about our story?" Sir Ander asked. "We will need to explain to the locals why we are there."

"Mr. Sloan and I discussed the matter," said Simon. "We concluded that you could pass for sporting gentlemen, out in the country to do some grouse shooting."

"And we would, of course, have our guns with us! Excellent idea," said Alan.

"I hoped you would approve," said Simon. "Mr. Sloan has already acquired clothing worn by the fashionable grouse hunter these days, as well as Father Jacob's disguise."

"Then we will go change," said Henry. "Mr. Sloan, if you would bring around the coach—"

"I took the liberty of anticipating your need, my lord. The coach is waiting for you outside," said Mr. Sloan.

"You gentlemen will be riding in my latest invention—the courier coach. Designed for speed, not comfort," Simon added.

Alan opened his mouth. Henry nudged him and Alan subsided.

"These coaches can be used by diplomats and couriers during those times when traveling by griffin is impractical, such as the cold months of the year," Simon went on. "I reduced the coach to the bare bones, removing the cushioned leather seats, lamps, and fold-down steps. Passengers sit on a wood bench. To keep from sliding, you hold on to hand straps that hang from the ceiling."

"Good God!" Alan exclaimed.

Henry glared at him.

"The body of the coach has been constructed of material chosen for its light weight. I've added magical constructs to increase its strength and durability."

The four men inspected the coach, which was parked on the small dock in front of the house. A handler was holding the two wyverns. For wyverns, they seemed unusually well behaved. When one started to act up, Mr. Sloan fixed the beast with a stern eye and it sullenly calmed down.

"Five will be a tight fit. Alan can sit with Mr. Sloan on the driver's box."

Alan noted the flimsy construction with dismay. "It will be like riding in a goddamn eggshell."

"The coach is perfectly safe," said Simon with pride. "Mr. Albright and I have ridden in it many times. The courier coach is the swiftest vehicle ever invented. Only griffins fly faster."

"Speed is of the essence, Alan," Henry observed.

"So is arriving at our destination in one piece," Alan muttered.

"Now," said Simon, "let me see how you look."

Henry, Alan, and Sir Ander were dressed in typical Freyan hunting costume: brown coat with long, full sleeves, white shirt and cravat, long waistcoat, brown breeches and lace up leather boots. Father Jacob wore his own cassock, the white dog collar around his neck, and the wide-brimmed black hat. Mr. Sloan had provided a variety of weapons, including the new bored rifles. Sir Ander was armed with his dragon pistol and his two nonmagical pistols. These fascinated Simon to such an extent that Sir Ander had some difficulty retrieving them. Mr. Sloan wore his usual attire.

"You look just like men expecting a jolly holiday in the countryside," said Simon.

"You should really have hunting dogs, my lord," said Mr. Sloan worriedly. "If you were truly going grouse hunting, you would have hounds with you to retrieve the birds. I regret that I could not arrange for them on such short notice."

"Never mind, Mr. Sloan," said Henry, hiding his smile. "We will make up some excuse for the lack of dogs. We can always say Alan is afraid of them."

"Very funny," Alan grumbled.

Sir Ander appeared to share Alan's distrust as to the safety of the coach. He noticed Father Jacob examining the constructs with interest.

"What do you think, Father?" Sir Ander asked in a low voice. "Is it safe?"

"As safe as any flying vehicle can be these days," said Father Jacob with unusual solemnity.

Sir Ander looked at him, wondering what he meant. Before he could ask, Father Jacob turned to talk to Simon.

"Remarkable work, Mr. Yates."

"Thank you, Father," said Simon. "I look forward to discussing contramagic with you. I hope you won't have to immediately return to Rosia after all this is over."

Father Jacob gave a wistful smile. "I will have time, Mr. Yates. A great deal of time."

Sir Ander shook his head, thanked Simon for his hospitality and helped Father Jacob into the carriage. Henry climbed in after them and Alan mounted the box to sit alongside Mr. Sloan.

"Safe adventures!" Simon called, waving. "I will see you in a few days. Mr. Albright and I are flying the *Contraption*."

"See you at the rendezvous site. I suggest you gentlemen take firm hold of the straps," Henry advised, shutting the door. "Simon tells me that setting forth can be rather jarring."

Mr. Sloan snapped the whip and shouted at the wyverns. They leaped off the dock, and the coach shook and rattled and tossed around those inside. Sir Ander clung to the strap for dear life, trying at the same time to keep Father Jacob from slamming into him. Sir Ander had told the priest three times to hold on to the strap, but the priest, lost in thought, was not paying attention. They could hear Alan swearing.

Once they had departed, the wyverns settled down and the flight grew smoother. Watching the city of Haever slide past rapidly beneath them, Henry had to admit he was impressed.

"What do you think, Father?"

"Brilliant," said Father Jacob, rousing at last from his thoughts. "Mr. Yates is a genius. But I suggest that once we land, we hire a horse-drawn vehicle."

Father Jacob ran his hand over the wood of the interior, his fingers idly tracing one of the magical constructs. "I would not want to be flying in this or in anything on Fulmea the first. According to Mistress Miri, that is when Xavier plans to launch his invasion fleet. He will most certainly use the drumming to first weaken our magic."

"You think the effect on magic will be as bad as that, Father?" Henry asked, startled.

"I fear it could be," said Father Jacob.

"The fiends have been drumming before now," said Henry, frowning. "You claim that drumming took down the Crystal Market. I find it hard to believe the fiends could knock ships out of the skies!"

"I noticed that the constructs on this coach are already breaking down," said Father Jacob. "The wizard storms Below have thus far blocked the full effect of the contramagic. If the princess and Mistress Gythe manage to stop the storms, the world will feel the full, terrible effect. Ships in the skies, buildings on the ground. Nowhere will be safe."

Sir Ander glanced out the window to see the landscape unrolling beneath them, far, far below. He hurriedly looked away. Henry slid his hand into his inner pocket, touched the letter from his wife.

Alan leaned down from the box to call to them. "Mr. Sloan says we are approaching the area where he found the boulder."

Henry drew out his pistol and checked to make certain it was loaded. Sir Ander did the same. Father Jacob did not carry firearms; his weapon was his magic. As Mr. Sloan slowed the wyverns' flight, the men looked down into a grassy field. Alan had brought along his spyglass. He held it to his eye, gazed through it and shook his head.

"Eiddwen's not there," he reported. "No one is there. At least that I can see. She might have left fiends to keep watch."

"I doubt it," Father Jacob said. "Why should she care if anyone finds a boulder? She is confident. She doesn't know yet that we have discovered her plan. She doesn't believe anyone can stop her."

"She may well be right," said Henry grimly.

The wyverns spiraled downward and brought the coach to a bumpy landing in the field. Mr. Sloan offered to remain on the coach with the wyverns, while the others climbed out and began tramping through the tall grass, heading for the boulder. They walked with their pistols drawn, their eyes sweeping the field.

Father Jacob was in the lead. He came to a sudden stop, raising his hand.

"Put away your weapons, gentlemen. We are too late," said Father Jacob. "Eiddwen has been and gone."

"How the devil do you know that?" Alan demanded.

"There is a trail someone left in the grass over there, heading off toward those trees. And I can see the contramagic constructs glowing on the boulder from here," said Father Jacob. "I am going to take a look. I would advise the rest of you to keep your distance. Including you, Sir Ander."

The rest of them stood where they were as Father Jacob proceeded toward the boulder. He walked around it, studying the constructs intently. At one point, he knelt down on the ground. The others stretched, trying to see.

"What is it, Jacob?" Henry called. "What have you found?"

"The detonator," said Father Jacob.

"Son of a bitch," said Alan.

Father Jacob remained on the ground a long time, studying the detonator. He reached out, taking care not to touch it, and cast some sort of spell. They could all see a faint blue glow of magic.

Alan grew fidgety. He slapped his cheek.

"I'm being eaten alive," he said irritably. "I don't see what good we're doing, standing here staring at the damn rock. I'm going back to the coach."

"We can all go back," said Father Jacob, standing up. "I was hoping to find some way to remove the fuse, but I don't want to tamper with it. I might inadvertently set it off. Eiddwen has been here recently. The blood used in the spell is still liquid—"

"Wait! I found a trail in the grass over here." Alan had gone only a few steps before he came to a stop.

"Oh, God," he said in an altered voice.

"What?" Henry demanded, alarmed. "What have you found?"

Alan didn't reply. He pointed. The others hurried over and gathered around him. The body of a young man lay in the grass that was trampled and wet with blood. His eyes were fixed and staring. His hands and feet were bound. His face was contorted in a grimace of pain and horror.

The young man was bare chested. His homespun shirt lay off to the side, near an empty wine bottle. His breeches were unlaced.

"Eiddwen lured the poor bastard here with the promise of a romp in the hay," Henry remarked bitterly.

"Instead she bound him, tortured him, and killed him. He was alive for a long time. He saw death coming," Father Jacob said.

"God have mercy on his soul," said Sir Ander.

Kneeling down, Father Jacob continued to examine the body. "She opened veins to let him bleed to death. See the cuts here on the thigh and here on the arm. Almost surgical in nature. Very skilled. Very precise."

"Why did she have to torture him?" Alan demanded harshly. "Some sick pleasure?"

Father Jacob looked up at his brother. "I take it you have never before seen a victim of a blood magic ritual. Blood magic requires not only blood. She needed the victim's fear and pain."

"The woman is a monster," said Alan.

Father Jacob closed the staring eyes, then rose to his feet. "There is nothing more we can do for him."

"We can report this to the authorities," said Alan.

Father Jacob and Henry glanced at each other.

"We can't tell anyone, Alan," said Henry. "At least not until this is finished."

"We can't have a bailiff and his men tromping about out here," Father Jacob added. "They might stumble upon the boulder and the detonator. If they touched it . . ."

"We can't leave him to rot!" Alan protested.

"We have no choice," said Father Jacob. "Sir Ander, your handkerchief."

Sir Ander took out his handkerchief and handed it to Father Jacob, who walked to the corpse, placed the handkerchief gently over the man's face and began to pray. Sir Ander bowed his head, and Henry respectfully removed his hat.

"Bugger it!" said Alan, suddenly angry.

He turned on his heel and stalked back to the carriage, viciously tramping the weeds beneath his boots.

Sir Ander was shocked and started to issue a stern reprimand. Father Jacob rested his hand on his friend's arm.

"Let him be," he said gently.

When Father Jacob had concluded his prayer, he looked back at his brother. Alan had climbed up onto the driver's box. He sat hunched over on the seat.

"This is hard for him," Father Jacob said.

"Alan is not squeamish," said Henry, defensive of his friend. "He's waded ankle-deep in blood and never flinched. But I know how he feels."

"You would think I would have become hardened to such grisly sights," said Sir Ander. "Every time I see a victim of blood magic, my gut twists."

"We accept the savagery of war as something honorable. Men go into battle with the willingness to sacrifice their lives for a cause greater than themselves," said Father Jacob. "The victim of murder is not given a choice. The murderer steals life, takes from her victim God's greatest gift. This man was nothing to Eiddwen, less than human. She used his cries of pain and his pleas for mercy only to fuel her magic."

As they walked back to the coach in silence, Henry reflected that his hands were far from clean. He had sanctioned murder, if he had not committed the deed. He absolved himself of any crime. He killed out of necessity, for a cause greater than himself, greater than them all. Someday, he would give his life in the same cause.

He noticed Father Jacob watching him. The priest's expression was grave, as though he had divined his thoughts.

"I sleep quite well at night, Father," said Henry. "Nothing on my conscience."

Father Jacob gave a slight smile and shook his head. "I leave you to God, sir."

They climbed into the carriage. Mr. Sloan snapped his whip over the heads of the wyverns and they flew off. The carriage circled over the boulder and the corpse lying in the flattened, bloodstained grass.

"A terrible sight," said Sir Ander.

"I fear we will see worse than that before we are finished," said Father Jacob.

27

God, fate, or coincidence, somewhere He, She, or It is laughing.

—Captain Alan Northrop

Waight was the town closest to the site of the boulder, one of a series of small towns located on the Longbow Highway that ran from Dunham in the south to Glenham in the north, following the fault line as Henry grimly noted. Originally small farming communities, these towns were becoming more prosperous with the expansion of the highway. Most of them had at least one inn. A few of the more up-and-coming villages offered the traveler the choice of two.

None of the men spoke much on the journey to Waight. They sat in silence, their thoughts dark, until the coach gave an unexpected lurch and began to lose altitude.

Henry opened the window and leaned his head out. He was about to ask what was wrong, when he could see the problem for himself.

He ducked his head back inside. "One of our wyverns has injured its wing and is having difficulty flying."

Since they were near their destination, Mr. Sloan deemed that they could keep going. They could hear him shouting encouragement to the laboring wyvern as the coach sank lower and lower. By the time they reached the inn, the coach was barely skimming the ground. The landing was bumpy, but safe.

Mr. Sloan unhitched the wyverns. After examining the injured wyvern, he looked at Henry and shook his head, then led the beasts to the stables. Henry stood in the yard, gloomily watching the wyvern limp away, dragging its injured wing.

"The wretched beast could not have picked a worse time to get hurt!" Alan remarked bitterly. "The nearest place we can hope to find another wyvern is in Dunham and that is twenty miles away."

"We planned to remain in Waight tomorrow anyway to conduct our investigations," said Father Jacob.

"Father Jacob is right," said Sir Henry. "Mr. Sloan can ride to Dunham tomorrow to purchase another wyvern. I will obtain rooms for the night."

"I don't like the looks of this place," Alan grumbled.

"Then you can sleep in the hayloft," said Henry. "This is the only inn around for miles. Here comes 'mine host.' Let me do the talking."

The master of the hostelry had observed the four well-dressed gentlemen traveling in an elegant wyvern-drawn coach and came hurrying out to greet them. He was a tall man with a bald head and a genial face. His well-rounded paunch was a testament to his wife, the inn's cook, or so he informed them, patting his belly with a broad smile.

"How can I be of service, gentlemen?" he added.

"I am supposed to meet my sister-in-law here. Should have arrived sooner but, as bad luck would have it, the damn wyvern came up lame," said Henry. "As you can see, the beast is not fit to travel. Could you provide us with accommodations until we can find a replacement?"

"If two of you would not mind doubling up, gentlemen,

I can do so," said the innkeeper. "We have only four rooms and one of them is occupied."

"Perhaps the occupant is my sister-in-law," said Henry. "She is Estaran, quite striking in appearance. She is of medium height with black curly hair and black eyes. She might be in company with a young man, her nephew."

The innkeeper shook his head. "I am sorry to disappoint you, sir. The lady currently residing here has chestnut hair and green eyes. She travels in company with two servants. She has been with us for several days."

"That's odd," said Henry, frowning. "I am certain my sister-in-law wrote to meet her at the"—he cast a swift glance at the sign—"Wyvern's Head inn. I trust nothing has happened to her."

"We can't go anywhere with the wyvern laid up, Sir Henry," said Father Jacob. "Perhaps you'll hear some word of her. We'll take a look at those rooms, Innkeep, if you would be so good as to show us."

The innkeeper was all smiles, talking affably as he accompanied them into the inn. His demeanor suddenly changed when he caught sight of Mr. Sloan returning from the stables. The innkeeper stopped talking in midsentence. He stared hard at Mr. Sloan. His brow creased, his eyes narrowed, his lips pursed.

"Who is that person?" he asked coldly.

"He is my manservant," said Henry, taken aback by the sudden change. "Why? What is wrong?"

The innkeeper regarded Henry with contempt.

"I cannot accommodate you, gentlemen."

The innkeeper walked off, leaving the men standing in the yard, staring at one another. They shifted their stares to Mr. Sloan.

"Is anything amiss, my lord?" Mr. Sloan asked worriedly.

"I was about to ask you the same question. What the

devil have you done, Mr. Sloan?" Henry demanded. "That man took one look at you and refused to provide us with lodging."

"Did you sleep with the bloke's wife, Mr. Sloan?" Alan asked, winking at Henry.

Mr. Sloan stiffened and drew himself up. "Certainly not, sir."

"He's jesting, Mr. Sloan," said Henry, casting Alan an exasperated glance. "Can you think of anything?"

"I confess I am baffled, sir," said Mr. Sloan. "I was in this part of the country investigating the boulders, but I took care not to come near the inn. My agents inquired after Mistress Eiddwen."

"Well, now, what do we do? Something is certainly very odd here. Father, you're looking grim. What do you think is going on?"

"I think the young woman staying here is in very great danger," said Father Jacob gravely. "We may already be too late to save her."

Alan blanched. "Good God! Not another bloody corpse! I'll put an end to this!"

He drew his pistol, cocked the hammer, and started for the door. Henry caught hold of him and dragged him back.

"We can't go in guns blazing, Alan. Keep your pistol handy. Let me do the talking. Are you armed, Sir Ander?"

The knight brushed aside his coat, revealing a pistol in his pocket. Alan kept a grip on his weapon, but he released the hammer. Mr. Sloan patted the inner pocket of his coat. Father Jacob folded his hands. He had only his magic and he was the most dangerous of them all.

Henry reached into his pocket, but he did not draw a pistol. He took out a leather case and entered the inn with Alan at his side. Father Jacob moved quickly to the foot of the stairs that led to the rooms on the second level. He peered up, looking and listening. Sir Ander and Mr. Sloan took up positions at the door.

The innkeeper glared at them.

"How dare you barge in here?" he demanded. "Get out of my establishment! I warn you! I will summon the bailiff—"

Alan raised his pistol. The innkeeper gulped. Holding his hands in the air, he backed away from his desk.

"Don't shoot! You can have all the money! It's in the strongbox—"

"We are not here to rob you," said Henry in disgust. He opened the leather case, drew out a card and laid it on the desk. "I am Sir Henry Wallace. You might have heard of me."

"Wallace!" The innkeeper went pale as death and began to wring his hands. "Please, your lordship. I am innocent! I have done nothing! Don't take me to prison. I have a wife, children—"

"All I want is information, my good man," said Henry in soothing tones. "How did you know of Mr. Sloan? Is there some connection to the young woman staying here?"

The innkeeper hesitated.

"Be quick, sir!" Father Jacob said urgently. "Her life may depend on it!"

"She . . . she arrived two nights ago, your lordship," said the innkeeper. "She's very young and pretty, sir. She told me she was fleeing her abusive husband and she begged for my help. She asked me to keep him away if he came."

The innkeeper cast a stricken glance at Mr. Sloan. "She gave me a description of the brute. I regret to say it matches you perfectly, sir."

"Very clever. She knew you were on her trail, Mr. Sloan," said Henry.

"Is this young woman traveling alone?" asked Sir Ander.

"Yes," said the innkeeper. "Except for her two servants. She has no visitors."

"And is she still in her room?"

"As far as I know, your lordship," said the quaking innkeeper. "I took luncheon up to her not long ago."

"What the devil difference does it make if she's in her room or not?" Alan asked impatiently. "The woman in that room can't be Eiddwen. She might be good at disguising herself, but she's not that good—"

"Not her," said Father Jacob sharply. "Her servants!"

"Two servants! Of course!" said Henry. "What room is she in?"

"Number four, the room at the end of the hall."

"Keep watch at the door, Mr. Sloan!" Henry ordered.

Father Jacob was already hurrying up the stairs. Henry and Alan and Sir Ander climbed quickly after him.

"Quiet!" Father Jacob ordered softly.

Arriving on the second floor, they moved down the hall, trying not to make any noise and not succeeding. Henry winced each time a floorboard creaked and groaned beneath his feet.

When they came to the door marked with the number *4* in brass, Henry motioned Father Jacob and Alan to stay back. Alan had his pistol drawn. Henry drew his pistol, then rapped at the door.

"Who is it?" a woman called.

"Is that her voice?" Alan mouthed.

Henry shook his head.

"Innkeeper," he said, doing a credible imitation of the man's voice. "I saw the man you warned me about, your brute of a husband."

"Oh, my heavens! Please come in and tell me what you saw," said the young woman. "The door is unlocked."

"Be careful!" Father Jacob warned softly.

Henry nodded. "We go on three! One, two, three—"

He flung open the door and sprang inside, pistol drawn. Alan ran in with him. The room's only occupant, a young woman, rose to her feet, regarding them with astonishment.

"Who are you?" she gasped. "What is the meaning of this?"

"We mean you no harm, mistress. Search the room, Alan," Henry ordered.

He looked behind the curtains. Alan opened the door to the wardrobe and peered inside. Father Jacob stood in the doorway. Sir Ander stayed near the priest.

"No one else here," Alan reported.

Henry turned back to the young woman. She was in her early twenties, or so he guessed. Her long chestnut hair was bound neatly around her head in braids. She was fair complected with a flush of rose on her cheeks. Her pretty frock was plain, but well made.

"Who do you expect to find? I am quite alone, as you see," she said haughtily.

Henry glanced out the window. "Where are your servants, madame?"

"I sent them on an errand," she replied. "Tell me, gentlemen, do you make a practice of barging into ladies' boudoirs with pistols? Or have I been specially singled out?"

Alan cast an accusing glance at his brother. "She's in no danger, Jacob. You've made us look like damn fools!"

Alan removed his hat and bowed. "We beg your pardon, madame. We have made a dreadful mistake. I hope you will forgive us."

The young woman regarded the handsome captain with a smile. She hesitated, then relented.

"How could I reject such a charming apology," she said. "We must be friends. I am Irene Fairchild."

She held out her hand to him.

"Don't touch her, Alan!" Father Jacob warned. "She's a sorceress!"

Henry didn't know if she was a sorceress or not, but he was suspicious of the young woman's calm demeanor. By rights, with four strange men invading her room, she should have been shrieking for help.

"Oh, for God's sake, Jacob, don't be an ass!" Alan said in disgust.

Taking hold of the young woman's hand, he bent to kiss it.

Irene smiled at him. "I am so pleased to meet you, Captain—"

Her hand darted from the folds of her skirt and thrust a dagger into his midriff. Alan gasped in shock and pain. He pressed his hand to his side and drew back his fingers, covered in blood. But the dagger meant to kill had merely sliced through his flesh. The magical constructs sewn into his weskit had saved him from serious harm.

"What the devil . . ."

"Alan, she has drawn blood!" Father Jacob cried, running toward his brother. "Get away from her—"

He was too late. Irene threw the dagger to the floor and flung her arms around Alan, using his blood to fuel her spell. Fiery red magic crackled from her body and twined about Alan. He screamed in agony. Writhing and twisting, he struck out at her, trying to break free of the deadly embrace.

Henry raised his pistol, but the two were so closely bound that he dared not fire for fear of hitting his friend.

"Jacob, do something!" Henry cried hoarsely.

Father Jacob seized hold of Irene's arms. "Release him!" he commanded.

"Go to the hell that spawned you, priest!" Irene snarled.

Her blood magic crackled. Father Jacob grimaced in

pain, but he kept fast hold of her. Blue radiance spread from his hand.

"Release him!" he said again.

The blue glow of his magic intensified. Irene cried out in anger and fell back, letting go. Alan dropped to the floor, groaning. Henry lowered his pistol and was going to help his friend when Irene suddenly sprang at him, her hands extended, her fingers covered in blood.

The sound of a pistol shot startled him. Irene gazed at him, smiled, then slumped to the floor. Blood poured from a bullet wound in her back. Sir Ander lowered his smoking pistol.

Henry knelt down beside the body of the young woman. Her fists remained clenched, even in death. He carefully pried loose the fingers of her right hand. A small glass bottle rolled out onto the floor.

Father Jacob passed his hand over it. The bottle began to glow with a bright green light. Henry jumped to his feet and scrambled back.

"We are quite safe," said Father Jacob. "Watch!"

The green light faded. The bottle broke with a loud crack, splitting into two pieces, spilling out a large quantity of crystals. Father Jacob sifted through them.

"Sulfur crystals laced with bitumen," he said. "When set on fire, they produce a lethal gas. Such a weapon was first used in the waning days of the Sunlit Empire, killing two hundred soldiers in less than two minutes—"

He was interrupted by a bellow from Mr. Sloan, who had been left to watch the front of the inn. "My lord, they're getting away!"

They could hear the pounding of horses' hooves and the sound of carriage wheels crunching over the gravel. Henry opened the window and leaned out to see a phaeton rolling past the front of the inn. A young man was driving. The female passenger, seated beside, looked up at him.

"Eiddwen!" he muttered.

She smiled at him, as if she had heard him. And then she was gone. The phaeton whirled off down the highway.

"We have to go after her!" said Henry.

"How?" Sir Ander demanded. "Our wyvern's hurt—"

"Mr. Sloan will find a suitable conveyance," said Henry. "Alan, can you stand?"

Alan tried to push himself to his feet, only to collapse, groaning.

"What is the matter with me?" he gasped. "I feel like my blood is on fire!"

"Her magic," said Father Jacob. "I can help."

Alan shrank from his brother's touch. "Not you. I am fine. I just need a moment to rest."

"Don't be a bloody fool, Alan!" said Henry sharply. "We don't have time for this nonsense. Let Father Jacob treat you."

Alan didn't like it, but he obeyed. Father Jacob knelt beside his brother and placed his hands on his breast. A soft blue glow spread over Alan and he breathed out a sigh of relief. Father Jacob started to put his arm around him to help him up. Alan pulled away.

"I can manage," he said tersely. He staggered to his feet. "Where's my pistol?"

"You dropped it over here," said Henry.

Alan was a bit woozy, but he could walk on his own. His weskit and the shirt beneath were stained with blood. He picked up the pistol and headed for the door. They were leaving the room, when Henry realized Father Jacob was not with them. He stopped to look back.

Father Jacob had removed his hat and was standing over the young woman, his hands folded.

"What the devil is he doing?" Henry demanded.

"Saying a prayer for the dead," said Sir Ander.

"A prayer! That blasted female tried to murder me!" Alan said angrily.

"As Father Jacob would say, she is one of God's children," said Sir Ander. "You gentlemen go on ahead. Father Jacob and I will catch up with you."

Alan cast Henry a grim glance. "And you talk to *me* about wasting time with nonsense."

He started down the hall. Henry looked back into the room.

Father Jacob began to pray. "Your power gives us life. By Your command, we return to dust. . . ."

Henry shrugged and went on, catching up to Alan.

Hurrying down the stairs, they came up short. The innkeeper was waiting for them at the bottom of the stairs, holding an ancient blunderbuss in a shaking hand.

"Don't move! I will shoot!" said the innkeeper. "So help me, God!"

The door to the inn stood open. Through it, Henry could see Mr. Sloan, his pistol drawn, standing alongside a luxurious landau drawn by a pair of matching black horses.

"Deal with this gentleman, will you, Alan?" said Henry.

Turning aside the muzzle of the blunderbuss, he walked past the innkeeper and out the door. Mr. Sloan was aiming his pistol at an enraged gentleman, his equally enraged wife, and their bewildered elderly coachman.

"I see you found us a carriage. Well done, Mr. Sloan," said Henry.

"Thank you, my lord," said Mr. Sloan.

Henry glanced at the coat of arms on the door of the landau and doffed his hat. "Sir Oswald Beckham, if I am not mistaken. I am Sir Henry Wallace and I am commandeering your landau in the name of the queen."

The nobleman went red in the face.

"I don't give a damn who you are—" he began.

Lady Oswald gasped and jabbed her husband in the ribs. "Henry Wallace! He's the queen's—"

She whispered something to her husband, who went from red to sickly yellow.

"Of course, you may have the carriage, Sir Henry," Lady Oswald said meekly, dropping a curtsy.

Her husband whipped off his hat and bowed.

"Thank you, madame. Mr. Sloan, go fetch the rifles from our carriage. I will keep an eye on Sir Oswald and his lady." Henry drew out his own pistol.

Mr. Sloan returned to the barn and came back armed with the rifles. Stowing these inside the landau, he climbed onto the driver's seat and took hold of the reins. Alan emerged from the inn. He glanced from Henry, who still held the pistol, to the quaking nobleman and grinned.

"I see Mr. Sloan found us a carriage."

"How is 'mine host'?" Henry asked.

"I took the gun away from him," said Alan. "Fool man might have shot someone. Speaking of fools, Jacob is right behind me."

Alan opened the half door and climbed into the landau.

Father Jacob and Sir Ander came hurrying out of the inn. Sir Ander held open the half door and helped the priest in. Alan was lowering the landau's cloth top, which was divided in half, so that the top could be opened with one half folding into the back and the other half into the front. Henry shoved his pistol into his coat and swung himself up onto the box alongside Mr. Sloan. He tipped his hat to the aggrieved nobleman.

"Her Majesty extends her grateful thanks! Ready when you are, Mr. Sloan."

Mr. Sloan slapped the reins on the backs of the horses and they lunged forward. The landau rolled out of the yard and onto the road.

"They were heading north, my lord," said Mr. Sloan.

"Very good, Mr. Sloan," said Henry, getting a firm grip on the seat irons.

A landau was a type of carriage meant to be driven around the park or taken for a leisurely drive through the countryside. The horses had probably never run faster than a slow walk. Mr. Sloan cracked the whip and the horses, startled, broke into a gallop.

"They are traveling down the highway in the direction of Dunham, my lord," said Mr. Sloan. "According to Master Yates, that is site of the last boulder."

The landau bounced up and down on its springs, making for an extremely uncomfortable ride.

"Indeed, Mr. Sloan," said Henry, trying to keep from biting his tongue.

"They have about a fifteen minute start on us, my lord," said Mr. Sloan. "They are traveling in a phaeton. I did not recognize the young man who was driving. I did recognize Mistress Eiddwen."

"So did I," said Henry grimly.

"She was dressed as a servant, as Father Jacob surmised. I assume the young man is her accomplice?"

"Twenties, dark hair, good-looking, walks with a limp?"

"I did not see him walk, but, yes, sir. That describes him."

"The Warlock," Henry stated. "Very dangerous, the pair of them."

"Did they kill the young woman, my lord?" Mr. Sloan asked.

"In a way. She was their accomplice. She tried to kill us. Sir Ander shot her."

Henry looked over his shoulder. Alan and Sir Ander were attempting to load the two rifled long guns, as well as an assortment of pistols, not an easy task, given the jouncing of the landau. Father Jacob clung to the sides, trying to keep his seat. The wind had carried away his hat. Henry clamped his own tricorn down hard on his head.

"Lucky for us Sir Oswald happened to be driving past," Henry commented.

" 'Ask and ye shall receive,' my lord," Mr. Sloan said gravely.

"You prayed to God to send us a carriage, Mr. Sloan?" Henry could not resist teasing his secretary. "You should have asked Him for one with a more comfortable ride."

"I fear that in my haste, my lord, I asked for a conveyance in which to pursue the criminals. I did not think to specify what type," said Mr. Sloan, adding. "I will know better next time."

Henry glanced in astonishment at Mr. Sloan, then saw the small smile on his lips.

"You made a jest, Mr. Sloan!" said Henry, chuckling.

"I trust my levity is not misplaced, my lord, given the gravity of our situation," said Mr. Sloan.

He slapped the reins on the horses' backs. They had attained their stride now, breaking into a mad gallop. Mr. Sloan had all he could do to keep them under control. Henry peered down the road, trying in vain to catch a glimpse of their quarry.

"Our time for laughter may be growing short, Mr. Sloan," said Henry with a sigh. "We should make the best of it."

28

God hath work to do in this world; and to desert it because of its difficulties and entanglements, is to cast off His authority.

—Franklin Sloan

The landau jounced and rattled down the dirt road. Mr. Sloan yelled and cracked the whip. The horses galloped madly, hooves pounding, nostrils flared. Henry hung on to the rails and stared ahead, trying in vain to see Eid-dwen's phaeton. The road was muddy from the recent rains and the tracks of the wheels were clearly visible, but there was no sign of the carriage itself.

The driver's seat was only slightly elevated above the seats of the passengers. Father Jacob was sitting directly behind Henry, and the priest's head collided with his back whenever the landau's wheels bumped over a rut.

"Pistol or rifle?" Alan shouted.

"Pistol," Henry yelled back. "You're a better shot than I am with the rifle!"

As he reached for the pistol, the landau bounced over a stone, almost throwing him off the seat and causing him to bite his lip. He spat blood and swore.

"I see the phaeton, sir," Mr. Sloan reported.

"Do you, by God?" Henry squinted down the road and shook his head. "I don't. You have eyes like a hawk, Mr. Sloan."

He turned to report to the others. "Our quarry is in sight."

Alan stood up, swaying perilously, steadying himself by placing his hand on Sir Ander's shoulder. "I see it. Too far away yet for a decent shot. What's the young man's name? The one you call the Warlock."

"I doubt he knows his true name. He was some guttersnipe Eiddwen picked up. He is known as Lucello."

Henry now had the phaeton in sight. A light, open-air carriage pulled by a single horse, the phaeton was the vehicle of choice for rash young men who dared each other to races on lazy Sunday afternoons.

"I fear we are not going to catch them, my lord," said Mr. Sloan. "They have only one horse to our two, but with five people in the landau, our horses will start to tire."

Father Jacob had twisted around to see, and he overheard Mr. Sloan.

"Slow the carriage!" he shouted. "Sir Ander and I will jump out!"

Startled, Mr. Sloan turned to Henry.

"He's right!" said Henry. "Slow the carriage."

Mr. Sloan slowed the horses. Sir Ander handed the rifle to Alan and with the wheels still rolling, he and Father Jacob leaped out. Mr. Sloan shouted and cracked the whip and the landau hurtled on faster than before. Alan, standing upright, spread his legs wide on the landau's floor for balance. His head was about level with Henry's shoulders.

Henry looked behind to see Father Jacob waving to them as he and Sir Ander trudged down the road.

"He's a decent fellow, your brother," Henry remarked to Alan. "That time I tried to kill him, I'm rather glad my pistol misfired."

Alan grunted. He lifted the rifle and put it to his shoulder.

They were gaining on the phaeton. Henry could see Eiddwen, her black curly hair whipping in the wind, sitting beside the Warlock. He saw her glance over her shoulder, gaze at them a moment, and then lean close to say something to her companion. Probably urging him to drive faster.

"Too far yet," said Alan, lowering the rifle. "You realize, Henry, that this shot is going to take more luck than skill."

"That's why you are doing the shooting, Alan," said Henry.

The pursuit continued. The horses' hooves pounded, flinging up clumps of mud that struck the landau and its occupants. Intent on watching those they were pursuing, excited by the chase, Henry paid no heed to the mud spattering his face and clothes. He leaned forward on the seat, his hands gripping the rails.

Mr. Sloan was intent on managing the horses and trying to avoid the deep ruts in the road. Alan stood with one hand braced against the seat, the other holding the rifle. He kept the barrel pointed down and focused intently on the ever-narrowing gap between the landau and the phaeton. Not one to waste a shot by firing wildly, he waited with the patience of the skilled marksman.

Lucello had his back to them, shoulders hunched, driving the horse, and Eiddwen was looking at the road ahead. As the landau drew closer, Alan lifted the rifle.

Eiddwen turned toward them again, and stretched out her right arm. Henry realized she was holding a pistol, but it was too late to duck. He saw a puff of smoke and heard a flat-sounding bang.

"She's shooting at us," said Henry.

Alan shook his head. "Waste of a bullet. The range is too far for a pistol."

He raised the rifle to his shoulder. The landau bounced and shook and he leaned his bent knee against the seat to steady himself. He had no choice but to hold the rifle so that the barrel thrust out between Henry and Mr. Sloan.

"This will be loud," Alan warned.

Henry covered his ears with his hands. Mr. Sloan leaned away from the rifle as far as he could. Alan aimed and fired.

They watched intently. Lucello looked back and kept driving, and Eiddwen was again facing forward as the phaeton drove on.

"Missed, damn it," said Alan.

He dropped the empty rifle and reached for the second.

They lost sight of the phaeton a moment as they crested a small hill, speeding past fields planted with wheat and corn. Then the road dipped down and they caught sight of the phaeton again, heading for an old stone bridge that spanned a small, sun-dappled stream.

The bridge had been built a hundred years ago to accommodate farm wagons and pedestrians and was so narrow only a single vehicle could pass, so anyone driving the opposite direction would have to pull over to wait. The stone surface had been paved over, but Henry could see the cracks in the surface even from here.

"The phaeton will have to slow down or risk breaking a wheel or crippling their horse," Henry remarked.

"Now we have them," said Alan.

As the landau hurtled down the hill, Henry could see Lucello had slowed the phaeton. Alan took careful aim, but just as he fired, the landau's front wheel hit a rock, throwing him off balance.

Henry had forgotten in the excitement to cover his ears, and the blast half deafened him. He watched the pair closely. The phaeton rolled across the bridge and then sped up. Henry shook his head.

"You must have missed."

Alan swore. "I'd have better luck throwing rocks at them!"

He crouched down in the landau to reload the rifles. Henry drew his pistol, planning to try for a shot himself. He then thought better of it. He wouldn't have time to reload and he would need his pistol if he did manage to capture Eiddwen. The landau wobbled from side to side. Alan was swearing again as he spilled gunpowder all over the floor.

As the landau came up on the bridge. Mr. Sloan hauled on the reins with all his strength, shouting at the horses. Henry kept his eyes fixed on Eiddwen; when she turned around and held up her hand, he thought she was going to shoot at them again. But she wasn't holding a pistol. The object glittered brightly in the sunlight reminding him of glass . . . a glass bottle . . .

"Alan! Shoot her!" Henry cried.

Alan rose to his feet, bringing the rifle to his shoulder. Before he could fire, Eiddwen flung the bottle at them. It landed on the bridge and rolled toward them.

"Stop!" Henry roared. "Stop the horses, Mr. Sloan!"

Mr. Sloan struggled to obey, but the maddened horses were out of control and rushed forward. The landau's wheels hit the rough surface of the stone bridge, shaking every bone in Henry's body.

"Look out, sir!" Mr. Sloan cried.

A red cloud of noxious gas blossomed right in front of them. Crackling red sparks erupted from the cloud, exploding beneath the horses' hooves. The animals shrieked in terror and reared up in the traces. One fell and landed on its side, hooves lashing, dragging the other down and causing the landau to roll over.

Henry hung on for dear life as the landau crashed. He heard wood splintering, horses screaming and the blast of Alan's rifle. Mr. Sloan, sitting next to him, disappeared.

And then with startling suddenness, everything stopped moving. The landau was on its side in the road, wheels spinning, with Henry still perched on the seat, still gripping the seat irons.

Alan appeared out of nowhere. "Henry, are you all right? Does anything hurt?"

"Everything hurts," said Henry, coughing in the smoke. He had to make a conscious effort to pry his fingers loose. "But I don't think anything's broken. What about Eiddwen?"

"They're getting away," said Alan bitterly, helping Henry to his feet.

Henry groaned. He was going to be one massive bruise. Blinking his eyes, he tried to see through the remnants of the red cloud, and could just barely glimpse the phaeton rolling down the road.

"You all right?" Henry looked at Alan.

"Not a scratch on me. I managed to jump out as we were tipping."

"What about you, Mr. Sloan?"

Hearing no answer, Henry glanced about. "Where *is* Mr. Sloan?"

"I lost sight of him," said Alan worriedly, looking around. He let out a cry. "There! In the water!"

They rushed to the edge of the bridge. Mr. Sloan was lying face-down in the creek. A stream of blood, flowing out from beneath his head, stained the water red. He was not moving.

"Good God! Alan, help me!"

The two men plunged down the embankment, slipping and skidding on loose rocks. They splashed into the shallow water and finally reached Mr. Sloan. Henry bent to examine him.

"His head struck a rock. He's not breathing!"

"We have to get him to shore," said Alan.

Between them, they took hold of Mr. Sloan by the shoulders and dragged him out of the water. Alan rolled Mr. Sloan over onto his back and thrust his hand down his throat. Water trickled out. Alan pressed his mouth over Mr. Sloan's and began breathing air into his lungs.

Henry watched anxiously and after a heart-stopping moment, Mr. Sloan coughed and gagged and drew in a breath. He moaned in pain, but did not regain consciousness. The deep, ugly gash on his forehead was bleeding freely. Henry, gently probing with his fingers, could feel the crack in the skull. His flesh was white, and as cold as a corpse.

Henry took off his coat and wrapped it around Mr. Sloan. "He's going into shock. We need to take him someplace warm."

"You stay with him," Alan said. "I'll go see if we can use the carriage."

Alan scrambled back up the embankment, and managed to untangle the traces and free the horses. Both beasts staggered to their feet, but one was limping and the other was clearly still in the grip of terror. Foaming at the mouth, eyes rolling wildly, the horse shied away whenever Alan came near. Once he finally had the horse under control, he tied both to the branch of a tree growing near the bridge and then went back to inspect the landau.

"Broken axle," he reported. "And the horses are finished. One has a bruised shoulder and the other is mad with fear. I'll go for help. There must be a farmhouse nearby."

Henry had pressed his handkerchief on Mr. Sloan's wound to try to stanch the bleeding, but the handkerchief was immediately soaked. He considered how far they had traveled from the last village, how far they had to travel before they reached Dunham and gave an inward sigh.

"I think I remember seeing—"

"Wait! Someone's coming!" Alan called, pointing to a farmer's wagon that had just topped the crest of the hill. He stood in the middle of the road, waving his arms and hallooing. The wagon came rolling to a stop. Father Jacob and Sir Ander jumped off the back. Seeing Mr. Sloan lying on the ground near the stream, they came running.

"Passing farmer," Father Jacob explained, kneeling beside Mr. Sloan. "We asked him for a lift."

"Can you help him, Father?" Henry asked.

"I am not a healer, unfortunately." Father Jacob shook his head gravely. "He needs expert medical attention. The farmer who drove us was telling us that his house is near here. We will take him there."

The farmer had been hauling hay and the bed was still covered with straw. Sir Ander and Alan carried Mr. Sloan between them and laid him in the wagon. While they were making the injured man comfortable, Henry questioned the farmer.

"Is there a physician in the area? A healer?"

"Little Sadie," said the farmer, nodding.

"What sort of healer is Little Sadie?" Henry asked, skeptical.

"Trundler, your lordship," said the farmer.

Henry scowled. "No one else?"

"Little Sadie's all we've ever needed, your lordship."

"The Trundlers have been practicing the healing arts for centuries," said Father Jacob.

Henry only shook his head. Alan obtained directions to Little Sadie's and set off at a run.

Sir Ander offered to take the injured horses to the farm. Neither could be ridden and so he walked, leading them by the reins. Father Jacob and Henry sat in the back of the wagon with Mr. Sloan. The farmer drove slowly to minimize jostling Mr. Sloan as much as possible.

Henry grasped Mr. Sloan's cold hand and gazed down

anxiously at the man who had been so much more to him than a secretary; who had rushed into a collapsing house to save him and his family; who had saved his life on more than one occasion.

"He is strong," said Father Jacob in a reassuring tone. "Do not lose hope."

"Spare me your platitudes, Father," Henry returned morosely. "You and I both know that men with cracked skulls sometimes never wake up."

"What happened? How did Mr. Sloan come to fall into the stream?"

"Eiddwen threw some sort of bomb at us. A red cloud of noxious gas and fireworks spooked the horses, causing the landau to crash. She escaped and now we have lost her."

"We know where she is going," said Father Jacob with quiet confidence. "Where she *has* to go, to put in place the final magical spell."

Henry gave a bitter snort. "The last boulder was hidden in the middle of a field miles from any town. We have no wyverns. We don't have even any bloody horses! The day after tomorrow is the first day of Fulmea, the day she is supposed to destroy Freya. How the devil are we supposed to stop her?"

"Certainly *not* by asking the devil," said Father Jacob with a half smile. "Mr. Yates and Mr. Albright are searching for the boulder from the air, aren't they?"

"They are. Simon may have found it, in fact. But the rendezvous site is outside of Dunham and we have no way to reach the site to find *him,*" said Henry, discouraged.

The wagon turned off the highway onto a road that was little more than two well-worn ruts. In the distance, they could see a modest farmhouse and outbuildings.

"You priests believe in miracles, don't you, Father?" Henry asked.

"A dead saint spoke to me," said Father Jacob. "Her voice was as clear to me as yours. She led me to the understanding of contramagic. Yes, I believe in miracles."

"We could use a miracle now. I suggest you pray to this dead saint of yours to work a miracle and send us some horses."

"I'm not sure Saint Marie is in the business of horse-trading," said Father Jacob. "But as we were riding here, the farmer was telling us about his master, the Earl of Brooking. The earl raises and trains griffins."

"I'll be damned," said Henry in almost reverent tones. "I am acquainted with the earl, Lord John Benedict, though I have never been to his estate. We are not friends. He is a bit of an eccentric, as well as being a member of the loyal opposition. But, now that I recall, he is known for keeping griffins."

Henry regarded Father Jacob in wondering silence for a moment, then shifted his gaze to Mr. Sloan. The wounded man had quit moaning. He was not responding to anything, even the bumping of the wagon. Henry had to rest his hand on his heart to make certain he had not died.

"Will you do something for me, Father?" he asked abruptly. "Will you say a prayer for Mr. Sloan?"

"I would be glad to, Sir Henry, but I fear my prayers might offend Mr. Sloan," said Father Jacob gently. "He does not approve of me or my religion."

"What he doesn't know can't hurt him," said Henry.

29

Despite the fact that our country deserted us, let it never be said that we deserted our country.

—Lord Haelgrund of the Dragon Brigade

Stephano rose early, far too preoccupied with all he had to accomplish today to stay in bed. Tomorrow the tugboats sent by the prince would arrive to haul the fortress out into the Breath, and the fortress was far from ready to fly. Rodrigo and his crafters were still working on the magic. Dag was not satisfied with the gunners so he was going to conduct yet another gunnery practice. Miri was working on the *Cloud Hopper,* which they were going to take with them. The unexpected arrival of supplies he'd been told not to expect meant that everything the sailors had previously stowed had to be shifted about to make room. And just when he thought he had thought of everything, he remembered something else.

Still in his shirtsleeves, he climbed the stairs to the battlements at the top of the fortress. Aside from those on watch, he was the only one awake and walking the battlements this early. Dawn was just breaking, and faint pinkish yellow light was starting to spread over the eastern sky. Soon the trumpet would sound and the world would wake and he would be plunged into the frantic chaos of preparing his fortress to descend into the Breath. But for now, the world was quiet. Still asleep.

A slight breeze sprang up, ruffling his hair and parting the morning mists. He was about to go back to his room, bathe and dress and prepare for the day, when movement caught his eye.

He gazed in that direction. His pulse quickened. His heart raced. His breath came fast.

The dragons had been hidden from view by pink-tinged mists of God's Breath. Now he could see them, flying in formation as they had flown so many times before. There were not many of them, only about twelve, a far cry from the thirty-six dragons that had once formed the Brigade. Haelgrund was leading them, flying proudly in front, with the other dragons in a *V* formation on either side of him.

"You came," said Stephano softly.

The soldiers would catch sight of the dragons any moment now and raise the alarm. But for just an instant, in the stillness of the morning, this moment of happiness was his own. The old loyalties remained; the past could be forgiven, if never forgotten.

Droal, the old quartermaster dragon, was the next to see the returning members of the Brigade. Wakened, perhaps, by stirrings of memories, he raised his head and saw the approaching dragons shredding the mists with their wings. He gave a trumpeting roar of welcome that woke Viola, Petard, and Verdi.

Petard was about to leap into the air and fly to join them—a serious breach of etiquette. Hroal hooted a command that stopped the young dragon in midleap. Viola added her own scolding and Petard slunk off, chastened, but Stephano saw the gleam of excitement in the young dragon's eyes. Viola herself was flustered, holding her head a little too high, trying to look as if the return of Haelgrund was of no interest to her. When Verdi saw her preening, he gnashed his teeth and dug his claws into the dirt.

The men on watch were shouting in astonishment, staring and pointing. Stephano had told them to be on the lookout for the members of the Dragon Brigade. He was fairly certain most had not believed him.

"Where's that piper?" Stephano called sharply.

"I'll fetch him, sir!" came a voice behind him.

Stephano turned to see the energetic and ubiquitous Master Tutillo running down the stairs, shouting for the piper at the top of his lungs. Stephano wondered how long the lad had been up and lurking about, hoping to be of use.

A short time later, Master Tutillo returned with the piper. The man had obviously been roused from his bed; his uniform coat flapped open, his hat wobbled on his head, his gaiters sagged.

"Play 'The Jolly Beggarman,'" Stephano ordered.

The piper blinked the sleep from his eyes, drew in a deep breath, brought the mouthpiece to his lips and began to play the rousing march. Prior to this, Master Tutillo had buttoned the man's uniform coat, straightened his hat, fixed his gaiters, and made him presentable.

Stephano gave the order to raise the colors. As the Rosian flag soared into the air, Stephano stood at attention. He noticed, out of the corner of his eye, Master Tutillo doing his best to imitate his captain, standing so stiffly he was in danger of falling over.

The dragons circled the fortress, dipping their wings in salute. Everyone in the fortress was awake now, hurrying from their quarters to witness the sight. Dag came running up the stairs, with Miri at his heels.

"They came, sir!" Dag exclaimed.

"I knew they would," said Miri, smiling at Stephano.

She wore a shawl wrapped around her shoulders, and her red curls were unbound, blazing in the sunshine. Dag was resplendent in his new lieutenant's dress uniform. The coat was the largest size he had been able to obtain from the admiralty at short notice and was still a tight fit. Stephano expected the shoulder seams to give way at any moment.

The dragons landed in the open field, starting with Haelgrund. Stephano missed the human members of the Brigade. Even if he'd known the dragons were coming, he would not have had time to summon them. But the dragons were here and that was what counted. They had all been trained to fight without riders.

"Should I fetch your coat and hat, sir?" Master Tutillo asked, diplomatically reminding his captain he was still in his shirtsleeves.

"Good God! I have to change!"

Stephano started down the stairs.

"And you might want to shave!" Miri called after him.

Once he was presentable, wearing his dress coat, Stephano made ready to leave the fortress to greet the dragons. He was taking Dag with him. He would have taken Miri, but she said she wasn't dressed to meet dragon nobility and she had work to do aboard the houseboat.

As they were leaving the officers' quarters, he and Dag nearly ran headlong into Rodrigo.

"Rigo!" Stephano exclaimed, amazed. "You're awake!"

"Don't remind me," Rodrigo muttered.

He was unshaven, with his hair straggling around his face and his shirt buttoned wrong. He was wearing two different style boots, and he stumbled along the corridor blindly, squinting against the sunlight streaming in through the main gate.

"What are you doing up at this hour?" Stephano asked.

"I have to finish working on the magic. It's taking longer than I anticipated. Why the hell does God have to make the sun so bloody bright! You'd think He'd have some consideration."

"Master Tutillo!" Stephano shouted.

"Here, sir!" said the midshipman, popping out from beneath Stephano's elbow.

"Fetch Monsieur Rodrigo a cup of strong tea."

"Yes, sir!" Master Tutillo dashed off, heading for the galley.

"Point me in the direction of the bridge," said Rodrigo groggily.

Stephano aimed his friend the right way and watched him stumble down the corridor, heading for the stairs that led up to the bridge, which overlooked the main gate.

"Rigo's done yeoman's work, sir," Dag remarked, adding in grudging tones. "I never dreamed I'd say it, but I've been mistaken about him all these years. I used to think he was a lazy, selfish bastard with the morals of a tomcat. But I was wrong. He's worked sunup to sundown, walking on scaffolding ten feet off the ground."

"He *is* accustomed to climbing out of the windows of ladies' bedrooms. I don't suppose he finds this much different," said Stephano, grinning. He grew more serious. "I'm glad you've come to value him, Dag. I've found that Rigo always rises to the challenge."

"Like pond scum, sir?" Dag suggested.

Stephano laughed. "For God's sake, don't tell him that!"

They left the fortress through the main gate and walked out into the field where the dragons were resting after their long flight. Haelgrund greeted them and made formal introductions, although Stephano remembered every one of them. His father had taught him that like people, dragons appreciate personal attention. Stephano took the time to ask about each dragon's family, and he carefully avoided politics.

With this formality concluded, Stephano introduced the three wild dragons. These noble dragons had not attended the Gathering, but they had heard what had happened and they observed their wild cousins with interest. The young dragons were abashed in such exalted company and kept their distance.

Stephano brought forth Hroal and Droal, who had been staying in the background. The two were common dragons of low rank, fit to supply the food the noble dragons required, but that was all. Stephano praised the fine work the brothers had done teaching the young dragons, bringing in deer meat, and helping with the refitting of the fortress. The noble dragons listened politely and asked when they could expect to be fed.

Finally, Stephano was able to talk privately to Haelgrund.

"I hope you won't be in too much trouble with the duke," said Stephano.

"He sanctioned our coming," said Haelgrund.

"Did he?" Stephano was amazed. "Why did he change his mind?"

"You have the Duchess of Talwin to thank. It seems her grace met with a priest, someone called Father Jacob. He told her about the Bottom Dwellers and explained how they were killing our young. She told her husband that he was wrong about them and argued that the dragons should stand with the humans in this battle. The duchess doesn't blaze up often, but when she does, the duke listens."

"God bless the duchess!" said Stephano, thinking she sounded a lot like his mother.

"And now, Captain, what is the plan?" Haelgrund asked.

The sun was fierce this morning; Stephano and Dag were both sweating in their heavy uniforms. Stephano proposed they walk over to stand in the shadow cast by the fortress walls. Master Tutillo appeared with camp chairs for the humans, and he unfolded them in the shade. Haelgrund settled down with his tail curled around his feet.

Stephano sent the midshipman to ask Sir Conal to join them. While they waited, Stephano asked Haelgrund if dragons had ever flown through the Breath down to the bottom of the world.

"I spoke to our loremasters," said Haelgrund. "During the end of the Sunlit Empire, one of the dukes asked dragon explorers to fly below the Breath, find out what was at the bottom of the world, see if it was suitable for habitation. This was during the time of turmoil in the human kingdoms, a time of turmoil for our kind as well. A time when our cousins left us."

Haelgrund cast a glance at the wild dragons. His gaze fixed on Viola, who happened to be lounging in the sunshine. The light caused her scales to glisten with jewel-like colors of amethyst and ruby.

Dag saw the male dragon's admiration and nudged Stephano. "I think romance is in the air," he whispered.

"I don't have time for romance," said Stephano curtly.

Dag raised an eyebrow. Stephano flushed.

"You know what I mean. Not dragon romance."

Dag grinned and shook his head. Stephano went back to business.

"You were saying, Haelgrund? About the Breath?"

"What? Oh, yes. The dragons were able to fly through the liquid part of the Breath, although the experience was not a pleasant one. It was very nearly disastrous. Some turned back, but others persevered and reached the bottom of the world. Of course, at that time, no humans were living there. Our explorers reported a land of shadows and swamp, of no value to anyone. Certainly no dragon would ever care to dwell in such a place."

At that moment, Sir Conal arrived and was introduced to the dragon. Stephano asked the knight to describe how he and Miri had sailed the Trundler houseboat through the Breath, particularly the part the Trundlers called the Aurora—a layer of the Breath stretching between Above and Below that was so cold the mists congealed and liquefied.

"So the difficult part for all of us will be to fly through the Aurora," said Stephano. "We have room for you dragons to shelter inside the fortress."

Haelgrund cast a glance at the fortress. The dragon's mane twitched.

"All of us, cooped up in there, penned in like cattle?"

"Just until we pass through the Aurora," said Stephano.

Haelgrund gave a grunt. "We will discuss it."

That was Haelgrund's polite way of saying Stephano should stay out of dragon business. But since it was his business to make certain the dragons arrived safely, Stephano was ready with another idea.

"My friend, Miri, had a suggestion. The fortress goes first and punches a hole through the liquid. You dragons would fly through it. This is how the Bottom Dwellers' ships pass through the Aurora," he added. "The hulls of their vessels are covered in contramagic constructs that disperse the liquid, opening up a hole."

"That sounds more sensible," said Haelgrund. "What do we do once we arrive at our destination?"

"If all goes according to plan, the fortress will remain hidden in the storm clouds as we descend." Stephano told the dragon the information he had received about the invasion fleet. He drew a crude map in the dirt. "There is a mountain not far from the city where the invasion fleet is located. We plan to set the fortress down on the other side of the mountain. Powerful wizard storms caused by the contramagic are sweeping the land. There are caves in the mountain where you and the others should be able to stay until the storms subside. Once that happens, we will attack the fleet and destroy it."

Haelgrund was eyeing Stephano. "Sounds far too easy, Captain."

"There might be one or two complications," Stephano admitted. He spread his hands. "The truth is, we don't know what we're going to find down there."

Haelgrund gave a grunt, his mane bristled and his eyes glinted. "I look forward to flying into action with you once again, Captain."

Stephano rose to his feet and stretched the kinks out of his back. Haelgrund returned to his comrades to apprise them of the plan.

"Could I have a moment of your time, Captain?" Sir Conal asked, as they were walking back to the fortress.

He relied on his cane to help him walk, though that did not seem to slow him down.

"Certainly, sir," said Stephano. "I have not had an opportunity to thank you for traveling with my mother, watching over and protecting her."

"Your mother is a remarkable woman," Sir Conal said, smiling. "A woman of courage and strong will. Extremely strong will. I still do not feel right about leaving her, but I could not very well disobey her direct order."

"Kings have bowed to my mother's will, sir," said Stephano, smiling.

"Your mother spoke of you often, Captain. She is very proud of you, and she loves you very much."

"I wish I was entitled to her love, sir," said Stephano. "I treated her badly."

"She intended you to feel the way you did. She was protecting you from her enemies at court. All that will change. As the priest said, no matter what happens, for good or for ill, Rosia will not be the same."

"I suppose not," said Stephano.

They had arrived at the fortress. Dag had hurried on ahead. Stephano could see Master Tutillo waiting for him, almost bursting to tell him news. Probably bad.

Stephano turned to the knight. "If you will excuse me—"

"Just a moment. Let me blunt, Captain," said Sir Conal. "I am doing nothing except taking up space and eating your rations. With your permission, I would like to return to the Mother House in Evreux. I have a presentiment I'm going to be needed there."

"You believe there will be war," said Stephano.

"Even if you do manage to stop the invasion fleet, the black ships are here, and they have struck Westfirth, Braffa, Estara, and God knows where else by now. Your mother foiled Eiddwen's plot to destroy the palace. They will attack Rosia again."

"Of course, you have my permission, sir. You may have your pick of the griffins we have stabled here."

"Thank you, Captain. I will leave immediately. I am honored to have met you. You are your mother's son and that is the greatest compliment I can think to give."

"The honor is mine, sir," said Stephano.

The two shook hands.

"Yes, Master Tutillo," said Stephano.

"Monsieur Rodrigo's compliments, Captain, and would you come speak to him. It's about the magic, sir."

Stephano went inside the fortress and climbed the stairs that led to the bridge. Once there, he had to lean out a window to view his friend, who was perched on his scaffolding directly below.

The Estaran crafters had transformed an island mountain into a fortress, magically planing the rough granite to form a smooth exterior. Stephano looked down to see Rodrigo passing his hand over the stone wall, murmuring words of magic. His eyes were half closed and, Stephano knew from having seen Rodrigo do this before, he was envisioning the construct in his mind and engraving his vision on the wall.

Stephano leaned his elbows on the window ledge and watched in admiration. He recalled another Rodrigo, whose only concerns were for the lace on his cuffs and the rosettes on his shoes; a Rodrigo who slept until noon, made love to a half dozen women at a time and never allowed himself to be caught by any of them; a Rodrigo who used his considerable magical talent for parlor tricks or to hide from jealous husbands.

He looked at this Rodrigo; grubby and dirty, his hands scratched and bleeding, perched on rickety scaffolding ten feet in the air, working to create magic that could mean the difference between victory over their foes and death and defeat.

Rodrigo let out a deep sigh and opened his eyes.

"Well . . . that's it," he announced. "The magical shield is in place. Now we wait to see if it works."

"Is there any way to test it?" Stephano asked.

"Not unless you have a few contramagic weapons lying about."

"Sorry, I'm afraid not," said Stephano.

Rodrigo left the scaffolding by means of a ladder. Reaching the bottom, he told the workmen they could start to dismantle it. He disappeared inside the fortress and a few moments later joined Stephano at the bridge. Master Tutillo arrived at the same moment, carrying two mugs of tea.

"What an estimable young man!" Rodrigo exclaimed. "Now if you had only thought to add a drop of brandy . . ."

"I did, sir!" said Master Tutillo, triumphant. "I thought you might need it. If there's nothing else, sir, I have an errand to run for Lieutenant Thorgrimson."

He saluted and dashed off, leaving Rodrigo to regard him with moist eyes. "That boy is a treasure. I think I shall adopt him. He will be the son I never had. Or at least the son I never *knew* I had."

"Don't let Dag hear you say things like that," said Stephano. "He's just starting to like you."

Rodrigo took a blissful sip of tea. "The Dragon Brigade flies again and I shall be part of it! I will wager that in your wildest dreams, Stephano, you never imagined that I would be heading into battle. Perhaps I shall earn a knighthood . . ."

Stephano regarded his friend with deep affection. "Rigo, you have done a wonderful job. I can't thank you enough. But I wish you would reconsider—"

"My dear fellow, I wouldn't miss this for the Duchess of Esterhausen's spring gala. Well, perhaps not the spring gala, which is the event of the season, but certainly for her winter gala, which is deadly dull—"

"Rigo, be serious for once in your life," Stephano said sternly. "This will be dangerous—"

"I understand the danger, my friend, probably better than you do," said Rodrigo softly.

"I shouldn't let you come," Stephano said.

"You have no choice, I'm afraid," said Rodrigo with a shrug and a smile.

Stephano gave up. "This magical shield you've created. Does it work like the protective magic Gythe cast on the *Cloud Hopper*?"

"It *should* be stronger than those Gythe cast," said Rodrigo. "Now that I understand contramagic."

Stephano looked back out the window. "So what is the magical construct you put on our fortress?"

"A combination of magic and contramagic."

"Won't one destroy the other?" Stephano asked, alarmed.

"Not if I've done this right. This is magic as God or science intended, depending on how you look at it," Rodrigo explained. He joined Stephano to gaze down on his work with pride. "I must admit that after talking to Father Jacob, I'm starting to think God and science are one and the same."

"So what is it you've put on my fortress?" Stephano asked. He looked down and could not see a thing.

"The seventh sigil," replied Rodrigo.

"And how do we know it works?"

"We don't," said Rodrigo.

30

The nations of the world warned us that if we did not stop the deprivations of my brother—the so-called Pirate King—they would destroy our island. I fear that none of us believed them.

—Xavier I, *Memoirs*

Stephano was wakened before dawn by Master Tutillo, who greeted him with a cup of hot tea and the news that the tugboats had arrived. Stephano thanked the excited midshipman and sent him to inform Dag.

When the lad was gone, Stephano sat on the edge of his bunk and blew on the steaming tea before taking a sip. He spent this moment as he always did before going into action: confronting Death, staring into the dark and empty eyes until fear subsided. He and Death then shook hands like gentlemen and parted.

Once the tea cooled, he drank it as he put on his dress uniform. His Highness, Prince Renaud was coming to see them off. Stephano looked forward with pride to introducing the prince to Haelgrund and the members of the Dragon Brigade. Perhaps he could start mending the schism between humans and dragons.

He walked out onto the battlements just as reveille was sounding. The early morning was clear, the air cool and refreshing. The dragons were still sleeping in the field, curled up into impossibly small balls, their tails wrapped around their noses.

Haelgrund had formally invited the wild dragons to join the ranks of the noble dragons and fly with them into battle. Stephano was pleased. This gesture meant the noble dragons had accepted their wild dragon cousins as equals. He had been displeased, however, to note that Haelgrund had not invited Hroal and Droal to join them. The old dragons were disappointed, but accepting of their lot. As common dragons of low rank, they knew their place. They were quartermasters, remaining "on the ground" as the dragons termed it.

Stephano knew the dragon brothers both dreamed of flying with the Brigade. But although he was their commander, he did not generally meddle in the dragons' internal politics.

The sailors and marines were in the mess, eating what would be their last hot meal. When the fortress embarked on the perilous journey, the cook would douse his fires and they would all live on cold food for the duration.

When Stephano had first taken command, he had kept their destination secret, fearing spies, not wanting word to get back to the enemy. He knew most of the men were assuming they were going to war with Freya. They were astonished when he had informed them yesterday that they would be traveling Below to fight the enemy that had attacked Westfirth, sunk the *Royal Lion* and destroyed the Crystal Market.

The men must have had their doubts about sailing to the bottom of the world; Stephano found it hard to believe himself at times, but most had friends who had served on the Royal Lion or family who had been in the Crystal Market and they gave him a rousing cheer at the end of his speech.

Dag walked along the battlements. He was grinning hugely and rubbing his hands, as happy and excited as a child on Yule.

"With your permission, sir, I'll meet with the tugboat captains, explain their duties," said Dag. "I was there when the Estarans first towed the fortress into place. She can be a bit tricky to handle. When is His Highness due to arrive?"

"In about an hour," said Stephano, glancing at his watch. "You'll need to be on hand for the welcome."

"All that bowing and scraping. Waste of valuable time, if you ask me, sir," Dag grumbled.

"We can spare him a few moments. Without the prince, I would be in prison in the Citadel. Have you seen Miri this morning?"

"The sailors are securing the *Cloud Hopper* to the dock. She's supervising." Dag shook his head. "God help the poor lads."

"I'll go rescue them," said Stephano.

The dragons were awake and, led by Haelgrund, they flew off to hunt what might be their last meal before arriving at their destination. He accompanied Viola, rousing Verdi's ire and causing Petard to tease his sister until she turned to snap at him. Hroal and Droal, not invited on the hunting party, flew off on their own.

Stephano walked around the fortress, inspecting the work, making certain all was ready. He then descended to the dock, where he found Miri swearing at his crew in Trundler. The sailors were attempting to secure the houseboat with ropes attached to iron rings embedded in the stone walls of the fortress and not doing it to her satisfaction. As he watched, she smacked one sailor on the head with the flat of her hand.

"Where did you find these lubbers?" Miri demanded angrily of Stephano, storming over to confront him.

"Prince Renaud sent his best men," he said in soothing tones. He consulted his watch and frowned. "Speaking of His Highness, he should be here by now. Do you have everything you require on board the houseboat? Did Rigo repair the magic? Did he add protecting constructs?"

"I have everything. The houseboat is covered in Gythe's protective constructs. He *thinks* they'll protect the boat on their own. He didn't want to do anything that might disrupt them."

"But he doesn't know for sure they will protect you."

"We can't know anything for sure, Stephano," said Miri.

Stephano sighed. "We're flying into this battle on a wing and a prayer. Once you're finished here, I'd like you to be up on the bridge. I'll need you to guide the helmsmen to our landing site. When we're in position, you can leave for the temple in the *Hopper* and bring back my mother and Gythe."

"Any message to your mother?"

"Yes," said Stephano softly. "Ask her to please forgive me."

"She's a mother, Stephano," said Miri. "There's nothing to forgive."

He took her hand and drew her off into a secluded hallway.

"Where are you taking me?" Miri asked, laughing.

"A kiss for luck."

He embraced her and was about to kiss her when Master Tutillo seemed to spring up out of the floor.

"Captain, sir, you're needed— Oh, uh, sorry, sir. I didn't mean to interrupt."

"What is it, Master Tutillo?" Stephano asked with all the patience he could muster.

"Yes, sir. Sorry, sir. Lieutenant Thorgrimson's compliments and you're wanted on the bridge. A griffin messenger just arrived. He says it's urgent."

"Thank you, I'll come."

Stephano turned back to Miri. "You know what's in my heart. I want to marry you. Why won't you give me an answer?"

"I'm still thinking."

"What's there to think about?" Stephano asked.

"You see?" said Miri. "*That's* the problem."

She kissed him gently on the cheek. "Go deal with your crisis. I have work of my own to do."

She pushed him away and ran back to the boat.

Stephano shook his head in frustration. Turning, he nearly fell over Master Tutillo.

"Women, sir," said the youngster with the wisdom of his fourteen years. "What's a fellow to do?"

Stephano smiled in spite of himself, though he took care to say sternly, "A 'fellow' can go about his duties."

"Yes, sir," said Master Tutillo, flushing and hurrying off.

Stephano left the dock and climbed the stairs to the bridge, reflecting as he walked through the fortress that the messenger was probably carrying bad news. One look at the griffin rider's dark expression confirmed his fears.

"Captain de Guichen," said the rider, saluting. "Prince Renaud sends his apologies. He will not be able to be with you. Evreux has come under attack."

"Bottom Dwellers?" Stephano asked.

He and Dag exchanged alarmed glances, both thinking that they were too late, and the invasion fleet had already launched.

"Yes, sir," the messenger replied. "His Highness believes these are the same ships that laid waste to Estara."

"They are softening us up, sir," said Dag grimly.

"Inflicting what damage they can before the arrival of

the invasion fleet, leaving them to finish us off," said Stephano. "Lieutenant Thorgrimson, we will make ready to launch immediately."

He turned back to the rider. "Corporal, can I offer you and your mount food and drink?"

"Thank you, no, sir. I must return to my post. His Highness bids you godspeed."

Stephano sent a message to the prince, wishing him the same. Dag left to inform the tugboat captains that they were ready to get under way. The helmsman was already on the bridge, sitting in his tall chair, his hands flying over the constructs engraved on the large brass helm.

The bridge was completely enclosed in stone except for a large portal made of thick, magically reinforced glass. Stephano gazed out into the orangish mists of the Breath to see the tugboats slowly sailing away from the docks. When the lines between them and the fortress grew taut, the helmsman sent magic flowing to the lift tanks, activating the crystals, the Tears of God.

God weeping for Evreux. Stephano pictured the black ships flying over the city and setting fire to the docks, with the royal palace in flames. He imagined the battle; the ships of the royal navy attacking the foe. The prince, as admiral of the fleet, would be on board his flagship, directing the assault. Stephano could see again, the sinking of the *Royal Lion* . . .

His dark thoughts were interrupted by the arrival of Rodrigo, who came rushing onto the bridge.

"I heard the fiends are attacking Evreux! Do you think Benoit will be safe?"

Stephano smiled. "The old man has a strong sense of self-preservation. He's probably hiding in the wine cellar where he can enjoy himself."

"I hope he took my handkerchief collection with him," said Rodrigo, sighing. "It's quite valuable."

He continued fondly recalling his handkerchiefs. Stephano wasn't listening. He glanced over at the helm. The magic should be flowing to the lift tanks by now. He waited for the lurch, the jolt that would send him staggering as the fortress sailed ponderously off the ground.

Frowning, he walked over to the helmsman. "Shouldn't the magic be working by now?"

"It is, sir," said the helmsman. "We left the ground a few moments ago."

"Did we?" Stephano was amazed. "I didn't feel a thing."

"Never had a smoother launch, Captain. This bloody, great hunk of rock floated off the ground like a bloody feather, if you'll forgive my language, sir."

Stephano looked out the porthole. Sure enough, the land was receding in the distance. All he could see beneath him were the mists of the Breath.

"I had my doubts about those crystals, Captain, but it seems they work as promised," the helmsman remarked.

The dragons returned, flying above the fortress, Haelgrund in the lead. The three wild dragons were in the rear of the flight, as was proper, given that they were new members of the Dragon Brigade. Viola caught sight of Stephano and gracefully dipped her head in acknowledgment. She was staying close to Petard, who must be chafing at being confined to the rear and forced to fly in formation. Haelgrund already had reprimanded Petard once for trying to edge his way up to the front.

The two dragon brothers, Droal and Hroal, flew with the wild dragons. Stephano had decided to promote the brothers, making them officers in the Brigade. Ordinarily he allowed the dragons to conduct their own affairs, but he knew the noble dragons would never promote the two common dragons and he believed they had earned their promotion through their valor and dedication. Haelgrund and the other noble dragons had not been pleased, but they had grudgingly agreed to accept the two brothers among the ranks of the elite.

"So long as the old boys keep out of our way," Haelgrund said dourly.

The tugboats pulled the fortress with relative ease. Fortunately the winds were calm in this part of the Breath. Stephano, pleased with the smooth launch, walked over to the chart table tucked into a corner of the bridge to study a map that marked the former location of Glasearrach, where it had been before it sank. According to Miri, the survivors of the sinking had claimed the island had plummeted straight down. He marked the location. A long way to go.

Filled with nervous energy, and with nothing to do except wait, Stephano roamed the fortress, making certain everything was secure, inspecting the walls and floors and ceilings to see if they had sustained any damage. Rodrigo had gone to take a nap to prepare himself for the rigors of battle, and Miri was with the helmsman, who was showing her the workings of the helm. Dag was on the dock, making certain the towlines were secure, with sailors ready to replace a line should it break. He had locked Doctor Ellington in the dry storage room. The cat was not as unhappy as usual, for the storage room was large and he was able to wage his own war on the fortress's rat population.

When they arrived at the location they'd targeted for the descent, the sailors cast off the lines. The tugboat captains wished Stephano godspeed and departed. Dag left to go to the mess hall. Stephano had ordered crafters to heat large rocks covered with magical constructs and place them in the mess hall. When the fortress sank into the coldest part of the Breath, he would send the men there to keep warm.

Stephano returned to the bridge. The helmsman looked at him expectantly, waiting for the command that would start the descent.

"Reduce the flow of magic to the lift tanks," said Stephano.

The fortress began to sink, and as it did, the sunshine soon vanished. Gray, dank fog closed in around them, and Stephano lost sight of the dragons. He could hear them repeatedly calling out to each other and see the red gouts of fire they breathed to make certain no one got lost.

Despite the fact that they had sealed up every crack, fog seeped inside the fortress, wisping down the corridors and forming eerie haloes around the lanterns. Walls glistened with moisture. Water dripped from the ceilings, and the temperature plummeted. The sailors put on warm coats, gloves, and snug hats and still stamped their feet and blew on their hands in vain attempts to keep warm as the damp chill crept through to the bone.

When the cold grew severe, Stephano ordered the men on watch to leave their posts and go to the mess hall. His order included Master Tutillo, whose teeth were chattering.

Stephano remained on the bridge with Miri and the helmsman. He was wearing his heavy Dragon Brigade coat and wool uniform and was still shivering. They had placed a warming rock on the bridge, but it did little to alleviate the cold. Miri was bundled up in a Trundler peacoat with a scarf tied around her head and mittens on her hands. The helmsman could not wear gloves because he had to work the magic. He alternated rubbing his hands and sitting on them to keep them warm.

Rodrigo appeared on the bridge, wrapped in a blanket, wearing every article of clothing he possessed. He had tied a gunnysack around his head for warmth, the sight of which made Stephano burst out in laughter.

"If only the ladies of the court could see you now!"

Rodrigo replied with a sneeze. He morosely gazed out the window. "Fire and brimstone, my ass! If this is hell, someone certainly got *that* wrong! I shall lodge a complaint with the grand bishop."

He huddled near the warming stone. "My ears are popping. It's quite painful. I can't think why I let you talk me into coming."

"The cold's only going to get worse," Miri said.

Rodrigo cast her a horrified glance and left, shivering, his blanket trailing on the floor behind him.

Fog changed to freezing fog, riming the fortress's walls with hoarfrost. Stephano worried about the dragons. He could still hear them calling and see the blasts of flame, so he knew they were managing to survive. Their bodies would grow sluggish in the cold; they would find it increasingly difficult to fly.

He had ordered the crew to stop ringing the ship's bells that marked the duty watches so that once they arrived Below, they would not give away their position. Time seemed irrelevant anyway. They were falling, sinking down and down into a gray-wrapped void. For a moment, he was horrified by the thought that they would never stop falling. It was such a terrifying thought, he couldn't repress a shudder.

Miri, standing by the window, cast a worried glance at him over her shoulder.

"Rigo was right," he said. "This *is* Hell."

"We are almost through the Fog Belt. Then we will enter the Aurora, the liquefied portion of the Breath."

"Strange name," Stephano remarked. "Aurora means 'dawn.' Light and beauty."

"You'll see," Miri promised.

Stephano left the bridge, descended the stairs to the ground level and went to the mess hall to see how his troops were faring. He had thought the bridge cold before entering the unheated corridor. This was much worse; he could see his breath in the air and frost on the walls.

Through the closed door he could hear the men grumbling. As he entered they quit grumbling and rose to their feet, but Stephano told them to sit down. Between the heated rocks and warm bodies, the mess hall was far more comfortable than the bridge. He told them that they were almost through the freezing fog and asked how they were faring. He warned them again to stay here and not to go roaming around.

"Once we are through the Aurora, we will be in the world Below. I'm doubling the watch and, in addition, I want every man who doesn't have a job to serve as lookout. Silence is crucial. When you man the cannons, do not load them. I don't want to risk a gun going off by accident. If you have to speak, keep your voice low. If you see or hear something, report quietly to the duty officer. He'll pass the word to me. Master Tutillo, you are with me. Lieutenant, a moment of your time, please."

Stephano and Dag stepped outside the door.

"How are the men holding up? I heard them complaining."

"The grousing is a good sign, sir," said Dag. "It's when the men *stop* grumbling that you can expect trouble."

"Good to know," said Stephano.

"Rigo's the worst of them all," Dag continued. "He's complained about everything from his frozen feet on up. You should have heard him when cook served cold beans and hardtack for lunch!"

"I'll take him back with me," said Stephano, smiling.

"Thank you, sir," said Dag, his sentiment clearly heartfelt.

"I'll let you know when we've passed through the Breath and into the skies above Glasearrach," Stephano added. "At that point, you can send the men to their posts."

Dag nodded and returned to the mess hall.

"Rigo," Stephano called out to his friend, "you're needed on the bridge."

"What for?" Rodrigo asked, huddled in his blanket.

"To boost morale," said Stephano.

31

It was as if God struck our island with His fist and knocked us from the sky.

—Xavier I, *Memoirs*

Arriving on the bridge, Stephano was relieved to see a pale, gray light glimmering through the porthole. He hoped that meant they were almost through the layer of fog. The return of the sun was cheering, though Rodrigo morosely pointed out that the pallid light did nothing to alleviate the cold.

"Come see this," Miri called from the porthole.

She stepped aside to make room for Stephano. He looked out, accompanied by Rodrigo, who rested his chin on Stephano's shoulder to get a better view.

Stephano gave a low, soft whistle. Rodrigo caught his breath.

Far below them, seeming to rise up as the fortress descended, myriad rainbows covered the surface of this part of the Breath, now so cold it had changed to liquid. The rainbows shimmered, spreading and receding, flowing across the surface of the Breath.

"My God! What is that?" Rodrigo asked, awed.

"That is the Aurora," said Miri. "The Trundlers on Glasearrach say that before the storms, on the rare days when the mists parted and the sun shone brightly, the sky was filled with rainbows."

"What a strange phenomenon," Stephano remarked.

"Not that strange," said Rodrigo. "The rainbowlike effect is produced by the angle of the rays of the sun as the world turns on its axis."

Stephano was impressed. "How do you know that?"

"I don't," Rodrigo said, grinning. "But all one has to do is talk of axis and angles and people assume you know whereof you speak."

"Could I see, sir?" Master Tutillo asked.

Stephano stepped aside. Master Tutillo gazed down at the glowing, multicolored lights.

"Coo, that's grand!" he said softly.

Stephano was relieved to see the dragons had survived the cold and were still flying overhead. Haelgrund was trumpeting commands to bring the stragglers back into formation. If all went according to plan, the fortress would crash through the Aurora, smashing a hole in the viscous Breath, and the dragons would follow, flying swiftly before the hole could close. The moment the fortress emerged from the Aurora, the dragons would be in the skies above Glasearrach.

"Should we brace for impact?" Rodrigo asked nervously. He was standing at the porthole, gazing down at the Aurora.

"There won't be an impact," said Miri. "We will glide through the liquid like a spoon through jelly."

"Now I feel nauseous," Rodrigo complained.

As they drew nearer the Aurora the rainbows faded and the liquid Breath became a gray, glistening, undulating mass rushing at the fortress with alarming speed.

Stephano was watching at the porthole, along with Miri.

Rodrigo sat on the floor, bracing his back against the wall.

"Here we go," said Miri softly.

Despite her assurance that they would feel no impact, Stephano flinched involuntarily as the fortress plunged into the Aurora. The fortress shuddered slightly, but glided right through, as Miri had predicted. The liquid Breath slid down the windowpane, a whitish gray in color that grew darker as they descended, for they were once more losing the sunlight. The liquid muffled sound; the silence was profound.

"How are the dragons?" Miri asked worriedly. "Can you see?"

Stephano pressed against the glass, looking up at the dragons. The sun illuminated the hole in the Breath created by the passage of the fortress, and the dragons were flying in the fortress's wake. They breathed flame on the liquid Breath, melting it, causing the hole made by the fortress to expand.

"They are still with us," said Stephano.

"We're nearing the end. I can see lightning," Miri reported. "Looks like we're going to be landing in a wizard storm."

"Perfect timing," said Stephano.

"Why in heaven's name would you say that?" Rodrigo asked, horrified.

"The fortress will be wrapped in rain clouds. No one will see us."

Rodrigo flung the blanket over his head.

Stephano spoke with a confidence he did not feel. The helmsman was going to have a difficult time steering the fortress through whipping winds and blinding rain toward their destination.

The fortress had never been intended to "fly." Air screws provided enough thrust to nudge the ponderous structure in one direction or another, but that was about all they could do. If the dragons had not agreed to join the fight, his alternate plan would have been to bring down the fortress in the midst of the fleet, crashing into the ships and blowing them apart with cannon fire. The dragons with their fiery breath and maneuverability could inflict far more damage.

Once on Glasearrach, he could maintain the fortress as a base of operations. Using Miri's calculations, Stephano had positioned the fortress to land near the mountain known as Gabhar Cloch or at least come so close to it they would need to travel only a short distance to reach the fleet.

The last of the liquid Breath slid down the window. Leaving behind silence and rainbows, the fortress plunged into the storm.

Wind beat on the walls, and lightning shattered the darkness. Thunderclaps shook the floor and rain rolled down the glass pane of the porthole in sheets.

"Miri, can you see where we are?" Stephano asked.

She had her face pressed against the porthole, peering out through cupped hands. "I can't see anything in this weather. We should hold our position, wait for the storm to pass."

"Helmsman, hold—"

"We can't," Rodrigo said in strangled tones. "We have to land . . . *now*!"

"Rigo, I know you're cold, but this is not the time—"

"Bother the cold!" Rodrigo jumped to his feet. Throwing off the blanket, he pointed at the walls. "The magic is failing!"

"Failing?" Stephano repeated, startled and uneasy. "How? Why?"

"The atmosphere is seething with contramagic," Rodrigo said. "It's attacking the magic in every part of the fortress, eating away at it."

He pointed at the wall. "Look! You can see the constructs starting to come apart—"

The fortress lurched and suddenly dropped, sending everyone in the room staggering. Stephano braced himself against the wall. He could not see the constructs coming apart, but he imagined them cracking beneath his fingers.

"Sir, helm not responding!" the helmsman reported.

The magic was no longer flowing from the helm to the air screws or—most important—to the tanks that contained the lift crystals. The fortress was in free fall. He pictured the building plummeting to the ground, splitting apart. The gunpowder stored in the powder magazine would explode. There would be nothing left.

"I thought God or science or that seventh something was supposed to protect the magic!" Stephano said.

"My dear fellow, if an arbusque blows off your head, a soothing balm will be of little help. I would guess that over time—"

"Stephano!" Miri cried from the porthole. "We're coming down in the wrong place. We're going to crash into the city! Come look!"

A brief respite in the rain allowed Stephano to see rows of buildings crowded together, homes and businesses that would be smashed when the fortress plowed into them. They would kill hundreds of innocents, including, perhaps, the families of those very resistance fighters who had agreed to join with them.

"Crash into the city . . . ," Rodrigo was muttering to himself. "Crash land . . . Stephano! This fortress has made a crash landing and survived!"

"By God, you're right. Master Tutillo, fetch Lieutenant Thorgrimson! At once!"

"Yes, sir!"

The midshipman ran out the door and almost collided with Dag, who was coming in. He caught hold of the young man, steadied him, and then thrust him to one side.

"What's happening, sir? I've got wounded—"

"The magic is failing," said Stephano. "We're off course and coming down too fast."

The fortress gave another lurch.

"Dag, you were in the fortress when the magic failed and it sank. What did Father Antonius do to save it, to keep it from crashing?"

"He did . . . magic," said Dag helplessly.

"Illustrative, but not helpful," Rodrigo growled.

Dag glared at him. "I'm not a bloody crafter!"

"Where was he?" Rodrigo asked suddenly. "Where did he work his magic?"

"Wait! Let me think . . . The helm! Father Antonius did something to the magic at the helm . . ."

"Of course," Rodrigo said, mulling this over. "The magic of the helm is likely to fail first, because it is far less complicated than the magic on the lift tanks, which would take some time to fail—"

"Can you fix it?" Stephano asked through gritted teeth.

"Maybe," said Rodrigo.

The helmsman moved aside to allow Rodrigo to take over the helm. Rigo studied the constructs inscribed on the brass.

"I understand the concept," said Rodrigo. "But I don't know how the helm works. Which constructs operate the air screws and which the lift tanks?"

The helmsman pointed them out, explaining briefly how the constructs worked. Rodrigo gave a terse nod and began to move his hands over the brass helm, muttering under his breath.

Miri left the window to watch. Stephano glanced around

and saw Master Tutillo white faced and shivering, but trying very hard to be brave. He clapped his hand comfortingly on the boy's shoulder.

"Go to the chief gunnery officer," Stephano said. "Tell him to make certain the cannons are secure and report back to me."

Master Tutillo managed to form the words, "Yes, sir" through fear-tightened lips and then ran off.

"I needed to give him something to do," Stephano said. "Keep his mind off his fear."

"Good thought, sir," said Dag. He gave a wry smile. "Could you give me something to do?"

Rodrigo moved his hands rapidly over the constructs. Finally, he paused, head cocked, as though listening. Miri gazed down at the helm, her hand pressed over her mouth. She gasped and flashed a relieved look at Stephano.

"Rigo's done it!"

"Helm answering, sir!" The helmsman returned to work, mopping sweat from his brow despite the chill in the air.

"Air screws and lift tanks both operating," the helmsman reported.

"Good work, Rigo!" Stephano said, regarding his friend with admiration.

Rodrigo shook his head. "My repair is only temporary. The contramagic will keep eating away at the constructs on the lines and when those fail . . ." He didn't finish the sentence. "Suffice it to say, we need to find a place to land and soon!"

Miri returned to the porthole. "We've flown past the city, but I'm not sure where we are. All I can see beneath us are trees and either a large ravine or a river."

"Keep searching for landmarks," Stephano said tersely.

"I am!" Miri retorted, glowering at him.

Stephano wisely refrained from saying anything else;

in the relative silence, he realized that the wind was lessening, the thunder had gone from a roar to a growl, and the rain had changed from torrents to a drizzle. The wizard storm was moving away, drifting off over the foothills.

"I know where we are!" Miri cried, pointing. "That's our destination, Mount Gabhar Cloch."

"What sort of name is that for a mountain?" Rodrigo whispered. "Sounds like a disease."

Stephano shot him a warning glance and went to the porthole to see for himself. The jagged peaks of the mountain were visible, black against a flaring sheet of purple lightning.

"We're way off course. The mountain is east of us," said Miri grimly. "It should be to the west. Our landing site is probably thirty miles that direction, on the far side of the mountain."

They all looked at Rodrigo.

"We'll never make it that far."

As if to confirm their fears, the helmsman reported, "Starting to sink, sir."

"We're near where the Trundlers dock their boats," Miri said, gazing out the porthole. "That's an open field. We could land there— Oh, no . . ."

Miri had stopped talking and was staring out, her face pressed against the glass.

"What's gone wrong now?" Stephano asked.

"Bat riders." Miri turned to face Stephano. "Two of them."

"Did they see us?"

"They changed course and flew off in haste," said Miri. "If I had to guess, I would say they saw us."

"We'd be pretty hard to miss," Rodrigo remarked.

"So much for the element of surprise," said Stephano grimly.

"Maybe not, sir," said Dag. "If they did see the fortress, they probably didn't see the dragons."

Dag had a point. Stephano sprang to the porthole and, craning his neck, looked into the sky. Rain spattered on the window, and the mountain was shrouded in the gloom, visible only when the occasional bolt of lightning flared. He saw no sign of the dragons. If he couldn't see them, the odds were good that the bat riders had not seen them either.

Of course, there was always the possibility the dragons had not survived the flight through the Breath, but he couldn't let himself think about that. He had more urgent problems.

"Still descending, sir," said the helmsman.

"There's open ground ahead," Miri told the man. "Four points off the port bow. Can we make it that far?"

The helmsman made the adjustment and the air screws nudged the fortress along. The movement was agonizingly slow, or so it seemed to Stephano.

Miri watched out the porthole, urging the fortress to keep going. "A little farther . . . just a little farther . . ."

The fortress crept ahead. Dark clouds clustered thick around the top of the mountain. If the dragons had survived, they might be there, hidden from view.

Rodrigo returned to the helm and looked at the constructs.

"How is the magic holding up?" Stephano asked.

Rodrigo shook his head. "Faltering."

"We're almost there," Miri said.

"Slow our rate of descent," Stephano ordered.

"I'm trying, sir," said the helmsman.

As the ground rose up to meet them, Stephano could see a few scraggly trees lining what he could now tell was a deep ravine. The rest of the land was open field.

"What sort of ground is it?" Stephano asked Miri.

If they landed in a swamp, the fortress might sink like the proverbial rock.

"The Trundlers dock their boats here because the area is solid bedrock." Miri glanced at Stephano in concern. "But we're coming down too fast."

"Trying to adjust the air screws, sir," said the helmsman. "They're still not responding."

As he swore beneath his breath, Rodrigo bent over the helm. His long, delicate fingers danced, almost as if he was playing one of his silent concertos that he occasionally performed on tabletops in the absence of a piano. When he looked up, his face was pale and his hair was falling into his eyes.

"That's done it!"

Their rate of descent slowed and the air screws shifted. Instead of pushing the fortress, they were creating a cushion of air. The fortress wobbled a moment, floating on the cushion. The helmsman decreased the power, and Stephano could hear the air screws slow down.

The fortress landed with a grinding thud, as the base scraped across the rock. After rocking for a few tense moments, the fortress finally settled.

Stephano could hear scattered cheers from the men. Miri sighed in relief. She brushed the sweat-damp curls out of her face and smiled at him.

"Welcome to Glasearrach," she said.

Stephano drew near her, their shoulders touching. He gazed out the window into the damp misty air and the realization struck him that his plan had succeeded. They were on the sunken island of Glasearrach.

Dag had vanished, having gone to give the command to run out the guns, while Rodrigo and the helmsman discussed the magic, neither sounding very happy. He could feel more than hear the gun ports creaking open and the rumble of the cannons moving into position.

But he stopped thinking about those things to breathe a sigh of relief when he saw the dragons spiraling down out of the Breath, flying in formation toward the mountain. Haelgrund would be keeping an eye on the fortress, and he must be wondering why they had landed so far from their original site.

A sudden worrying thought occurred to Stephano.

"Rigo, dragons are made of magic, so to speak. What effect will the contramagic have on them?"

Rodrigo waved him to silence. He had left the helm and was down on his hands and knees, squinting at the wall. The matter must be serious, given that Rodrigo was risking serious damage to his trousers.

Stephano made a mental note to bring up the matter of the dragons later. He had the feeling he wasn't going to like the answer anyway.

He looked back toward the mountain. The peak was still shrouded in clouds that shifted and roiled uneasily. One of the dragons had perched on an outcropping of rock, wings folded at its sides. Haelgrund had stationed a lookout.

Stephano was still watching the dragons when he became aware that Miri was trying to slip away.

He caught hold of her. "You can't leave the fortress. It's too dangerous."

"I have to set sail now, Stephano," said Miri. "Before there's another storm."

"Xavier could know we're here—"

"All the more reason for me to go," said Miri. "I can find out what he plans."

"The magic on the helm will be damaged, like ours. You should let Rigo look—"

"The helm has Gythe's magic to protect it," said Miri.

She faced him, her lips tight and her green eyes narrowed. Stephano knew that look well. The only way he could stop her would be to lock her in the storage room with the cat. And then he'd have to tie her up.

"Take this," said Stephano. He held out the dragon pistol.

Miri's eyes opened wide. "Your pistol . . . No, Stephano, I couldn't . . ."

"Take it. I like to think part of me will be with you, watching over you."

Miri flushed deeply. Taking the pistol, she thrust it into the waistband of her skirt, then kissed him on the cheek and left the bridge, just as Master Tutillo returned. He bounded through the door with his usual energy, apparently fully recovered.

"Surgeon's report, sir. One man in the infirmary with a broken arm and another with a cracked skull."

Stephano gave an absent nod. His thoughts were on Miri. He looked out the porthole, down onto the dock below. He could see her in her oilskin coat, climbing on board the *Cloud Hopper*. Sailors stood by, ready to cast off the lines. Master Tutillo continued with his report.

"Lieutenant Thorgrimson says the fort suffered some minor damage—cracks in the walls and ceilings. And one of the cannons broke loose, but the men are securing it now. Oh, and I'm to tell you that the powder magazine is dry. No water leaked in."

"Thank you. My compliments to the lieutenant. I will be making my inspection shortly."

Master Tutillo saluted and ran off.

He saw Miri raise the *Cloud Hopper*'s sails, and the sailors cast off the lines. Miri grabbed them, coiled them up, and laid them on the deck. She hurried to the helm sending lift gas to fill the balloon. The sails caught the wind, as the *Cloud Hopper* floated off the dock.

Stephano could see Miri at the helm, waving good-bye, her red hair a bright beacon in the bleak gray land. He waved back, although he knew she couldn't see him, and watched as the sturdy little Trundler houseboat sailed into the mists and was lost to sight.

"So what do you think of Glasearrach?" asked Rodrigo, coming up behind him.

Stephano gazed out at the desolation: the windswept, rain-soaked ground, empty and lifeless; the roiling clouds trailing ugly tendrils. In the distance, purple flickers of lightning presaged another storm.

"Not much," Stephano grunted. "Why do you ask?"

"Because the magic is failing and there is no way to stop it," said Rodrigo. He added with a shrug, "In other words, we may as well get used to this place. We can't leave."

32

God has abandoned me, Julian. You are dead and my heart dies with you. I cling to life for the sake of our son, who must grow up thinking me cold and heartless, for fear our enemies will destroy him.

—Countess Cecile de Marjolaine, diary

Cecile sat with her back against the wall, on her pallet in the prison cell, listening to the soft breathing of Gythe and Sophia. The hour was past midnight, and they were both asleep. But Cecile remained awake, gazing into the flickering light of a small oil lantern she had placed in a corner of the cell to comfort Sophia, who was frightened of the dark.

The princess huddled beneath the blanket, her arm around Bandit. The drumming had started at noon and with it came a wizard storm. When the drumming eventually stopped, several hours later, the storm stopped, as well. The night was quiet. The pounding of the drums had made Sophia ill; her headaches so bad she was screaming and writhing in pain. The guards had sent for Brother Barnaby.

He had treated her with soothing words and a cooling poultice. Cecile was not certain which helped the most, the brother's gentle touch or his herbs. Sophia had finally fallen into a restful sleep.

Gythe slept on a pallet near Sophia. Her sleep was peaceful. She even smiled, as though dreaming of something pleasant. Cecile envied her.

She was not able to find rest. Sleep was more disturbing than being awake. When she was awake, she could discipline her thoughts, keep fear caged. Sleep unlocked the door to worry and fear. Not for herself. She had survived two assassination attempts and thwarted efforts by the queen and others to have her exiled or even beheaded. She spent her store of fear on those she loved: Sophia and Gythe, Miri and Stephano, the gentle Brother Barnaby. Even Bandit.

Days had passed since Miri's escape, and Cecile's plan had succeeded. She had been able to persuade Xavier that she and the girls were innocent, that they had known nothing of Miri's activities. Their argument was helped by the fact that Gythe and Sophia had been the first savants to show they could control the storm with their magic, if only for a short time. Twice more, Xavier had asked them to work their magic on the wizard storms. Twice more Gythe and Sophia had slowed the wind and stopped the rain, though again, only for a short time.

Xavier had been pleased that his theory was proven right. According to Brother Barnaby, however, the Blood Mage had not been impressed. He had observed the Blood Mage, standing with his drummers, watching with a hungry expression as Gythe and Sophia quieted the thunder claps and tamed the lightning.

According to rebel spies, the Blood Mage was said to have told his drummers, "When these young women fail to stop the storms and his fleet is forced to remain on the ground, Xavier will know that his theory about savants is wrong and this foolish experiment will end."

Sophia flinched and shuddered in her sleep. Cecile pulled the meager blankets up over the princess's thin shoulders and smoothed her tangled hair. Her movement disturbed Bandit, who opened one eye, regarded her with drowsy displeasure, and then rolled over on his back and closed his eyes again.

Cecile fell asleep sitting up, only to wake with a start, jolted from her doze by the sound of a trumpet blaring, tinny and flat sounding in the rain. After a few moments, she heard voices coming from outside the prison walls. She wondered at first if it was morning. The cell was dark, however, except for the glow of the lantern. The voices continued, loud and excited, and the trumpet continued to blare. Uneasy, she hurried to the window.

The temple was ablaze with light. The drummers were running from the dortoir, some of them hastily flinging on their cloaks against the rain. The voices she had heard belonged to soldiers hurrying past the prison, heading for their posts.

Gythe sat up, clutching the blanket to her chest.

"What is going on?" she signed.

"The drummers are being summoned to the temple," Cecile replied. "Something is happening."

"The invasion?" Gythe asked, making a sign of a soldier firing a weapon.

"Too early," said Cecile, frowning. "The fleet is not supposed to launch until tomorrow."

If Miri had succeeded in reaching Stephano, he should arrive in time to stop the fleet. Brother Barnaby and the rebels were planning to help her and Gythe and Sophia escape at that time.

"What is wrong?" Sophia murmured; she, too, was now sitting up.

"Perhaps nothing, Your Highness," said Cecile. "Go back to sleep—"

The drumming started, shattering, loud and insistent, pounding with anger, thundering defiance. The sound thudded inside Cecile, set her teeth on edge. Gythe paled, and Sophia screamed once, as though she had been struck a physical blow. She clutched her head and moaned, and Bandit, also awake now, barked and howled his protest.

Gythe put her arms around Sophia to comfort her. Cecile ran to the cell door and began to bang on it.

"Send for Brother Barnaby!" she pleaded. "The princess has fallen ill!"

The key rattled in the lock. Startled, Cecile sprang back. The door opened, and Xavier walked in.

He was wearing a cloak with the hood drawn up against the rain and he carried a lantern. He sent the light flashing around the cell and paused when the light found Sophia, huddled in Gythe's arms. He gazed at the two a moment, then shifted the light to shine in Cecile's face.

"The girl is ill," he said.

"Yes, *Naomh,*" Cecile replied, recovering herself. She lifted her hand to block the bright light. "The drumming affects her. It is strangely loud tonight."

"The drums will be loud," Xavier said, his voice grating. "Our enemies will hear the drums in every city and village and hamlet. They will hear us and shudder for they will hear our wrath."

He glanced around, shifting the light impatiently. "Where are you, monk?"

"I am here, *Naomh,*" said Brother Barnaby.

Cecile had not seen him in the darkness. He gazed steadily at her, his dark eyes shining in the light. He lowered his eyelids, hooding his eyes, warning her of trouble.

"Go do whatever you do to help the young woman," said Xavier. "In a few hours, it will be dawn," he continued. "The girl must be well by then, for she and the other savant will stop the wizard storms. They will stop them so that my fleet can launch," he added, his voice hardening.

"The girls are not ready," Cecile protested. "You said the invasion was scheduled for tomorrow."

"Our foe has come to Glasearrach," Xavier said. He was burning cold, like wet fingers touching ice. "Bat riders reported seeing a fortress sail down from above, manned by an army."

Cecile struggled to keep her composure. Joy and hope surged, even as fear constricted her throat. Joy that Stephano's plan had succeeded, hope that they would be rescued, and suffocating fear.

"My people are fighting back, *Naomh,*" she said. "This cannot come as a surprise to you."

"Nor to you, Countess," Xavier said softly.

He lowered the lantern, as if he had wearied of holding it, and set it on the floor between them. The room grew very quiet. Bandit stopped barking and Sophia quit sobbing. Even the sound of the drumming faded away.

"I suppose I have only myself to blame," Xavier remarked. Folding his arms across his chest, he gazed thoughtfully into the light of the lantern. "I should have never tried this experiment with the savants or permitted the capture of prisoners. I should have foreseen that I was providing a means for your people to infiltrate our world. But what else could I do? I had to find a way to stop the storms."

He lapsed into silence, his head bowed. Cecile pitied him. Xavier was a weak man, like King Alaric, vacillating, lacking purpose of his own. He hated because he had been told it was his duty to hate. He had committed his life to seeking a revenge he had never wanted. His tragedy was that, unlike Alaric, Xavier was a good man grieving over the terrible deeds being done in his name, yet lacking the strength to put a stop to them.

He raised his eyes and looked at Cecile. Perhaps he saw the pity in her eyes, for he frowned, seemed to plead for her understanding.

"When I was young, Countess, I believed I could help my people to a better life. I was hopeful, full of plans. But I am Xavier. The hands of all the Xaviers before me reached out of the pit, seized hold of me, and dragged me down."

"It's only a name," said Cecile.

He glowered in sudden anger, and glanced around the cell. "The red-haired Trundler woman. She was not abducted by rebels. The rebels helped her escape. Do not try to deny it. My brother suspected as much. He captured one of the rebels and made him confess. The Trundler woman sailed through the Breath, then led this army down here. You women arranged her escape between you."

"The idea was mine," Cecile said swiftly. "Gythe and Sophia knew nothing. You should not blame them."

The lantern light held only the two of them. His world had contracted around him until all that was left was this circle of light surrounded by darkness. He eyed her, seeming now more puzzled than angry.

"What can your people hope to do against my fleet? The fort has landed far from the docks. My ships are not within range of the cannons. This strategy does not make sense. Yet your people are not fools."

The image of a dragon loomed so large in Cecile's mind that she was half afraid he would see it.

"Lead your people to that better life, *Naomh*," she said. "End this war."

"They won't let me." Xavier wasn't talking about his people. He looked into the darkness that, for him, was crowded with ghosts; all the Xaviers, stretching back generations, pushing him toward his fate. His smile was bitter. "There is a reason I dressed my soldiers to look like fiends from Hell."

He picked up the lantern. The circle of light wobbled wildly and flashed around the cell until it fell on Gythe and Brother Barnaby and finally Sophia, who was holding Bandit with her hand over his muzzle. Xavier stared at them and then, shifting the light, he walked over to the prison door and indicated to the guards he was ready to come out.

"I will launch the fleet ahead of schedule, as soon as it is light. Whatever this fort's commander has planned, I will steal a march on him. Bring the two girls to the square at dawn. The countess will remain in prison, serve as hostage for their cooperation."

"I stay with Her Highness," Cecile said, her voice grating.

"You are my prisoner!" Xavier shouted, rounding on her. "The only reason I have not ordered your execution is because I need these two to stop the storms!"

He paused, regaining control. "If the girls fail this time, my brother will use them in his blood magic ritual. I will not be able to stop him."

He slammed out the door, taking the lantern with him. She was aware, once more, of the relentless beating of the drums.

Cecile sighed. What was done was done. Stephano was here on Glasearrach. She allowed herself to smile, in a moment of maternal joy and pride. Then, accustomed to keeping her feelings hidden, she wrapped up that joy and locked it away.

"Xavier is launching the invasion fleet early, hoping to catch Stephano unprepared. You two have to stop the storms." Cecile spoke to the young women in matter-of-fact tones. "You have to appear to be cooperating with

Xavier, though in reality you will be clearing the skies for Stephano and his forces."

She turned to Brother Barnaby. "You must take word to the resistance that the plans have changed. They have to be ready to rescue Sophia and Gythe this morning, after they have calmed the storms."

"But what about you, Countess?" Sophia asked anxiously. "They have to rescue you, as well."

"Of course. They will have to do that, my dear," said Cecile, smiling. "You must not worry about me."

The drumming continued, so loudly that the walls of the building seemed to pulse to the beat. Cecile could see the pain on Sophia's face, in her trembling lips, in the lines on her forehead. She still suffered, but she made a valiant attempt to smile.

Cecile fixed her gaze on Brother Barnaby, letting him know silently that her own fate was not as important as those of Sophia and Gythe.

"I understand, my lady," he said gravely.

Sophia picked up Bandit, hugged him close, kissed him on his head, and then held him out to Brother Barnaby. "Take Bandit, please, Brother. Take him somewhere safe."

Bandit guessed what was happening and struggled to return to his mistress. Brother Barnaby spoke soothingly to him and Sophia promised him cakes on her return. Eventually Bandit calmed down and even tucked his nose into the monk's arm. Cecile accompanied Brother Barnaby to the cell door.

"I will find a way to free you, my lady," said Brother Barnaby.

"You and your friends must concentrate your efforts on saving Sophia and Gythe," Cecile said, adding with a shrug, "I am accustomed to fending for myself."

"You are not alone, my lady," said Brother Barnaby. "God is with you."

Cecile made no reply. The monk was a simple soul. He would be sad to learn that she had dismissed God long ago, as she would have dismissed an inept servant.

The drumming in the temple boomed and thundered, rivaling the sounds of the storms. Sometimes the drumming would stop, and the silence was dreadful, almost worse than the drumming. Brother Barnaby had told them the silence after the drumming was when they held the blood magic rites and sacrificed the victims.

No one could go back to sleep. To take their minds off their fear, Cecile talked cheerfully of what they would do when they were back home.

"I will take you to visit my château in the beautiful countryside of Marjolaine," she said.

She described the gardens and the fountains, the bedrooms, twelve turrets, and four hundred lead-paned windows.

"The countess takes me every year, when my father goes for hunting season. I have my own room in one of the turrets," said Sophia. "I can see ever so far, all the way to the mountains. The windows are tiny squares of glass that sparkle like diamonds in the sunlight. Bandit loves to visit. He barks at the swans . . ."

Her eyes filled with tears. "I miss him."

"He will be fine," Gythe signed. "We will introduce him to Doctor Ellington."

She gave herself whiskers and made her hands into cat claws. Sophia laughed. She had started translating for Gythe now that Miri was gone. Sophia began telling Gythe about the time Bandit had chased the Duchess of Waverly's cat. Cecile had been waiting for dawn. Watching the darkness fade to dismal gray, she was not surprised to hear voices outside their cell, the strident tones of the Blood Mage.

"It is time," Sophia said, turning quite pale. She flung her arms around Cecile. "I don't want to leave you here alone!"

"Hush, my dear, I will be fine. You are not to worry about me," Cecile said, smiling.

"You and Bandit and my father and I will go to Marjolaine together, won't we," said Sophia, clinging to her. "As soon as we get back."

"As soon as you want, my dear," said Cecile.

She looked at Gythe, whose eyes were shimmering in the lantern light.

"Take care of her!" Cecile said softly.

Gythe nodded, biting her lip.

The door opened to reveal the Blood Mage standing in the doorway. He was dressed in his crimson robes, and though he had washed his hands the odor of blood clung to him.

"I am here for the savants," he said. His lip curled slightly.

Cecile hugged Sophia close. Reaching out to Gythe, she drew her into the embrace.

"Give Stephano my love and a mother's blessing," said Cecile. "And a mother's blessing to both of you, my dear ones."

"Make haste, you two!" the Blood Mage said impatiently. "Our saint wants you in the square by dawn!"

"You must go," said Cecile.

Sophia clung to her, but Cecile gently freed herself. Gythe pulled Sophia away, and the Blood Mage stood aside to let them pass, the two young women holding fast to each other. When they reached the door, Sophia looked over her shoulder at Cecile. The countess smiled and pressed her fingers to her lips.

The cell door shut behind them.

Almost immediately, a flash of lightning lit the cell, followed by a low, roaring boom.

Cecile sank to her knees and gripped the small gold ring. She remembered another prison cell, long ago. A last kiss, a final embrace.

"Julian, watch over those I love," Cecile said softly. "Guard and protect them, since I cannot. Be with our son. Be with me, my love. Give me strength."

She held the ring and conjured up his face, so like Stephano's. She felt Julian's presence, even seemed to feel the touch of his hand brush against her cheek.

He was so close that when the voice spoke, she thought it was his.

"My lady," the voice whispered.

Cecile looked up and gasped. "Brother Barnaby!"

He reached down, helped her to her feet.

"How did you get in?" she asked. "What about the guards?"

"They are napping," said Brother Barnaby.

He held out a hooded cloak. Cecile stared at him, incredulous, then seized the cloak and hurriedly put it around her shoulders. Her hands were shaking so she had difficulty with the clasps.

"Gythe and Sophia," she said urgently.

"I will take you to them, my lady," said Brother Barnaby. He reached into his pouch and drew out a gun. "Mistress Miri sent you this."

Cecile recognized Stephano's prized dragon pistol. She thrust the pistol into the waistband of her skirt and made certain the folds of her cloak covered it, then she and Brother Barnaby hurried out of the cell.

The guards lay on the floor, slumbering peacefully to judge by their snoring. Brother Barnaby closed the cell door behind them, locked it, keeping the key. Once outside, he tossed the key over the wall surrounding the enclave. They heard it land with a plop in a puddle.

"The only key to the cell. It will be some time before they find you missing," he remarked.

The rain fell in torrents. Purple lightning flared and the thunder shook the heavens. Dragons could not fly through this. Sophia and Gythe would have to stop the storm, as the saints had done so long ago.

"I am sorry I had to interrupt you when you were praying, my lady," said Brother Barnaby.

"You did not interrupt my prayers, Brother," said Cecile. "You came in answer to them."

33

God must have important work for Father Jacob to do, otherwise I do not know how He puts up with him.

—Sir Ander, letter to Cecile, Countess de Marjolaine

The hour was long past midnight. Father Jacob and Sir Henry had reached the farmer's house late in the afternoon, and the farmer and Sir Henry had carried the unconscious Mr. Sloan from the wagon into the farmer's house. Alan had arrived with the Trundler healer, and under her ministrations, Mr. Sloan had briefly regained consciousness. He was disoriented and in considerable pain. He did not recognize Henry, though he did remember his own name, which the healer said was a good sign.

She dosed the patient with a tincture made of skullcap, oats, St. John's wort, and hot pepper, saying this would ease his pain and help the blood flow to his brain. She left them with orders to wake the patient every three hours, promising she would return in the morning.

Father Jacob had been keeping watch by Mr. Sloan's bedside. He must have fallen asleep in his chair, for he woke with a start, awakened by a strange sound. He waited to hear the sound again, hoping to identify it, but the house was quiet. He checked on his patient. Mr. Sloan slept peacefully.

Father Jacob wondered about the sound. He was certain he had not dreamed it. He left the bedchamber, treading softly so as not to disturb Mr. Sloan, and stood in the hallway of the farmhouse, listening. He peeped in on Sir Ander, who was comfortably ensconced in a blanket in a chair by the kitchen fire, his legs stretched out, his feet on the hearth. He was deeply asleep.

Alan Northrop was not here. He had ridden to the estate of the Earl of Brooking in quest of griffins. The farmer and his wife, son, and little daughter were all in bed. The house was quiet.

Father Jacob shook his head and returned to his chair. Unable to fall asleep, he gazed down at Sir Henry Wallace lying on a straw mattress on the floor, and mused on the dichotomies of human nature.

Sir Henry Wallace was the most powerful, dangerous, and feared man in Freya, maybe in the world. He had killed men by his own hand or issued orders that sent men to their deaths. Father Jacob marveled to see the cold, calculating, ruthless man meekly obeying the instructions of a humble Trundler healer, tending to Mr. Sloan's needs with gentle care and refusing to leave his side. When Father Jacob had prayed for God to keep Mr. Sloan in His care, Sir Henry stood with bowed head.

How does one judge such a man? Father Jacob wondered. He was thankful he didn't have to.

Mr. Sloan stirred in his sleep. He was breathing easier and some color had returned to his face. Father Jacob reached out to take the man's pulse, but he stopped, his hand in midair. He heard the sound again, not so much with his ears as with his being. The drumming thrummed in his blood. His heart echoed it, mirrored it. He could feel it thumping in his head, shaking him to the core of his being.

"Father, what is it? Is something wrong?" Sir Henry jumped from the mattress and sprang to the side of the bed, gazing anxiously at Mr. Sloan.

Father Jacob didn't answer. He sank back down in his chair.

Sir Henry placed his hand on Mr. Sloan's shoulder and gently shook him.

"Mr. Sloan, Franklin. Wake up!"

Mr. Sloan's eyes fluttered open, he groaned and fully opened his eyes. He gazed at Sir Henry and blinked in confusion.

"My lord? . . . What is . . . what is going on? Where am I?"

"You recognize me, Mr. Sloan!" Sir Henry exclaimed, delighted.

"Yes, my lord. Of course, my lord." Mr. Sloan's brow creased in puzzlement as he gazed in confusion at his surroundings. "Where am I, my lord? What happened?"

"What do you remember?"

Mr. Sloan frowned. "I seem to recall driving a carriage. We were chasing after Mistress Eiddwen, going down a hill. I fear that is all I can recollect, my lord."

"Eiddwen tossed some sort of magical bomb that spooked the horses, the carriage tipped over, you went flying into the river and hit your head on a rock, cracked your skull," Sir Henry said. "You must drink more of this foul stuff."

He poured the tincture into a cup and handed it to Mr. Sloan, who grimaced at the smell, but drank it down. He then lay back weakly on the pillows.

Sir Henry's eyes grew moist and his expression softened. He reached out to clasp Mr. Sloan's hand.

"You gave me a bad few moments, Franklin," said Sir Henry gruffly. "I feared I had lost you."

Mr. Sloan gave a faint smile. "I am sorry to have been the cause of such distress, my lord."

He closed his eyes and drifted back to sleep. Sir Henry stood gazing at him for long moments, then he brought out his handkerchief, blew his nose and, turning his back, walked over to look out the window. Lightning flared in the distance.

"Still several hours to dawn." Sir Henry consulted his watch. "Mr. Sloan appears to be making a good recovery, wouldn't you say so, Father?"

Father Jacob looked up. He was aware of Sir Henry and of Mr. Sloan, aware of what was happening around him. But he was more aware of the drumming. Voices floated on the surface, like leaves on dark and turgid water.

"What is the date?" Father Jacob asked.

Sir Henry glanced over his shoulder, startled. "The thirtieth of Soles. Why do you ask?"

"A day early," Father Jacob muttered, talking to himself. "And yet . . . the drums are beating. The storm is brewing. Xavier is on the move. But why now? Something must have happened . . . Ah, of course!"

Father Jacob slammed his hand down on the arm of his chair. "Captain de Guichen! He has reached Glasearrach!"

"What are you babbling about, Father?" Sir Henry asked irritably. "Keep your voice down. You will wake Mr. Sloan."

"Xavier is not going to wait until Fulmea the first to attack," said Father Jacob. "He is launching the invasion fleet today. The arrival of Captain de Guichen's fortress has forced his hand."

Sir Henry regarded him with surprise. "How the devil do you know this?"

"Because I hear the drums," Father Jacob said. "I have heard them before, but I didn't know what they were, not until Miri told me. These are Xavier's drums, the drums that shattered the Crystal Market."

A streak of purple lightning lit the sky. Sir Henry saw it and shook his head.

"A storm is coming. What you heard was the thunder, Father."

Father Jacob left his chair and went to the window.

"That is no ordinary storm. That is a wizard storm. The waves of contramagic are causing a disruption in the Breath. We have to leave! Now! We have to have those griffins!"

Sir Henry raised an eyebrow. "It is three in the morning! You are not seriously proposing we knock at the earl's door at this ungodly hour."

"If I hear the drums, so does Eiddwen," said Father Jacob grimly. "She has to act today to set off the final bomb. She needs the contramagic generated by the drumming. The contramagic from Below is the fire that will light the fuse."

"I wish to God I understood what you were talking about, Father."

Father Jacob shrugged. "You either trust me or you don't, Sir Henry. If you don't, then we have all gone to a great deal of trouble for nothing."

"I trust you," said Sir Henry. "More's the pity."

Father Jacob hurried off to wake Sir Ander, while Sir Henry gathered up their equipment and went to rouse the farmer and his wife. Sir Henry did not like having to leave Mr. Sloan, but the farmer's wife assured him she would care for him as though he were a member of the family.

"Keep your coin, sir," she said, when Sir Henry offered her money. "I would do the same for the poorest tramp on the highway."

Sir Henry gave her his grateful thanks. Father Jacob noted that when she wasn't looking, Sir Henry slipped the money beneath her flour canister.

When the farmer had fetched the wagon, Sir Ander took a seat up front and Sir Henry and Father Jacob sat in the wagon's bed. Before they could leave, the farmer's wife came hurrying out of the house, holding out a basket of food.

"You'll need something in your bellies if you're going to be chasing miscreants," she said.

Father Jacob took charge of the basket, the farmer clucked to the horses and the wagon rolled off. The sky was a strange sight: sheets of purple lightning spread across dark clouds boiling up from Below, while the sky above them was calm, bright with stars and a three-quarter moon. The worst of the storm was probably hundreds of miles away, out beyond Khendrun Island, deep in the Breath. But the wind was picking up, blowing out of the east.

Sir Henry passed round their equipment, which Mr. Sloan had carried in a leather satchel. Each man had a dark lantern, known as a bull's-eye, which could be worn around the neck. He had brought along two extra pistols and the two rifles, wrapped in oilcloth. He offered Sir Ander a knife, but Sir Ander shook his head. He was wearing his sword. Father Jacob refused to accept any weapons.

Sir Henry smiled. "I hope God shoots straight."

"I have trusted in His aim thus far," said Father Jacob.

Sir Ander watched with concern as Sir Henry thrust the pistols into his belt. "Remember what the contramagic does to magical pistols."

"Not much I can do about that now," said Sir Henry wryly.

Sir Ander reached into his coat and drew out a pistol. "Take one of these. It works without magic. I had them specially made."

"Works without magic?" Sir Henry regarded the pistol with interest and some skepticism. "How?"

Sir Ander smiled. "That's my secret. And I'll be asking for that pistol's return when this is finished."

Father Jacob opened the basket to find oat cakes, grapes, and cheese wrapped in a cloth. He doled out the rations, sharing them with the farmer. The road ran through fields of wheat that rippled in the strengthening breeze. Father Jacob looked back to see the shadowy figure of the woman watching them, her arm around her little daughter.

"If we fail, that mother and her family will be dead before nightfall," Sir Henry remarked gravely. "Along with thousands of other women and children."

He sat hunched over, gazing at the flaring lightning. His expression grew grim, his face drawn, haggard. He tossed his bread aside, uneaten.

"Are they somewhere safe?" Father Jacob asked.

Sir Henry looked at him, startled.

"Your wife and child," said Father Jacob.

Sir Henry gazed out over the fields of wheat to the storm clouds and the flaring purple lightning.

"They are safe for the moment. But if these fiends win, there will be no safe place anywhere."

Father Jacob sighed. He very much feared Sir Henry was right.

They arrived at the magnificent residence of Lord John Benedict, Earl of Brooking, long before any of the noble family or the servants were awake. Even in the darkness they could see the storm clouds were drawing nearer, creeping slowly inland. The wind carried the scent of rain.

Sir Henry pulled the bell rope and banged loudly on the door. After several long moments, a bleary-eyed footman in his nightcap, carrying a lamp in one hand, opened the door and peered out. He stared at Sir Henry, too amazed to speak.

"Is Captain Northrop a guest in this house?" Sir Henry demanded.

"Yes, s-s-sir," said the footman, stuttering.

"I am Sir Henry Wallace," said Sir Henry, handing the stupefied footman his card. "This is Reverend Northrop and Sir Ander Martel. We are friends of Captain Northrop's. We must speak to the earl."

Shouldering past the footman, Sir Henry barged into the house with Father Jacob and Sir Ander following close behind.

They entered a large foyer. The light of the footman's lamp shone on marble floors adorned with the earl's crest, a griffin rampant over a blue-green river. The fragrance of fresh-cut flowers filled the room. At the far end, they could make out the gleaming wood railing of a spiral staircase.

By this time, the butler had arrived, bristling with indignation.

"Who are these gentlemen, Charles?" he said, addressing the footman.

"He's Sir Henry Wallace, Mr. Smyth," said the footman in a loud whisper.

At the mention of Sir Henry's name, Mr. Smyth regarded him with a frozen look of disdain.

"I must ask you to leave, Sir Henry. The earl is not in the habit of receiving guests at three of the clock—"

"He'll damn well receive me," said Sir Henry shortly.

Strolling over to the foot of the spiral staircase, he

shouted Alan's name in ringing tones, the sound reverberating through the house. The horrified butler protested volubly. Sir Henry responded by shouting again, this time even more loudly. They could hear doors opening and the people asking in sleepy, irritated voices what was going on.

Alan appeared on a landing three floors above them. He must have been accustomed to such emergencies, for he was already dressed. He ran down the stairs, buttoning his jacket as he came.

"Henry, what the devil are you doing here at this hour? Did something happen to Mr. Sloan? He's not dead—"

"No, no. He is recovering," said Sir Henry.

"Good news," said Alan. He glanced at the angry butler and shook his head. "You should not have come, Henry. The earl doesn't like you. He very nearly tossed me out on my ear when he found out you were with me. Only the lateness of the hour and the pleas of his very charming wife and daughters induced him to let me stay the night. Why *are* you here?"

"We have reason to believe that Eiddwen will act today, not tomorrow," said Sir Henry.

"Today!" Alan stared at him. "How do you know that?"

"I hear the drums beating," Father Jacob said. "Captain de Guichen's arrival has caused Xavier to advance his plans."

Alan gaped at him in astonishment, then rounded on Henry. "You woke the household because my brother hears beating drums? I swear to God, Henry, I think Jacob has put you under some sort of spell—"

"You are a crafter, Alan," said Father Jacob. "Listen. You can hear the drumming."

Alan turned away in disgust, only to stop. His body stiffened. He looked back at his brother in shock.

"We need the griffins," said Sir Henry urgently. "Did you present our case to the earl?"

"I'm afraid it's hopeless," said Alan. "The beasts are not for sale at any price and the earl won't even consider lending them, especially to you. When I mentioned your name, he called you, among other things, a 'bounder' and a 'rogue.' "

"Astute judge of character," Sir Ander whispered in Father Jacob's ear.

Father Jacob frowned and shook his head. "This is not good. We need those griffins."

Sir Ander glanced up the stairs. "You can talk with the man yourself. Unless I am much mistaken, that must be the earl."

A man wearing a dressing gown descended the stairs, quivering with outraged dignity. Lord John Benedict was tall and well built, in his late forties, with dark hair. He was stern-faced, his cheeks flushed with anger. He had his right hand in his pocket.

"Wallace, you reprobate!" the earl said, glowering. "What do you mean by invading my house? Get out at once. All of you!"

"Watch him, Henry. He has a pistol," Alan warned. "He isn't afraid to use it."

"Damn right, I'm not afraid!" the earl said angrily. "I would consider shooting you, Wallace, to be a service to my country."

Sir Henry was losing patience. "We are on opposite sides when it comes to politics, Sir John, but we are both loyal subjects of Her Majesty. We are in pursuit of dangerous criminals. One of our wyverns went lame and we are in urgent need of transportation. We would like to borrow your griffins. I can pay you whatever you want—"

"You could offer me the crown jewels and the answer

is no," said the earl. "I want you and your friends out of my house and off my land this instant."

"My lord, our need is very great—" Alan began.

The earl cast him a scathing glance. "I am sorry to find you keep such low company, Captain Northrop. I once thought you a hero. You have dropped considerably in my estimation."

"I could commandeer the griffins in the queen's name, my lord," said Sir Henry.

"You could try," the earl snarled.

He took the pistol from his pocket of his dressing gown and aimed it at Sir Henry; in response, Sir Ander and Alan both drew their pistols and aimed them at the earl. Father Jacob thrust himself between the antagonists.

"Gentlemen, this is madness! Every second that passes brings us closer to disaster!" Father Jacob said urgently. "There is no time for a lengthy explanation, Sir John. Suffice it to say that the fate of Freya hangs in the balance—"

The front door burst open. A man rushed inside with such haste, he nearly knocked over the butler. He ran straight to the earl, ignoring the drawn pistols or perhaps so agitated he didn't even notice. He had a bloody gash on his head and he staggered where he stood, almost falling to his knees.

"Sir John, we've been robbed!"

"Robbed?" The earl stared at him. "Jenkins, pull yourself together. What do you mean, robbed?"

Jenkins was trying to catch his breath and talk at the same time, his words coming in gasps. His face was pale beneath his tan, beaded with sweat mingling with the blood.

"I flew here on griffin back, as fast as I could. Two of the griffins were stolen in the night!"

The earl went a ghastly white, the flush of anger draining from his face. "Stolen . . . How?"

"The thieves killed Richard and I think they took young Ralph, the groom with them. They clouted me over the head. When I came to myself, I found Richard murdered, his throat slashed, and blood everywhere."

Jenkins shuddered and his voice cracked. "A horrible sight, my lord. And Ralph's gone missing, along with two of the griffins."

The earl was bewildered. "But . . . but . . . how could someone *steal* a griffin? The beast would fight, tear a thief apart!"

"Blood magic," said Father Jacob.

The earl stared, baffled.

"I believe your griffins were stolen by the very criminals we are tracking, my lord," Father Jacob explained. "The woman is a sorcerer. She murdered the groom, then used his blood to cast a magical spell on the griffins, inducing them to obey her. She would cast her spell on either a fresh deer haunch she brought with her or perhaps even parts of the unfortunate man's body and then feed that to—"

"We understand, Father," said Sir Ander hurriedly, seeing Jenkins on the verge of collapse. "No need to go into detail."

"But why would Eiddwen need to steal griffins?" Alan asked. "She has her carriage—"

"Because Xavier's sudden move took *her* by surprise," Father Jacob said excitedly. "Think about it. After she set the bombs, Eiddwen would need a way to escape Freya before the bombs exploded. She probably planned to depart on one of the black ships. But Xavier upset her plans by launching his attack early. Like me, she can hear the drumming. Perhaps she can even feel the waves of contramagic. She knows she has to act now, but she has no way to contact the black ship, no way to escape this doomed continent. Thus she has to steal griffins."

"That makes sense," Sir Henry conceded.

"Not to me! What the devil are you talking about?" the earl demanded. "Someone called Eiddwen . . ." He paused, then said, frowning, "I know that name. She was companion to Lord Brobeaton's mother. Damn fine-looking woman. She was here, in my house. I took her to see the griffins."

"Which is how she knew where to find them," said Sir Henry.

"I don't believe it!" the earl said stoutly. "That handsome woman, stealing griffins and murdering people. Bosh!"

"That handsome woman is responsible for countless murders, Sir John. I have reason to know," said Father Jacob somberly. "These gentlemen and I have chased her across two continents. She is planning a devastating attack on Freya."

The earl snorted. "Tomfoolery! A woman attack Freya? Bosh! I don't believe it."

"And yet your griffins are gone, my lord," Sir Henry pointed out impatiently. "A groom has been abducted and another murdered."

The earl grumbled, eyeing Sir Henry distastefully. Then he asked in a gruff tone of voice, "Can you save my griffins, Wallace?"

"I believe we can, my lord," said Sir Henry. "But we will need griffins of our own to pursue the criminals."

"I suppose I have no choice," said the earl ungraciously. "Jenkins, escort these men to the eyries."

He added, as they were starting to leave, "Save my griffins, Wallace, and I might change my opinion of you."

"How very kind of you, my lord," said Sir Henry, his lip curling.

Once they were on the porch and out of earshot, Alan declared, "Damn son of a bitch! I wish I had shot him! Never mind stopping Eiddwen from blowing us up or rescuing that poor devil of a groom. Just save his goddamn griffins."

"At least we got what we came for," said Sir Henry. He clapped his hand on Alan's shoulder. "I feared for a moment your notorious luck had failed us."

"Not so lucky for the grooms, poor devils," Alan said, shaking his head.

Jenkins hurried out to join them. "I'm going to fly on ahead, gentlemen, warn the griffins you're coming. They are in such a state they are likely to attack strangers."

Jenkins mounted his griffin. The beast was clearly upset, gnashing its beak, tail lashing. The lion paws had gouged a large hole in the gravel drive.

"You'll find the eyries about half a mile to the north in that stand of oaks. You can see some of the griffins now. Go across the lawn and around the lake. On the other side is a path that will take you straight there."

Jenkins flew off, heading for the grove of trees.

"How did this earl come to own griffins?" Sir Ander asked, as they trudged across the smooth, well kept lawn. "I never heard of anyone who kept them like chickens."

"For God's sake, don't let the griffins hear you say that," said Sir Henry. "They'll snap off your head. The earl doesn't really own his griffins. During the Dark Ages, dragons and griffins living in the Sountral Mountains fought over the dwindling food supply. As you can imagine, the dragons always won. Several major griffin families formed pacts with wealthy humans, agreeing to serve them in return for food and a safe place to raise their young. Generations of the Brooking family have kept griffins. That might come to an end," Sir Henry added grimly.

"Does he mean the griffins or the earl?" Sir Ander asked Father Jacob in a low voice.

Father Jacob didn't reply. He was keeping a wary eye

on the storm. The wind was growing stronger, snatching at their hats and whipping their coattails. The black, boiling clouds were slowly advancing, blotting out the stars to the west. Sir Henry and Alan began arguing over whether Alan should go to the rendezvous site to find Simon. Alan protested that he didn't want to miss out on the action. Sir Henry was endeavoring to persuade him when Alan came to a sudden stop.

"What is it?" Sir Henry asked. He reached for his pistol.

Alan was peering into the sky. "Look there. Above the trees. I think Simon has come to us."

A strange-looking vessel sailed into view, black against the stars. The vessel flew low to the ground, barely skimming the treetops. Two men were seated in what appeared to be two comfortable armchairs that had been welded onto a cigar-shaped metal lift tank with wings.

"What in heaven's name is that thing?" Sir Ander asked, staring in amazement.

"The *Contraption*!" Alan replied, laughing.

"How does it stay airborne?"

"Each wing has an air screw and a small lift tank, plus a larger lift tank for ballast." Alan raised the lantern, signaling with the light, and began to shout. "Simon! Down here!"

Apparently one of the occupants saw him, for the vehicle veered off its course and flew in their direction. After circling several times, the *Contraption* made a gentle landing on the lawn, bumping twice, then coming to a halt.

"Simon!" Sir Henry exclaimed, running over to meet his friend. "What are you doing here?"

"I could ask you the same question. When you didn't arrive at the rendezvous point, we went searching for you.

There has been a development. Mr. Albright and I have been using the other boulders as guides to the final one, taking measurements and such like. When we flew over one of the boulders this morning, we noticed that the contramagic constructs had started to glow green."

He looked at Father Jacob, whose expression had darkened.

"That's bad, isn't it," said Simon.

"I'm afraid so," said Father Jacob. "The drumming has lit the fuse, so to speak."

"Drumming," said Simon thoughtfully. "Of course. That's the beating sound I've been hearing in my head."

"What about the last bomb?" Father Jacob asked urgently. "You said you made calculations. Does this mean you know where it is located?"

"I believe I do," said Simon. "I can lead you to it." He paused, looking around, then frowned. "What has happened? Where is Mr. Sloan?"

"I will tell you the short version," said Henry. "Eiddwen cast a spell that caused our carriage to crash. Mr. Sloan tumbled into a brook and nearly drowned. He is in bed with a cracked skull. Eiddwen came here to steal griffins. We came here to be insulted by the earl."

"So just another day at the office for you, Henry," said Simon, grinning.

"We *did* manage to obtain the loan of the earl's griffins," said Sir Henry. "Without shooting the earl. Though we came close."

"Of course, you did. Well, mount your griffins and follow me. We'll have to hurry. I don't like the looks of that wizard storm."

The *Contraption* returned to the air. Father Jacob and the others hastened to the eyries, where the earl housed his griffins or, as the griffins viewed it, the residences they deigned to inhabit.

The griffins built their eyries at the tops of enormous, ancient oak trees, some probably dating back to the time of the first earl. The nests were so high in the trees, they were impossible to see from the ground. A few outbuildings below housed the grooms, the saddles and bridles and other equipment.

The griffins were flying in circles above the trees, shrieking in anger, upset, no doubt, over the loss of members of their family. Jenkins and two of his stable hands had two of the beasts saddled and were working on the other two. After finishing, Jenkins provided helmets and urged the men to be careful.

"I explained to the griffins that you gentlemen know the people who are responsible for the abduction and that you are going after them. I have no idea if they understood me or not. The earl, Lord bless him, thinks griffins understand every word he says. I'm not so certain myself. At least they didn't bite off my head when I brought out the saddles."

Sir Henry and Alan went to talk to the grooms and inspect the saddles. Simon and Mr. Albright, in the *Contraption,* circled overhead. Father Jacob stood braced against the buffeting wind, his cassock whipping around him. Lightning flared, spreading purple flame over the surface of the advancing clouds. He could hear the thunder now, a low rumble that seemed to roll over the ground. He felt a few cold spatters of rain on his face.

"There was a storm the night I fled my home," said Father Jacob.

Sir Ander looked at the priest, startled. Father Jacob had never talked about that period of his life.

"Alan followed me out of the house, his angry voice

shrill above the cracks of thunder. I tried to explain why I had to leave. My brother, who had never known God, could not possibly understand. With the soldiers closing in, I turned and ran. Alan chased after me until he slipped in the mud and fell to his knees. He cursed me, 'Traitor, coward.' I heard his cries." Father Jacob sighed. "But God's voice was louder."

"A good thing for us all that you listened, Father," said Sir Ander.

"Was it?" Father Jacob shook his head. "I brought my family to ruin, broke my father's heart, lost my brother's love. Did I ever feel a sliver of doubt? A pricking of my conscience?"

Sir Ander said nothing. Father Jacob was not talking to him anymore.

"Sometimes, many times, I argued with God, fought with God. I struck at Him with my fists like a prize fighter in the ring. He fended me off, let me flail away until I grew weary and my rage died and I could again hear His voice in my heart. I never doubted Him. Always I have believed."

Father Jacob reached into the breast of his cassock to touch the slim volume he always carried with him. Saint Marie's *Confession.* He remembered her words, written at the very end before she started on the journey that would end in her martyrdom.

" 'And now it seems that the tears and the curses and the blessings have led me to this moment,' " Father Jacob murmured. " 'God stands with me and if I fall He will raise me up and my soul will shine as a star in His firmament.' "

A hand touched his arm. Father Jacob turned, half expecting to see the saint. Instead he saw Sir Ander.

"The griffins are saddled, Father. We're waiting only for you. We need to leave before the storm hits."

"I'm coming," said Father Jacob.

But before he could go, Sir Ander stopped him, his hand grasping his shoulder.

"God has more than enough stars, Jacob," Sir Ander said. "He doesn't need another."

"I'll bear that in mind," said Father Jacob.

34

God stands with me and if I fall, he will raise me up . . .

—Sister Marie Elizabeth

Morning's pale glow spread across the sky, making the massive cloud formations boiling out of the east seem that much darker by contrast. The wizard storm dogged them, following them slowly, inexorably. Outrider clouds spat rain at them.

Sir Ander tore his gaze away from the purple, lightning-shot clouds. There was nothing to be gained by staring at them. He concentrated on the ground rolling below him, only faintly illuminated by the coming of the new day—maybe the last day. Sir Ander sternly stopped such dark thinking.

"Between Father Jacob and Sir Henry, we have God and the devil both on our side," Sir Ander said to himself with a grim smile "That must count for something."

Simon flew ahead of them in the *Contraption*. According to his calculations, the boulder that was the final link in the deadly chain was about ten miles to the north. Scanning the ground below, Sir Ander could barely make out large structures, such as houses or barns, in the gloaming. He wondered gloomily how he was supposed to find a boulder.

In order to see, he was forced to lean over the griffin's leonine shoulders, bracing himself against the feathered eagle neck. The griffin didn't like such familiarity, apparently, for it kept glancing back at him, black eyes glinting.

Sir Ander wished the beast would watch where it was going. He was not impressed with the earl's griffins and neither were the others. Jenkins had used the word "spoiled" in reference to these griffins, though not within their hearing, of course. The earl rode to the hunt on occasion, but mainly he reveled in the pride of ownership.

"Though there's some question of who owns who," Jenkins had told them. "The earl gives the beasts every luxury and the griffins do almost nothing in return. I must warn you, gentlemen. I have worked with griffins for nigh on thirty years and it's my feeling you dare not trust these beasts. They're using you to find their own. Once they do, they'll leave you high and dry."

Sir Ander straightened his back, grimaced at the stiffness, and looked over at Father Jacob, who was flying to Sir Ander's left and slightly ahead of him.

Father Jacob enjoyed riding griffin-back. He would sit braced in the saddle, the short, knee-length "traveling" cassock flapping in the wind; his helmet straps dangling behind. He would kick at the griffin with his heels, urging the beast to fly faster, much to the irritation of the griffin.

This morning, Father Jacob sat motionless in the saddle, holding the reins loosely, as if he wasn't aware he was holding them at all. He did not search the ground, but gazed ahead, far ahead, past Sir Henry and Alan. Past Simon sailing along in his *Contraption*. Sir Ander wondered what the priest was seeing.

A vision of heaven? Or of hell?

Whatever it was, Sir Ander didn't like it. He had overheard Father Jacob quoting Saint Marie about going to God. For the first time since he'd met the priest, he wondered if Father Jacob was afraid. Sir Ander had never known Father Jacob to fear anything. As he had once put it, Father Jacob didn't have enough sense to be afraid.

The idea that he might now be afraid was upsetting.

They followed the highway, flying over fields of grain and oak groves, lush lawns and rolling hills, homes and villages. After miles of this, the *Contraption* veered away, flying in a more southerly direction that would take them closer to the edge of the continent.

The southeastern shoreline of Freya was undeveloped, unlike the southern part of the continent. The jagged cliffs of granite that jutted out into the Breath were dangerous to shipping, and the wind swirling around the cliffs was so unpredictable that it would suck ships too close to the coastline or blow them far off course. There were no natural harbors, like those in the major shipping ports of Haever and Westfirth, in Rosia.

Looking down, Sir Ander saw a land that was desolate, empty, and windswept, dotted by stunted trees bent double by the wind and sparse outcroppings of saw grass and brush.

Sir Ander looked back to see that the storm was closing on them. Boiling up from below, the ragged black clouds were slowly starting to obliterate the sunlight. The spitting rain had stopped and the wind had lessened in force, but there was an ominous feeling, as if the storm were sucking in a huge breath. Scudding wisps of fog drifted between him and the ground, making it more difficult to see.

The *Contraption* flew on, undeterred. They were nearing the coast, the continent's sharp-toothed shoreline lit by the glow of the sun. The *Contraption* began to slow its speed. Simon thrust out his arm and waved and pointed, motioning downward.

Sir Ander searched the area, but he could not see a boulder and concluded that they must have arrived at the general location where Simon hoped to find it.

The *Contraption* descended, accompanied by the griffin riders. Sir Ander started to give the order to descend, then noticed Father Jacob continuing on, apparently unaware that they were landing. Sir Ander shouted at him and pointed to the *Contraption.* Father Jacob came back to reality with a start, nodded and signaled his griffin to follow the others.

Alan was the first to find the boulder and the activity around it. Once he had pointed it out, Sir Ander wondered with chagrin how he could have missed it. The boulder looked completely out of place in the midst of the empty, barren landscape. They glided nearer, keeping to the cover of the mists of the Breath.

The two stolen griffins were tethered to some scrubby pine trees not far from the boulder. Four men formed a perimeter around the boulder, each posted at a compass point. The dwindling sunlight glinted off metal helms and the barrels of their long guns.

"She brought soldiers," Sir Ander muttered. "She knows we're coming."

A fifth man was leaning against the boulder. Sir Ander guessed that was Lucello. He searched for Eiddwen, but couldn't see her.

The wizard storm that he had cursed now proved to be a blessing. The mists of the Breath mingled with the advancing clouds to effectively hide Ander and the others from the view of those on the ground as they descended.

They had devised a plan before they left. Sir Ander, Sir Henry, and Alan would swoop down, bursting out of the clouds, fire at Eiddwen and her guards at close range, killing or wounding them before they knew what hit them. Once the area was secure, Father Jacob would defuse or dismantle the bomb.

Alan flashed the light from his dark lantern, giving them the signal. Sir Ander looked at Father Jacob to see if he knew what was happening, if he was even paying attention.

Father Jacob shouted something. It was hard to hear with the wind rushing in his ears, but Sir Ander thought he said, "God go with you!"

Taking that for a "yes," Sir Ander drew his dragon pistol. He would fire his first shot with that magical weapon, saving the nonmagical pistol for whatever followed.

He and the others flew lower, still shrouded in mist. Every so often, Sir Ander would catch a glimpse of the guards, who were keeping watch for enemies on the ground, not expecting trouble to swoop down on them from above.

They had only a few more yards to go when a blast of rain-laden wind shredded the mists and left them without cover. Nonetheless, they kept going. So far the guards had not noticed them.

Unfortunately, the two stolen griffins did. Once they caught sight of their fellows in the air, the hobbled griffins began shrieking and thrashing about.

The alarmed guards looked up at the griffin riders, as did Lucello. He sprang from his place by the boulder and shouted something Ander couldn't make out. Eiddwen, who must have been on the opposite side of the boulder, came into view. She, too, was looking at the descending griffins, who were screeching and hooting at their fellows.

"Attack!" Alan bellowed.

He really had no need to give the command, Sir Ander thought bitterly. The fool griffins were going to attack whether their riders willed it or not. The guards, seeing the threat, raised their long guns, took aim and fired. Green fireballs soared into the air. The fireballs had a greater range than a bullet, but lacked the velocity, making them relatively easy to dodge. The griffins instinctively avoided them and the fireballs sailed past harmlessly.

It was then Sir Ander realized his griffin was not intending to land, allowing him to dismount. The stupid beast was going in for the kill!

He pulled on the reins and shouted and cursed, trying to stop it, but the griffin ignored him. With claws extended and beak snapping, the beast dove down on its prey. Sir Ander wondered briefly if he would survive the collision.

He fired his pistol at the guard, then flung both arms around the griffin's neck and gripped with his thighs, hoping desperately to hang on. Green fire burst in front of him and the griffin screamed in pain. He could feel the beast shudder and smell the nauseating stench of burnt feathers. The enraged griffin slammed into the Bottom Dweller, its claws striking the man in the chest. Sir Ander lost his grip and flew out of the saddle.

For a moment he lay dazed and stunned on the stony ground, trying to catch his breath. Overhead, a sheet of purple lightning blossomed among the clouds, followed almost instantly by deafening thunder and a deluge of rain. The sun disappeared, vanquished by the storm.

He caught a glimpse of the *Contraption*. Overtaken by a squall, the vehicle was being tossed about. He saw it go into a steep dive, plummeting toward the ground, and then day grew dark as night and he lost sight of it.

Two pistol shots went off not far from him. He heard Alan swearing and Sir Henry shouting. Sir Ander lurched to his feet and yanked off his helm, trying to see through the roaring darkness.

"Henry!" Alan shouted out of the night. "Behind you!"

A dazzling sheet of lightning flared. Sir Ander drew his pistol and turned to see one of the soldiers taking aim at Sir Henry. At Alan's shout, the soldier whipped around, shifting his aim to the captain.

Alan raised his rifle.

"Drop it, Alan!" Sir Ander warned. "The magic!"

He was too late. A blazing ball of green contramagic struck the rifle and wrapped the barrel in sizzling tendrils of flame. The rifle blew apart in a ball of orange fire. Alan gave an agonized cry and fell to the ground, writhing in the mud.

Sir Ander raised his pistol, but before he could fire, he heard a shot behind him. The soldier jerked and spun and then crumpled to the ground.

"I'll go to Alan," Sir Henry cried, running past. "You stay with Father Jacob!"

"I can't find him! Have you seen him?" Sir Ander shouted.

Sir Henry shook his head and kept running.

Sir Ander fought his way through the wind-driven rain, searching for the priest in the light of every lightning strike. Father Jacob must be here somewhere, caught in the storm, unarmed save for his magic and in a strange, fey mood.

While he was looking, Sir Ander stumbled upon the soldier who had fired at him—or what was left of the man. The enraged griffin was holding the man like a mouse in its eagle claws, tearing him apart with its razor-sharp beak.

Sir Ander thrust his pistol into his belt inside his coat, hoping to keep it as dry as possible. Drawing his sword, he kept searching.

Lightning arced across the clouds in a dazzling array. He glanced back to see Sir Henry standing protectively over his fallen friend, aiming his pistol at something in the darkness. He saw a flash, but no shot rang out. Either the gun had misfired or the powder was wet.

In the next lightning strike, he saw Sir Henry pick up Alan's sword and spring at his attacker. Green fire blazed, blue constructs on the sword flared briefly, then went out. Darkness and sheets of rain dropped like a curtain. Sir Ander heard muffled sounds, a cry and a groan.

"Henry!" Sir Ander risked calling.

No response.

Sir Ander's instinct was to go to the aid of a comrade, even if that comrade was Henry Wallace. His duty, however, was to Father Jacob, as Sir Henry himself had reminded him.

Sir Ander stood in the rain, grimly taking stock of the situation. Between them, they had disposed of three of the guards, perhaps four, he couldn't be certain. But the cost had been high. Alan was gravely wounded, perhaps dead and God alone knew what had become of Sir Henry.

And the two most dangerous people, Eiddwen and Lucello, were still at work, presumably working to arm the bomb. He and Father Jacob were the only people left to complete the mission, and he had no idea what had happened to the priest.

Sir Ander continued his search. Whenever the lightning flared, he scanned the area. All he could see was the desolate landscape of mud, brush, and stunted trees. All he could hear was the thunder and, from deep inside him, the sound of the drums.

Sir Ander was no crafter and yet he could hear drumbeats pounding in his ears like the pulsing of his heart's blood.

"If *I* can hear them, then we're in trouble," Sir Ander muttered beneath his breath.

Thunder rumbled, shaking the ground. Sir Ander realized he was walking about aimlessly and he forced himself to stop, wait for the next lightning flash, find landmarks, get his bearings.

Raucous, joyous cawings sounded in the distance. The cawings grew louder, coming from overhead. Sir Ander looked up to see the griffins winging their way through the storm, returning to their eyries.

All the griffins, including those they had ridden, still wearing their saddles.

They'll leave you high and dry. Sir Ander smiled grimly.

Purple lightning billowed across the sky and in the flash he located the huge, misshapen lump that was the boulder. He had been walking in the wrong direction, away from it.

Still no sign of Father Jacob.

Sir Ander cautiously retraced his steps. He had caught only that one glimpse of the boulder, but it was enough for him to be able to tell that it was massive. He stood over six feet tall and the boulder topped him by several feet. Roughly round in shape, it measured probably a good ten feet across. Judging from the grass growing around the base and the fact that it was partially buried in the ground, the boulder had been here for some time.

A beam of light, as from a dark lantern, came from behind the boulder, jabbing through the rain. The beam flashed for only a few seconds, then went out.

Sir Ander stopped dead. He wiped his hands on his shirt, drying them as best he could, to get a good grip on the hilt of his sword. He waited where he was, ears and eyes straining. Light suddenly blazed, catching him full in the face.

"Sir Ander!"

"Shut off that light, Father!" Sir Ander hissed, shading his eyes. "You've damn near blinded me!"

"Sorry, I had to be sure it was you."

Father Jacob slid shut the dark lantern's panel, dousing

the light. He was hunkered down beside the boulder, trying to find shelter from the wind and rain.

Sir Ander sheathed his sword and ran toward him. Reaching the boulder, he crouched down with a grunt.

"Thank God I found you, Father. I've been—"

"Lower your voice. Have you seen Eiddwen?" Father Jacob asked urgently. "I heard gunshots."

"Alan and Sir Henry dealt with three of the guards. My griffin tore apart the fourth." Sir Ander frowned. "The fiendish woman has to be here somewhere. We saw her griffins leaving—"

"She *is* here," said Father Jacob, his voice grating. "I just don't know where."

"Maybe not," Sir Ander suggested, hoping he was right. "Maybe she fled. Her guards are dead, and her griffins flew off without her. If she blew up Freya now, she would have no way to escape death herself."

"Escape does not matter to her," said Father Jacob. "She always knew death was a possibility."

He slid back the panel on the bull's-eye lantern and flashed the light on the rain-slick rock. The boulder was covered with constructs that, like the others, seemed to have been etched onto the rock with acid. But she had not used acid. She had used blood. Father Jacob slid the panel shut.

"The constructs aren't glowing," he said. "She isn't finished. We interrupted her work. Think of this boulder as a powder keg. Eiddwen has placed the fuse. She is out there in the darkness, biding her time, waiting for the opportunity to strike the match."

"Don't forget the Warlock. He's out there, too, the murderous bastard," said Sir Ander.

"Lucello is probably with her. Where are the others, my brother and Sir Henry? You said they killed the guards."

Sir Ander had been dreading this question. He didn't immediately answer.

Father Jacob saw his expression. "They're both dead . . ."

"I hope not," said Sir Ander.

He briefly described what had happened, telling how Alan's rifle had blown up in his hands and Sir Henry's pistol had misfired.

"I called his name. There was no answer. I'm sorry, Father."

Father Jacob drew in a breath, let it out in a sigh. "If they are dead, it is up to us to save the country for which they died. Do your pistols work?"

"I have no idea," said Sir Ander. "I've been trying to keep them dry, but in this downpour . . ." He didn't finish the sentence; there was no need.

"You keep watch. I have to study these constructs and, to do that, I have to have light," said Father Jacob.

He opened the panel of the dark lantern. Light flared, shining on the wet rock. As he ran his fingers over the constructs. Sir Ander felt his skin crawl. He could almost see the blood running down the boulder.

"The constructs form a chain," Father Jacob explained. "Every construct is a link in that chain connecting each one to the next, just as this boulder is the link in the chain of boulders stretching across Freya. I need to find the last construct."

"And I need to stand up," Sir Ander grunted, rubbing his aching thighs.

He stood, took a step backward and stumbled over something, losing his balance. Putting out his hand to stop his fall, he touched what felt like flesh and bone.

He snatched back his hand and opened the panel on the lantern. The light shone on bare feet, bare legs: a naked man, sprawled on the ground. Sir Ander felt bile rise in his throat.

The man's belly had been sliced open and the blood was still pumping, the rain washing it in rivulets around him. The green light gleamed hideously on the entrails. As Sir Ander looked, the man's hands clenched into fists from what must have been terrible pain, began twitching. His eyes opened, and his mouth worked soundlessly.

Sir Ander switched off the light, overcome with horror and loathing. "Father, come quickly! He's still alive! We need do something—"

"God have mercy!" Father Jacob whispered.

The priest quickly knelt at the man's side and, placing one hand on his forehead, took hold of the other hand.

"Go to God, my child. He will grant you ease."

The man grimaced and gave a final gasp. His tortured body shuddered, then relaxed, his eyes staring into the storm. Father Jacob murmured a prayer, then placed his hands over the man's eyes to close them.

The hair on the back of Sir Ander's neck prickled as he sensed someone was behind him. With his hand on his pistol, he started to turn. A knife plunged into his back, the blow hitting him between the shoulder blades.

Magical constructs on his coat flared blue, thwarting the attack, turning the blade aside. He heard a sharp hiss of anger and a muttered curse.

In one swift, trained move Sir Ander drew his pistol and pivoted. He faced his attacker, Lucello, known as the Warlock. The young man had handsome features, large melting eyes, and a full, sensuous mouth that was twisted in a disappointed scowl.

Lucello's crimson robes crackled with magical protective constructs, his bloodstained fingers curled around the handle of a butcher knife. He began chanting a spell, ugly words drenched in blood.

Green glowing magic flickered at the Warlock's fingertips, aiming at the pistol.

"Magic, meet contramagic!" Lucello laughed as green jagged bolts shot from his hands and flared around the pistol.

He waited expectantly for the weapon to explode. When nothing happened, he frowned.

"No magic," said Sir Ander. He raised his pistol. "Meet your God."

He cocked his pistol, waited a split second, long enough to give Lucello time to see his own death. The melting eyes widened in fear.

Sir Ander fired.

The bullet hit Lucello in the forehead. He went over backward, landed in the mud and lay there, unmoving. The rain beating on his face washed away the blood that oozed from the hole between the terror-filled eyes.

Sir Ander looked up to see Father Jacob standing, watching.

"If you ask God to save this bastard's soul, Father, I may shoot you."

Father Jacob gazed a moment at the body, then went back to studying the constructs on the boulder. Sir Ander returned the pistol to his pocket with a silent, heartfelt prayer of thanks to God and Cecile.

Eiddwen was alone. Her four soldiers and now her apprentice were dead. But she was the most dangerous of all. Sir Ander could feel her eyes on them. Father Jacob was the threat. She was watching the priest, waiting for her chance.

A bolt of lightning streaked across the heavens turning the stormy night as bright as day. And there was Eiddwen, only a few feet away, holding a pistol in her hand.

"Father, behind you!" Sir Ander shouted.

Father Jacob, startled, looked over his shoulder. Eiddwen raised the pistol. It was not an ordinary pistol. The barrel was long, like a horse pistol. She aimed.

Sir Ander flung himself in front of the priest. Eiddwen fired.

Green light flared from the muzzle, and the green glowing bullet slammed into Sir Ander's left hip, knocking his leg out from under him. He landed heavily in the mud and lay there groaning.

He had heard the bullet hit bone. The contramagic glowed. He could smell the stench of his own flesh burning. The pain was excruciating. He rolled over onto his right side, clutching his hip, and choking off a cry of agony. He'd die before he'd give Eiddwen the satisfaction of hearing him scream.

"Sir Ander! My God!" Father Jacob dropped down beside him and grasped hold of him. "Where are you hit?"

Sir Ander shifted his head.

"Never mind me, Father!" he gasped through clenched teeth. "Stop her!"

Eiddwen emerged from the darkness, coming to stand over them.

"A noble sacrifice, Knight Protector," she said to Sir Ander. "But useless."

She drew a second gun from the folds of her capacious cloak. Sir Ander fumbled for his pistol, only to find it soaking wet. He bit his lips to keep from screaming.

"The good thing about these new contramagic pistols is that rain has no effect on them," Eiddwen remarked.

She raised the pistol and pointed it at Father Jacob's head.

"Jacob!" Sir Ander struggled to rise.

"Rest easy, my friend."

Father Jacob lifted his hand. Dazzling blue shot from his fingertips and arced through the air. The blue fire bolts struck the pistol and began to sizzle around the barrel. Eiddwen stared in shock for an instant, then flung the pistol from her with a cry.

The gun exploded in midair. Chunks of it fell to the ground, glowing blue in the mud.

The shocked expression on Eiddwen's face at seeing magic destroying contramagic instead of the other way around was almost comical. Sir Ander would have laughed, but the pain of his wound was all-consuming. He was dreadfully cold and a strange lethargy crawled over him, the grayness of obliteration. He started to sink beneath it, then felt strong hands shaking him.

"Stay with me, Sir Ander!" Father Jacob ordered sharply. "Do not leave me!"

Hands, strong and comforting, grasped him tightly.

"I do not have Brother Barnaby's skills at healing, my friend," said Father Jacob. "But perhaps I can stop the bleeding and ease the pain."

A soothing warmth spread through Sir Ander, dulling the pain's knife-sharp edge and driving back the gray.

Eiddwen was watching Father Jacob through narrowed eyes, pondering, reevaluating.

"You surprise me, priest," she said abruptly. "You have studied contramagic, committed a mortal sin, forfeited your soul. But, at least now, you can appreciate my work."

She reached out her hand to touch the boulder. Brilliant green light flared beneath her fingers. The bright light dazzled Sir Ander's eyes.

Magical constructs on the boulder came to life. One by one, they burst into flame, lighting the surroundings, shining through the rain. The light cast a lurid green glow over the stony ground, illuminating the scrub bushes, the scraggly trees, the tortured corpse, the dead Warlock.

Father Jacob said quietly, "I have to leave you now, Sir Ander."

Fear for his friend gripped the knight. He struggled, reached out his hand to try to stop him.

"Father—" Sir Ander was too weak. His hand fell to his side.

"God be with you, my friend," Father Jacob said.

He regarded Sir Ander with deep affection, then rose to his feet to face Eiddwen.

"The sin lies with those who named contramagic evil and then used it to sink the island of Glasearrach," Father Jacob told her. "Xavier has compounded that sin, corrupting the contramagic with blood magic, sacrificing his own people to achieve his terrible goal of revenge. Sacrificing you . . ."

The harsh, cold, aloof lines of Eiddwen's face softened. Her black curls were wet and tangled, straggling down her back. Her cloak was soaked. She shivered beneath it and drew near the glowing boulder for warmth. She smiled, a faraway smile.

"The father of this Xavier held me in his arms when I was a child and told me of the sinking, of the fall through the cold, the descent into darkness. He told of the prayers that were wasted. He named *me* 'holy' and said that I would be his Son's Avenging Angel. His Angel of Death. He did not sacrifice me. He gave me purpose, a reason to live."

"With God's help, I will stop you," said Father Jacob.

Eiddwen began to laugh. "God?" She jabbed her finger at the boulder. "This is contramagic, blood magic! What has God to do with it?"

"Everything," said Father Jacob.

He laid his hand upon the boulder and drew a single sigil.

The sigil shone a soft blue. Eiddwen eyed it, frowning.

"What is that?" she asked scornfully.

"The seventh sigil," said Father Jacob. "God."

The sigil was pale in comparison to the bright green glowing constructs around it and, as they watched, the blue glow dimmed and wavered.

"God. Fading away . . . ," said Eiddwen.

Dismissing it with a shrug, she knelt down beside the body of Lucello. His sightless eyes seemed to stare at her. She rested her hand on his forehead, dipped her hand in his blood.

"Stupid boy," she said. "To get yourself killed. Yet you are still of use to me."

She drew back her hand, wet with blood, then smeared the blood, mingled with the rain, over the boulder, down near the bottom. She began to etch constructs into the stone. The contramagic hissed and burned. She glanced at Sir Ander and smiled.

"The end of Freya will be quite dramatic, Sir Knight. Too bad you will die in the explosion."

"So will you," Sir Ander said harshly.

She shrugged.

"Do you hear the beat of the drums?" she asked. "Far below, in a grand temple, a hundred people beat drums made of human skin taken from the blood magic sacrifices. The Blood Mage says the beating drums echo the beating heart of revenge. When I finish this construct, the boulder will radiate contramagic."

She continued to talk as she worked.

"Amplified by the drumming, the spark will leap from this boulder to the next in the chain, setting off a spark that will leap to the next and so on in a line that spreads across Freya. When the spark hits the last boulder, they will all explode, sending waves of contramagic through the ground, splitting the fault line. The streets will crumble, buildings fall, fires erupt, and people will die by the thousands. The ground will shudder and crack, and with a horrendous roar of splitting, shattered rock, the continent of Freya will break apart and fall, as Glasearrach fell—"

She stopped talking, drawing in her breath with a hiss. The seventh sigil blazed into a radiant blue light. The blue flame spread from one contramagic sigil to another, expanding rapidly, flowing over the green constructs like sparkling rainwater. The green glow was starting to go out.

"Very clever of you, Father," Eiddwen said, watching closely. "I see what you've done. You have altered the structure of my constructs with that single sigil."

"Not only the structure," Father Jacob said. "The very nature of the magic."

Sir Ander listened, appalled. The two were discussing magic as if they were standing in a school room, and all the while, their world was about to explode. He wanted to leap to his feet, shake sense into Father Jacob, throttle Eiddwen. Sir Ander had all he could do, however, to keep breathing.

"The seventh sigil transforms contramagic so that it is now as God intended it to be," Father Jacob continued in a scholarly tone. "Contramagic becomes magic's opposite, a mirror image that strengthens, does not corrupt."

"Clever, as I said," Eiddwen remarked. "But your holy tinkerings won't work."

She spread her bloodstained hands over the magical constructs and began to chant, her voice low and harsh. The contramagic blazed, shining brighter and brighter.

Father Jacob kept his hand on the seventh sigil. The blue fire burned steadily, never wavering. The blue glow continued to spread, pure and shining.

Eiddwen ran her hands over her contramagic constructs, refining, mending, repairing. When the two met, the magic sparked and flared. Magic crackled, blazing like a raging fire. Contramagic flamed. The warring magicks soared to heaven, dimming the lightning and drowning out the thunder.

Father Jacob and Eiddwen dwindled, as though the powerful magicks were consuming them. Sir Ander squinted against the awful radiance, trying to see as tears ran down his cheeks.

The green magical light began to slowly diminish and flicker out, and the blue light grew stronger, spreading across the boulder, splashing over it, mingling with the blood, reminding Sir Ander of the water that had cleansed the altar of the blood of the martyred nuns.

Eiddwen gave a shrill cry of disbelief that devolved into rage. She was a shadow against the gleaming light, a body without substance. She clutched at her constructs, trying to strengthen them. She beat her hands on the rock until they bled, then used her own blood to spur the contramagic. Sometimes she was rewarded with a spurt of green flame, but that quickly died. The green light continued to drain, flowing out of the constructs, leaving them empty, nothing but lines etched in a rock.

The seventh sigil glimmered in the darkness. Father Jacob stood near it, and the radiant blue light shone on his face, weary, haggard, at peace. Thunder rumbled, but distantly. The rain stopped. The wizard storm was moving on, out into the Breath.

Sir Ander was about to thank God.

Eiddwen tore his prayer from his lips.

He didn't understand the words she used, but he didn't need to; they crawled into his brain like maggots, burrowing and twisting. Her chanting sounded with the beating of the drums, growing louder and louder, trying to drown out the voice of God.

Eiddwen picked up the butcher's knife that had fallen from Lucello's hand. Her fingers curled around the handle. Chanting the words of the spell, she bent over Sir Ander and plunged the knife into the gaping wound in his hip.

White hot pain lanced through him, and he screamed, writhing in agony.

"Sir Ander!" Father Jacob cried and started toward him.

"Don't take another step, Father. If you do, your knight dies."

Eiddwen raised her knife, wet with his blood, and pressed the tip to his throat.

Through the searing pain, Sir Ander realized dimly that she was using his agony and his fear to enhance her blood magic and he was helpless to stop her. She gazed down at him, her lips parted, drinking in his torment.

Bending close, she spoke softly into his ear, her words emphasized by each beat of the drums. "You would have spent your last drop of blood for him. How ironic that now, Protector, your blood will end his life."

She rose to her feet, the blood dripping from her hand, and flung his blood on Father Jacob. Each droplet of blood swiftly melded together, forging a chain of green fire. The magical constructs on the priest's cassock blazed blue, countering the contramagic spell. The links of the chain began to break. But, as Sir Ander saw in growing fear, with every beat of the drums from Below, the blue constructs started to fade.

Eiddwen patiently watched and waited, holding the bloody knife in her hand. The last blue construct flickered out.

"Cast another spell, Father," Sir Ander managed to gasp through clenched teeth. "Keep fighting!"

A trickle of blood ran from the priest's nose. He winced in pain and dabbed at the blood with his hand.

He has no more spells to cast, Sir Ander realized in despair.

Eiddwen walked toward the priest, slowly, deliberately. If she was expecting to feed off his fear, she must have been disappointed. Father Jacob stood calm, unafraid. Blood ran out of his ear and more blood from his nose. He wiped it away with his sleeve. Glancing at Sir Ander, he gave a rueful smile.

"I never seem to have a handkerchief . . ."

"Father . . ." Sir Ander choked on his grief and fear.

The knife gleamed a fiery red. Eiddwen threw herself at Father Jacob, striking wildly, hitting him in the face, slashing at his arms, at his chest, at any part of him she could reach. He tried in vain to defend himself. His face was bloody, his breathing ragged. He staggered and nearly fell.

Sir Ander gritted his teeth, gathered what strength he had left. He dug his hands into the mud and dragged his body over the ground, swallowing the moans of agony each movement cost him. He thrust out his hand, grabbed hold of Eiddwen's ankle, and yanked her off her feet. She fell to her knees in the mud.

Father Jacob staggered and sagged against the boulder. "It is over."

Eiddwen's head bowed. She did not look up. Her hand closed around the knife's hilt.

Father Jacob cried out in horror and sprang to stop her. He was too late. Eiddwen plunged the knife into her stomach. She gasped, groaned, then slumped down, her body curling around the blade.

Father Jacob swiftly knelt beside her, to see if he could save her.

"Don't trust her, Father!" Sir Ander warned. "Let her be!"

Of course, Father Jacob paid no heed. She was one of God's children.

He gently shifted Eiddwen, but there was nothing to be done. She moaned as he touched her. The blade was buried deep in her belly. Her hands clutched the handle.

She looked up at Father Jacob and smiled.

"Xavier gave me my name," she whispered, wrenched with the pain. "My name means 'holy.' "

Her stiffening lips began to chant. She uncurled her blood-clotted fingers from the knife and placed her bloody palm on Father Jacob's chest.

She cast her final spell, using her own blood, her own torment. A bright and hideous red glow spread from her hand over the priest's breast. Father Jacob's face turned deathly pale and he shuddered in pain and gasped, fighting to breathe. The thudding drums became the thudding of the priest's heart, wild and spasmodic, lurching and heaving.

Eiddwen's hand clenched in agony. She cried out, stiffened, and died. The red glow died with her. Her hand went limp and fell lifelessly into the mud. Her lifeless eyes remained fixed on Father Jacob and there was a smile on her lips.

He clutched his chest and sagged to the ground. Reaching into his rain-soaked, blood-drenched cassock, he drew out a book, a slender volume, the *Confessions of Saint Marie.* Sighing deeply, as though he could finally take his ease after a long day's work, he clasped the book, closed his eyes and lay still, his hand resting on his breast, over his heart.

A faint blue glow shone from beneath his fingers.

"Father . . . ," Sir Ander called frantically. "Jacob! God in heaven, don't let him die!"

Sir Ander felt a pulse in his friend's neck, thin and weak. He needed help.

"Henry! Are you there?"

All he heard was the beating of the drums. Sir Ander gritted his teeth. The pounding thudded in his head as if he would never be rid of it. He tried again.

"Alan! Alan Northrop!"

No answer.

The wind was starting to rise, as another wizard storm massed on the horizon. Purple lightning streaked from cloud to cloud, followed by distant thunder.

He looked back at Father Jacob. His skin was cold and clammy, his breathing ragged. He was dying. Sir Ander rested his hand on his friend's shoulder, holding fast to him, as though he could keep him from leaving.

The drums raged Below, beating out the cadence of war. Somewhere down there, Stephano and his dragons were fighting to stave off endless night, deafening silence.

Sir Ander was wet and shivering. He could no longer feel pain, only a bitter cold. He shifted his body in an effort to offer what shelter he could give, protect Father Jacob from the coming storm.

35

The drums—the voice of our rage—will drown out the voice of their God and forever silence Him.

—Ian Meehan, the Blood Mage, to his followers

The men in Fort Ignacio remained on alert throughout the night. Stephano doubled the watch and mounted the battlements himself. The enemy had seen them sailing down out of the sky. Logic dictated Xavier must know by now that he had to contend with an invasion force from Above. The question was: What would he do? Would he attack the fortress? Would he continue with his plans to launch his invasion fleet? Would he do both? Given the severity of the wizard storms, could he do either?

Which begged the question, what could Stephano do? The answer was: nothing. Miri had warned him the storms were ferocious, unlike any storm he had ever encountered. Even then, Stephano had not been prepared for the reality: the driving rain, the lashing winds, the fierce lightning and heart-stopping thunder. Dragons could not fly in such weather, and ships could not sail. He and his enemy could only hunker down and wait while a wrathful God pounded on them both.

To add to his worries, Miri had sailed off in the *Cloud*

Hopper, hoping to make contact with the rebels and to hear some news of Gythe and his mother. Miri had not returned. She was somewhere out there, alone.

The wizard storms had abated for the moment. The darkness was thick and smothering, the air wet and heavy. He wished the night would end, though he was not certain he wished for day to begin.

"What time do you have?" he asked Dag.

The two stood huddled near the wall of the fallen guard tower, trying to find a modicum of shelter from the wind. The rain drizzled down, running off his tricorn in rivulets. He wore a cloak, but it was soaked through. He was so wet, he didn't notice anymore.

"About five minutes from when you asked me the last time, sir," Dag replied. "I looked at my watch before I came outdoors. It was thirty past two then. Must be getting close to three."

"Miri should be back by now," said Stephano.

At the sound of feet splashing through the puddles, he and Dag both turned.

"Who's there?" Dag called in a low voice.

"Tutillo, sir," Master Tutillo returned softly.

The midshipman emerged out of the rain, keeping one hand on the wall of the battlement as he groped his way through the darkness. Stephano had given the order that there were to be no lights and no noise. If someone saw something, he was to pass the word.

"Lookouts sighted the running lights of a boat, sir, coming this way," he reported in a smothered voice. "The boat gave the correct signal. It's the *Cloud Hopper,* sir."

"Thank God!" Stephano breathed.

He and Dag entered the fort, heading for the stairs that led down to the dock.

"I could go on ahead, sir, see if I can help," Master Tutillo offered.

Stephano gave him permission and he dashed off, tumbling down the stairs at breakneck speed. Dag carried a dark lantern and, once they were inside the fortress, they used its light to navigate the corridors.

"He's a good lad," said Stephano. "I admire his energy."

"He'll make a good officer," said Dag. "He wants to be a dragon rider."

"In a Brigade that doesn't exist," said Stephano.

"The prince thinks well of you, sir," said Dag. "He might persuade the king to reinstate it."

Stephano shook his head. He was in a gloomy mood. This place was oppressive.

"We may not have a king, or even a country anymore. Who knows what is happening while we're down here? We could find chunks of Freya falling on our heads. You go to the bridge. I'll join you there."

Arriving at the dock, he stood in the rain waiting for Miri. He ordered the men to shine a beacon light to guide her in, flashing it on and off at intervals. The *Cloud Hopper* looked like a ghost ship gliding through the night, dark and silent. When she landed on the dock, the men were waiting, running to secure the boat.

"Don't tie it down," Miri called to them. "I'm not staying long."

Wearing her oilskin coat and hat, she was making final adjustments at the helm. She didn't lower the gangplank so Stephano had to pull himself up and over the rail to board. As he did, he heard what sounded like muffled barking.

"Do I hear a dog?" he asked, puzzled.

"In the storage closet," said Miri.

"Why is there a dog in the storage closet?" Stephano was mystified.

"I'll explain in a minute."

They stood in the light cast by a lantern mounted above the helm. Miri had removed her hat. The light glistened on her wet oilskin coat, set fire to her red hair and shone in her eyes. He loved her so much his heart ached.

"Are you listening to me?" Miri demanded. "I don't have much time. I have to be back before dawn. I've talked to Brother Barnaby. He's been in contact with your mother. Xavier knows we are here."

"I figured as much," said Stephano. "It's not every day a fortress drops out of the sky and lands in your backyard. What is he going to do? How is my mother? How is Gythe?"

"Fine, for the moment. According to Brother Barnaby, Xavier has accelerated his plans. He is going to launch his invasion fleet today, this very morning. Not tomorrow. As we planned. Can you be ready?"

"We'll have to be," Stephano said grimly. "Tell me about Gythe and my mother. Are they all right?"

"Xavier has told Gythe and Sophia they have to stop the storms. If they fail, he's threatened to give them to the Blood Mage, who will kill them. But don't worry! The rebels and I are going to free them."

"How?" he asked.

"We don't know yet," said Miri. Seeing his expression darken, she added tersely, "Now don't you look at me like that, Stephano! While I'm here, Patrick and his friends are making plans to save them. I came to warn you about the fleet. Oh, and to deliver the dog. He belongs to the princess. I brought him here for safekeeping. I'll go fetch him."

She left the helm, heading below.

"Miri, wait—"

But she was gone, descending down into the living area of the *Cloud Hopper.*

Stephano paced the dock in the rain. He longed to go back with Miri to rescue Gythe and his mother and the princess. He had to face the fact that he had a far more important mission—as his mother would have been the first to remind him. He had to stop the fleet, put an end to this war.

Miri emerged carrying a drenched, scruffy, and extremely miserable spaniel.

"His name is Bandit," said Miri, handing him to Stephano.

"What am I supposed to do with him?" Stephano asked helplessly.

The dog squirmed in his arms and tried to bite him.

"I'll take charge of him, sir," Master Tutillo offered. "I like dogs."

Stephano handed Bandit over the rail to Master Tutillo, who stroked the dog's head. "He looks hungry. Where should I put him, Captain?"

"The safest place would be in the storage room with the cat."

"The Doctor will probably claw out his eyes," Miri predicted darkly. "It would be just like that cat to fight with the royal dog."

Miri stood close to Stephano and looked at him with fixed intensity. "You have to trust me," she said. "You have your job to do and I have mine."

He couldn't say everything that was in his heart, not standing on board the *Cloud Hopper* in the rain with magic failing and all his carefully laid plans in ruins. He took her in his arms and held her tight.

"Thank you, Stephano," said Miri. "I won't fail you!"

"You never could," he said.

They held on to each other for another moment, then Miri pulled away and told the men to let loose of the ropes. Waving at Stephano as the *Cloud Hopper* took to the air, she pressed her fingers to her lips in a kiss. As the boat disappeared into the night, Stephano watched until he could no longer see her and even then he waited another moment before he went back into the fortress.

Once there, he took out his watch. According to Miri, he had about two hours until dawn.

Stephano climbed the stairs that led to the bridge. He found Dag gazing out the window through the spyglass. When Stephano relayed what Miri had told him, Dag nodded, his attention focused on something out the window.

"Miri's information was right. You should see this, sir." Dag handed the spyglass to Stephano. "Over that way. Straight ahead."

"What I am supposed to be looking for?" Stephano raised his spyglass, searching the blackness. At first he couldn't see anything and then lightning flared. He saw the ships of the invasion fleet silhouetted against the brilliance. He watched a moment, waiting for another lightning strike, then lowered the spyglass.

"They're inflating the balloons."

"Yes, sir. Looks like the fleet is making ready to set sail."

"But they can't!" Rodrigo protested.

Stephano turned to see his friend hunched in the doorway, yawning over a cup of tea and looking very ragged. His hair straggled over his face. He had not shaved and he was wearing his shirt inside out. His eyes were red and bleary.

"It's too soon!" Rodrigo continued. "*Tomorrow* is the first of Fulmea. They're not sailing until tomorrow. I have until tomorrow to work on the magic!"

"What are you doing awake?" Stephano asked. "It's not morning."

"Those fornicating drums!" Rodrigo groaned. He staggered over to the helmsman chair and slumped down.

"Pound, pound, pound in my head. All the fornicating night. Pardon my language."

"Drums?" Stephano glanced at Dag, who shook his head. "I don't hear any drums."

"Because you are both magically benighted, which makes you fortunate. These are the drums Miri was telling us about. Made of human skin from the victims of blood magic rituals. They are the source of the contramagic that is destroying us."

"Drums," said Stephano skeptically.

Rodrigo regarded him with frowning exasperation. "I have explained this to you before."

Now that he mentioned it, Stephano did remember Rodrigo talking about resonance, synchronous vibrations, prolongations of sound, reflections from surfaces, and harmonics. He also remembered dozing off.

"If you could refresh my memory," Stephano suggested.

Rodrigo gave him an aggrieved look. "You were snoring."

"Rigo, it's important. I have an idea. Just a brief explanation. Leave out the part about the glass harmonicas."

Rodrigo sighed deeply. "As you recall, music has always been an integral part of Trundler magic. Miri sings when she is concocting her ointments, for example. Gythe sings when she casts her protections spells. These people have taken that to a new and frightening level. The drums are imbued with constructs that cause them to resonate with contramagic. As the drummers beat the drums, they are pouring power into the contramagic. The drumming provides a way to gather all that raw power into one coherent wave. The use of blood magic allows for the collection of an even greater amount of power."

He stopped to rub his eyes and take a sip of tea.

"One drummer begins and as more join in they synchronize until they are all in perfect unison. The drummers sit on a wooden platform splashed with blood that acts like a soundboard on a pianoforte. Enhanced by blood magic, the board projects the wave of contramagic outward. These waves of base contramagic are breaking apart our magic down here and also the magic above."

"So if we could stop these drummers, we stop the effects of the contramagic," said Stephano. He hurried over to the chart table and pointed to a place on the crude map of the city he had drawn from Miri's directions. "The drummers are here, in the temple. The temple complex is located here, on the outskirts of the city."

"What are you thinking, sir?" Dag asked. "We can't attack the temple. We have to stop the fleet."

"Maybe we can do both," said Stephano, more ideas forming in his head.

"What about Miri and Gythe and the princess?" Dag asked. "According to Miri, they will be in the temple square trying to stop the storms."

"Miri and the rebels are going to rescue them," said Stephano. His mind boiled over with plans. "I need to talk to Lord Haelgrund. Dag, wake the brigade piper. Rigo, I'm glad you're here. I want you to inspect the magic on the cannons—"

"You want me to inspect cannons?" Rodrigo repeated, appalled. "My dear fellow, you usually won't let me within ten feet of a pistol."

"I need you to examine the magic. Tell me if it is failing—"

"I can tell you that now," Rodrigo said grimly. "The magic is failing. And there is another problem. Have you considered how the contramagic will affect the dragons?"

"I was going to ask you about that . . ." said Stephano. He could see by his friend's expression that the answer wasn't good.

"According to Father Jacob, dragons have both magic

and contramagic in their systems, holding them in balance with what you might think of as a natural form of the seventh sigil. The contramagic is having an effect on the dragons Above, but that is mainly with the young. Down here, the dragons will essentially be bombarded with contramagic, which will upset the balance."

"And the result would be . . . ," said Stephano impatiently.

"I'm not certain exactly what will happen because I am not a dragon. You would need to ask them. I would imagine, however, that after a time, they will start to feel weak, lethargic, short of breath."

"How long will that take?" Stephano asked abruptly.

"There are so many variables—"

Stephano had been looking at the map. Now he rounded on his friend. "How long, damn it, Rigo? How long before the dragons and ourselves and every bloody thing in the fortress starts to fall apart?"

"Lower your voice, sir," Dag advised.

Stephano forced himself to calm down.

"I'm sorry, Rigo. I didn't mean to yell at you. It's not your fault. Do I have an hour, six hours, a day, a month . . ."

"Twelve hours," Rodrigo answered. "That's a guess."

"Thank you," said Stephano. "That should give us time. I want you in the gun rooms. You need to show the gunnery crafters how to fix the magic that reinforces the iron. And if they can't fix it, how long they can fire before the barrels overheat."

"You realize I know nothing at all about cannons," said Rodrigo. "That I never *wanted* to know anything about cannons."

"You do remember that you volunteered to come with us," said Stephano, resting his hand on Rodrigo's shoulder. "As our master crafter."

"I know," Rodrigo replied glumly, as he was leaving.

"I'm admitting myself into the Asylum of Saint Charenton the moment we are home."

Outside the pipes began to skirl, playing "The Jolly Beggarman," the battle march of the Brigade. The music always stirred the blood. Stephano felt his heartbeat quicken. His confidence returned. Fear and doubt did not leave, but they backed off, gave him room to maneuver.

Stephano watched out the window, waiting to see Lord Haelgrund. Black against a backdrop of lightning, the dragon came flying out from the mountain caves where the dragons had taken shelter.

"He's not going to be happy when he hears my plan," Stephano remarked.

"Why not, sir?" Dag asked.

"It involves Hroal and Droal."

Lord Haelgrund and the other noble dragons had been trained to fight. The common dragons had been trained to work: lift heavy cannons into place, clear boulders from landing fields. Stephano would need that very engineering skill and knowledge for his plan to work and he blessed his decision to bring them over Lord Haelgrund's objections.

Lord Haelgrund landed on the ground outside the fortress and settled down to wait. On the cliffs above, another dragon stood watch. Stephano changed into the uniform coat of the Dragon Brigade, put on his hat and cloak, and hurried out, hoping to be able to finish explaining his plans to the dragon before the next wizard storm struck.

He looked at his watch. One hour until dawn.

36

Hope that we will be rescued has fallen into despair and despair, I fear, will sink into hatred.

—Xavier I

Cecile and Brother Barnaby joined the throng of people entering the temple by way of the back door. Drummers pushed past them, putting on their blood-red robes, carrying their drums, hastening to the amphitheater to swell the ranks of those already at work. Soldiers jostled them, running to their posts, weapons in hand.

The atmosphere was tense. The walls themselves seemed to vibrate in and out to the deafening throb of the drumming. Cecile had the eerie impression that the temple was a living thing, with the drums the beating heart.

Torches mounted on sconces in the walls cast pools of light on the floor, leaving the rest of the corridor in shadow. Cecile kept to the shadows and pulled the hood of her steward's golden cloak over her face. Not that her precautions mattered. People were far too worried and apprehensive about this sudden alarm and what it might portend to notice a steward and a monk.

Cecile's main concern was to reach the temple square before Gythe and Sophia started working their magic, and then somehow find a way to let them know she was there. Brother Barnaby had to make contact with the resistance who would be waiting for them in the plaza. On their way to the Temple he told Cecile about his meeting with Miri.

"She is going to carry word to Stephano about the change in plans. And I gave her Bandit to take back to the fortress."

"Have you spoken with the rebels?" Cecile asked.

"I spoke to Patrick, my lady. The resistance has been thrown into confusion by Xavier's sudden change in plans."

"Will they help us?"

"Miri promised she would be there," Brother Barnaby said. "As for the Resistance, they have much do, my lady, and few people to spare. They planned to time their attacks on Xavier's forts all over the island to coincide with the launching of the fleet. The members of the resistance who are here now have to carry word to our people throughout Glasearrach."

What this meant was that Cecile couldn't count on the rebels for help. She was on her own with a monk who had vowed that he would not kill. While she honored Brother Barnaby for his faith and his courage, she did not see how he would be of much use to her in a fight.

People pressed around her. The stench of blood and fear and sweat was suffocating. She longed to break free of the crowd, yet she had to keep hold of Brother Barnaby's arm to avoid being separated and losing each other.

They were nearing the front of the temple. Cecile could see a glimmer of gray light and she caught a breath of fresh air. Before she and Brother Barnaby could reach the exit, several drummers swarmed around them, backing them into a wall. Cecile tried to find a way through the drummers, afraid that the ceremony would start, but she and Brother Barnaby were trapped.

One of the drummers pulled open a door behind her. A blaze of light flooded out into the darkened hallway. Looking inside, she could see drummers milling about the room, finding their places. Suddenly, a man's agonized scream rose from somewhere in the center of the room and echoed through the hall.

"My God, what is happening?" Cecile said, gasping.

"One of the sacrifices being put to death," Brother Barnaby said softly. "That chamber is the *Croi na Xavier.* The Heart of Xavier. Look inside and you will see what we are fighting to end."

The large circular room had a high ceiling and wood-paneled walls polished to a rich glow. Carved stone buttresses met directly above the center of a wooden platform that was raised about four feet off the floor. The walls, the floor, the ceiling, the columns were covered with glowing constructs, some green and some red. Drummers sat cross-legged on the platform beating the drums with either their hands or with sticks, while others stood around an altar in the center and the bloody corpse that lay spread across it.

Blood mages were draining his blood, carrying it off in small bowls to pour on the drums, on the platform, and the stone floor below, feeding the magic.

Suddenly, by some unseen, unheard signal, the drumming stopped. The silence was almost worse, for it was thick with the echoes and the smell. From inside the room came another terrible, gurgling scream, then the sound of the drummers beating softly on their drums in approval. Cecile shuddered.

Brother Barnaby clasped her hand. "God is with us, my lady," he said firmly.

"Even in this dark and evil place?" Cecile asked.

"*Especially* in this place," said Brother Barnaby.

He smiled at her in reassurance. He had been tortured

in this building, perhaps in this very chamber. He had avoided becoming one of the sacrifices by proving himself more valuable as a healer than as a victim. His suffering must have been unendurable and yet, he had not only found the strength to survive, he had forgiven his tormentors and helped to mend them.

"I envy you, Brother," Cecile said. "I envy your faith."

He cast her a surprised glance. "But when I entered the prison, you were praying."

"I do not pray to God," said Cecile.

She saw his gaze go to her left hand, to the golden ring she wore. She placed her hand over it, drawing strength from the touch.

"You turn to love for strength, my lady," said Brother Barnaby with a quiet smile. "I turn to God. There is no difference. Ah, we may leave now."

The drummers had moved out of their way and into the drumming chamber. Someone closed the door and Brother Barnaby and Cecile hastened to the exit. A contingent of armed guards stood blocking the door. Cecile was afraid they would not let them pass, but apparently the soldiers were posted at the entrance to the temple to keep people from entering, not leaving.

One of the soldiers recognized Brother Barnaby and greeted him in a friendly manner.

"A momentous day, Brother," he said.

"Indeed it is," Brother Barnaby agreed. "Steward Cecile and I would like to be part of this historic occasion. Are we permitted to go out onto the square?"

"Of course! Our saint wants all to witness his triumph."

The soldier opened the door. Cecile looked outside and gasped in dismay.

The temple square was packed with people. Word had apparently spread among the residents of Dunlow that this day their saint was going to stop the destructive wizard storms and launch the invasion of the world Above. It seemed the entire population had turned out in the gray dawn. Cecile could not see the center of the plaza for the mass of bodies, nor could she see Xavier, Gythe, or Sophia. She had no idea how they would ever reach them.

"Stay close to me, my lady," said Brother Barnaby with a calm certainty she could not understand.

As he led her into the crowd she realized that this crowd was unusually quiet, and also that there were no children. Only adults. Everyone stood in the rain, waiting with grim faces in grim silence.

"People are expecting trouble," Cecile said softly.

Brother Barnaby glanced at her and nodded. "That is why they left the children at home."

The beating of the drums increased to its former intensity, thudding in Cecile's head, a vibrant pounding that made it hard even to think. Rain soaked her cloak. The wind was rising, threatening to blow off her hood. A wizard storm was brewing.

She kept her head down and took firm hold of Brother Barnaby's arm as he began again to move through the crowd. Everyone was facing the square, craning their heads to see, standing on tiptoe, their backs to them. Brother Barnaby pushed through the press of people, tapping them on the shoulder with his hand to draw their attention, offering murmured explanations and apologies.

"Pardon, let us pass," he said over and over. "Please let us pass."

People turned their heads, some startled or frowning in annoyance until they saw it was him. Then they smiled and moved aside. More than that, they quietly sent the word to those ahead to make way. Cecile followed in his wake, keeping fast hold of him. As she passed, she heard whispered comments.

"That is Brother Barnaby. He delivered my wife's baby . . . He nursed me through a fever . . . He gave my child a balm for the pain . . ."

Many wished him well as he passed. Some reached out to touch him, as if for luck. He seemed to recognize them all, addressing many of them by name, but always moving, and keeping her in tow. Cecile regarded the young monk with newfound respect. Brought here a prisoner, he had given love for hatred, hope for fear.

As more and more people made way for them, they moved steadily toward the center of the square. Trying to find Sophia and Gythe, Cecile did not realize that Brother Barnaby had stopped to talk to a woman in a heavy cloak until she nearly bumped into him. The two held a brief conversation, then Brother Barnaby walked quickly on.

"Our friends are here," he said to her softly. "Those wearing green. Miri is with them."

Glancing around, Cecile saw a man wearing a drab green cloak, a woman with a light green kerchief around her neck, another man in a green slouch hat. None of them looked her way, but Cecile sensed they were aware of her and her companion.

"Where is Miri?"

"She is here, among the crowd," said Brother Barnaby. "She left the *Cloud Hopper* waiting on the outskirts of town. But there is a problem. The Blood Mage feared the rebels would attack, and has placed Gythe and Sophia under armed guard."

She could finally see the center of the square. Xavier stood on a crude stage with his brother, the Blood Mage, behind him, his crimson robes a lurid splash against the gray, dreary morning. At least twenty soldiers in demonic armor and carrying long guns formed a ring of steel around the base of the stage. They faced the crowd, weapons raised, while bat riders circled in the air overhead.

Almost lost to view, Gythe and Sophia, looking very small and forlorn, huddled together behind Xavier.

Cecile was sick with despair. "What can we do, Brother? How can we save them?"

"I do not know," said Brother Barnaby. "We did not expect this."

Xavier stepped to the edge of the stage and raised his hands, calling for silence.

"My friends," he said. "Thank you for coming."

He spoke in the Trundler language. Cecile had learned a fair number of words from Sir Conal on their journey, and she had learned more Trundler during her recent captivity, so she could follow his speech, which was simple and direct.

"At last, the wronged people of this doomed island will have their revenge!"

He described how his agents were planning to destroy Freya and bring down the king of Rosia; how they had captured the refineries in Braffa and brought economic ruin to the trade cartels of Travia; how the coast of Estara was in flames.

"Those nations that came together to slaughter our children are now weeping over their own dead sons and daughters. Our drummers are beating out mayhem, destroying magic, causing buildings to crumble and nations to fall. Wizard storms will light their skies with fire and fill the air with the thunder. No ship will dare to set sail. They will know what it is to live in darkness!"

He stopped, expecting the crowd's enthusiastic response.

But the crowd was silent. Instead of showering him in adulation, their utter silence was a bitter rebuke.

Xavier gazed out at them grimly.

"What is the matter with you people?" he asked, suddenly, going off script. "For hundreds of years, you have demanded vengeance. I am your saint! I am giving you what you want. I have done it all for you!"

The silence resounded like thunder. His brother was regarding him with angry disapproval. In the temple, the drums began to beat anew, as if they had been waiting for this moment to be heard.

Xavier put his hands to his head, pressing his fingers to his temples.

"Stop the drumming, Brother!" he ordered. "The sound is maddening. I cannot hear myself think."

Lightning flared, filling the sky with purple fire. Thunder cracked. Raindrops spattered.

"Go on with your speech, *Naomh,*" said the Blood Mage, frowning.

Xavier shook his head impatiently.

"I ordered you to stop the drumming!"

The Blood Mage drew back, stepping away from his brother. His lips compressed. He made an abrupt gesture with his hand, and a ram's horn blew a single blast, a signal to the drummers to stop. The drummers were thrown into confusion, the rhythmic beating faltered until it eventually petered out.

"When I was young," Xavier said in a low voice, repeating what he had once told Cecile, "I thrilled to hear the drums. My father told me the sacrificed went to their deaths willingly, proud to be chosen. Now I hear their screams and I know my father was lying."

In the quiet, Cecile could hear the raindrops dripping from drenched garments onto the wet cobblestones.

"The drumming will end," Xavier said harshly. "The sacrifices will end. The blood magic will end. Release these young ones." He gestured to Gythe and Sophia, standing in the background, forgotten until now. "I don't need them. The storms will end when the drumming ends."

The Blood Mage was livid. "You do not know what you are saying, *Naomh* . . ."

Cecile heard the menace in his voice and she saw, with shock, that the Blood Mage gripped a knife, his hand wrapped around the blade, deliberately driving the sharp edges into his flesh. Blood welled from between his fingers.

Xavier faced the crowd, holding out his hands in supplication. "At last I can hear the words you do not speak. I will do what I should have done, what my father and grandfather and all the other Xaviers should have done. I will find a way to improve lives, not destroy them. I will end this war, sue for peace—

"By my command, the blood magic will end!" Xavier flung his arms wide and raised his voice to be heard by everyone in the square. So still was the crowd, his voice might have been heard in heaven. "You will obey! I am Xavier!"

The Blood Mage dropped the knife to the ground, then raised his bloody hand. The drops burst into green flame.

"You are not Xavier!" he said. "You never were."

He flung the drops of blood onto his brother. The drops exploded, tearing into Xavier's body like bullets. He stared at his brother in amazement, then his face contorted in agony. His own blood blossomed on his chest and arms and legs, pouring from a dozen wounds. He sagged to his knees on the stage and doubled over, gasping.

No one moved except Brother Barnaby. He shoved aside the shocked guards and jumped onto the stage. Kneeling beside Xavier, Brother Barnaby gently lifted him in his arms.

Xavier looked into the sky, into the storm clouds. He

tried to speak, coughed, choked, and shuddered. His body sagged. Brother Barnaby lowered him down onto the stage that was soaked with blood and rainwater.

Xavier lay unmoving, staring into the storms.

A murmur of shock and disbelief ran through the crowd, rippling over them like a breath of wind across a still and silent sea.

Their saint was dead. And no one knew what to do.

37

When we sing, the magic sings.

—Princess Amelia Louisa Sophia

The crowd was no longer silent. Some began to shout in anger; some wailed in grief. Their rumbling vied with the thunder of the coming storm. The soldiers guarding the stage raised their long guns, but they seemed uncertain. Who was the enemy?

The Blood Mage had only moments to recover, to take command. He stepped to the front of the stage and raised his bloody hands.

"I am not Xavier!" Ian cried. "But I am the true heir of my father and my grandfather and all those saints who came before me! My brother was weak, like that first Xavier, who worshipped a God that cast us into darkness and despair. I, Ian Meehan, will lead you to war against our foes!"

He seized the ram's horn and blew a blast. The drumming recommenced with renewed vigor, and the pounding beat seeming to shake the ground.

"Let our rage rise up and engulf them. Our despair will become their despair. Our darkness will become their darkness. Let the drums sound! We will shatter their magic, shatter their world."

As if by his command, the wizard storm broke overhead, lashing out in fury. Lightning blazed and thunder boomed almost continuously. The rain beat down on Xavier's body, washing away the blood.

In the confusion and turmoil, the Blood Mage seemed to have forgotten about Gythe and Sophia. They stood at the back of the stage, holding fast to each other, staring in horror and shock at the body of the murdered man. Any moment, Cecile feared, he would remember them and he would take them away.

The Blood Mage continued his harangue, but the crowd wasn't listening. They were in a dangerous mood, surging and heaving, some cheering, others enraged. Kneeling beside the body, Brother Barnaby tried to find Cecile. She could see him searching for her, even as he prayed.

Cecile tried to reach the stage, but she was caught in the turmoil of people around her pushing and shoving. She lost her balance and almost fell. A hand gripped her arm, steadied her.

"My lady! Are you all right?"

"Miri! Thank God!" Cecile clutched at her gratefully.

"I saw you from a distance. I have been trying to reach you!" Miri gasped.

"All hell is going to break loose," said Cecile grimly. "We have to get Gythe and Sophia to safety."

"We will," said Miri. "My friends are here. They will help. Did Brother Barnaby give you the pistol?"

Cecile nodded and motioned to the pistol tucked into the waistband of her skirt.

"I have my own," Miri added. "Remember, these pistols are magic, so we must be careful."

Miri fixed her gaze on her sister. "Gythe, dear! I am here."

Gythe suddenly raised her head and scanned the crowd.

Miri gave a little wave, and Gythe whispered something to Sophia, who looked around for them. Cecile drew her hood back from her face, and Sophia almost immediately saw her. The princess's face brightened.

"We're going to come to your rescue," Miri mouthed. "Be ready."

Gythe shook her head vehemently. "No, sister, you must not!" She raised a warding hand, motioning Miri to keep away. She said something to Sophia, who, seemingly in response, reached out to Gythe and resolutely clasped her hand. Cecile didn't know what was going on, but she could see plainly that neither young woman had any intention of leaving the stage.

"What are they doing?" Cecile asked, dismayed.

"They are going to do what Gythe came here to do. They are going to stop the storms," said Miri.

"We cannot let them," Cecile said firmly. "It is too dangerous. They don't understand—"

"They *do* understand. They understand that the dragons cannot fly, that Stephano cannot attack the fleet unless the skies are clear."

"If they fail—" Cecile stopped, realizing that Miri understood the peril as well as she did. "We have to move closer."

She and Miri began to push through the crowd, fighting their way slowly toward the stage. Men and women wearing green joined them, shouting as they went, stirring up trouble, inflaming an already volatile situation.

"He killed our saint!" the rebels were shouting. "Stop him! Stop the drumming!"

The soldiers had scrambled onto the stage in an effort to keep from being trampled by the mob. Waves of angry people lapped at the foot of the stage, and thus far the soldiers were keeping them at bay, but the sea of humanity was likely to soon break over their heads.

The Blood Mage stood glaring at the crowd. He had acted on impulse, and probably had not considered how the people would react to the assassination of their saint. Or perhaps he had assumed they would follow him.

He cast a glance at his temple, a safe haven standing on the opposite shore. Between him and the temple, though, stood a raging sea of fury.

"Clear the way for me!" the Blood Mage ordered. "Disperse these people!"

The soldiers raised their long guns, and green light flared. Fireballs burst over the heads of the crowd.

Some drew back, frightened, but the attack seemed to embolden others.

"They can't kill us all!" shouted a man wearing a green hat.

One of the soldiers lost his nerve and fired directly into the crowd. A woman screamed and fell, then one of the rebels drew a gun and shot back, the green glowing bullet felling the soldier.

At that, some of the soldiers turned and ran. Flinging off their helms, they threw down their arms and jumped from the stage. As if waiting for a signal, the people surged forward. The Blood Mage shouted angry commands to the bat riders circling overhead, and bats swept down on the crowd, striking with their claws, driving people back and adding to the chaos. All the while, Brother Barnaby remained on the platform, crouched protectively over Xavier's body.

Cecile and Miri found themselves caught in a human riptide, in danger of being dragged under. They held on to each other, struggling to keep from falling and being trampled. A familiar-looking man in a green cloak carrying one of the long guns, seeing their distress, pushed and shoved and knocked people aside to reach them.

"Patrick, help us!" Miri cried, catching sight of him. "We are trying to reach Gythe and Sophia!"

"Keep close!" he ordered.

They followed in his wake. When a guard sought to block their way, someone behind Cecile shot him, the fireball half blinding her as it blazed past. The soldier tumbled off the stage into the crowd.

Three steps led from the ground up to the stage. Miri pushed past Patrick, prepared to dash up the stairs to rescue the women.

"Don't go! Not yet!" Cecile warned.

One of the bat riders wearing a crimson emblem had landed in front of the Blood Mage and offered his mount to him. As he was about to climb into the saddle, the Blood Mage pointed at the body.

"Bring my brother to the temple."

The soldier advanced toward the corpse. Brother Barnaby rose to his feet and moved to stand between bat rider and Xavier's body.

"You will not defile the dead," said Brother Barnaby.

He had no way to defend himself and was so slight of build, a breath could have knocked him over. His robes were wet and bloodstained and hung from his thin body. Yet he stood and spoke with such dignity that the soldier stopped, hesitant to carry out his orders.

Gythe and Sophia joined the monk, presenting a solid front of faith, innocence, and love.

The Blood Mage shoved the soldier aside and walked toward them. People in the crowd began chanting Xavier's name. Brother Barnaby did not move. Gythe and Sophia stood with him. The body lay at their feet.

Cecile drew her pistol. She had no clear idea of what she was going to do. She knew only she had to stop the Blood Mage. Miri seized hold of her.

"Watch!"

Radiant blue strands of magical fire whirled and danced in the air above Gythe. The crowd hushed, watching in awe.

Gythe plucked the sparkling magical tendrils from the air and began to weave a spider's net of blue light around herself, Sophia, and Brother Barnaby. The net glistened, shimmering and sparkling in the rain.

The bat shrieked and flew off the stage, leaving its rider and the Blood Mage stranded. He looked to his soldiers, those who were left. He would get no help from them. They were as mesmerized by the magic as those in the crowd.

The Blood Mage seemed uncertain what to do. Cecile watched him, the pistol hidden in the folds of her cloak. He cast a narrow-eyed glance at the people—his people—trying to gauge their reaction. The brawling and tumult had ceased, and they gasped in wide-eyed wonder as the blue magical light spread over the stage, glittering in the falling rain so that it seemed they were standing amid a shower of sapphires. The blue light surrounded Xavier's body with a soft blue glow.

Cecile kept watching the Blood Mage. He couldn't leave the stage; if he did so, the crowd might tear him apart. He could try to fight the magic with his own. Cecile saw the thought cross his mind. His brows drew together. He rubbed his fingers, still gummy with blood.

"Signal the drummers," he ordered the man with the ram's horn. The man blew a blast and the drumming boomed.

The Blood Mage focused his attention on Sophia and Gythe, observing them with keen, shrewd eyes that glittered with the blue light.

Cecile relaxed for a moment, released the hammer of the pistol and thrust it back into her belt. Patrick looked over at Miri and frowned.

"What are they doing? What is going on?"

"They're going to stop the storms," said Miri.

Gythe began to sing in the Trundler language. Her beautiful voice soared over the pounding drums, and was quickly joined by Sophia's voice. She knew the song and she sang it in Rosian. Cecile recognized an old hymn, one she especially loved.

She had learned it as a child; a simple song in praise of God, describing mankind bowing in reverence, listening to His voice. The rain poured down on the already sodden, drenched crowd, but people did not leave. They listened to the song entranced, with softened expressions.

The tempest increased in fury with lashing rain and buffeting winds. Lightning leaped from cloud to cloud. The thunder seemed to boom in time with the frantic beating of the drums.

Gythe and Sophia kept singing. They seemed in a world of their own, neither Above nor Below, far from the storms of nature or man. Sophia knew this hymn well. She had sung it many times, seated in the church pew between her vacuous mother, who would be fretting at her daughter's lace and fussing with her hair, and her self-absorbed father, fuming over some fancied insult by the grand bishop. Sophia had scarcely dared raise her voice above a whisper then. Now she was singing with joyous abandon, her face upturned to the rain, the blue magic glowing in her hands.

Gythe was serene, ecstatic. Where had she learned this hymn? From Brother Barnaby? He was singing silently, his lips moving. The two young women continued to work their magic. The Blood Mage stood in the background, hidden behind a curtain of rain, his crimson robes all that could be seen.

Gythe stopped singing the hymn and switched to a tune popular with jongleurs and street performers. She began to sing "The Pirate King," the song that told of his exploits and made him into a hero. There was no doubting her intent. People in the crowd looked toward the Blood Mage, their expressions grim. They all knew the truth—how the

Pirate King had tortured his brother, Xavier, forcing him to reveal the secrets of contramagic, then corrupting the magic and using it for killing.

As Gythe sang about the Pirate King, Sophia continued to sing the hymn. The two melodies blended well, twining about each other. The young women raised their cupped hands. Sophia held a blazing ball of blue flame. Gythe reached out to the people. Her hands burned with green fire. She raised her voice in the rousing chorus and the people began to sing with her. She flung the ball of fiery contramagic into the air. Sophia lifted her shining blue flame to meet it.

The green and blue magical glow twined and twisted and began to swirl about Sophia and Gythe. The two women continued to sing, their voices carrying with surprising clarity over the roar of the storm and the pounding of the drums. People gazed in rapt joy.

The green magic and blue flames blended together, yet remained separate. Whirling and shining, the magic spiraled upward, rising to the heavens. The two magicks touched the purple lightning-laced clouds until they dissipated shredded, and wafted away in wisps of gray. The thunder rumbled and was silent. The lightning flared and then vanished. A pale, glistening shaft of sunlight broke through the clouds and shone down on the stage, on Gythe and Sophia, on Brother Barnaby, on the body of the saint.

The eyes of the dead man opened, and Xavier gazed into the sun. The shimmering rainbow colors of the Aurora unfurled, rolling out like bright silken banners flung across the sky. He seemed to smile.

"A miracle . . . Look! Did you see? Our saint! His eyes opened!"

The awed whispers swept like wind over the crowd, creating a ripple in the vast sea. The people turned wondering faces to the sunlight and watched with tears the lights of the Aurora dancing across the sky.

All the while, the Blood Mage stood in the background, his face impassive. He did not look at the sun, nor did he look at his brother. He tapped the blood-gummed fingers of his hand against his thigh in time to the beat of drumming that grew louder, replacing the thunder.

The two young women were pale, drained, exhausted. The blue glow and the green faded, diminishing. Lightning from another wizard storm flickered on the horizon. The magic was starting to fade.

Brother Barnaby gently closed Xavier's eyes.

People in the crowd looked at each other uncertainly, wondering what would happen now.

The Blood Mage wiped the blood from his hand on his robes. "Give the signal to launch the fleet."

His aide with the ram's horn blew it again, three times. Green flares soared from the temple and burst in the clearing sky. But the captains of the ships had not waited for the signal; they already had taken advantage of the clear skies to order their ships into the air.

One by one, the ships of the invasion fleet released their mooring lines and rose into the sky. Sails billowed as they caught the wind. The sight was breathtaking and awful.

"Where are the dragons?" Cecile asked softly. "Where is Stephano? Do you think something has happened?"

"I hope not!" Miri said worriedly, anxiously scanning the skies. "Stephano should be here now!"

All they saw were more bat riders, flying low over the crowd, coming from the direction of the temple. The riders were wearing the same demonic helms, but these were emblazoned with crimson badges.

"The Blood Guard," Patrick said grimly. "Soldiers loyal to Ian and skilled in his magic."

The Blood Mage advanced to the center of the stage. He raised his hands, that were now cleansed of blood, to draw the attention of the crowd away from the body of his brother.

"The invasion has begun," he shouted. "*I* will be the one to lead our armies. Go back to your homes! Await word of our victory!"

The Blood Mage rested his hands on Gythe and Sophia, placing one hand on the shoulder of each young woman. Sophia shuddered at his touch. Gythe paled and flinched and looked at her sister. The Blood Mage shouted orders to the circling bat riders.

"He's ordered them to fly him to his flagship," said Patrick. "He's going to take the girls with him. Probably use them as sacrifices."

One of the bats landed near the Blood Mage. Another bat rider flew close to Gythe. Leaning down from the saddle, he reached out to grab her.

Miri started to run up onto the stage, but both Patrick and Cecile stopped her.

"You can't go up there," said Patrick. "If the Blood Mage didn't kill you, the bats would rip you apart!"

"Let go of me!" Miri cried, struggling. "I have to do something! I can't just stand here."

Cecile drew her pistol.

"I'm a fair shot. I can stop one, at least—"

Gythe gave a sudden, joyous, inarticulate cry.

A dragon soaring out from the clouds gave a wild, hooting call in response. The other dragons of the Dragon Brigade were behind him, flying in their *V* formation.

"Petard!" Miri exclaimed. "*That* is why Gythe sang 'The Pirate King.' She was calling to him."

Petard went into a steep dive, flying toward the plaza. Flames shot from his mouth, and plumes of smoke trailed after him.

The people of Glasearrach knew stories about dragons, but they were creatures of long ago, from before the sinking. Such fearsome beasts had never been seen Below. The sight of a dragon bearing down on them, fire flaring from his jaws, sent people fleeing in panic.

"There's Stephano!" Miri shouted, pointing to a sleek dragon with purplish red scales, flying at the head of his brigade.

Cecile watched him, her heart aching with love and pride. She knew him by the way he sat in the saddle, tall and proud, so much like his father. He blew a shrill call on the bosun's pipe, and the dragons broke formation and singly or in pairs, veered toward the ships of the invasion fleet.

Petard flew low over the crowd, scattering them like a wolf in the sheep fold, emptying the square as people ran for their lives. Petard circled around and then came back, flying toward the bat rider who had been reaching for Gythe. The bat shrieked and flew off, dumping his startled rider out of the saddle. The other members of the Blood Guard were having similar difficulty controlling their mounts.

The Blood Mage cast a baleful glance at the dragon and another at Gythe, who was clapping her hands and laughing.

The bat on the stage was flapping its wings and jumping about, trying to escape. The soldier holding the reins shouted for the Blood Mage to hurry, he couldn't hold the frantic creature much longer.

The dragon was a terrifying sight, his eyes blazing, flames flickering from his jaws.

The Blood Mage turned and ran to the bat, and the soldier helped him into the saddle. Once he was safely mounted, the soldier let loose.

"Kill the beast!" he shouted to the Blood Guard, pointing toward Petard.

His bat flapped its wings, rose into the air and sped off. Petard blew a blast of flame after him, but missed.

A few members of the Blood Guard had managed to control their bats and now they flew to the attack, shooting at Petard with the long guns. As green fireballs burst around him, Petard sucked in a breath and blew out a gout of flame. The fire engulfed a soldier and his bat, sending them plunging, screaming, to the ground.

"The countess and I are going to save Gythe and Sophia, Patrick," said Miri. "Have your people ready."

Patrick was watching the dragon, his expression dark. "How do I know the beast won't kill us all?"

"Because he's our friend," said Miri.

Patrick appeared reassured, yet he kept a wary eye on the dragon, shouting to his people, as Miri ran up the stairs onto the stage. Cecile had thrust her pistol back into her waistband and was right behind her. Petard circled menacingly overhead, keeping the bat riders at bay and Brother Barnaby stood protectively beside the two young women. The square was nearly empty; only a few people remained and they were wearing green.

Cecile ran to embrace Sophia, taking her into arms and hugging her close.

"I am so proud of you, my dear one!" Cecile said fiercely. "So very proud!"

"I was frightened, my lady," Sophia said, talking breathlessly. "The fear was terrible. I thought it might kill me. But then I started to sing and the magic sparkled all through me . . . like sunlight. . . . We stopped the storm! With our magic!"

"You were wonderful, my dear, but now we must take you somewhere safe," said Cecile.

She was worried about Sophia, whose eyes shone with wonder. She obeyed Cecile, but she moved slowly, her feet wandering, as if she was in a daze. Cecile led her across the platform, past the body of Xavier. Sophia looked back at the corpse.

"He heard God's voice," she said softly.

"Make haste, Miri!" Patrick called. "It's not safe here!"

The battle was above them now as enemy ships tried to escape the dragons, who were blasting them with their flaming breath and doing extensive damage. Smoke filled the air, stinging the eyes. Parts of the burning ships broke off and fell to the ground below. As if to emphasize Patrick's warning, a blazing spar crashed in a flurry of flames and cinders right in front of them.

Petard flew overhead, torn between joining the battle and protecting his friends. He was obviously eager to fight.

"Go on, you great ugly beast!" Miri shouted up at him.

Petard's lips pulled back from his fangs in what might have been a grin. He made one more pass and then flew off, nodding his head in salute.

"I'm afraid something's wrong with Her Highness," said Cecile. "She seems lost. I can't bring her back."

Sophia was happily humming the hymn to herself, gazing around and smiling as black smoke filled the air and fire rained down from the skies.

"She's drunk, my lady," said Miri.

Cecile stared at her.

"Drunk with the magic. I've seen it before. I know how to handle her. *You* need to talk to Brother Barnaby," Miri added. "Gythe won't stir without him and it doesn't look to me as if he's planning to leave."

Miri took off her cloak, wrapped it around Sophia and began talking to her in a low voice. Patrick was shouting at them to come quickly before the bat riders realized the dragon was gone. A burning piece of debris crashed onto the platform, smashing the wooden planks and setting them on fire.

Coughing in the smoke, Cecile found Brother Barnaby

kneeling beside the body. "Brother, you must come with us! It's not safe for you to stay!"

Brother Barnaby shook his head. "If I leave him, the Blood Guard will use his body in their evil magic."

Cecile could not argue. He was undoubtedly right. She wondered how to persuade him.

"We will guard him," said Patrick. "Step aside."

Brother Barnaby stood in his way. "You hated him. You rebels were going to kill him yourselves."

"He tried to do right at the end, Brother," said Patrick. "He failed, but we won't forget."

He jumped onto the stage. Dropping the long gun, he flung off his cloak and deftly wrapped it around the bloody corpse like a shroud. With Brother Barnaby's help, Patrick lifted the corpse into position over his shoulder. Cecile hurried down the stairs ahead of them.

"I sent my people ahead to make certain the boat is safe," said Patrick. "Keep watch, all of you. The Blood Guards will be roaming the city, looking for victims. The drums are still beating."

"The *Cloud Hopper* is not far," Miri added. "I left it on the outskirts of the city. I'll lead the way. Gythe, you stay with Sophia."

They left the plaza and hurried down a street, following Miri's lead. Gythe had her arm around Sophia and was pulling her along. Cecile stayed near the two, her pistol in her hand. She had not thought about the drumming until Patrick's warning caused her to hear the sound again. It dinned in her ears, swelling with the drummers' increased fervor.

As they hurried through the deserted streets, Cecile thought she caught a glimpse of soldiers walking down an alley. Judging by his baleful glance, Patrick saw them, too. "Keep moving," he said.

The sky continued to rain fire from the battle raging

overhead. Cecile tried to find Stephano, but the smoke was so thick all she could see was the orange flames of the dragons and the deadly green beams of the black ships' weapons.

Miri kept them moving at a rapid pace, taking them down side streets and alleys, avoiding major thoroughfares and the smoldering, burning parts of ships that had fallen into the street. She kept saying encouragingly that they had only a short distance to go, but then she would turn down yet another street that was seemingly endless.

Under Gythe's care Sophia had come out of her daze, was aware of her surroundings and talking rationally. But she was pale with fatigue, and her strength was flagging. Gythe was exhausted. Her shoulders slumped and her steps lagged, she struggled to keep going. Patrick labored under the weight of the body. Brother Barnaby stayed near him, doing what he could to help. Cecile wondered how long they could keep going.

"There! Ahead!" Miri cried. "You can see the balloon."

They straggled to a weary halt. They had reached the outskirts of the city, where the paved streets ended in dirt and mud. If there had once been buildings here, they had either been torn down or had fallen down, for piles of broken wood and a few bricks were all that remained. Beyond was swampy grassland. Few people ever came here, which was why Miri had chosen the landing site. The bright colors of her balloon were visible through the smoke.

Miri raised her voice. "Hello, the boat. Who is your captain?"

The answer came back. "Doctor Ellington."

Gythe laughed and Miri smiled. Patrick heaved a sigh of relief and, with the help of Brother Barnaby, lowered the body to the ground. Brother Barnaby knelt beside the corpse, rearranging the cloak so that it covered the face.

"Let me go check with my people, Miri, just to be certain," Patrick said. "The rest of you stay here. I will send someone back to help carry the body."

"I'm going with you," said Miri firmly. "It's my boat. If anything's wrong I need to know. Gythe, you stay with the others."

Gythe shook her head, tapped herself on the chest, and then excitedly motioned to the boat, indicating that she was coming.

"I will stay with Sophia and Brother Barnaby," Cecile offered. "We need to rest anyway."

"I just need to catch my breath," said Sophia, sitting on what was left of a stoop.

Cecile sat down beside her. A breeze began to blow, carrying with it the smell of rain from the distant storm, wafting away the smoke. Sophia gazed off into the distance. Her expression was grave, solemn.

She was no longer the girl who romped with Bandit and played waltzes on the piano and wore ribbons in her hair to please her mother. The girl was a woman and she was a stranger, not only to Cecile, but perhaps to herself.

"I have been thinking, my lady."

"What about, Your Highness?" Cecile asked.

"About going home," Sophia replied. Her voice ached with sorrow. "I long to go back and yet I dread it. How can I tell Mama and Papa that I have changed? That I am not going to be the daughter they want?"

"You won't have to tell them, Sophia," said Cecile with a gentle smile. "They will know when they look at you—"

A scream cut off her words, a scream of such panicked terror that it nearly stopped her heart. The scream came from the direction of the boat.

"Barnaby! Barnaby, look out!"

Turning, Cecile saw a lone bat rider diving down on Brother Barnaby, who was kneeling in the street, holding vigil over Xavier's body. The soldier wore the red emblem of the Blood Guard.

Cecile drew the dragon pistol.

"Run for the boat, Your Highness!"

Sophia looked back fearfully at the bat rider and then ran down the street toward the *Cloud Hopper*.

Cecile raised the dragon pistol, all too mindful of the fact that if the powder was wet the weapon might not work. She aimed and fired, hitting the bat in the head.

The bat dropped out of the air, but the rider managed to jump from the saddle just before the bat crashed to the ground. The soldier landed heavily, falling to his knees and dropping his long gun.

Brother Barnaby rose to his feet.

"Run, Brother!" Cecile cried.

He ignored her cries and remained standing protectively over Xavier's body as the soldier drew a curved blade sword and advanced on the unarmed monk. Cecile was helpless. She was out of ammunition. She looked back, hoping desperately to see Patrick or one of his men.

No one was coming.

The soldier said something that Cecile could not make out. Brother Barnaby shook his head, and the soldier advanced on him, sword raised.

Brother Barnaby drew a small sack from his robes and hurled it into the man's face.

Fine, sparkling blue powder flew inside the soldier's helm. The powder went down his throat, up his nose, and into his eyes. He gave a strangled cry, coughing and wheezing. Flinging away the sword, he ripped off his helm, coughing and frantically rubbing his burning eyes.

Patrick came running, carrying a pistol that he aimed at the guard.

"Let him be," said Brother Barnaby. "He cannot harm us now."

The man had dropped to his hands and knees and was heaving up his guts.

Patrick stared at him, irresolute. He wasn't happy, but he did as Brother Barnaby asked and thrust the pistol into his belt. Patrick picked up the soldier's long gun and slung it over his shoulder, then broke the sword over his knee and tossed back the pieces.

"The boat is secure," he reported. "We should board quickly. If this soldier found us, so can others."

Patrick lifted the body of Xavier in his arms and walked toward the boat.

"Thank you, my lady," said Brother Barnaby, catching up with Cecile. "You saved my life."

"Whoever shouted that warning saved your life, Brother," Cecile replied with a faint smile.

She saw Brother Barnaby about to add something and fearing he would grow effusive in his thanks, she hurriedly changed the subject. The sight of Patrick boarding the *Cloud Hopper* carrying Xavier's body gave her the opportunity.

"What will happen with Xavier now? To his memory? Will the rebels make him a symbol for their cause?"

"I think he will be more than that. I believe he will become a true saint for his people," Brother Barnaby replied. "Not just a saint in name only. He died trying to give back what he had taken away."

"As good a measure for sainthood as any, I suppose," Cecile reflected. "Perhaps better than most."

The sturdy little Trundler boat, with its gaily colored silk balloon, stubby mast, and pocket-handkerchief sails looked more wonderful to Cecile than her own elegant yacht. Climbing the gangplank, she saw Sophia smiling radiantly at something and wiping away tears. Miri sat on a stool, sobbing, her face buried in her hands. Gythe stood apart, looking frightened and confused.

Cecile stopped and glanced about fearfully. Nothing seemed amiss. The body of Xavier lay on the deck, covered by a blanket. Patrick and the rebels stood ready to cast off the lines.

"What has happened?" Cecile asked in alarm. "What is wrong?"

"Nothing is wrong, my lady," Sophia said. "It was Gythe who warned Brother Barnaby. She called to him."

At first Cecile was still confused. Why should Gythe warning Brother Barnaby cause this upheaval? And then she understood.

She had not recognized the voice that had cried out Brother Barnaby's name because she had never heard that voice speak. No one had heard Gythe speak, not for many long years.

Gythe touched Miri on the shoulder. Miri lifted her tear-stained face and reached out to embrace her sister. Gythe started to gesture. Miri caught hold of her hands and held them tightly, lovingly.

"You don't need to be silent anymore, Gythe," she said. "You can say what is in your heart."

"Stop . . . crying," Gythe said, speaking haltingly.

Miri laughed and brushed away her tears. Standing up, she walked over to the helm.

"I must get us out of here! Gythe, be ready to take up the gangplank. Patrick, stand by with those lines. Make haste, Brother Barnaby," Miri added in scolding tones. "Come on board! Why are you dawdling?"

Brother Barnaby remained on the ground, standing near the gangplank, but not on it.

"I am not sailing with you, Mistress Miri," said Brother Barnaby. He spoke to her, but his eyes were on Gythe. "I am staying in Dunlow with Patrick and the resistance. I will do what I can to help them. Thank you, Gythe, for saving my life and giving your people hope."

She stood gazing at him, stricken. Her lips trembled, her body was rigid.

"I found my voice," she said. "Only to say good-bye."

"Good-bye, Gythe. God go with you," said Brother Barnaby gently.

Gythe gave him a long, last look, then she smiled and, blinking back tears, hauled in the gangplank. Patrick cast off the lines. Miri sent the magic running into the lift tank. The *Cloud Hopper* rose into the air.

"God go with you all!" Brother Barnaby called, waving to them.

Miri was busy with the helm. Gythe had climbed nimbly up a mast and was doing something with the sails. As the *Cloud Hopper* skimmed over the treetops, Cecile looked back toward Dunlow. Dragons and ships still fought, the battle still raged. Green beams lit the thick smoke and orange fire glowed. And above the boom of the cannon fire, she could hear the beating of the drums. Somewhere amid the smoke and fire, Stephano was fighting. Wounded. Maybe dead or dying.

Julian is with Stephano, Cecile reminded herself. He is riding by his side, watching over him with a father's love.

"Bring our son safely home, my love," Cecile prayed softly.

38

Soaring above. Ever vigilant below.

—Motto of the Dragon Brigade

The members of the Dragon Brigade waited in the shelter of the caves the dragons were using for refuge, watching the rain and listening to the booming thunder that shook the mountain. Stephano was mounted on Viola; Dag was on Verdi. Haelgrund and the other dragons, including the immensely proud dragon brothers, Hroal and Droal, were there, too, all of them waiting for the wizard storm to end.

Haelgrund had stated that he and the other dragons could fly in the wizard storm. It was clear that he was reluctant, however, and Stephano had his own reservations. The driving rain reduced visibility to such an extent that Stephano feared they might lose their way. The lightning strikes could be deadly, the whipping winds perilous. He decreed that they would remain in the caves and trust that Gythe and the princess would find a way to stop the storms.

Haelgrund was skeptical. He considered ludicrous the idea of a human, even a savant, stopping the storms with magic. Rodrigo had assured his friends that Gythe could work miracles. The saints had stopped the storms centuries ago, and he believed that Gythe and the princess, both savants, could do the same. But he was alone in his belief.

Even Dag was dubious.

"I love Gythe dearly and I've learned to just about tolerate Rigo, but if ever there were two weak reeds in this world, sir, you're leaning on both of them."

And so Stephano waited in a cave, mounted in the saddle, listening to the drums. Even here, miles from the city, he could hear the beating, feel it in his body, thudding in his heart. He was having difficulty shaking off an oppressive sense of gloom and foreboding, feelings he had never before experienced when flying into battle. He wondered if the contramagic could be having an effect on him, as well as on the dragons of the Brigade.

"The sooner we stop that racket, the better," he muttered grimly to himself.

Viola turned her head to look back at him, her eyes glinting. She could hear a whisper, it seemed, or maybe his thoughts. He smiled at her reassuringly and wished the storm would end. He hated waiting.

When the sky began to lighten, at first he said nothing, fearing he was seeing a product of his overeager imagination. The rain stopped, the lightning flickered out, the thunder rumbled away. The sun broke through the clouds.

Stephano smiled broadly and grinned at Dag. "Now what do you say?"

"God bless Gythe and Rigo," Dag replied solemnly, putting on his helm. Stephano put on his own, and gave the order to fly.

The dragons soared out of the cave, led by Stephano and Viola, with Dag and Verdi on his right flank. Haelgrund flew behind, leading the Brigade.

Petard came to grief immediately. He had been told he was to fly in the rear of the formation, as befitted his status as a new recruit. But in his excitement and impatience with his slower elders, he thrust his way to the front of the cave and flew out ahead of everyone, including Stephano.

Haelgrund bellowed furiously, and Stephano was angry at this breach of discipline. He was about to order the young dragon grounded when Viola twisted her head to look back at him, pleading for understanding.

"Gythe calls to him," she said.

Viola's language skills had vastly improved since Haelgrund had taken it upon himself to teach her. He would have taught the other two, but Petard could not be bothered and Verdi was too bitterly jealous of his rival to take advantage of the offer.

"Are Gythe and Miri and the others all right?" Stephano asked worriedly.

Viola shook her head. She didn't know.

Stephano let Petard go. He could not do much else, given that the dragon was already far ahead of them, out of earshot.

The Dragon Brigade flew from the cave into the pale, watery sunlight. Stephano had left Gunnery Officer Vega in command of the fort. Stephano had been planning to leave the fort under Dag's command, but those plans had changed with his idea to attack the temple. He would need Dag to lead the attack on the fleet, leaving Stephano free to accomplish his mission.

Vega was a competent, though unimaginative officer. Stephano might have been worried about him, but he did not consider it likely the fortress would come under assault. From what Sir Conal had learned, Xavier had allocated the majority of his forces to the invasion fleet, leaving his forts and outposts only sparsely defended.

As they flew over the fortress, he looked down to see the Rosian colors flying from the flagpole above the bridge and Rodrigo's magical construct, the mysterious seventh sigil, which had been hammered and chiseled directly into the stone below the bridge. The last Stephano had seen of Rodrigo, his friend had been working to activate the magic. Stephano knew nothing about magic, so he had no idea if this seventh sigil was in any way meaningful. Haelgrund, however, had been amazed and impressed.

"Ingenious," he had said, eyeing the construct. "Finally you humans have come to your senses."

The Brigade flew on, leaving the fortress behind. They could now see the ships of the Bottom Dwellers with the naked eye. The fleet was made up of a hodgepodge of various types of ships the fiends had captured over the years. Stephano counted twenty warships, including a Freyan warship, ten smaller ships that were probably used to transport troops, and a couple of what were likely supply ships. Among these were several Travian merchants, a Rosian passenger ship, and even a Freyan trawler.

He wondered if the warships still had their cannons, if the Bottom Dwellers knew how to operate cannons or if they would use only their powerful green beam weapons. If the ships had cannons, the captains had not yet run them out.

Stephano smiled grimly. He truly had the element of surprise.

The ships had inflated their balloons preparatory to launch. Now that the skies were clearing, they were preparing to set sail. The Brigade would soon be flying into range. He pictured the reaction of the lookouts when they first saw dragons—creatures that had not been seen on Glasearrach in hundreds of years: shock and disbelief, terrified calls to officers who would react the same way. Thereafter, confusion and fear and frantic haste; precious moments of time lost during which the dragons could strike with impunity.

He could now see the temple square in the distance. He put his spyglass to his eye. Petard was almost there. On the ground below, people were massed around a stage. He was too far away to be able to tell who was on the stage, but from what Miri had told him, Xavier would be there with Gythe and Sophia. He watched as Petard swooped down on the terrified crowd, sending them fleeing in fear.

Stephano was pleased and surprised to see Petard actually giving some thought to what he was doing. He had listened as Stephano and Haelgrund discussed the plan, which Haelgrund had been supposed to carry out. He was to cause confusion, give Gythe and Sophia time to escape, and clear the temple square of as many civilians as possible. As Stephano watched the crowd scatter, he could only hope those he loved were among them.

Stephano blew the signal on the bosun's pipe, sending the dragons, led by Dag on Verdi and Haelgrund, to attack the ships. He and Droal and Hroal broke off from the main body. Flanked by the dragon brothers, Stephano took a moment to watch with pure pleasure the Dragon Brigade in action.

The dragons were trained in assaulting ships. They attacked in pairs. Haelgrund and a veteran dragon, Lady Teloreau, were the first to attack, and they caught their victim completely unprepared. No one manned the green beam weapon, and none of the crew was even armed.

Haelgrund, flying above the ship, breathed a broad swath of fire on the main deck to clear it, aiming especially for the officers, either killing them or forcing them to run for their lives.

Lady Teloreau followed, specifically targeting the green beam weapon mounted on the ship's prow, directing a narrow stream of flame at the beam weapon. It would be protected by magical constructs, in this case, contramagic, but dragon fire had the ability to break down all magical constructs and eventually destroy them, which is what made dragons far more effective than cannons in battle.

Stephano had no idea how effective dragon breath would be against contramagic, so he took a moment to observe as dragon fire engulfed the entire platform on which the weapon stood, blackening the barrel, setting the wooden truck alight and toppling the weapon over on its side. He could not tell if the dragon had eroded the contramagic, but even if she hadn't, the fiends would have to take time to put out the flames. Teloreau flew off to allow her partner to swoop in again.

By this time, surviving members of the ship's crew were arming themselves, firing green balls of contramagic at the dragons. Although the fireballs were ludicrously small compared to the immense size of the dragons, they could inflict a great deal of damage, far more than a bullet or even a cannonball, as Hroal could attest. He was still recovering from wounds he had received during the attack on the Westfirth. The contramagic in the green fire broke down the natural magical constructs on a dragon's scales and skin, burning through to the flesh beneath. Such wounds were extremely painful, debilitating, and slow to heal.

The frightened soldiers were firing in haste, and the flaming balls fell short of their target. Haelgrund breathed a blast of flame that incinerated many of the soldiers and sent the rest diving for cover. This done, he set fire to the masts and the rigging. Teloreau dove toward the ship, raking the balloon with her claws, shredding it and cutting through the lines that held it in place.

"She's a goner, sir!" Droal bellowed.

Stephano agreed. All three of the ship's masts were on fire, as well as the rigging, and the balloon was in tatters. Men were fleeing the burning ship, some of them desperate enough to jump over the rails as the ship plunged out of the sky, raining burning debris on the ground below.

Stephano knew better than to declare victory. He could see that the dragons attacking other ships were having a more difficult time. Due to the fact that some of the ships of the fleet were docked in close proximity to one another, the dragons were not able to fly as close as Haelgrund and his partner for fear they would foul their wings on the rigging. The smaller ships were taking to the air as fast as they could, and the warships were readying their defenses. One, at least, was running out its cannons. The others were manning their green beam weapons and sending armed soldiers to fire at the dragons. Fortunately, the ships would be also hampered by the close proximity to their fellows. They would not want to risk destroying another ship.

This battle was going to be bloody and one Stephano was not certain they could win. The drumming would have a debilitating effect on the dragons unless he could stop it. He waved at Dag, signaling he was going off on his mission. Dag acknowledged the wave and flew off on Verdi to join the battle.

Stephano eyed the line of ships, searching for one that would suit his purposes. He settled on an old-fashioned Guundaran merchant vessel built along the same lines as the *Sommerwind*, the ship that had rescued the sinking *Cloud Hopper* after they left the island.

Designed to carry cargo, the ship was big and bulky and slow moving. Merchant ships of that period were not armed, so he would not have to contend with cannons, although this one had a green beam weapon mounted on the bow, and soldiers with long guns lined the rails. The ship had the additional advantage of flying near the temple and slightly apart from its fellows.

As he had arranged in advance, Stephano left the two

dragon brothers behind as he and Viola flew to the attack. Smaller and faster than the two elder dragons, Viola could dart in, breathe fire, and dart out again with remarkable speed. She had also learned how to twist and roll to avoid enemy fire. Stephano made certain the straps that held him in the dragon saddle were cinched snug.

They flew in below the bowsprit, then banked upward at the last moment, rising over the forecastle with a blast of flame. The soldiers died instantly as the dragon's breath rolled over them.

Stephano guided Viola down the starboard side of the ship; her fiery breath clearing a path before them. Sailors and soldiers had to scramble for cover, with no chance to return fire.

When they cleared the stern, Viola banked hard into a twisting roll that brought them around to repeat their strafing run, only in reverse. She breathed fire onto the deck, setting it ablaze and making certain the remaining soldiers were pinned down.

When Viola flew off a short distance, leaving the ship in flames and the crew in chaos, Stephano gave the signal for the dragon brothers to take over. The smoke from the burning ship provided cover for Hroal and Droal. Hroal sank his claws into the hull and Droal unleashed a blast of fire that destroyed the green beam weapon, then latched on to the forecastle.

The brothers had served in the quartermaster corps for most of their naval career and had often had to keep damaged ships afloat until they could safely land. They had pushed supply barges and hauled away wrecks. The two massive dragons, wings pumping and tails lashing, expertly maneuvered the burning ship in the direction of the temple.

Stephano ordered Viola to fly over the damaged ship's large balloons. She swept along the port side and using her claws, she ripped small holes in a few of the chambers of each of the balloons. Stephano wanted to scuttle the ship, but he needed it to stay afloat long enough to reach the temple.

He was about to make another pass when he heard a voice shouting his name.

"Stephano!" the man called urgently. "Look to the west!"

Stephano turned, startled, his hand on his pistol. The only other human member of the Brigade was Dag and he was far off, in the thick of the battle.

A dragon rider was flying alongside him, on his left flank, and now the unknown rider raised the visor of his helm. Stephano opened his mouth, but he had no breath to speak. He could only stare, in disbelief at the shadowy figure. The dragon rider was his father.

Julian de Guichen looked grim. He pointed urgently. "To the west, Stephano! Look to the west!"

Shaken and wondering, Stephano tore his gaze from his father and looked in the direction he had indicated. He saw, to his shock and dismay, one of the enemy ships had managed to escape and was sailing away from the battle. The ship flew a blood-red flag different from those on the other ships. He had no idea what that meant or who was captaining that vessel, but the intent was obvious. The ship was sailing straight for the fortress.

Stephano looked back at his father. He wanted to thank him. He wanted to tell him so much . . .

His father wasn't there.

"Of course, he isn't there! Good God. Now I'm seeing ghosts!" Stephano muttered.

Yet the ship Julian de Guichen had pointed out was most certainly there.

Stephano could not take time to wonder. He gazed grimly at the ship heading toward the fortress, and tried to think what to do. Not fearing an attack, he had left the fortress only lightly manned. His men could hold out, but for how long? Dag and the other dragons were fighting their own battles, too far away to help.

He could not go himself. Not now. His task was to destroy the temple, stop the drumming that was wreaking havoc on humans and dragons the world over.

The boom of cannon fire caught Stephano's attention. A warship that seemed to have come out of nowhere was firing her guns at him and the dragons. The ship was a small Travian frigate, maybe eighteen guns, and from the sound, no bigger than nine pounders. Stephano could only watch as each gun belched fire and iron. Normally he would not worry about such small cannonballs hurting a dragon, whose scales were tough as steel plating. Unfortunately Hroal was still missing scales from wounds received in the battle at Westfirth.

The warship was only three hundred yards away, a relatively easy shot for a trained gun crew. An effectively fired broadside aimed right at the dragons could have killed or seriously maimed both of them. This crew was not trained, however. The cannons were firing sporadically as they came to bear and thus far they had missed the dragons and hit the merchant ship, tearing through the rigging, and knocking holes in the hull.

Stephano briefly considered flying over to attack the warship, at least to put an end to the cannon fire, but he discarded the idea. He and Viola still had work to do with the balloons, because while the ship was sinking, its rate of descent wasn't fast enough. And down on the deck below, the captain was urging his men to attack.

This time, the cannon shot hit its mark. Hroal's body shuddered as three cannon balls smashed into his wounded flank, causing him to momentarily lose his hold on the ship. Droal roared a question, asking his brother how he was. From the dragon's angle, he could not see the extent of the injuries.

"I'm fine!" Hroal roared back. "Keep pushing!"

Droal nodded. "Together, brother!"

Stephano guided Viola past Hroal and saw that blood ran from the dragon's side. The impact of the cannonballs had blasted apart flesh and muscle, exposing the bone. Hroal managed a grin that was meant to be reassuring, but Stephano could see blood on the dragon's teeth, and his breathing was labored.

They were gradually increasing the distance between themselves and the warship, but he feared they weren't traveling fast enough. Inept though the gun crews might be, they were once again running out the cannons. He dared not leave to try to stop them; they were too close to the temple. He looked about to see if he could signal one of the other dragons.

Viola must have been thinking along the same lines, for catching sight of Petard, she let out a deafening roar that got his attention. The young dragon turned his head, saw the cannons and understood their danger. Stephano blessed those afternoons of telling the wild dragons stories of the Dragon Brigade, describing their battles. Petard had never been in this situation, but he had heard the tales.

He sped through the smoke-filled air like a rocket, turning his body at the last moment to aim at the guns and the open gun ports. When he raked the cannons with fire, flames burst through the gun ports and explosions rocked the warship. Elated, Petard spun around in midair and just for fun snapped a yard off the mizzenmast. Stephano shook his head, but he signaled to Petard that he had done a good job.

Hroal's strength was starting to flag. Blood was dripping from his jaws.

"Hroal, stop. Let Viola take over," Stephano ordered.

Hroal eyed the sleek, slender dragon and gave a snort. "Too puny. Bird bones."

Hroal cast a fierce, pleading look at Stephano. "Great honor, Captain. Won't let you down."

Viola, hearing this, turned to look at Stephano, begging him to order Hroal to quit the battle.

The blood was flowing freely from the dragon's horrific wounds. Every flap of his wings cost Hroal a great effort. Yet he persevered, making no complaint. Indeed, he was doing his damnedest to hide his pain. Stephano remembered the flash of pride in the old dragon's eyes when he had been given this assignment. All his life, Hroal had wanted to fly into battle with the Brigade. He may well have taken his death wound in this fight. If so, he had made his choice of how he wanted to die.

"Carry on, Hroal," Stephano said curtly.

He ignored Viola's pleading eyes. She was young; she would learn.

Droal, on the other side of the massive ship, eyed Hroal worriedly and shifted his position to take over the greater share of the ship's weight.

"Hurt? How bad?" Droal called worriedly.

"Keep working," Hroal growled. "Lord Captain watching."

They had only a short distance farther to carry the ship; once they had it in position over the temple, Viola, Hroal, and Droal would turn their flaming breath on the ship and send it crashing down onto the temple dome. Parts of the ship were already on fire. The captain must have given the order to abandon ship, because sailors, including the captain, were jumping into the lifeboats and setting sail.

Stephano let them escape. His task was to stop the drumming. He shifted in the saddle, looking to the west, where he thought he heard cannon fire. He could not see the enemy ship. He guessed that it was attacking the fort.

He knew the frustration of needing to be in two places at once. The task at hand could not be hurried. The dragon brothers were moving the huge ship as fast as possible, faster than he had reason to expect, given that one was severely wounded. Looking again to the west he concluded that yes, that was definitely cannon fire.

Below him the square was empty. Buildings hit by debris were burning. Soldiers massed around the temple, which was located on the north end of the plaza. Miri had told the rebels the temple would be a target, warned them to keep their distance. From inside the temple, the drums thundered, pounding until he thought the sound might drive him mad.

He could feel a shudder of pain ripple through Viola's body, see her grit her teeth. The drumming was having a debilitating effect on her and all the dragons.

He put the spyglass to his eye and shifted in the saddle, trying to observe the battle. His view was obscured by smoke rolling off the burning ships and by the roiling clouds of another storm, wielding its own weapons of wind and rain and deadly lightning.

Eyeing the storm's advance, Stephano judged they had maybe a half hour before its full fury broke. He concentrated on the fighting; once the storm was fully upon them the dragons would have a much more difficult time of it. But for now, they were doing damage to the enemy. The warship Petard had attacked was sinking, trailing smoke and fire. He spotted Dag and Verdi in the thick of the battle, along with Petard and two other dragons, fighting one of the larger warships. A green beam lanced out, illuminating the smoke with an ominous glow. A rain squall mingled with the smoke blocked the dragons from view. He stared until his eyes started to ache with the strain, but the smoke was too thick for him to see what had happened.

Stephano looked down. He and the dragons were close to their destination. The ship was almost in position. With no other enemy ships near, he decided to leave. He could trust Droal and Hroal to follow through. All they had to do was haul the ship a little farther, then destroy the lift tanks and drop it on the temple.

He was about to tell Droal, when a powerful explosion tore through the merchant ship, upending his world. The shockwave struck Viola and flipped her, head over tail. Stephano hung upside down, held in the saddle by nothing more than the leather straps. Blood rushed to his head and the straps dug painfully into his legs. Just when he feared the straps would break, Viola flew into the roll, as she had been taught, and managed to right herself.

Stephano clung to the saddle. Dizzy and light-headed, and gasping for breath, he watched his plan to destroy the temple go up in flames.

The merchant ship was now a fire ship, the silk balloons having gone up with a whoosh. Fire danced along the spars, blazed up the masts and rolled over what was left of the deck. The rigging was gone. No wonder the captain and crew had fled, Stephano thought grimly. The hold must have been packed with gunpowder. The ship was sinking and it was coming down in the wrong place.

The blast had sent both dragon brothers reeling, and Droal had been injured. His neck and chest were bloody, his scales charred, and though he was still airborne, he had lost altitude and was far below, struggling to reach Hroal, who had broken a wing in the blast, and whose head, neck, and chest were covered in blood.

He looked at his brother and gave a little nod. Droal bellowed, anguished. Viola cried out in horror.

Hroal lurched toward the fire ship, latched on to the

remnants of the hull and with a final, desperate beating of his crippled wings, carried it over the temple. The blazing ship fell, taking Hroal with it.

The burning ship landed on the temple's roof. The building imploded and smoke, dust, and fire rolled up in a billowing cloud. Hroal was gone. Droal roared out his grief and then hung listlessly in the sky, gazing down at the blazing ruin that had become his brother's funeral pyre.

They had accomplished their mission. Stephano was free to leave, to fly to see if the fortress was under attack. He did not need Viola's agonized look to tell him that he could not fly off and leave Droal here by himself. Then there was the battle still raging in the skies. He could see little through the smoke and rain squalls: purple flashes of lightning, green beams and fireballs, orange flames. Dragons wheeled amid the clouds and ships sank, trailing fire. Yet Stephano could not tell if they were winning a glorious victory or going down in ignominious defeat.

He forced himself to wait precious minutes until he at last located Dag and Verdi.

"Sergeant Droal!" Stephano called.

The bereft dragon did not reply or even look up. He was slowly sinking, his wings barely moving. He might well follow his brother. Stephano and Viola flew close, hovered near.

"Sergeant Droal!" Stephano shouted angrily.

The dragon turned his head to look up at him.

"Your brother died a hero," Stephano said. "His name will be honored in the rolls of heroes of the Brigade. But this fight is not over! Lives hang in the balance. I need you to carry a message to Lieutenant Dag."

Droal blinked, and for a moment Stephano feared he had lost him. Then the massive dragon's head snapped up. Blood covered his chest and neck, his scales were burned, but he was still flying.

"Sad later. Duty now."

Stephano smiled. "Tell the lieutenant an enemy ship is attacking the fortress and I'm going to go help them."

"Yes, Captain!" Droal hesitated, then added, "Thank you, Captain. Hroal died proud."

The dragon soared into the midst of the storm and the raging battle.

Stephano gave his orders to Viola; as they flew toward the fortress he thought of Rodrigo. He would be terrified; Master Tutillo, the boy who wanted to be a dragon rider, had never been in combat before; Miri and Gythe were there, too; and so were his mother and the Princess Sophia, who would be looking to the fortress as a safe haven.

"Fly as fast as you can!" Stephano ordered Viola.

He hunkered down in the saddle as the dragon spread her wings and the wind and rain rushed over him.

Sad later. Duty now.

That could be the motto of the Brigade this day.

39

In mathematical terms, one could say that the seventh sigil is God plus Man equals Magic. Without the seventh sigil, the equation is Magic divided by Man minus God equals destruction.

—Father Jacob Northrop, *Notes from Prison*

Rodrigo stood on the second story parapet that encircled the fortress just below the bridge that jutted out at a right angle from the side of the beehive-like fort. A single window on the bridge allowed the helmsman to view his surroundings and take readings. Rodrigo's head was about level with the bottom of the window.

He examined the construct he and his crew of crafter masons had carved onto the stone wall.

The fortress already had protective magical constructs designed by Father Antonius, now of the Arcanum. Rodrigo and the masons had been impressed with the priest's work. Even after all these years, though the magical constructs he had inscribed were weakened—as was happening to all magical constructs these days—they hadn't been significantly damaged. Indeed, Rodrigo noted that they had survived better than most constructs were surviving these days.

The crafters were dubious about the new construct, which was extremely simple in design, consisting of a circle formed by the six basic sigils on top and their mirror images on the bottom.

The masons could not understand why they were told to carve the six sigils backward. Rodrigo had said this was modern thinking, all the rage at court instead of telling them the simple truth, that the constructs were contramagic. If he had told them that, he would have faced a revolt. Rodrigo said the seventh sigil was his own design, a magical theory he was testing.

The masons had sent their foreman to protest to Captain de Guichen that Rodrigo's construct wouldn't work and was, in their professional opinion, a waste of valuable time. Stephano had curtly told them they were to follow Rodrigo's instructions without question or they would all find themselves reduced in rank and pay. He had been so grim and so formidable that the foreman had retired precipitously. There were no more complaints after that.

Rodrigo had been so busy trying to repair the damaged constructs in other critical parts of the fortress, such as those that operated the cannons, that he had not had the time to see if the seventh sigil construct was surviving the barrage of contramagic from the drumming. The cannons were now as good as they were ever going to be, which meant they might or might not fire.

Given the devastating effect the drumming was having on magical constructs throughout the fortress, Rodrigo was concerned about the amount of damage the seventh sigil had sustained. Stephano had ordered him to activate it, on the chance the fortress might come under attack.

"I don't think that will happen," Stephano had said soothingly, seeing Rodrigo go quite pale. "The dragons will keep the Bottom Dwellers occupied; they'll be fighting for their lives. But since you added the construct in order to protect the bridge, you might check to see if it works."

Rodrigo frowned at the construct carved in the wall. Not being able to work the magic with his mind like a savant, he would have to touch the sigil to activate it. He had told the crafters to carve the uppermost sigil in the circle close to the parapet, so that all he had to do was lean over the low wall and put his hand on that sigil.

He regarded the wet wall with distaste, then heaved a sigh and braced himself, and was about to do his part for king and country by sacrificing his last clean shirt, when he was joined by Master Tutillo, lugging a tarp.

"I thought you could use this, sir."

"Bless you, lad! You know what I need before I need it," Rodrigo remarked. "Just fling that over the wall, will you?"

Master Tutillo spread the tarp over the wall.

"Do you mind if I stay to watch, sir?"

"Be my guest," said Rodrigo, studying the construct.

"What does it do?" Master Tutillo asked, leaning over the roof to see.

"It is supposed to protect the bridge in case we're attacked," said Rodrigo. "Stephano says an attack isn't the least bit likely, but he thought it well to be prepared."

"Good idea," said Master Tutillo. "If he and Lieutenant Dag and the dragons are all killed, the enemy would throw everything they had at us."

Rodrigo stared at the young man in shock.

"You . . . you don't think that's likely, do you?" Rodrigo asked, shaken.

"Well, you never know, do you, sir? Just as well to be prepared," said Master Tutillo cheerfully.

Rodrigo looked out toward the battle. He couldn't see much, given the smoke and the first rain squalls of an advancing wizard storm. Sometimes he could see a dragon or an enemy ship, but mostly it was orange fire and green beams flaring among the clouds. Rodrigo had no idea who was winning. He was reminded of the terrible time during the failed revolution when he had waited for Stephano to return from battle. He remembered vividly the news that his friend was lost and presumed dead.

He shook off the unhappy memory and dropped down flat on the tarp. Stretching out his hand, he touched the very top sigil, which was the sigil of fire done backward. He spoke words of contramagic that Father Jacob had taught him and felt the energy flow through him and into the construct.

"I've never seen anything like that, sir!" said Master Tutillo in awe. "How do you make the magic glow green?"

"Do you have some magic in you, Master Tutillo?" Rodrigo asked.

"I'm a fair channeler, sir. Our parish priest wanted me to go to school to study it, but I never wanted to do anything except sail the Breath. My father was captain of the *Glow Worm* until he got his leg blowed off by a cannonball in the battle of Blue Angel. A captain friend of his offered to take me on. I've never seen green magic . . . Wait!"

Master Tutillo stared at Rodrigo with wide eyes. "Yes, I have! The weapons those fiends use shoot balls of fire and it's green! Is that devil magic, sir?"

"There is no such thing as 'devil' magic," said Rodrigo.

The working of the magic made him feel better, warmed away the chill of the fear in his gut. He watched as the green contramagic spread from one sigil to the other. He had no need to touch the six magic sigils. He reached down to touch the first magical sigil and spoke the word, "fire." They all began to glow blue.

That left only the seventh sigil.

"The one in the middle is still dark," said Master Tutillo.

"That's stating the bloody obvious," Rodrigo muttered.

He had expected the seventh sigil to light up with the others. It was in the center, where he couldn't reach it. A flaw in his planning, he had to concede.

"But, damn it, I thought it would work with the others. Why isn't it? It *must* be working. The rest of them aren't devouring each other."

Though he did notice they were starting to glow more faintly.

Rodrigo considered that seventh sigil and gnawed his lip. He rarely took anything in life seriously and that included religion. He enjoyed teasing the deeply devout Dag, who made no secret of the fact that he believed Rodrigo was damned for all eternity.

When it came to magic, he had always believed that it was rooted in science, and scoffed at those who claimed magic was miraculous. But then Father Jacob had revealed his discovery of the seventh sigil that allowed magic and contramagic to work in harmony, neither destroying the other. Father Jacob had said the seventh sigil was God. Rodrigo was certain he would eventually come up with a scientific explanation, but at the moment he couldn't.

"Must I pray over it?" Rodrigo had asked the priest. "No offense, Father, but I haven't said a prayer since I was a prattling lad at Nanny's knee. I'm afraid God would hear me and burst out into a hearty guffaw."

"Say what is in your heart," Father Jacob had replied, smiling. "God or science. It's all the same."

Rodrigo had his doubts about that. Still, he didn't seem to have much choice and he had the feeling that if he gave the matter some thought and sorted it all out, the priest might actually be right. Rodrigo nervously considered a prayer that wouldn't cause God to smite him with a thunderbolt, and he thought of his friends out there in the battle, fighting for their lives. Rodrigo said the words he had said long years ago during that last terrible battle, when he was waiting for Stephano.

"Bring them home."

The seventh sigil began to glow with a shimmering blue-green radiance.

"You did it, sir!" Master Tutillo cried triumphantly. He looked expectantly at Rodrigo. "What does it do?"

Rodrigo gazed at the construct. "Damned if I know."

"Don't worry, sir," said Master Tutillo. "Captain de Guichen and the Dragon Brigade will send those fiends to the bottom of the world. Except I guess we are at the bottom of the world, aren't we? Never thought about that before. Would you like a cup of tea laced with a little Calvados, sir?"

"I would love one," said Rodrigo gratefully. "Except just leave the tea out, will you? I'll be in my room."

Master Tutillo dashed off. The tarp having offered only minimal protection, Rodrigo went to change his muddy, wet shirt. He was walking down the shadowy, dimly lit corridor, heading for his room, when he thought he saw a flash of blue-green light slither along on the wall.

Rodrigo glanced at it, startled. The light vanished. He shrugged and went back to wondering if he would be able to clean the mud off the lace of his shirt cuffs. A flash of the same color appeared right in front of him, shining from a construct on the interior wall.

"That's odd," Rodrigo remarked.

He stopped to examine the wall, but the glow had vanished and, with all the various constructs covering the stone, he couldn't tell which had been glowing.

He walked on, keeping a watch for blue-green flashes,

and saw them again, going off seemingly at random, appearing and then disappearing.

Maybe something to do with that bloody drumming, he thought grimly. It's playing merry hell with the magic and giving me the most frightful headache.

Master Tutillo arrived with Calvados and news. "Lookout's spotted the *Cloud Hopper,* sir. Sailing this way."

"Thank God!" Rodrigo exclaimed. He glanced up at heaven, thinking he should explain. "I'm not really taking Your name in vain, this time. I truly mean it."

He drank off the Calvados at a gulp and between the liquor and the return of the *Cloud Hopper,* he felt better. Half a prayer answered.

Rodrigo made a dash for the parapet. Standing in the shadow of the bridge, he looked out over the sodden and depressing landscape. "The *Cloud Hopper*! Where is it? I don't see her."

The lookout was watching through a spyglass. "Caught a glimpse of the boat, sir. Gone now. Lost her in the trees."

"Lost!" Rodrigo gasped.

"Lost sight of her, sir," said the lookout. "She's sailing too low. Looks like she's having difficulty maintaining altitude."

"The magic is breaking down," said Rodrigo unhappily. "Because of the drumming. Could you see who is on board?"

If Gythe was with them, she could repair the broken magic, at least enough to keep the little boat sailing.

The lookout shook his head. "No, sir. Sorry. Too far away."

Rodrigo heaved a sigh and paced back and forth along the wall. He saw a few more blue flashes from constructs on the walls and one on the ceiling. He was too preoccupied with worrying about his friends to go investigate.

"There she is, sir!" the lookout reported.

The *Cloud Hopper* was back in the air and now that he knew where to look, Rodrigo could see the sturdy little boat trundling along, dipping and bobbing just above tree level. The boat was sailing at an agonizingly slow speed, but at least she was sailing.

Gythe *must* be aboard! Rodrigo told himself. Aloud he asked the lookout, "Can you tell what's happening with the battle? Are we winning or losing?"

"Hard to see, sir," the lookout reported. "The smoke is too thick."

Rodrigo could do nothing except wait, and he had never been good at waiting. He thought back to the time he had waited for his duel with that Estaran count, knowing with terrible certainty that in a few hours he would be dead. He hadn't died. The count had died, killed by Sir Henry's hired assassin. The startling realization came to Rodrigo that the duel and events surrounding it had led them to this moment in time.

"How extraordinary," Rodrigo murmured.

He watched the *Cloud Hopper*'s faltering advance, willing the boat to keep going. The wizard storm, off in the distance, was crawling closer. He could hear rumbles of thunder. Master Tutillo hovered at his elbow, waiting for news.

"Four women on board!" reported the lookout.

"Let me see!" Rodrigo cried eagerly.

The lookout handed over his spyglass. Rodrigo put it to his eye and after swinging the glass around wildly and making himself dizzy, he eventually found the *Cloud Hopper.*

Rodrigo breathed a deep sigh of relief. "They all appear safe! Badly dressed, but safe!"

The lookout had been watching Rodrigo's gyrations

with alarm. He deftly removed the spyglass from his hand before Rodrigo could drop it.

"Master Tutillo, we are expecting the arrival of the Countess de Marjolaine and Her Royal Highness, the Princess Sophia—"

"The royal princess!" Master Tutillo repeated, staggering. "Coming here?"

"We will want a room made ready for her; refreshments, of course," Rodrigo continued. "What do we have in the larder? Ordinarily I would suggest champagne, tea cakes, sweetmeats, cucumber sandwiches . . ."

"We have salt pork, dried fish, hardtack, and Calvados, sir," said Master Tutillo. "I can show Her Highness how to knock the hardtack on the table to make the weevils jump out."

Rodrigo shuddered.

"Perhaps soaking the hardtack in Calvados . . . ," he began, only to find the young man had dashed off. He was wondering if there was some way he could make salt pork taste like duck à l'orange when a soldier shouted, "God's balls! Look at that!"

An enormous cloud of dust and smoke, shot through with flame, roiled into the sky over Dunlow, rising higher and higher. The gigantic boom from the blast hit them, sounding like an enormous, extremely close-by thunder clap. The men standing on the parapet began shouting and cheering.

All Rodrigo noticed was the sudden silence. The drumming. The drumming had stopped.

"Captain's done it!" the soldiers were shouting exultantly. "He blew up the temple!"

Rodrigo breathed a deep sigh. With the temple no longer spewing forth contramagic, the destruction of the magical constructs would cease, and he could start to make repairs. The work would take a long time, perhaps months, but at least there was hope they might someday be able to leave this godforsaken place and return home.

"What's all the bloody shouting about?" demanded Gunnery Officer Vega as he emerged from a door onto the parapet.

The gunnery officer was a short, stolid, humorless Guundaran mercenary who lived, breathed, and perhaps even ate gunpowder, or so Rodrigo believed. Stephano had left Vega in command during his absence. The soldiers told him about the temple. Vega viewed the cloud of dust and debris through a spyglass.

"Destroying the temple means we've won, doesn't it?" Rodrigo asked, hoping he was right. He nudged Vega's elbow, much to the man's ire. "Stephano—that is, Captain de Guichen, and the others will be back soon, won't they?"

"Not bloody likely!" Vega snorted.

"Why? Why not? What's wrong?" Rodrigo asked, alarmed.

"Still have the whole bloody invasion fleet to deal with," Vega muttered.

Rodrigo looked back to see the *Cloud Hopper* sailing slowly through the air. He could imagine Gythe nursing the magic, urging the boat to sail just a little farther. She would have an easier time of it now that the contramagic wasn't breaking down the constructs as fast as she could fix them.

Feeling a presence at his back, Rodrigo turned to see Master Tutillo, resplendent in his best parade uniform. He had even washed his face.

"How do I look, sir? I've always wanted to meet the princess. I saw her ride past in a carriage once. She smiled and waved at me. Will Her Highness let me kiss her hand?"

Rodrigo was so preoccupied by his concerns for the *Hopper* that he let this most unforgiveable breach of etiquette slip past him. He was watching the boat when the mists lifted and several of the lookouts called simultaneously.

"Enemy ship off the port bow! Closing rapidly!"

Every man with a spyglass clapped it to his eye. Officer Vega shouted orders and left the parapet in haste to return to his cannons. Men ran to their posts, bumping into Rodrigo. Having never learned his starboard from his port, he wasn't sure where to look. While he was searching for the enemy, he caught sight of the *Cloud Hopper* bobbing into the air to clear a stand of trees.

"Miri!" he gasped and pointed. "The *Cloud Hopper*! She's out there alone!"

The men shifted around to watch the little boat sailing with agonizing slowness toward the safety of the fortress. Rodrigo could see the enemy ship now, heading straight for the fortress. He didn't know one vessel from another so he had no idea what type of ship this was. All he knew was this ship was extremely large, it was flying a blood-red flag, and it was bearing down on them rapidly.

"We have to do something to help Miri! She can't fight back," Rodrigo cried. "We have to stop that ship!"

"We can't, sir," Master Tutillo said with maddening calm. "The enemy isn't in range of our guns yet."

"There must be something!" Rodrigo said helplessly.

Master Tutillo shook his head. "Sorry, sir. Maybe the enemy won't waste their ammunition shooting at an unarmed boat."

The hope seemed a faint one to Rodrigo. He wondered if Miri had seen the danger. His question was answered when he saw the *Cloud Hopper* began to radiate glowing blue light. Gythe was working her magic, activating the constructs that protected the boat. Her magic had worked the last time the *Hopper* had come under attack by the Bottom Dwellers, but then they had faced only the green fireballs. This enemy ship undoubtedly was carrying one of the fearsome green beam weapons that had taken out the side of a mountain. Rodrigo doubted if even Gythe's magic could protect against a direct hit of contramagic.

The *Cloud Hopper* lurched and jounced slowly toward safety. The ship with the red flag was rapidly closing in. A rumbling sound beneath Rodrigo's feet indicated the cannons were being run out. He wondered if this was a good idea. A blast of contramagic hitting the cannons would destroy their protective and strengthening constructs and most likely detonate the powder and cause them to explode.

Rodrigo had pointed this out to Stephano. "The cannons are as great a danger to us as they are to the enemy."

"If all goes as planned," Stephano had said, "we won't need the cannons."

But nothing had gone as planned.

He glanced at the seventh sigil, pulsing with a faint bluish green or greenish blue light.

"God or science, I could use the help of either right now," Rodrigo muttered.

"Oh, no, sir!" Master Tutillo gasped, clutching Rodrigo's arm. "Look!"

A green beam streaked across the sky and struck the *Cloud Hopper* amidships. Blue light flared, flashed, and then vanished. The *Cloud Hopper* dropped like a sparrow hit by a stone and disappeared among a stand of scrubby trees. A flicker of orange flame quickly became a conflagration. Smoke trailed upward.

Fire spread rapidly across the deck and climbed the masts, devouring the gaily colored balloon and feeding on the sails. For an instant, the *Cloud Hopper* seemed to be made of bright, blazing fire, with flames for the masts and sails. And then it all collapsed into a blackened heap of cinders and ashes and billowing smoke.

The *Cloud Hopper* was gone.

40

Blood magic gives us power over life and death, makes us gods.

—Anonymous

Several soldiers on the parapet began to fire their rifles at the enemy ship, more out of rage and frustration than with the hope of hitting anything, for the ship was still out of range.

A wave of nausea washed over Rodrigo. He leaned against the parapet until the spell passed, leaving him shivering with cold. He turned away and walked toward the stairs.

"Are you all right? Where are you going, sir?" Master Tutillo asked.

"To help them," said Rodrigo. "They could be hurt."

"Sir! You can't go out there, sir!" Master Tutillo cried, startled. "You'd be a sitting duck!"

"I found Stephano on the battlefield," Rodrigo replied. "He was dying. I can't leave them to die."

"No, sir! I won't let you!" Master Tutillo flung his arms around Rodrigo and yelled for help.

The feel of hands being laid roughly on his person brought Rodrigo to his senses. He gazed out at the wide stretch of empty marshland that lay between him and the place where the *Cloud Hopper* had gone down. The fire was a roaring inferno now, setting several of the nearby trees ablaze.

Rodrigo pushed away the hands, trying to free himself. "I'm not going anywhere. You can release me."

The soldier slowly let go of him.

Master Tutillo still kept hold of his sleeve.

"Are you sure you're not going to run off, sir?" he asked, eyeing Rodrigo doubtfully.

"I'm sure," said Rodrigo wearily.

He slid down the wall to sit on the floor and lowered his head to his hands.

"How will I tell Stephano? How will I tell Dag? I stood here and watched them die!" Rodrigo said in despair.

"Don't give up hope, sir," said Master Tutillo, who was squatting down beside him. "The ship is sailing on by, leaving them be. It's not shooting at them anymore."

That's because there's no one left alive to shoot at, Rodrigo thought. He was about to say this to Master Tutillo, when he took a good look at him. The young man was trying to be brave, but his eyes were red rimmed. He was pale, his lip quivered. Rodrigo managed a faint smile and pulled himself up off the floor. He smoothed his hair, adjusted the cuffs of his sleeves, and twitched his coat into place.

"You should find some place to hunker down, sir, keep yourself safe," said the lookout. "We're going to be coming under fire soon."

He sounded very cool at the prospect.

"I might be needed," said Rodrigo. "To repair the magic."

"You can't stay here, sir," said Master Tutillo. "You should go to the bridge. It's protected and you can see what's happening from there."

"That's true," Rodrigo said. He started off, then realized Master Tutillo wasn't with him. He turned around. "Aren't you coming?"

"I have my orders," said Master Tutillo. "Don't worry, sir! Our gun crews are the best in the navy. We'll blast the fiends out of the sky. Send her straight to kingdom come."

Rodrigo didn't like thinking about kingdom come, which might be coming far too soon. He left the parapet and made his way to the bridge. The helmsman wasn't there. Since the fortress was not sailing, he wasn't needed and must have duties elsewhere. Rodrigo located the helmsman's spyglass and put it to his eye. He looked for the *Cloud Hopper.* All he could see was a charred, burnt-out wreck.

Rodrigo's mouth was dry and his hands shook. He had to lower the glass because tears were stinging his eyes.

He couldn't find a handkerchief and so he wiped his eyes with his shirtsleeve and raised the glass again to see the enemy ship, a big hulking vessel covered in some sort of strange-looking constructs. At first Rodrigo thought they were contramagic, but then he realized that they weren't, because he recognized them. He looked at the blood-red flag and went cold all over.

"Blood magic!"

He was jolted by the unexpected boom of the cannons firing a broadside and the shaking of the building beneath his feet as the twelve cannons went off simultaneously. Smoke drifted past the window and the acrid smell of gunpowder filled the air.

He put the glass to his eye again and looked out, hoping to see the ship blow up or fall out of the sky, or do whatever enemy ships did when they were hit. He watched in despair, his hopes dashed. The ship kept coming straight for them. He dimly recalled Officer Vega saying something about having to find their range.

Unfortunately, the enemy had found his range.

A brilliant beam of green light flashed through the air and struck the fortress. Rodrigo couldn't see where it had hit, but he could feel the building shudder like a living thing.

The seventh sigil on the wall right below the bridge flared brightly—radiating green and blue light. Flashes of blue light flickered on the stone walls, running along the protective constructs that had been built into the stone. Rodrigo was cheered by the sight. The shield was working just as he had planned, protecting the fortress. But when he looked around, his good mood evaporated. The constructs on the walls that had been battered by the drumming were being destroyed by the blast of contramagic. He could see the cracks spreading as he watched. Some of the constructs simply disappeared.

He reached out to repair them and then let his hand fall. What was the use? Magical constructs were breaking down all over the fort. He could not rush about repairing them all. The next green beam blast or the one after that would bring the fortress down around their ears.

Rodrigo started to turn away, then he stopped, blinked and rubbed his eyes. He dropped to his hands and knees to stare intently at the constructs on the wall. He touched them with his fingers, marveling, and then sat back on his heels to consider his discovery.

The broken part of the constructs were glowing with a blue-green light so faint it was barely visible. He would not have noticed the change if he hadn't been staring straight at it. He leaped to his feet and looked outside to see the seventh sigil shining blue-green. He looked back at the construct. There was only one explanation. The magic from the seventh sigil was seeping through the broken constructs, rebuilding them, making them whole.

Rodrigo felt his knees go weak and he sat down rather

suddenly in the helmsman's chair. Father Jacob had made a scientific breakthrough, much like early man's discovery that sigils could be combined to form a construct. Forces seemingly bent on destroying each other had joined together to nourish and restore.

Another broadside shook the walls and sent a cascade of dust down on Rodrigo's head, but he scarcely reacted, other than to irritably brush the dust out of his eyes so he could watch the constructs. The blue-green magic moved slowly, almost a trickle, like water seeping through a hair-thin crack. He wondered if the magical repairs were happening in other parts of the fortress or just on the bridge. He recalled, suddenly, the odd blue-green flashes he had seen on the walls. He had not paid much attention, but now he wondered if those had been signs of the seventh sigil at work.

Completely forgetting the fortress was under fire, Rodrigo left the bridge, ran down the stairs and into the corridor. He was planning to go to the lower level near the gun emplacements. The magic had been badly damaged there and he wanted to see if the seventh sigil was repairing it.

A horrific blast shook the fortress, and the next thing he knew, he was lying on the floor with no clear memory of how he'd come to be there. His head hurt abominably, he couldn't see for the dust and the smoke and he was having trouble breathing as he coughed and retched, which made his head hurt more. Terrible screams of the wounded and dying echoed through the corridor.

Rodrigo staggered to his feet. The screams tore at his heart. He should go help, but he had no idea which way to go. Nothing looked the same. The corridor was choked with dust. He stumbled off in one direction, only to find his way blocked by a pile of rubble; so he turned around and walked in the other direction.

Soldiers covered in dust and blood, looking like ghosts, shoved past him, while the screaming went on and on . . . until suddenly it stopped. Rodrigo eventually made his way back to the stairs that led to the bridge. He climbed them slowly, hanging on to the rail, trying not to pass out. He made it to the bridge and looked out the window. Flames were shooting out of what had once been a gun emplacement and was now a cavernous hole.

The enemy ship was in front of the fort, hovering above the ruined guard towers on the top. Rodrigo could look up and see the keel above him. Smoke poured out of a gaping hole.

A few soldiers with rifles were sniping at the ship from the parapets. The fiendish soldiers on the ship were firing back, raining green fire balls down on the walls. Rodrigo waited in a kind of dazed terror for the green beam to shoot again and kill them all.

The ship didn't fire at them. Rodrigo found that odd. He watched the ship with a horrible fascination and realized after a moment that it was descending, drifting down to the ground. The ship had caught fire and was going to land.

"Monsieur Rodrigo! Where are you? Monsieur!"

Someone was calling him, and he realized the person had been calling his name for quite some time.

"I'm here, on the bridge!" Rodrigo shouted, wincing in pain.

He heard someone running up the stairs, then Master Tutillo burst through the door. He was covered in dust, his uniform was torn and smeared with blood, and his face beneath the dust was white. He was carrying a rifle that was as tall as he was. The stock bumped along the ground.

"Officer Vega is dead!" he gasped.

Rodrigo wondered with a sick feeling in his gut if it was Vega who had been screaming. "I'm sorry—"

"That means I am in command!" Master Tutillo blurted out. He was trembling. He repeated the words as though attempting to convince himself of the reality. "I am in command."

"Merciful heavens!" Rodrigo exclaimed, shaken.

Stephano had once attempted to explain the various ranks. A midshipman was an officer, hoping someday to be promoted to lieutenant. With Vega dead, Master Tutillo, at age fourteen, was now the only officer in the fortress and that meant he was in command.

Rodrigo realized the young man was looking to him for reassurance.

"I am certain you will do fine," he said, not knowing what else to say. Congratulations on his promotion didn't seem to be in order.

"Thank you, sir," said Master Tutillo with a gulp. "I hope so."

The boy pulled himself together. Carefully resting the rifle against the wall, he straightened, threw back his shoulders and then, with an air of authority, walked over to the window. He even managed to deepen his voice.

"I came to reconnoiter, sir. That means to see what the enemy ship is doing."

"It's landing," said Rodrigo.

Master Tutillo looked out, and his eyes widened. His voice cracked. "It's landing!"

"Coming down almost on top of us," Rodrigo remarked.

"Look at that, sir!" Master Tutillo cried excitedly. "See the hole in her hull? Her lift tanks are failing. We sunk her, by God!"

He paused a moment and added with a terrible calm, "The fiends are going to try to take the fort."

Ranks of soldiers formed up on the decks, preparing to abandon the sinking ship and swarm into the fortress. Their uniforms were red, not like the demonic armor. They were not carrying the long guns they had been using against the soldiers on the parapets. They were now armed with curved-blade swords. A body covered in blood lay on the deck beside the green beam weapon. Near the body stood a man dressed in a red surcoat and cloak, carrying the same type of curved-blade sword as the others. He was giving the orders.

"Swords!" Master Tutillo scoffed. "No soldier fights with a sword anymore. We'll make short work of these fiends—"

"They're not soldiers," said Rodrigo, his voice tight. He was sick with horror. "They are blood mages."

"Huh?" Master Tutillo stared at him. "What's that?"

The ship lowered a gangplank, and the blood mages began to descend. Rodrigo shrank back with a sickening sense of dread. He looked into the sky, past the ship, hoping against hope to see Stephano flying to the rescue.

Shots rang out. Riflemen posted in the ruins of the guard towers were firing at the green beam weapon in an attempt to disable it. A red fog billowed out from the ship, spewing from iron tubes set with crystal panels on the deck. The fog had the effect of hiding the ship and the green beam weapon, making it difficult for the fort's soldiers to find a target.

The green beam shot out from the red fog and hit the guns guarding the main docks. The blast blew up a chunk of wall, knocked out the cannons, and rocked the bridge. Rodrigo caught hold of Master Tutillo, who nearly tumbled into the helm. The air was thick with smoke and dust and a noxious odor from the red fog. Rodrigo coughed and wiped his eyes.

As the riflemen continued to shoot into the fog, hoping for a lucky hit, the enemy fired the green beam again. It streaked through the red cloud toward the iron-banded wooden doors on the dock below. Rodrigo braced himself as a brilliant flash of blue light lit the interior of the bridge and the fortress shivered. The doors held.

The magical shield was working to protect them, at least for the time being. But the green beam was like a battering ram; all they had to do was keep firing. Eventually the shield would fall and the Blood Mage and his troops would enter the fortress.

"I have to go, sir," Master Tutillo said, heading for the door. "The men will be going to guard the doors, preparing to repel the invaders. I need to be there—"

"Good God, no!" Rodrigo cried. "You have to order the men back. Tell them to run—"

"Retreat in the face of the enemy? Never, sir!" said Master Tutillo indignantly.

"I wouldn't use the term 'retreat,' " Rodrigo said nervously. "Leaving by the back door. Not the same thing at all. Stephano and I have done it when occasion demanded."

"We can't let the enemy seize the fortress, sir," Master Tutillo pointed out. "How would we get back home?"

"You're right," Rodrigo said. "The problem is . . ."

He tried to think how best to explain. "Those men are blood mages. The more people they kill, the more powerful they become."

"We have rifles, sir," said Master Tutillo patiently, as though talking to a child. "They just have those funny swords—"

"They have magic! Blood magic!" said Rodrigo. He couldn't make this lad understand. He made up his mind. "Our men can't fight that. At least not by conventional means. I have to stop them."

He left the bridge and ran down the stairs. The green beam must have fired again, because he felt the walls shake. Master Tutillo grabbed his rifle and came pounding after him.

"Sir, you can't!"

Rodrigo halted just inside the stairwell and peered cautiously out the door. Across the hall were the officers' quarters. The main dock was down the corridor and to his right. A blast, coming from that direction, shook the floor and the walls and knocked Rodrigo off his feet. He toppled backward, landing on his rump on the stairs. Master Tutillo tumbled over him and went sprawling, dropping the rifle. The corridor filled with smoke and debris rained down on top of them.

When the building quit shaking, Rodrigo checked himself quickly for injuries and found nothing serious. His head still hurt, but apparently gut-clenching fear was an effective medicine; that pain seemed to have receded. Master Tutillo was on his hands and knees, searching for the rifle in the smoke.

"Sir! You should go back to the bridge!" Master Tutillo urged.

Rodrigo ignored him. He peered out to survey the damage.

The main doors leading to the dock were gone, blown apart, along with a portion of the wall and the ceiling. He could see sunlight filtering through the dust and the smoke. Soldiers had taken up positions behind the large piles of rubble, aiming their muskets at the entryway. They were calm, confident. They had plenty of ammunition and would be firing at point-blank range.

"They have no idea of the nightmare that is about to walk through that door," Rodrigo said. "And I can't tell them."

Now that he was here, he had to face facts. He could urge these men to flee, but they wouldn't listen to him. Why should they? He was, after all, the captain's foolish friend, the foppish gentleman who whined over the bad food and worried about soiling his lace.

"Sir, if you won't go to the bridge, go to the storage

room. My boys can deal with the fiends," Master Tutillo said proudly.

The blood guard marched down the gangplank, armed with their "funny" swords. They wore leather armor, probably made from the skin of their victims, and they were covered head to toe with magical constructs. They had no helms and their bald heads were marked with constructs. Before they left the ship, each man dipped his hand into the blood of the sacrifice and smeared it on his face.

The Blood Mage led them. His hands and face were bloody, his cloak and surcoat covered with intricate magical patterns. Rodrigo thought he could see the magic glowing a lurid red, but that might be his terrified imagination.

"Please! Order the men to retreat," Rodrigo begged Master Tutillo.

The lad shook his head. "I can't do that, sir."

He started walking toward the gaping hole in the wall.

Rodrigo ran after him and caught hold of him by the cravat he wore around his neck, half choking him. He dragged the young man kicking and protesting into a corridor directly across from the main dock, near the officers' quarters. Crouching behind the wreck of a door, Rodrigo pulled the angry and indignant Master Tutillo down with him and held on to him.

The soldiers opened fire, and the bullets hit the armor of the Blood Guard, knocking some down, but doing little damage. They kept coming. The soldiers reloaded, glancing at one another uncertainly. They had never faced a foe like this. Master Tutillo quit struggling. He looked questioningly at Rodrigo.

"Blood magic," Rodrigo answered.

The soldiers fired another volley. Bullets struck the blood mages, wounding some and killing others. The blood mages smeared their hands with their own blood or that of their comrades and marched on.

The Blood Mage seemed impervious to bullets. He fairly crackled with magic, brushing off bullets as if they were annoying gnats. He strode through the rubble, stepping over fallen beams and twisted iron, kicking aside splintered boards.

One of the soldiers stood up, aimed his rifle at point-blank range at the Blood Mage's head. Before he could fire, the Blood Mage lifted his hand, and the rifle barrel burned red hot, forcing the soldier to drop it with a cry. The Blood Mage made a backhanded slash with his sword across the soldier's neck, nearly severing the head from the body and sending blood spurting from the gruesome wound.

Seeing his comrade lying dead at his feet, another soldier tried to run. The Blood Mage pointed at him, and red magic snaked out and wrapped around the soldier's legs, tripping him. He fell on his back on the blood-covered floor. The Blood Mage slashed open his gut, exposing his entrails, as the soldier screamed in agony.

Rodrigo had seen enough. He knew what had to be done; he was the only one who could do it. He caught hold of Master Tutillo, who was crouched beside him, white faced, his lips quivering.

"Where are the rest of the men?"

Master Tutillo didn't answer. He was staring at the Blood Mage, who was lathering himself in the blood of the dying soldier. Behind him, the rest of the Blood Guard was now entering the fortress. They cut down soldiers with their swords or bound them with hideous magicks, and within mere moments, the troops defending the door were either dead or horribly dying.

Rodrigo grabbed Master Tutillo, hauled him to his feet, and ran for the interior door that led from the officers' quarters to the enormous chamber where the dragons sheltered. Feeling exposed in the cavernous room, he ducked into the privies and closed the door.

Master Tutillo stumbled along beside him. He seemed in a horror-stricken daze.

Rodrigo gave the boy a shake. "The rest of the men! Where are they? Master Tutillo, you are in command. These men are depending on you. *I'm* depending on you!"

Master Tutillo gulped and shivered. "There are twenty-two men with the cannons and six manning the gun emplacements, plus Cook and his helpers . . ."

"Order all of them to leave the fortress!" said Rodrigo urgently. "They can run for the caves in the mountain where the dragons were living."

"They won't want to go, sir," said Master Tutillo.

"You are in command. You have to make them obey you," said Rodrigo sternly. "You've seen for yourself what will happen to them."

"Yes, sir," said Master Tutillo in a whisper. He started off, then turned back. "Aren't you coming with me?"

"No," said Rodrigo. "They have to be stopped."

He could still hear screams of the dying men from the main entrance. He tried to blot out the sound.

"How are you going to do that, sir?" Master Tutillo demanded. "You have to tell me. I'm in charge."

Rodrigo didn't answer. He opened the door, looked out. The dragon room was empty. The Blood Mage and his fiends were busy torturing and killing, enhancing their magical power. He shut the door.

"The way is clear. You should go."

"Not until you tell me, sir," said Master Tutillo stubbornly.

Rodrigo drew in a deep breath, wiped the sweat from his face with the sleeve of Stephano's shirt.

"I'll be in the powder magazine."

Master Tutillo didn't understand at first and then he gasped. "Sir! You can't!"

"It's only a bluff," said Rodrigo. "I won't really do it. Now, you have to go. We're running out of time."

Master Tutillo cast an agonized glance at Rodrigo and then he flung open the door to the privies and ran off. Rodrigo heard his footfalls echo down the corridor.

He looked out the door again. Seeing no sign of the Blood Guard, he made a dash for the powder magazine. Reaching it, he found it was locked.

"Bloody hell!" Rodrigo muttered.

He forced himself to calm down and think. Making one's way in court depended not only on who you knew, but what you knew about them. Locked doors, locked desks, locked diaries. Rodrigo had learned to open them all. He removed the lantern hanging from the wall and shone it on the lock. It was only a simple padlock, with no magical spells to interfere.

He twitched his fingers, muttered a few words. Blue sparks hit the lock and it clicked open. Rodrigo entered the powder magazine. His nose wrinkled at the smell. The light from the lantern revealed barrels of gunpowder stacked on one side of the chamber; rifles and other weapons were arranged on the opposite side.

Outside, the screaming had stopped. The Blood Mage would be on the prowl, but it would take him time before he found this place.

Rodrigo shut the door and hung the lantern from a hook on the wall. He had work to do.

41

It has been my experience that heroes are those who bloody well do what damn well needs to be done.

—Admiral Randolph Baker

Miri yanked open the door that led to the deck of the *Cloud Hopper.* She had prepared herself for the worst, but not for this—flames spreading across the deck and the brass helm in ruins.

The *Cloud Hopper* had suffered a direct hit from the green beam weapon. The moment Miri had sighted the enemy ship, she'd ordered the others to the safety of the hold below. She had stayed at the helm as long as she could, nursing the *Cloud Hopper* along, running below deck just before the green beam struck, and slamming the door shut behind her.

The little boat had withstood the blow far better than she expected. Gythe's magical protection spells had done their work, keeping the boat in one piece, even though the hull was staved in, saving the women huddled below deck. In the end, however, the contramagic had overwhelmed Gythe's spell, causing the magic to fail, and the *Cloud Hopper* had gone down. Fortunately it had not been sailing very high off the ground, and it landed with a thud in a tangle of scrub trees and bushes. The four women had been knocked around a bit in the landing, but were otherwise unhurt.

"I can . . . put out the fire," said Gythe.

She raised her hands, preparing to cast a spell that would smother the flames. Miri drew in a breath, closed her eyes, and crushed her hand over Gythe's.

"No," Miri said. "Let it burn."

Gythe stared at her in dismay.

"The Blood Mage is on that boat," Miri said harshly. "We have to make him think he killed us or he will try again. We will use the smoke as cover to escape."

Miri turned and made her way through the smoke to Cecile and Sophia, who were waiting in the same cabin where Dag and Stephano had once hung their hammocks. The hammocks lay rolled up in a corner. Miri looked away. Smoke was rolling through the open door and wafting down the corridor.

"We are abandoning ship," Miri said crisply. "We have to leave now. Gythe will guide you."

She indicated her sister, who was crouched in the doorway, beckoning to them as she covered her nose and mouth against the smoke.

"Go along, Your Highness," said Cecile. "I will be right behind you."

Sophia made her way to Gythe, who grabbed her hand and pulled her up onto the deck. Cecile took a moment to squeeze Miri's hand in silent sympathy, then she left, hurrying after the princess.

Miri took a last look around the boat that was alive with memories of her friends: Dag's thundering snore, Stephano's laugh, Rodrigo's complaining, Doctor Ellington yowling from the storage closet. Her eyes filled with tears and she dashed them away, muttering about the smoke, and returned to the deck.

Only the starboard side was on fire. The flames were spreading, but not very rapidly.

Cecile and Sophia had climbed safely over the rail and were waiting for them, hidden among the broken tree branches. The ground was soft and wet, part of the marshland that lapped up against the bedrock of the mountain. They stood up to their ankles in muck.

The Blood Mage's ship was sailing slowly above them. Miri could not see the green beam weapon, but she could not take the chance that they might fire again.

"Go join the countess and Sophia," Miri told her. "Stay with them."

Gythe shook her head. "I can't lose you, too!" she said, her newfound voice shaky and uncertain.

"You haven't lost me," said Miri. "I'll be along. First, I have to spread the fire."

"Our home!" Gythe said bleakly.

"It's only a boat," said Miri, shrugging.

Gythe cast her an unhappy glance. She started to leave, then turned back.

"What about him?" She pointed to Xavier's corpse that lay on the forecastle, shrouded in a blanket.

Miri shook her head. They would be lucky to escape without trying to lug the body with them. Wherever Xavier was, he would understand.

Gythe made her way along the canting deck and climbed over the rail. Miri dashed back down below. Running to the kitchen, coughing in the smoke, she grabbed up a bottle of Calvados, and ran back on deck. She flung the liquor about. The fire drank it thirstily.

The flames spread to the mast and crawled upward, igniting the balloon. Smoldering shreds of silk began to rain down on the deck, and the flames licked at the cloak covering Xavier's body. She doused the corpse with the remainder of the Calvados—a fitting Trundler burial—

spoke a brief blessing, and watched as the flames began to consume it.

She stayed on the *Cloud Hopper* as long as she could, coughing and choking in the thick smoke, reluctant to leave. When the hem of her skirt caught fire, she knew she had to go. She clambered up onto the rail and jumped, landing in the muck on her hands and knees.

Now fully engulfed in flame, the *Cloud Hopper*'s last act was to protect those who had sailed her, hiding them from view of the enemy with thick, roiling clouds of black smoke.

The Blood Mage's ship sailed on past them. The green beam fired again, but not at them. It was aimed at the fortress.

The four women huddled beneath the trees and took stock of their situation.

"The fortress is under attack. We won't find refuge there," said Cecile.

"The fort will hold," said Miri. "They'll repel the attack."

"You don't know that, my dear," said Cecile gently. "Think what the Blood Mage would do if he got hold of Sophia and your sister . . ."

Miri pressed her lips together. Rodrigo was inside that fortress, and so was young Master Tutillo. It would hold. But as if to confirm Cecile's words, an explosion shook the ground, and smoke and flame belched out of the side of the fortress. The green beam had hit one of the gun emplacements.

"We can go to the caves in the mountains," said Miri, reluctantly agreeing. "We'll be safe there."

The women started their trek over the soggy ground, heading toward the mountain. Miri paused to cast one last look back at the *Cloud Hopper*. The boat was now little more than a blackened skeleton, lying on its side, smoke and flames pouring from the hull. She turned her back and kept going.

The mud spattered their skirts and sucked at their boots, sapping their strength. Luckily, though, they did not have to go far, before they struck solid ground, the stony feet of the mountain. Gythe came to a sudden halt and dragged Miri to a stop.

"What is it?" Miri asked, alarmed.

Gythe pointed to the fortress, to a magical construct on the wall, shining bright blue and green.

"Rodrigo did that," said Miri, hoping with all her heart that he was somewhere safe, perhaps hiding in the storage room with Doctor Ellington and Bandit. "He calls it the seventh sigil. Papa Jake taught him."

"The magic is very powerful," said Gythe, gazing at the construct with wide, solemn eyes. "I wonder what it does."

"Not even Rigo knew for certain," said Miri.

They gave the fortress a wide berth, heading for the caves. They lost sight of the ship, which had landed on the ground, and they had no idea what was happening. They heard another massive explosion and then there was silence. Reaching the entrance to one of the caves, they stopped, looking at one another in consternation, not knowing if the silence boded good or ill.

"Maybe they blew up the Blood Mage's ship," said Sophia hopefully.

"No," said Miri. "Look at that."

A rocket soared into the air, trailing flame, and burst over the fortress in a ball of yellow.

"A distress signal," said Cecile.

"Soldiers coming!" Gythe warned.

"They're ours," said Miri, after a moment. "I recognize the uniforms. They'll tell us what has happened."

"*I* can tell you what has happened," said Cecile softly. "They're in retreat."

The soldiers had been in full flight, seemingly, for their coats were awry, their stockings ripped, their hats missing. But they had slowed to a dismal walk, their heads down, their shoulders slumped. In the lead was a big man wearing his uniform coat over his apron. His round, usually jovial face was grim. He wore a rifle slung across his shoulder and moved doggedly, looking back constantly at the fortress.

"Cook, what is going on?" Miri called.

He stopped dead, reaching for his rifle.

"Cook, it's me! Miri!" she said.

His eyes bulged, then his face broke into a smile.

"Mistress Miri! We saw your boat go down. We thought you were dead!" Cook walked forward to shake her hand. He glanced at the other women and made a little bow. "Ladies."

"What has happened?" Miri asked. "Where are you going?"

"We've been ordered to the caves," said Cook, adding with a scowl, "I don't like it, running from the enemy, but orders is orders. You ladies best come with us. The fort's not safe. The demons got inside. They've butchered our boys. They aim to escape in the fortress, sail off with it, leastwise that's what Master Tutillo says. He and the captain's friend, the foppish gentleman, are going to try to stop the fiends."

"Rodrigo!" Miri gasped. "He's there? With the Blood Mage? How is he going to stop him?"

"Danged if I know," said Cook, shaking his head.

"He can't fight them alone," said Miri. "Gythe, take the countess and Her Highness to the caves."

"You're going to help Rigo, aren't you?" Gythe said accusingly.

"I am. And, no, you can't come with me. You have to stay with Sophia."

Gythe started to argue, saw Miri's grim expression, and fell silent.

"Orders be damned!" said Cook. "We'll go back with you!"

"No, you will not, sir," said Cecile. "This young lady is Her Royal Highness, Princess Sophia of Rosia. I am her guardian, the Countess Cecile de Marjolaine. Her Highness has just escaped from an enemy prison. She requires your protection. Miri, you will need this."

She handed Miri the dragon pistol. The amazed soldiers, after staring blankly at the princess, provided Miri with powder and shot. She loaded the pistol, then tucked the bullets and the powder horn into her pockets.

"Stephano will come," said Gythe.

Miri looked back over her shoulder at the battle raging above the city. She saw a confusion of burning ships and dragons flying around them, green fireballs arcing through the air, green beams blasting.

Even if Stephano can leave his command, he won't, Miri thought. She didn't say this aloud, however. She smiled at Gythe and nodded agreement.

Gythe eyed her sister narrowly.

"You don't believe me. I know by that silly smile you wear when you're lying. I'm right. You'll see." Gythe tossed her head, her wet hair flipping around her shoulders.

"I liked you better when you couldn't talk," said Miri, laughing shakily.

She embraced her sister, holding her tight, then left, making her way among the rocks down to the fortress.

By the time Rodrigo had everything arranged, he was covered in grime and dirt and gunpowder. He had carefully removed his coat and laid it on a large metal chest. His shirt was ruined, as were his trousers. His stockings had long since met their end. He smelled of saltpeter. He sadly gazed at his hands—black with grime—and wondered if he would ever manage to clean them.

He had opened the door to the powder magazine a crack to hear what was going on in the fortress. A terrible scream sounded close by. He felt suddenly weak and he sat down on a metal gun case. He'd been trying to concentrate on his work to keep from hearing the screams and, what was worse, the sounds of voices raised in hideous chants.

The Blood Mage and his demonic forces were steeping themselves in blood, enhancing their power before advancing. They undoubtedly thought they were facing an army of soldiers who were preparing to stop them. But there were no soldiers. Only Rodrigo, armed with magic and chicanery.

"But those," Rodrigo said to himself, "are in the hands of a master."

He could regard his work with satisfaction and that was some comfort. The long trail of magical constructs leading to a cluster of gunpowder barrels looked quite impressive. He had altered the magical constructs in the lantern. That, too, was ready. Now all he had to do was wait and keep from throwing up.

The screaming stopped. The chanting continued for a moment, and then the voices fell silent. He had no idea what was happening, but he pictured the Blood Mage and his Blood Guard fanning out, searching for resistance.

When he heard the sound of footfalls coming down the corridor, his heart failed him. A hand pushed on the door. It opened, creaking on its hinges.

"Monsieur Rodrigo?" came a whisper. "Are you inside?"

"Master Tutillo!" Rodrigo gasped in relief. "What are

you doing here? You're supposed to be with the others in the caves."

"I'm in command of the fortress, sir," Master Tutillo replied, stepping into the lantern light. "I can't leave my post. You know that."

Rodrigo, usually so glib, found himself without words. The young man looked so very young. His best uniform, that he had put on to meet the princess, was covered in dust and dirt and blood. One sleeve was torn, his hair fell around his face and beads of sweat glistened across his upper lip.

"Can I help, sir?" Master Tutillo asked, looking about curiously.

"It would look more impressive if we pushed those barrels closer together," said Rodrigo. "I couldn't manage it on my own."

They pushed and shoved at the barrels filled with gunpowder until they stood clustered together in the center of the room.

"Did all the men leave safely?" Rodrigo asked as they worked.

"Only after I threatened Cook with a flogging," said Master Tutillo. "I sneaked a look at the enemy ship, sir. Her crew is transferring that green beam weapon to the fortress. And I did something else, sir. I set off a distress flare."

Rodrigo regarded Master Tutillo with admiration.

"An excellent idea! Stephano or Dag or someone will be sure to see it!" Rodrigo exclaimed eagerly.

Master Tutillo shook his head. "I think it's a long shot, sir, what with the dragons blasting fire and the ships burning and all. The captain would have to be looking this direction when the flare went up. But I thought it was worth a try."

"Good lad," said Rodrigo. "You've done an excellent job

as commander. Stephano—that is, Captain de Guichen—will be very proud of you."

"If something happens, if we lose the fight, I hope the captain will know I didn't abandon my post," said Master Tutillo with a little quaver in his voice.

"We haven't lost yet," said Rodrigo.

Master Tutillo was about to reply when, cocking his head, he whispered loudly, "Someone's coming!"

They could both hear booted feet of what sounded like several people moving slowly and cautiously down the corridor. Reaching the door to the powder magazine, they stopped. Two voices conferred in the Trundler language. Rodrigo couldn't understand them, but he could guess by the tone that they were questioning what was inside the room.

Rodrigo picked up the lantern. His mouth was so dry he had trouble speaking the words that would activate the constructs. He licked his lips and managed to get the words out. The lantern, that had been shining with a bright yellow light, began to glow a soft blue.

Master Tutillo set his jaw and stood ramrod straight, every inch the commander.

One of the Blood Guard kicked the door open and peered inside. Catching sight of the blue glow, he hissed something at his comrade and jumped back, expecting an ambush. When nothing happened, he cautiously entered the doorway and stopped to look around.

What he saw caused his eyes to first widen, then narrow suspiciously. Rodrigo was holding a blue glowing lantern near a great many barrels of gunpowder. He was flanked by Master Tutillo.

"Both of us appear scared, but courageous and resolute," Rodrigo said to himself, thinking how he would write this in his memoir.

The two blood guards stepped into the pale blue light.

Their faces, hands, and arms were smeared with fresh blood, the smell of which made Rodrigo gag. Raising their swords, the two guards started to approach.

"Stop right there!" said Rodrigo, gulping. "Don't come any closer."

The two guards looked at him, then at each other, frowning.

Rodrigo suddenly saw the fatal flaw in his plan.

"Good grief! They don't understand me!" he said frantically, out of the corner of his mouth. "They don't speak our language!"

"What do we do?" Master Tutillo asked in dismay.

"I don't know!" Rodrigo said helplessly.

The guards shook their heads, shrugged, and once more started to move toward them. Master Tutillo pointed desperately at the barrels of gunpowder, then pointed to the lantern, and said breathlessly, "Boom!"

Apparently "boom" was a word that was universally understood. The guards came to a halt and stood frozen in place.

"We want to talk to the Blood Mage," said Rodrigo, using the imperious tone of voice that had often curdled the blood of some rude lordling at court. "Go fetch him."

Whether the two understood or whether they deemed that this situation called for their commander, Rigo couldn't tell. But they conferred briefly, and then one of the Blood Guards departed. The other retreated, removing himself to the doorway. He watched them with a scowl.

Rodrigo lowered his arm, which had started to ache from holding up the lantern. He shifted the lantern to the other hand, and wiped his sweating palm on his trousers. He tried to think about something else besides his twisting gut and the god-awful taste in his mouth.

To bolster his courage, he pictured Stephano catching

sight of that distress flare and ordering Viola to fly to the fortress as fast as her wings could carry her. Rodrigo could almost see the dragon winging her way toward the fort.

He just had to keep the Blood Mage occupied a little longer.

"He's here," said Master Tutillo in a smothered voice.

The Blood Mage entered and took a moment to assess the situation. He glanced around the shadowy room lit only by the lantern's magical blue glow. He gazed at the barrels of gunpowder, the stores of weapons, the two men standing near the barrels. His eyes glittered and his brows came together.

Master Tutillo was the one who had suggested the Blood Mage might want to sail off in the fortress, use it to escape. Perhaps the Blood Mage had been up to the bridge, trying to figure out how to operate the helm. That wouldn't take him long, Rodrigo reflected. The seventh sigil was busy repairing the magic. The Blood Mage wasn't alarmed. He was annoyed.

"I am told you two are threatening to blow up my fortress," he said. "Who the devil are you?"

He spoke Rosian. Rodrigo was relieved. The word "boom" could take him only so far.

"This is Master Tutillo, the fortress's commander," Rodrigo answered. "I am Rodrigo de Villeneuve, a gentleman of Rosia. Return to your ship. If you don't, I will destroy 'your' fortress. And you."

The Blood Mage snorted. "And yourselves. This is a trick."

"You deal in magic," said Rodrigo. He found himself growing surprisingly calm. He had detected a note of doubt in the man's voice. "Even though my magic is pure and uncorrupted, you must still be able to identify the constructs. Look at those I have placed on the lantern, on the floor, and on the barrels of gunpowder. Then tell me if this is a trick. Or if I am sincere."

The Blood Mage's eyes were hooded, the glitter gone. He took a step toward them.

"If you come one step closer, I will drop the lantern," Rodrigo warned.

The Blood Mage smiled grimly. "No, you won't, monsieur. You are a 'gentleman,' as you say. I know your kind. I have been around many like you in my travels Above. You think too highly of yourself to commit suicide. Give me the lantern and I will let you live. I need a crafter to repair the magic."

Master Tutillo had turned quite pale, and his lips were clamped tight to suppress his fear. His body trembled.

Rodrigo was no longer calm. He was shaking and sweating and sick with fear. His trick had not worked. The Blood Mage was not going to be duped, frightened off.

Where is Stephano? Rodrigo thought wildly. Why doesn't he come?

The Blood Mage drew close, so close Rodrigo could smell the revolting stench of the fresh blood that covered his face. His robes were spattered with blood. His eyes were empty and seemed to suck the life out of Rodrigo, needing his blood to fill the void.

The Blood Mage reached out to take the lantern. He smiled, patronizing, as to a naughty child. He no longer had any doubt. He was confident, sure of himself.

Anger stirred deep inside Rodrigo, an anger that was, perhaps, another word for courage. Rodrigo had felt this anger before: once when he defied the king and risked his life to find Stephano on the field of battle; and once when he stood his ground at that strange duel that had been the beginning of this end.

I may not be overly burdened with courage, but I am not a coward.

His own words came back to him. This Blood Mage and his followers were demented murderers. He could not let them continue their atrocities. He knew, too, the truth of what they would do to him and to the boy beside him.

If I have done nothing else good in my life, Rodrigo said to himself with a sigh and a faint smile, I will do this.

"You misjudge me, sir," he said aloud and he flung the lantern to the floor.

The lantern crashed in a shower of glass and flaring blue sparks. The magical constructs on the floor burst to life. Blue fire flashed along the trail, spreading rapidly to the barrels.

Master Tutillo's hand closed over his. "Will it be quick, sir?"

"Yes," said Rodrigo.

The Blood Mage grunted in surprise and cast a startled glance at the flaring magic.

"Run!" he shouted. "Back to the ship!"

The Blood Guards made a desperate dash. Their feet pounded down the hall. The Blood Mage followed, disdaining to run, although he did move at a rapid walk, his coat flowing behind him. He paused in the door to look back at Rodrigo, his eyes reflecting the blue glow, were dark and malevolent. And then he was gone.

The magical fire reached the barrels of gunpowder. The magical constructs on the barrels flared. Rodrigo shut his eyes tightly and waited for the blast that he imagined as a white-hot sun turning him inside out.

He waited.

And waited.

No blast. Nothing happened. Rodrigo opened one eye.

The blue magic had gone out. The barrels of gunpowder stood untouched, safe and secure, in no danger of exploding. Rodrigo opened both eyes, staring.

"I guess your magic didn't work," said Master Tutillo.

Rodrigo was shocked and indignant. "My magic always works! This should have blown up! We should be dead!"

He felt quite annoyed and was about to go examine the constructs to see what had gone wrong.

"Sir!" Master Tutillo seized hold of his arm. "That Blood Mage! He'll know the magic didn't work when the fortress doesn't blow up! He'll be back!"

"Good God! You're right!"

Rodrigo jumped to his feet and started toward the exit, with Master Tutillo behind him. Reaching the door, Rodrigo stopped. The fortress was crawling with members of the Blood Guard. Not to mention the Blood Mage, who would be justifiably angry at Rodrigo for the fright he had just given him.

"We can't go out there," he said.

"We can't stay in here either, sir," Master Tutillo pointed out.

"Rigo! I can hear you!" Miri called from the darkness. "I can't see you, though. Where are you?"

Rodrigo blinked. "That sounded like Miri."

"It *is* Mistress Miri, sir!" Master Tutillo said, elated. He pointed the opposite direction from where they were standing. "She's at the door to the armory! We can go out that way!"

"I didn't know there was a door to the armory," Rodrigo said. "But then I didn't know there was an armory. Lead the way."

Master Tutillo started off. Rodrigo was about to follow. He glanced back at the barrels of gunpowder, the constructs on the floor, and saw them glimmer with faint blue-green glow. Rodrigo came to a halt. He stared at the constructs and then he began to laugh.

"The seventh sigil!"

Master Tutillo came running back in search of him. He eyed Rodrigo with concern. "Sir, are you hysterical?"

Rodrigo shook his head and wiped his eyes. Master Tutillo latched on to him and began to lead him through a maze of muskets stacked like corn stalks and cases of ammunition and what-not. Miri was waiting for them at the door, looking grim, a pistol in her hand.

"What's so funny?" she asked, glaring at Rodrigo.

"The seventh sigil," he explained. "It's working." He began to laugh again.

Miri snorted and went back to keeping watch out the door. "I'll pretend to care later. Right now, we have to get out of here. If we can make it to the privies, we can go from there out the back door. But that's not going to be easy."

To reach the privies they had to cross the large, cavernous corridor, about thirty yards with no cover.

A loud voice echoed down the corridor. The Blood Mage was redeploying his troops, sending them to secure the fortress.

"And if you find that fop, bring him to me—alive. I will be on the bridge."

Rodrigo stopped laughing.

Miri eyed him. "You are the fop in question, I assume."

"I'm afraid so," said Rodrigo with a self-deprecating smile. "He's going to try to escape in the fortress. He said he needed me to help with the magic."

"But he can't raise it off the ground," Miri said, frowning. "The magic was failing."

"But the seventh sigil is working. That's what's so funny." said Rodrigo. "The seventh sigil has been repairing the magic. We have to stop him."

"We can't, Rigo," said Miri. "This place is crawling with his soldiers. We might have a chance—a slim one—to escape out the back door. But that's all we have."

Rodrigo and Master Tutillo exchanged glances. Master Tutillo had armed himself with a rifle. He gave a tight-lipped nod. Rodrigo sighed deeply.

"Miri, we have to try—"

"Hush!" Miri gripped hold of him, digging her fingernails into his wrist. She looked back into the powder magazine. "I heard voices."

"Blood Guards!" Rodrigo said. "They're searching for me."

"And there are more coming from this direction," said Miri, looking out the door. "We're cut off."

A huge, bellowing roar resounded through the fortress.

Rodrigo recognized Viola. He sighed deeply and thought to himself that angels must roar like that dragon.

The Blood Guards who had entered the powder magazine jerked their heads around in alarm and then hurriedly fled.

"We have to find Stephano," Rodrigo said. "Warn him about the Blood Mage—"

"No," said Miri firmly. She slammed shut the door and leaned her back against it. "We're staying put, right where we are. Master Tutillo, go shut that other door. Shove something up against it and stand guard. Rigo, help me drag that crate over."

He and Miri hauled a large crate across the floor and positioned it in front of the door. Master Tutillo shifted a metal crate and stood beside it, rifle ready. Sounds from outside grew muffled.

"We're safe for the moment," said Miri. She smiled at Rodrigo. "You can stop being a hero now."

"Thank God," he said in heartfelt tones. "I'm simply not cut out for it."

Miri drew close to him, putting her arm through his arm. She leaned her head on his shoulder. He put his arm around her.

"I hope it's over soon," he said.

"It will be," said Miri. "One way or the other."

42

In my experience, being a hero is bad for the complexion. I don't recommend it.

—Rodrigo de Villeneuve, journal

Stephano left the battle in the skies over Dunlow with mingled feelings: sorrow over the death of Hroal, grim satisfaction in the destruction of the temple, and cautious optimism that they had succeeded in stopping the invasion fleet. He could not yet know with certainty they had won, but he could see many ships on fire and more sinking to the ground.

His concern now was the fortress. He had heard the cannons firing, then a loud blast, and then nothing. He could only assume that the green beam weapon had destroyed at least one of the gun emplacements.

He was so desperate to see that he released the straps holding him in the saddle and stood up, balancing himself precariously as he held his spyglass to his eye. The ship with the red flag had landed in front of the fortress, and he could not tell from this angle, but he assumed its crew had the fort under siege.

Lowering his spyglass, he noticed smoke rising from a

patch of trees off to his left. He looked more closely and sharply ordered Viola to fly over to investigate.

The dragon flew low over the trees as a gentle rain fell. Heavy gray clouds seemed more sorrowful than threatening. Smoke rose from the blackened, smoldering wreckage of a boat. All that was left was a strip of gaily colored silk caught on a tree branch. The silk fluttered gallantly like a tattered flag, refusing to surrender.

Stephano recognized the *Cloud Hopper.*

Bleak, bitter pain tore at his heart; rage and anger burned in his throat. Viola also recognized Miri's boat, and she turned her head to stare at him in anguish. He indicated with a hand signal she should circle, looking for survivors, although he knew that was hopeless. No one could have survived that fire.

The land around was empty.

"Fly to the fort," he ordered harshly. "The ship first."

Viola banked, wheeling in the air, and flew toward the ship. Stephano expected to come under fire from the green beam weapon, and braced himself for the attack. He was surprised when nothing happened. Drawing near the ship, he saw the reason. Six fiends in garish red uniforms were hauling the green beam weapon down the gangplank with the apparent aim of taking it into the fortress. Stephano had no need to give Viola orders. The two were a team; she knew what to do.

The dragon dove swiftly and silently on the enemy. The soldiers were so busy with their work they did not see Viola coming until one of them glanced up and saw death swooping down. Stephano had to give the fiends credit. They did not flee in terror, as he expected. They tried frantically to shift the barrel of the weapon, bring it to bear on the dragon.

Viola breathed a blast of fire that incinerated the weapon

and its crew, who died before they could even scream. The dragon flew up out of her dive and soared over the walls of the fortress, leaving behind a mass of twisted metal and charred flesh.

Stephano studied the ship, which was flying a red flag with a black sun pierced by a curved-bladed sword. He found this odd. The ships of the invasion fleet had all flown a different flag, what he assumed was the flag of Glasearrach: a golden tree against a background of green and white stripes.

The same blood-red flag was now flying over his fortress.

Stephano blamed himself. When the fortress had come down in the wrong place, he had known it might come under attack. He should have made better provisions for its defense, though even as he thought this he asked himself what more he could have done. He had needed Dag and Verdi to lead the assault on the ships. He had needed every one of his dragons to attack the fleet.

His men had not given up without a fight. He could see the gaping hole in the wall, the twisted remains of the cannons, and the smoldering remnants of the main gate, destroyed by enemy fire. He ordered Viola to set fire to the ship. They made several passes and soon the masts were burning brightly and the deck was in flames.

"Fly over the fort," Stephano told her.

He examined the bridge as they flew past and was pleased to see that it had not suffered any damage. The constructs of the seventh sigil, Rodrigo's pride and joy, were intact. But if it had been supposed to protect the fort, it had failed. Rodrigo would be unhappy. Stephano tried not to think about Rodrigo lying dead in that fort, and comforted himself with the thought that his friend had a strong sense of self-preservation. He would have found someplace safe to hide. Perhaps he was in the storage room with Doctor Ellington.

As Viola circled the fortress, she began picking off the red-uniformed soldiers manning the parapet that encircled the top. Drawing in an enormous breath, she spewed out a slow, steady stream of fire down on the fiends as she passed overhead. Some broke and ran, while others stood their ground, returning fire, shooting green fireballs at the dragon.

One of the blasts hit Viola in the shoulder, and Stephano felt her flinch with the pain. Having run out of breath by this time, she killed the fiend who had shot at her with a swipe of her claws, ripping him apart and taking out a chunk of the parapet.

The walls of the fort were now empty except for the bodies of the dead. Those who had managed to survive had fled inside. Stephano nudged Viola with his legs, and she rose into the air, making a wide circle above the fortress. As he considered whether or not to wait for Dag, Viola suddenly shifted her head. Stephano looked to see what she had spotted.

A group of men wearing Rosian uniforms were marching down out of the foothills. Sighting the dragon, they began waving wildly to draw his attention. Stephano signaled Viola to land, and she flew down to the ground.

Stephano freed himself from the saddle and dismounted. The men approached as close as they dared, taking care not to come too close to the dragon. Viola stood aloof and proud, her wings folded at her sides, her tail slightly brushing the ground. She kept a narrow-eyed watch on Stephano, who fairly radiated anger.

Stephano removed his helm and eyed the soldiers grimly. "Why have you men abandoned your posts?"

They all began to talk at once. Stephano silenced them

with a baleful look. One man stepped forward. Stephano recognized Cook. He had apparently made himself their leader.

"What have you to say for yourself?" Stephano asked coldly.

"It was Master Tutillo's orders, Captain," said Cook. "He's in command now, sir."

"He told you to retreat?"

Stephano couldn't believe it. The midshipman might be young, but he had always proven himself to be an exemplary soldier.

"It was that friend of yours, Captain. The foppish gentleman."

"Rodrigo?"

"Yes, sir. He told Master Tutillo that these demons were . . . what did he call them . . ."

"Blood mages," several of the men called out.

"That's it, sir. They murdered our boys and then used their blood to make themselves more powerful. Master Tutillo said that if we stayed, they would kill us and use our blood the same way."

Stephano remembered Miri telling him about blood mages, how they tortured and then slaughtered the sacrificial victims.

"We did as Master Tutillo ordered, sir, though we didn't like it," Cook went on.

"Where is Master Tutillo?" Stephano looked around.

"He and your friend are in the fort. The foppish gentleman said he knew how to fight the demons."

"You're talking about Monsieur Rodrigo? Fighting demons?" Stephano repeated. "Are you certain?"

"That's what Master Tutillo told us, Captain. We did as he ordered, came out here and found the women," Cook continued.

Stephano stared in confusion. "What women?"

"Mistress Miri and her sister, a countess and the princess," said Cook.

For a moment Stephano couldn't speak or even breathe as joy and relief overwhelmed him. "Are they . . . all right?"

"Wet, worn out, and hungry, but otherwise fine. The countess and the princess and Mistress Miri's sister are back in the caves," Cook said, jerking his thumb in that direction. "I left men to guard them."

"Where's Mistress Miri?"

"When she found out your friend, the foppish gentleman, was still in the fortress, she went to fetch him. I tried to stop her, sir," Cook added hurriedly. "She gave me such a look. It's a wonder I'm not burnt to a crisp.

"After she left, the rest of us talked it over and decided to join her, go back to the fort. We know we're disobeying orders, Captain, but we're not going to give up without a fight. We were on our way when we saw you."

Cook and the other men anxiously watched Stephano. He had only been half listening. He had planned to wait for Dag and the dragons to attack the fort, but couldn't do that now, not with Miri and Rodrigo and Master Tutillo still inside.

Stephano turned to the dragon. "Viola, these men and I are going to enter the fortress on foot. I need you to keep watch from the air, give us cover."

As Viola lifted her wings, bounded off with her powerful hind legs, and soared into the sky, Stephano shifted his attention to the terrain around the fort. He and his men were in the foothills, hidden from view of anyone inside the fort by trees and boulders. Once they descended, the ground they would have to cross was devoid of cover, with not so much as a single tree or a ditch. Even the rain, which would have obscured their movements, had stopped. The sun was trying to break through the clouds.

Stephano ordered the men to fall into line. Taking the lead, he walked beside Cook.

"Tell me about these blood mages," Stephano said. "How do they fight?"

"They use demon magic, sir," he said, sounding awed. "They smear themselves with blood and bullets bounce right off them."

Stephano wondered if that was true. He had fought Bottom Dwellers before and knew they were hard to kill. But bullets bouncing off them? He didn't consider that likely, magic or no magic.

He looked back at the line of marching men, fifteen in all, carrying rifles. "How are the men fixed for powder and ammunition?"

Cook shook his head. "We have what we carried with us. And likely the powder's damp by now, sir."

Stephano nodded. He was armed with two empty pistols and his sword. He had long since run out of ammunition.

"We'll go to the armory first," he said, deciding on the spot. "Pick up extra muskets, powder, and ammunition. I hope the enemy hasn't raided it."

"I doubt they would, sir. Their guns shoot fire and they have their accursed swords *and* their demon magic. All we have is bullets," Cook concluded morosely.

When they arrived at the edge of the woods near the fort, Stephano halted the men just before they broke cover.

"We're going to make a run for it."

Drawing his sword, he led the charge, bounding over the soggy ground, splashing and squishing, slipping in the mud. The men ran after him, carrying their muskets high, trying to keep their powder dry. When they reached the stony ground, they could run faster, but those in the fort with an outside view would be able to see them coming.

Viola flew overhead, keeping watch, ready to attack any of the enemy that dared show themselves.

No one appeared. No one fired a shot.

Stephano and his small contingent reached the back entrance safely. If he hadn't known better, he would have thought the fortress was deserted. He should have been elated, but he wasn't. He was fighting demons with blood magic and he had no idea what he would be facing.

He ordered the men to stand close to the walls. Looking them over, he chose one he remembered as being an excellent shot. He, Cook, and the sharpshooter moved cautiously toward the door.

They found it unlocked, standing slightly ajar.

"This is too bloody easy, sir," Cook whispered.

Stephano agreed. "Keep alert."

Gripping his sword, he gave the door a push and it swung open, creaking on rusty hinges. This door opened onto the main corridor. If he turned to his right, the corridor would lead to the officers' quarters, the stairs to the bridge and the dock. Down the corridor to his left was the door that led into the dragon chamber, and from there he could reach the armory and powder magazine.

The interior was dark. The lanterns mounted on the wall were growing dim and, in some instances, had gone out. Their magic needed to be renewed on a regular basis. When he looked left and right and saw the corridor was empty he motioned for the rest of the men to come forward.

"You two, stand guard. Keep a lookout for Lieutenant Thorgrimson and his dragon. If you see them, signal to Dag to land and let him know where we are."

The two men took up their positions at the door and Stephano motioned the rest of the men inside and led them along the corridor. They had not gone far when he heard the sound of beating drums. The sound sent a cold shiver through his body, raising the hair on his arms and the back of his neck. He looked questioningly at Cook.

"Each of the demons carries a drum, sir," Cook said softly. "Not sure why or what it's for."

Stephano had a pretty good idea. The drumming in the temple had something to do with contramagic, and he'd bet these did, too. He brought his men to a halt and listened to hear if the drummers were on the move. The sound remained constant, the drums beating in rhythm.

"Sounds like it's coming from the direction of the bridge, sir," Cook said.

Stephano agreed. An ominous thought. "Let's keep moving."

They continued down the corridor and had just reached the door that led to the dragon chamber when the floor suddenly shifted, the walls shook, and dust rained down from the ceiling. The quaking lasted only a few unnerving seconds and then stopped.

Stephano looked at those behind him, a question in his eyes.

"We felt it, too, sir," said Cook.

The fortress had landed on solid bedrock, but Stephano supposed the massive structure still could be shifting, settling. Gripping his sword, he opened the door.

He continued on, walking cautiously down the short, dark hallway adjacent to the privy, which led to the dragon chamber. He knew by the smell he was in the right place. Halfway down the shadowy hall, he felt the floor and the walls shake again, and everyone halted until the fort quit shaking and everything settled.

All the while the beating of the drums continued, never stopping. If anything, the sound was growing louder.

The dragon chamber was pitch black, except for a sliver of light shining out from beneath the door to the armory.

"You men stay here," Stephano ordered. "Keep watch."

He ran across the chamber and fetched up against the armory door. He listened, but he couldn't hear anyone inside. He tried to open the door, but it wouldn't budge. He motioned for the stout, heavy cook to join him, and they slammed into the door with their shoulders. They didn't gain much except bruises.

They were about to try again when someone on the other side of the door shouted, "Break down that door, you fiend, and I will blow off your head!"

43

Plans are useless, but planning is everything.

—Julian de Guichen

Stephano recognized the voice.

"Miri! Don't shoot! It's me, Stephano!"

He heard a glad cry, then the sound of scraping, as though someone was dragging something heavy across the floor. Miri yanked the door open and both she and Rodrigo flung themselves at Stephano with such force they nearly knocked him over backward.

"We have to stop him, Stephano!" Miri cried.

"Do you hear the drums?" Rodrigo cried frantically. "We don't have a moment to lose!"

"Wait a moment! Where's Master Tutillo?"

"Here I am, sir!" a voice called from across the room of the powder magazine. "I'm guarding this door!"

Stephano looked worriedly from Miri to Rodrigo. Both were covered in grime, Miri's skirt was muddy and charred. Rodrigo's face was smeared with gunpowder and he smelled of saltpeter. But both seemed to be well and unharmed. Stephano breathed easier.

"Now, what's this about the drums? Who are we trying to stop from doing what?"

"Did you feel the walls shake?" Rodrigo asked.

"Yes," said Stephano with a sudden sense of dread. "Why? What does that mean?"

"The fortress's magic is working again," Rodrigo said. "The seventh sigil must have repaired it. I don't understand . . . well, I *do* understand. I just didn't foresee . . . I should have known . . . It's my theory that the elemental base structure of the magic and contramagic being brought into balance by the seventh sigil causes the magicks to be drawn together, their sigils completing each other instead of destroying. Thus—"

"Devil take your theories!" Miri elbowed Rodrigo aside. "All you need to know, Stephano, is that the magic is working again, and the Blood Mage has gone to the bridge and is trying to escape in the fortress!"

"Is that possible?" Stephano asked, alarmed.

"Sadly, yes," Rodrigo replied. "The shaking you felt was the magic starting to flow from the helm to the lift tanks. The magic is weak, so far. That's why we haven't flown off. Probably some constructs still need mending."

"What about the drumming?" Stephano asked.

"The drums are an ancient part of the blood magic rituals. Drumming enhances the magical power of the mages. Probably what gave these fiends the idea to use drums and blood magic to enhance the power of contramagic. They're using the drumming to try to help the Blood Mage power the magic of the helm. It might be having the opposite effect, though," Rodrigo said, frowning. "I need to consider this."

"All we need to consider is that the Blood Mage is on the bridge and his troops are with him. That's why no one was guarding the door, why no one fired on us," said Stephano in sudden realization. "They don't care if we're inside the fortress or out."

"They are probably *glad* we are here," said Miri, shivering. "They can kill us and use our blood."

The thought was chilling. The drumming continued. The sound was grating, teeth jarring. Stephano found it hard to concentrate with the drums beating in his head.

"Master Tutillo!" Stephano called.

There was no response. The door to the powder magazine stood wide open.

"Damn it!" Stephano was about to send men to look for him when the midshipman popped up out of the shadows like an imp.

"I'm here, sir! I went to reconnoiter, see what the fiends are doing. I thought you'd want to know."

"That was extremely dangerous!" Stephano glared at him.

"I'm sorry, sir," said Master Tutillo. "But it wasn't really, begging your pardon. I just ran down the corridor by your quarters, peeked around the corner, and ran back. No one saw me."

"What did you see—?"

"It doesn't matter what he saw. I have an idea!" said Rodrigo. "We can remove the crystals from the lift tanks! Then the Blood Mage can't go anywhere! All we have to do is sneak down to the lower level and unlock the door that leads to the fueling chamber and . . . what's wrong?"

"How do you plan to unlock the door?" Miri asked.

"With the keys . . . which are on the bridge with the Blood Mage." Rodrigo sighed. "And the door is by the bridge. Never mind."

"What did you see?" Stephano asked Master Tutillo again.

"The Blood Guard are assembled in the corridor leading up to the bridge. There must be twenty of them, sir. All banging on their drums. They're covered in blood, and the walls and the floors are glowing red. I went all wobbly at the sight, sir."

"Blood magic," Rodrigo explained, "inspires fear and terror. Drains the will to fight."

Stephano swore beneath his breath. "So the only way to reach the bridge is down that corridor and up the stairs now being defended by mages armed to the teeth with blood magic, not to mention green fireball guns and swords."

"What about Viola?" Miri suggested. "The dragon could destroy the bridge with a blast of fire."

"And if she destroys the bridge, how do *we* get home?" Rodrigo asked.

"You were the one who was going to blow up the fortress," Miri retorted.

"I was under duress. Stephano is here and he will have a plan. He always has a plan."

Stephano did have a plan, or at least the beginning of one. He was trying to think through the pounding in his head when he heard the sound of heavy, booted feet running across the dragon chamber.

Dag burst into the doorway, carrying his rifle. His long, leather dragon-riding coat was covered in grime and ashes and spattered with blood. One spot over his breast was charred black. Stephano, glancing down at his own coat, realized he himself didn't look much better.

Dag came to a halt. "Are you all right, sir? What's going on? I saw the *Hopper.* Where's Gythe? Is she all right?"

"She's safe. She's in the caves with Stephano's mother. We lost the *Cloud Hopper,* but something wonderful happened," Miri said with a faint smile. "You'll find out. Gythe wants to tell you herself."

Dag looked confused; he must be wondering why Miri wouldn't tell him anything more.

"What about Doctor Ellington?" Dag asked.

"He's in the storage closet, sir," said Master Tutillo. "I'm afraid he's not getting along well with the princess's dog."

Stephano explained their situation, how the Blood Mage planned to steal their fort. "The fiends are guarding that corridor so we can't reach the bridge to stop him. They outnumber us and they're whipping up some sort of fear-inducing magic."

"So what's the plan, sir?" Dag grinned. "I know you have one."

"I remember you telling me that at the siege of the *Royal Sail,* you shifted one of the cannons so that you could fire it down a hallway."

Dag nodded. "Fired canisters filled with lead balls."

"It won't work," said Rodrigo.

"Rigo, this is no time—" Stephano began impatiently.

"The cannons rely on magic," Rodrigo continued, "and the seventh sigil is playing merry hell with the magic."

"Huh?" Dag stared at him. "What's he talking about, sir?"

Stephano heaved a sigh and ran his hand through his hair. "I'm afraid he's right. Don't ask him why."

"Well, sir," said Dag thoughtfully. "If we can't fire the canisters from the cannon, maybe we can throw them. We'll make grenades. Pack the canisters with shot and gunpowder, add a slow burning fuse, and toss them into the corridor."

"Then, during the chaos, you and I can enter the corridor, charge the door, run up the stairs, and kill the Blood Mage," said Stephano.

"And how do you propose to do that?" Rodrigo asked.

"Shoot the bastard," Dag growled.

"This man is a blood mage, one of the most powerful wizards in this or any world. He is skilled in the use of blood magic *and* contramagic. Shoot him? You'd be dead before you got in the door."

"He's right, Stephano," said Miri unhappily. "I saw him kill a man with a flick of his hand."

Stephano looked at Dag, who shook his head.

"Don't look at me, sir. I never had to fight a wizard."

"Neither have I," Stephano muttered.

They all fell silent. The drumming was growing increasingly louder, or so it seemed. Miri was watching him anxiously. Master Tutillo shuffled his feet.

"I have another idea regarding the lift crystals," said Rodrigo cautiously. "You only used one or two of them in each of the lift tanks, right?"

"Right," said Miri. "That's all we need."

"I remember you saying you stored the barrel containing the rest of the crystals here, in the armory, where it would be safe in case of attack."

"The barrel is right behind you. What do you plan to do with the crystals?" Stephano asked.

"Do you remember my balloon filled with lift gas that I used to protect the pinnace from the Bottom Dwellers' attack? I covered the silk with magical constructs and the lift gas gave them the power to work. I might be able to do the same with the seventh sigil and the crystals. It would protect you from the Blood Mage's magic. There's only one problem."

"*You* had to be physically connected to the balloon to make the magic work," Miri pointed out.

"That's the problem," said Rodrigo. "If I was a savant, I could work the magic with my mind alone. As it is, I would need to be on the bridge with you—"

"Good God, no!" Dag protested. "You'd get us all killed!"

"I'm afraid that wouldn't work, Rigo," said Stephano.

"Dag and I are going to have to fight our way onto the bridge. We wouldn't be able to protect you."

"There might be a way," said Miri slowly. "You brought the seventh sigil to life, Rigo; you figured out the mystery of contramagic. You may not be a savant, but you are one of the most skilled crafters I know."

"I'm one of the most skilled crafters *I* know," said Rodrigo. "I don't see how that helps."

"I believe you are more talented than you imagine. I've seen you do wondrous things with your magic." Miri put her hand on his arm and looked up at him earnestly. "You could inscribe the seventh sigil on the crystal, throw it onto the bridge and then concentrate on the construct, use your mind to make the magic work."

"I *did* send the grand bishop's miter sailing around the dining hall," Rodrigo reflected. "That took considerable mental concentration, not to mention about six glasses of wine. Let me think about this."

He began pacing back and forth, muttering to himself.

"How would he throw the crystal onto the bridge?" Stephano asked. "He can't get close enough."

"He could if he and I were riding Viola," said Miri.

"Absolutely not," Stephano said sharply. "You may have flown a dragon once, but that was under different circumstances—"

"You're right," Miri returned heatedly, putting her hands on her hips. "*This* time I would be riding a *trained* dragon with a saddle! Not an untrained dragon bareback!"

Stephano smiled. "You have a point," he conceded.

"Viola could handle the mission, sir," said Dag. "Miri could sit in the saddle with Rodrigo in front of her."

All three of them looked at Rodrigo, who saw them and stopped his pacing.

"I just thought of something. How do I get to the bridge?"

"We think we have a way," said Stephano. "You can ride Viola—"

"Viola? Me? A dragon?" Rodrigo exclaimed in horror. "You have all gone stark raving mad. I'm not even certain I can control the magic with my mind. I *know* I can't if my mind is shivering in terror!"

"Rigo, you were ready to blow yourself up—"

"A far quicker death than falling off the back of a dragon," Rodrigo observed, shuddering.

The fortress lurched, rose into the air, hung there for a few terrifying moments, then sank back down.

"He's at the helm. He's learning how to control the magic," said Miri in grim tones. "You won't fall off, Rigo. I'll be there to hold on to you."

Rodrigo sighed deeply. "If I ever want to see home again, I suppose I will have to. Someone pry open the lid of this barrel. I'll need a knife and one of the empty cans from the whirly gun."

"Canisters from the swivel gun," Stephano translated.

They set to work. Rodrigo began to carefully scratch magical constructs onto the outside of an empty canister. Under Dag's direction, Cook and the rest of the men removed the lead balls from a standard canister round and replaced them with a powder charge from one of the cannons. They then packed as many of the lead balls into the canister as possible.

Miri made fuses out of thin strips of cloth cut from Cook's shirt that she rubbed with a paste of black powder and Calvados, then braided them together. Using a bayonet to punch a hole in the top of the canister, Dag fed the fuse through the hole into the powder charge.

The fortress shook twice more, causing everyone to look at one another with strained expressions, wondering if this time would be the time it rose into the air and didn't come back down. Each time it landed, but the periods of flight were lasting progressively longer.

Stephano joined Miri, who was slicing up Cook's shirt. He looked over at Rodrigo, bent over the canister, scratching on it with a knife, moving his lips as if he were also scratching the constructs onto his mind.

"He's been a true hero today, Stephano," said Miri.

"That doesn't surprise me," said Stephano, regarding his friend with deep affection.

"We're ready, sir," Dag reported.

"Rigo?" Stephano looked at his friend.

Rodrigo was tamping down the lid of the canister with the hilt of the knife.

"Half a second," he said.

He gazed intently at the constructs of the seventh sigil, tracing them over and over with his finger, murmuring to himself.

"Here, take the bosun's pipe," Stephano said to Miri. "Use this to summon Viola. You sit in the saddle. Be sure to strap yourself in. You'll need to hang tight on to Rodrigo."

Miri nodded gravely at each of his instructions.

"Rigo and I will be fine, Stephano," she said, trying to smile. "Don't worry about us. We have the easy task."

"Not necessarily," he said drily. "You have to wrestle Rodrigo onto the back of a dragon."

Miri laughed a little shakily. "I'll manage."

Stephano tried to embrace her, but she slipped out of his arms.

"I don't want to say good-bye again."

"After this is over, we will never have to tell each other good-bye again," Stephano promised.

Miri turned to Rodrigo. "We'd best be going. Rigo, are you ready?"

"As ready as I'll ever be. There better be a knighthood in this," Rodrigo grumbled.

He and Miri departed. Stephano sent men to escort them and watched until they had disappeared into the darkness of the dragon chamber and he lost sight of them. No one spoke. Stephano waited tensely until he heard the shrill whistle of the bosun's pipe, summoning the dragon.

"That's the signal," said Stephano. "Move out."

44

I do not fear death so much as I fear failing those who have been loyal to me.

—Joseph Voyou, Duke of Bourlet

Armed and ready, Stephano and his men gathered near the double doors that opened from the dragon chamber onto the hallway leading to the officers' quarters. Beyond that were the main gates, which had been destroyed, and the corridor to the bridge. He opened the doors a crack and looked into the hallway. Ordinarily, it would have been dark, but now pale sunlight crept inside the hole where the gates had been. The light waxed and waned as mists and clouds obscured the sun, but even that small amount of light allowed them to see that the corridor was filled with debris: chunks of stone, pieces of twisted metal. Walking would be treacherous.

Stephano looked at his men. They were quiet, determined, resolute. Prince Renault had given Stephano sailors from his own flagship, some of his very best. Stephano did not make a speech. They all knew what was at stake.

"Cook, Gunner's Mate, you both ready?"

The men replied with grunts and tight-lipped nods. Stephano had chosen the two best bocce players in the fortress to toss the canisters. Cook was deemed to have the strongest arm, so he was tasked with tossing the canister that had to travel the farthest. The gunner's mate—said to be the most accurate—would throw the other.

Stephano nodded. Dag thrust open the doors and the men entered the hallway, moving as quietly as they could. Now Stephano blessed the incessant drum beats that drowned out the sounds of booted feet shuffling down the corridor. Debris from the blast that had taken out the main gate covered the floor, forcing them to climb over and around the rubble.

About halfway down the hall, Stephano came upon the grisly remains of three fallen comrades. The men had died in agony, bellies ripped open, hands and feet chopped off while they were still alive. The floor and the walls and even the ceiling were wet with blood. Stephano had seen many horrible sights in war, but this deliberate and cold-blooded butchery brought him to a halt, shaken. Next to Stephano, Master Tutillo clamped his teeth down on his quivering lower lip and clutched his rifle so tightly his knuckles were chalk white.

"Keep moving!" Stephano ordered in a harsh whisper.

He led the way, and as he walked in the blood of the fallen the stench filled his nose and mouth. His gut twisted, and behind him, he heard the muffled sounds of someone heaving. The drumming grew louder.

As he passed the door of his own quarters, nearing the end of the hall, he raised his hand, ordering the men to halt. A few feet ahead, the hall ended in a *T,* intersecting with the corridor that to his right led to the bridge and to his left continued around the fort. Stephano flattened himself against the wall and inched forward. When he reached the end of the *T,* he risked a quick glance down the corridor to his right.

The drummers had formed into two rows in the hallway,

their backs against the wall. Their drums must have been part of their equipment, for they were attached to harnesses slung over their shoulders, allowing each drummer to hold a drum in one hand while pounding on the drum with the other. No one was guarding the corridor; no one had drawn a weapon. They were all chanting loudly, oblivious to the danger.

Far too oblivious.

He ducked back and motioned to Dag.

"It's a trap," he whispered. "They know we have to try to reach the bridge. They're waiting for us to enter that corridor."

"I guess we should oblige them," Dag said.

"I guess we should," said Stephano grimly. "Cook, Gunner, light the fuses. Be ready to throw on my command."

Cook and Gunner lit the fuses. They had only moments now to toss the grenades or risk blowing themselves up.

Stephano and Dag, both carrying rifles, jumped out into the hallway, preparing to fire. Blood mages were waiting for them and a green glowing cloud of contramagic roiled down the corridor and over Dag and Stephano. When the contramagic struck the magic in their rifles, the barrels sizzled.

"Now!" Stephano ordered.

He and Dag flung their rifles as far as they could and dove for cover back down the hallway. Cook rushed past them, holding the canister, the fuse blazing, dropping showers of sparks. He heaved it as far as he could. The gunner was right behind him, and the moment Cook let go, the gunner sent his canister rolling along the floor toward the nearest drummers.

Both he and Cook came racing back around the corner to the safety of the hall.

Stephano risked a glance to see what was happening.

The first canister landed in the middle of the corridor, lying on the floor, hissing and sputtering while the drummers stared in amazement and sudden horrified understanding. Before they could react, the first canister blew, followed almost immediately by the second.

The force of the two blasts took Stephano by surprise. The air was suddenly thick with black smoke, but he could hear the grapeshot rattling off the walls and the floor and the screams of the victims. The drumming stopped abruptly, and the green cloud of contramagic vanished.

"Ready, sir?" Dag asked.

He was armed with two pistols, one in each hand. Stephano was armed with his two pistols and wore his sword on his baldric.

"Ready."

He and Dag dashed into the hall, holding their breath, trying to keep from breathing in the smoke. They ran down the corridor, heading for the door that opened onto the stairs leading up to the bridge. The corridor was awash in blood, the floor littered with bodies of the wounded and dying. Here and there, men were rising up, reaching for their swords or their drums. Stephano left them to Master Tutillo and his small force, who would be on their heels.

Dag kicked aside bodies and battered down the door. He and Stephano entered, pistols drawn, hammers cocked. Smoke rolled in behind them. The stairs were dark and the smoke didn't help. The door to the bridge itself was closed. Stephano started to climb the stairs.

"Look out, sir!" Dag cried, firing his pistol.

Red streaks of crackling lightning flashed out of the darkness, striking Dag, hitting him in the shoulder and knocking him sideways into the wall. Constructs on the dragon coat burst into a blue glow, protecting him from serious harm. Shining brightly in the darkness, they also made him an excellent target.

Stephano couldn't see anyone, but he heard the man chanting and fired his pistol at the sound. The man cried out and toppled over. The body thudded down the stairs. Apparently bullets didn't bounce off him.

"Go, sir!" Dag yelled. "I'll hold the door!"

Stephano jumped over the body and dashed up the steps, taking them two at a time. Dag planted himself in the doorway, a pistol in each hand. Rifle shots echoed in the corridor. Master Tutillo raised his young voice, leading the charge.

Stephano expected the door to the bridge to be locked. He hurled himself against it, crashing into it to force it open. To his surprise, the door unexpectedly gave way, sending him staggering into the room.

On the bridge, the sounds of the battle raging down below were muffled. Sunlight shone through the single window, gleaming on the brass helm and the man standing over it.

The Blood Mage was tall and spare. His red cloak, crimson surcoat, breeches, and shirt were wet with gore. Magical constructs seemed to crawl on his face, and every change of expression caused them to move. His hands, on the helm, were stained with blood.

Stephano raised his pistol. A gentleman would have demanded this man's surrender, but Stephano had waded through the blood of his victims. He started to pull the trigger.

The Blood Mage did not move; and did not say a word. A lurid red glow suffused the bridge. Both pistols grew as hot as if they had been dipped in fire. Stephano dropped them with a curse and reached for his sword, only to snatch back his hand, for the hilt, too, blazed red hot.

The Blood Mage continued to study the helm. When

Stephano saw him make a casual movement with his hand he remembered Miri saying how she had seen him kill a man "with the flick of his hand." Stephano dropped to the floor, as the puffs of red smoke struck the wall behind him with explosive force. He looked up to see holes punched into the stone. Those puffs would have taken off his head.

He remained on the floor, on his belly, wondering what the devil to do now, while the Blood Mage continued to be absorbed in whatever problems he was having with the helm. He had not even really looked at Stephano.

A drop hit Stephano on the back of the hand. The liquid looked like blood, but it seared his flesh as if it had been a droplet of boiling lead. Stephano gasped in pain and tried to wipe off the drop, but another hit him on the back of his neck and yet another on the top of his head, causing him excruciating pain. He frantically wiped them away, only to see the ceiling covered with the red droplets of blood that were now falling like rain.

The hands of the Blood Mage and the scars on his face began to glow red. He looked at Stephano now, raised his eyebrows and said in flawless Rosian, "You come as a gift, sir. My magic was starting to wane." The Blood Mage moved his hands over the helm.

Stephano choked back a cry. Everywhere a drop hit him, his skin burned as if struck by a red-hot poker. Pulling the collar of his dragon coat up over the back of his neck, he dove for cover underneath the chart table and crouched there, helpless to stop this man, equally helpless to save himself. He looked down at his hand to see an ugly, gaping wound where the first drop had struck him. More wounds covered his body, all of them bleeding and burning with a pain he could not have imagined.

He clenched his fist to keep from passing out and, tilting his head, looked at the window, hoping to see Viola. Clouds were gathering and the room grew darker, but there was no sign of the dragon.

The Blood Mage muttered something, and suddenly the stone floor beneath Stephano began to glow red and grow warm, then unpleasantly warm, and then blazing hot. Stephano stood it as long as he could, praying Viola would appear. When at last the heat was unbearable, he crawled out from under the chart table.

He looked up to see the Blood Mage standing over him, curved sword drawn. Stephano made a desperate lunge, struck the Blood Mage around the shins, and carried him down.

The Blood Mage went over backward, narrowly missing striking his head on the helmsman's chair. He lay still a moment, shaken. Stephano, on his hands and knees, made a grab for the curved sword. The Blood Mage raised his hand, and puffs of smoke slammed into Stephano, hitting him in the chest, shoulders, and arms. The constructs on his coat protected him, but the impact sent him flying. He crashed into the wall beneath the window, where he lay gasping for air. His coat was smoldering, the magical constructs were starting to fail. He wouldn't survive another hit.

Dazed, he thought he saw movement in the window above him. Then he caught a brief glimpse of Viola's head and before he could blink, saw a gigantic clawed foot lunging for the window. Still reeling, Stephano flung his arms over his head as the claw smashed through window, covering him with shattered glass. Dimly, he saw the canister containing the crystal marked with the seventh sigil sail through the window and land on the floor with a metallic clatter.

The Blood Mage was just starting to rise and he jumped back, thinking the canister was going to explode. When nothing happened, he eyed the canister warily.

Stephano pulled himself to his feet, crunching on broken glass. Raindrops spattered in through the opening, and he glanced over his shoulder to see Viola hovering slightly above the window, her wings scarcely moving. Rodrigo sat on her back, in front of Miri with both arms wrapped around the dragon's neck in a deathlike grip. He was staring intently at the canister that lay in the middle of the floor.

The canister kept on doing nothing, at least as far as Stephano could tell. He tried to draw his sword, only to feel the hilt still red hot.

The Blood Mage was growing impatient. Retrieving his own sword, he walked purposefully across the room, heading for Stephano. Sounds of fighting came up from the corridor. He heard Dag bellowing and the bang of gunfire. Stephano warily kept his gaze divided between the Blood Mage inside and Rodrigo outside, who now was lying on the dragon's neck, his face pale, drawn, intent.

The canister started to glow with a faint blue-green light. Stephano breathed an inward sigh. "God bless you, Rigo!"

The Blood Mage had his back to the canister, and couldn't see the glow. He raised his hand. Red magic blazed . . . and then died.

The Blood Mage frowned, confused. He looked out the window to see Rodrigo working his magic, then he turned to stare at the canister. He lowered his hand, amazed at what he was seeing.

The seventh sigil. Contramagic complementing magic, not destroying it. The blue-green light spread over the bridge like a soothing balm. Stephano grasped the hilt of his sword and, feeling it cool to the touch, slid it from its scabbard.

When the Blood Mage heard the scrape of metal, his body stiffened. He carried a sword, but he probably only used his weapon for slitting throats and chopping off body parts, so he would be no match for an experienced swordsman.

Stephano advanced, his sword drawn, watching the eyes of his foe. The Blood Mage circled around the helmsman's chair, keeping the helm between him and Stephano. The Blood Mage gripped his sword. His eyes were hooded, calculating.

Stephano tried to dart around the chair. The Blood Mage kept moving, keeping the chair always between them. He raised his sword, but instead of attacking, he slashed the sleeve of his own shirt and cut open a large vein in his upper arm.

Blood spurted, flowing fast, and the Blood Mage began to chant, very softly.

Stephano stared, appalled. Blood spilled down the sleeve of the man's shirt and dripped onto the floor. The Blood Mage fixed Stephano with a look of venomous hatred and continued to chant.

The canister's glow began to fade. The magic was failing. Either Rodrigo was losing his concentration, or the blood magic was overwhelming.

The chanting continued, the blood flowed, and the Blood Mage's magic began to work again. Stephano felt the magical, debilitating fear twist inside him, choking him with bile, squeezing his chest. His palms were wet, his mouth dry. His hands shook so that he had trouble holding his sword.

He once more tried to dash around the helm, but his movements were slow and sluggish, mired in fear. The Blood Mage no longer tried to evade him. Grasping his sword with both hands, he rushed at Stephano, swinging his blade in great, sweeping, slashing arcs.

Stephano stood his ground, letting go of thought and fear, letting instinct and his body meld with his blade.

Ducking the vicious stroke that was meant to decapitate him, he thrust his blade into the man's chest.

The rapier slid deep, biting bone, piercing lungs, puncturing the heart. Stephano jerked his sword free and the Blood Mage fell, sliding off the blade to land on the floor.

He was almost assuredly dead, but Stephano wasn't taking any chances. Kicking the body over, he stabbed the Blood Mage in the throat. The scarred face froze in a strange and hideous smile; the eyes, still dark with hatred, stared straight at him.

Stephano sagged back against the chart table. He was covered in blood. Blood glistened on the floor, the helm, the walls and the ceiling. The stench of blood was sickening. Blood spatter covered the canister, which had gone dark. Stephano pushed himself off the table, planning to go to the window, to breathe some fresh air and let Viola and his friends know all was well. He could see the dragon, gazing anxiously inside the broken glass, trying to see what was going on.

He was arrested by a strange sizzling sound. He turned to see the dead man's blood starting to bubble. And now, all the blood in the room, from the spatters on the ceiling to the pools of blood on the floor, began to boil, giving off a red, noxious vapor.

The vapor hung in the air, seeped into Stephano's mouth and nose, seized him by the throat. His lungs burned, his eyes watered. He couldn't see, and he couldn't breathe. He tried to reach the window, to find fresh air, but the vapor dragged him down. He collapsed, gasping for breath, only to draw in more of the poison.

His vision blurred, his body convulsed. He could hear voices . . . but he couldn't answer.

He couldn't breathe.

45

Never despair.

—Motto of the Cadre of the Lost

Dag stood in the doorway leading to the bridge, pistols drawn, watchful and wary. The Blood Guards who had survived the blast had first tried to fight, but Master Tutillo and his men had surged into the corridor, firing rifles and pistols with deadly effect. When the few remaining Blood Guards tried to flee, Master Tutillo and his soldiers had gone after them.

Dag could not see what was happening, but he could hear Verdi hooting the alarm, then sporadic gunfire, calls, and shouts. The Blood Guards must have run outside. The dragon had seen them and attacked, driving them back inside the fortress where the riflemen waited.

The battle was not prolonged. After the sound of gunfire stopped, Dag did not relax. He did not trust these fiends, and he waited for more to come out of nowhere and attack. He tried to hear what was happening on the bridge, hoping to figure out what was going on. When he heard Stephano cry out in pain it was all Dag could do to stay at his post. He hoped the sound of glass breaking was the dragon smashing the window; after that came muffled shouting, but he couldn't understand what the man was saying.

Then came the clash of steel. Dag smiled grimly and nodded in satisfaction. Rodrigo's magic must have worked. The Blood Mage had only his sword and Stephano was an expert swordsman. He would make short work of the fiend. Dag pictured the fight in his mind. He didn't think it would last long; the thud as of a body hitting the floor seemed to prove him right.

Dag waited for Stephano to emerge the victor.

When Stephano didn't come out, Dag wondered what he could be doing up there.

"Captain!" Dag shouted.

No answer. He was starting to grow worried and was just about to go find out when he heard someone moving. The sunlight, dim at best, was gone. He could see only a shadow. He raised his pistol.

"Who's there?" he demanded.

His answer was a fiery ball, hurtling straight for him. Dag ducked into the doorway. The blazing glob sizzled past him. He jumped back out and fired his pistol in the direction of the shadow. He didn't hear a scream and he began to fear he'd missed.

A great and terrible bellowing came from outside the bridge, accompanied by the sound of Miri blowing frantically on the bosun's pipe.

Dag forgot the fiend and raced up the stairs, calling Stephano's name and getting no response. The door stood open, and he got a whiff of the vapor before he was half-way up the stairs. The fumes bit into his throat and stung his eyes; he coughed, choked. Feeling dizzy, he stumbled back down the stairs, out of range.

The vapor filled the room; it was noxious, possibly deadly.

Dag sucked in a huge breath, covered his nose and

mouth with his hand, and dashed back up the stairs and into the room. He could barely see through the blood-red mist, but finally found Stephano lying on the floor.

The vapor stung Dag's eyes painfully, and his lungs were about to burst. He ran to the window, thrust his head out, and sucked in a deep breath. Viola was hovering distractedly, and Miri cried out, asking about Stephano, while Rodrigo shouted something about poison.

Dag didn't have time to respond. He drew in another breath, turned, reached down and picked up Stephano by the shoulders, dragged him across the floor and out the door, onto the stairs.

Dag's head spun, his vision was blurry, and the stairs seemed to jump up at him. He missed his step, lost his hold on Stephano, and went crashing down the stairs, fetching up against the wall. Stephano tumbled limply down the stairs and ended in a crumpled heap at the bottom.

Dag crawled over to him and laid his ear on Stephano's chest. He thought he was breathing, but he couldn't really tell. He felt for a pulse and found it, eventually, but it was very weak.

A gun blast went off, and Dag swore with what breath he had left. He had forgotten about the fiend in the hall. Master Tutillo appeared in the doorway, a smoking pistol in his hand.

"Oh, my God! Is the captain dead?" Master Tutillo gasped. He started gagging. "What's that awful smell?"

"Poison!" Dag grunted. "Help me get the captain away from the bridge."

By this time, Cook and the rest of the men had arrived. They picked up Stephano by his shoulders and legs and had carried him as far as the dock when they, too, started choking.

"I can still smell it, sir!" Master Tutillo said, coughing.

"It's in his clothes and on his skin," Dag said, coughing. "Cook, go fetch a blanket."

He and Master Tutillo stripped Stephano of his dragon coat, his breeches and shirt, and wrapped him in a blanket. This done, Cook and his gunner partner carried Stephano to his quarters. Dag kicked the pile of clothes out the door and into the rain.

He posted the rest of the men at either end of the corridor, warning them that poisonous fumes were coming from the bridge and that no one was to go near it.

Feeling his own breathing start to ease, Dag hurried to Stephano's quarters. He found his captain lying in his bed with Master Tutillo hovering helplessly, fussing with his pillow. Cook stood in a corner, twisting his apron in his big hands.

"What do we do for him, sir?" Master Tutillo cast a stricken glance at Dag. "I think he's dying!"

Dag had no idea. He could have treated a battlefield wound—dug out a bullet, tied a tourniquet around a bleeding limb. But this was beyond him.

"Fetch Miri," he ordered.

Cook offered to go, glad to have something to do. Dag sat down in a chair and grimaced, feeling the painful results of his tumble down the stairs. He gingerly touched a rising lump on the back of his head.

The room was growing dark. Master Tutillo lit a lamp and placed it on the nightstand. Dag looked at Stephano and willed him not to die.

"Keep breathing, sir," he said softly.

Stephano lay on his back, his face ghastly pale and his eyes sunken. He made no sound and didn't move.

Master Tutillo sat huddled in a chair. His face was black with grime, and he had a nasty burn on his forehead. His best uniform was in shambles. He blinked his eyes rapidly and wiped his nose when he thought Dag wasn't looking.

The boy needed something else to think about.

"Is the fortress secure, Master Tutillo?" Dag asked sternly. "All the enemy accounted for? Did we suffer any casualties?"

Master Tutillo drew in a deep breath and stood up. Shoulders back, standing at attention, he made his report.

"The survivors tried to escape, Lieutenant. They ran out the door. One of the dragons swooped down on them, killing two of them. The others ran back inside, where we were waiting for them. Two of our men were wounded in that attack, sir. Mostly burns and such. Nothing as bad as the captain." He cast an unhappy glance at Stephano.

"Excellent work, Master Tutillo," said Dag.

"Thank you, sir," said Master Tutillo dispiritedly. "Is there anything else I should be doing? If not, I'd like to wait here."

"You may stay," said Dag gruffly.

Master Tutillo nodded and huddled back down in his chair again.

Miri appeared in the doorway. "Oh, my God!" she cried. "Stephano!"

She was wet and bedraggled, her hair wildly tangled, and white to the lips. She put her hand on the door frame for support.

"What happened to him, Dag? Tell me what happened!"

"Some sort of foul blood magic," said Dag, shaking his head. "Something in the room was giving off a red vapor. I took one whiff of the stuff and it was like breathing liquid fire."

Miri pushed herself away from the door frame and walked unsteadily into the room. She reached out a trembling hand to Stephano, smoothed back his hair to feel his forehead. His skin was cold and clammy to the touch. She felt for his pulse and bit her lip.

"Where's Rigo?" she asked, glancing around. "He was right behind me."

"I'm here," said Rodrigo in a small voice. He had been standing outside the room. "Is Stephano . . . Is he . . ."

"No," said Miri sharply. "He isn't. I need Gythe, Rigo. I need her right now! She's in the cave."

Rodrigo tried to move. He staggered and almost fell. Dag caught hold of him, eased him into a chair.

"I'll go fetch Gythe," Dag offered gently. "You stay here."

Rodrigo nodded. His clothes were soaking wet. His hair straggled over his face. He was almost as pale as Stephano.

"You should bring the countess, too," he said in a low voice. "She should be with him in case . . ."

Miri rounded on Rodrigo. Her red hair flared, her eyes flashed. She shook her fist in his face.

"He's not going to die! Do you hear me?"

She began to sob. Dag took hold of her and she sagged against him, beating on his chest with her clenched hands and repeating over and over. "He's not going to die!"

Rodrigo looked up at Dag. "Bring the countess."

Dag found Cecile, Gythe, and Sophia standing at the mouth of the cave waiting impatiently for news. Dag didn't have to say a word. One look at his face and the countess put her hand to her mouth to stop a cry. The princess put her arm around her.

"He's not dead, your ladyship," Dag hastened to reassure her. "But you should come."

"He won't die. He's Stephano. He knows he can't go off and leave us," said Gythe, smiling. She gazed into the sky and pointed. "Look there. The dragons are returning. The battle is over. Stephano will need to know. We have to go tell him."

Dag stood stock still and stared at Gythe.

"Girl, dear!" Dag said, amazed. "You spoke!"

"The soldier was going to kill Brother Barnaby," Gythe added in a matter-of-fact tone of voice. "I had to warn him."

Dag gazed at her in wonder, but she only laughed and ran off.

The rain had stopped and the clouds had moved off, revealing the sun glimmering through the mists.

They hurried down the hill. Dag had brought his rifle, just in case. He didn't really know why. Verdi was keeping watch above the fortress, and Viola circled, waiting to hear word of Stephano. The other dragons flew overhead, heading for the caves near the mountain peak. They had all of them suffered wounds, but they were coming home; all except one.

Droal flew alone, behind the others. The old dragon flew slowly, his head bowed. Viola, catching sight of him, went to join him, and said something to him that made the old dragon lift his head and fly a little more strongly.

Dag took the others to Stephano's room. Rodrigo had retreated to a chair in a corner, where he sat listlessly, staring down at the floor. Miri was seated on Stephano's bed, holding his hand. She had recovered herself, wiped away her tears. She rose when Cecile entered and moved aside so that Cecile could take her place.

Cecile stood gazing down at her son. She was pale, but composed. Dag noticed her hand twisting a little ring she wore.

Gythe crept softly into the room and put her arm around her sister.

"I've tried and tried to think what spells, what potions

might help him," said Miri brokenly. "Can you think of something?"

Gythe's eyes welled up.

"This is blood magic, sister. We can do nothing. He has to fight this battle himself. But he will. He won't die."

Sophia had not entered the room, but stood in the doorway, looking very alone and forlorn. Hearing a cheerful barking, she turned around to see Master Tutillo carrying Bandit in one arm and an irate Doctor Ellington in the other.

Sophia gave a glad cry and took hold of Bandit.

"Thank you so much for taking care of him," she said.

Master Tutillo could only gaze at her, tongue-tied. He lost his hold on Doctor Ellington, who jumped out of his arms and ran straight for Dag. Scooping up the cat, Dag put him in the usual place on his shoulder.

"The captain's in bad shape," said Dag, petting the Doctor, who purred in resounding triumph. "We have to pull him through."

Cecile bent down to kiss Stephano on the forehead. When she rose, her lips were moving. Dag thought she was praying and he bent his head in his own pleading, desperate prayer.

And then he heard her say, "Julian . . ."

The sunlight shone brightly through the window. Stephano opened his eyes, dazzled by the brilliance.

It was only Benoit, drawing the curtains, as he did every morning. They had no maids, no housekeepers. Benoit wouldn't have them. He prided himself on looking after Stephano and his father. The old man began puttering around the bedroom, pretending to dust.

It was Stephano's old bedroom in the old château. He was back at home. He blinked at the light and realized suddenly that the sun was high in the sky. He was going to be late for training.

"Why didn't you wake me earlier, Benoit?" he demanded. "Father will be furious!"

Benoit smiled and faded away.

Stephano started to throw off the bedclothes and climb out of bed. Instead, he lay back down. He drew the blanket up over himself and snuggled down underneath it. His bed was warm and comfortable, he was so tired, and his whole body ached. He closed his eyes and basked in the warmth and sunshine.

"Our son fought bravely today," said a woman.

Stephano opened his eyes again. A man and a woman stood at the end of the bed. The woman was holding fast to the man's arm, and the man clasped her hands in his own. Stephano stared from one to the other.

"Mother?" he said, astonished. "Father?"

"I was proud of him," said Julian. "I fought at his side. He didn't see me. He never does."

"He knows you are there," said Cecile.

"Father, Mother," Stephano repeated, bewildered. "What are you doing here?"

"He has been grievously wounded," said Cecile sadly. "This final fight is hard for him. He is tempted to give up."

"He is my son," said Julian proudly. "I taught him better than that."

"I'm sorry I'm late, Father. I'm sorry."

Stephano kept repeating the apology over and over, just as he kept trying to throw off the bedclothes and kept trying to get out of bed. Someone kept pushing him back down.

He was growing angry and frustrated. He needed to find his father, apologize.

"Damn it, Benoit! Let me up! I have to go—"

Hands, strong, but firm, rested on his shoulders and shoved him back in the bed.

"You're not going anywhere, Stephano de Guichen," Miri said in stern tones. She used his full name, which meant he was in trouble. "We nearly lost you once. We're damn well not going to lose you again."

Stephano opened his eyes. The bright sunlight was gone, and the room was dark except for the light of a lamp.

His mother stood at the end of the bed, exactly where she had been standing before. This time she was alone. She smiled at him.

Stephano smiled back.

Miri was at his side, ready to block any attempts he might make to get out of bed. Stephano lay back, giving up the fight. He was so weak, even smiling was an effort. Gythe stood beside her sister, her hand on Miri's shoulder. Dag was close by, as always guarding and protecting them both.

"Glad to have you back, sir," Dag said gruffly. "We thought you'd left us."

Doctor Ellington gave a loud meow.

"The Doctor says he is glad, too," said Gythe.

Miri sniffed. "The fool beast is just hungry."

"Viola has been so worried about you she couldn't eat," Gythe continued. "Petard tried to fly into the fort to see you. Dag wouldn't let him."

"The dragons have given us no peace, sir," Dag added, "wondering how you are."

"Tell them I am fine and I will be with them soon," said Stephano. He was missing someone.

"Where's Rigo?"

"I'm here," Rodrigo replied in a choked voice. He had been keeping to the shadows. His hair was uncombed, his clothes disheveled. He held a crumpled handkerchief in his hand. "I am glad you are here, too, dear friend."

Clasping hold of Stephano's hand, Rodrigo pressed it tightly.

"You look terrible," said Stephano.

Rodrigo heaved a doleful sigh and sank down on the edge of the bed. "I feel terrible. I've had the most frightful day. You can't imagine!"

Stephano began to laugh. Laughing hurt, but he couldn't help it. At first Miri tried to stop him, then she began to laugh. And soon everyone was laughing, a little shaky, laughter mixed with tears. Stephano looked at them lovingly. His friends.

He was very tired. He didn't remember much of what had happened to him, but that didn't matter. For now he was content to lie here with his friends around him.

"I'm going to sleep now," he said. "Just for a little while. We have lots of work to do to get this fortress ready to go back home."

"You rest, sir," said Dag. "The work will take care of itself."

"We will be here when you wake," Miri promised.

Stephano closed his eyes.

Easy, restful, healing sleep crept over him.

We will be here when you wake. And so they would.

The Cadre of the Lost.

Not lost anymore.

46

Our evils can never be so great as to oppress us, for His power is great to deliver us.

—Franklin Sloan

Henry Wallace woke to find himself lying on a slab of cold stone with raindrops hitting him full in the face. Given the cold stone, his first thought was that he was in the morgue. The rain splashing in his face was a relief to him at first, proving he was not dead, but then started to become a damn nuisance. He found this situation highly uncomfortable, and he couldn't think why he was in it. He tried to sit up and fell back with a stifled cry. Movement brought pain and remembrance. He didn't know which was worse.

Above him, the sky boiled with black clouds shot through with purple lightning. Thunder pounded on the rocks. He had a dim recollection of Sir Ander shouting his name, pleading for help. That did not bode well. Neither did this wizard storm beating down on him. He wondered if Father Jacob had managed to stop Eiddwen or if the ground on which he lay was about to fall from underneath him.

There was nothing he could do about it either way. He

lay still, catching his breath, not wanting to move again, yet knowing he had to. He shifted his head, looking for Alan. The last he had seen of him, his rifle had blown up in his hands. Henry had been running to his aid when he'd been hit by a green fireball, and that was the last thing he remembered.

Another flash of lightning revealed Alan, lying only a short distance away, deathly pale and unmoving. Henry's breath caught at the sight of his friend's mangled arm. Blood oozed from the horrific wound. Henry called his name, but Alan didn't stir.

"Got to . . . stop that bleeding," Henry muttered.

Which meant he had to move, when even breathing hurt.

The worst of his pain was on his right side. Gritting his teeth, he raised his head to observe the damage. The right side of his coat hung in charred tatters, where it wasn't burned away altogether. What was left of his shirt and weskit was plastered to his body with blood.

He blessed the magical constructs Simon and Mr. Sloan's friend, the magically talented seamstress, had placed on his clothes. They had undoubtedly saved him from a face-to-face meeting with his creator. Henry managed to move his left hand, reach in and gingerly touch the wound. He felt burnt flesh and warm blood and, when he touched his ribs, searing pain.

He fell back, letting the pain subside, then thrust his left hand inside the breast of his coat, fumbling about until he managed to draw a small vial from an inner pocket. He pulled out the cork with his teeth, shuddering at the pain, and tossed the liquid inside the vial down his throat. He waited for it to take effect.

The elixir was a concoction of Simon's. He had offered to explain what was in it, but since it involved illegal experimenting with corpses, Henry didn't want to know. He waited until he felt the elixir's desired effect start to work in his body. The foul-tasting stuff also had undesired effects, but those would come later.

Henry felt a hot flush run through his body and then a surge of energy. The pain subsided from a shrieking howl to a gasping whimper, but he knew better than to try to stand. He could crawl, and that was enough. Blinking rainwater out of his eyes, he hauled himself over the rain-swept ground until he managed to reach Alan's side. Once there, he collapsed from the pain, but hung on to consciousness with grim determination.

Alan was in bad shape. Splintered edges of the broken bones in his arm protruded through the skin, and what remained of his right hand was attached by only a strip of flesh. Blood poured from the wound, taking his life with it.

Henry needed a strip of cloth and a stick to make a tourniquet. The strip of cloth was easy. He had only to rip up what was left of his shirt. The stick was a different matter. The only trees in this godforsaken part of the world were too far away for him to reach. Then he remembered he had a knife in his boot. Clenching his teeth against the pain, he struggled to reach it and finally got hold of it.

Alan's skin was cold to the touch. If he had a pulse Henry couldn't find it. The fact that the blood was warm and oozing was a good sign that he was still alive.

He tied the cloth around Alan's arm, knotted it over the hilt of the knife, and twisted. When he deemed it was tight enough, he tied the ends of the tourniquet around the knife to keep it from loosening. Then Henry rolled over on his back as the pain crashed down on him.

He cried out for help, but no one answered, and he forced himself to face harsh reality. No one was coming to help because no one knew they were here. No one would even find their bodies. His wife and little son would never know what had happened to him. He hoped she would know that he was thinking of them at the end.

He passed out again.

When he woke, the rain had stopped. The wizard storm had moved out into the Breath. By the distant rumbling of thunder, another storm was on the way. The first of many in an age of endless storms, endless darkness. He looked at Alan.

No change. The tourniquet was holding. The bleeding had more or less stopped. He was alive, but he wouldn't be for much longer. Not unless they could get him some place warm and dry.

Henry smiled bitterly and said into the silence, "And that's not bloody likely."

From behind him came a gentle cough. "Perhaps I might be of service, my lord."

Henry closed his eyes. A shudder ran through his body. He feared he might be hallucinating. Simon had warned that could be a side effect of the adrenaline.

"Tell me you are real, Mr. Sloan!" Henry said brokenly.

He stretched out his hand.

A strong, firm hand closed over his.

"I am very real, my lord," said Mr. Sloan.

Henry clung to Mr. Sloan's hand. He couldn't speak for long moments. When he did, his voice was choked. "How did you find us, Mr. Sloan? How did you get here? Angel wings?"

"I trust those are in my future, my lord. I flew here on griffin-back. I regained consciousness not long after you left. The farmer's wife told me where you had gone, and she provided me with a horse. I rode to the earl's to find that his griffins had all safely returned. I persuaded them to bring me to the location where they had left you."

Mr. Sloan took off his heavy coat and, ignoring Henry's

feeble protests, tucked it around him. "If you can hold on a little longer, my lord, the earl's wife is coming behind me with a carriage."

"The earl's wife?" Henry was confused. "Sir John Benedict's wife?"

"Yes, my lord. That would be Lady Elaine. Her husband forbade her to come to your aid, but the lady is quite spirited and told him he was a silly ass, if you will forgive the expression. She was deeply concerned about Captain Northrop. It seems he made quite a favorable impression on her."

Henry started to laugh, caught his breath with a gasp and held very tightly to Mr. Sloan until the pain had eased. He looked worriedly at Alan, who had not regained consciousness. He lay unmoving, wrapped in a saddle blanket taken from the griffin.

"How is he, Mr. Sloan?"

"Touch and go, my lord. I fear he will lose the hand."

"Better than his life," said Henry.

"Indeed, my lord."

"How are *you,* Mr. Sloan?" Henry asked, remembering his friend's own injury. Talking hurt, and his words came in gasps. But talking was less painful than the dreadful silence. "Should you be riding griffins and gallivanting about the countryside with a cracked skull?"

"I have a slight headache, my lord. Nothing to speak of."

Henry eyed him grimly. Mr. Sloan was dressed only in his shirtsleeves and weskit and those were soaking wet from riding here through the driving rain. His head was still bandaged and there was fresh blood from the head wound. His face was pale and drawn.

"I think you are a damn liar, Mr. Sloan. I should sack you immediately."

"Yes, my lord," said Mr. Sloan.

"What's become of Father Jacob?" Henry struggled to

sit up, trying to see. "We haven't all fallen into the Breath, so I assume he managed to stop Eiddwen?"

"Mistress Eiddwen is dead, my lord," said Mr. Sloan, pushing him gently back down. "Father Jacob was grievously hurt in the battle, as was Sir Ander. I did what I could to help, but the sooner they receive the ministrations of a healer, the better."

"And Simon? I saw the *Contraption* go down."

"Mr. Yates and Mr. Albright suffered bumps and bruises, but they are otherwise unhurt. Mr. Albright is attempting to repair the vehicle under Mr. Yates's direction. Prior to my arrival they were planning to fly off to seek help. You should rest, my lord."

Henry was shivering with the cold. Mr. Sloan drew the coat more closely around him, but given that he was lying on cold, wet stone, the coat wasn't much help. Henry turned his head so he could keep an eye on Alan. Father Jacob and Sir Ander both badly hurt! They had managed to stop Eiddwen, but it might have been at a grievous cost. And that didn't mean they had stopped the Bottom Dwellers. They might have won the battle, only to lose the war.

He must have dozed off, for he woke to the sound of wyverns shrieking and the clattering, harness-jingling thud of a carriage landing on the ground.

"Ah, that will be her ladyship," said Mr. Sloan. "If you will excuse me, my lord, I will go meet her, explain what needs to be done."

"Of course, Mr. Sloan," said Henry weakly.

He heard Mr. Sloan conferring with Lady Elaine, who spoke in brisk, no-nonsense tones. The two talked briefly, then Mr. Sloan returned.

"She has arrived in a coach-and-four, my lord, with enough room to carry litters. The man who tends the griffins is following with another conveyance. They are going to take you back to the earl's estate. Lady Elaine sent for physicians to meet us there."

"Tell her to transport Alan first. I can wait," said Henry.

"I have taken the liberty of doing so. Drink this, my lord," said Mr. Sloan. "Lady Elaine brought it, along with blankets and other supplies. She is a woman of considerable foresight."

"Wonder how she came to marry the earl," Henry muttered.

Mr. Sloan held a flask to Henry's lips. He swallowed a sweet syrupy drink and felt soothing warmth spread through him. Lady Elaine brought two servants bearing a litter over to Alan. She was a tall woman with big bones, fair skin, and hair the color of ripe wheat. Henry was reminded of the paintings he had seen of the queens of the Sunlit Empire.

She apparently had some knowledge of the healing arts, for she adjusted Alan's tourniquet, gently wrapped his mangled hand and arm and supervised the servants as they lifted him onto the litter. She escorted Alan to her carriage, telling Mr. Sloan to wait with Henry.

He next saw her accompanying a litter bearing Father Jacob, with her servants following, carrying Sir Ander. The lady's carriage departed, and another carriage landed almost immediately.

By this time, Mr. Sloan had removed Henry's wet clothing and wrapped him in blankets with magically heated stones placed at his feet for warmth. He remained with him, kneeling on the wet ground.

"The men are coming with the litter, my lord. I am afraid you will find the journey to be quite painful—"

Mr. Sloan suddenly stopped talking. He sat back on his heels, his head cocked, listening.

"What is it, Mr. Sloan?" asked Henry, alarmed.

"The drumming, my lord. I no longer hear it."

"The devil you say!" Henry looked at him with intense interest.

"I believe the drumming has stopped, my lord. The wizard storms have stopped, as well. You can see sunlight off to the east, shining beneath that bank of clouds."

Mr. Sloan gently shifted him so that he could see. The clouds were drifting away, being blown apart by the Breath. God's Breath, if one believed in that sort of thing.

The servants appeared, carrying the litter, which they laid down on the ground next to Henry. Mr. Sloan fussed over him, giving them instructions, tucking the blanket around Henry more securely

"Do you know what that sunlight means, Mr. Sloan?" Henry asked with a catch in his voice. "It means that Captain de Guichen and his dragons have been victorious."

"God be praised, my lord," said Mr. Sloan solemnly.

Henry smiled. "Don't be too quick to praise Him. We shall probably have to go to war against the gallant captain and his Dragon Brigade sometime in the future. They will be formidable foes, Mr. Sloan."

"I trust you are not planning to rush off to war any time soon, my lord," said Mr. Sloan, keeping a close eye on the litter bearers. "I was thinking that if you have no further instructions for me, I could go fetch Lady Anne. I am certain she would want to be with you."

"Thank you, Mr. Sloan," said Henry.

His voice thick with emotion, he couldn't say anything else. He gripped Mr. Sloan's hand to express his gratitude and then braced himself for the pain he knew would come when the men lifted him onto the litter and carried him to the carriage.

The men picked up Henry and bore him slowly to the waiting carriage. The pain was shattering, but the poppy syrup took off the edge. Mr. Sloan stayed close to his side.

The sun burst out brightly. He could see the light shining on the boulder. No longer a bomb, it was now nothing more than a large rock. He noticed activity around it and realized that the inimitable Mr. Sloan had thought to organize a burial detail to deal with the bodies of Eiddwen and the Warlock. Men were wrapping the corpses in tarps, to be hauled away, burned, and forgotten.

Henry felt himself starting to grow sleepy. When he woke, he would look up to see his Mouse, smiling down on him. She would cry over him and tend to him, refusing to leave his side. He pictured himself in his convalescence, resting in an overstuffed chair with his feet propped up, while Anne read to him and fluffed the pillows and fed him beef soup and chamomile tea.

Captain de Guichen and his damned Dragon Brigade. They had done it.

Henry smiled and drifted off.

War could wait.

47

If only I could talk . . .

—Doctor Ellington, the cat

King Alaric was dead. Long live the king.

Alaric died a hero, defending his people from an attack by the Bottom Dwellers, who sent four black ships to destroy Evreux. Refusing to heed the pleas of his son to remain in the palace, King Alaric and the Knight Protectors sailed in the ship of his youngest son, Prince Alessandro, a naval captain. The Bottom Dwellers captured and boarded his ship.

The king met his end fighting valiantly alongside his crew and his Knight Protectors who gave their lives in a vain effort to save him. Among those who died was Sir Conal O'Hairt, whose body was found lying beside Alaric's.

The battle ended when a flight of dragons, led by the Duke and Duchess of Talwin, came to fight alongside their former allies. The dragons destroyed the black ships of the Bottom Dwellers, saving Rosia, although they were too late to save the king. His son, Alessandro, survived, though he was grievously wounded.

King Alaric was entombed in the family vault in the cathedral. King Alaric II, known to most as Renaud, ascended the throne upon the death of his father in a brief and solemn ceremony. The people of Evreux had suffered grievous losses and he had to tell them that Rosia and the other nations of the world were still in danger. During the ceremony, he announced publicly, for the first time, that his father had sent the famed Dragon Brigade to stop a fleet of black ships. The king and the world waited in dread to hear news of them.

A fortnight following the battle of Evreux, a young dragon landed on the palace grounds. He had braved the perils of flying through the Breath to carry a letter from Captain Stephano de Guichen, announcing that the Dragon Brigade had been victorious. A private letter, for Renaud alone, told him that his sister, Sophia, and the Countess de Marjolaine were safe.

Bells rang out in the cities and towns and villages of Rosia and, as the news spread, in every church in Freya, Travia, and Estara and Guundar, and all the other nations of the world, united for once, if not for long.

A month later, the Fortress of the Dragon, as Stephano had renamed it, flanked by the members of Dragon Brigade, rose out of the mists of the Breath and landed on Rosian soil. The new king was there to greet them, to embrace his sister and do honor to the men and women and dragons who had fought so valiantly.

King Renaud announced that he would wait to hold the coronation until after the official period of mourning for the former king had ended. He named a date six months from then, and gave Stephano, Rodrigo, Dag, Miri, and Gythe each a personal invitation to attend the coronation and the coronation ball that would follow. He issued another invitation to Lord Haelgrund and all the dragons, thanking them for their service and expressing his hope that the dragon duchies would once more consider themselves a part of Rosia.

He left Stephano in command of the fort until it could be repaired and refitted for its eventual return to Glasearrach—not to wage war, but to bring much needed supplies to ease the suffering of the people.

Rodrigo and Gythe repaired the fort's magic, with Rodrigo spending much of his time studying contramagic and the seventh sigil and making notes in his journal.

Dag was in charge of repairs to the walls and replacing the cannons, while Doctor Ellington, having vanquished the annoying spaniel, Bandit, proudly roamed the fort, the victor.

Miri nursed Stephano until he was able to return to duty. After that, she volunteered to lead the crew responsible for the grim task of cleaning the halls of blood and gore. Cleaning meant more to her than scrubbing away all traces of the battle. She sang under her breath as she worked, and burned bundles of dried sage and lavender to cleanse the fort of evil. Everyone felt their spirits rise, except Rodrigo, who complained that the smoke made him sneeze.

Cecile spent time with Stephano during his illness and recovery, answering all his questions, telling him the truth about her love affair with his father and the circumstances surrounding his birth, why she gave up her child, and why she had returned to court to become the king's lover.

Stephano was able to express his gratitude to his mother, now that he understood—or tried to understand—how she had used her power and influence to protect and benefit him. If he had hoped his mother would express regret and remorse for the past, he was disappointed.

Cecile made no apologies. She had done what she needed

to do for him, for herself, and for her country. When he expressed his hope that she could now retire to live a peaceful life at her estate, he was disappointed in that, as well. At the request of the new king and the urging of Princess Sophia, Cecile was planning to return to the royal court, prepared to go back to her duties as His Majesty's adviser.

"And spymaster," Stephano grumbled.

"I cannot ride to battle on a dragon, my dear," his mother responded.

In one way, she pleased him greatly. She was warm in her praise of Miri and gave her blessing to Stephano for his marriage, although her response was guarded.

"I want you to think, Stephano. You are asking her to live your way of life," his mother said. "You plan to live in your château and ask her to take over the duties of lady of the manor."

"Yes, of course," Stephano replied.

"How would you feel if it were the other way around?"

"You mean if I ran off to become a Trundler?" Stephano laughed.

His mother did not find it amusing. She regarded him gravely. Stephano decided that his mother was being pretentious and he walked away before he could say something he would regret.

After his mother left, Stephano tried to talk to Miri about their future together, but she was always too busy to discuss it.

"Wait until we are back at home in Evreux," she said. "Then we can make plans."

"You are always putting me off," he protested. "First Gythe, then the war. Gythe is safe and the war is over."

Miri seemed remorseful. She kissed him tenderly. "I love you, Stephano. I will be proud and happy to be your wife. You make the arrangements. I have no idea how such fancy events take place. Unless you want a Trundler wedding," she added with a laugh.

She was teasing, of course. The lord captain of the Dragon Brigade could not very well be married onboard Miri's uncle's houseboat. Stephano turned to Rodrigo, thinking his friend would delight in the chance to plan a fashionable wedding.

"Ordinarily, I would be only too pleased, dear fellow, but I am far too busy with my study of the seventh sigil and contramagic. I am writing a monograph, you see. When it's finished, I suppose I shall have to submit it for publication." Rodrigo fetched a deep sigh.

"You are serious, aren't you?" Stephano regarded his friend in amazement. "You are actually working at this."

"I believe I am what they term 'inspired,'" Rodrigo said. "I found myself up before noon this morning writing away."

"Before noon." Stephano smiled.

"Shocking, isn't it," said Rodrigo gloomily. "I am sure I shall wreck my health."

About a month following their return to Rosia, Lord Haelgrund and the other dragons announced that they were going to fly back to their homeland, after having remained at the fort to rest and heal their wounds. Lord Haelgrund invited Stephano to travel with them, and he was glad to go. He wanted to personally thank the Duke and Duchess of Talwin for their help and hoped to persuade them to rejoin the royal court and reestablish relations.

Stephano flew on Viola with Verdi and Petard accompanying them, for the wild dragons also wanted to pay their respects. Lord Haelgrund was still attempting to woo Viola, though, as far as Stephano could tell, the dragon was having little success. Viola appeared flattered by his attention, but she seemed to have no desire to settle down and said she was looking forward to riding with the Dragon

Brigade, even though the future of the Dragon Brigade was up in the air.

Stephano met with the duke. While gracious, he was noncommittal. The dragons had been deeply insulted and they wanted to take the measure of the new king before they made any decisions.

Stephano and the three wild dragons flew from the duchies to his château, convenient for Viola, Petard, and Verdi, who were going to make their home in the nearby mountain range. Droal was there to welcome them, and though the old dragon had aged a great deal, he was cheered by the sight of the young dragons and the knowledge that they had decided to make their homes here with him and not in the dragon realms.

"I expect you to keep an eye on them, Lieutenant Droal," Stephano said. "Especially Petard. He seems to fly from one disaster to another."

"Pleased, Captain," said Droal. He added with a snort, "And continue their training. Need improvement."

Stephano heard a wistful note in the dragon's voice. "You must miss your brother."

"I do," said Droal, his head drooping a little. He straightened. His head snapped up. "These young ones. His legacy."

Stephano spent the night in the château, making plans for his return with Miri as his wife. Together they would rebuild it as he had always dreamed. He could afford to do so, now that his mother had insisted on giving him a portion of his inheritance. He slept in his old bed, then, the next day, he traveled from Argonne to Evreux to be home for the coronation. Dag and Rodrigo, Miri and Gythe and Benoit were all there to welcome him.

The old man was back in his usual chair by the fire. He was perfectly healthy, according to the physician. Benoit professed himself still weak, especially when there was any work to be done. As Miri noted, Benoit had no trouble making frequent trips to the beer barrel, but he was too feeble to put on the teakettle.

"You old faker," Miri scolded, then stopped to give him a kiss on the top of his head as she and Gythe fixed the tea.

Since the *Cloud Hopper* was gone, Miri and Gythe were residing with Stephano. In an unusual fit of energy, Benoit had opened and cleaned out one of the upstairs rooms for their use. Dag was back in his boarding house, along with Doctor Ellington, who was indignant to discover that the mouse population had flourished in his absence.

The first night of Stephano's return, they gathered around the kitchen table for an official ceremony.

"I hereby declare the Cadre of the Lost disbanded," said Stephano.

Rodrigo closed the strongbox, which was empty anyway, and tossed the accounts ledger into the fire.

"We have known hard times, danger, and despair," said Rodrigo. "We were marooned on an island. We flew with dragons. We fought demons."

"We came through it all because we were true to each other," said Gythe softly.

Everyone grew somber. Miri brushed her hand over her eyes, Dag cleared his throat with a loud rumble that scared the cat, and Rodrigo gazed into the fire, watching his accounts burn. Stephano knew what they were all thinking.

"Our friendship won't end," he said insistently. "I officially declare that we are now the Cadre of the Found."

Everyone laughed, but no one said anything. Change was coming and they all knew it.

King Renaud's coronation was a magnificent affair. Heads of state came from every nation of Aeronne. Queen Mary traveled from Freya, the Estaran king and a great many Travian princes also attended. Frau Madeleine Aalder represented the Braffan council, and all the bishops were in attendance, except the grand bishop, who sent his regrets, lamenting the illness that kept him bedridden. The archbishop of Westfirth conducted the ceremony in the cathedral in Evreux, which drew thousands of Rosians who came to cheer their new king.

That evening, Stephano was in his room, dressing for the coronation ball. He stood in front of the mirror, wrestling with his cravat, and suddenly realized he was smiling. Only a few months ago, the thought of having to endure an evening at the palace would have filled him with dread. Tonight, he was happy, looking forward to the evening with eager anticipation.

The reason for the change was Miri. She was attending the ball with him tonight. He was going to take her to the palace and introduce her into society. Miri, who would soon be Lady Miri.

Rodrigo poked his head into Stephano's room. "Are you ready? The carriage is at the door."

Stephano gave up. "It's this damn cravat! I think something's wrong with it."

"*You* are what is wrong with it," said Rodrigo severely.

He was wearing a sky-blue silk knee-length waistcoat with a flared waist. The coat was adorned with silver buttons, silver embroidery around the upturned cuffs, and a silver embroidered waistcoat. He smiled at himself in the mirror, pleased with the result.

Stephano was wearing a new dress uniform coat. He was now able to afford the finest material and the coat was made of merino wool, soft and luxurious. The dragons on the front were stitched in silk, embroidered in golden thread.

Rodrigo deftly tied the cravat, regarded him with a

frown, then whisked off several infinitesimal bits of dust from his shoulder.

"Such a refreshing change to see you cheerful at the thought of attending a ball. Generally you look as if you were being marched to your execution."

Stephano smiled at his own reflection in the mirror. "Is Miri ready? I am eager to see her in her new gown."

He had wanted to purchase a new dress for Miri to wear to the ball, but there had not been time to have one made. His mother had offered one of her own dresses, emerald green to match Miri's eyes.

Cecile had brought in her dressmaker to fit the gown. Miri had made trips to the palace for fittings, learning how to wear the hoop that went beneath the skirt. She described the hoop to Stephano as being like a large wooden birdcage that tied around her waist. Added to that were the silk stockings with the ribboned garters, tight shoes with two-inch heels, the petticoat, the chemise, corset, and God alone knew what else.

Cecile's maid, Maria, gave Miri lessons in deportment, teaching her how to curtsy, how to properly greet dukes, earls, counts, duchesses, princesses, and marchionesses, each of which had to be addressed differently. Miri was in despair. Stephano assured her she would be fine.

"After all, your curtsy is far better than Dag's bow," said Stephano.

Rodrigo had tried to teach Dag the proper way to bow to the king as he went through the royal reception line.

"You are going to be introduced to the King. You have to show your respect. This leg extended, bow at the waist, a graceful flourish of the hand," said Rodrigo.

"I can't," Dag protested, watching Rodrigo demonstrate. "I'm not built for that."

"Just try," Rodrigo pleaded.

When Dag extended one leg, his other foot slid out from underneath him and he toppled over heavily, almost landing on the cat. Gythe collapsed on the floor with laughter and Doctor Ellington fled the room, hissing. Rodrigo declared the lesson over.

"When you arrive at the palace, just stand in a corner and don't move," Rodrigo advised Dag.

Stephano could hear Dag's nervous pacing downstairs. He was wearing his new uniform coat. As he bitterly termed it, he was "dressed to the eyeballs." His new ceremonial sword—a gift from the king—kept tripping him.

"I knocked on Miri's door and told her the carriage was waiting," Rodrigo said. "She answered with a Trundler expression, which I am fairly certain does not mean 'Oh, joy!' You had better go find out what is wrong. I don't want to be late. Not tonight of all nights."

Stephano looked at his friend more closely. He had been so absorbed in his own affairs, he had not paid much attention to Rodrigo. Now he saw that his friend was glowing with some inner happiness.

"Rigo, what is it? You are beaming," Stephano said.

Rodrigo flushed with pleasure. "I wasn't going to say anything. I am supposed to keep this confidential. But I am bursting to tell someone."

He reached into his inner breast pocket and drew out a letter. Handing it to Stephano, he pointed at the last sentence: *conferring upon you a knighthood*.

"My dear fellow!" Stephano exclaimed, choked with emotion. "Congratulations! No one deserves this more!"

He embraced Rodrigo, who shed a few tears, and then hastily recovered himself, drawing one of his innumerable handkerchiefs from his sleeves.

"My mother will be so pleased," he said, dabbing at his eyes. "Her ne'er-do-well son finally amounts to something. I hope the poor dear lady doesn't faint from the shock. I must go adjust my lace. You fetch Miri."

Stephano ran up the stairs, taking them two at a time. He reached the room that Miri shared with Gythe and knocked at the door.

"Miri, the carriage is here."

"Come in, Stephano," Miri called.

Stephano entered, expecting to be dazzled.

Miri was sitting on the bed. She was wearing her homespun Trundler dress with the pantaloons and the white blouse. The green silk dress was laid out on the bed, along with the petticoat, chemise, boned corset, the hoop, the silk stockings, and the shoes with ribbons and elegant little heels.

"Miri!" Stephano gasped. He felt as if someone had doused him with a bucket of cold water. "What's wrong? You can't go to court dressed like that."

Miri looked at him. "I'm not going, Stephano."

Gythe rose to her feet and glided out of the room. As she passed Stephano, she gave him a gentle kiss on the cheek, then closed the door behind her.

"Miri," said Stephano, a tight, painful feeling in his chest. "What does this mean?"

Miri patted the beautiful dress with her hand, then she sighed and stood up.

"I love you, Stephano. I have from the moment I found our lads beating you to a pulp. And I always will love you. But I can't be your wife. I have tried. I really have. If I thought I could make you happy—"

"You do! You will!" said Stephano, grasping her hands.

Miri shook her head, her red curls gently brushing her shoulders. "The corset pinches me. I can't breathe. The shoes are too tight. I trip over the skirt. And when I sit down, the hoop flips up and hits me in the face."

"Miri, it's only a damn dress!" Stephano said impatiently.

"Don't you understand what I'm trying to say, Stephano? The life you want me to lead is like this dress. It would pinch me and trip me and make me miserable."

Stephano let go of her hands.

"Did my mother put you up to this?" he demanded angrily. "Did she tell you not to marry me?"

Miri drew back. Her red hair bristled. Her green eyes flashed fire. She put her hands on her hips.

"Stephano de Guichen, you should know both me and your mother better than that!"

He had never seen her so angry.

"I'm sorry. You're right. The hell with the dress and the court and the king. I will give all this up. I will come live with you . . ."

"And do what?" Miri asked gently. "Sell Calvados?"

"If I have to!" Stephano said recklessly. "At least I will be with you."

"I love you for saying that, Stephano," Miri said with a smile. "You think you mean it. But you don't. Your dream has come true. Someday you will meet your lady. She will be gracious and lovely—"

"*You* are my dream. You are my lady. Change your mind," Stephano pleaded. "I need you."

Miri drew close to him, nestled in his arms. "Close your eyes, Stephano. Now, I want you to picture me. Where am I? Am I sailing the mists of the Breath or walking the halls of a palace in shoes that hurt my feet?"

Stephano closed his eyes, but he did not try to picture her. He closed his eyes because he knew she was right and he could not bear for her to see the knowledge in his eyes. He embraced her, held her close to his heart.

"I will be gone when you return," said Miri. "Gythe and I are going to Westfirth to live with our uncle. We leave tonight."

Stephano opened his eyes and saw her on the boat, her red curls blowing in the wind, the sunlight shining in her eyes, the mists of the Breath pink and gold behind her.

"I'm glad you understand," said Miri. A tear rolled down her cheek.

"I wish I didn't," said Stephano. He brushed the tear away.

The pain was almost unbearable. He turned and made his way blindly to the door. Flinging it open, he stumbled into Rodrigo.

"Eavesdropping?" Stephano demanded angrily.

"Of course," said Rodrigo, raising his eyebrows. "I'm surprised you even have to ask. My dear fellow, I am so sorry—"

"So am I," said Stephano.

He slammed the door shut behind him and walked down the stairs. Entering the kitchen, he found Gythe and Dag talking. When they fell silent, he knew they had been talking about him.

"You know," said Stephano.

"Yes, sir. Gythe told me. I'm sorry, sir," said Dag.

Doctor Ellington gave a harsh meow.

"Even the damn cat has something to say," Stephano muttered.

Gythe looked at him sadly. "Will you be all right?"

Stephano managed a stiff smile. "Of course. Dag, I was thinking you should accompany Miri and Gythe to Westfirth. You will have to miss the ball—"

"I don't mind, sir," Dag said earnestly. "Truly I don't."

"Thank you, Dag. I will make your excuses to His Majesty."

"Good luck, sir," said Dag.

"I will meet you back at the fortress," said Stephano. "We still have a lot of work to do."

He grabbed his hat from the bust of the late King Alaric and was almost out the door when he felt Gythe's hand on his arm.

Gythe took hold of his hand, turned it over, and drew a symbol on his palm—a Trundler good luck charm. She kissed his palm, then closed his fingers over it.

"Good-bye, dear brother."

Stephano kissed her on the forehead, then entered the hall and found Benoit standing there holding his cloak and hat. The old man's eyes were red rimmed.

"Don't say a word," said Stephano.

"No, sir," said Benoit. "Monsieur Rodrigo is waiting in the carriage."

He helped Stephano on with his cloak. Stephano went out to join Rodrigo in the carriage that was drawn by horses, not wyverns. The Sunset Palace was on the ground now, and Renaud had decreed the palace would remain on the ground. No longer would the king float above his subjects.

"Do you want to talk?" Rodrigo asked.

"No," said Stephano.

They rode to the palace in silence.

The Sunset Palace or, as one wit jocularly termed it, the Sun*down* Palace, now stood on the shore of the lake over which it had once sailed so grandly.

Only a very few people knew the truth about Eiddwen's sabotage or the fact that the palace had been in danger of crashing. Renaud told the people his father had ordered the palace to the ground due to the threat of attack from the Bottom Dwellers.

Those nobles who resided in the palace had returned

from their summer revels to complain that with the palace on the ground, their magnificent view of the countryside had been ruined. They did not complain in the king's hearing, however.

Everyone was in awe of King Renaud. The former naval officer had stated he intended to "run a tight ship." He was a family man, not a bon vivant like his father. He put an end to what he considered frivolous pursuits: hunting parties, drinking bouts, and games of baccarat. The former king's young mistress and her family left hurriedly in the night. Several of his licentious companions also departed in haste.

Lights shone from every window this night, their reflection glittering in the lake. Carriages rolled up to deposit their bejeweled and dazzling occupants. The ships of the royal navy patrolled above the palace, no longer floating beside it.

Stephano viewed the glittering lights and wondered how long he would be forced to stay before he could escape and go back home. His enjoyment of the evening had been ruined. He had looked forward to proudly walking with Miri on his arm. His dreams dashed, he faced another tedious event, one in which he would be constantly looking at his watch.

When their carriage rolled up to the front, he opened the door and jumped out, nearly bowling over the footman. He rudely brushed past the perfumed throng gathered in the entryway, pretending he did not hear the praise and congratulations that followed in his wake. He went immediately to the grand ballroom, leaving Rodrigo to bask in the smiles of the ladies, all of whom had missed him terribly.

He waited impatiently to be announced. At the name of "Lord Captain Stephano de Guichen," many people stopped talking and turned to regard with admiration the heroic leader of the Dragon Brigade. All Stephano saw was that the ballroom was hot and crowded.

A quartet played from a balcony while people milled about, gathering in small groups, laughing and talking. He searched for his mother and found her talking to a short, rotund little man dressed all in black, looking very much like a clerk.

"Stephano, I believe you know Monsieur Dubois," said his mother.

"Captain de Guichen, I am pleased to see you safely returned from your mission," Dubois said, making his bobbing bow.

"Monsieur Dubois, I understand I have you to thank for much of my good fortune," said Stephano gratefully.

His mother flashed him a warning look, but he knew better than to refer to his arrest.

"A small favor," said Dubois, gently waving his hand to brush it away. "I was glad to help. And now, if you will excuse me, Countess, I must go pay my respects to the archbishop."

Dubois made another bobbing bow and scurried off, looking more like a clerk than ever.

"There you see the leader of the Church of the Breath," Cecile commented.

"What? Dubois?" Stephano asked, shocked.

"Keep your voice down, my son," said Cecile. "No one is supposed to know, of course. Grand Bishop Montagne suffered a severe apoplectic attack. He is confined to his bed in the Citadel and speaks to no one except Dubois. The Council of Bishops are quite beside themselves. Montagne cannot be removed while he still lives, and Dubois claims that all the decisions he is making come from the mouth of the grand bishop."

Cecile fanned herself and said with a wry smile, "If so, the grand bishop has gained a good deal of sense since his illness. He has repealed the edict that condemned the study of contramagic."

"Rodrigo will be glad to hear that. He's writing a monograph on the subject." Stephano sighed and lapsed into silence. Standing with his head bowed, his hands behind his back, he thought of Miri. She and Gythe had probably left by now. He would return to a cold, dreary, and empty house. A cold, drear, and empty life.

"I am sorry, my dear," Cecile said, gently touching his arm.

She was elegant in a wine-colored silk dress, adorned with tiny red rosebuds and black lace; her neck was graced by a necklace of jet and diamonds. She was too thin and her hair had gone white, but she was still, Stephano thought, the most beautiful woman in the room.

"How did you know? Did Miri tell you?"

"Not in so many words," said Cecile. "I came to know her well. Look around this room, Stephano. Ask yourself, would she be happy here?"

Stephano looked about the room, at the glittering throng, gossiping, chattering, bowing and fawning and flattering. He tried to imagine Miri among them, afraid to sit down for fear her hooped skirt would fly up over her head. He had to smile, and came perilously close to crying.

"She would much rather be on her boat, sailing free among the clouds," Cecile continued with a little sigh.

"You envy her," he said.

"I must admit, now that Her Highness is safe, I did enjoy my adventure," said Cecile.

"I was sorry to hear about the death of Sir Conal," said Stephano.

"He was a good friend, a brave man," said Cecile. "He died as he would have wanted, fulfilling his vow, protecting his king. Her Highness and I both owe him a great debt."

Her fond gaze went to Princess Sophia, who was talking animatedly with a group of young men. Among them, Stephano was pleased to see, was Master Tutillo, now Lieutenant Tutillo. He had been given the honor of holding Bandit, who had been discovered stealing chicken wings from the buffet table.

"You heard the queen dowager has left the palace," Cecile said.

"I heard that she and her children had a falling out," said Stephano.

"Sophia told her mother that she was not going to be married. She planned to attend university to study magic and if she did ever marry, she would marry for love. The dowager appealed to the king, and he concurred with his sister's decision. The dowager burst into a flood of tears, told them both they were ungrateful children, packed up and took herself off to her summer palace."

Cecile pressed his hand and suddenly smiled at him. Her smile was warm, loving, as if she knew some wonderful secret.

"What is it, Mother?" he asked. "Is my cravat crooked?"

"You look very handsome. I am so proud of you, my son," she answered. "Ah, there is the Travian ambassador. I promised I would speak with him."

She glided off in a rustle of silk and a faint fragrance of jasmine. Stephano stood by himself in a corner, fidgeting and tugging at his cravat. The room was stifling. Rodrigo had entered, surrounded by a bevy of women, and catching Stephano's eye, he waved gaily and pointed him out. The women turned to look, smiling and whispering behind their fans. He was a hero now, celebrated in story and song, as the saying went.

Stephano turned away, pretending to be fascinated by a vase of late summer roses. He wondered if he could slip away, leave the palace without being noticed. Feeling a presence at his shoulder, he turned from the roses to see D'argent, hovering.

"I am glad you are safely returned, sir," said D'argent.

"I am glad to see you, D'argent." Stephano regarded him with concern. D'argent was thin and haggard, his face worn with care. "Have you been unwell?"

"I have found the last few months quite trying, sir," said D'argent. "But I must not keep you. His Majesty asked me to find you. He would like to speak to you."

"Speak to me?" Stephano repeated, astonished. "Now?"

"If you will accompany me, I will take you to him," said D'argent.

D'argent led Stephano to a room that had once been King Alaric's office. A large window provided a magnificent view of the lights of Evreux, sparkling in the distance. Paintings of ships adorned the walls. In the place of honor above the desk was a painting of Renaud's flagship.

The king sat at his desk, going through some paperwork. He looked up when D'argent announced Stephano's name and immediately rose to his feet.

D'argent departed, closing the door behind him. Stephano bowed deeply, wondering why he had been summoned to the king's presence. He stood in silence, waiting to be told. Renaud was not one for idle chitchat. He came straight to the point.

"I have just been reading your report on the victory in Glasearrach, Captain," said the king. "Amazing tale. You must tell me all the details."

"I would be glad to do so, Your Majesty," said Stephano. "I fear I am keeping you from your party."

Renaud grimaced. "To tell you the truth, Captain, I would rather be standing on the deck of my ship enduring a broadside than attending one of these silly affairs."

Stephano didn't know what to say. He murmured something unintelligible.

"But I didn't ask you to come listen to me grouse," Renaud continued. "First I have news of the Dragon Brigade. The Council of Dragons has agreed that the Brigade will be reinstated, and it will be needed soon. The fiends still hold the refineries in Braffa and that blasted monastery whose name I can never remember."

"That is excellent news, Your Majesty!" Stephano said, pleased. He would have an excuse to leave Rosia, fly to battle with Dag and the dragons.

"I am removing you from command, Captain," Renaud went on. "Before you leave, you will recommend someone to be the Brigade's new commander."

Stephano gasped. He had to struggle through his bitter disappointment to find his voice.

"Have I done something to offend Your Majesty?"

Renaud turned away without answering. "Come over here. I want your opinion on a matter."

Stephano didn't want to give his opinion on anything. He wanted only to leave. He would have to stand and watch as the Dragon Brigade took to the air under the leadership of some other commander. He dared not insult the king, however, so he followed listlessly as Renaud led him to a chart table. Renaud unrolled a large map of Rosia and jabbed a finger on the map.

"The duchy of Bourlet. I am much concerned about it. The region has been too long neglected. Wouldn't you agree?"

Stephano stiffened, his facial muscles tight, careful to give no hint of his outrage. The reason the duchy of Bourlet had been long neglected was that King Alaric had done everything in his power to punish the people of Bourlet for supporting the Lost Rebellion.

"Argonne is the largest city on Rosia's southern coast," Renaud went on, seeming not to notice. "Important port city, but the population is dwindling, businesses closing. The port's defenses are outdated and falling to ruin."

"Yes, Your Majesty," said Stephano coldly. His fists were clenched behind his back, nails digging into his flesh.

"The long and short of it is, de Guichen," said Renaud, turning to him. "I want you to take charge."

Stephano stared, confused. He wondered if they were back to discussing the Dragon Brigade. "I am sorry, Your Majesty, I don't understand. Take charge of what?"

Renaud gave a loud snort. "Hah! As my wife always tells me, I expect people to know what I am thinking. What I am thinking is this: de Guichen, I am conferring upon you the dukedom of Bourlet."

Stephano saw the lights in the room waver and the walls seem to expand and then shrink. The floor shifted beneath his feet, so that he had to rest his hand on the back of a nearby chair to steady himself.

Renaud chuckled. "You look as if you'd been hit with a belaying pin, Captain."

"I feel as if I have been struck by a fireball, Your Majesty," said Stephano dazedly. He drew in a deep breath. "Do I understand you correctly, sir? You are saying I am to be . . ."

He couldn't finish. The words were sacred, fraught with memories of friendship, memories of a great man.

"The Duke of Bourlet," said Renaud with a smile. His voice softened. "I am saying exactly that, de Guichen. I can think of no one who deserves the honor more."

Stephano didn't know what to say. He couldn't yet fathom that this was real. Renaud went on talking, perhaps realizing that Stephano needed time to adjust to this astonishing change in his life.

Stephano caught a word here and there. Only later would he recall everything the king was saying.

"The duke had no heirs, so the lands and revenues reverted to the crown upon the duke's death. A small portion of the money went into the royal coffers, but there remains a considerable sum. Revenue from the tenants. Vast amount of farmland and forests. Three castles—the largest in Argonne . . ."

The castle in Argonne. When Stephano heard that his breath caught. The castle was a magnificent structure, built on a cliff overlooking the city and the mists of the Breath. He and his father had visited many times. As a boy, Stephano had often imagined what it must be like to be a duke and live in such a grand and beautiful palace.

"I suppose you will live in Argonne," the king went on. "Restoring the castle will be good for the city, encourage growth. I will have all the proper paperwork drawn up later. Damn paperwork. Never ends."

Renaud stood looking at Stephano, who was still leaning on the chair. "Everything I have told you is confidential, de Guichen, mind you. Must wait for it to be official. Your mother is the only one who knows."

"Yes, Your Majesty . . ." Stephano faltered. He was still finding it hard to speak for his roiling emotions. "Thank you."

"Oh, and tell your red-haired Trundler friend that I have commissioned a new boat for her and her sister. I'm having it built in the shipyard in Westfirth if she'd like to go see it."

"That will please Mistress Miri immensely, Your Majesty," said Stephano.

"Good! Now I suppose we must return to that damn ball," said Renaud. "My wife will have me keelhauled if I don't dance with her."

Stephano never knew how he left the king's presence or how he managed to find his way back to the ballroom.

He seemed to float on the air, wrapped in a golden cloud. He had to take a quiet moment to compose himself before he felt he could face people.

He sought out the chapel and got down on his knees, bowing his head, feelings of joy mingled with sorrow. He asked God to make him worthy of the memory of the duke and of his father; worthy of the trust the king had placed in him; worthy of the trust of the people who would look to him for wise rule.

Once he felt that he could appear as if nothing out of the ordinary had happened, he made his way back to the ballroom. He searched for his mother, longing to share his elation, if only in an exchange of smiles and glances. Not watching where he was going, he bumped into a gentleman from behind. He was making his apologies when the man turned around.

"Sir Henry!" Stephano exclaimed.

He shook hands, honestly glad to see him.

"Captain de Guichen," said Sir Henry, smiling in turn. He leaned over to whisper, "Or should I say, *Monsieur le Duc.*"

Stephano was astonished. "How did you know?"

Sir Henry gave a sly smile, and Stephano remembered to whom he was talking.

"I beg your pardon, sir. That was a foolish question. Speaking of spying, I am surprised to find you in Rosia. Isn't there a warrant for your immediate arrest?"

Sir Henry chuckled. "I am one of the party escorting Her Majesty, Queen Mary. I have been given diplomatic immunity. Which reminds me, I was just talking with your charming mother. The countess was telling me the tale of your victory, Captain. How you very nearly died."

"And she told me you nearly died saving Freya from Mistress Eiddwen's plot to destroy your country," said Stephano gravely.

A shadow crossed Sir Henry's face.

"Indeed," he said quietly. "That was a terrible experience, one I hope to God I am not asked to repeat. We survived, Freya survived, thanks to Father Jacob."

"My mother said that Captain Northrop lost his hand in the battle," said Stephano. "The captain is a gallant foe. I trust he will be all right."

"Alan?" Sir Henry smiled at the thought of his friend. "He will be fine. Our friend Simon is working on fitting him with some sort of new mechanical hand he's invented."

"I am glad to hear it. Speaking of Captain Northrop," Stephano added with feigned innocence, "what news do you hear of Braffa, sir? The king told me the Bottom Dwellers still hold the refineries."

"I am sure I know nothing about Braffa, sir," said Sir Henry. "We Freyans have no interest at all in the matter."

He winked at Stephano, who laughed.

"Ah, I see Her Majesty looking for me," said Sir Henry. "I must go attend her. My sincere congratulations, Captain. And my thanks for your brave service."

He paused, became thoughtful. "I find I am heartily sick of war, Captain."

Stephano was watching Sir Henry depart and thinking that he, too, was heartily sick of war, when he was engulfed in a bear hug of an embrace. He managed to extricate himself and turned to see Sir Ander and Father Jacob.

"Congratulations, Stephano," said Sir Ander. He regarded him with pride. "My godson, the Duke of Bourlet!"

"Does everyone in this room know?" Stephano demanded, exasperated. He noticed that Sir Ander was walking with the aid of a cane. "The news is supposed to be confidential."

"We won't breathe a word," said Father Jacob, shaking Stephano's hand.

"I am glad to see you at liberty, Father. My mother said the charges of heresy were dropped," said Stephano.

"His Eminence, the grand bishop, has pardoned both Sir Ander and myself," said Father Jacob.

Stephano followed his gaze and saw him looking at Dubois. The little man was standing in a corner, almost eclipsed by a potted plant.

"Not only that," Sir Ander added. "The grand bishop offered Father Jacob a position in the university, teaching the new courses in contramagic. A safe life, one of ease and contentment. Of course, he turned it down."

"We are joining those traveling in the fortress back to Glasearrach. We are going Below to visit Brother Barnaby," said Father Jacob.

"I knew he had written to you," said Stephano. "I was sorry I didn't have much chance to see him while we were there. He was busy among the wounded."

"The rebels are trying to set up a new government, and Brother Barnaby has asked if I would lend my aid. He has found a new saint, it seems, Saint Xavier the Martyr. The fortress will be packed with supplies. The nations of the world have come together to pledge their help and support."

"Guilt is a wonderful thing," Sir Ander remarked drily.

"You are accompanying Father Jacob, I presume, Sir Ander," said Stephano.

"He insists upon it," said Father Jacob, frowning at Sir Ander and his cane. "I told him there was no need. I am perfectly capable of taking care of myself."

"And I told him I took an oath," said Sir Ander patiently. "God won't let me off the hook."

They spent a few more moments together talking of the fortress. Father Jacob asked about Miri and Gythe.

"They are both well, Father," Stephano answered

steadily. "They have gone to Westfirth to live with Miri's uncle."

Father Jacob studied him. Seeming satisfied by what he saw, he took Stephano's hand and clasped it warmly.

"You will hold in your care the lives and happiness of your people, Stephano. They will look to you for guidance. Always remember that if *you* need guidance, you can look to the One who is ruler of us all. May God walk with you all your days, my son."

"I will remember. Thank you, Father," said Stephano softly.

Sir Ander embraced him. "Julian would be so very proud of you. I wish he could be here."

Stephano remembered his father standing at the foot of his bed when he had been so ill. He remembered the ghostly image of his father riding at his side during the battle. Julian was here. He had never left his son's side.

Father Jacob and Sir Ander moved on, walking over to speak to Dubois. Stephano stood alone in the crowded ballroom. His mother, seated in a chair and talking with Sir Henry Wallace, must have felt Stephano's gaze upon her, for she smiled at him and touched her left hand, with the little golden ring, to her heart.

Stephano searched for Rodrigo and found him sitting at a pianoforte, accompanying himself as he was telling some scandalous story, to cries of horrified delight from his audience.

He waved to Stephano to join them.

"My dears," said Rodrigo to the women gathered around him, "I want you to meet Stephano de Guichen. He's—"

Rodrigo dropped his voice to a whisper. The women leaned closer, then gasped and looked back at Stephano with fan-fluttering adoration.

"This is supposed to be confidential," said Stephano.

"Oh, we know," said Rodrigo solemnly. He looked around the women. "We won't say a word, will we?"

The women promised they would die before they told, and gathered around Stephano, begging to hear his adventures. He cast Rodrigo a baleful glance.

Rodrigo grinned, then motioned him to come close. "Seriously, my dear fellow, I am immensely pleased for you. Consider the strange ways of fate. All this happened because we were hired to find a missing journeyman."

Stephano managed to disentangle himself from the bevy of admirers and was finally able to make good his escape. He needed to go somewhere quiet, to think and reflect. At home, Benoit would be awake, waiting for him. He would tell him the news, which would make the old man gloriously happy. Benoit could spend the remainder of his days sitting in front of a fire in the kitchen of the castle in Argonne, ordering about a staff of hundreds.

The Dragon Brigade. The king had asked him to name his replacement. Stephano did not have to look far for a commander. Captain Dag Thorgrimson would make his home in the de Guichen château near the dragon training grounds, and the old dragon, Droal, would be on hand to assist. Dag's first new recruit would be Lieutenant Tutillo. He and Petard would make a good pair.

Viola would be unhappy, for she would have to find a new rider. Stephano promised himself he would still make time for her. The two of them were a team; he would always be a part of the Dragon Brigade, even if he was retired from combat.

Roaming the gardens outside the palace, Stephano gazed up at the myriad stars. The Breath of God was soft on his face, telling him of a future that held a wife, the "lovely and gracious lady," and sons and daughters. He would teach them all to ride dragons.

Feeling a tickle on his palm, where Gythe had traced the good luck charm, he gently closed his hand over it.

He thought back to the last time he had been in the castle of Argonne, sitting between his father and the Duke of Bourlet; he looked forward to a time when his family and friends would gather around the same table.

Lord Captain Dag Thorgrimson would tell them stories of his latest triumph of the Dragon Brigade. The elderly Doctor Ellington would be sitting proudly on Dag's shoulder, plotting, in spite of his advanced years, to get to the butter. Miri and Gythe would talk of their latest adventures as they sailed the Breath in their new boat, the *Dragon Song.* And Sir Rodrigo would impart the latest court scandals and show them the book titled *The Seventh Sigil,* that bore his name.

Stephano could hear the sound of laughter, see the sparkle of the crystal goblets in the candlelight, feel the warmth and camaraderie. Beneath his hand was fine linen, silver knives and forks and spoons, porcelain plates painted with dragons.

He looked around the table at his family and friends and knew that he was blessed.

ABOUT THE AUTHORS

MARGARET WEIS attended the University of Missouri, Columbia, graduating in 1970 with a B.A. in literature and creative writing. In 1983, she moved to Lake Geneva, Wisconsin, to work as a book editor for TSR, Inc., producers of the Dungeons & Dragons® role-playing game. She is the author or coauthor of a number of *New York Times* bestselling series, including the Dragonlance® Chronicles, Darksword, Rose of the Prophet, Star of the Guardians, The Death Gate Cycle, Sovereign Stone, Dragonvarld, and The Lost Chronicles. She recently contributed to a role-playing game set in the popular Firefly universe. She lives in Wisconsin with her four dogs. Discover more at www.margaretweis.com.

ROBERT KRAMMES lives in southwest Ohio with his wife, Mary, and their two cats. He is a longtime member of the Society for Creative Anachronism, an avid Cincinnati Bengals fan, and a backyard bird-watcher.

The Seventh Sigil is their third collaboration, following *Shadow Raiders* and *Storm Riders,* the first two novels of the Dragon Brigades.

Turn the page for a sneak peek
at the next exciting adventure in the world of
The Dragon Brigade . . .

SPYMASTER

BOOK ONE OF
THE DRAGON CORSAIRS

MARGARET WEIS
AND
ROBERT KRAMMES

Coming from Tom Doherty Associates in 2017

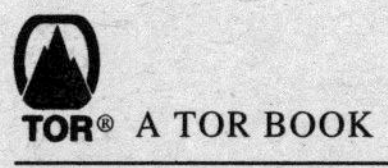

A TOR BOOK

PROLOGUE

Kate sat on the deck, her back against the lift tank, playing at a game of knucklebones and watching her father meet with the revenue agent, who had come aboard to inspect the ship for contraband. The ship's crew were old hands at their business and went about their duties as they normally did: lowering the sails, deflating the balloons, making ready to dock the ship. Those who had no work leaned over the railing to barter, with Trundler men offering to sell their potent liquor, Calvados, or with fancily dressed women.

"Hey, little boy, want to become a man tonight?" a shrill voice called out.

"You talking to me?" Kate demanded, turning to see a gaily colored barge filled with enterprising whores nudge alongside the ship. One of the whores stood up in the barge and lifted her skirt to display her wares.

"Come to the Perky Parrot, little boy," she said. "I'll give you a closer look."

"Did you say the Poxy Parrot?" Kate shouted back.

The crew roared and even the revenue agent laughed. The offended whores sailed off.

"You tell 'em, li'l captain," said one of the sailors, regarding her with the fond pride of a parent whose child has done something clever.

Kate grinned and went back to her game and to keeping an eye on her father and the revenue agent. She didn't have to concentrate on the game; she was an expert at knucklebones, having quick reflexes and deft hands. The crew had quit playing knucklebones with her for money when she was ten. She kept an eye on her father, ready to spring into action if something should go amiss.

Her father and the agent shook hands and then exchanged pleasantries. Watching closely, Kate saw that after the handshake, the agent slid his hand into his pocket, no doubt depositing the five silver Rosian coins her father had just slipped to him to keep inspection of the ship brief.

The *Barwich Rose* was a merchant ship with two masts and an especially wide beam, following the style they had used in the old days for sailing the open Breath. Short wings swept back along the length of the hull, ending with a large air screw on either side. A cargo hold ran the full length of the ship with a smaller hold located under the sterncastle and other holds hidden in secret places.

The revenue agent, sweating in his blue uniform beneath the midday sun, was glad to make quick work of the inspection so that he could return to his cool office on shore. He approached Kate, who jumped to her feet and respectfully knuckled her forehead. She was dressed in loose-fitting trousers and shirt. With her sun-bleached blond hair cut short and her skin burned brown, Kate looked like just another ship's boy, and she knew how to act the part.

"You are a clever lad," said the agent.

"Thankee, sir," said Kate.

The agent walked on and Kate cast a sly glance at Olaf, the ship's crafter and mechanic, who had been loitering nearby, ready with his magic in case the revenue agent had taken it into his head to ignore the bribe and inspect the lift tank. Olaf winked at her and nodded. All was well.

The agent asked them to open the hatch to the hold. Glancing down, he saw a great many barrels marked TAR. Noting that they were listed on the manifest, he gave

Captain Morgan Fitzmaurice permission to enter the harbor. The agent departed, jingling the coins in his pocket.

The *Barwich Rose,* named for Kate's late mother, sailed into the Rosian harbor city of Westfirth, joining the traffic in the busy harbor. Kate's father celebrated their good fortune by buying a bottle of Calvados from one of the Trundlers. The bottle in hand, he walked over to Kate and clapped her on the shoulder.

"I heard you give the Perky Parrot a new name," he said, grinning. "The Poxy Parrot! Agent Rouchard was most amused."

Morgan reached out to cup his daughter's chin with his hand. He turned her face to the sun slanting through the mists of the Breath.

"Damn, but you look like your mother, Kate. Poxy Parrot!" Morgan was suddenly downcast. He stroked Kate's hair, shook his head, and sighed. "A girl your age shouldn't talk of such things or even know about such things. Your mother would be shamed by us both if she were alive. Damn if I know what to do about you, though."

Taking off his hat, he ran his sleeve across his forehead while he regarded Kate with a look of mingled regret, fondness, and perplexity.

"I suppose you could go to school back in Freya," he said. "You're a fair crafter. The crown would pay for your schooling, or so I hear. Probably so they can keep an eye on those who study magic."

Kate felt a little fear. Her father had talked of sending her off to school ever since her mother had died. So far, he hadn't carried through on his threat, but she noticed he was starting to bring it up more often now that she was growing older. He had not known what to do with his daughter when she was six, and he was completely flummoxed over what to do with her now that she was developing into a young woman.

Captain Morgan Fitzmaurice, born to a family of merchant seamen who had used their influence to gain him an officer's commission in the royal navy, had lost his commission and barely escaped court-martial when the navy suspected him of using their ships to transport contraband. He was guilty, of course, but they were never able to prove it. A handsome man with a ready smile and glib tongue, Morgan had one goal in life, and that was to make as much money as he could with as little effort as possible.

He might have done well, for he was clever and skilled, but a fondness for baccarat always seemed to prevent him from achieving that goal. Morgan was optimistic, however, and never failed to believe that the next voyage would make his fortune. When Kate was little she had adored her father, and she tried hard to keep on adoring him, even after she was old enough to know better.

She had always known how to handle him. Grabbing a section of silk from a balloon that was being mended, Kate wrapped it around her slim body and then went mincing about the deck, while the crew looked on.

"My dear sweet papa wants to send me to school to learn to be a fine lady," said Kate, talking through her nose. "I'm to be presented to the queen."

Her exaggerated curtsy drew hoots of laughter from the crew. Morgan laughed as loudly as any of them and Kate dropped the silk to run to him.

"I don't need schooling," Kate said persuasively. "Mama taught me to read and write and cipher. I'm better at keeping the account books than you are. I can do everything there is to be done around the ship. I'm as good a crafter as Olaf—"

"You are not!" Olaf roared, pleased.

"Well, almost," Kate amended. "I can do ship's crafting—repairing the magical constructs on the lift tanks, for example, to keep us aloft, and I know how to use a sextant. I can read navigational charts, I know the weather signs, when there's going to be a storm and when it's going to be fine for sailing. I can take the helm—in fine weather, at least. And, most important, I'm your luck, Father."

"She is that, Cap'n!" called several members of the crew. "She's our luck!"

"She brings us fair winds and a prosperous voyage," said another.

"And revenue agents who take bribes!" said a third.

"Remember when I was sick with the measles and you had to leave me with the nuns at Saint Agnes and sail on without me? You remember what happened, Papa?" Kate asked.

The crew remembered and dourly shook their heads.

"Only time we was ever boarded," said one.

"Had to dump the cargo," said another.

Kate gave her father a kiss on his cheek. "You're the best father a girl could have and you know you can't get along without me, so don't talk nonsense."

Morgan allowed himself to be persuaded; particularly in the matter of her being his luck. No one is more superstitious than a sailor, and he and the crew firmly believed Kate really was their lucky charm. As they said, the one voyage she had missed ended in disaster.

"You're a good daughter to me, Kate," said Morgan, adding with a shrug and a grin, "You're growing up wild as a catamount and God knows what will become of you, but you are a good daughter."

He clapped her on the shoulder and went to take over the helm to steer the ship into port. Kate gave a sigh of relief as she neatly folded up the piece of silk sail and stowed it.

"Come here, Katydid," Olaf called, using his pet name for her. "Come look at this."

Grateful for the distraction, Kate joined her friend at the rail. The sights of Westfirth were new to her. Morgan's usual smuggling runs generally took him to remote and isolated coves along the coastlines of Rosia and Freya. He had recently made some new friends among the notorious

Westfirth gangs, who didn't like the bother of having to travel long distances to obtain their shipments. They made all the arrangements for delivery of their cargo, including making certain the right revenue agent was on hand to clear the ship, and telling Morgan what dockyards the police didn't bother to patrol.

Kate was impressed by the huge gun emplacement guarding the harbor. She had never seen so many cannons, and she was staring at them when Olaf nudged her elbow and pointed to the top of the enormous cliff that towered high above the city. Kate craned her neck to see.

"Dragons," he said.

"Oh, Olaf, they're wonderful!" she breathed, awed.

She had heard of dragons all her life, but never seen any before now, for there were no dragons in her homeland of Freya. And here were three of the magnificent creatures, flying in wide circles above the cliff.

"Those aren't just any dragons," said Olaf. "Those are members of the famed Dragon Brigade. The Brigade has its headquarters, the Bastion, atop that cliff. Those would be young recruits, I'm guessing. Probably in training."

"You're talkin' heresy, Olaf!" said one of the sailors, scowling. "Don't pay heed to him, Kate. Dragons are evil creatures. Foul serpents. Minions of the devil. That's why they do the bidding of the damn Rosians."

Kate looked at Olaf and saw him roll his eyes in disgust. She turned her gaze back to the dragons—huge, monstrous beasts, yet so graceful in flight. The sunlight glittered on their scales and shimmered through the membrane of their wings.

"No creature that beautiful could be evil," Kate said softly. "Look, Olaf! There's a man riding on the back of a dragon!"

"He'll be one of the officers," said Olaf.

They watched as a fourth dragon took to the air, the officer riding on its back seated just below the neck, ahead of the massive shoulders and the flashing wings.

"The riders sit in specially designed saddles that keep them strapped in, even when the dragon flips over in midair," said Olaf. "Saw it myself at the Battle of Daenar when I was apprentice to a gunnery crafter. Let me think, that must have been nigh on thirty years ago."

"Tell me about it!" said Kate.

"We were holed up in this fortress when the Dragon Brigade attacked us. It was a terrible sight, Katydid, to see the beasts fly so close that you could feel the heat of their fiery breath. It was worse yet to watch their magical fire burn clean through our magic and see the walls start to crumble around us. Terrible, but, as you say, beautiful."

Olaf fell silent, watching the dragons, his chin resting on his hand on the rail. He was a short man, about five foot, with grizzled hair and a gap-toothed smile, large shoulders and arms and undersized legs. He had worked for a blacksmith in his youth and his face and hands were black from the soot ingrained in his skin. He didn't know his age, but had a vague idea that he was somewhere between fifty and sixty.

He had been a ship's crafter employed by the Fitzmaurice Shipping Company. When it had gone down in financial ruin, he'd gone to work for Morgan, and he'd known Kate since she was born. Most of what Kate knew about her family—or at least the truth of what she knew—came from Olaf. She had learned not to believe anything her father told her.

"How do you suppose people reach the top of the cliff?" Kate asked nonchalantly.

Olaf gave her a sharp glance, which she pretended not to notice.

"Those who have permission to be in the Bastion fly there on the backs of their dragons," said Olaf. "The area is restricted. They don't encourage visitors."

"Pooh, there must be some other way to reach it," said Kate, taking a practical view of the matter. "What if someone was sick and they needed a healer? And how do they get food up there? I know you know, Olaf," she added in wheedling tones. "You know everything."

"I know you could charm a wyvern with those blue eyes," Olaf grumbled. "You see the Old Fort, that big building surrounded by the *wall* with the *guard towers* near the gun emplacements. The Admiral of the Western Fleet lives there in that part of the building that looks like a palace. I've heard there's a walking path that leads from his garden to the Bastion."

Kate heard his emphasis on the words "wall" and "guard towers," but dismissed those as unimportant. She differed from her father, who tended to be easygoing and take life as it came. Kate was a fighter, like her mother. When Rose Cascoyne had decided to do something, she had let nothing stand in her way.

After the *Barwich Rose* docked, the crew would begin to unload the tar, the legitimate cargo, while it was daylight. Tonight they'd unload the barrels of whisky marked TAR and the Brandywine bottles stashed in the fake lift tank. Her father would meet with the buyers when they came to take delivery.

Kate had to be back on board ship at that time to see to it there was money enough to pay the crew and make the repairs the ship needed for the voyage home. Otherwise the profits would end up on the baccarat table.

The buyers wouldn't arrive until midnight and that left her with the afternoon and evening free. The merchant ship slowed as a harbor tug pushed the *Barwich Rose* into a berth barely larger than the ship itself. As soon as the ship was secured to the dock, her father paid the tug's owner, who then sailed off to the next ship.

The moment the crew started to lower the gangplank, Kate raced along it, reaching the end before the plank had touched land. She waved back at the crew and with ease made the leap from the plank to the shore.

She heard both her father and Olaf yelling that Westfirth was a wicked place and she should stay on board ship. Ignoring them, she made her way along the wharf, and turned into a street lined with warehouses, markets, and taverns.

The street was named Canal Street. Kate had looked at one of her father's maps and it seemed Canal Street would lead her to where she wanted to go. She made certain by stopping to ask for directions. She spoke enough Rosian to get by, and although the fishmonger appeared to wonder why a ship's boy needed to know how to reach the Old Fort, he told her to just keep following Canal.

She did so and found the Old Fort. As Olaf had warned her, the fort was surrounded by a high brick wall punctuated with guard towers. Although known as the Old Fort, the residential part of the building did resemble a palace more than a fortress, just as Olaf had said.

Kate was impressed. She considered her family's estate, Barwich Manor, to be the most beautiful house she had ever seen, but she allowed that this building would come in second, and she was somewhat daunted by the prospect of trying to sneak inside the garden. The street and sidewalks were crowded with people coming and going. The women were elegantly dressed, wearing hooped skirts and elaborate hats. Most of the men were officers in the Rosian navy, splendid in their uniforms. Kate wasn't even wearing shoes.

Pilfering an apple from a vendor, she ate it and walked around the wall, mulling over what to do. Her mother's daughter, she refused to give up and soon found a solution to her problem: a large oak tree growing near the wall. The lowest branches were far above her head, but she had been climbing the rigging since she was little. Digging her bare feet into the bark, she shinnied up the trunk with ease, crawled along a large branch that extended over the wall, and dropped down into the garden.

She was annoyed to find that the garden was crowded, with a great many elegantly dressed people promenading up and down the paths. Kate circled about the ornamental fish ponds, dodging behind hedges and trees, always keeping her goal—the Bastion at the top of the cliff—in sight.

She had no trouble locating the flagstone stairs that led up the side of the cliff. They had been cut into the cliff in a zigzag pattern, interspersed with flowers and rosebushes that were both decorative and functional. Ascending the stairs gradually was far easier than climbing straight up. True, the stairs were easily visible to anyone looking at them, but the rosebushes would provide cover.

Kate ran up the hundreds of flagstones with the strength and energy of her twelve years, fueled by her eagerness to obtain a close-up view of the dragons. Reaching the top of the cliff, she saw the Bastion and stopped to catch her breath and marvel.

The Bastion was built in a circle; halls and rooms radiated from an enormous courtyard made of stone. In the center of the courtyard a tile mosaic glittered. It featured a blue-green dragon in flight, wings extended, set against a red and golden sun.

She guessed some of the buildings were barracks for the humans, for she could see men in long leather uniform coats and tricorns walking about or stopping to observe the maneuvers being performed by the dragons. The humans were far away and not likely to notice her, leaving Kate free to admire the dragons. Three of the enormous beasts were standing at the edge of the cliff, not far from her, poised to take flight.

An officer stood alongside a fourth dragon, both of them watching the three youngsters. He would sometimes make comments to his dragon, who either nodded in agreement or said something back. Kate couldn't hear what they were saying for the wind blew their words away, at one point nearly taking the officer's hat with it.

She was enthralled to know that dragons could talk with humans. Wyverns couldn't talk; not that they would have much anyone would care to hear, being stupid, nasty beasts. Griffins could talk, according to her father, but chose not to, thinking themselves above having to communicate with humans.

When she had seen them from the ship, in the Breath far below the top of the cliff, the dragons had seemed as small as birds. Viewed up close, the dragons were huge. She could not fathom the height of the beasts, but she guessed that if the dragons were standing alongside the cathedral of Saint Agnes, their heads would be about level with the tops of the spires.

The older dragon's shimmering scales changed colors in the sunlight, sometimes looking blue and sometimes green. His head, with elongated snout and sharp fangs, was mounted on a long, graceful neck. A spikey mane started at the top of his head and ran the length of his neck, ending at his shoulders, leaving a gap that was used for the saddle, then flowed down his back to the tip of his tail.

One dragon, Kate noticed, had a twisted spike on top of his head; an oddity, for all the rest of spikes on his mane were smooth, as were the spikes on the other dragons.

Kate knew what it was to be an oddity and she chose him for her favorite, naming him Twist. She watched in awe to see the dragons take flight, one after another, spreading their wings, pushing off with their powerful legs, and sailing effortlessly off the cliff into the wind.

Plunking herself down on the ground, she hugged her knees to her chin and watched the dragons dip and roll and turn somersaults in the air. She thought they were simply playing, until she saw the officer closely observing them and making notes in a book.

After about an hour, the officer said something to the dragon at his side, who gave a hooting, booming call. This must have been some sort of signal, for the three dragons started to spiral downward, and Kate realized with a thrill they were going to land in the courtyard only a few yards away.

She held her breath to see the first dragon hit the ground with his back legs and tail, then drop down on his front legs. Wings folded, the dragon shook its mane and then walked off, as the officer nodded and called to the dragon that he could rest, training had ended for the day.

The second dragon followed the first. She also got a nod from the officer, and went to join her fellow.

Twist was next. Kate was excited to see him land, and she looked up into the sky and was disappointed not to see him. Wondering where he was, she ventured out from the tree line. She searched the skies, not watching where she was going, and not realizing she had strayed out into the landing site.

The dragon standing beside the officer suddenly gave a deafening shriek. The officer whipped around. Dropping his book, he shouted a warning. Kate turned to see Twist almost on top of her, preparing to touch down.

The dragon saw her at the last moment and frantically beat his wings, trying to gain altitude. The officer raced toward her, yelling at her to run. Kate bolted, tripped on a loose flagstone, and sprawled flat on her face. The officer flung himself on top of her and the dragon missed, but came so close that Kate felt a blast of air and a jarring thud. She couldn't see, for her face was plastered against the stone, but she knew by the thud the dragon must have hit the ground.

The officer picked himself up and turned to help Kate.

"Are you all right?" he asked, speaking Rosian.

Kate nodded a little shakily and scrambled to her feet. She was scraped, cut, and bruised, and had the wind knocked out of her, but otherwise was unharmed. She was far more worried about the dragon than for herself. She could see him now, tumbling and rolling over the ground, raising a cloud of dust. He finally came to a stop and lay still a moment, dazed.

Kate gasped. "Will Twist be all right?"

"Twist?" the officer asked.

"My dragon. Will he be all right?"

The dust settled and Twist raised his head and started to move, albeit a little unsteadily. The dragon who had been watching with the officer hastened over to check on him, along with his two comrades and some of the men that had been in the barracks.

"Lady Cam," the officer shouted, "how is Dalgren?"

Before Lady Cam could reply, the dragon himself responded, "A few bumps, Lieutenant. Nothing broken. I remembered what you taught me, sir," he added with faint pride. "If you're going to crash land, tuck in the wings, go limp and roll."

"Well done, Dalgren," said the officer. "Don't move until Lady Cam has examined you."

Reassured that Twist was not hurt, Kate shifted her gaze to the man standing in front of her. He was perhaps in his midtwenties. He had removed his hat and his heavy uniform coat in the heat and was in his shirtsleeves, uniform trousers, and tall, black riding boots. He wore his blondish brown hair tied back from his face. He was about to say something, but Kate interrupted him.

"It was my fault, sir!" she said breathlessly. "I was trying to see Twist land and I didn't realize the wind had changed direction and that he would come in behind me. He won't get into trouble, will he?"

The officer glanced over his shoulder, saw the dragon staggering to his feet, and looked back at Kate.

"I'm glad you're thinking of the dragon," he said, regarding her sternly. "You realize, son, that you could have been killed. The Bastion is a dangerous place, which is why access is restricted to the dragons and their riders. You've broken the law, young man. I could have you arrested."

Kate had a lie on the tip of her tongue. All she had to do was claim that she had gotten lost, wandered up here by accident. The lie died on her lips and she wasn't sure why. She lied to her father all the time and never thought twice. She found she couldn't lie to this man gazing down at her with cool, appraising eyes. He, a fine gentleman, had risked his life to save her.

Her father never put much stock in a man's honor, saying that only the wealthy could afford it. In that moment, Kate learned her father was wrong. This man had been willing to die to save her and she was bound, by honor, to repay him. She had nothing to give in return except the truth.

Hanging her head, she lowered her eyes.

"I broke the law and sneaked in, sir. I . . . I wanted to see the dragons."

When he didn't say anything, Kate was frightened. Peeking up, she saw his lips twitch.

"I see," he said finally. "What's your name, son?"

"I'm a girl. My name is Katherine Cascoyne-Fitzmaurice," she said and, remembering her lessons from her mother, gave a bobbing, awkward curtsy.

The man's smile broadened. "A girl with a name that's bigger than she is."

"They call me Kate, sir."

"Very well, Kate. You're Freyan. You're not a spy, are you?"

"Oh, no, sir!" Kate assured him. "My father is a merchant seaman, Captain Morgan Fitzmaurice. He has his own vessel, the *Barwich Rose.* We're in port making a delivery."

"So you are a sailor," said the officer. "That's how you knew about the shift in the wind. I am Lieutenant Stephano de Guichen of the Dragon Brigade."

"Pleased to meet you, sir," said Kate with another curtsy. "Thank you for saving my life. You didn't have to do that."

"Well, of course, I did," said Stephano, laughing. "Otherwise you would have left an ugly splotch of blood and brains all over our nice clean flagstones."

He grinned at her and Kate, feeling a little better, gave a tentative smile back.

"So I'm not in trouble?"

"We will overlook the infraction this once," said Stephano. "And now, since you're not a Freyan spy and you've come all this way, would you like to meet Dalgren? I'm sure he's worried about you."

"Oh, yes, sir!" said Kate. "I'd like to apologize."

"You speak Rosian like a native," said Stephano, as they walked toward Dalgren, who had been watching them all this time.

"My father does business with people from all over the world," said Kate and hurriedly changed the subject. "What is that picture?"

She pointed to the mosaic.

"The emblem of the Dragon Brigade. Dragons and humans working together, living together, fighting together for our country."

Kate sighed with longing. "I suppose someone would have to be Rosian to join the Dragon Brigade?"

"I'm afraid so, yes," said Stephano. "Lord Dalgren is a young dragon, one of our new recruits, hoping to join the Brigade."

"*Lord* Dalgren?" Kate questioned.

"Dragons and men must be of noble birth to be officers in the Brigade," said Stephano.

"My grandfather was a viscount," said Kate.

She remembered, as a little girl, growing up in her beloved Barwich Manor, how the servants had called her mother "my lady"—right up to the time they left because they hadn't been paid.

She looked at the lieutenant to see if he was going to laugh. He did smile, but with understanding and a shadow in his eyes.

Dalgren stood stiffly to attention as they approached. When Kate noticed that he was favoring his left foreleg, trying not to put his weight on it, she felt horrible.

"At ease, Lord Dalgren," said Stephano. "May I introduce Lady Katherine Cascoyne-Fitzmaurice, the young woman you almost flattened. You will be glad to know that although shaken up, she is not injured."

"I am so sorry, Lady Katherine," said Dalgren, lowering his head to speak to her. "I did not see you standing there."

"It was all my fault, your lordship," said Kate. "I wanted to watch you land and I didn't realize the wind had shifted—"

They were interrupted by someone shouting from the barracks. "Stephano! Officer's meeting!"

"I have to go," he said. "Lord Dalgren will show you the way out. A pleasure meeting you, Lady Katherine. Please, *don't* come again."

He grinned and she grinned back, then he turned and walked off. He had taken only a few steps when he stopped and turned back. "Fight for your dreams, Kate! Never sound retreat!"

He waved, then hurried to the barracks on the run, motioning for Lady Cam to join him.

"I know the way out, your lordship," said Kate, embarrassed. "Your leg is hurt. You don't have to show me."

"But I'd like to," said Dalgren. He lowered his head to say in a low voice, "Otherwise I have to return to barracks and listen to Lady Cam scold me for my mistakes."

They walked together, the dragon moving at a crawl in order not to outdistance her as he explained what he had been doing.

"We were practicing maneuvers used in attacking ships and fortresses, and the proper way to land."

Kate listened, fascinated, and asked one question after another.

When they reached the wall, Dalgren flattened down on his belly and rested his head on the ground to bring himself at eye level with Kate. They continued talking until a bugle call caused Dalgren to lift his head.

"That's evening mess. I have to go. You should leave, Kate, before it gets dark."

"Good-bye, Dalgren," said Kate. "This has been the best day of my life. I wish we could meet again."

"I'm afraid that's not likely," said Dalgren regretfully. "If you came back, Lieutenant de Guichen would have no choice but report you to the authorities." After a moment's thought he added, "We could write letters."

"Can dragons write?" Kate asked, trying to picture Dalgren holding a pen in an enormous claw.

"Well, no." Dalgren rumbled deep in his throat, which Kate took for laughter. "Human scribes do the writing for us."

"I'd love to get a letter. The problem is that I don't have an address," said Kate. "We live on our ship and we never stay any place very long, and we don't generally know where we're bound until my father gets his next shipment."

"Sounds like a wonderful life," said Dalgren, adding in rueful tones, "I *always* know where I'm bound. I have no say in the matter."

Kate thought he was just being kind and didn't respond. She was busy thinking.

"We do stop in one place a few times a year," she said. "The Abbey of Saint Agnes. The nuns are kind to us, and whenever we are in Rosia, father spends the night exchanging news and visiting with them. The nuns would hold letters for me."

"What a good idea! I'll write to you care of the Abbey of Saint Agnes," said Dalgren. "And you must write back. I'll send you my address."

She waved to Dalgren and then hurried down the path. Reliving over and over every glorious moment of this wonderful day, she ended up getting lost in the admiral's garden and was nearly caught by one of the gardeners, who chased her until she reached the oak tree and climbed over the wall. He stood beneath it, shaking his fist at her.

Kate paid attention to where she was going after that and reached the ship just as the sun was setting. She longed to tell Olaf her adventure, but decided not to risk it. He was her friend, but he was also her father's friend and might betray her. If he did that, her father would then talk again about sending her off to school and this time might go through with it.

Late that night, her father delivered the goods. The customer was satisfied and not only paid, but wanted to order more. Kate managed to wheedle the money she needed out of her father. He took the rest and went to the gambling dens. The crew, except for those on watch, set out for the taverns and the whorehouses.

Kate snuck into her father's cabin. Cutting a blank page from the ship's log book, she sat down at his desk, opened the ink bottle, and picked up a pen and began to write. When she was finished, she let the ink dry, then carried the paper with her to the storage closet that Olaf had transformed into a small cabin of her own.

Kate lay on her bed and read over what she had written.

Before this day, her one dream in life had been to buy back Barwich Manor. She now had another dream: joining the Dragon Brigade. Folding the paper, she tucked it under her pillow. She would keep the paper with her always, as a reminder of this day.

Fight for your dreams. Never sound retreat.